PENGUIN CANADA

THE RETURN OF INSPECTOR BANKS

Peter Robinson grew up in Leeds, Yorkshire. He emigrated to Canada in 1974 and attended York University and the University of Windsor, where he was later writer in residence. He received the Arthur Ellis Award in 1992 for *Past Reason Hated*, in 1997 for *Innocent Graves* and in 2001 for *Cold Is the Grave*. *Past Reason Hated* also won the 1994 TORGI Talking Book of the Year Award, and in 2001, Robinson won the Edgar Award for the best short story. His books have been published to critical acclaim in Canada, the United States and the United Kingdom. Peter Robinson lives in Toronto.

Other Inspector Banks mysteries

Gallows View

A Dedicated Man

A Necessary End

The Hanging Valley

Past Reason Hated

Wednesday's Child

In a Dry Season

Cold Is the Grave

Aftermath

The Summer That Never Was

Playing with Fire

Other Inspector Banks collections

Meet Inspector Banks
(includes *Gallows View, A Dedicated Man* and *A Necessary End*)

Inspector Banks Investigates
(includes *The Hanging Valley, Past Reason Hated* and *Wednesday's Child*)

Also by Peter Robinson

Caedmon's Song

No Cure for Love

PETER ROBINSON

The Return of Inspector Banks

Innocent Graves

Final Account

Dead Right

PENGUIN
CANADA

PENGUIN CANADA

Published by the Penguin Group

Penguin Group (Canada), 10 Alcorn Avenue, Toronto, Ontario, Canada M4V 3B2
(a division of Pearson Penguin Canada Inc.)

Penguin Group (USA) Inc., 375 Hudson Street, New York, New York 10014, U.S.A.
Penguin Books Ltd, 80 Strand, London WC2R 0RL, England
Penguin Ireland, 25 St Stephen's Green, Dublin 2, Ireland (a division of Penguin Books Ltd)
Penguin Group (Australia), 250 Camberwell Road, Camberwell, Victoria 3124, Australia
(a division of Pearson Australia Group Pty Ltd)
Penguin Books India Pvt Ltd, 11 Community Centre, Panchsheel Park, New Delhi – 110 017, India
Penguin Group (NZ), Cnr Airborne and Rosedale Roads, Albany, Auckland, New Zealand
(a division of Pearson New Zealand Ltd)
Penguin Books (South Africa) (Pty) Ltd, 24 Sturdee Avenue, Rosebank, Johannesburg 2196, South Africa

Penguin Books Ltd, Registered Offices: 80 Strand, London WC2R 0RL, England

Innocent Graves first published in Viking Canada hardcover, 1997;
published in Penguin Canada paperback, 2002

Final Account first published in Viking Canada hardcover, 1994;
published in Penguin Canada paperback, 2003

Dead Right first published in Viking Canada hardcover, 1997;
published in Penguin Canada paperback, 1998

Published in this edition, 2004

1 2 3 4 5 6 7 8 9 10 (WEB)

LIBRARY AND ARCHIVES CANADA CATALOGUING IN PUBLICATION

Robinson, Peter, 1950–
The return of Inspector Banks / Peter Robinson.

Contents: Innocent graves — Final account — Dead right.
ISBN 0-14-305027-3

I. Title. II. Title: Innocent graves. III. Title: Final account.
IV. Title: Dead right.

PS8585.O35176R47 2004   C813'.54   C2004-902820-0

Visit the Penguin Group (Canada) website at **www.penguin.ca**

CONTENTS

INNOCENT GRAVES

For Sheila

ACKNOWLEDGMENTS

I would first of all like to thank several people for reading and commenting upon the manuscript through its several drafts: my agent, Dominick Abel; Cynthia Good, from Penguin Books Canada; Natalee Rosenstein, from Berkley; and my copy editor, Mary Adachi.

I would also like to acknowledge expert help from a variety of sources. Thanks, as ever, to Detective Sergeant Keith Wright, of Nottingham CID, who answered my frequently silly questions with his characteristic patience and humour. Thanks also to Pamela Newall, from the Centre for Forensic Sciences, for saving me from sounding like a complete idiot on DNA, to Paul Bennett for reading and commenting on the trial scenes, to John Halladay for further information on legal procedure and to Dr Marta Townsend for the displacement.

In addition, I would like to offer special thanks to Elly Pacey and Nancy Gali´c for the Croatian insults and to Emily Langran for the Yorkshire schoolgirl slang. And, last but not least, I must thank John Irvine for keeping my computer going through thick and thin, and for the occasional wicked line.

As usual, any mistakes are entirely my own and are made in the interests of the story.

ONE

I

The night it all began, a thick fog rolled down the dale and enfolded the town of Eastvale in its shroud. Fog in the market square, creeping in the cracks between the cobbles; fog muffling the sound of laughter from the Queen's Arms and muting the light through its red and amber panes; fog rubbing and licking against cool glass in curtained windows and insinuating its way through tiny gaps under doors.

And the fog seemed at its thickest in the graveyard of St Mary's Church, where a beautiful woman with long auburn hair wandered barefoot and drunk, a wineglass full of Pinot Noir held precariously in her hand.

She weaved her way between the squat, gnarled yews and lichen-stained stones. Sometimes she thought she saw ghosts, grey, translucent shapes flitting among the tombs ahead, but they didn't frighten her.

And she came to the Inchcliffe Mausoleum.

It loomed ahead out of the fog, massive and magnificent: classical lines formed in marble, steps overgrown with weeds leading down to the heavy oak door.

But it was the angel she had come to see. She liked the angel. Its eyes were fixed on heaven, as if nothing earthly mattered, and its hands were clasped together in prayer. Though it was solid marble, she often fancied it was so insubstantial she could pass her hand right through it.

She swayed slightly, raised her glass to the angel and drained half the wine at one gulp. She could feel the cold, damp earth and grass under her feet.

"Hello, Gabriel," she said, voice a little slurred. "I'm sorry but I've sinned again." She hiccupped and put her hand to her mouth. "'Scuse me, but I just can't seem to—"

Then she saw something, a black-and-white shape, sticking out from behind the mausoleum. Curious, she squinted and stumbled towards it. Only when she was about a yard away did she realize it was a black shoe and a white sock. With a foot still in it.

She tottered back, hand to her mouth, then circled around the back of the tomb. All she could make out were the pale legs, the fair hair, the open satchel and the maroon uniform of St Mary's School for Girls.

She screamed and dropped her glass. It shattered on a stone.

Then Rebecca Charters, wife of the vicar of St Mary's, fell to her knees on the broken glass and started to vomit.

II

The fog tasted of ashes, thought Detective Chief Inspector Alan Banks, as he pulled up his raincoat collar and hurried down the tarmac path towards the faint, gauzy light. Or perhaps he was being fanciful. Even though he hadn't seen the body yet, he felt that familiar clenching in his stomach that murder always brought.

When he reached the scene, just off a narrow gravel path past the shrubbery, he saw the blurred silhouette of Dr Glendenning through the canvas screen, bent over a vague shape lying on the ground, like a dumb-show in a Jacobean drama.

Fog had played havoc with the usual order of arrival. Banks himself had been at a senior officers' meeting in Northallerton when he got the call, and he was consequently almost the last person to arrive. Peter Darby, crime-scene photographer, was there already, and so was Detective Inspector Barry Stott, who, for reasons clear to anyone who saw him, was more commonly known as "Jug-ears." Stott, who had recently been transferred from Salford upon his promotion from detective sergeant, was a temporary replacement for DS Philip Richmond, who had gone to Scotland Yard to join a special computer unit.

Banks took a deep breath and walked behind the screen. Dr Glendenning looked up, cigarette dangling from his mouth, its smoke indistinguishable from the fog that surrounded them.

"Ah, Banks ..." he said in his lilting Edinburgh accent, then he shook his head slowly.

Banks looked down at the body. In all his years in Eastvale, he hadn't had to deal with a crime like this. He had seen worse in London, of course, which was part of the reason he had left the Met and transferred up north. But you clearly couldn't hide from it any more now. Not anywhere. George Orwell was right about the decline of the English murder, and this was exactly the kind of thing it had declined into.

The girl, about fifteen or sixteen by the look of her, lay on her back in the long grass behind a huge Victorian sepulchre, upon which stood a marble statue of an angel. The angel had its back turned to her, and through the fog Banks could make out the chipped feathers of its wings.

Her eyes stared into the fog, her long blonde hair lay fanned out around her head like a halo, and her face had a reddish-purple hue. There was a little cut by her left eye and some discolouration around her neck. A trickle of blood the shape of a large teardrop ran out of her left nostril.

Her maroon school blazer lay bunched up on the ground beside her, and her white blouse had been ripped open at the front; her bra had then been removed—roughly, by the looks of it.

Banks felt the urge to cover her. In his job, he had already seen far more than a man should, and it was little things like this that sometimes affected him more than the blood and guts. The girl looked so vulnerable, so callously violated. He could imagine her shame at being exposed this way, how she would blush and hurry to cover herself if she were alive. But she was beyond shame now.

Below her waist, someone had pulled her skirt up to reveal her thighs and pubic region. Her long legs lay open at a forty-five-degree angle. Her white socks were down around her ankles. She wore shiny black shoes with buckles fastened at the sides.

Lying beside her was an open satchel. The strap had come free of the metal ring at one end. Using his pen, Banks pushed back the flap and read the neatly inked address:

Miss Deborah Catherine Harrison
28 Hawthorn Close
Eastvale
North Yorkshire
England
United Kingdom of Great Britain and Northern Ireland
European Community
Earth
Solar System
Milky Way
The Universe.

He smiled sadly to himself. It was a typical teenager's sense of playfulness, exactly the same thing he had done at school.

Hawthorn Close meant money, as did St Mary's in general. It was an area of large, mostly detached houses, each with an acre or two of garden, long drives and croquet lawns shaded by copper beeches. To live there, you had to make enough money to employ a gardener, at the very least. St Mary's School required money, too—about £1200 per term. Banks had checked when he first arrived in town, but soon found he couldn't afford to send his daughter, Tracy, there.

Banks cadged some evidence bags from one of the SOCOs and, holding the satchel by its edges, tipped the contents inside one of them. All he found were a couple of exercise books with the name "Deborah Catherine Harrison" written on the cover, a portable chess set, a few cosmetic items and three loose tampons in cellophane wrappers. But why had the satchel been open? he wondered. The buckles seemed strong enough, so he doubted it came open during a struggle. Had someone been looking for something?

Glendenning directed one of his underlings to take oral, vaginal and anal swabs and comb the pubic hair. Then he groaned and got to his feet. "I'm getting old, Banks," he said, massaging his knees.

"Too old for this sort of thing." He jerked his head towards the body. Tall and white-haired, with a nicotine-stained moustache, the doctor was probably in his late fifties, Banks guessed.

They moved away, letting the screen block their view of the victim. Every so often, Peter Darby's flash exploded, creating a strobe-light effect in the fog. Banks accepted one of Glendenning's Senior Service. Normally he smoked Silk Cut tipped, but he had cut down drastically on his smoking over the last few months and wasn't even carrying a packet with him. Well, he thought, as Glendenning proffered a gold, initialled lighter, cutting down had been easy enough to do in a lazy summer with no murders to investigate. Now it was November and there was a body at his feet. He lit up and coughed.

"Ought to get that cough seen to, laddie," said Glendenning. "Might be a touch of lung cancer, you know."

"It's nothing. I'm just getting a cold, that's all."

"Aye ... Well, I don't suppose you dragged me out here on a mucky night like this just to talk about your health, did you?"

"No," said Banks. "What do you make of it?"

"I can't tell you much yet, but judging by her colour and the marks on her throat, I'd say asphyxia due to ligature strangulation."

"Any sign of the ligature?"

"Off the record, that satchel strap fits the bill pretty nicely."

"What about time of death?"

"Oh, come off it, laddie."

"Vaguely?"

"Not more than two or three hours ago. But don't quote me on that."

Banks looked at his watch. Eight o'clock. Which meant she was probably killed between five and six. Not on her way home from school, then. At least not directly.

"Was she killed here?"

"Aye. Almost certainly. Hypostasis is entirely consistent with the position of the body."

"Any sign of the rest of her underwear?"

Glendenning shook his head. "Only the brassiere."

"When can you get her on the table?"

"First thing in the morning. Coming?"

Banks swallowed; the fog scratched his throat. "Wouldn't miss it for the world."

"Fine. I'll reserve you the best seat in the house. I'm off home. You can get her to the mortuary now."

And with that, Glendenning turned and faded into the fog.

Banks stood alone for a moment trying to forget the girl he had just seen spread-eagled so cruelly before him, trying desperately not to see Tracy in her place. He stubbed out his cigarette carefully on the side of the Inchcliffe Mausoleum and pocketed the butt. No point leaving red herrings at the crime scene.

A couple of yards away, he noticed a light patch on the grass. He walked over and squatted to get a closer look. It looked and smelled as if someone had been sick. He could also make out the stem and fragments of a wineglass, which seemed to have smashed on the stone edging of a grave. He picked up one of the slivers carefully between thumb and forefinger. It was stained with blood or wine; he couldn't be certain which.

He saw DI Stott within hearing range and called him over.

"Know anything about this?" he asked.

Stott looked at the glass and vomit. "Rebecca Charters. Woman who discovered the body," he said. "Bit of an oddball. She's in the vicarage. WPC Kemp is with her."

"Okay. I'll talk to her later." Banks pointed to the mausoleum. "Anyone had a look in there yet?"

"Not yet. I sent PC Aiken to see if he could come up with a key from the vicar."

Banks nodded. "Look, Barry, someone's got to break the news to the girl's parents."

"And seeing as I'm the new lad on the block ..."

"That's not what I meant. If you're not comfortable with the job, then get someone else to do it. But get it done."

"Sorry," said Stott, taking his glasses off and wiping them on a white handkerchief. "I'm a bit ..." He gestured towards the body. "Of course I'll go."

"Sure?"

"Yes."

"Okay. I'll join you there soon. Before you go, call in DC Gay and DS Hatchley and tell them to get down here. Someone might have to drag Jim out of The Oak."

Stott raised his eyebrows. Banks noticed his little moue of distaste at the mention of Detective Sergeant Hatchley. Well, he thought, that's *his* cross to bear.

"And get as many officers out on the streets as you can. I want every house in the area canvassed as soon as possible. It's going to be a long, busy night, but we'd better work fast. People forget quickly. Besides, by tomorrow the vultures will be here."

"Vultures?"

"Press, TV people, sightseers. It's going to be a circus, Barry. Prepare yourself."

Stott nodded. PC Aiken turned up with the key to the mausoleum. Banks borrowed a torch from one of the search team, and he and Stott trod carefully down the weed-covered steps.

The heavy wooden door opened after a brief struggle with the key, and they found themselves in the dark with the dead; six sturdy coffins rested on trestles. A few tentacles of fog slid down the stairs and through the door after them, wreathing around their feet.

The small tomb didn't smell of death, only of earth and mould. Fortunately, there were no fresh Inchcliffes buried there; the family had left Eastvale fifty years ago.

All Banks could see on his first glance around were the spider-webs that seemed to be spun in the very air itself. He gave a little shudder and shone his torch over the floor. There, in the corner furthest from the entrance, lay two empty vodka bottles and a pile of cigarette ends. It was hard to tell how recent they were, but they certainly weren't fifty years old.

They found nothing else of interest down there, and it was with great relief that Banks emerged into the open air again; foggy as it was, it felt like a clear night after the inside of the tomb. Banks asked the SOCOs to bag the empty bottles and cigarette ends and search the place thoroughly.

"We'll need a murder room set up at the station," he said, turning to Stott again, "and a van parked near the scene; make it easy for people to come forward. Exhibits Officer, phone lines, civilian staff, the usual thing. Get Susan Gay to see to it. Better inform the Chief Constable, too," Banks added with a sinking feeling.

At the moment, Banks was senior man in Eastvale CID, as Detective Superintendent Gristhorpe had broken his leg while fixing his drystone wall. Technically, Detective Chief Superintendent Jack Wormsley, from North Yorkshire Regional HQ at Northallerton, was supposed to be in charge of a murder investigation. However, Banks knew from experience not to expect much beyond the occasional phone call from DCS Wormsley; he was rumoured to be far too close to finishing his scale matchstick model of the Taj Mahal to be bothered with a mere murder. If it came from anywhere, Banks knew, the main hindrance would come from the new chief constable: Jeremiah "Jimmy" Riddle, a high-flier of the pushy, breathe-down-your-neck school of police management.

"We'll also need a thorough ground-search of the graveyard," Banks went on, "but we might be better doing that in daylight, especially if this fog disperses a bit during the night. Anyway, make sure the place is well secured." Banks looked around. "How many entrances are there?"

"Two. One off North Market Street and one off Kendal Road, just by bridge."

"Should be easy to secure, then. The wall looks high enough to deter any interlopers, but we'd better have a couple of men on perimeter patrol, just to make sure. The last thing we need is some intrepid reporter splashing crime-scene photos all over the morning papers. Is there any access from the riverside?"

Stott shook his head. "The wall's high there, too, and it's topped with broken glass."

"Welcoming sort of place, isn't it?"

"I understand they've had a bit of vandalism."

Banks peered through the fog at the lights in the vicarage. They looked like disembodied eyes. "You're a bit of a churchman, aren't you, Barry?"

Stott nodded. "Yes. St Cuthbert's, though, not St Mary's."

Banks nodded towards the vicarage. "Do you know who the vicar is here?"

"Father Daniel Charters."

Banks raised his eyebrows. "I thought so. I don't know all the details, but isn't he the one who's been in the news a bit lately?"

"He is," Stott said through gritted teeth.

"Interesting," said Banks, "Very interesting." And he wandered off towards the vicarage.

III

The woman who answered Banks's knock at the back door was in her mid-thirties, he guessed, with a lustrous cascade of auburn hair spilling over her shoulders, an olive complexion, large hazel eyes and the fullest, most sensuous lips he had ever seen. She also had a stunned, unfocused look on her face.

"I'm Rebecca Charters," she said, shaking his hand. "Please come through."

Banks followed her down the hall. A tall woman, she was wearing a heavy black shawl draped over her shoulders and a loose, long blue skirt that flowed over the swell of her hips almost down to the stone flags of the hallway. Her feet were bare and dirty, with blades of grass stuck to her ankles and instep. There was also a fresh cut by the Achilles tendon of her right foot. As she walked, her hips swayed just a little more than he would have expected in a vicar's wife. And was it his imagination, or did she seem a little unsteady on her pins?

She led him into a living-room with a high ceiling and dull, striped wallpaper. WPC Kemp stood by the door, and Banks told her she could leave now.

Bottle-green velour curtains were drawn across the bay window against the fog. An empty tiled fireplace stood directly across from the door, and in front of it lay a huge bundle of brown-and-white fur that Banks took to be a large dog of some kind. Whatever it was, he hoped it stayed there. Not that he disliked dogs, but he couldn't stand the way they slobbered and fussed over him. Cats were much more Banks's kind of animal. He liked their arrogance, their independence and their sense of mischief, and would have one for a pet were it not that Sandra, his wife, was violently allergic.

The only heat was provided by a small white radiator against the far wall. Banks was glad he hadn't taken off his raincoat yet; he was thankful for the extra layer of warmth.

A three-piece suite upholstered in worn brown corduroy ranged around the coffee-table, and in one of the armchairs sat a man with thick black eyebrows that almost met in the middle, a furrowed brow, a long, pale face and prominent cheekbones. He had the haunted look of a troubled young priest from an old movie.

As Banks came in, the man stood up, a manoeuvre that resembled some large, long-limbed animal uncurling from its lair, and reached out his slender hand.

"Daniel Charters. Would you like some coffee?"

Shaking his hand, Banks noticed the carafe on the table and nodded. "Love some," he said. "Black, no sugar."

Banks sat on the sofa, Rebecca Charters next to him. Also on the coffee-table stood an empty bottle of Sainsbury's Romanian Pinot Noir.

As Daniel Charters poured the coffee, Rebecca walked over to a glass-fronted cabinet, brought out a bottle and a brandy balloon and poured herself a large one. Banks noticed her husband give her an angry look, which she ignored. The coffee was good. Almost as soon as he sipped it Banks felt the scratchiness in his throat ease up a little.

"I realize you've had a terrible shock," Banks said, "but do you think you could answer a few questions?"

Rebecca nodded.

"Good. Did you report finding the body immediately?"

"Almost. When I saw the shape, what it was, I ... I was sick first. Then I ran back here and telephoned the police."

"What were you doing in the graveyard at that time, on such a miserable night?"

"I went to see the angel."

Her voice was such a low whisper, Banks didn't believe he could have heard right. "You what?" he asked.

"I said I went to see the angel." Her large, moist eyes held his defiantly. They were red-rimmed with crying. "What's wrong with that? I like graveyards. At least I did."

"What about the glass?"

"I had a glass of wine. I dropped it, then I fell. Look." She lifted her skirt as far as her knees. Both of them were bandaged, but the blood was already seeping through.

"Perhaps you should see a doctor?" Banks suggested.

Rebecca shook her head. "I'm all right."

"Did you disturb the body in any way?" Banks asked.

"No. I didn't touch anything. I didn't go near her."

"Did you recognize her?"

"Just that she was a St Mary's girl."

"Did you know a girl called Deborah Catherine Harrison?"

Rebecca put her hand to her mouth and nodded. For a moment, Banks thought she was going to be sick again. Her husband didn't make a move, but Banks could tell from his expression that he recognized the name, too.

"Is that who it was?" Rebecca asked.

"We think so. I'll have to ask you not to say anything to anyone until the identity has been confirmed."

"Of course not. Poor Deborah."

"So you knew her?"

"She sang in the choir," Daniel Charters said. "The school and the church are very closely linked. They don't have a chapel of their own, so they come here for services. A number of them also sing in the choir."

"Have you any idea what she might have been doing in the graveyard around five or six o'clock?"

"It's a short cut," Rebecca said. "From the school to her house."

"But school finishes at half past three."

Rebecca shrugged. "They have clubs, societies, activities. You'd have to ask Dr Green, the head." She took another gulp of brandy. The dog on the hearth hadn't moved. For a moment Banks thought it might have died, then he noticed the fur moving slowly as it breathed. Just old, most likely. The way he was feeling.

"Did either of you see or hear anything outside earlier this evening?" he asked.

Daniel shook his head, and Rebecca said, "I *thought* I did. When I was in the kitchen opening the wine. It sounded like a stifled cry or something."

"What did you do?"

"I went over to the window. Of course, I couldn't see a damn thing in this fog, and when I didn't hear anything else for a couple of minutes I decided it must have been a bird or a small animal."

"Can you remember what time that was?"

"Around six o'clock, maybe a few minutes after. The local news was just starting on television."

"And even though you thought you heard a cry, you still went out into the dark, foggy graveyard alone forty minutes later?"

Rebecca cast her eyes on the empty wine bottle. "I'd forgotten all about it by then," she said. "Besides, I told you, I assumed it was an animal."

Banks turned to Daniel Charters. "Did you hear anything?"

"He was in his study until I came back screaming about the body," Rebecca answered. "That's the other room at the front, the far side. He couldn't have heard a thing from there."

"Mr Charters?"

Daniel Charters nodded. "That's right. I was working on a sermon. I'm afraid my wife is correct. I didn't hear anything."

"Have either of you seen any strangers hanging around the area recently?"

They both shook their heads.

"Has anyone been inside the Inchcliffe Mausoleum lately?"

Charters frowned. "No. As far as I know no-one's been in there for fifty years. I just gave the key to one of your men."

"Where do you usually keep it?"

"In the church. On a hook in the vestry."

"So it's accessible to anyone?"

"Yes. But I can't see—"

"Someone's been down there recently. We found vodka bottles and cigarette ends. Have you any idea who it might be?"

"I can't ..." Then he stopped and turned pale. "Unless ..."

"Unless what, Mr Charters?" Banks drank some more coffee.

"As you probably know," Charters said, "I've been under a bit of a cloud these past two months. Do you know the details?"

Banks shrugged. "Only vaguely."

"The whole thing *is* only vague. Anyway, we employed a Croatian refugee here as a sexton. He turned out to be a complete mistake. He drank, he was abusive and he frightened people."

"In what way?"

"He used to leer at the schoolgirls, make lewd gestures. One girl even saw him urinating on a grave." Charters shook his head. "That sort of thing. He never actually touched anyone as far as we know, but some of the girls complained to Dr Green, and she and I had a long talk. The upshot was, I decided to get rid of him. As soon as he'd gone, he went to the church authorities and claimed that I fired him because he refused to have sex with me."

"And the church authorities believed him?"

"It doesn't matter what they believed," said Charters, with a bitter glance at his wife. "Once the accusation is made, the wheels start to grind, enquiries have to be made. And the accused is put immediately on the defensive. You ought to know how it works, Chief Inspector."

"Like 'when did you stop beating your wife?'"

"Exactly."

"And you think he might have been in the mausoleum?"

"He's the only one I can think of. And he had better access to the key than most. Also, as I remember, vodka was his drink of preference because he believed people couldn't smell it on his breath."

"What do you think of all this, Mrs Charters?"

Rebecca shook her head, looked away and drank more brandy.

"My wife, as you can see," said Charters, "has been a pillar of strength."

Banks decided to leave that one well alone. "What's he called, this man you fired?"

"Ive Jelačić. It's pronounced *eaver yell-a-chitch*."

"How do you spell that?"

Charters told him, explaining the diacritical marks. Banks wrote it down.

"What does he look like?"

"He's tall, about my height, solidly built. He has black hair, which always needed cutting, a dark complexion, a slightly hooked nose." He shrugged. "I don't know what else to say."

"Where is he now?"

"Leeds."

"Has he ever threatened or bothered you at all since you fired him?"

"Yes. He's been back a couple of times."

"Why?"

"To offer me a deal. He suggested that he would drop the charges if I gave him money."

"How much?"

Charters snorted. "More than I can afford, I'm afraid."

"And how would he get the charges dropped?"

"Say he misinterpreted my gesture. Cultural differences. I told him to go away. The man's a liar and a drunk, Chief Inspector. What difference does it make?"

"It might make a lot of difference," said Banks slowly, "if he had a reputation for bothering the St Mary's girls and he had a grudge against you. Do you know his address?"

Charters went over and opened a sideboard drawer. "I ought to," he muttered, flipping through a pile of envelopes. "There's been enough correspondence on the matter. Ah, here it is."

Banks looked at the address. It was in the Burmantofts area of Leeds, but he didn't recognize the street. "Mind if I use your phone?" he asked.

"Go ahead," said Charters. "There's an extension in my study, if you want some privacy. It's just across the hall."

Banks went into the study and sat at the desk. He was impressed how tidy it was—no papers scattered all around, no chewed pencils, no reference books open face down, no errant paperclips or rubber bands, the way his own desk usually looked when he was working on something. Even the ruler was lined up parallel with the edge of the blotter. A neat man, the Reverend Charters. So neat that he had even tidied his desk *after* his wife came in screaming about a murder in the graveyard?

Banks consulted his notebook and phoned Detective Inspector Ken Blackstone at home. Blackstone, a good friend, worked for West Yorkshire CID out of Millgarth, Leeds. Banks explained what had happened and asked Blackstone if he could arrange to have a couple of officers go around to the address Charters had given him.

First, he wanted to know if Jelačić was at home, and secondly, whether he had an alibi for this evening. Blackstone said it would be no problem, and Banks hung up.

When he went back into the living-room he obviously interrupted Daniel and Rebecca Charters in the midst of a hissed argument. Rebecca, he noticed, had refilled her brandy glass.

Banks had nothing more to ask, so he knocked back the rest of his lukewarm coffee and headed out into the graveyard.

IV

As soon as Banks had gone, Daniel Charters looked disgustedly at the empty wine bottle and the remains of the brandy, then at Rebecca. "I asked you why you did that," he said. "Why on earth did you lie to him?"

"You know why."

Daniel leaned forward in his chair, hands clasped between his knees. "No, I don't. You didn't even give me a chance to answer. You just jumped right in with your stupid lie."

Rebecca sipped her brandy. "I didn't notice you rushing to correct me."

Daniel reddened. "It was too late by then. It would have looked suspicious."

"Shpicious? Oh, that's a good one, Daniel. And how do you think it looks *already?*"

Daniel's face contorted in pain. "Do you think I did it? Do you really believe I killed that girl out there?" He pointed a long, bony finger towards the graveyard. "Is that what you think you were protecting me from? Giving me an alibi for?"

Rebecca turned away. "Don't be silly."

"Then why did you lie?"

"To make things easier."

"Lies never make things easier."

Oh, don't they? Rebecca thought. Shows what you know. "We've got enough problems," she said with a sigh, "without having you as a suspect in a murder investigation."

"Don't you want to know where I was?"

"No. I don't care where you were."

"But you lied for me."

"For us. Yes." She ran her hand through her hair. "Look, Daniel, I saw something horrible out there in the graveyard. I'm tired, I'm upset and I feel sick. Can't you just leave me alone?"

Daniel remained silent for a moment. Rebecca could hear the clock ticking on the mantelpiece. Ezekiel stirred briefly then settled down to sleep again.

"You think I did it, don't you?" Daniel persisted.

"Please, Daniel, just let it drop. Of course I don't think you did it."

"Not the murder. The other business."

"I don't think anything of the kind. I told you. Haven't I stuck by you? Do you think I'd still be here if I thought you did it?"

"*Here*? You're not *here*. You haven't been *here* since it happened. Oh, you may actually be physically present in this room. Yes, I'll admit that. But you're not really *here*, not with me. Most of the time you're in the bottle, the rest you're ... God knows where."

"Oh, right, and we all know you're such a bloody saint you haven't touched a drop throughout all our troubles. Well, maybe I'm not as *strong* as you, Daniel. Maybe we're not all so bloody *devout*. Some of us might just show a little human *weakness* every now and again. But you wouldn't know about that, would you?"

Rebecca topped up her brandy with a shaking hand. Daniel reached forward and knocked the glass out of her hand. The brandy spilled on the coffee-table and the sofa, and the glass bounced on the carpet.

Rebecca didn't know what to say. Her breath caught in her throat. It was the first time since she had known him that Daniel had shown even the slightest sign of violence.

His face was red, and his frown knitted his thick dark eyebrows together at the bridge of his nose. "You have your doubts don't you?" he insisted. "Go on. Admit it. I'm waiting."

Rebecca bent down, picked up the glass and poured herself another shot with shaking hands. This time Daniel did nothing.

"Answer me," he said. "Tell me the truth."

Rebecca let the silence stretch, then she took a long sip of brandy and said, in a parody of a prostitute's tone, "Well, you know what they say, don't you, ducky? There's no smoke without fire."

V

Banks left his car parked on North Market Street, outside St Mary's, and set off on foot to Hawthorn Close. The fog appeared less menacing on the main road than it had in the unlit graveyard, though the high amber street-lights and the flashing Belisha beacons at the zebra crossing looked like the Martian machines out of *War of the Worlds*.

Why had Rebecca Charters lied for her husband? She *had* lied, of that Banks was certain, even without the evidence of the tidy desk. Was she giving him an alibi? Perhaps tomorrow he would call on them again. She was certainly an odd one. *Going to see the angel*, indeed!

Banks looked at his watch. Luckily, it was just after nine o'clock, and he still had time to nip into the off-licence at the corner of Hawthorn Road and buy twenty Silk Cut.

After he had walked about two hundred yards down Hawthorn Road, he took Hawthorn Close to the right, a winding street of big, stone houses that traditionally housed Eastvale's gentry.

He found number 28, stubbed out his cigarette and walked up the gravel drive, noting the "O" registration Jaguar parked outside the front door. On impulse, he put his hand on the bonnet. Still a little warm.

Barry Stott answered the door, looking grim. Banks thanked him for doing the dirty work and told him he could return to the station and get things organized; then he walked down the hall alone into a spacious white room, complete with a white grand piano. The only contrasting elements were the Turkish carpets and what looked like a genuine Chagall on the wall over the Adam fireplace, where a thick log burned and crackled. A white bookcase held Folio Society editions of the classics, and French windows with white trim led out to the dark garden.

There were three people in the room, all sitting down, and all, by the looks of it, in a state of shock. The woman wore a grey skirt and a blue silk blouse, both of a quality you'd be hard-pushed to find in Eastvale. Her shaggy blonde hair was the expensive kind of shaggy, and it framed an oval face with a pale, flawless complexion, pale blue eyes and beautifully proportioned nose and mouth. All in all, an elegant and attractive woman.

She got up and floated towards him as if in a trance. "Has there been a mistake?" she asked. "Please tell me there's been a mistake." She had a hint of a French accent.

Before Banks could say anything, one of the men took her by the elbow and said, "Come on, Sylvie. Sit down." Then he turned to Banks. "I'm Geoffrey Harrison," he said. "Deborah's father. I suppose it's too much to hope there *has* been a mistake?"

Banks shook his head.

Geoffrey was about six foot two, with the long arms and broad shoulders of a fast bowler. In fact he looked a bit like a famous test cricketer, but Banks couldn't put a name to him. He was wearing grey trousers with sharp creases and a knitted green V-neck sweater over a white shirt. No tie. He had curly fair hair, with some grey visible around the ears, and a strong, cleft chin, a bit like Kirk Douglas. Everything about his movements and features spoke of power, of someone used to getting his own way. Banks put his age at about forty-five, probably a good ten years older than his wife.

All of a sudden, the realization hit Banks like a bucket of cold water. Christ, he should have known. Should have been able to add it all up. This damn cold must be addling his brain. The man in front of him was Sir Geoffrey Harrison. *Sir*. He had been knighted for services to industry—something to do with leading-edge computers, electronics, microchips and the like—about three years ago. And Deborah Harrison was his daughter.

"Do you have a recent photograph of your daughter, sir?" he asked.

"Over there on the mantelpiece. It was taken last summer."

Banks walked over and looked at the photograph of the young girl posing on the deck of a yacht. It was probably her first year in a bikini, Banks guessed, and while she hardly had the figure to fill it out, it still looked good on her. But then anything would probably have looked good on such youth, such energy, such potential.

Deborah was smiling and holding the mast with one hand; with the other she held back a long strand of blonde hair from her face, as if the wind were blowing it out of place. Even though the girl in the picture glowed with health and life, it was the same one who now lay in Eastvale mortuary.

"I'm afraid it's not a mistake," he said, glancing at the photograph beside it. It showed two smiling young men in cricket whites, one of them unmistakably Sir Geoffrey, standing together in a quadrangle. The other man, who had his arm casually draped over Sir Geoffrey's shoulder, could easily have been the other person in the room about twenty-five years ago. Even now, he was still slim and good-looking, though the sandy hair above his high forehead was receding fast and thinning on top. He was wearing what looked like very expensive casual clothes—black cords and a rust-coloured cotton shirt—and a pair of gold-rimmed spectacles hung around his neck on a chain. "Michael Clayton," he said, getting up and shaking Banks's hand.

"Michael's my business partner," said Sir Geoffrey. "And my oldest friend. He's also Deborah's godfather."

"I live just around the corner," said Clayton. "As soon as Geoff heard the news ... well, they phoned me and I came over. Have there been any developments?"

"It's too early to say," said Banks. Then he turned to Sir Geoffrey and Lady Harrison. "Did you know if Deborah was planning on going anywhere after school?"

Sir Geoffrey took a second to refocus, then said, "Only the chess club."

"Chess club?"

"Yes. At school. They meet every Monday."

"What time is she usually home?"

Sir Geoffrey looked at his wife. "It's usually over by six," Lady Harrison said. "She gets home about quarter past. Sometimes twenty past, if she dawdles with her friends."

Banks frowned. "It must have been after eight o'clock when Detective Inspector Stott came to break the bad news," he said. "But you hadn't reported Deborah missing. Weren't you worried? Where did you think she was?"

Lady Harrison started to cry. Sir Geoffrey gripped her hand. "We'd only just got in ourselves," he explained. "I was at a business reception at the Royal Hotel, in York, and the damn fog delayed me. Sylvie was at her health club. Deborah has a key. She *is* sixteen, after all."

"What time did you get back?"

"About eight o'clock. Within minutes of each other. We thought Deborah might have been home and gone out again, but that wasn't like her, not without letting us know, and certainly not on a night like this. There was no note, no sign she'd been here. Deborah's not ... well, she usually leaves her school blazer over the back of a chair, if you see what I mean."

"I do." Banks's daughter Tracy was just as untidy.

"Anyway, we were worried she might have been kidnapped or something. We were just about to phone the police when Inspector Stott arrived."

"Have there ever been any kidnap threats?"

"No, but one hears about such things."

"Could your daughter have been carrying anything of value? Cash, credit cards, anything?"

"No. Why do you ask?"

"Her satchel was open. I was just wondering why."

Sir Geoffrey shook his head.

Banks turned to Michael Clayton. "Did you see Deborah at all this evening?"

"No. I was at home until I got Geoff's phone call."

Sir Geoffrey and Lady Harrison sat on the white sofa, shoulders slumped, holding hands like a couple of teenagers. Banks sat on the edge of the armchair and leaned forward, resting his hands on his knees.

"Inspector Stott says Deborah was found in St Mary's graveyard," Sir Geoffrey said. "Is that true?"

Banks nodded.

Anger suffused Sir Geoffrey's face. "Have you talked to that bloody vicar yet? That pervert?"

"Daniel Charters?"

"That's him. You know what he's been accused of, don't you?"

"Making a homosexual advance."

Sir Geoffrey nodded. "Exactly. If I were you, I'd—"

"Please, Geoffrey," Sylvie said, plucking at his sleeve. "Calm down. Let the chief inspector talk."

Sir Geoffrey ran his hand through his hair. "Yes, of course. I apologize."

Why such animosity towards Charters? Banks wondered. But that was best left for later. Sir Geoffrey was distraught; it wouldn't be a good idea to press him any further just now.

"May I have a look at Deborah's room?" he asked.

Sylvie nodded and stood up. "I'll show you."

Banks followed her up a broad, white-carpeted staircase. What a hell of a job it would be to keep the place clean, he found himself thinking. Sandra would never put up with white carpets or upholstery. Still, he didn't suppose the Harrisons did the cleaning themselves.

Sylvie opened the door to Deborah's room, then excused herself and went back downstairs. Banks turned on the light. It was bigger, but in much the same state of disarray as Tracy's. Clothes lay tossed all over the floor, the bed was unmade, a mound of rumpled sheets, and the closet door stood open on a long rail of dresses, blouses, jackets and jeans. Expensive stuff, too, Banks saw as he looked at some of the designer labels.

Deborah's computer, complete with CD-ROM, sat on the desk under the window. Beside that stood a bookcase filled mostly with science and computer textbooks and a few bodice-rippers. Banks searched through all the drawers but found nothing of interest. Of course, it would have helped if he had known what he was looking for.

Arranged in custom shelving on a table by the foot of the bed were a mini-hi-fi system, a small colour television and a video— all with remote controls. Banks glanced through some of the CDs. Unlike Tracy, Deborah seemed to favour the rough, grungy style of popular music: Hole, Pearl Jam, Nirvana. A large poster of Kurt Cobain was tacked to the wall next to a smaller poster of River Phoenix.

Banks closed the door behind him and walked back down the stairs. He could hear Sylvie crying in the white room and Sir Geoffrey and Michael Clayton in muffled conversation. He couldn't hear what they were saying, and when he moved close, they saw him through the open door and asked him back in.

"I have just one more question, Sir Geoffrey, if I may?" he said.

"Go ahead."

"Did your daughter keep a diary? I know mine does. They seem to be very popular among teenage girls."

Sir Geoffrey thought for a moment. "Yes," he said, "I think so. Michael bought her one last Christmas."

Clayton nodded. "Yes. One of the leather-bound kind, a page per day."

Banks turned back to Sir Geoffrey. "Do you know where she kept it?"

He frowned. "I'm afraid I don't. Sylvie?"

Sylvie shook her head. "She told me she lost it."

"When was this?"

"About the beginning of term. I hadn't seen it for a while, so I asked her if she'd stopped writing it. Why? Is it important?"

"Probably not," said Banks. "It's just that sometimes what we don't find is as important as what we do. Trouble is, we never really know until later. Anyway, I won't bother you any further tonight."

"Inspector Stott said I'd have to identify the body," Sir Geoffrey said. "You'll make the arrangements?"

"Of course. Again, sir, my condolences."

Sir Geoffrey nodded, then he turned back to his wife. Like a butler, Banks was dismissed.

VI

What with one thing and another, it was after two in the morning when Banks parked the dark-blue Cavalier he had finally bought to replace his clapped-out Cortina in front of his house. After Hawthorn Close, it was good to be back in the normal world of semis with postage-stamp gardens, Fiestas and Astras parked in the street.

The first thing he did was tiptoe upstairs to check on Tracy. It was foolish, he knew, but after seeing Deborah Harrison's body, he felt the need to see his own daughter alive and breathing.

The amber glow from the street-lamp outside her window lit the faint outline of Tracy's sleeping figure. Every so often, she would turn and give a little sigh, as if she were dreaming. Softly, Banks closed her door again and went back downstairs to the living-room, careful to bypass the creaky third stair from the top. Despite the late hour, he didn't feel at all tired.

He turned on the shaded table lamp and poured himself a stiff Laphroaig, hoping to put the image of Deborah Harrison spread-eagled in the graveyard out of his mind.

After five minutes, Banks hadn't succeeded in getting his mind off the subject. Music would help. "Music alone with sudden charms can bind / The wand'ring sense, and calm the troubled mind," as Congreve had said. Surely it wouldn't wake Sandra or Tracy if he played a classical CD quietly?

He flipped through his quickly growing collection—he was sure that they multiplied overnight—and settled finally on Richard Strauss's *Four Last Songs*.

In the middle of the second song, "September," when Gundula Janowitz's crystalline soprano was soaring away with the melody, Banks topped up his Laphroaig and lit a cigarette.

Before he had taken more than three or four drags, the door opened and Tracy popped her head around.

"What are you doing up?" Banks whispered.

Tracy rubbed her eyes and walked into the room. She was wearing a long, sloppy nightshirt with a picture of a giant panda on the front. Though she was seventeen, it made her look like a little girl.

"I thought I heard someone in my room," Tracy muttered. "I couldn't get back to sleep so I came down for some milk. Oh, Dad! You're smoking again."

Banks put his finger to his lips. "Shhh! Your mother." He looked at the cigarette guiltily. "So I am."

"And you promised."

"I never did." Banks hung his head in shame. There was nothing like a teenage daughter to make you feel guilty about your bad habits, especially with all the anti-smoking propaganda they were brainwashed with at school these days.

"You did, too." Tracy came closer. "Is something wrong? Is that why are you're up so late smoking and drinking?"

She sat on the arm of the sofa and looked at him, sleep-filled eyes full of concern, long blonde hair straggling over her narrow shoulders. Banks's son, Brian, who was away studying architecture in Portsmouth, took after his father, but Tracy took after her mother.

They had come a long way since the bitter arguments over her first boyfriend, long since dumped, and too many late nights over the summer. Now Tracy had determined not to have a boyfriend at all this year, but to put all her efforts into getting good A-level results so she could go to university, where she wanted to study history. Banks couldn't help but approve. As he looked at her perching so frail and vulnerable on the edge of the sofa his heart swelled with pride in her, and with fear for her.

"No," he said, getting up and patting her head. "There's nothing wrong. I'm just an old fool set in his ways, that's all. Shall I make us both some cocoa?"

Tracy nodded, then yawned and stretched her arms high in the air.

Banks smiled. Gundula Janowitz sang Hermann Hesse's words. Banks had listened to the songs so many times, he knew the translation by heart:

The day has tired me,
and my spirits yearn
for the starry night
to gather them up
like a tired child.

You can say that again, thought Banks. He looked back at Tracy as he walked to the kitchen. She was examining the small-print CD liner notes with squinting eyes trying to make out the words.

She would find out soon enough what had happened to Deborah Harrison, Banks thought. It would be all over town tomorrow. But not tonight. Tonight father and daughter would enjoy a quiet, innocent cup of cocoa in the middle of the night in their safe, warm house floating like an island in the fog.

TWO

I

Chief Constable Jeremiah Riddle was already pacing the lino when Banks arrived at his office early the next morning. Bald head shining like a new cricket ball freshly rubbed on the bowler's crotch, black eyes glowing like a Whitby jet, clean-shaven chin jutting out like the prow of a boat, uniform sharply creased, not a speck of fluff or cotton anywhere to be seen, and a poppy placed ostentatiously in his lapel, he looked alert, wide-awake and ready for anything.

Which was more than Banks looked, or felt for that matter. All told, he had got no more than about three hours' uneasy sleep, especially as an early telephone call from Ken Blackstone had woken him up. Though the fog was quickly turning to drizzle this morning, he had walked the mile to work simply to get the cobwebs out of his brain. He wasn't sure whether he had succeeded. It didn't help that his cold was getting worse, either, filling his head with damp cotton wool.

"Ah, Banks, about bloody time," said Riddle.

Banks removed his headphones and switched off the Jimi Hendrix tape he had been listening to. The breakneck arpeggios of "Pali Gap" were still ringing in his stuffed-up ears.

"And do you have to go around with those bloody things stuck in your ears?" Riddle went on. "Don't you know how silly you look?"

Banks knew a rhetorical question when he heard one.

"I suppose you're aware who the victim's father is?"

"Sir Geoffrey Harrison, sir. I talked to him last night."

"In that case you'll realize how important this is. This … this … terrible tragedy." Never at a loss for a cliché wasn't Jimmy Riddle,

Banks reflected. Riddle slid his hand over his head and went on. "I want a hundred per cent on this one, Banks. No. *Two* hundred per cent. Do you understand? No shirking. No dragging of feet."

Banks nodded. "Yes, sir."

"Now what about this Bosnian fellow? Jurassic, is it?"

"Jelačić, sir. And he's Croatian."

"Whatever. Think he's our man?"

"We'll certainly be talking to him. Ken Blackstone has just reported that Jelačić's known to the Leeds police. Drunk and disorderly, one charge of assault in a pub. And he didn't get home until after two this morning. They've got his prints, so we should be able to compare them if Vic gets anything from the vodka bottle."

"Good." Riddle grinned. "That's the kind of thing I like to hear. I want a quick arrest on this one, Banks. Sir Geoffrey's a personal friend of mine. Do you understand?"

"Yes, sir."

"Right. And take it easy on the family. I don't want you pestering them in their time of grief. Am I clear?"

"Yes, sir."

Riddle straightened his uniform, which didn't need it, and brushed imaginary dandruff from his shoulders. Wishful thinking, Banks guessed. "Now I'm off to give a press conference," he said. "Anything I ought to know to stop me looking a prize berk?"

Nothing could stop you from looking like a prize berk, Banks thought. "No, sir," he said. "But you might like to drop by the murder room and see if there's anything fresh come in."

"I've already done that. What do you think I am, a bloody moron?"

Banks let the silence stretch.

Riddle kept pacing, though he seemed to have run out of things to say for the present. At last he headed for the door. "Right, then. Remember what I said, Banks," he said, pointing a finger. "Results. Fast."

Banks felt himself relax and breathe easier when Riddle had gone, like a Victorian lady when she takes her corsets off. He had read about "Type A" personalities in a magazine article—all push and shove, ambition and self-importance, and bloody exhausting to be in the same room with.

Banks lit a cigarette, read the reports on his desk and looked at the *Dalesman* calendar on his wall. November showed the village of Muker, in Swaledale, a cluster of grey limestone buildings cupped in a valley of muted autumn colours. He walked over to the window where the early morning light was leaking through the cloud cover like dirty dishwater.

The market square, with its Norman church to his left, bank, shops and cafés opposite and Queen's Arms to the right, was a study in slate-grey, except for one bright red Honda parked by the weathered market cross. Banks watched a bent old lady hobble across the cobbles under a black umbrella. He checked his watch with the church tower clock: five to eight, time to gather his papers and head for the morning meeting.

DI Stott was already waiting and raring to go in the "Boardroom," so called because of its well-polished oval table, ten matching stiff-backed chairs and dark-burgundy wallpaper above the wainscoting.

Detective Constable Susan Gay arrived two minutes later. Her make-up almost hid the bags under her eyes, the gel made her short curly hair look as if it were still wet from the shower, and her subtle perfume brought a whiff of spring to the room.

Detective Sergeant Jim Hatchley, big and heavy, like a rugby prop-forward gone to seed, came in last. He hadn't freshened up. His face looked like a lump of dough with tufts of stubble sticking out of it, his eyes were bloodshot and his strawy hair uncombed. His navy-blue suit was creased and shiny.

"Okay," said Banks, shuffling the papers in front of him, "we've got two new pieces of information to deal with. I'd hesitate to call them leads, but you never know. First off, for what it's worth, one of our diuretically challenged constables found the missing underwear while nipping behind a handy yew to drain the dragon. They're with the rest of her clothing at the mortuary. The second item might be even more significant," he went on. "Some of you may already know that a Croatian refugee called Ive Jelačić was recently fired by Daniel Charters, vicar of St Mary's, and subsequently brought charges of sexual harassment against him. By the sound of it, this Jelačić's an unsavoury character. According to West Yorkshire CID, Mr Jelačić didn't get home until after two o'clock last night, plenty of time to get back from committing a murder in Eastvale, even in the fog. He said he'd been playing cards with some fellow countrymen at a friend's house."

Hatchley grunted. "These foreigners would lie as soon as look at you," he said. "Especially to cover up for one another."

"West Yorkshire CID are already checking it out," Banks went on, "but I'm afraid Detective Sergeant Hatchley has, in his inimitable fashion, probably put his finger on the truth of the matter. So we'll take this alibi with a large pinch of salt. DI Blackstone said they'll sit on Jelačić until we get there. I think we'll let him sweat for a couple more hours.

"Now we don't have anything in from the lab yet, but from my observations of the scene, what we've got here looks like a sex murder. There was an *arranged* quality to it all. But I want to stress *looks like*. Right now, we just don't know enough. There are several other avenues we simply can't afford to overlook." He counted them off on his fingers. "School, family, Jelačić, boyfriends and the couple at the vicarage, for starters. Rebecca Charters lied to me last night when I asked where her husband had been at the time of the crime. She gave him a false alibi and I'd like to know why he needed it, especially given the recent scandal involving him. We also need to know a lot more about Deborah Harrison's life. Not just her movements yesterday, but her interests, her activities, her sex life, if she had one, and her past. We need to know what made her tick, what kind of person she was. Any questions?"

They all shook their heads.

"Good. Barry, I'd like you and Sergeant Hatchley to spend the morning going through the records of all known sex offenders in the county. You know the procedure. If anyone sounds likely, make enquiries. After that, ask around at some of the restaurants and cafés in the St Mary's area, places that might have been closed after eight or nine last night, when the uniforms did their house-to-house. You never know, our man might have stopped off for a cup of tea on his way to the graveyard."

Stott nodded.

"And, I'd also like you to try and find out anything you can about Jelačić from records, immigration, wherever. Does he have form back home? Has he ever committed a sex offence of any kind there?"

Stott scribbled notes on his pad.

"Susan, I'd like you to team up with me and check out a few things closer to home. For a start we've got to find out exactly what Deborah's movements were yesterday, who saw her last. Okay?"

"Yes, sir."

"So if there's nothing else," Banks said, "let's get on with it. Everyone check in with the murder room at regular intervals."

Given their tasks, they drifted away. Except DC Susan Gay, who topped up her milky coffee and sat down again.

"Why me, sir?" she asked.

"Pardon?"

"Why am I teamed up with you on this? I'm only a DC. By rights it should—"

"Susan, whatever your rank, you're a good detective. You've proved that often enough. Think about it. Taking Jim Hatchley around to a girls' school, a vicarage and Sir Geoffrey Harrison's … It would be like letting a bull loose in a china shop."

Susan's lips twitched in a smile. "What exactly will we be doing?"

"Talking to the family, friends, teachers. Trying to find out if this isn't just the sex murder it seems, and if someone had a *reason* to want Deborah Harrison dead."

"Are you going to check her parents' alibis?"

Banks paused for a moment, then said, "Yes. Probably."

"The chief constable won't like it, will he?"

"Won't like what?"

"Any of it. Us going around poking our noses into the Harrison family background."

"Maybe not."

"I mean, it's pretty common knowledge around the station that they're in the same funny-handshake brigade, sir. The chief constable and Sir Geoffrey, that is."

"Oh, is it?"

"So rumour has it, sir."

"And you're worried about your career."

"Well, I've passed my sergeant's exam, as you know. I'm just waiting for an opening. I mean, I'm with you all the way, sir, but I wouldn't want to make enemies in the wrong places, not just at the moment."

Banks smiled. "Don't worry," he said, "it's my balls on the chopping-block, not yours. I'll cover you. My word on it."

Susan smiled back. "Well, that's the first time not having any balls has ever done me any good."

II

When she woke up shortly after eight o'clock on Tuesday morning, Rebecca Charters felt the hammering pain behind her eyes that signalled another hangover.

It hadn't always been like this, she reminded herself. When she had married Daniel twelve years ago, he had been a dynamic young cleric. She had loved his passionate faith and his dedication just as she had loved his sense of humour and his joy in the sensual world. Lovemaking had always been a pleasure for both of them. Until recently.

She got up, put on her dressing-gown against the chill and walked over to the window. When they had first moved to St Mary's six years ago, her friends had all said how depressing and unhealthy it would be living in a graveyard. Just like the Brontës, darling, they said, and look what happened to them.

But Rebecca didn't find it at all depressing. She found it strangely comforting and peaceful to consider the worms seething at their work just below the overgrown surface. It put things in perspective. It also reminded her of that Marvell poem Patrick had quoted for her just on the brink of their affair, when things could have gone either way:

But at my back I always hear
Time's wingèd chariot hurrying near;
And yonder all before us lie
Deserts of vast eternity.

Thy beauty shall no more be found;
Nor, in thy marble vault, shall sound
My echoing song; then worms shall try
That long preserv'd virginity:
And your quaint honour turn to dust;
And into ashes all my lust.
The grave's a fine and private place,
But none I think do there embrace.

What an easy seduction it had been, after all. The poem worked. Marvell would have been proud of himself.

Rebecca pulled back the curtain. Some fog still drifted around the yew trunks and the heavy grey headstones, but the drizzle seemed to have settled in now. From her window, she could see uniformed policemen methodically searching the ground around the church in a grid pattern.

Deborah Harrison. She had often seen Deborah taking a short cut through the churchyard; she had also seen her in church and at choir practice, too, before the trouble began.

Deborah's father, Sir Geoffrey, had deserted St Mary's at the first hint of a scandal. The school had stuck with Daniel, but Sir Geoffrey, to whom appearances were far more important than truth, had made a point of turning his back, taking his family and a number of other wealthy and influential members of the congregation with him. And St Mary's was the wealthiest parish in Eastvale. Had been. Now the coffers were emptying fast.

Rebecca rested her forehead against the cool glass and watched her breath mist up the window. She found herself doodling Patrick's name with her fingernail and felt the need for him burn in her loins. She hated herself for feeling this way. Patrick was ten years younger than she was, a mere twenty-six, but he was so ardent, so passionate, always talking so excitedly about life and poetry and love. Though she needed him, she hated her need; though she determined every day to call it off, she desired nothing more than to lose herself completely in him.

Like the drinking, Patrick was an escape; she had enough self-knowledge to work that out, at any rate. An escape from the poisoned atmosphere at St Mary's, from what she and Daniel had become, and, as she admitted in her darkest moments, an escape from her own fears and suspicions.

Now this. It didn't make sense, she tried to convince herself. Daniel couldn't possibly be a murderer. Why would he want to murder someone as innocent as Deborah Harrison? Just because you feared a person might be guilty of one thing, did that mean he had to be guilty of something else, too?

As she watched the policemen in their capes and wellingtons poke through the long grass, she had to face the facts: Daniel had come home only *after* she had gone to see the angel; he had gone out *before* she thought she heard the scream; she hadn't known where he was, and when he came back his shoes were muddy, with leaves and gravel stuck to their soles.

III

The mortuary was in the basement of Eastvale General Infirmary, an austere Victorian brick building with high draughty corridors and wards that Susan had always thought were guaranteed to make you ill if you weren't already.

The white-tiled post-mortem room, though, had recently been modernized, as if, she thought, the dead somehow deserved a healthier environment than the living.

Chilled by the cooling unit rather than by the wind from outside, it had two shiny metal tables with guttered edges and a long lab bench along one wall, with glass-fronted cabinets for specimen jars. Susan had never dared ask about the two jars that looked as if they contained human brains.

Dr Glendenning's assistants had already removed Deborah Harrison's body from its plastic bag, and she lay, clothed as she had been in the graveyard, on one of the tables.

It was nine o'clock, and the radio was tuned to "Wake up to Wogan." "Do we have to listen to that rubbish?" Banks asked.

"It's *normal*, Banks," said Glendenning. "That's why we have it on. Millions of people in houses all around the country will be listening to Wogan now. People who aren't just about to cut open the body of a sixteen-year-old girl. I suppose you'd like some fancy classical concert on Radio 3, wouldn't you? I can't say that the thought of performing a post-mortem to Elgar's *Enigma Variations* would do a hell of a lot for me." Glendenning stuck a cigarette in the corner of his mouth and pulled on his surgical gloves.

Susan smiled. Banks looked at her and shrugged.

The girl on the slab wasn't a human being, Susan kept telling herself. She was just a piece of dead meat, like at the butcher's. She remembered June Walker, the butcher's daughter, from school in Sheffield, and recalled the peculiar smell that always seemed to emanate from her. Odd, she hadn't thought of June Walker in years.

The smell—stale and sharp, but sweet, too—was here, all right, but it was buried under layers of formaldehyde and cigarette smoke, for both Glendenning and Banks were smoking furiously. She didn't blame them. She had once seen a film on television in which an American woman cop rubbed some Vick's or something under her nose to mask the smell of a decomposing body. Susan didn't dare do such a thing herself for fear the others would laugh at her. After all, this was Yorkshire, not America.

Still, as she watched Glendenning cut and probe at the girl's clothing, then remove it for air-drying and storage, she almost wished she were a smoker. At least that smell was easier to wash away than the smell of death; that seemed to linger in her clothes and hair for days after.

Deborah's panties lay in a plastic bag on the lab bench. They weren't at all like the navy-blue knickers, the "passion-killers," that Susan had worn at school, but expensive, silky and rather sexy black panties. Maybe such things were *de rigueur* for St Mary's girls, Susan thought. Or had Deborah been hoping to impress someone? They still didn't know if she'd had a boyfriend.

Her school blazer lay next to the panties in a separate bag, and beside that lay her satchel. Vic Manson, the fingerprints expert, had sent it back early that morning, saying he had found clear prints on one of the vodka bottles but only blurred partials on the smooth leather surface of the satchel. DI Stott had been through

Deborah's blazer pockets and found only a purse with six pounds thirty-three pence in it, an old chewing-gum wrapper, her house keys, a cinema ticket stub and a half-eaten roll of Polo mints.

After one of his assistants had taken photographs, Glendenning examined the face, noting the pinpoint haemorrhages in the whites of the eyes, eyelids and skin of the cheeks. Then he examined the weal on the neck.

"As I said last night," he began, "it looks like a clear case of asphyxia by ligature strangulation. Look here."

Banks and Susan bent over the body. Susan tried not to look into the eyes. Glendenning's probe indicated the discoloured weal around the front of the throat. "Whoever did this was pretty strong," he said. "You can see how deeply the strap bit into the flesh. And I'd say our chappie was a good few inches taller than his victim. And she was tall for her age. Five foot six." He turned to Susan. "That's almost 168 centimetres, to the younger generation. See how the wound is deeper at the bottom, the way it would be if you were pulling a leather strap upwards?" He moved away and demonstrated on one of the assistants. "See?" Banks and Susan nodded.

"Are you sure the satchel strap was the weapon?" Banks asked.

Glendenning nodded. He picked it up and held it out. "You can see traces of blood on the edge here, where it broke the skin. We're having it typed, of course, but I'd put money on this being your weapon."

Next, he set about removing the plastic bags that covered the hands. Gently—almost, Susan thought, like a manicurist—he held up each hand and peered at the fingernails. Deborah's nails had been quite long, Susan noticed, not the bitten-to-the-quick mess hers had been when she was at school.

When Glendenning got to the middle finger of her right hand, he murmured to himself, then took a shiny instrument from the tray and ran it under the top of the nail, calling to one of his assistants for a glassine envelope.

"What is it?" Banks asked. "Did she put up a fight?"

"Looks like she got at least one good scratch in. With a bit of luck we'll be able to get DNA from this."

Passing quickly over the chest and stomach, Glendenning next picked up a probe and turned his attention to the pubic region. Susan looked away; she didn't want to witness this indignity, and she didn't care what anyone said or thought of her.

But she couldn't shut out the sound of Glendenning's voice.

"Hmm. Interesting," he said. "No obvious signs of sexual interference. No bruising. No lacerations. Let's have a look behind."

He flipped the body over; it slapped against the table like meat on a butcher's block. Susan heard her heart beating fast and loud during the silence that followed.

"No. Nothing," Glendenning announced at last. "At least nothing obvious. I'm waiting for the test results on the swabs but I'd bet you a pound to a penny they'll turn up nothing."

Susan turned back to face the two of them. "So she wasn't raped?" she asked.

"Doesn't look like it," Glendenning answered. "Of course, we won't know for sure until we've had a good look around inside. And in order to do that ..." He picked up a large scalpel.

Glendenning bent over the body and started to make the Y incision from shoulders to pubes. He detoured around the tough tissue of the navel with a practised flick of the wrist.

"Right," said Banks, turning to Susan. "We'd better go."

Glendenning looked up from the gaping incision and raised his eyebrows. "Not staying for the rest of the show?"

"No time. We don't want to be late for school."

Glendenning looked at the corpse and shook his head. "Can't say I blame you. Some days I wish I'd stayed in bed."

As they left Glendenning to sort through the inner organs of Deborah Harrison, Susan had never felt quite so grateful to Banks in her life. Next time they were in the Queen's Arms, she vowed she would buy him a pint. But she wouldn't tell him why.

THREE

I

St Mary's School wasn't exactly Castle Howard, but it certainly looked impressive enough to be used as a location in a BBC classic drama.

Banks and Susan turned through the high, wrought-iron gates and drove along a winding driveway; sycamores flanked both sides, laying down a carpet of rust and gold leaves; double-winged seeds spun down like helicopter blades in the drizzle.

Through the trees, they first glimpsed the imposing grey stone building, with its central cupola, high windows and columns flanking the front entrance. Statues stood on the tops of the columns, against a frieze, and double stairs curled out at the front like lobster claws.

St Mary's School for Girls, Banks had read, was founded in 1823 on forty acres of woodland by the River Swain. The main building, completed in 1773, had been intended as a country house but had never been lived in. Rumour had it that Lord Satterthwait, for whom the house had been built, lost much of his fortune in an ill-advised business venture abroad, along with the money of a number of other county luminaries, and was forced to flee the area in disgrace for America.

The grounds were quiet this morning, but a group of girls in maroon blazers saw Banks pull up and started whispering among themselves. The car was unmarked, but Banks and Susan were strangers, and by now everyone must know that Deborah Harrison had been murdered.

Banks asked one of the girls where they might find the head, and she directed him through the front door, right down to the back of the building, then along the last corridor to the right. Inside, the place was all high, ornate ceilings and dark, polished wainscoting. Susan's footsteps echoed as they walked. It was certainly a far cry from the institutional gloom of Eastvale Comprehensive, or from Banks's old redbrick school in Peterborough, for that matter.

They walked along the narrow corridor, noting the gilt-framed paintings of past heads on the walls. Most of them were men. When they reached the door marked "Dr JS Green: Principal," Banks knocked sharply.

Expecting to be asked into an anteroom and vetted by a secretary first, Banks was surprised when he and Susan found themselves in the head's office. Like the rest of the building, it had a high ceiling with elaborate cornices, but there its ancient character ended.

The wainscoting, if there had been any, had been removed and the walls were papered in an attractive Laura Ashley print. A shaded electric light hung from the old chandelier fixture, and several gun-metal filing cabinets stood against the wall. The bay window dominated the room, its window seat scattered with cushions that matched the wallpaper. The view through the trees to the river, Banks noticed, was magnificent, even on a drizzly November morning. Across the river was St Mary's Park, with its pond, trees, benches and children's playground.

"What do you think?" Dr Green asked, after they had introduced themselves and shaken hands.

"Pardon?" said Banks.

She took their raincoats and hung them on a rack in the corner. "I couldn't help but notice that you were 'casing the joint' as they say," she said.

"Hardly," said Banks. "That's what the bad guys do."

She blushed slightly. "Oh, dear. My gaffe. I suppose criminal parlance is not my forte."

Banks smiled. "Just as well. Anyway, it's very nice."

The tall, elegant Dr Julia Green looked every bit as Laura Ashley as her walls. The skirt and waistcoat she wore over her white blouse were made of heavy cloth; earth colours dominated, browns and greens, mixed with the odd flash of muted pink or yellow, like wildflowers poking their way through the undergrowth.

Her ash-blonde hair lay neatly piled and curled on her head, with only one or two loose strands. She had a narrow face, high cheekbones and a small nose. There was also a remote, unattainable quality about her that intrigued Banks. She might be one of the pale and distant beauties, but there was no mistaking the sharp glint of intelligence in her apple-green eyes. Right now, they also looked red from crying.

"This is a terrible business," she said. "Though I suppose you have to deal with it all the time."

"Not often," said Banks. "And you never get used to it."

"Please, sit down."

Banks and Susan sat in the two chairs opposite the small, solid desk. Susan took her notebook out.

"I don't know how I can help you," Dr Green went on, "but I'll do my best."

"Maybe you could start by telling us what kind of a girl Deborah was."

She rested her hands on the desk, tapered fingers laced together. "I can't tell you very much," she said. "Deborah is ... was ... a day-girl. Do you know how the system works?"

"I don't know much about public schools at all."

"*Independent* school," she corrected him. "Public school sounds so Victorian, don't you think? Well, you see, we have a mix of day-girls and boarders. The actual balance changes slightly from year to year, but at the moment, we have 65 day-pupils and 286 boarding. When I say that Deborah was a day-girl I don't describe her status in any way, just note the simple fact that she came and went each day, so one didn't develop any special relationship with her."

"Relationship?"

"Yes. Well, when you live in such close proximity to the pupils, you're bound to get to know more about them, aren't you?"

"In what way?"

"In any number of ways. Whether it be the crisis of Elizabeth's first period, Meredith's parents' divorce or Barbara's estrangement from her mother. These things can't help but come out from time to time with the boarding pupils."

"So you'd soon find out who's a troublemaker, for example?"

"Yes. Not that we have any troublemakers. Nothing serious, anyway. We did catch one girl smoking marijuana in the dorm last year, and some years ago one of our upper-sixth girls got pregnant. But these are extremes, you understand, quite rare."

"Have you ever had any inkling of widespread problems here?"

"Such as what?"

"Drugs, perhaps, or pornography."

"Chief Inspector, this isn't a comprehensive, you know."

"Perhaps not. But girls will be girls."

"I don't know what you mean by that, but to answer your question, no, there's been nothing of that nature at St Mary's."

"Do you live on the school grounds?"

Dr Green nodded. "There's a small block of flats for members of staff—for some of us, anyway—and I live there."

"Alone?"

"Yes. Alone."

"So what can you tell me about Deborah Harrison?"

Dr Green shrugged. "Just superficial things, really. She was a bright girl. Very intelligent. I don't think there's much doubt she would have ended up at Oxford or Cambridge, had she lived."

"Where did her strengths lie?"

"She was something of an all-rounder, but she excelled in the sciences—maths and physics, in particular. She was also good at modern languages. She had just entered the lower sixth this year. The school offers twenty-three subjects at A-level. Deborah was taking four: mathematics, French, German and physics."

"What about her personality?"

Dr Green leaned back and put her hands on the arms of her chair. "Again, I can only be fairly superficial."

"That's all right."

"She always seemed cheerful and lively. You know, some girls can get very moody and withdrawn in the lower sixth—they go through a very difficult period in their lives—but Deborah seemed to be outgoing. She was an outstanding athlete. Swimming, tennis, running, field events. She was a good equestrian, too."

"I understand she belonged to the chess club?"

"Yes. She was a fine player. A superb strategist."

"You sound as if you play, yourself."

She smiled. "Moderately well."

"I'd appreciate it if you could provide me with a list of the other members."

"Of course." Dr Green searched through one of the filing cabinets and handed Banks a sheet of paper with ten names on it. Then she paused, scratched her cheek, and said, "I must admit, Chief Inspector, the questions you're asking surprise me."

"They do? Why?"

"Well, I know nothing of police work, of course, but I fail to understand why you should require my impressions of Deborah in order to apprehend the criminal who attacked and murdered her."

"What kind of questions do you think I should be asking?"

She frowned. "I don't know. About strangers in the area, that sort of thing."

"Have you noticed any suspicious strangers hanging around the area lately?"

"No."

Banks blew his nose. "Sorry. Well, that covers that one, doesn't it? Now, what about Deborah's faults?"

"Faults?"

"Yes, was she mischievous, disobedient, dishonest, wilful?"

"No more than any other child of her age. Less than most, actually." She thought for a moment. "No, I'd say if Deborah did have a fault it was that she tended to show off her abilities to some extent. She could sometimes make the other girls feel small, or awkward and clumsy. She had a tendency to belittle people."

"Was she boastful?"

"Not at all. No, that's not what I mean. She never boasted about her abilities, she just used them to the full. She wasn't the kind to hide her light under a bushel. Half the time it was as if she didn't even realize she was so much brighter and more fortunate than many. She liked the way her quickness with figures impressed people, for example, so she would add up or multiply things in her head quicker than some of the other girls could do it with a calculator."

"That's one good way to make enemies." Banks remembered his

own school maths reports: *Could do better than this; Harder work needed; Watch that arithmetic!*

"It was hardly serious," Dr Green went on, shrugging. "Simply a matter of girlish exuberance, a young woman taking full joy in her talents." Her eyes sparkled for a moment. "Have you forgotten what it was like to be young, to be popular, gifted?"

"I don't know that I was ever gifted or popular," Banks said, with a sidelong glance at Susan, who was smiling down into her notebook. "But I do remember what it was like to be young. I thought I would live forever."

After the awkward silence that followed, Banks asked, "Was Deborah popular with the other girls?"

"What do you mean?"

"She sounds like a right little madam to me, a proper pain in the neck. I was wondering how she got on with her classmates."

"Really, Chief Inspector," Dr Green said through tight lips. "These were very minor faults I'm talking about. Mostly, Deborah was friendly, cheerful and helpful."

"Was there any friend in particular?"

"Yes. Megan Preece. Her name's on the list I gave you."

"I understand from Daniel Charters," Banks went on, "that there was some trouble with Ive Jelačić, the sexton."

"Yes." Julia Green rubbed her cheek. "He'd been bothering the girls. Saying things, making lewd gestures, that sort of thing."

"Had Deborah, in particular, complained about him?"

"I believe she had."

"Did she continue going to the church after Mr Jelačić made his accusations against Daniel Charters? It was my impression that her father seemed more upset about what Charters had been accused of, rather than what Jelačić *did*."

Julia Green paused for a moment, then said. "Yes, yes he was. I don't understand it myself. The school stands one hundred per cent behind Father Charters, but Sir Geoffrey forbade Deborah from singing with the choir or attending any services."

"Why do you think he did that?"

"I don't know. Some people are just ... well, very funny about any hint of homosexuality in the ministry."

"Did Deborah obey him?"

"As far as I know she did. I never saw her there, anyway."

"Did Deborah keep any of her belongings here at school?"

"All the girls have desks."

"No lockers or anything?"

She shook her head. "Not the day-girls. They bring what they need from day to day, mostly."

"Might we have a look?"

"Of course. We've cancelled classes for the day, so the room should be empty."

She led them through a maze of high corridors to a small room. It wasn't like any classroom Banks had even seen before, with its well-polished woodwork and nicely spaced desks.

"This one," said Dr Green, pointing to a desk.

Banks lifted the hinged flap. He hadn't expected much—school desks are hardly the most private of places—but he was disappointed by how little there was: a couple of school exercise books, a computer magazine, textbooks, pens and pencils. There was also a tattered paperback Jeffrey Archer. Deborah's intelligence obviously hadn't stretched as far as her literary taste.

Under the flap, Deborah had taped a photograph of a scruffy pop star Banks didn't recognize.

Dr Green saw it and said, with a smile, "We discourage such things, but what can you do?"

Banks nodded. Then he examined the desk surface to see if Deborah had carved any initials, the way he had at school. Again, nothing. Strongly discouraged, no doubt.

"Thanks," he said to Dr Green. "Can we have a word with Megan Preece now? Is she here?"

Dr Green nodded. After stopping back at her office for their raincoats and her umbrella, she led them outside.

"Where are we going?" Banks asked.

"The school infirmary. That's where Megan is. I'm afraid she had rather a nasty turn when I broke the news in assembly this morning."

II

The brick shattered the vicarage window at nine-thirty that morning, waking Rebecca from the uneasy doze she had slipped into after taking three aspirin and a glass of water.

At first she lay there terrified, fearing that someone had broken in. Then, slowly, so as not to make the bedsprings creak, she sat up, ears pricked for any sounds. But nothing came.

She put on her dressing-gown and looked out of the bedroom window. Nothing but the drizzle on the trees and graves, and policemen in capes searching the grounds. She tiptoed downstairs, and when she got to the front room she saw the damage.

Shards of glass lay all over the floor, and some had even got as far as the sofa and coffee-table. The brick had clearly been thrown from the river path, beyond the small garden, an area that was unguarded because it didn't provide access to the graveyard.

The brick had bounced off the coffee-table and ended up in the far corner by the sideboard. It had a piece of paper wrapped around it, fixed by a rubber band. Slowly, Rebecca bent, picked up the brick and unfolded the paper:

Once you let the devil into your heart he will corrupt every cell in your body and this is what has happened it is clear. You must confess your sins. It is the only way. Or else we must take things into our own hands.

Someone knocked at the back door. Crumpling the note in her pocket, Rebecca gathered her dressing-gown around her and went to see who it was.

"Is everything all right, ma'am?" asked one of the uniformed constables who had been searching the graveyard. "I thought I heard breaking glass."

"You did," Rebecca said. "But everything's fine. Just a little domestic accident."

"Are you sure?"

"Yes." Rebecca started closing the door on him. "Thank you, everything's fine." When she had shut the door she leaned her back against it and listened. In a few seconds, she heard his footsteps going along the path.

She took out a dustpan and broom and busied herself sweeping up the glass, wondering what she could use to cover the broken window before she caught a chill and died. Maybe that would be best for everyone, she thought. It would be very fitting, too. Hadn't Emily Brontë died after catching a chill at her brother's funeral? But no. She wasn't going to give the miserable, mean-spirited bastards the satisfaction.

Just as she was trying to tape up a piece of cardboard over the window, the phone rang.

"Can you talk?" the familiar voice asked.

"Patrick. Yes. Yes, I can."

"We've been given the day off, pupils and staff. That terrible business with the girl. It must have been especially awful for you. How are you bearing up?"

"Oh, not bad, I suppose."

"Is Daniel ... ?"

"He's out. Meeting in York. Said he couldn't get out of it."

"Could we see one another? I could come over."

"I don't know," Rebecca said, feeling herself flush with desire like a silly schoolgirl as she spoke. "No, I don't think we should. Not the way things are around here."

"But I want you."

Rebecca put her hand over the mouthpiece and took a deep breath.

"Don't you want me?" he went on.

"Of course I want you, Patrick. You know I do. It's just ... there's police all over the place."

"We could go for a drive."

Rebecca paused and looked around her. She couldn't stay here, not with this mess, not after the threatening note; she would go insane. And she couldn't deal with the police, either. On the other hand, the very thought of Patrick made her tingle. God, how she hated herself, hated the way her body could so easily betray her morality and her good intentions, how her defective conscience found ways of rationalizing it all.

"All right," she said. "But you mustn't come here. I mean it about the police. We shouldn't be seen together."

"I'll pick you up at the—"

"No. Let's meet at the hotel." She looked at her watch. "There's a bus at ten-fifteen."

"All right. I'll be waiting for you."

III

"These are the dormitories for the boarding pupils," Dr Green pointed out as they walked through the school grounds. The two large buildings ahead were of far more recent construction than the main school building, redbrick for the most part, with some stone at their bases, functional rather than aesthetically pleasing. "As I said earlier, we have 286 boarders. They have showers, central heating, all the comforts the modern child requires. You'll also notice we have installed a number of lamps along all the major pathways. They're kept on until ten o'clock every night, by which time all the girls are expected to be in bed. This isn't Lowood or Dotheboys, you realize. Parents spend a lot of money to send their children here."

"Television?"

She smiled. "Yes, that too."

"What's that building over there?" Banks pointed through the trees to a three-storey rectangular building that seemed to be made of some sort of prefabricated concrete the colour of porridge.

"That's the staff residence, I'm afraid," said Dr Green. "Ugly isn't it? Actually, it's quite nice inside. The flats are quite spacious: living-room, bedroom, storage heaters. Luxury."

"Who lives there, apart from you?"

"At the moment, six of the flats are occupied. It all depends. We have thirty members of staff, a very good ratio, and some of our teachers live in or near town. The flats are essentially for single members of staff who have recently moved into the area, or, as in my case, single teachers who want to maintain close contact with the school." She tilted her umbrella and gave Banks a challenging glance from under the rim. "You asked me rather impertinently not so long ago whether I lived alone. The school is my life, Chief Inspector. I have neither the inclination nor the time for anyone or anything else."

Banks nodded. Then he sneezed. Susan blessed him.

"Here we are," Dr Green went on, stepping under the porch of the dormitory and lowering her umbrella. She shook it carefully before rolling it up. "The infirmary is on the ground floor. We have one full-time nurse on staff and a local doctor on call."

They walked down the hall and entered the infirmary. It smelled of disinfectant. After a brief word with the nurse, Dr Green directed Banks and Susan towards a row of curtained cubicles, in one of which Megan Preece lay on a narrow bed.

"Megan's fine, nurse says," Dr Green whispered. "But she's had a terrible shock and she's been given a mild tranquillizer, so please go slowly."

Banks nodded. There clearly wasn't room for all of them in the cubicle, yet Dr Green seemed to want to stay.

"It's all right," Banks said, ushering Susan to Megan's bedside chair. "We'll find our own way out when we've finished."

Dr Green stood for a moment and frowned, then she nodded, turned on her heel and clicked away down the corridor.

When Banks found a chair for himself, Susan was already talking to Megan, reassuring her that everything would be all right. From what Banks could see of the head poking above the grey blanket, Megan was a slight, thin girl of about Deborah Harrison's age, with dark curly hair and a tanned complexion.

But Megan's features lacked whatever cohesion or symmetry it took to make her conventionally pretty, unlike her friend Deborah, who had been beautiful in that lissom, blonde, athletic sort of way. Megan's nose was a little too big, and slightly crooked; her lips were too thin, and her mouth was too small for her teeth. But her big, serious earth-brown eyes were striking; they seemed to capture you at first glance and draw you to her.

Banks introduced himself, noting that Megan seemed comfortable enough in the presence of a male policeman, and said he wanted to ask her a few questions about Deborah. Megan nodded, eyes turning a little glassy at the mention of her friend's name.

"Were you very close friends?" he began.

She nodded. "We're both day-girls and we've known each other for years. We both live in the same area."

"I thought you must be boarding," said Banks. "Why aren't you at home?"

"I had a dizzy spell at assembly, then I ... I got all upset. Nurse says I should rest here for a while, then I can go home at lunch-time. There'll be nobody there, anyway. Mummy's away in America and Daddy's at work."

"I see. Now can you tell me what happened yesterday after the chess club. Go as slowly as you want, there's no hurry."

Megan chewed her lower lip, then began, "Well, when we'd put all the boards and pieces away in the cupboard and made sure the room was tidy, we left the school—"

"Was this the main building?"

"Yes. We hold the chess club in one of the upstairs classrooms."

"What time?"

"Just before six o'clock."

"How many attended last night?"

"Only eight. Lesley and Carol are doing a play with the theatre department, so they had rehearsals. The others are all boarders."

"I see. Was there anyone else around?"

"A few people, coming and going, as usual. The school is always well lit and there are always people around."

"Okay. Go on."

"Well, we walked down the drive to Kendal Road. There's only one main gate, you see. The school's surrounded by woods, and there's the river on the west side. It was so foggy we could hardly see the trees around us. I must admit I was getting a bit scared, but Debs seemed to be enjoying herself."

"What do you mean?"

"Oh, she liked things like that. Spooky things. She liked to tell ghost stories in graveyards, just for fun."

"Do you know if she ever went inside the Inchcliffe Mausoleum?"

"She never said anything to me about it if she did."

"Okay. Go on."

"We crossed the road. I live on St Mary's Hill, behind the shops, so Debs and I always said goodbye at the bridge." She put her hand over her eyes.

"Take it easy," Susan said. "Take your time." When Banks looked down, he noticed that Megan was gripping Susan's hand at the side of the bed.

Megan took a deep breath and went on. "That's all," she said. "We said goodbye. Debs was running backwards, just showing off, like, then she disappeared into the fog." She frowned.

"Was there something else?" Banks asked. "Did you notice anyone else around?"

"Well, like I said, it was so foggy you couldn't really see more than a few feet, but I saw a shape behind her. I remember thinking at the time there was something odd about it, but I put it down to the way Debs had been scaring me with her stories of ghosts taking shape from the fog."

"You mean you thought you were imagining it?"

"Yes. Seeing things. But I know I wasn't, if that makes any sense."

"You're doing fine, Megan. What kind of shape was it?"

"It was a man's shape. A tall man."

"What was he doing?"

"Nothing. He was just standing on the bridge looking down the river towards the town." She paused and her eyes lit up. "That's it. That's what was strange. He was looking over the bridge towards the town, but he couldn't possibly see anything, could he, because of the fog. So why was he standing there?"

"Did you think that at the time?"

"No. It just came to me."

"Did you see what he looked like?"

"Not really, because of the fog. I mean, he was like a silhouette, a dark figure. His features weren't clear, and he was in profile. He did have a bit of a big nose, though."

"Could you see what he was wearing?"

"An anorak, I think. A bright colour. Orange or red, maybe."

"Did you see him approach Deborah?"

"No. He was just behind her. I don't think she'd seen him because she was still running backwards and waving goodbye. I remember thinking if she wasn't careful she'd bump into him and that would give her a shock, but I really didn't think much of it. I mean, it wasn't the only person we'd seen."

"Who else did you see?"

"Just ordinary people, you know, crossing the road and such. I mean, life goes on, doesn't it? Just because it's foggy you can't stop doing everything, can you?"

"That's true," said Banks. "Can you remember anything else?"

Megan squeezed her eyes shut. "I think he had dark hair," she said. "Then I turned away and went home. I never thought anything of it. Until ... until this morning, when I heard ... I should have known something was going to happen, shouldn't I?"

"How could you?"

"I just should. Poor Debs. It could have been me. It *should* have been me."

"Don't be silly, Megan."

"But it's true! Debs was so good, so wonderful and pretty and talented. And just look at me. I'm nothing. I'm not pretty. She should have lived. I'm the one who should have died. It's not fair. Why does God always take the best?"

"I don't know the answer to that," Banks replied softly. "But I do know that *every* life is important, every life has its value, and *nobody* has the right to decide who lives and who dies."

"Only God."

"Only God," Banks repeated, and blew his nose in the ensuing silence.

Megan took a tissue from the box on the table beside her and wiped her eyes. "I must look a sight," she said.

Banks smiled. "Just like me first thing in the morning," he said. "Now, when we found Deborah, she had about six pounds in her purse. Did she ever have a lot of money to flash around?"

"Money? No. None of us ever carried more than a few pounds."

"Do you know if she kept anything valuable in her satchel?"

Megan frowned. "No. Just the usual stuff. Exercise books, text-books, that sort of thing."

"Did she say if she was intending to meet anyone after the chess club or go anywhere else before she went home?"

"No. As far as I know, she was going straight home."

"Can you tell us anything else about her?"

"Like what?"

"You were her best friend, weren't you?"

"Yes."

"Did you ever fall out?"

"Sometimes."

"Why?"

"Nothing, really. Maybe Debs would tease me about a lad she thought I liked, or something, or about not being good at arithmetic, and I'd get mad. But it wouldn't last long."

"Is that all?"

"Yes. She can be quite a tease, can Debs. She gets her little needle in where she knows it hurts and just keeps pushing." She put her hand to her mouth. "Oh, I didn't mean that to sound as bad as it did, honest I didn't. All I mean is that she had an eye for a weakness and she could be a bit nasty about it. It was never anything serious."

"Do you know if anything had been bothering her lately?"

"I don't think so. She'd been a bit moody, that's all."

"Since when?"

"The beginning of term."

"Did she say why?"

"No. We have a lot on our minds. A lot of work. And she's been moody before."

"She didn't mention any problems, anything that might have been worrying her?"

"No."

"Did she have any enemies, anyone who might have wanted to harm her?"

"No. Everyone loved Debs. It must have been a stranger."

"Did she even mention Mr Jelačić, the sexton at St Mary's?"

"The man who got fired?"

"That's the one."

"She said he was gross, always sticking his tongue out and licking his lips when she went past."

"Did he ever bother you?"

"I never went in the churchyard. I live this side of the river, over Kendal Road. It was a short cut for Debs."

"Are you sure Deborah didn't have any other problems, any worries? Maybe at home?"

"No. She didn't complain about anything in particular. Only the usual stuff. Too much homework. That sort of thing."

Banks realized that Deborah Harrison would probably have fewer practical causes for concern than his own daughter, Tracy, who, at one time anyway, had been constantly moaning about some new style of jacket or jeans she just had to have because everyone else was wearing it, and the Doc Martens that were just *essential* these days.

Banks had been like that himself, and he gave Tracy the same answer his mother and father gave him when they bought him a pair of heavy workboots for school instead of the thin-soled winkle-pickers he had asked for. "We can't afford it. You'll just have to make do. These will last a lot longer."

But Deborah Harrison had wanted for nothing, at least nothing that had a monetary value.

"What about boyfriends?" Banks asked.

Megan blushed. "We don't have time, not in the lower sixth. And Debs was always involved in some school event: equestrian, sports or quizzes or whatever."

"So she didn't have a boyfriend?"

"I'm not saying she *never* had one."

"When was the last one?"

"In the summer."

"What was his name?"

"She told me his name was John, that's all. They didn't go out together for long. She said he was really cool but too thick, so she chucked him."

"Did she tell you anything else about him?"

Megan blushed. "No."

"Are you sure?"

"Yes. That's all I know. His name was John and he was a thickie."

"Where did she meet him?"

"I don't know. She didn't say. I was away in America all summer with my parents, so I didn't see her until school started. By then she'd already chucked him."

"Was he her first boyfriend?"

"I don't think so, but there was never anyone serious."

"How do you know?"

"She would have told me."

"Does she tell you everything?"

Megan considered the question seriously for a moment or so, then said, "No, I don't think so. She can be secretive, can Debs. But she'd tell me if she had a boyfriend. Or I'd just *know*."

"Was she being secretive about anything recently?"

Megan frowned. "Yes, she was. I was getting fed up of it."

"Did she tell you anything about it?"

"No. It wouldn't be a secret then, would it?"

"Did she tell you who or what it concerned?"

Megan shook her head. "No."

"Did she say *anything* about it?"

"Just that she thought it was time to tell someone, and then to watch what happened when the sh—. Just to see what happened."

"When did she tell you this?"

"Just as she was leaving, on the bridge."

"While she was running backwards?"

"Yes. It's … it was the last thing she said." Her eyes filled with tears. "I'm tired."

"All right," said Banks. "I'm sorry, Megan. You're doing really well. I'll try not to be much longer. But you must realize how important it is. If it was a secret about somebody who didn't want it known … And if that somebody knew that Deborah knew … Do you see what I mean?"

Megan nodded.

"How long had she been talking about this secret?"

"Since the beginning of term."

"That's quite a long time."

"Yes. She'd let it drop for a week or two, then bring it up again."

"Would she have told anyone else?"

"No. I'm her *best* friend."

"Is there anything else you can tell us, Megan? Anything at all."

Megan shook her head. "I don't think so."

Banks and Susan stood up. "Get some rest now," Banks said. "And believe me, we'll be doing our best to find out who did this."

They said goodbye to the nurse, picked up their raincoats and headed out into the drizzle.

"What did you think?" Banks asked Susan as they walked back to the car.

"About Megan? I think she told us pretty much all she knew."

"Notice the way she blushed and turned her eyes away when I pushed her about the boyfriend? I'd say there's more to that relationship than she's told us."

"Well, sir," said Susan, "from my experience I'd say Deborah probably said he had his uses but he was thick."

"You think Deborah might have slept with this John?"

"She might have, but that's not what I mean. What I mean is, she'd say that, or hint that she had, the way kids do. It doesn't mean they actually *did* anything."

"And Megan was embarrassed by it?"

"Yes. I'd guess Megan is a bit shy around boys."

"Would you agree she was the ugly one in that relationship?"

"I wouldn't put it quite that way, sir."

Banks smiled. "I'm sorry. It must be something to do with being on school grounds again. It takes me back. But when you were a teenager and you met two girls, one of them was bound to be the ugly one."

"And when you met two boys, one of them was certain to be a drip and the other an octopus. If you were really lucky, you got a combination of the two."

Banks laughed.

"I'm sorry, sir," Susan went on, "I don't get your point. Surely you're not suggesting that Megan Preece had anything to do with Deborah's murder?"

"No. Of course not. Just thinking out loud, is all."

They got in the unmarked police car. When it started up, Vaughan Williams's *Suite for Viola and Orchestra* was playing on the radio: the beautiful, melancholy "Ballad." It suited the falling leaves and the November drizzle perfectly, Banks thought.

"I'm just trying to understand the relationship so that I can understand the way Deborah related to people," he said. "The way

I see it is that Megan was the less attractive of the two friends. That would probably make her adoring and resentful in equal measures. She knew she was overshadowed and outclassed by Deborah's looks and talent, and for the most part she was probably content to bask in the glory of being the chosen one, best friend of the goddess. Are you with me so far."

"Yes, sir. Megan was the kind of friend who could only make Deborah look even better."

"Right. But it also sounded as if Deborah could twist the knife, too, could be cruel. If she could annoy her best friend the way she did, then she could have angered a more dangerous enemy, don't you think?"

"It's possible, sir. But a bit far-fetched, if you don't mind me saying so. I still say we're looking for a stranger. And from what we know already, that stranger on the bridge could have been Ive Jelačić."

"True," said Banks. "It could also have been a figment of Megan's imagination, at least in part. But we'll sort out Mr Jelačić later. He's not going anywhere. Ken Blackstone's got him under surveillance. What do you think about the secret?"

"Not much. A lot of schoolkids are like that. As Megan said, it probably didn't mean anything."

"Not to her, perhaps. But maybe to someone else. Look, isn't that ..." He pointed.

As they were turning left onto North Market Street, Banks noticed a woman in a long navy raincoat standing at the bus-stop over the road.

"Isn't it who?" Susan asked.

"Oh, I forgot. You haven't met her. Rebecca Charters, the vicar's wife. I'm sure it was her. I wonder where she's going?"

"Curioser and curioser," said Susan.

FOUR

I

"Well, sir," said Sergeant Hatchley, looking at his watch. "Don't you think we might as well have a spot of lunch?"

Barry Stott sighed. "Oh, all right. Come on."

This was the detective inspector's first major case after his promotion and transfer, and he intended to make the most of it. The only thorn in the ointment was this idle, thick lump of Yorkshire blubber beside him: Detective Sergeant Hatchley.

Stott would have preferred DC Susan Gay. Not because she was prettier than Hatchley—he didn't find her attractive in that way—but because she was smarter, keener and a lot less trouble.

Like now. Left to himself, Stott would have skipped lunch, or bought a take-away from one of the cafés on North Market Street. The morning had been a waste of time; they had found no leads in the sex offender files, and all Stott could find out from immigration about Jelačić was that he was an engineer from Split, who had come to England two years ago. And since then, he had worked at a variety of odd jobs, never lasting long in any one place. Short of going to Croatia himself, Stott thought, it didn't look as if it would be an easy task getting hold of a criminal record, if there was one.

At least out here, near the crime scene, he felt he had a good chance of scoring some success. *Somebody* had to have noticed a stranger in the area, fog or no fog. Or a car parked where it shouldn't be. St Mary's was, after all, an upper-crust area, and people who could afford to live there were very wary of strangers. And Stott was sure that a stranger had murdered Deborah Harrison.

They were standing in the rain outside the Nag's Head at the north-west corner of Kendal Road and North Market Street, diagonally across from St Mary's Church, and Stott was ready to do just about anything to shut Hatchley up.

It wasn't the kind of pub you'd expect in such a wealthy area, Stott thought: no thick carpet, polished brass and gleaming wood, pot of mulled wine heating on the bar. In fact, it looked distinctly shabby. He guessed it was probably a travellers' pub, being situated at such an important junction. In one form or another, Kendal Road ran all the way from the Lake District to the east coast and Market Street was a major north-south route. The locals would have their own tasteful pubs hidden away in the residential streets. Either that or they drove out to the country clubs.

There were about six people in the lounge bar. Stott noted with distaste that the room smelled of smoke and beer. This certainly wasn't his kind of pub, if there were such a place. He far preferred churches. Pubs, as far as Stott was concerned, were simply breeding grounds for trouble.

Pubs were where fights started—and he had a couple of scars from his beat days to prove that—they were where crooked deals took place, dodgy goods traded hands, places where drugs were openly sold, where prostitutes plied their filthy trade, spreading disease and misery. Close all the pubs and you'd force the criminals into the open, right into the waiting arms of the police. At least that was what DI Barry Stott thought as he turned up his nose in the Nag's Head that lunch-time.

Sergeant Hatchley, on the other hand, looked quite at home. He rubbed his ham-like hands together and said, "Ah, this is better. Nowt like a bit of pub grub to take away the chill, don't you think, sir?"

"Let's make it quick, Sergeant."

"Yes, sir. Alf! Over here, mate. Let's have a bit of service. A person could die of thirst."

If there were a landlord Hatchley didn't know by name in all of the Eastvale—nay, all of Swainsdale—Stott would have been surprised.

When Alf finally turned up, Stott waited while he and Hatchley exchanged a few pleasantries, then ordered a ham and cheese sandwich and a cup of tea. Alf raised his eyebrows but said nothing.

"I'll have one of those bloody great big Yorkshire puddings full of roast beef, peas and gravy," said Hatchley. "And a pint of bitter, of course."

This seemed to please Alf more.

Pint in hand, Hatchley marched over to a table by the window. Through the streaked glass, they could see the rain-darkened trees in the park and the walls of St Mary's Church across the intersection, square tower poking out above the trees.

The drizzle hadn't kept the ghouls away. Here and there along the six-foot stone wall, people would jump up every now and then and hold themselves up by the fingertips for a glimpse into the graveyard.

A group of about ten people stood by the Kendal Road entrance. Journalists. One of them, a woman, stood talking into a microphone and looking into a video camera wrapped in a black plastic bag to protect it from the rain. Someone else held a bright light over her head. Yorkshire Television, Stott thought. Or BBC North. And newspaper reporters. Pretty soon they'd be doing re-enactments for "Crimewatch." Banks was right; the vultures had come.

"We haven't had much of a chance to get to know one another since you got here, have we, sir?" said Hatchley, lighting a cigarette. "And I always find it helps to know a bit about one another if you're going to work together, don't you?"

"I suppose so," said Stott, inwardly grimacing, trying to sit downwind of the drifting smoke. It didn't work. He thought it must be one of those laws, like Sod's and Murphy's: wherever a non-smoker sat, the smoke was going to come his way, no matter which way the draught was blowing.

"Where are you from, sir?" Hatchley asked.

"Spalding, Lincolnshire."

"I'd never have guessed it. Not from the accent, like."

"We moved away when I was just a boy."

"Where?"

"All over the place. Cyprus, Germany. My father was in the army." Stott remembered the misery of each move. It seemed that as soon as he had made friends anywhere, he had to abandon them and start all over again. His childhood had consisted of a never-ending succession of new groups of strangers to whom he had to prove himself. Cruel strangers with their own initiation rights, just waiting to humiliate him. He remembered the beatings, the name-calling, the loneliness.

"A squaddie, eh?"

"Major, actually."

"Pretty high up, then?" Hatchley swigged some beer. "Where does he live now?"

"Worthing. He retired a few years ago."

"Not a dishonourable discharge, I hope, sir."

"No."

"Look, sir," said Hatchley, "I've been wondering about this here inspector's exam. I've been thinking of giving it a go, like. Is it easy?"

Stott shook his head. All promotional exams were tough and involved several stages, from the multi-choice law test and the role-playing scenarios to the final oral in front of an assistant chief constable and a chief superintendent. How Hatchley had even passed the sergeant's exam was a mystery to Stott.

"Good luck," he muttered as a pasty-faced young woman delivered their food and Stott's pot of tea, which was actually just a pot of lukewarm water and a teabag on a string to dunk in it. And they were stingy with the ham, too. "About one in four get through," he added.

How old was Hatchley? he wondered. He couldn't be older than his mid-thirties. Maybe five or six years older than Stott himself. And just look at him: unfit, a bulky man with hair like straw, piggy eyes, freckles spattered across his fleshy nose, tobacco-stained teeth. He also seemed to own only one suit—shiny and wrinkled—and there were egg stains on his tie. Stott could hardly imagine Hatchley going up before the chief for his formal promotion dressed like that.

Stott prided himself on his dress. He had five suits—two grey, two navy blue and one brown herring-bone—and he wore them in rotation. If it's Thursday, it must be herring-bone. He also wore his father's old striped regimental tie and, usually, a crisply laundered white shirt with a starched collar.

He always made sure that he was clean shaven and that his hair was neatly parted on the left and combed diagonally across his skull on each side, then fixed in place with spray or cream if need be. He knew that the way his ears stuck out still made him look odd, especially with his glasses hooked over them, just as they had when he was a young boy, and that people called him names behind his back. There was an operation you could have for sticking-out ears these days, he had heard. Maybe if it wasn't too late he'd have his ears done soon. A freakish appearance could, after all, be detrimental to one's career path. And Barry Stott felt destined for the chief constable's office.

Hatchley tucked into his Yorkie with great relish, adding a gravy stain to the egg on his tie. When he had finished, he lit another cigarette, inhaled deeply and blew out the smoke with a sigh of such deep satisfaction as Stott had never encountered before over a mere physical function—and an unpleasant one at that. One of nature's true primitives, Sergeant Hatchley.

"We'd better be getting along, Sergeant," he said, pushing his plate aside and standing up.

"Can't I finish my fag first, sir? Best part of the meal, the cigarette after, if you know what I mean." He winked.

Stott felt himself flush. "You can smoke it outside," he said rather harshly.

Hatchley shrugged, slurped down the rest of his pint, then followed Stott towards the door.

"Bye, Alf," he said on the way to the door. "I hope our lads didn't catch you serving drinks after hours last night."

"What lads?" said Alf.

Hatchley turned and walked towards the bar. "Police. Didn't they come and ask you questions last night? Whether you'd seen any strangers, that sort of thing?"

Alf shook his head. "Nah. Nobody in last night. I shut up at ten o'clock. Filthy weather."

By the time Stott got to the bar, Hatchley seemed to have magically acquired another pint, and his cigarette had grown back to its original length.

Stott swallowed his anger.

"Were you open earlier?" Hatchley asked.

Alf snorted. "Aye, for what it were worth."

"Any strangers?"

"We get a lot of strangers," he said. "You know, commercial travellers and the like. Tourists. Ramblers."

"Aye, I know that," said Hatchley. "But how about yesterday, late afternoon, early evening?"

"Nah. Weather were too bad for driving."

"Anyone at all?"

Alf scratched his stubbly cheek. "One bloke. He had nobbut two pints and a whisky and left. That were it."

"A regular?"

"Nah. Don't have many regulars. People round here are too stuck-up for the likes of this place."

Stott was beginning to feel frustrated. This Alf was obviously a moron; they would get nothing useful out of him. "But you said you hadn't had any strangers in lately," he said.

"He weren't a stranger, either."

"Who was he, then?"

"Nay, don't ask me."

"But you said you knew him."

Alf looked over at Hatchley and gave a sniff of disgust before turning back to Stott and answering. "No, I didn't," he said. "I said he weren't a regular, but he weren't exactly a stranger, either. Different thing."

"So you've seen him before?"

Alf spat on the floor behind the bar. "Well, of course I bloody have. Stands to reason, doesn't it? He'd have been a stranger if I hadn't seen him before, wouldn't he?"

Hatchley took over again. "All right, Alf," he said. "You're right. Good point. How often have you seen him?"

"Not often. But he's been in three or four times this past year or so. Used to come in with a lass. A right bonnie lass, and all. But not the last few times."

"Do you know who he is?"

"No. He always stuck to himself."

"Any idea where he lives?"

"Could be bloody Timbuktu, for all I know."

"Are you saying he was African-English?" Stott cut in.

Alf gave him a withering look. "It's just a saying, like. Summat me mother used to say."

"What did he look like?" Hatchley asked.

"Well, he were a tall bloke, I remember that. A bit over six foot, anyroad. Thick black hair, a bit too long over t'collar, if you ask me. Bit of a long nose, too."

"Did you talk to him?"

"No more than to serve him and make a few remarks about the weather. He didn't seem to want to talk. Took his pint over by the fire and just sat there staring into his glass. Muttered to himself now and then, too, as I recall."

"He talked to himself?"

"Well, not all the time. And not like he was having a conversation or anything. No, he'd just say something once in a while, as if he were thinking out loud, like you do sometimes."

"Did you hear anything he said?"

"Nay. He were too far away."

"Did he have any sort of an accent?" Stott cut in.

"Couldn't say."

"Did you know Ive Jelačić, the sexton over the road at St Mary's."

"Nah. He drank at t'Pig and Whistle."

"How do you know?"

"Landlord, Stan, told me, after it was in t'papers, like, about him and that dodgy vicar."

"Did you ever see Mr Jelačić?"

"Only from a distance."

"Could this have been him?"

"Could've been, I suppose. Same height and hair colour."

"Do you know if this customer had a car?"

"How would I know that?" Alf rubbed his chin. "Come to think of it, he looked more like he'd been walking. You know, a bit damp, short of breath."

"What time was this, Alf?" Hatchley asked.

"About five o'clock."

"What time did he leave?"

"Just afore six. Like I said, he had nobbut two pints and a double whisky. One for the road, he said, and knocked it back in one, then he was out the door." Alf mimicked the drinking action.

Stott pricked up his ears. The timing worked, assuming the girl had been killed on her way home from the school chess club. Was that the way a person might act before raping and murdering a sixteen-year-old schoolgirl in a foggy graveyard? Stott wondered. A dram of Dutch courage? He tried to remember what he'd learned in the criminal psychology course.

The trouble was, you could justify just about any sort of behaviour if you were talking about a psycho. Some of them liked to sit and have a beer and a fag before a nice little dismemberment; others liked to buy a box of chocolates or bunch of flowers for their mothers. You could never predict. So maybe the killer would have dropped in at the Nag's Head. Why not? Maybe he just needed to sit there for a while, have a little chat with himself about what he was going to do?

"Did you see which direction he went?" Stott asked.

"Nay. You don't expect me to chase outside after my customers and see which way they're going, do you?"

"What was he wearing?" Stott asked.

"Orange anorak. Expensive type, by the looks of it. That Gore-Tex stuff. Lots of pockets and zips."

"Can you remember anything else about his appearance?"

"I'm not good at describing people. Never was."

"Do you think you could work with a police artist?"

"Dunno. Never tried it."

"Will you give it a try?"

Alf shrugged.

"Sergeant," Stott said, "go and see if you can get a police artist out as soon as possible, will you? I'll wait here."

It was almost worth suffering the stale smoke and booze atmosphere of the Nag's Head for another hour or so to see the expression on Sergeant Hatchley's face as he trudged out into the rain.

II

They had made love in every position imaginable: sideways, backwards, forwards, upside down. They had also done it in just about every place they could think of: her bed, his bed, hotels, a field, his cramped Orion, up against a wall, under the kitchen table. Sometimes, it seemed to last forever; other times, it was over almost before it began. Sometimes, the foreplay went on so long Rebecca thought she would burst; other times, they were overtaken by a sense of urgency and didn't even have time to get all their clothes off.

This time, it had been urgent. Afterwards, Rebecca lay on the bed of a hotel room in Richmond panting for breath, covered by a film of sweat. Her skirt was bunched up around her waist, her knickers down, still hanging around one bare ankle; her blouse was open at the front, a couple of the buttons torn off in the heat of the moment, and her bra was pushed up to expose her breasts.

Patrick's head lay against her shoulder. She could feel his breath warm against her skin. Both their hearts were beating fast. Rebecca rested one hand over his broad, strong shoulders, and with the other she stroked the hair over his ear, felt the stubbly down at the back of his neck, where it had been recently cut. It wasn't love—she knew enough to realize that—but it was one hell of a fine substitute.

But all too soon the sense of shame and melancholy that always came to her after sex with Patrick began to descend like a thick fog, numbing the nerve-ends that, only minutes before, had thrilled to such exquisite pleasure, and guilt began to overwhelm the vestiges of her joy.

Patrick moved away and reached for a cigarette. It was the one thing she disliked, his smoking after sex, but she didn't have the heart to tell him not to. He also put his glasses on. She knew he couldn't see a thing without them, but sometimes she laughed because he looked so funny naked except for his glasses.

"What is it?" Patrick asked, clearly sensing something was wrong. "Didn't you enjoy it?"

"Of course I did. You know that. I always do … with you. No … it's just that I feel so … so damn guilty."

"Then leave him. Come and live with me."

"Don't be foolish, Patrick. Just imagine the scandal. School-teacher shacks up with minister's wife. You'd lose your job, for a start. And where would we live?"

"Oh, don't be so practical. We'd manage. We'll get a flat in town. I can get another job. We'll move away."

Rebecca shook her head. "No. No. No."

"Why not? Don't you love me?"

Rebecca didn't answer.

"You do love me, don't you?" he persisted.

"Of course I do," Rebecca lied. It was easier that way.

"Then leave him."

"I can't."

"You don't love him."

"I ... I ... don't know." Rebecca *did* love Daniel. Somewhere inside her, the feeling was still there, she knew: battered, bruised, half-evaporated, but still there. She couldn't explain that to Patrick.

"I shouldn't tell you this, but ..."

Rebecca felt a tingle run up her spine at the words, nothing to do with sex. "Yes?" she prompted him. "Go on."

"Yesterday evening your husband came to see me."

"Daniel went to see you? Why?"

"He came to talk to me."

Rebecca sat up. She quickly slipped her bra down and rearranged her skirt to cover herself, holding the front of her blouse together as best she could. "What about?" she asked, feeling awkward and stupid.

"About us." Patrick flicked his ash into the ashtray on the bedside table. It was a small room, with the curtains drawn, and Rebecca already felt claustrophobic.

"But he doesn't know about us."

"Oh, but he does. He says he's known for a while. He suspected something, then he watched you. He's seen us together."

"My God."

"He told me not to tell you he'd been to see me."

"What did he want?"

"He asked me to stop seeing you."

"What did you say?"

"I told him the truth. That we were in love. That you were discovering for the first time your true erotic nature. And that as soon as we could manage it you were going to leave him and we were going to live together."

Rebecca couldn't believe what she was hearing. Daniel knew? Had known for ages? "You bloody fool." She swung her legs over the side of the bed and pulled up her knickers. Then she buttoned her blouse, put on her jacket over it and went to the wardrobe where her raincoat was hanging. "You bloody fool," she muttered again under her breath. "Daniel. I must go to him."

Patrick sat up and stubbed out his cigarette. "What do you mean? It *is* the truth, isn't it?"

"You idiot. You've ruined everything."

He got up and walked over to her. She thought he suddenly looked ridiculous with his glasses on, the limp penis hanging between his thin, hairy legs.

"Rebecca," he said, grasping her arms. "He's only concerned about how it looks. With appearances. Don't you see? He wants everything to seem normal, for you to act like the dutiful vicar's wife. But it's not you. It's really not you. I know you, Rebecca. I know your true nature. We've discovered it together. You're a wild, passionate, sensual creature, not a bloody dried-up vicar's wife."

"Let me go!"

She tore herself out of his grasp, finished putting her raincoat on and grabbed the door-handle.

"Don't do this, Rebecca," he said. "Stay with me. Don't be afraid of finding out who you really are. Follow your passion, your *feelings*."

"Oh, shut up, you pompous bastard. It was just a fuck, that's all. You don't know a bloody thing, do you?"

"Wait. I'll drive you," he called out as she walked through the door.

"Don't bother," she said over her shoulder. "I'll catch a bus." And she slammed the door behind her.

III

A couple of uniformed policemen kept the press away from Sir Geoffrey's house. When Banks and Susan got there early in the afternoon, there were only about six reporters hanging around at the end of the driveway. They fired off a few questions, but Banks ignored them. Too early to start giving statements to the press. Unless you were Chief Constable Riddle, of course.

The only new information Banks had was that the swabs taken from Deborah had revealed no traces of semen, and he certainly wasn't going to tell the media that. He had also discovered that Sir Geoffrey's reception at the Royal Hotel in York had ended at four o'clock, plenty of time to get back home by six, even in the fog. Lady Harrison had, indeed, been at the health club; but she hadn't arrived there until almost six-thirty.

Banks hadn't noticed in the fog last night, but the house had a large lawn and beautiful flower-beds, clearly the work of a gardener. Even keeping the lawn trimmed would have been a full-time job. The house itself was an ostentatious pile of Victorian stone, complete with gables, probably built for one of the get-rich-quick wool merchants in the last century.

Sir Geoffrey himself answered Banks's ring and beckoned the two of them in. Banks introduced Susan.

"Is there any news?" Sir Geoffrey asked.

Banks shook his head. "Not yet, sir. Sorry."

Sir Geoffrey looked drawn and stooped, and he had large bags, like bruises, under his eyes. Banks followed him through to the white room with the bookcases, the Chagall and the grand piano. Michael Clayton was sitting in one of the armchairs, also looking as if he had gone without sleep for a week.

"Michael, I believe you met Detective Chief Inspector Banks last night," Sir Geoffrey said.

"Yes," said Clayton, "and I know Detective Constable Gay, too. I don't know if I ever thanked you."

Susan smiled. "All part of the service, sir."

Banks gave her a quizzical look.

"Mr Clayton had his car and a valuable notebook computer

stolen in August," she explained. "We got them back for him. Someone was trying to sell the computer at Eastvale market."

"I don't think I explained last night," Sir Geoffrey went on, "but in addition to being a dear friend, Michael's the scientific genius behind HarClay Industries. I simply provide the sales and marketing strategies." He clapped Clayton on the shoulder. "I don't know what we'd do without him. Please, sit down."

"Where's your wife, sir?" Banks asked.

"Sylvie's resting. She ... we didn't get much sleep last night. She's exhausted. Me, too. Look, we ... er ... I'm sorry. Things are a bit of a mess around here. How can I help you?"

"We won't keep you long. Just a couple of questions."

Sir Geoffrey nodded wearily. "I'll do the best I can."

"Thank you," said Banks. "We've talked to a few people at Deborah's school, and everyone seems to agree that Deborah was a cheerful and talented girl."

Sir Geoffrey nodded. "Sylvie and I are very proud of her."

"But even the best of people make enemies," Banks went on. "Often inadvertently. Can you think of any enemies Deborah might have made?"

Sir Geoffrey closed his eyes and thought for a moment, then shook his head. "No. She got along well with her schoolfriends and teachers—I'm sure they'll all bear that out—and there wasn't really anyone else in her life aside from family."

"I heard that she had a tendency to show off at times. Would you say that's fair?"

Sir Geoffrey smiled. "Yes, Deborah can be a show-off, and a bit of a devil at times. But what child can't be?"

Banks smiled, thinking of Tracy. "And Deborah was still a child in some ways," he said. "She might not always have realized the effects of her actions on others. Do you see what I mean?"

Sir Geoffrey nodded. "But I can't see us getting anywhere with this," he said. "Unless you're implying that someone at the school had something to do with her death. Or that bloody minister at St Mary's."

"Daniel Charters?"

"That's the one."

"Why do you dislike him so?"

"The man's a pervert. He abused his power."

Banks shook his head. "But nothing's been proved against him. Isn't he entitled to be presumed innocent until proven guilty?"

"In theory, perhaps. But a man in his position should be above suspicion."

"The man who accused Father Charters is called Ive Jelačić. Would it surprise you to know that he made lewd gestures towards your daughter, and that she complained to Dr Green, the head of St Mary's?"

"She never told me that. If she had, I'd have broke his bloody neck."

Banks turned to Clayton. "Did Deborah ever confide in you about anything?"

Clayton raised his eyebrows. "Me? Good heavens, no. I suppose I was just as uncool as her parents as far as she was concerned."

"Uncool?"

"You know teenagers, Chief Inspector. We're ancient and decrepit creatures to them."

"I suppose we are." Banks took a deep breath and turned back to Sir Geoffrey. "This is a little delicate, I'm afraid, but I have to ask where you went after the Royal Hotel reception ended at four o'clock yesterday."

"Good God, man! You can't poss—"

"Geoff, he has to ask. He's just doing his job," said Michael Clayton, putting his hand on Sir Geoffrey's arm. "Offensive though it may be."

Sir Geoffrey ran his hand over his hair. "I suppose so. I had a private meeting with a client, if you must know. A man from the government called Oliver Jackson. It's a very confidential matter, and I don't want *anyone* else to know about the meeting. Things like this can have an effect on share prices and any number of market factors. Not to mention international affairs. Do you understand?"

Banks nodded. "There is just one more thing ..."

Sir Geoffrey sighed. "Go ahead, if you must."

"I was wondering about any boyfriends Deborah might have had."

"Boyfriends?"

"Yes. It would be perfectly natural for a girl of sixteen to have an interest in the opposite sex. Perfectly innocent things, like going to the pictures with a boy, maybe. She did have a ticket stub from the Regal in her blazer pocket."

Sir Geoffrey shook his head. "She used to go to the pictures with her mother a lot. The two of them ... Deborah didn't have any boyfriends, Chief Inspector. You're barking up quite the wrong tree there. She didn't have time for boys."

"Had she never had a boyfriend?"

"Only Pierre, if that counts at all."

"Pierre?"

"In Bordeaux, or rather at Montclair. My wife's family owns a chateau in the country near Bordeaux. We often spend holidays there. Pierre is a neighbour's son. All quite innocent, of course."

"Of course," Banks agreed. "And a long way away."

"Yes ... well. Look, about this Jelačić character. That's a disturbing piece of news. Are you going to bring him in?"

"We're pursuing enquiries in a number of directions," Banks said as he and Susan walked to the door, annoyed at himself for sounding as if he were talking to the press.

Outside, they ducked through the reporters beyond the gate and got back into Banks's car out of the rain.

"Interesting, don't you think?" Banks said. "About the boyfriend."

"Yes, sir. Either he really didn't know, or he was lying."

"But why lie?"

"Perhaps Deborah really did keep it a secret from him? If he's a strict father, I could see her doing that."

"Possibly. What about his alibi?"

"Very plausible," said Susan. "I noticed you didn't ask his wife for hers."

"One at a time, Susan. One a time. Besides, I hardly think Sylvie Harrison murdered her own daughter. She's not tall or strong enough, for a start."

"If she goes to a health club, she's probably strong enough," Susan pointed out. "Maybe she stood on a stone?"

Banks sneezed into his handkerchief.

"Bless you, sir," Susan said.

They headed towards North Market Street. "You know," said Banks, "I think there's a lot more to Deborah's life than people know, or are saying. I'd like to have another talk with her mother, alone if possible. Michael Clayton was right, teenagers don't have a lot of time for adults, but daughters do sometimes confide in their mothers. And I'd like to find this John, if he exists."

"Oh, I'm sure he does, sir. Deborah was an attractive girl. And she was sixteen. I'd be very surprised indeed if she had nothing at all to do with boys."

Banks's car phone beeped. He picked it up.

"DI Stott here."

"What's up, Barry?"

"I think we should meet up back at the station. We've got a description of a possible suspect in the Deborah Harrison murder, and it could be Jelačić. Vic Manson called, too. Jelačić's prints are all over the vodka bottles."

"We're on our way." Banks switched off the phone and put his foot down.

IV

All the way home on the rickety bus, Rebecca chewed her nails. She didn't look once at the fading autumn scenery beyond the rain-streaked windows: the muted gold, russet and lemon leaves still clinging to the roadside trees, fragile and insubstantial as the moon's halo; the soft greens and browns of the fields; the runic patterns of the drystone walls. She didn't notice the way that the dale to her west, with its gradually steepening valley sides, was partially lost in mist and drizzle, making it look just like a Chinese water-colour.

Rebecca just chewed her nails and wished that tight, tearing, churning feeling inside her would go away. She felt constantly on the verge of screaming, and she knew if she started she could never stop. She took deep breaths and held them to calm herself. They helped.

By the time the bus lumbered into Eastvale, she had regained some control of her emotions, but she still felt devastated, as if her world had been suddenly blown apart. She supposed it had to happen, that she had been living a lie, living on borrowed time, or whatever other cliché she could come up with to describe the last few months of her life.

Looking at it now, her life had simply become one hangover after another; either from booze or infidelity, it didn't seem to make any difference. What pleasures she had found in getting drunk or having sex were so fleeting and so quickly overwhelmed by the pains—headaches, stomach-ache, guilt, shame—that they no longer seemed worthwhile. But was it too late now? Had she lost Daniel?

Almost there.

She pushed the bell and felt the driver and other passengers giving her strange looks as she waited for the bus to stop. What could they sense about her? Could they smell sex on her? She hadn't washed before leaving Patrick in Richmond; she had simply pulled her clothes on as quickly as possible and left. But her rain-coat covered the torn blouse. God, what could she do about that? If Daniel were home, he would notice. But what did it matter now? He knew anyway. Even so, she couldn't stand the thought of his knowing she had been with Patrick this afternoon.

As the bus approached the stop, she saw the knot of reporters hanging about by the church walls and knew why the passengers were looking at her. She was getting off at St Mary's, the scene of the most horrible crime Eastvale had experienced in decades.

The bus came to a sharp halt and Rebecca would have tumbled forwards if she hadn't been holding onto the metal pole. When the doors opened, she jumped off and dashed past the policeman at the gate, then ran through the churchyard to the vicarage.

When she got there she flung open the door and called out for Daniel. Silence. Thank God, he wasn't home. Pulling off her torn blouse, she ran upstairs to the bathroom to wash the smell of sex from her body. Then she would be ready to face Daniel. She would have to be.

V

Ive Jelačić lived on the sixth floor of a ten-storey block of flats in Burmantofts, off York Road. In the grey November drizzle, the maze of tall buildings reminded Banks of a newspaper picture he'd seen of workers' quarters in some Siberian city.

"Charming, isn't it?" said Detective Inspector Ken Blackstone, waiting for them outside. He looked at his watch. "Do you know, the council had to put slippery domes on all the roofs to stop kids climbing down on the upper balconies and breaking in through people's windows?"

Immaculately dressed as usual, Blackstone made Banks aware that his top collar button was undone and his tie a little askew. Blackstone looked like an academic, with his wire-rimmed glasses, bookworm's complexion and thinning sandy hair, a little curly around the ears, and he was, in fact, something of an expert on art and art fraud. Not that there was often much call for his area of expertise in Leeds. Nobody had knocked off any Atkinson Grimshaws recently, and only an idiot would try to fake a Henry Moore sculpture.

"Jelačić's alibi checks out," Blackstone said as they walked towards the entrance. "For what it's worth. And we've had a poke about his flat. Nothing."

"What do *you* think it's worth?" Banks asked.

Blackstone pursed his cupid's-bow lips. "Me? About as much as a fart in a bathtub. There were three of them—all Croatian. Stipe Pavič, Mile Pavelič and Vjeko Batorac. They'd probably swear night was day to protect one another from the police. Here it is. Take my word, the lift doesn't work."

Banks looked through the open sliding doors. The walls of the lift were covered in bright, spray-painted graffiti, and even from where he stood he could smell glue and urine. They took the stairs instead, surprising a couple of kids sniffing solvent on the third-floor stairwell. The kids ran. They knew the only people dressed like Blackstone in that neighbourhood were likely to be coppers.

There were a few times when Banks regretted smoking, and the climb to the sixth-floor flat was one of them. Puffing for breath and sweating a little, he finally arrived at the outside walkway that went past the front doors.

Number 604 had once been red, but most of the paint had peeled off. It also looked as if it had been used for knife-throwing practice. Jelačić answered on the first knock, wearing jeans and a string vest. His upper body looked strong and muscular, and tufts of thick black hair spilled through the holes in the vest. With his height, longish hair and hooked nose, he certainly resembled the descriptions of the man seen in St Mary's yesterday evening.

"Why you bother me?" he said, standing aside to let them in and letting his eyes rest on Susan for longer than necessary. "I tell you already, I have done nothing."

Inside, the flat was small enough to feel crowded with four people in it and tidy enough to surprise Banks. If nothing else, Ive Jelačić was a good housekeeper. An ironing board stood in one corner, with a shirt spread over it, and there was a small television set in the opposite corner. No video or stereo equipment in sight. The only other furniture in the room consisted of a battered sofa and a table with three chairs. Family photographs and a couple of religious icons stood on the mantelpiece over the electric fire.

"How are you making a living now, Mr Jelačić?" Banks asked.

"Dole."

"Do you own a car?"

"Why?"

"Just answer the question."

"Da. Is old Ford Fiesta."

"Did you drive it to Eastvale yesterday?"

Jelačić looked at Blackstone. "Ne. I tell him already. I play cards. Vjeko tells you. And Stipe and Mile."

Jelačić sat down on his sofa, taking up most of it, and lit a cigarette. The room quickly began to fill with smoke. Blackstone stood with his back against the door, and Banks and Susan sat on the wooden chairs. Banks soon noticed the way Jelačić was sliding his eyes over Susan's body, and he could tell Susan noticed it too, the way she made sure her skirt was pulled down as far over her knees as it would go and the way she kept her knees pressed tight together. But still Jelačić ogled.

"The thing is," Banks said, "that people will often lie to cover for their friends, if they think a friend is in trouble."

Jelačić leaned forward aggressively, muscles bulging in his arms and shoulders. "You call my friends liars! *Jebem ti mater!* You tell that to their face. Fascist police. *Šupak.*"

Banks held out a photograph of Deborah Harrison. "Did you know this girl?"

Jelačić glared at Banks for a moment before glancing towards the photo. He shook his head.

"Are you sure."

"*Da.*"

"She went to St Mary's, sang in the church choir, used to walk through the graveyard on her way home."

He shook his head again.

"I think you're lying, Mr Jelačić. You see, she complained about you. She said you used to make lewd, sexual comments and gestures towards her. What do you think about that?"

"Is not true."

"Father Charters said you were drunk most of the time, you didn't do your job properly and you bothered the girls. Is that true?"

"*Ne.* He is liar. All St Mary's people lie, get Ive in trouble, make him lose job."

"Did you ever enter the Inchcliffe Mausoleum?"

"*Nikada.* Is always locked."

Banks looked at Ken Blackstone and rolled his eyes. "Oh, come on, Ive. We found your fingerprints all over the empty vodka bottles in there."

"*Vrag ti nosi!*"

"We know you went down there. Why?"

Jelačić paused to sulk for a moment, then said, "All right. So I go down there sometime in summer when it get too hot. Just for cool, you understand? Maybe I have a little drink and smoke. Is not crime."

"Did you ever take anyone else down there? Any girls?"

"*Nikada.*"

Banks waved the photograph. "And you swear you didn't know this girl?"

Jelačić leaned back on the sofa. "Maybe I just see her, you know, if I am working and she walk past."

"So you do admit you might have seen her?"

"*Da.* But that is all."

"Mr Jelačić, what were you wearing last night?"

Jelačić pointed towards a coat-hook by the door. A red windcheater hung on it.

"Shoes?"

Frowning, Jelačić got to his feet and picked up a pair of old trainers from the mat below the hook. Banks looked at the soles and thought he could see gravel trapped in the tread and, perhaps, bits of leaves. There was also mud on the sides.

"How did your shoes get in this state?" he asked.

"I walk back from Mile's."

"You didn't drive?"

Jelačić shrugged. "Is not far."

"We'd like to take your shoes and windcheater in for testing," Banks said. "It would be easiest if you gave us permission. You'll get a receipt."

"If I do not?"

"Then we'll get a court order."

"Is okay. You take them. I have nothing to hide."

"Were you standing on the Kendal Road bridge around six o'clock yesterday evening?"

"*Ne.* I go to Mile's house. We play cards until late."

"Did you have two pints of beer and a double whisky in the Nag's Head, opposite St Mary's Park?"

"I tell you. I go to Mile's and we play cards and drink."

"Daniel Charters told us you'd been back to Eastvale to extort money from him. Is that true?"

"*Vražje!* I tell you, that man, he is Satan's tool, an evil liar."

"So it's not true that you offered to withdraw the charges in exchange for money?"

"Is not true. *Ne.* And I have nothing more to say." Jelačić looked at Susan again, letting his eyes travel slowly from her feet all the way up to her breasts, where they lingered. He didn't exactly lick his lips, but he might as well have done. Banks saw Susan flush with embarrassment and rage.

"Well, let me just get clear what you *have* told us," Banks said. "Last night, you were playing cards with friends who will vouch for you, right?"

Jelačić nodded.

"You didn't know the girl in the photograph, though you might have seen her in passing."

"*Da.*"

"But you certainly didn't leer at her or make any suggestive gestures."

"*Ne.*"

"And after you were unjustly fired you never went back to Eastvale and tried to extort money out of Father Daniel Charters."

"*Nikada.*"

"Fine, then," said Banks, standing up. "That'll be all. We'll be off now."

Jelačić looked surprised. "You leave now?"

"Don't worry, we'll take good care of the clothing and get it back to you as soon as we've run our tests. Thank you for your co-operation, Mr Jelačić. Good day."

And they left him gaping after them.

"Biggest load of bollocks I've ever heard in my life," said Ken Blackstone as they walked down the stairs. A dog went on pissing nonchalantly against the wall as they passed by.

Banks lit a cigarette. "Yes, it was, wasn't it? What do you think Susan?"

"Whether he did it or not," Susan Gay said between gritted teeth, "I think the bastard should be hung over the balcony by his balls. Sir."

FIVE

I

It was after six and Daniel still wasn't back. Rebecca paced. She should make a start on dinner. At least it would take her mind off things. Had all this happened just a couple of days ago, she would have gone to see the angel, blabbed her fears and feelings out to its marble heaven-ward gaze, but the Inchcliffe Mausoleum was soured for her now by what she had seen there.

She put on her striped butcher's apron—a birthday present from Daniel, when he still had his sense of humour—and searched in the fridge for the remains of the weekend's roast. She would make shepherd's pie. There was a bottle of Marks and Sparks Sauvignon Blanc in the fridge, lying on its side near the front. After a moment's hesitation, Rebecca opened it and poured herself a generous glass before setting about grinding the leftover meat.

She was halfway through her second glass, and had just put the potatoes on, when she heard the door open. Daniel. Her legs turned to water. Suddenly she couldn't face him, didn't know what to say. He called out her name and she managed to tell him she was in the kitchen. Quickly, she knocked back the rest of the wine and poured herself another glass. Her hand was shaking so much she spilled some of it on the table. Sometimes you just couldn't get drunk enough quick enough.

"What happened to the front window?" Daniel asked when he came through.

Rebecca stared down at the potatoes in the pan, waiting for the water to boil. "Someone chucked a brick through it," she said. She didn't tell him about the note.

"Where were the police?"

"Up around the Inchcliffe Mausoleum."

"Isn't it marvellous? Police all over the place but still a crime gets committed." Daniel rested the backs of his thighs against the solid wood table.

"Daniel, a young girl's been killed. And I found her."

Daniel rubbed his brow. "I know. I'm sorry. I wasn't thinking clearly. Bad day."

"How was the meeting?"

"At least they're resolved on not kicking me out for the present," Daniel said. Over the past month, he had developed a tic beside his left eye. It was jumping now. "But the bishop is very upset about the murder, especially about its happening on church property. That's another nail in my coffin. Things could hardly get much worse."

"Don't tempt providence."

"Providence? Hah. I don't know if I still believe in providence any more. Or in anything, for that matter. I'm hungry." He went to the fridge, found some old Cheddar and cut himself a chunk. "How about you?"

Rebecca shook her head. The way her stomach felt, she thought she might never be able to eat again. The potatoes came to a boil. She turned down the heat and wiped her hands on her apron. The tension inside her had built so high that she felt like a volcano about to erupt. She couldn't stand it any longer.

"Daniel?" She turned to face him.

"What?"

"I ... I don't ... Today. I—"

The front doorbell rang.

"Damn!" Rebecca banged her fist on the table. "Who could that be?"

"I'll go and see." Daniel went off to answer it.

Rebecca grasped the edge of the table. She could feel the room spinning around her, and it wasn't the booze this time.

"Becky!" The note of concern in his voice brought her back. "Are you all right?"

She closed her eyes and shook her head. Not so bad. "I'm fine. Sorry. I just came over a bit funny, that's all." When she opened her eyes, she saw Daniel standing next to the detective who had visited them last night.

He was smaller than you'd expect for a policeman, she noticed, compact, lean and wiry, with an aura of pent-up strength. His closely cropped black hair showed just a little grey at the temples, and his blue eyes danced and sparkled with energy. There was a little crescent scar beside his right eye.

"Detective Chief Inspector Banks is back," Daniel said. "He wants to ask us some more questions."

Rebecca nodded, took off her apron and followed them through to the living-room. She left the glass of wine on the kitchen table. Another postponement. Maybe she could drink herself through yet another night of guilt and misery.

"I'm sorry to intrude again," Banks said when they had all sat down. He sneezed, took out a large handkerchief and blew his nose. "Sorry. I seem to be catching a cold. Look, I'll come straight to the point. I can see you were busy getting dinner ready. I was just wondering if maybe you'd decided to tell me the truth about last night?"

For a moment, Rebecca was stunned by the matter-of-fact way Banks spoke. "The truth?" she echoed.

"Yes. You're a poor liar, Mrs Charters. And you can take that as a compliment." He glanced towards Daniel. "When I asked your husband where he had been at the time you said you heard a cry, you jumped in a bit too quickly and answered for him."

"I did?"

"Yes. Then he felt duty-bound to lie to cover for you. It's all very admirable in some ways, but it won't do. Not when there's a sixteen-year-old girl lying dead in Eastvale mortuary."

Rebecca felt completely tongue-tied. What the hell was going on? Her mind whirled, searching for things to say, but before she could say anything a voice far calmer than her own cut in.

"Chief Inspector," Daniel Charters said. "I'm afraid that's my fault. I should have corrected Rebecca rather than let the deceit stand. Believe me, there was no need for a lie. I have nothing to hide."

Banks nodded. He seemed to be waiting for something else.

Daniel sighed and went on. "Yes, I was out at the time my wife heard the cry, but I can assure you that my whereabouts had absolutely nothing at all to do with the poor girl's murder."

"Where were you?" Banks asked.

Rebecca noticed Daniel's lips tighten for a moment as he tensed in thought. "I'd rather not say."

"It would help us a lot if we could verify your story."

Daniel shook his head. "I'm afraid I wouldn't be able to prove my alibi, even if I told you."

"You could let *us* try."

He smiled sadly. "It's a kind offer, but—"

The doorbell rang again.

"I'll go," said Rebecca.

"Whoever it is," Daniel told her, "get rid of them."

Leaving them in silence, Rebecca went to open the front door. Patrick Metcalfe was standing there. He looked as if he had been walking around in the rain without a raincoat for hours.

"Oh, my God," Rebecca cried, trying to shut the door against his shoulder. "Please, go away. Can't you see you've caused enough trouble already?"

"Let me in, Rebecca. I want to come in. I must come in. I want to talk to both of you. You must listen to me."

He kept pushing at the door and Rebecca wasn't strong enough to hold him back. Suddenly, Banks's calm voice behind her said, "Why don't you let him in, Mrs Charters? Whoever he is. The more the merrier."

II

Even Barry Stott was almost ready to call it a day by six-thirty. The drizzle that, at one time, had looked like ending, had turned into a much harder downpour as darkness fell, and now both he and Sergeant Hatchley were soaked to the skin. Even the best raincoat and shoes, which Stott's were, could only take so much without springing leaks. If only Jelačić had broken down and confessed instead of stubbornly protesting his innocence, the way Banks said he had, how much easier life would have been.

They were showing the police artist's impression, based on Alf's description—and what a lengthy and frustrating experience getting that done had been—along the rather twee row of shops set back from Kendal Road opposite the school. The newsagent hadn't seen anyone, the grocer was closed and the hairdresser gave a lengthy opinion as to the sorry state of the suspect's locks, but said she was closed on Mondays, and no, she hadn't noticed anyone strange hanging around on any other days.

The teashop was also closed, the way most Yorkshire teashops close at teatime, but the Peking Moon, the Chinese restaurant next door, had just opened. It was, as Hatchley explained, a rather pricey, up-market sort of Chinese restaurant, not the kind of place that yobbos go for a quick chop suey after a skinful of ale on a Friday night.

"I wonder why they don't change the name," Sergeant Hatchley said as they approached the door. "Isn't Peking called Beijing now? A real Chinaman wouldn't have a clue where he was if he saw this."

Stott turned to Hatchley before he pushed the door open. "I know what you're thinking, Sergeant. And you can forget it. We're not staying here for dinner. Definitely not. Got it?"

Hatchley looked hurt. "Furthest thing from my mind, sir. I don't even like Chinese food. It's got no sticking power. I'm always hungry again ten minutes after I've eaten it."

"Right. Just as long as we understand each other ..."

The bell at the top of the door jingled as they went in. Like many Chinese restaurants, its decor was simple and relaxing, with a series of ancient Chinese landscapes—tiny human figures dwarfed by evergreen-covered mountains—on the walls, and plain red tablecloths. Soft, tinkling music played in the background. So soft that Stott couldn't even figure out whether it was pop or classical. Or Chinese. Not that he cared much for music.

A waiter in a white jacket walked towards them. "Jim, me old mate. What can I do you for?" he asked in a cockney accent you could cut with a knife, despite the oriental eyes and complexion.

"DI Stott," Hatchley introduced them. "This is Well Hung Low." He laughed, and the waiter laughed with him.

Stott seethed inside, his rage, as it always did, crystallizing quickly from fire to ice.

"Just a joke, sir," Hatchley went on. "His name's Joe Sung. Deserted the bright lights of Whitechapel for the greener pastures of Eastvale. Joe wanted to be a copper once, too, sir, but I managed to persuade him he was better off where he was. His father owns this place. It's a little gold-mine."

"Perhaps you should reconsider," Stott said with a smile, shaking Joe's hand. "We need more ... a more ethnically diverse police force. Especially in Yorkshire."

"Aye," said Hatchley. "I told him he wouldn't know what was worse, the prejudice or the patronizing."

Joe laughed.

Again, Stott felt his anger boil up and freeze. Oafs like Hatchley symbolized all that was wrong in today's police force. His type's days were numbered. "I wonder if we might ask you a few questions?" he said to Joe Sung.

"Fire away, mate." Joe gestured to the empty restaurant. "See how busy we are. Here, take the weight off." He beckoned them to join him at one of the tables.

"Remember what I said, Sergeant," Stott hissed in Hatchley's ear as they followed. "This isn't another meal break."

"No, sir." But Hatchley took the ashtray on the table as an invitation to light up.

"What is it, then?" Joe asked when they'd sat down. "Official business? About that murder?"

"Yes," said Stott.

Joe shook his head. "Terrible business. I knew the girl, too, you know."

"Knew her?"

"Well, not in the real sense of the word. Not to talk to, like. I mean she'd eaten in here with her mates, that's all. I couldn't believe my eyes when I saw that photo in the *Evening Post*."

Stott couldn't understand how it happened, but a tray of appetizers suddenly appeared on the table in front of them:

spring rolls, garlic shrimp, chicken balls. All Stott noticed was the retreating back of another waiter. He hadn't heard a thing. Hatchley picked up a shrimp and popped it in his mouth between drags on his cigarette.

"When did she eat here?" Stott asked.

"They come here every now and then. A bunch of girls from the school, that is. Maybe when one of their daddies sends the monthly cheque. Anyway, they generally keep quiet, don't cause any trouble, and they don't expect to be served beer. She was with them once or twice, that Deborah Harrison who got killed. I recognized her."

"Do you remember anything about her?"

"Nah, not really. 'Cept that she was a good-looking girl. That's why I remembered her in particular."

"Ever noticed anyone take an unusual interest in her, or the other St Mary's girls?"

"Well, they've caught the odd eye or two. There's a couple of right corkers among them, and there's always something about a girl in a school uniform. Sorry. That was in bad taste."

"Not at all, Joe," said Hatchley. "I know what you mean, and I'm sure the inspector does, too."

Stott said nothing. Three bottles of beer materialized with three glasses on the table before them, as if by magic.

"Somefink to wash the food down," Joe said with a grin. "My treat."

Stott ignored the beer. Hatchley grabbed a bottle and ignored the glass. Well, let him drink it, Stott thought. Fine. He wasn't going to touch any, himself. Give Hatchley enough rope and he'll surely hang himself. If only he didn't have a strong ally in Chief Inspector Banks. Stott couldn't understand that relationship at all. Banks seemed like an intelligent, civilized sort of copper. What could he possibly see in a boor like Hatchley?

Right now, though, there were more important things to think about than Hatchley's eating and drinking habits. "So you noticed nothing unusual about the girl and nobody taking any undue interest in her or her friends?" Stott asked.

"That's right," said Joe. "Noffink out of the ordinary."

"Did she ever meet anyone here? Anyone other than her school-friends?"

"No. They always came and left together as a group. Never had any boys with them, if that's what you mean. Too close to the school, if you ask me. You never know when one of the teachers might drop in and catch them. They eat here, too, sometimes."

Stott glanced over at Hatchley, who took out the artist's impression of the stranger in the Nag's Head. "Ever seen this man?" he asked.

Joe stared at the picture, shaking his head. "It doesn't look much like him, except for the hair," he said, "but we had a bloke looked a bit like that in here just last night."

Stott's pulse began to race. "What was he wearing?"

"An orange anorak."

"Tall?"

"Yeah, tall-ish. Bit over six feet, anyway."

"What time did he come in?"

"About half six. I remember because he was the only one in at that time. Miserable night."

The time fit, Stott thought, feeling his excitement rise. The killer had a couple of drinks at the Nag's Head, murdered Deborah Harrison, and then he came here for dinner.

"Did he do or say anything unusual?"

"He seemed a bit restless. I saw him muttering to himself once or twice."

"Hear what he said?"

"Sorry."

"Who waited his table?"

"I did. We were short-staffed because of the fog. He was certainly hungry, I'll say that. First he had spring rolls, then he ordered orange beef *and* Szechuan shrimp, a bowl of rice and a pint of lager. Ate it all, too."

"Did you talk to him?"

"Only to take his order. He didn't seem communicative, so I didn't push it. You learn how to behave in this business, who wants to chat and who just wants to be left alone. This bloke wanted to be left alone."

Stott saw his bottle of beer disappear into Hatchley's hand. He let it pass. "Did you notice anything else about him?"

"Yeah. He had a little cut, just up there, high on his left cheek." Joe touched the spot on his own cheek.

Stott could hardly contain his excitement. The post-mortem had reported skin and tissue under the middle fingernail of Deborah Harrison's right hand. She had scratched her attacker. It had to be Jelačić. "How long did he stay?" Stott asked.

"Just as long as it took to order and eat. About three-quarters of an hour."

"Did he have a car?"

"If he did, I didn't see it. Somehow, I got the impression he was on foot. I mean, who'd take the car out by himself on a night like that, just to go out alone for a Chinese meal? Fine as the food here is. Me, I'd order a take-away and let some other poor bugger do the driving."

"Good point," said Stott. "See where he went?"

"Afraid not."

From the corner of his eye, Stott noticed the last spring roll disappear between two sausage-like fingers.

"Had you ever seen him before?" he asked.

Joe shook his head.

Stott smiled. "I don't suppose he happened to mention his name, did he?"

Joe grinned back. "Sorry. Didn't mention his address, either. No. Like I said, some of them are chatty, this one wasn't." He paused. "I'll tell you what, though."

"What?"

Joe stood up. "If my memory serves me right, he paid by card. You might be able to get his name from that. I haven't done the returns yet. Shall I go get it for you?"

Stott sent up a silent prayer of thanks to God.

Joe came back with a sheaf of Visa slips in his hand and started going through them. "Not this one. Not that ... no ... no. Yeah. Right, this is the one." And he passed it over.

Anxiously, Stott grabbed the slip of paper, but as soon as he looked at it, his spirits sank. He couldn't read the signature—that was just a mess of loops and whirls—but the name was printed clearly enough in the top left corner. And it *wasn't* Ive Jelačić.

Beside him, he heard the glug of an emptying beer bottle followed by a resonant burp.

III

"Right," said Banks, "now that we've all calmed down a bit, maybe we can play truth or consequences. And I'm telling you, the consequences will be bloody severe if you don't play. Got it?"

The three pale, miserable-looking people in the chilly vicarage living-room nodded in unison. The brown-and-white bundle of fur on the hearth scratched and fell still again.

As soon as Banks had appeared in the hall, Patrick Metcalfe had tried to make a break for it. Perhaps he believed that the power of his love could vanquish unhappy husbands, but he must have known it didn't stand a chance against the long arm of the law. As he turned to run away, he slipped on the doorstep and fell down three stone steps onto the garden path, sprawling in the rain on the worn paving-stones, holding his knee and cursing. Banks helped him inside with a firm hand and sat him down in one of the armchairs.

Now he sat there, hair plastered to his skull, looking sullen. The "consumptive" look wasn't hard for him to cultivate, given his lanky frame and hollow cheeks. He kept giving Rebecca Charters significant stares with his soulful eyes, but she averted her gaze.

By this time, Rebecca had brought the bottle of wine from the kitchen and topped up her glass. She was beginning to look a little blurred around the edges. Daniel Charters, permanent frown etched in his high brow, muscle twitching beside his left eye, just sat there, long legs crossed, his face growing steadily paler, looking like a man old before his time.

"Now, then, Mr Charters," Banks said. "You were trying to tell me where you were last night before we were so rudely interrupted."

"He was with me," the newcomer burst out.

"And you are?"

"Patrick Metcalfe. I'm the history teacher at St Mary's."

"So you knew Deborah Harrison?"

"I wouldn't say I *knew* her. I taught her history last year."

"And you say Mr Charters was with you yesterday evening?"

"He was."

"What time did he arrive?"

Metcalfe shrugged. "About a quarter to six. I was just thinking about putting something in the microwave for dinner, and I usually eat at about six."

"Does that time sound right to you, Mr Charters?"

Charters nodded glumly.

Banks turned back to Metcalfe. "Where do you live?"

"One of the school flats. On St Mary's grounds."

"Alone?"

"Yes. Alone." Metcalfe looked longingly at Rebecca Charters, who stared down into her wineglass.

"What time did Mr Charters leave?" Banks asked.

"Around ten to six. He didn't stay more than five minutes. He could see I wasn't interested in what he had to say."

Which meant that Charters was unaccounted-for during the crucial period around six o'clock. Banks could see Rebecca frowning at this information. She had lied for her husband, only to have someone give him what seemed like an alibi, then immediately snatch it away again. Did *she* know where he had been between ten to six and whenever he got back home?

And, Banks realized, this also left Patrick Metcalfe without an alibi. Rebecca, too, for that matter; he only had her word that she had heard something like a cry around six o'clock.

"What were you wearing?" Banks asked Charters.

"Wearing? A raincoat."

"Colour?"

"Beige."

"May I see it."

Charters went and brought the raincoat in from the hall closet. Banks examined it closely but could see no traces of blood or earth. "Do you mind if I take this for further testing?" he asked. "I'll give you a receipt of course."

Charters looked alarmed. "Should I call my lawyer?"

"Not if you've got nothing to hide."

"I've got nothing to hide. Go ahead. Take it."

"Thank you."

"Where did you go after you left Mr Metcalfe?"

"Nowhere in particular. I just walked."

"Where?"

"In the school grounds. By the river."

"Did you see anyone?"

"There were a few people about, yes."

"What about on or near the bridge?"

He thought for a moment, then said, "Yes, come to think of it, I did see someone. When I came out of the main school gate and crossed the road, there was a man in front of me walking along Kendal Road towards the bridge."

"Did you get a good look at him?"

"No. He stopped on the bridge and I walked past him. He was about my height—six foot two—and he was wearing an orange anorak. I could see that much from behind. His hair was dark and rather long."

"Are you sure it was a man?"

"Certain. Even in the fog I could tell by the way he walked. There's something ... I don't know how to explain it ... but I'm *certain* it was a man."

Another sighting of the mysterious stranger that Stott and Hatchley had unearthed in the Nag's Head. Interesting. "Can you tell me anything more about him?"

"I'm afraid not," said Charters. "I had other things on my mind."

"Could it have been a red windcheater rather than an orange anorak?"

Charters frowned. "I suppose it *could* have been. I wasn't paying really close attention."

"I hope you realize, Mr Charters, that if you'd continued lying to us you would also have been withholding what could be an important piece of evidence."

Charters said nothing.

"Where did you go next?" Banks asked.

"I walked up to North Market Street, carried along there for a while, then took Constance Avenue back down to the river path and home." He looked at Rebecca, then looked away again. "But when I got here I ... I ... didn't want to go in and ... Not just yet. So I kept on walking for a good ten minutes or so, then turned back and came home."

"Is that everything?"

"Yes."

"Did you go into the churchyard at any time?"

"No. I wish I had. I might have been able to prevent the poor girl's murder."

"What time *did* your husband get home, Mrs Charters?"

"He was home when I got back from the graveyard."

"And that was about a quarter to seven?"

"Yes."

"And what did you do after Mr Charters left your flat?" Banks said to Metcalfe.

"Nothing much. Heated up my dinner. I considered coming over here and putting an end to the ridiculous charade, but decided against it."

"What ridiculous charade?"

They were all silent for a moment, as if someone had finally gone too far and they were deciding how to cover up, then Daniel Charters spoke up. "I went to talk to Metcalfe," he said, "to try to persuade him to stop seeing my wife."

Banks looked at Metcalfe. "Is this true?"

"Yes."

"And what was your response?"

Metcalfe sneered at Charters. "I told him I wasn't interested, that it was too late. Rebecca and I are in love and we're going away together."

Banks looked towards Rebecca. She had lowered her head, so he couldn't see her expression, only the mass of auburn hair hanging down to her knees. Her glass of wine had sat untouched for several minutes on the table.

"Tell him," Metcalfe urged her. "Go on, Rebecca. Tell him it's true. Tell him how this marriage is a sham, how it's stifling you, destroying your true nature. Tell him you don't love your—"

"No!"

"What?"

Rebecca Charters held her head up and stared directly at Metcalfe. Her dark eyes flashed with angry tears. "I said no, Patrick." She seemed to gain control of the situation; the welling tears remained at the edges of her eyes. She spoke quietly: "I tried to tell you before, but you wouldn't listen. You didn't want to understand. I'm not defending myself. What I've done is wrong. Terribly wrong." She looked at her husband, who showed no expression, then back at Metcalfe. "But it's *my* guilt, *my* sin. If I wasn't strong enough to stand by my husband when he needed me most, if I let a hint of scandal and suspicion poison our marriage, then it's my mistake, my fault. But I won't compound it with lies."

She turned to Banks. "Yes, Chief Inspector, I had an affair with Patrick. I met him at a social evening we put on for the staff and upper sixth of St Mary's School around the middle of last month. He was charming, interesting, passionate, and I became infatuated with him. Daniel and I were already going through a difficult time, as I think you know, and when I should have been strong, I was weak. I'm not proud of myself, but I want you to know that's why I lied to you, because I was afraid that too many questions would lead to exactly this kind of situation. Now it's happened, I'm glad, believe me, though I've been trying to avoid it at all costs. There's been far too much distrust and suspicion around this house lately. I can't believe that my husband had anything to do with this murder, any more than I can believe he's capable of doing what that vile man accused him of."

She turned back to Metcalfe, tears still hanging on the rims of her eyes, dampening the long, dark lashes. "I'm sorry, Patrick, if I misled you. I didn't intend to. Just put it down to a foolish woman seeking temporary escape. But you were only a distraction. I didn't mean for you to fall in love with me. And, if you're honest with yourself, I think you'd have to admit that you're not in love with me at all. I think you're in love with the idea of being in love, but you're far too self-absorbed to ever love anyone but yourself."

Metcalfe stood up. "It's not true, Rebecca. I do love you. Can't you see how you're blinding yourself? If you stay, you'll wither up and die before your time, before you've even—"

A harsh sound came from one of the armchairs, and Banks saw Daniel Charters bend forward, cup his head in his hands and start to cry like a child. Rebecca jumped up and went over to him, putting her arm around his shoulder.

"He doesn't even like women," Metcalfe went on. "You can't possibly—"

Banks picked up Charters's raincoat, grasped Metcalfe by the back of the collar and shoved him towards the front door. Even though Metcalfe was a few inches taller than Banks, he didn't put up much of a struggle, just muttered something about police brutality.

Once outside, Banks shut the door behind them, guided Metcalfe down the path and tossed him out of the gate onto the river path. "On your bike," he said.

Still muttering, Metcalfe walked towards the school. Banks glanced back as he closed the gate and saw Rebecca and Daniel framed in the window. Rebecca was cradling her husband's head against her breast, like a baby's, stroking his hair. Her mouth was opening and closing, as if she were uttering soothing words.

Banks had unfinished business at the vicarage—they weren't off the hook yet—but it could wait. He looked up into the dark sky, as if searching for enlightenment, but felt only the cool raindrops on his face. He sneezed. Then he pulled his collar up and set off along the river path for the Kendal Road bridge.

SIX

I

Owen Pierce had just opened a bottle of wine and taken the heated remains of last week's beef stew out of the oven when the door-bell rang.

Muttering a curse, he put his stew back in the oven to keep warm and trotted to the front door. At the end of the hall, he could make out two figures through the frosted glass: one tall and heavy-set, one shorter and slim.

When he opened the door, he first thought they were Jehovah's Witnesses or Mormons—who else came to the door in pairs, wearing suits? But these two didn't quite look the part. True, one of them did look like a bible salesman—sticking-out ears, glasses, not a hair out of place, freshly scrubbed look—but the other looked more like a thug.

"Mr Pierce? Mr Owen Pierce?" asked the bible salesman.

"Yes, that's me. Look, I was just about to eat my dinner. What is it? What do you want? If you're selling—"

"We're police officers, sir," the man went on. "My name is Detective Inspector Stott and this is Detective Sergeant Hatchley. Mind if we come in?" They flashed their warrant cards and Owen stood back to let them in.

As soon as they got into the living-room, the big one started poking around.

"Nice place you've got," Stott said, while his partner prowled the room, picking up vases and looking inside them, opening drawers an inch or two, inspecting books.

"Look, what is this?" Owen said. "Is he supposed to be going through my things like that? There are no drugs here, if that's what you're looking for."

"Oh, don't mind Sergeant Hatchley. He's just like that. Insatiable curiosity."

"Don't you need a search warrant or something?"

"Well, Owen" said Stott, "the way it works is like this. We *could* go to a magistrate, and we *could* apply for a warrant to search your premises, but it takes a lot of time. Sergeant Hatchley would have to stay here with you while I took care of the formalities. I think this way is much better all round. Anyway, you've nothing to hide, have you?"

"No, no, it's not that. It's just ..."

"Well," said Stott with a smile. "That's all right, then, isn't it?"

"I suppose so."

"Mind if I sit down?"

"Be my guest."

Stott sat in the chair by the fake coals and Owen sat opposite him on the sofa. A mug of half-finished coffee stood between them on the glass-topped table beside a couple of unpaid bills and the latest *Radio Times*.

"Look," Owen said, "I'm afraid you've got me at a disadvantage here. What's it all about?"

"Just routine inquiries, sir. That's a nasty scratch on your face. Mind telling me where you got it?"

Owen put his hand up to his cheek. "I've no idea," he said. "I woke up this morning and there it was."

"Were you in the St Mary's area of Eastvale yesterday evening?"

"Let me think ... Yes, yes, I believe I was." He glanced at Hatchley, who seemed fascinated by the print of Renoir's *Bathers* over the fireplace.

"Why?"

"What? Sorry."

"Look, just ignore Sergeant Hatchley for the moment," Stott said. "Look at me. I asked you *why* you were in St Mary's."

Owen shrugged. "No particular reason. I was just walking."

"Walking? On a miserable night like that?"

"Well, if you let the weather dictate it, you wouldn't get much walking done in Yorkshire, would you?"

"Even so. St Mary's is quite a distance from here."

"No more than three miles each way. And it's a very pleasant walk along the river. Even in the fog."

Hatchley fished a copy of *Playboy* out of the magazine rack and held it up for Stott to see. Stott frowned and reached over for it. The cover showed a shapely blonde in skimpy pink lace panties, bordered in black, a flimsy slip, stockings and suspender belt. She was on her knees on a sofa, and her round behind faced the viewer. Her face was also turned towards the camera: glossy red lips, eyes an impossible shade of green, unfocused, as if she had just woken from a deep sleep. One thin strap had slipped over her upper right arm.

"I bought it because of one of the stories I wanted to read," Owen said, immediately feeling himself turn red. It wasn't so much that he had been caught with something warped and perverted, but with something sub-literary, something beneath his intelligence and dignity. "It's not illegal, you know. You can buy it at any newsagent's. It's not pornography."

"That's a matter of opinion, sir, isn't it?" said Stott. He handed the magazine back to Hatchley as if he were dropping something in a rubbish bin, holding it between his thumb and forefinger.

"And there's a video tape full of what sounds like sexy stuff to me, sir, judging by the titles," said Hatchley. "One of them's called *School's Out*. And you should have a butcher's at some of the poses in these here so-called art books."

"I'm an amateur photographer," Owen said. "It's my hobby. For Christ's sake, what do you expect? Is that what all this is about? Pornography? Because if it is—"

Stott waved his hand. "No," he said. "It's of no matter, really. It might be relevant. We'll have to see. Do you live here by yourself, Mr Pierce?"

"Yes."

"What kind of work do you do?"

"I'm a lecturer at Eastvale College. English."

"Ever been married?"

"No."

"Girlfriends?"

"Some."

"But not to live with?"

"No."

"Videos and magazines enough to satisfy you, eh?"

"Now just a min—"

Stott held up his hand. "Sorry," he said. "Sorry, I shouldn't have said that. Tasteless of me. Out of line."

Why couldn't Owen quite believe the apology? He sensed very strongly that Stott had made the remark on purpose to nettle him. He hoped he had passed the test, even though he couldn't be sure what the question was. Feeling more like Kafka's Joseph K every minute, he shifted in his chair. "Why do you want to know all this?" he asked again. "You said you were going to tell me what it's all about."

"Did I? Well, first, would you mind if we had a quick look around the rest of the place? It might save us coming back."

"Go ahead," Owen said, and accompanied them as they did the rounds. It wasn't a thorough search, and Owen felt that by granting them permission he had probably saved himself a lot of trouble. He had seen on television the way search teams messed up places. They gave the bedrooms, one of which was completely empty, a cursory glance, poked about in his clothing drawers and wardrobe. In the study, Stott admired the aquarium of tropical fish and, of course, Hatchley rummaged through some of Owen's photo files and found the black-and-white nude studies of Michelle. He showed them to Stott, who frowned.

"Who's this?" Stott asked.

Owen shrugged. "Just a model."

"What's her name?"

"I'm sorry. I don't remember."

"She looks very young."

"She was twenty-two when those were taken."

"Hmm, was she now?" muttered Stott, handing the photos back to Hatchley. "Must be artistic licence. Notice any resemblance, Sergeant?" he asked Hatchley.

"Aye, sir, I do."

"Resemblance to who?"

"Mind if we take these, too?" Stott asked.

"As a matter of fact, I do. They're the only prints I've got, and I've lost the negatives."

"I understand, sir. You want to hang onto them for sentimental reasons. We'll take good care of them. Wait a minute, though ... didn't you say she was just a model?"

"I did. And I didn't say I wanted to keep them for sentimental reasons. They're part of my portfolio. For exhibitions and such like."

"Ah, I see. Might we just take one of them, perhaps, then?"

"Oh, all right. If you must."

Hatchley leafed through some more art books on a shelf over the filing cabinet. One of them dealt with Japanese erotic art, and he opened it at a charcoal sketch of two young girls entwined together on a bed. They had either shaved off their pubic hair, or they were too young to have grown any. It was difficult to tell. He shoved it under Stott's nose.

"A bit like those books in the other room, sir," he said.

Stott turned up his nose.

"And some of them novels he reads have been on trial," Hatchley went on. *"Lady Chatterley's Lover, Naked Lunch, Ulysses, Delta of Venus, a bit of De Sade ..."*

"For Christ's sake!" Owen cut in. "I can't believe this. I'm an English teacher, you fucking moron. That's what I do for a living."

"Now, you look here, mate," said Hatchley, squaring up to him. "The last bloke used that kind of language with me had a nasty accident on his way down the police station steps."

"Are you threatening me?"

Hatchley thrust his chin out. "Take it any way you want."

"Stop it, Sergeant!" Stott cut in. "I'll not have you talking to a member of the public this way. Apologize to Mr Pierce at once."

"Yes, sir," said Hatchley. He looked at Pierce and said, "Sorry, sir."

"If you ask me," Owen said, "you're the ones who are sick. Like witch-hunters, seeing the devil's work everywhere."

"Maybe it is everywhere," Stott said calmly. "Have you ever thought about that?"

"It's just hard to believe there's someone who still thinks *Lady Chatterley's Lover* and *Ulysses* are dirty books, that's all."

They sat down in the living-room again. "Now why don't you tell me all about what you did in St Mary's yesterday evening," Stott said. "Sergeant Hatchley will take notes. No hurry. Take your time."

Owen told them about his walk, the drinks at the Nag's Head, the meal at the Peking Moon and the walk home. As he spoke, Stott looked directly at him. The stern, triangular face showed no expression; and the eyes behind the lenses seemed cool. The man's ears almost made Owen want to laugh out loud, but he restrained himself. The big one, Hatchley, scribbled away in a spiral-bound notebook. Owen was surprised he could even write.

"Are you in the habit of talking to yourself, Mr Pierce?" asked Stott when he had finished.

Owen reddened. "I wouldn't say *talking* to myself exactly. Sometimes I get lost in thought and I forget there are people around. Don't you ever do that?"

"No," said Stott, "I don't."

Finally, after they had asked him to go over one or two random points again, Hatchley closed his notebook and Stott got to his feet. "That'll be all for now," he said.

"For now?"

"We might want to talk to you again. Don't know. We have to check up on a few points first. Would you mind if we had a look in your hall cupboard on the way out?"

"Why?"

"Routine."

"Go ahead. I don't suppose I can stop you."

Stott and Hatchley searched through the row of coats and jackets and pulled out Owen's new orange anorak. "Is this what you were wearing last night?"

"Yes. Yes, it is. But—"

"What about these shoes?"

"Yes, those too. Look—"

"Mind if we take them with us, sir?"

"But why?"

"Purposes of elimination."

"You mean it might help clear this business up?"

Stott smiled. "Yes. It might. We'll let you have them back as soon as we can. Do you think you could get me a plastic bag while the sergeant here writes out a receipt?"

Owen fetched a bin-liner from the kitchen and watched Stott put the shoes and anorak inside it while Hatchley wrote out the receipt. Then he accepted the slip of paper and signed a release identifying the items as his.

Stott turned to Hatchley. "I think we'd better be off, then, Sergeant," he said. "We've already taken up enough of Mr Pierce's valuable time."

Hatchley took the plastic bag while Stott slipped the photograph into his briefcase, then they walked towards the door.

"Aren't you going to tell me what it's all about?" Owen asked again as he opened the front door for them. It was still raining.

Stott turned and frowned. "That's the funny thing about it, Owen," he said. "That you don't know." Then he shook his head slowly. "Anybody would think you don't read the papers. Which is odd, for an educated man like yourself."

II

Tracy Banks's bedroom, lit by a shaded table lamp, was a typical teenager's room, just like Deborah Harrison's, with pop-star posters on the wall, a portable cassette player, a narrow bed, usually unmade, and clothes all over the floor.

Tracy also had a desk against one wall and perhaps more books on her shelves than many girls her age. They ran the gamut from *The Wind in the Willows* to the *Pelican History of the World*. A row of dolls and teddy bears sat on the bookcase's lowest shelf; they always reminded Banks that his daughter wasn't that far away from childhood things yet. One day, they would disappear, as had most of his own toys: the fort with its soldiers, the Hornby train set, the Meccano. He had no idea where they had gone. Along with his childhood innocence.

Tracy herself sprawled on the bed in black leggings and a sloppy sweatshirt. She looked as if she had been crying. When Banks had got the message from his wife, Sandra, at his office, saying that Tracy was upset and wanted to talk to him, he had hurried straight home.

Now Banks sat on the edge of the bed and stroked his daughter's hair, which was tied back in a ponytail. "What is it, love?" he asked.

"You didn't tell me," Tracy said. "Last night."

"Are you talking about the murder?"

"Yes. Oh, it's all right. I know *why* you didn't tell me." She sniffled. "You wanted to spare my feelings. I don't blame you. I'm not mad at you or anything. I wish you had told me, though. It wouldn't have been such a shock when all the girls at school started talking about it."

"I'm sorry," said Banks. "I knew you'd find out eventually and it would upset you. I suppose I was just trying to give you one more night of peace before you had to deal with it. Maybe it was selfish of me."

"No. Really. It's all right."

"So what *is* wrong?"

Tracy was silent a moment. Banks heard laughter and music from downstairs. "I knew her," she said finally.

"Knew who?"

"Deborah Harrison. I knew her."

Apart from both being attractive blonde teenagers, Tracy and Deborah Harrison were about as far apart as you get in background and class. Deborah went to the expensive, élite St Mary's School, where she was carefully groomed for Oxford or Cambridge, and Tracy went to Eastvale Comprehensive, where she had to fight her way through overcrowded classes, massive apathy and incompetent teaching to get decent enough A-levels to get into a redbrick university. Now here was Tracy saying she *knew* Deborah.

"How?" he asked.

Tracy shifted on the bed and sat cross-legged. She pulled the duvet over her shoulders like a shawl. "You won't get mad at me, will you, Dad? Promise?"

Banks smiled. "I've a feeling I'm not going to like this, but you've got my word."

Tracy took a deep breath, then said, "It was in the summer. A few times I hung around with the crowd at the Swainsdale Centre down by the bus station."

"You hung around with those yobs? Jesus Christ, Tracy, I—"

"See! I knew you'd be mad."

Banks took a deep breath. "Okay. I'm not mad. Just surprised, that's all. How could you *do* that? Those kids are into drugs, vandalism, all sorts of things."

"Oh, we didn't do any harm, Daddy. It was just somewhere to go, that's all. And they're not so bad, really. I know some of them look pretty weird and frightening, but they're not really. What did you used to do when you were a kid with nowhere to go?"

Banks would like to have to answered, "Museums, art galleries, long walks, books, classical concerts." But he couldn't. Mostly he and his friends had hung around on street corners, on waste ground or in empty schoolyards. Sometimes they had even broken into condemned houses and played there.

"Okay," he said. "We'll let it pass for now. Carry on."

"Deborah Harrison was down there shopping one day and one of the girls in the group knew her vaguely from dressage or swimming competitions or something, and they got talking. She came down a couple of days later—dressed down a bit—and started to hang out. I think she was bored with just staying at home and studying so she thought she'd slum it for a while."

"What about her own friends?"

"I don't really think she had any. She said most of her schoolfriends were away for the summer. Most of the boarders had gone home, of course, and the day-girls had all jetted off to exotic places like America and the south of France. Why can't we go to places like that, Dad?"

"You were in France earlier this year."

She slapped his arm. "I'm only teasing. It wasn't a serious question."

"When did Deborah first start joining in with the group?"

"Early August, I think."

"And how did the others treat her?"

"They'd tease her about being a bit lah-de-dah, sometimes, but she took it well enough. She said somebody had to be, and besides, it wasn't all it was cracked up to be."

"What did she mean by that?"

"It was just her way of talking about things."

"Did she ever flaunt her wealth, flash it about?"

"No. Not that I saw."

"How long did she hang around with the group?"

"About three weeks, on and off."

"Have you seen her since then?"

Tracy shook her head. "Well, she wouldn't want to be seen dead with the likes of us now, would she? Not now she's back at St Mary's." Then she put her hand over her mouth. "I'm sorry, Dad. I just haven't got used to the idea that she's dead yet."

Banks patted her arm. "That's all right, love. It takes time. How well did you know her?"

"Not very well, but we chatted once or twice. She wasn't so bad, you know, when you got to know her a bit. I mean, she wasn't so snobbish. And she was quite bright."

"Did you ever talk about school?"

"Sometimes."

"What did she think of St Mary's?"

"She thought it was all right. At least the teachers were pretty good and the classes weren't too big. She said they had a staff to pupil ratio of one to ten. It must be more like one to five hundred where I go."

"Did she mention any teachers in particular?"

"Not that I can remember."

"Patrick Metcalfe. Does that name sound familiar?"

Tracy shook her head. "No."

"What kind of things did she say about school?"

"Nothing much, really. Just like, 'You'd be surprised if you knew some of the things that go on there.' That sort of thing. Very melodramatic."

"What did you think she meant?"

Tracy looked down and rubbed her hand against her knee. "Well, there's a lot of girls live in, you know, all together in the dormitories. I thought she meant, like, lesbians and stuff."

"Did she imply that any of the teachers had any sort of sexual relations with the pupils?"

"No, Dad. Honest, I don't know. I mean, she never really *said* anything. Not specific. She just implied. Hinted. But she was like that about everything."

"Like what?"

"As if she knew more than she let on. And as if we were poor fools who saw only the surface, and she knew what *really* went on underneath. Like, *we* all swallowed the illusion, but she knew the underlying truth. I'm not trying to paint her in a bad way. She was really nice, but she just had this sort of tone, like, as if she knew more than everyone else."

"Did she ever speak about her family?"

"She mentioned her father's business now and then."

"What did she say about that?"

"I said once that it must be interesting having a father as famous as Sir Geoffrey Harrison, being knighted and all that."

So much for having a mere detective for a father, Banks thought, swallowing his pride. "What did she say?"

"The usual. Something like, 'Oh, you'd be shocked if you knew some of the things I know.'"

"And she didn't elaborate?"

"No. I just shrugged it off. I thought she meant the bad side of technology, all the war stuff, missiles and bombs and that. We all know Sir Geoffrey Harrison's companies are involved in things like that. It's in the papers nearly every day."

"And she didn't say any more about it?"

"No."

"Did she ever mention Father Daniel Charters or Ive Jelačić?"

"The people from St Mary's Church?"

"Yes."

"Not to me. If you ask me, she was more interested in boys than anything else."

"Boys? Anyone in particular."

"Well, she sort of took up with John Spinks." Tracy pulled a face. "I mean, of all the boys ..."

Banks leaned forward. The bedsprings creaked. "Tell me about John Spinks," he said.

SEVEN

I

Eastvale College of Further Education was a hodgepodge of ugly redbrick and concrete buildings on the southern fringe of the town, separated from the last few houses by a stretch of marshy waste ground. There was nothing else much around save for the Featherstone Arms across the road, a couple of industrial estates and a large riding stable, about half a mile away.

The college itself was a bit of a dump, too, Owen thought over his lunch-time pint and soupy lasagna, and he wouldn't be teaching there if he could get anything better. The problem was, with only a BA from Leeds and an MA from an obscure Canadian university, he *couldn't* get anything better. So he was stuck teaching the business, secretarial and agriculture students how to spell and write sentences, skills they didn't even want to know. It was a long way from the literary ambitions he had nursed not so many years ago.

But he had more immediate problems than his teaching career: he had lied to the police, and they probably suspected as much.

It wasn't much of a lie, admittedly. Besides, it was none of their business. He had said he never lived with a woman, but he had. With Michelle. For five years. And Michelle was the woman in the black-and-white nude photographs.

So Owen wasn't exactly surprised when Stott and Hatchley walked into the pub and asked him if he would mind going to the station with them to clear up a few points. Nervous, yes, but not surprised. They said the department head had told them where they were likely to find him, and they had walked straight over.

Nobody spoke during the first part of the journey. Sergeant Hatchley drove the unmarked Rover, and Inspector Stott sat beside him. Owen could see the sharp line of his haircut at the back of his neck and the jug-handle shape of his ears, glasses hooked over them. As they approached the market square, Owen looked out of the window at the drab, shadowy figures hurrying from shop to shop, holding onto their hats.

"I wonder if you'd mind very much," Stott said, turning slightly in his seat, "if we arranged to take a couple of samples?"

"What kind of samples?"

"Oh, just the usual. Blood. Hair."

"Do I have to?"

"Let me put it like this. You're not under arrest, but the crime we're investigating is very serious indeed. It would be best all around if you gave your permission and signed a release. For elimination purposes."

"And if I refuse? What will you do? Hold me down, pull my hair out and stick a needle in me?"

"Nothing like that. We could get the superintendent to authorize it. But that wouldn't look good, would it? Especially if the matter ever went to court. Refusing to give a sample? A jury might see that as an admission of guilt. And, of course, as soon as you're eliminated from the enquiry, the samples will all be destroyed. No records. What do you say?"

"All right."

"Thank you, sir." Stott turned to face the front again and picked up his car phone. "I'll just take the liberty of calling Dr Burns and asking him to meet us at the station."

It was all handled quickly and efficiently in a private office at the police station. Owen signed the requisite forms, rolled up his sleeve and looked away. He felt only a sharp, brief pricking sensation as the needle slid out. Then the doctor pulled some hair out of his scalp. That hurt a little more.

The interview room they took him to next was a desolate place: grey metal desk; three chairs, two of them bolted to the floor; grimy windows of thick wired glass; a dead fly smeared against one institutional-green wall; and that was it.

It smelled of stale smoke. A heavy blue glass ashtray sat on the desk, empty but stained and grimy with old ash.

Stott sat opposite Owen, and Sergeant Hatchley moved the free chair and sat by the wall near the door, out of Owen's line of vision. He sat backwards on the chair, wrapping his thick arms around its back.

First, Stott placed the buff folder he'd been carrying on the desk, smiled and adjusted his glasses. Then he switched on a double-cassette tape recorder, tested it, and gave the date, time and names of those present.

"Just a few questions, Owen," he said. "You've been very co-operative so far. I hope we don't have to keep you long."

"So do I," said Owen, looking around the grim room. "Shouldn't I call my lawyer or something?"

"Oh, I don't think so," said Stott. "Of course, you can if you want. It's your right." He smiled. "But it's not as if you're under arrest or anything. You're free to leave anytime you want. Besides, do you actually have a solicitor? Most people don't."

Come to think of it, Owen didn't have a solicitor. He knew one, though. An old university acquaintance had switched from English to law after his first year and now practised in Eastvale. They hadn't seen each other in years, until Owen had bumped into him in a pub a few months back. Gordon Wharton, that was his name. Owen couldn't remember what kind of law he specialized in, but at least it was a start, if things went that far. For the moment, though, Stott was right. Owen hadn't been arrested, and he didn't see why he should have to pay a solicitor.

"Let me lay my cards on the table, Owen. You have admitted to us that you were in the area of St Mary's on Monday evening. Is that true?"

"Yes."

"Why?"

"I told you. I went for a walk."

"Shall we just go over it again, for the record?"

Owen shrugged. "There's really nothing to go over." He could see the sheet of paper in front of Stott, laid out like an appointment book. Some of the times and notes had question marks in red.

"What time did you set off on this walk?"

"Just after I got back from work. About four. Maybe as late as half past."

"How far is it to St Mary's?"

"Along the river? About three miles from my house. And the house is about half a mile from the river."

"About seven miles there and back, then?"

"Yes. About that."

"Now, before you ate at the Peking Moon you drank two pints of bitter and a Scotch whisky at the Nag's Head, right?"

"I wasn't counting, but yes, I had a couple of drinks."

"And you left the pub at about a quarter to six?"

"I wasn't especially aware of the time."

"That's what the landlord told us."

"I suppose it must be true, then."

"And you ate at the Peking Moon at approximately six-thirty, is that correct?"

"About then, yes. Again, I didn't notice the actual time."

"What did you do between a quarter to and half past six?"

"Walked around. Stood on the bridge."

"Did you go into St Mary's graveyard?"

"No, I didn't. Look, if you're trying to tie me in to that girl's murder, then you're way off beam. Why would I do something like that? Perhaps I *had* better call a solicitor, after all."

"Ah!" Stott glanced over Owen's shoulder towards Sergeant Hatchley. "So he *does* read the papers, after all."

"I did after you left. Of course I did."

Stott looked back at him. "But not before?"

"I'd have known what you were talking about, then, wouldn't I?"

Stott straightened his glasses. "What made you connect our visit with that particular item of news?"

Owen hesitated. Was it a trick question? "It didn't take much," he answered slowly, "given the kind of questions you asked me. Even though I know nothing about what happened, I know I was in St Mary's that evening. I never denied it. And while we're on the subject, what led you to me?"

Stott smiled. "Easy, really. We asked around. Small, wealthy neighbourhood like St Mary's, people notice strangers. Plus you were wearing an orange anorak and you used your Visa card in the Peking Moon."

Owen leaned forward and slapped his palms on the cool metal surface. "There!" he said. "That proves it, then, doesn't it?"

Stott gave him a blank look. "Proves what?"

"That I didn't do it. If I *had* done it, what you seem to be accusing me of, I would hardly have been so foolish as to leave my calling card, would I?"

Stott shrugged. "Criminals make mistakes, just like everybody else. Otherwise we'd never catch any, would we? And I'm not accusing you of anything at the moment, Owen. You can see our problem, though, can't you? Your story sounds thin, very thin. I mean, if you were in the area for some real, believable reason ... Maybe to meet someone? Did you *know* Deborah Harrison, Owen?"

"No."

"Had you been watching her, following her?"

Owen sat back. "I've told you why I was there. I can't help it if you don't like my reason, can I? I never thought I'd have to explain myself to anyone."

"Did you see anyone acting suspiciously?"

"Not that I remember."

"Did you see Deborah Harrison?"

"No."

"About that scratch on your cheek," Stott said. "Remember yet where you got it?"

Owen put his hand to his cheek and shrugged. "Cut myself shaving, I suppose."

"Bit high up to be shaving, isn't it?"

"I told you. I don't remember. Why?"

"What about the nude photos, Owen? The ones we found at your house?"

"What about them? They're figure studies, that's all."

Sergeant Hatchley spoke for the first time, and the rough voice coming from behind startled Owen. "Come on lad, don't be shy. What's wrong with you? Don't you like looking at a nice pair of tits? You're not queer, are you?"

Owen half-twisted in his seat. "No. I didn't say I didn't like looking at naked women. Of course I do. I'm perfectly normal."

"And some of the girls in that magazine seemed very young to me," said Stott.

Owen turned to face him again. "Since when has it been a crime to buy *Playboy*? You people are still living in the middle ages. For Christ's sake, they're models. They get paid for posing like that."

"And you like videos, too, don't you, Owen? There was that one in your cabinet, your own private video to keep, to watch whenever you want. Including *School's Out*."

"A friend gave me it, as a sort of joke. I told him I'd never seen any porn—any sexy videos before, and he gave me that, said I'd enjoy it."

"Well, I'll tell you, Owen," said Stott. "I've got to wonder about a bloke who watches stuff like that and likes the sort of art books and pictures you like. Especially if he takes nude photos of young girls, too."

"It's free country. I'm a normal single male. I also happen to be an amateur photographer. And I have a right to watch whatever kind of videos I want as long as they're legal." Owen felt himself flushing with embarrassment. Christ how he wished Chris Lorimer at the college hadn't given him the bloody video.

"*School's Out*," Hatchley said quietly from behind him. "A bit over the top, that, wouldn't you say?"

"I haven't even watched that one."

"You can see what Sergeant Hatchley's getting at, though, can't you, Owen?" said Stott. "It looks bad: the subject-matter, the image. It all looks a bit odd. Distinctly fishy."

"Well, I can't help that. It's not fishy. I'm perfectly innocent, and that's the truth."

"Who's the girl in the photographs? The one who looks about fifteen."

"She was twenty-two. Just a model. It was a couple of years ago. I can't remember her name."

"Funny, that."

"What is?"

"That you remember her age but not her name."

Owen felt his heart pounding. Stott scrutinized him closely for a few seconds, then stood up abruptly. "You can go now," he said. "I'm glad we could have our little chat."

Owen was confused. "That's it?"

"For the moment, yes. We'll be in touch."

Owen could hardly stand up quickly enough. He banged his knee on the underside of the metal desk and swore. He rubbed his knee and started to back towards the door. His face was burning. "I can really go?"

"Yes. But stay available."

Owen was shaking when he got out of the police station and turned down Market Street towards home. Could they really treat you like that when you went along with them of your own free will? He had a feeling his rights were being trampled on and maybe it was time to look up Gordon Wharton.

The first thing he did when he got into the house was tear up the copy of *Playboy* and burn the pieces in the waste-bin, Cormac McCarthy story and all. Next, he took the video that Chris Lorimer had given him, pulled the tape out, broke the plastic casing and dumped it in the rubbish bin to burn too. At least they couldn't use it as evidence against him now.

Finally, he went into the spare room and took the rest of the nude photographs of Michelle from his filing cabinet. He held them in his hands, ready to rip them into tiny pieces and burn them along with the rest, but as he held them he couldn't help but look at them.

They were simple, tasteful chiaroscuro studies, and he could tell from the way Michelle's eyes glittered and her mouth was set that she was holding back her laughter. He remembered how she had complained about goose-bumps, that he was taking so long setting up the lighting, then he remembered the wine and the wild lovemaking afterwards. She had liked being photographed naked; it had excited her.

His hands started to shake again. God, she looked so beautiful, so perfect, so young, so bloody innocent. Still shaking, he thrust the photos back in the cabinet and turned away, tears burning in his eyes.

II

While Stott and Hatchley were interviewing Owen Pierce, Banks drove out to St Mary's to see Lady Sylvie Harrison. He would have liked Susan with him, for her reactions and observations, but he knew he was risking Chief Constable Riddle's wrath by having anything more to do with the Harrisons, and he didn't want to get Susan into trouble.

She was right; she had worked hard and passed her sergeant's exam, all but the rubber stamp, and he wouldn't forgive himself easily if he ruined her chances of a quick promotion. He would be sad to lose her, though. Detective constables were rarely promoted straight to the rank of detective sergeant, and almost never in the same station; they usually went back in uniform for at least a year, then they had to reapply to the CID.

Before setting off, Banks had phoned the Harrison household and could hardly believe his luck. Sir Geoffrey was out with Michael Clayton, and Lady Harrison was at home alone. No, she said, with that faint trace of French accent, she would have no objections to talking to Banks without her husband present.

As he drove along North Market Street past the tourist shops and the community centre where Sandra worked, Banks played the tape of Ute Lemper singing Michael Nyman's musical adaptations of Paul Celan's poems. It was odd music, and it had taken him some time to get used to it, but now he adored them all, found them pervaded by a sort of sinister melancholy.

It was a chilly day outside, grey and windy, skittering the leaves along the pavements. But at least the rain had stopped. Just as "Corona" was coming to an end, Banks pulled up at the end of the Harrisons' drive.

Lady Harrison must have heard him coming because she opened the large white door for him as soon as he got out of the car. She wore jeans and a blue cashmere pullover. She hugged herself against the cold as she stood in the doorway.

She had done her best to cover up the marks of misery and pain on her face, but they were still apparent through the make-up, like distant figures looming in the fog.

This time, instead of heading for the white room, she hung up his overcoat and led him to the kitchen, which was done in what Banks thought of as a sort of rustic French style: lots of wood panelling and cupboards, copper-bottomed pots and pans hanging on hooks on the wall, flower-patterned mugs on wooden pegs, a few potted plants, a vase of chrysanthemums on the table and a red-and-white checked tablecloth. The room smelled of herbs and spices, cinnamon and rosemary being the two most prominent. A kettle was just coming to the boil on the red Aga.

"Please sit down," she said.

Banks sat on a wooden chair at the kitchen table. Its legs scraped along the terracotta floor.

"Tea? I was just going to make some."

"Fine," said Banks.

"Ceylon, Darjeeling, Earl Grey or Lapsang Souchong?"

"Lapsang, if that's all right."

She smiled. "Exactly what I was going to have."

Her movements were listless and Banks noticed that the smile hadn't reached her eyes. It would probably be a long time before one did.

"Are you sure you're all right here alone, Lady Harrison?" he asked.

"Yes. Actually, it was *my* idea. I sent Geoffrey out. He was getting on my nerves. I needed a little quiet time to ... to get used to things. What would be the point of us both moping around the house all day? He's used to action, to doing things. And please," she added with a fleeting smile, "call me Sylvie."

"Fine," he said. "Sylvie it is."

She measured out the leaves into a warmed pot—a rather squat, ugly piece with blue squiggles and a thick, straight spout—then sat down opposite Banks and let it brew.

"I'm sorry to intrude on your grief," Banks said. "But there are still a lot of questions need answering."

"Of course," said Sylvie. "But Geoffrey told me this morning that you already have a suspect. Is it true?"

Interesting, Banks thought. He hadn't realized there was a lodge meeting last night. Of course, as soon as Stott had tracked down

Owen Pierce and sent his anorak off to the lab for analysis, Banks had let the chief constable know what was happening, and Riddle obviously hadn't wasted much time in reporting to Sir Geoffrey. Ah, privilege.

"Someone's helping us with our enquiries, yes," he said, immediately regretting the trite phrase. "I mean, last night we talked to someone who was seen in the area on Monday evening. Detective Inspector Stott is interviewing him again now."

"It's not that man from the church, the one who was fired?"

"We don't think so, but we're still keeping an open mind about him."

"Do you think this other person did it?"

"I don't know. I haven't talked to him yet. We're playing it very cautiously, very carefully. If he is the one, we want to be certain we don't make any mistakes that will come back to haunt us when the case goes to court."

"Sometimes," mused Sylvie, "it seems that the system favours the criminal rather than the victim. Don't you think?"

Tell me about it, thought Banks wearily. If they did think they'd got their man, next they would have to convince the Crown Prosecution Service they had a case—not always an easy job— then, after they had jumped through all the hoops, as often as not they could look forward to watching the accused's lawyer tear the evidence to shreds. "Sometimes," he agreed. "Did Deborah ever mention anyone called Owen Pierce?"

Sylvie frowned. "No. I've never heard the name before."

Banks described Pierce, but it meant nothing to her.

She poured the tea, tilting her head slightly and biting the end of her tongue as she did so. The Lapsang smelled and tasted good, its smoky flavour a perfect foil for a grey, cold November day. Outside, the wind whistled through the trees and rattled the windows, creating dust devils and gathering the fallen leaves into whirlwinds. Sylvie Harrison put both hands around her mug, as if keeping them warm. "What do you want to know from me?" she asked.

"I'm trying to find out as much as I can about what Deborah was like. There are still a few gaps."

"Such as?"

"Boyfriends, for example."

"Ah, boyfriends. But Deborah was far too busy at school for boys. There was plenty of time for that later. After she finished her education."

"Even so. There was the summer."

Sylvie held his gaze. "She didn't have a boyfriend."

Banks paused, then said slowly, feeling as if he were digging his career grave with every word, "That's not what I heard. Someone told me she had a boyfriend in August."

Sylvie paled. She pressed her lips so tight together they almost turned white.

"*Did* she have a boyfriend?" Banks asked again.

Sylvie sighed, then nodded. "Yes. In the summer. But she finished with him."

"Was his name John Spinks?"

She raised her eyebrows. "How did you know that?"

"You knew about him?"

She nodded. "Yes. He was a most unpleasant character."

"Why do you think a bright, pretty girl like Deborah would go out with someone like that?"

A distant look came into her eyes. "I don't know. I suppose he was good-looking, perhaps exciting in a way. Sometimes one makes mistakes," she said, with a shrug that Banks thought of as very Gallic. "Sometimes one makes a fool of oneself, does something with the wrong person for all the wrong reasons."

"What reasons?"

She shrugged again. "A woman's reasons. A young woman's reasons."

"Was Deborah having sex with John Spinks?"

Sylvie paused for a moment, then nodded and said with a sigh, "Yes. One day I came home unexpectedly and I caught them in Deborah's bedroom. I was crazy with anger. I shouted at him and threw him out of the house and told him never to come back."

"How did he react?"

She reddened. "He called me names I will not repeat in front of you."

"Was he violent?"

"He didn't hit me, if that's what you mean." She nodded in the direction of the hall. "There was a vase, not a very valuable vase, but a pretty one, a present from my father, on a stand by the door. He lifted it with both hands and threw it hard against the wall. One small chip of pottery broke off and cut my chin, that's all." She fingered the tiny scar.

"Did he leave after that?"

"Yes."

"Did you tell Sir Geoffrey about him?"

"No."

"Why not?"

She paused before answering. "You must understand that Geoffrey can be very Victorian in some ways, especially concerning Deborah. I hadn't even told him she was seeing the boy in the first place. He would have made things very uncomfortable for her if he'd known, given Spinks's character and background. I ... well ... I'm a woman, and I think in some ways I understood what she was going through, more than Geoffrey would have, anyway. I'm not saying I approved, but it was something she had to get out of her system. Stopping her would only have made her more determined. In the long run it would probably have resulted in even more damage. Do you know what I mean?"

"I think so. Did Deborah go on seeing Spinks?"

"No. I don't think so. Not after he threw the vase. She was very upset about what happened and we had a long talk. She said she was really sorry, and she apologized to me. I like to think that she understood what I was telling her, what a waste of time seeing this Spinks boy was. She said she realized now what kind of person he was and she would never go near him again. She'd heard him curse me in the most vile manner. She'd seen him throw the vase at the wall, seen the sliver cut me, draw blood." Sylvie touched the small scar again. "I think it truly shocked her, made her see him in a new light. Deborah is a good girl inside, Chief Inspector. Stubborn, wilful, perhaps, but ultimately sensible too. And like a lot of girls her age, she is very naïve about men."

"In what ways?"

"She didn't understand the way they use women, manipulate them, or the power of their lust. I wanted her to learn to value herself. In sex, when the time came, as much as in everything else. Unless a woman respects her sexual self, she's going to be every man's victim all her life. Giving herself away to that ... that *animal* was a bad way for her to start. You men don't always understand how important that time of a woman's life is."

"Was she a virgin before she met Spinks?"

Sylvie nodded and curled her lip in disgust. "She told me all about it that night after the row. He stole a car, like so many youths do these days. They went for a ride out on the moors ..." Her fists clenched as she talked. "And he did it to her in the back of the car."

"Had you met him before that time?"

She nodded. "Just once. It was two or three weeks earlier. Deborah brought him to the house. It was a sunny day. They were out making a barbecue when I got back from shopping in Leeds."

"What happened?"

"That time? Oh, nothing much. They were drinking. No doubt at the boy's instigation, Deborah had taken a bottle of my father's estate wine from the cellar. I was a little angry with them, but not too much. You must remember, Chief Inspector, that I grew up in France. We had wine with every meal, taken with a little water when we were children, so drinking under age hardly seems the great sin it does to you English."

"What was your impression of John Spinks?"

"He was very much a boy of single syllables. He didn't have much to say for himself at all. I'll admit I didn't like him right from the start. Call me a snob, if you like, but it's true. After he'd gone, I told her he wasn't good enough for her and that she should consider breaking off with him."

"How did she react to that?"

Sylvie smiled sadly. "The way any sixteen-year-old girl would. She told me she'd see who she wanted and that I should mind my own business and stop trying to run her life."

"Exactly what my daughter said in the same situation," said Banks. "Is there anything else you can tell me about Spinks?"

Sylvie sipped some tea, then she went to fetch her handbag. She slipped her hand inside and pulled out a packet of Dunhill. "You don't mind if I smoke, do you?" she asked. "Why I should ask permission in my own house, I don't know. It's just, these days ... the anti-smoking brigade ... they get to you. It's only in moments of stress I revert to the habit."

"I know what you mean," said Banks, pulling his Silk Cut out with a conspiratorial smile. "May I join you?"

"That would be even better. Geoffrey will go spare, of course. He thinks I've stopped."

The phrase "go spare" sounded odd with that slight French lilt to it; such a Yorkshire phrase, Banks thought.

"Your husband told me you're from Bordeaux," Banks said, accepting a light from her slim gold lighter.

Sylvie nodded. "My father is in the wine business. A *négociant*. One of *la noblesse du bouchon*."

"I'm afraid my French is very rusty."

"Literally, it means 'the bottle-cork nobility.' It's a collective term for the *négociants* of a great wine centre, like Bordeaux."

"I suppose it means he's rich?"

She wrinkled her nose. "Very. Anyway, I met Geoffrey when he was on a wine-tasting tour of the area. It must have been, oh, seventeen years ago. I was only nineteen at the time. Geoffrey was thirty."

"And Sir Geoffrey fell in love with the *négociant*'s daughter? How romantic."

Sylvie dredged up another sad smile. "Yes, it was romantic." Then she drew deep on her cigarette and let the smoke out of her nose. "You asked if there was anything else about Spinks, Chief Inspector. Yes, there was. Things had been going missing from the house."

"Missing? Like what?"

She shrugged. "A silver snuffbox. Not very valuable, though it might look antique to the untrained eye. Some foreign currency. A pair of silver earrings. Little things like that."

"Since Deborah had been seeing Spinks?"

She nodded. "Yes. I'm almost certain of it. Deborah wouldn't do anything like that. I'm not saying she was a saint—obviously not—but at least she was honest. She was no thief."

"Did you challenge her about the stolen articles?"

"Yes."

"And what did she say?"

"She said she didn't know about the missing things but she would talk to him."

"Did she tell you what he said?"

"She said he denied it."

"Did Spinks ever bother either of you after that day you threw him out?"

Sylvie frowned and stubbed out her cigarette. She rubbed the back of her hand over her lips as if to get rid of the taste. "He made threats. One day, he came to the house when both Deborah and Geoffrey were out."

"What did he do?"

"He didn't *do* anything. Nothing physical, if that's what you mean. If he had, I wouldn't have hesitated to call the police. I tried to close the door on him, but he pushed his way in and asked for money."

"Did you give him any?"

"No."

"What did he say?"

"He said if I didn't give him money, he would keep on seeing Deborah, and that he would get her pregnant, make himself part of the family." She shuddered. "He was disgusting."

"And you still didn't give him anything?"

"No. Then he said if I didn't give him money he would start spreading the word around that he had deflowered Sir Geoffrey Harrison's daughter. That she was nothing but a slut. He said he would spread it around St Mary's and get her expelled, and he would make sure people in the business community knew so that they would all laugh at Geoffrey behind his back."

"What did you do?"

"Nothing. I was too shocked. Luckily, Michael was here at the time. He handled it."

"What did he do?"

"I don't know. You'll have to ask him. I was so upset I went upstairs. All I can say is that I heard nothing more of the matter after that. Spinks disappeared from our lives just as if he had never been there in the first place. Not without leaving some damage, of course."

"Did he ever threaten to harm Deborah physically?"

Sylvie shook her head. "Not that I heard."

"But he certainly seemed capable of acting violently?"

She touched her scar again. "Yes. Do you think … ?"

"I honestly don't know," said Banks. "But anything's possible. Did Mr Clayton know about Spinks from the start?"

"Yes. He dropped by the house that time when they were having the barbecue. He said something to Spinks about the drinking and Spinks was very rude. Michael agreed with me then that Deborah was wasted on the boy. And I told him about … when I found them together in bed. I had to tell someone."

Clayton seemed to be dropping by Sir Geoffrey's house an awful lot, Banks thought. Especially when Sir Geoffrey wasn't there but Sylvie was.

"Does Mr Clayton have any family of his own?" he asked.

"Michael? No. He and his wife, Gillian, split up three years ago. It was a childless marriage." She smiled. "I think part of the problem was that Michael is married to his work. Sometimes I think he has his computers wired directly to his brain. He has a girlfriend in Seattle now, and that seems ideal for him. Long-distance romance. He travels there quite often on company business."

"How long have he and Sir Geoffrey known one another?"

"Since Oxford. They've always been inseparable. In fact, Michael was with Geoffrey when we met."

Banks paused for a moment and sipped some lukewarm tea. "Do you know any of the teachers at St Mary's?" he asked.

"Some of them. When you pay as much money to send your child to school as we do, you tend to have some say in the way the place is run."

"And?"

"And St Mary's is an excellent school. Wonderful facilities, good staff, a healthy atmosphere … I could go on."

"Did you ever get the sense there was anything unpleasant going on there?"

"Unpleasant?"

"I'm sorry I can't be any more precise than that. But if anyone, or any group, was up to something at school—something illegal, such as drugs—and if Deborah found out about it ... She was attacked on her way home from school, after all. Someone could have followed her from there."

Sylvie shook her head slowly. "The things you policemen dream up. No, I never heard the slightest hint of a rumour of anything wrong at St Mary's. And I believe one *does* hear about these things, if they are going on."

"Did you have any reason to think John Spinks or anyone else might have introduced Deborah to drugs?"

She sighed. "I can't say I didn't worry about it." Then she shook her head. "But I don't think so. I never saw any signs. Deborah was a very active girl. She valued her physical health, her athletic prowess, far too much to damage it with drugs."

"Do you know Patrick Metcalfe?"

"I've met him, yes."

"Did Deborah ever talk about him?"

"No, not that I recall."

"Did she like him?"

"She didn't say one way or the other. She did quite well at history, though it wasn't her best subject. But why do you ask?"

"He's just part of the tapestry, that's all. Maybe not an important part. Did Deborah have any contact with the church after you and your husband stopped going?"

"I don't think so. Geoffrey was quite adamant that we all stay away. But the school and the church remained close. She may have had some contact." She rubbed her eyes and stood up. "Please excuse me, Chief Inspector, but I'm feeling very tired. I think I've told you all I can for the moment. And I hope you'll be discreet. I'd prefer it if you didn't let Geoffrey know about what I've told you today."

Banks smiled. "Of course not. Not if you don't tell him I've been here. I'm afraid my boss—"

But before he could get the words out, the front door opened and shut and Sir Geoffrey shouted out, "I'm home, darling. How is everything?"

III

At the back of Eastvale bus station, past the noise of revving engines and the stink of diesel fumes, a pair of heavy glass doors led past the small newsagent's booth to an escalator that rarely worked.

At the top of the staircase, a shop-lined corridor ended in an open, glass-roofed area with a central fountain surrounded by a few small, tatty trees in wooden planters. The Swainsdale Centre.

Several other corridors, leading from other street entrances, also converged like spokes at the hub. There were shops all around— HMV, Boots, W.H. Smith, Curry's, Dixon's—but at six-thirty that Wednesday evening, none of them were open. Only the small coffee shop was doing any business at all—if you could call two cups of tea and a Penguin biscuit in the last two hours "business."

The teenagers hung out around the fountain, usually leaning against the trees or sitting on the benches that had been put up for little old ladies to rest their feet. No little old ladies dared go near them now.

A number of pennies gleamed at the bottom of the pool into which the fountain ran. God knew why people felt they had to chuck coins in water, Banks thought. But the small pool was mostly full of floating cigarette ends, cellophane, Mars bar wrappers, beer tins, plastic bags containing traces of solvent, and the occasional used condom.

Banks experienced a brief flash of anger as he approached, imagining Tracy standing there as one of this motley crowd, smoking, drinking beer, pushing one another playfully, raising their voices in occasional obscenities or sudden whoops, and generally behaving as teenagers do.

Then he reminded himself, as he constantly had to do these days, that he hadn't been much different himself at their age, and that as often as not, beneath the braggadocio and the rough exteriors, most of them were pretty decent kids at heart.

Except John Spinks.

According to Tracy, Spinks was a hero of sorts among the group because of his oft-recounted but never-detected criminal exploits. She thought he made most of them up, but even she had to admit that he occasionally shared his ill-gotten gains with the others in the form of cigarettes and beer. As he didn't work and couldn't have got very much from the dole, he clearly had to supplement his income through criminal activities. And he never seemed short of a few quid for a new leather jacket.

He lived with his mum on the East Side Estate, a decaying monument to the sixties' social optimism, but he never talked much about his home life.

He had boasted of going to an "Acid House" party in Manchester once, Tracy said, and claimed he took Ecstasy there. He had also tried glue-sniffing, but thought it was kids' stuff and it gave you spots. He was proud of his clear complexion.

Spinks, standing a head taller than the rest, was immediately recognizable from Tracy's description. His light-brown hair was short at the back and sides, and long on top, with one long lock half-covering the left side of his face. He wore jeans, trainers with the laces untied and a mid-length flak jacket.

When Banks and Hatchley approached, showed their warrant cards and asked for a private little chat, he didn't run, curse them or protest, but simply shrugged and said, "Sure," then he gave his mates a sideways grin as he went.

They went into the coffee shop, took a table, and Hatchley fetched three coffees and a couple of chocolate biscuits. The owner's face lit up; it was more business than she'd done in ages.

In a way, Tracy was right; Spinks did resemble someone from "Neighbours." Clean cut, with that smooth complexion, he had full lips, perhaps a shade too red for a boy, brown eyes that could probably melt a young girl's heart, and straight, white teeth, the front ones stained only slightly by tobacco. He accepted the cigarette Banks offered and broke off the filter before smoking it.

"You Tracy Banks's dad, then?" he said.

"That's right."

"She said her father were a copper. Nice bit of stuff, Tracy is. I've had my eyes on her for a while. Come to think of it, I haven't seen her for a few weeks. What's she up to, these days?"

Banks smiled. It hadn't taken long to get past the good looks to the slimy, vain and cocky little creep underneath. Now he knew he wouldn't feel bad, no matter what he had to do to get Spinks to talk.

When Banks didn't answer, Spinks faltered only slightly before saying, "Why don't you ask her to drop by one evening? She knows where I am. We could have a really good time. Know what I mean?"

"One more remark like that," Hatchley cut in, "and you'll be mopping blood from your face for the rest of our little chat."

"Threats now, is it?" He shrugged. "What's it matter, anyway? I've already had the little bitch and she's not—"

The woman behind the counter looked over just after Spinks's face bounced off the table, and she hurried over with a cloth to stem the flow of blood from his nose.

"That's police brutality," Spinks protested, his words muffled by the cool, wet cloth. "Broke my fucking nose. Did you see that?"

"Me?" said the woman. "Didn't see nothing. And there's no call for that sort of language in here. You can keep the cloth." Then she scurried back behind the counter.

"Funny," said Banks, "I was looking the other way, too." He leaned forward. "Now listen you little arse-wipe, let's start again. Only this time, I ask the questions and you answer them. Okay?"

Spinks muttered a curse through the rag.

"Okay?" Banks asked again.

Spinks took the cloth away. The flow of blood seemed to have abated, and he only dabbed at it sulkily now and then throughout the interview. "You've broken my tooth," he whined. "That'll cost money. I was only joking, anyway, about your—"

"Deborah Harrison," Banks said. "Name ring a bell?"

Spinks averted his eyes. "Sure. It's that schoolkid from St Mary's got herself killed the other day. All over the news."

"She didn't 'get herself' killed. Someone murdered her."

"Whatever." The lock of hair kept slipping down over Spinks's eye, and he had developed the habit of twitching his head to flick it back in place. "Don't look at me. I didn't kill her."

"Where were you on Monday around six o'clock?"

"Was that the day it was really foggy?"

"Yes."

"I was here." He pointed to the group outside. "Ask anyone. Go on, ask them."

Banks nodded at Sergeant Hatchley, who went out to talk to the youths.

"Besides," Spinks went on, "why would I want to kill her?"

"You went out together over the summer and you parted on bad terms. You were angry with her, you wanted revenge."

He probed his tooth and winced. "That's a load of old knob-rot, that is. Besides, they wasn't supposed to tell you that."

"Who wasn't?"

"*Them*. The French tart and that bloody Clayton. They went to enough trouble to stop me from telling anyone, now they go and tell you themselves. Bloody stupid, it is. Doesn't make sense. Unless they just wanted to drop me in it." He dabbed at his red nose.

Hatchley came back inside and nodded.

"They telling the truth?" Banks asked.

"Hard to say. Like Jelačić's mates, they'd probably say black was white if young Lochinvar over here told them to."

Banks studied Spinks, who showed no emotion, but kept dabbing at his nose and probing his tooth with his tongue. "What did Michael Clayton do to stop you from talking?" he asked.

Spinks looked down into the bloodstained rag. "Imagine how it would sound if some newspaper got hold of the story that an East Side Estate yobbo like me had been sticking it to Sir Geoffrey Harrison's daughter."

"That's *why*. I asked you *what*."

"Gave me some money."

"Who did?"

"Clayton."

"Michael Clayton gave you money to stay away from Deborah?"

"That's what I said."

"How much?"

"Hundred quid."

"So you admit to blackmailing Lady Harrison?"

"Nothing of the sort. Look, if you sell a story to the papers, they pay you for it, don't they? So why shouldn't you get paid if you *don't* sell the papers a story?"

"Your logic is impeccable, John. I can see you didn't waste your time in school."

Spinks laughed. "School? Hardly ever there, was I?"

"Was Deborah there when you went to ask for money?"

"Nah. Just the two of them. Clayton and the old bag." He put on a posh accent. "It was Deborah's day for riding, don't you know. *Dressage*. Got a horse out Middleham way. Always did like hot flesh throbbing between her legs, did Deborah."

"So the two of them had a talk with you?"

"That's right."

"And after Lady Harrison had gone upstairs, Michael Clayton hit you and gave you a hundred pounds."

"Like I said, we came to an arrangement. Then her ladyship came back and said if she ever heard I'd been talking about her daughter, she *would* tell Sir Geoffrey and he'd probably have me killed."

"You blackmailed her and she threatened you with murder?"

"Yeah. Get away with anything, those rich fuckers. Just like the pigs."

"You've been listening to too many Jefferson Airplane records, John. They don't call us pigs now."

"Once a pig, always a pig. And it's compact discs now, not *records*. Jefferson Airplane, indeed. You're showing your age."

"Oh, spare us the witty repartee. Did you see Deborah again after that?"

"No."

"Did you ever have anything to do with St Mary's Church, with Daniel Charters and his wife, or with Ive Jelačić?"

"Church? Me? You must be fucking joking."

"Did Deborah ever mention an important secret she had?"

"What secret?"

"You're not being very co-operative, Johnny."

"I don't know anything about no secret. And my name's John. What you gonna do? Arrest me?"

Banks took a sip of coffee. "I don't know yet. If you didn't kill Deborah, who do you think did?"

"Some psycho."

"Why are you so sure?"

"I saw it on telly. That's what they said."

"You believe everything you hear on telly?"

"Well if it wasn't a psycho, who was it?"

Banks sighed and lit another cigarette. This time he didn't offer Spinks one. "That's what *I'm* asking *you*." He snapped his fingers. "Come on, wake up, John boy."

Spinks dabbed at his nose; it had stopped bleeding now. "How should I know?"

"You knew her. You spent time with her. Did she have any enemies? Did she ever talk to you about her life?"

"What? No. Mostly we just fucked, if you want to know the truth. Apart from that, she was boring. Always on about horses and school. And always bloody picking on things I said and the way I said them."

"Well, she was an educated woman, John. I realize it would have been hard for you to keep up with her intellectually."

"Like I said, she was only good for one thing."

"I understand you once stole a car and took Deborah for a joyride?"

"I ... Now, hang on just a minute. I don't know who's been spreading vicious rumours about me, but I never stole no car. Can't even drive, can I?" He took a pouch of Drum from his flak-jacket pocket and rolled a cigarette.

"What about drugs?"

"Never touch them. Stay clean. That's my motto."

"I'll bet if we had a look through his pockets," said Sergeant Hatchley, "we'd probably find enough to lock him up for."

Banks stared at Spinks for a moment, as if considering the idea. He saw something shift in the boy's eyes. Guilt. Fear.

"No," he said, standing up. "He's not worth the paperwork. We'll leave him be for the moment. But," he went on, "we'll probably be back, so don't wander too far. I want you to know you're looking good for this, John. You've got quite a temper, so we hear, and you had every reason to hold a grudge against the victim. And one more thing."

Spinks raised his eyebrows. Banks leaned forward, rested his hands on the table and lowered his voice. "If I ever catch you within a mile of my daughter, you'll think that bloody nose Sergeant Hatchley gave you was a friendly pat on the back."

IV

At home later that evening, after dinner, when Tracy had gone up to her room to do her homework, Banks and Sandra found a couple of hours to themselves at last. With Elgar's first symphony playing quietly on the stereo, Banks poured himself a small Laphroaig and Sandra a Drambuie with ice. He wouldn't smoke tonight, not at home, he decided, even though the peaty bite of the Islay almost screamed out for an accompaniment of nicotine.

First, Banks told Sandra about John Spinks and his visit to Sylvie Harrison.

"I thought the chief constable ruled the family off-limits," she said.

"He did." Banks shrugged. "Actually, I just escaped by the skin of my teeth. Sir Geoffrey came in and caught me talking to her. A word in Jimmy Riddle's ear and my name would be mud. Luckily, Lady Harrison didn't want him to know we'd been talking about Deborah's boyfriend, so she told him I'd just dropped by to give them a progress report. He was more annoyed that she'd been smoking than he was about my presence."

"This Spinks," Sandra said. "He sounds like a bad character. Do you think Tracy had anything to do with him?"

Banks shook his head. "He was part of the crowd, that's all. She's got more sense than that."

"Deborah Harrison obviously didn't have."

"We all make mistakes." Banks stood up and walked towards the hall.

"Oh, go on," Sandra said with a smile. "Have a cigarette if you want one. It's been a tough day at the gallery. I might even join you." Sandra had stopped smoking some years ago, but she seemed able to cheat occasionally without falling back into the habit. Banks envied her that.

As it turned out, Banks hadn't been going for his cigarettes but for the photograph that Stott and Hatchley had got from Owen

Pierce. Still, not being one to look a gift horse in the mouth, he weakened and brought the Silk Cut from his overcoat pocket.

Once they had both lit up and the Elgar was moving into the adagio, Banks slid the photograph out of the envelope and passed it to Sandra.

"What do you think?" he asked.

"Very pretty. But not your type, surely. Her breasts are too small for your taste."

"That's not what I meant. And I've got nothing against small breasts."

Sandra dug her elbow in his side and smiled. "I'm teasing."

"You think I didn't know that? Seriously, though, what do you think? Professionally."

Sandra frowned. "It's not *her*, is it? Not the girl who was killed?"

"No. Do you see a resemblance, though?"

Sandra shifted sideways and held the photo under the shaded lamp. "Yes, a bit. The newspaper photo wasn't very good, mind you. And teenage girls are still, in some ways, unformed. If they've got similar hair colour and style, and they're about the same height and shape, you can construe a likeness easily enough."

"Apparently she's not a teenager. She was twenty-two when that was taken."

Sandra raised her dark eyebrows. "Would we could all look so many years younger than we are."

"What do you think of the style?"

"As a photograph, it's good. Very good in fact. It's an excellent composition. The pose looks natural and the lighting is superb. See how it brings out that hollow below the breasts and the ever-so slight swell of her tummy? You can even see where the light catches the tiny hairs on her skin. And it has a mood, too, a unity. There's a sort of secret smile on her face. A bit Mona Lisa-ish. A strong rapport with the photographer."

"Do you think she knew him?"

Sandra studied the photograph for a few seconds in silence, Elgar playing softly in the background. "They were lovers," she said finally. "I'll bet you a pound to a penny they were lovers."

"Women's intuition?"

Sandra gave him another dig in the ribs. Harder this time. Then she passed him the photo. "No. Just look at her eyes, Alan, the laughter, the way she's looking at him. It's obvious."

When he looked more closely, Banks knew that Sandra was right. It *was* obvious. Men and women only looked like that at one another when they had slept together, or were about to. He couldn't explain why, certainly couldn't offer any proof or evidence, but like Sandra, he *knew*. And Barry Stott had said that Pierce denied knowing the woman. The next job, then, was to find her and discover why. Banks would wait for the initial forensic results, then he'd have a long chat with Owen Pierce himself.

EIGHT

I

The man who sat before Banks in the interview room at two o'clock that Saturday afternoon looked very angry. Banks didn't blame him. He would have been angry, himself, if two hulking great coppers had come and dragged him off to the police station on his day off, especially with it being Remembrance Day, too.

But it couldn't be helped. Banks would rather have been at home listening to Britten's *War Requiem* as he did every 11 November, but it would have to wait. New information had come in. It was time for him to talk to Owen Pierce in person.

"Relax, Owen," said Banks. "We're probably going to be here for a while, so there's no point letting your blood pressure go right off the scale."

"Why don't you just get on with it," Owen said. "I've got better things to do with my time."

Banks sighed. "Me, too, Owen. Me too." He put new tapes in the double-cassette recorder, then he told Owen that the interview was being taped, and, as before, stated the names of everyone in the room, along with the time, place and date.

Susan Gay was the only other person present. Her role was mostly to observe, but Banks would give her the chance to ask a question or two. They were taking a "fresh team" approach—so far only Stott and Hatchley had interviewed Pierce—and Banks had already spent a couple of hours that morning going over the previous interview transcripts.

"Okay," Banks began, "first let me caution you that you do not have to say anything, but if you do not mention now something which you later use in your defence, the court may decide that your failure to mention it strengthens the case against you. A record will be made of anything you say and it may be given in evidence if you are brought to trial."

Owen swallowed. "Does this mean I'm under arrest?"

"No," said Banks. "It's just a formality, so we all know what's what. I understand you've been informed about your right to a solicitor?"

"Yes."

"And you've waived it?"

"For the moment, yes. I keep telling you, I haven't done anything. Why should I have to pay for a solicitor?"

"Good point. They can be very expensive. Now then, Owen, can we just go over last Monday evening one more time, please?"

Owen sighed and told them exactly the same as he had told Stott the last time and the time before that.

"And you never, at any time that day, had contact with the victim, Deborah Harrison?"

"No. How could I? I had no idea who she was."

"You're quite sure you didn't meet her?"

"I told you, no."

"Why were you in the area?"

"Just walking."

"Oh, come on. Do you think I was born yesterday, Owen? Hey? You had a meeting with Deborah, didn't you? You knew her."

"Don't be ridiculous. How could I know someone like her?"

Banks reached down into his briefcase and pushed the photograph across the desk. "Who's this?" he asked.

"Just a model."

"Look at it, Owen. Look closely. You *know* her. Any idiot can see that."

Banks watched Owen turn pale and lick his lips. "I don't know what you mean," he said. "She was just a model."

"Bollocks she was just a model. Have you noticed her resemblance to the murdered girl?" Banks set a photograph of Deborah Harrison next to it.

Owen looked away. "I can't say I have."

"Look again."

Owen looked and shook his head. "No."

"And you still maintain that you've never met Deborah Harrison?"

"That's right." He looked at his watch. "Look, when is this farce going to end? I've got work to do."

Banks glanced over at Susan and nodded. She leaned forward and placed two labelled packages on the desk. "The thing is, Owen," Banks said, "that this evidence shows otherwise."

"Evidence? What evidence?"

"Hair, Owen. Hair." Banks tapped the first envelope. "To cut a long story short, this envelope contains samples of hairs taken from those we found on the anorak you were wearing on Monday evening when you went for your walk, the one you gave us permission to test. There are a number of hairs that our experts have identified as coming from the head of Deborah Harrison."

Owen grasped the edge of the desk. "But they can't be! You must be mistaken."

Banks shook his head gravely. "Oh, I could bore you with the scientific details about the medulla and the cortex and so on, but you can take my word for it—they match."

Owen said nothing. Susan pushed the other package forward. "Now this," Banks said, "contains hair samples taken from Deborah Harrison's school blazer. Oddly enough, some of these hairs have been positively identified as yours, again matched with the samples you freely allowed us to take the other day." Banks sat back and folded his arms. "I think you've got quite a bit of explaining to do, haven't you, Owen?"

"You're trying to set me up. Those hairs aren't mine. They can't be. You're lying to get me to confess, aren't you?"

"Confess to what, Owen?"

Owen smiled. "You're not going to catch me out as easily as that."

Banks leaned forward and rested his palm on the desk. "Read my lips, Owen," he said. "We're not lying. The hairs are yours."

Owen ran his hand through his hair. "Wait a minute. There must be some simple explanation for this. There's got to be."

"I hope so," said Banks. "I'd really like to hear it."

Owen bit his lip and concentrated. "The only thing I can think of," he said after a few moments, "is that when I was on the bridge, someone bumped into me. It all happened so fast. I was turning from looking over the river, and she knocked the wind out of me. I didn't get a really good look because she disappeared into the fog and I only saw her from behind, but I think she had long fair hair and wore a maroon blazer and skirt. It could have been her, couldn't it? That *could* have been how it happened, couldn't it?"

Banks frowned and looked through the notes in front of him. "I don't understand, Owen. When you talked to DI Stott and DS Hatchley you didn't say anything about this."

"I know." Owen looked away. "At first I just forgot, then, well ... when I remembered, when I'd seen the paper and knew why they'd been questioning me ... Well, I'd already not said anything, so I suppose I was worried it would look bad if I spoke up then."

"Look bad? But how could it, Owen? How could it look bad if you simply said the girl might have bumped into you? What were you afraid of?"

"Yes, but I mean, if it really *had* been Deborah Harrison ... I don't know. Besides, I couldn't be *sure* it was her. It just seemed like the best thing to do at the time. Keep quiet. It didn't seem important. I'm sorry if it caused you any problems."

"Caused *us* any problems? Not really, Owen. But it has caused you quite a few. It's funny you should mention it now, though, isn't it, now we've matched the hair samples?"

"Yes, well ... I told you. Look, you can check, can't you? Didn't her friend see me? I could just see her through the fog."

Banks tapped the two envelopes. "What if she did see you? That doesn't help your case at all, does it? In fact, it makes things worse."

"But I never denied being on the bridge."

"No. But you led us to believe you didn't see Deborah Harrison. Now you're changing your story. I'd like to know why."

"I was confused, that's all."

"I understand that, Owen. But why didn't you tell the detectives who first interviewed you that you'd seen Deborah that night?"

"I told you. It slipped my mind. After all, I had no idea *why* the detectives were talking to me. Then later, when I knew ... well, I was worried that this was exactly the kind of thing that would happen if I did tell you, that you would misconstrue it."

"Misconstrue?"

"Yes. Misinterpret, distort, misunderstand."

"I know what the word means, Owen," said Banks. "I don't need a bloody thesaurus, thank you very much. I just don't see how it applies in your case."

"I'm sorry. Just put it down to an English teacher's pedantry. What I mean is, I thought you'd read more into it, that's all. When you get right down to it, it's not very much in the way of evidence, is it? You have to admit." Owen attempted a smile, but it came out crooked. "I mean, a couple of hairs. Hardly enough to stand up in court, is it?"

"Don't get clever with me, sonny."

"I … I wasn't. I was just pointing out, that's all."

"But we don't know *how* the hairs got where they did, do we?"

"That's what I'm saying. Maybe it happened when she bumped into me."

"If it was her who bumped into you."

"I can't think of any other explanation."

"But I can. See, you've lied to us before, Owen. To DI Stott and DS Hatchley. Why should we believe you now?"

Owen swallowed. His Adam's apple bumped up and down. "Lied?"

"Well, you never told us about seeing Deborah, or about bumping into her for that matter. That's a lie of a kind, isn't it? You might call it a lie of omission. And you also said you didn't know the girl in the photo, but you do know her, don't you?"

"No. I—"

Banks sighed. "Look, Owen, I'm giving you a chance to dig yourself out of this hole before it's too late. We've talked to the landlord of the Nag's Head again, showed him the picture of this 'model.' He says you've been in the pub with her on a number of occasions. He's *seen* you together. What do you have to say about that?"

Banks noticed the sweat start beading on Owen's forehead. "All right, I know her. Knew her. But I don't see how it's relevant in any way. She was my girlfriend. We lived together. Does that satisfy you?"

"Who is she? Where is she now? What happened to her?"

Owen put his hands over his ears. "I don't believe I'm hearing this. Surely you can't think that I've killed Michelle, too?"

"Too? As well as who?"

"For Christ's sake. It's a figure of speech."

"I'd have thought a pedantic English teacher like yourself would be more careful with his figures of speech."

"Yes, well, I'm upset."

"This Michelle, what happened?"

"We lived together for nearly five years, then we split up over the summer. Simple as that."

"And where is she now?"

"She lives in London. In Swiss Cottage."

"Why did you split up?"

"Why does anyone split up?"

"Irreconcilable differences?" Banks suggested.

Owen laughed harshly. "Yes. That'll do. Irreconcilable differences. You could call it that."

"What would *you* call it?"

"It's none of your business. But there is something else. It's got nothing to do with this at all, but if it'll help ..."

"Yes?"

"Well, it's the reason I was out walking. It was the anniversary. The anniversary of the day we met. I was a little down, a bit sad. We used to go for walks by the river, as far as St Mary's, or even further, and we'd sometimes drop in at the Nag's Head to wet our whistles. So I just went for that long walk to get it out of my system."

"You were upset?"

"Of course I was upset. I loved her."

"And did you get it out of your system?"

"To a certain extent."

"How did you get it out of your system?"

"Oh, this is absurd. You've got a one-track mind. There's no point talking to you any more."

"Maybe not, Owen. But you've got to admit things are looking pretty bleak. You lied to us *four* times." He counted them off on his fingers. "Once about why you were out walking, once about never meeting Deborah Harrison, once about not knowing the girl in the photo and once again about never having lived with anyone. All lies, Owen. You see what a position it puts me in?"

"But they were all so ... such small lies. Yes, all right, I lied. I admit it. But that's all. I haven't harmed anyone."

At that point came the soft knock at the door that Banks had arranged earlier. He turned off the tape recorders and told the person to come in. DI Stott entered, nodded quickly at Owen Pierce and apologized for disturbing them. Then he handed a report to Banks and stood by the door.

Banks glanced over the sheets of paper, taking his time, pretending he didn't already know the information they contained. When he had finished, he passed them to Susan. All the time, he was aware of Owen's discomfort and restlessness. Susan read the report and raised her eyebrows. Banks thought they were overacting a bit, behaving like doctors who had just looked at the X-rays and found out their patient had an inoperable tumour. But it was working. Pierce was really sweating now.

Banks turned the tape recorders on again, explaining briefly why he had turned them off and adding that DI Stott was now also in the room. "Results of the blood tests," he said to Owen.

"What blood tests?"

"Remember, we took samples the other day?"

"Yes, but ..."

"With your permission."

"I know, but—"

"Well, we also found a small dried bloodstain on your anorak, and according to this report, Owen, it's Deborah Harrison's blood group, not yours. Can you explain that?"

"I ... I ..."

The three detectives remained silent for a few moments as Owen struggled for an explanation. Then Banks spoke up again. "Come on, Owen," he said. "Tell us about it. It'll do you good."

Owen slammed his fist on the table. "There's nothing to tell! I saw a girl. She bumped into me. Then she ran off. She *might* have been Deborah Harrison. It was foggy. I didn't get a clear enough look. That's all that happened. I don't know how her blood got there. You're trying to frame me. You're planting evidence."

"You're starting to sound a bit desperate now, Owen," Banks said. "Clutching at straws. Why don't you calm down and tell us all about it?"

"But *why* would I have killed the girl? What possible reason could I have? Why don't you believe me?"

"Because you didn't tell us the truth. That means you had something to hide. And there's something else, too."

"What?"

"We found your blood under Deborah Harrison's fingernails. What do you have to say to that?"

"Nothing," Owen said, "I want a solicitor. Now. I'm not saying another word until I get a solicitor."

"That's your right," said Banks. "But just hear me out for a moment before you do or say anything else. You'll feel much better if you just tell us what happened. And it'll go better for you in the long run. When you saw Deborah Harrison on the bridge, she reminded you of this Michelle, didn't she? The girl you were upset about. Were you punishing Michelle through Deborah, Owen? Is that what all this was about? What did she do to you?"

Owen broke off eye contact. "Nothing," he said. "This is all just speculation. It's rubbish."

"You followed her into the graveyard and you approached her, didn't you?" Banks went on, resting his elbows on the desk and speaking softly. "Maybe you offered her a fiver to toss you off so you could pretend it was Michelle doing it. Whatever. It doesn't matter. But she reacted badly. She got scared. You dragged her off the path, behind the Inchcliffe Mausoleum. It was dark and foggy and quiet there. You were going to give her what for, weren't you? Give it to her good and proper just to show her she couldn't do what she did to you and get away with it? All your anger burst out, didn't it, Owen? What happened? Couldn't you get it up? What did Michelle do to you? It *was* her you were strangling, wasn't it? Why did you lie about knowing her?"

Owen put his head in his hands and groaned. Banks packed up his papers, stood and nodded to Stott, who said, "Owen Pierce, you have already been cautioned and now we're going to put you under arrest. I'm going to ask you to come with me to the custody officer. Do you understand me, Owen?"

II

Stott had called it the "custody suite" on the way down, and the sign on the door said "Charge Room," but to Owen it resembled nothing less than the entrance to hell. Abandon all hope ...

It was a cavernous room in the basement of the old Tudor-fronted Eastvale Regional HQ, full of noise and activity. Saturday afternoon was one of the busiest times in the Eastvale custody suite. Today, in addition to the usual Saturday bouts of shoplifting, hooliganism and drunkenness, Eastvale United were playing at home to arch-rivals, Ripon, and there had already been plenty of violence both on and off the field.

The flaking paint had obviously once been an attempt at a cheerful lemon colour; now it looked like a nicotine stain. Owen sat between Stott and Hatchley on a hard bench opposite elevated, joined desks, screwed to the floor, that ran the whole length of the room like a counter. Behind the desks, about six or seven uniformed police officers typed, bustled about, shouted, laughed, filled in forms and questioned people, presided over by the custody sergeant himself. The contrast between the real smell of fear and this slick, bureaucratic activity brought, for Owen, its special brand of terror, like a hospital casualty department where ripped flesh bleeds and pristine machines hiss and beep.

At the moment, a drunk with a bloody face leaned over the desk singing "Danny Boy" at the custody sergeant, who was trying to get his personal details. On the benches near Owen sat a couple of gloomy skinheads, laces missing from their bovver boots; a man who resembled nothing more than a bank clerk, perhaps an embezzler, Owen thought; and a nervous-looking young woman, smartly dressed, biting her lip. A kleptomaniac?

Another man at the desk started arguing with one of the officers about being picked on because he was black. The drunk paused in his song to look over and shout, "Bloody right, too. Ought to go back to the bloody jungle where you came from, Sambo," then he emitted a technicolour whoosh of vomit all over the desk and sank to his knees on the floor to clutch his stomach and whimper. The sergeant swore and jumped backwards, but he wasn't quick enough to prevent some of the vomit from spattering the front of his uniform.

"Get that bastard out of here!" he yelled. In the room's eerie acoustics, his voice rose, echoed wildly, then fell dead.

Adrenalin pumped through Owen's system. He took a couple of deep breaths to calm himself and almost gagged on the stink of vomit and ammonia cleaning fluid that permeated the stale air.

An officer filled in names, numbers, charges and times with a black marker on a white board. Posters covered the walls: one gave a graphic warning about the possible consequences of driving while drunk; one informed prisoners of their rights; a third showed sign language; another advised officers to wear gloves when dealing with vomit and blood due to possible AIDS and Hepatitis B exposure.

Two officers dragged the drunk out and another started clearing up the mess with a mop, cloth and a bucket of Lysol. He was wearing plastic gloves. Blood had dripped on the pale green linoleum. Even the skinheads looked cowed by it all.

Owen kept trying to convince himself that the nightmare would end any moment and he would wake up and find himself out shopping with the rest of the Saturday crowd. Perhaps he would go to HMV in the Swainsdale Centre and buy the new Van Morrison CD. Then, maybe a pint or two and a nice dinner out, Chinese or Indian, just to celebrate. Alone, the way he liked it best.

Or perhaps the policemen would rip off their uniforms to reveal clowns' costumes underneath, and Stott would break into a song and dance number, like characters out of a Dennis Potter play.

As soon as the custody sergeant was free, Stott went over and had a brief word, then gestured for Owen to approach the desk. Stott disappeared through the far door.

"Empty your pockets, please, sunshine," said the sergeant, after taking Owen's personal details.

Owen emptied his pockets onto the desk. There wasn't much in them: keys, wallet, three pounds sixty-eight pee in change, cheque book, bank machine and credit cards, a few crumpled shopping lists and old bus tickets that had been through the washer and dryer a couple of times, his gold Cross fountain-pen, the small Lett's appointment diary-cum-address book with the pencil tucked down the spine, three pieces of Dentyne chewing-gum and a few balls of fluff.

The sergeant flipped through Owen's diary. It was empty apart from a few addresses. Next he looked through Owen's wallet. "Nothing much there," he said, placing it in the plastic bag with the other items. He held the pen between thumb and forefinger and said, "Gold-looking fountain-pen."

"It *is* gold," Owen said. "It's not just gold-looking."

"Well we're not going to get a bloody appraiser in, mate, are we?" the sergeant said. "Gold-looking." He dropped it in the bag.

Before they sealed the bag, a constable patted Owen down to see if he had anything else hidden.

"Shall we have a look up his arse, sir?" he asked the custody sergeant when he had finished.

The sergeant looked at Owen, then back at the constable, as if he were seriously considering the proposition. "Nah," he said. "I never did like rectal searches, myself. Messy business. Never know what you might find. Take him to the studio."

Jesus Christ, thought Owen, they're enjoying this! They don't need to be rude, violent and brutal; they get their kicks better this way, the vicious tease, the cruel joke. They had already judged and condemned him. In their minds, he was guilty, and the rest would be mere formality. And if they believed it, wouldn't everyone else?

When they put him jail, he thought with a stab of fear, it would be even worse. He had heard about the things that went on, how people like the Yorkshire Ripper and Dennis Nilsen had to be kept in solitary for their own good, how Jeffrey Dahmer had been murdered in prison and Frederick West had hanged himself.

Solitary confinement would probably be better than a poke up the bum from a three-hundred-pound Hell's Angel with tattoos on his cock, Owen thought. But could he stand the loneliness, the feeling of being hopelessly cut off from everything he held dear, abandoned by the whole civilized world? He liked the solitary life, but that was his choice. Could he stand it when it was imposed on him?

The constable led him into another room for fingerprinting and mug shots taken by a mounted camera. The "studio." Another cruel joke.

"Now then, mate," the constable said, "let's have your belt and shoelaces."

"What? Why on earth—"

"Regulations. So's you don't top yourself, see."

"But I'm not going to do away with myself. I've told you all. I'm innocent."

"Aye. Well, it doesn't matter. It's more than my job's worth. We'd have your tie too if you were wearing one. Saw a fellow once topped himself with his tie. Polka-dot tie it was. A nice one. You should've seen him, eyes all bulging and his tongue sticking out. And the pong, you wouldn't believe it! Aye, nasty business, it was. Don't worry, mate, you'll get your things back—that's if you're ever in a position to need them again."

He had a good laugh at that while Owen took the belt off his jeans and the long white laces from his trainers.

Back at the desk, the custody sergeant gave Owen a pamphlet on legal aid and sheet of paper that advised him of his rights: to call a solicitor, to inform a friend, and to consult the Codes of Practice. Then he went over to scrawl details on the board.

"I want to call my solicitor," Owen said.

The sergeant shrugged and gestured to the constable again, who escorted Owen to a telephone. He felt in his inside pocket for his address-book, where he had politely jotted down Wharton's number, but realized it had been taken away along with all his other possessions. He turned to the constable.

"The phone number," he said. "It's in my diary. Can I get it back for a minute?"

"Sorry," the constable replied. "Against regulations. It's all been entered and bagged."

"But I can't remember my solicitor's number."

"Best try this, then." He pulled a dog-eared telephone directory from the desk drawer. "It usually works."

Owen flipped through and managed to find Gordon Wharton's office number. He got an answering machine, and even though it was late on Saturday afternoon, left an urgent message anyway, just in case. Then he tried the listed home number, but got no answer. "What now?" he asked the constable.

"Cells." Another constable appeared beside them. They took Owen gently by the elbows and led him back into the corridor. "Nothing to worry about," the first officer said. "Quite comfortable really. More like a hospital ward. Most modern part of the whole building."

Police boots echoed from the greenish-blue walls and high ceiling as the three of them walked down the hallway. At the end, the constable took out a key and opened a heavy, hinged door.

True, the cell wasn't the dank, dripping dungeon Owen had imagined; it was actually very clean, all white tiles, like a public urinal, and bright light from bulbs covered by wire mesh.

It contained a narrow bed, fixed to the wall and floor, with a thin mattress, a washstand and a seatless toilet made of moulded orange plastic. There was only one window, set high and deep in the wall, about a foot square and almost as thick. The door had a flap for observation. A faint odour of dead skin and old sweat lurked under the smell of disinfectant.

"Sorry there's no telly," said one of the jailers, "but you can have something to read if you like. A book, maybe, or a magazine?" He turned to his companion. "Jock here's probably got an issue or two of *Playboy* hidden away at the back of his desk."

Owen ignored the taunt. He simply shook his head and stared around in amazement at the cell.

"Owt to eat?" the jailer asked.

When he thought about it, Owen realized that he was hungry. He said yes.

"The special's steak and kidney pud today. Or there's fish and chips, sausage and—"

"Steak and kidney pud sounds just fine," Owen said.

"Mug of tea? Milk and sugar?"

Owen nodded. This is bloody absurd, he thought, almost unable to contain his laughter. Here I am, sitting in a cell in the bowels of the Eastvale police station putting in an order for steak and kidney pudding and a mug of tea!

"You won't be here long," said the jailer. "And if it wasn't a weekend we'd have you up before the beak tomorrow. Anyway, just so's you know, you'll be well treated. You'll get three square meals a day, a bit of exercise if you want it, reading material, pen and paper if you want—"

"We can't give him a pen, Ted," said Jock. "He might ... you know ... Remember that bloke who ... ?" He drew his forefinger across his throat and made a gurgling sound.

"Aye, you're right." Ted turned back to Owen. "We had a bloke once tried to cut his throat with a fountain-pen. Messy. And another jabbed a pencil right through his eye socket. A yellow HB, if I recollect it right." He shook his head slowly. "Sorry lad, you'll have to wait for writing privileges. It's our responsibility, see. Anything else you want, though, just let us know. As I always say, just ring the bell and ask for room service."

They laughed and walked out into the corridor. The heavy door slammed shut behind them.

III

"So what do you think, sir?" Susan Gay asked over the noise, handing Banks the pint she had just bought him.

"Thanks. Looks like I was wrong, doesn't it?" Banks said, with a shrug.

The Queen's Arms was buzzing with conversation and ringing with laughter that Saturday evening. Rumours had leaked out that the "Eastvale Strangler" was in the holding cells and all was well with the world. Parents could once again rest easy in their beds; just about every phone, fax and modem in town was tied up by the press; and those police who were off duty were celebrating their success. The only things missing were the fireworks and the brass band.

Banks sat next to Susan Gay, with Hatchley and Stott not far away. Stott looked like the cat that got the cream.

Chief Constable Riddle had visited the station earlier, patting backs and bragging to the media. He hadn't wasted the opportunity to admonish Banks for pestering the Harrisons; nor had he neglected to praise Stott for his major role in what was probably the quickest arrest of a sex murderer ever.

This time, Riddle was going to go and tell the Harrisons personally that he had a man in custody for Deborah's murder, largely due to the efforts of new member of Eastvale CID, DI Barry Stott. Of course, Riddle wouldn't be seen dead drinking in a pub with the common foot-soldiers, even if he didn't have a couple of TV interviews lined up. Thank God for small mercies, Banks thought.

As he sipped his pint and let the conversation and laughter ebb and flow around him, Banks wondered why he felt so depressed. Never one to shy away from self-examination, he considered professional jealousy first.

But was that really true? Banks had to admit that it would only look that way to the chief constable and one or two others who had it in for him. As far as the media were concerned, Detective Chief Inspector Alan Banks had headed the most successful investigation in the history of Eastvale Divisional Headquarters. *His* troops had won the battle. He was the general. So why did he feel so depressed?

"The evidence is pretty solid, isn't it, sir?" Susan shouted in his ear.

Banks nodded. It was. Nothing on the shoes that Pierce couldn't have picked up on the river path, but positive blood and hair matches both ways. His and hers. Suspect a bit of an oddball. A liar, to boot. Seen in the area, with no good reason, around the time of the murder. Oh, yes, Banks admitted, even the Crown Prosecution Service should have no trouble with this one. What could be better? And if the DNA results were positive when they came through ...

He looked at Susan. Earnest expression on her round face, with its peaches and cream complexion; short, slightly upturned nose; tight blonde curls. She had a glass of St Clement's in front of her.

Banks smiled, trying to shake off his gloom. "Let me buy you a drink, Susan," he said. "A *real* drink. What would you like?"

"I shouldn't, sir, really ..." Susan said. "I mean, you know, officially ..."

"Bugger *officially*. You're off duty. Besides, this is your senior officer telling you it's time you had a real drink. What's it to be?"

Susan blushed and smiled, averting her blue-grey eyes. "Well, in that case, sir, I'll have a port and lemon."

"Port and lemon it is."

"Let me go, sir."

"No, stay there. Save my seat."

Banks got up and edged his way through the crowd, nodding and smiling a hello here and there. One or two people clapped him on the back and congratulated him on the speed with which he had caught the killer.

With his pint in one hand and Susan's port and lemon in the other, he excuse-me'd his way back. Before he had got halfway he felt a tap on his shoulder and turned around to see Rebecca Charters standing there, long auburn hair framing her pale face.

Banks smiled. "A bit off the beaten track, aren't you?" he said.

"I dropped by the police station first. The man on the front desk said you were all over here celebrating. I've heard that you've got someone under arrest for Deborah Harrison's murder. Is it true?"

Banks nodded. "Yes. A suspect, at least."

"Does that mean you'll be leaving us alone now? Things can get back to normal?"

"Whatever that is," Banks said. "Why? What are you worried about?"

"I'm not worried about anything. It would just be nice to know we could get on with our lives in private now rather than sharing every significant emotional event with the local police."

"That was never my intention, Mrs Charters. Look, it's a bit silly just standing here like this. Would you like a drink?"

He could see Rebecca consider the offer seriously, needily. She eyed the bottles ranged behind the bar, then suddenly she shook her head. "No. No thank you. That's another thing I'm trying to put behind me."

"Good," said Banks. "Good for you."

"How the hell would *you* know?" she said, and stormed out.

Banks shrugged and headed back to the table, where everyone, even DI Stott, was laughing at one of Hatchley's jokes. Banks didn't mind missing it; he had heard them all before, at least five times.

When he slid into his seat again, Susan thanked him for the drink. "What was all that about?" she asked.

"I'm not sure," said Banks. "I think I offended her. Or maybe abstinence has made her irritable."

"As long as she doesn't complain to the chief constable. What next, sir?"

"Next, I think we've got to find out a bit more about what makes Pierce tick. We've still got no motive, have we? He asked us why he should have committed such a crime, and I think we have a duty to try and answer that. If not for his sake, then for a jury's."

"But, sir, if it was a sex murder we don't really need a motive, do we? We wouldn't expect a rational one."

"Did Owen Pierce seem mad to you?"

"That's a very difficult question," Susan said slowly. "The kind of thing experts argue about in court."

"I'm not asking for an official statement. This is off the record. Your personal observations, your copper's intuition."

Susan sipped her port and lemon. "Well, to start with, he was nervous, edgy, hostile and confused."

"Isn't that how you would feel if you were accused of murder and subjected to an interrogation?"

Susan shrugged. "I don't know, sir. I've never been in that position. I mean, if you've got nothing to hide ... If you're telling the truth ... Why get upset?"

"Because everyone *thinks* you did it. And they've got all the power. We have the power. We basically bullied Pierce until he was so confused he acted like a guilty man."

"Are you saying you still don't think he did it, sir?"

Banks scratched the scar beside his right eye. It was itching; sometimes that meant something, sometimes not. He wished he knew which was which. "No. All I'm saying is that everyone's got *something* to hide. Everyone starts to feel guilty when they're stopped and questioned by the police, whether they've done anything or not. Almost anyone would react the way Pierce did under that sort of pressure." Banks lit a cigarette and blew out the smoke slowly, careful to blow it away from Susan, then he took a long swig of beer.

"But you still have doubts?"

Banks clicked his tongue. "I shouldn't, should I? I mean, I *did* arrest him. This is just perfect: signed, sealed and delivered. I'm still confused, that's all. All this business with Pierce has happened so quickly. There are still too many loose ends. There was so much going on around Deborah. Remember? Jelačić's alibi still doesn't really hold water. Then there's that triangle of Daniel and Rebecca Charters and Patrick Metcalfe. That's a pretty volatile combination if ever I've seen one. There's John Spinks, another character capable of violence. Add to that the open satchel, Michael Clayton spending half his time with Sylvie Harrison while her husband is out, and you've still got a lot of unanswered questions."

"Yes, sir, but are any of them relevant now we've got Pierce with the hair and blood?"

Banks shrugged. "Hair and blood aren't infallible. But you're probably right. Sometimes I wish I could just accept the official version."

"But you agree Pierce *could* have done it?"

"Oh, yes. He probably *did* do it. We found no trace evidence at all on either Charters's or Jelačić's clothing. And Pierce *was* in the area. There's also something about him that *harmonizes* with the crime in an odd sort of way. I don't know how to put it any better than that."

"You struck a nerve in him there, sir. I must admit, he gives me the creeps."

"Yes. There's a part of him that has some sort of imaginative sympathy with what happened to Deborah Harrison. What I tried to do in that room was make contact with his dark side." Banks gave a little shudder.

"What is it, sir?"

"Everyone has a dark side, Susan. Doesn't Owen Pierce make you wonder about your own?"

Susan's eyes widened. "No, sir. I don't think so. I mean, we've done our job. We've got the evidence, we've got a suspect in custody. I think we should just let it lie and move on."

Banks paused, then smiled. "You're right, of course," he said. "But we've still a fair bit of work to do. How do you fancy a trip to London on Monday?"

"London? Me, sir?"

"Yes. I'd like to pay this Michelle a visit, see what her story is. He did his best to keep their relationship from us, so there has to be something in it. Besides, I'd like your impressions, woman to woman, if that's not a terribly sexist thing to say."

"It isn't, sir. Of course. I'd love to come."

"Good." Banks looked at his watch and finished his pint. "I'd better get home. Have a nice lie-in tomorrow. You'll enjoy it."

Susan smiled. "I think I will, sir, good-night."

Banks put his overcoat on, said farewell to everyone and acknowledged a few more pats on the back as he walked through the crowd to the door. He stood for a moment on Market Street by the cobbled square watching his breath plume in the clear, cold air.

So much had happened today that he had hardly had time to notice the clear blue sky, the autumn wind stripping leaves from the trees. Now it was dark and the stars shone for the first time in days. A line from last month's Eastvale Amateur Dramatic Society production tripped through his mind: "The fault, dear Brutus, is not in our stars, / But in ourselves." Again, Banks thought of that foggy night in the graveyard and wondered what had really happened there. Perhaps he would never know.

It was a cold night to walk home, but he had drunk three pints, too much for driving, and he decided he wanted to clear his head anyway. With numb hands, he managed to put on his headphones and flip the switch of the Walkman in his pocket. After a second or two of hiss, he was shocked by the assault of a loud, distorted electric guitar. He had forgotten about the Jimi Hendrix tape he had put in earlier in the week to wake him up on his way to work. He hadn't listened to it since then. Then he smiled and started walking home. Why not? "Hear My Train a' Coming" would do just fine; he would listen to Britten's *War Requiem* later.

NINE

I

The 9:36 InterCity from York pulled into London King's Cross at 12:05 on Monday, 13 November, twenty minutes late. A problem with points outside Peterborough, the conductor explained over the PA system. Not for the first time, Banks regarded the bleak, post-industrial landscape of his hometown with a mixture of nostalgia and horror. *Peterborough*. Of all the places to come from. Even if the football team he had supported as a teenager had recently edged about halfway up the second division.

As forecast, the rain came. Not a shower or a storm, but steady November drizzle that looked as if it would keep falling forever from a leaden sky. It was raining in Eastvale when Banks and Susan drove out to York that morning; it was raining in York when they caught the train; and it was raining in London when they got off the underground at Oxford Circus. At least it was a little warmer than the weekend: raincoat weather, not heavy overcoat.

To make it easy all around, Michelle Chappel had suggested over the telephone that she talk to them during her lunch-hour, which started at 12:30, in a small pasta restaurant off Regent Street, near where she worked as office administrator for a quality stationery company.

As the questioning was to be informal, and Michelle herself certainly wasn't suspected of any crime, Banks agreed. It meant they could get the job done and be back in Eastvale by late afternoon if they were lucky.

As usual, Regent Street was crowded, even in the rain, and Banks found he had to dodge many an eye-threatening umbrella spoke as he and Susan made their way to the rendezvous in a side-street not far from Dickins & Jones.

They got there about five minutes late, and Banks spotted Michelle Chappel at a window table. With a skill that Peterborough United could have used the previous weekend, he managed to side-step the waiter, who was blocking the way, holding out large menus and muttering about a fifteen- to twenty-minute wait.

The restaurant was unpretentious in appearance—rickety tables and chairs, plenty of scratched woodwork, gilt-framed water-colours of Venice and Florence, stained white tablecloths—but when Banks looked at the list of specials chalked on the black-board, he soon realized it was the kind of London unpretentious-ness you pay for through the nose.

The small dining-room was crowded, but Michelle had saved two places for them. Waiters scurried around, sweaty-browed; carafes of wine appeared on tables; and the smell of garlic, toma-toes and oregano permeated the air. Despite the bustle, though, it wasn't unduly noisy, and when they had introduced themselves and sat down, they didn't have to shout to be heard.

"I've told Mr Littlewood I might be a few minutes late getting back," Michelle said. "He said he didn't mind."

"Good," said Banks. "We'll certainly try not to take up too much of your time."

"That's all right."

Physically, Michelle resembled her photograph very closely except for her hair, which was now cut short, razor-sculpted around her delicate ears, and hung in a ragged fringe. The strong bone structure was still apparent in her cheeks and jaw, the pale, almost translucent skin still flawless, and although she was sitting, it was clear that she maintained her slim, athletic figure. She wore a tailored red jacket over a black silk blouse buttoned up to the hollow of her long, swan-like neck. From her tiny, pale ears two silver angel earrings danced every time she moved her head.

"You said on the telephone that you would recognize me from one of Owen's photographs," Michelle said to Banks, clearly aware of his scrutiny. "That was two years ago. Have I changed very much?"

Banks shook his head.

"It was one of the nudes, I suppose."

"Yes."

"Then I'm afraid you'll have to take my word on the rest." She smiled, and the humour flickered in her eyes for a moment just as Owen Pierce had captured it on film. She touched her hair. "I had this cut six months ago. Just for a change. Would you like to eat?"

Both Banks and Susan had skipped the train food and were starving. After much study and some consultation, Banks decided on the gourmet pizza with goat cheese, olives, sun-dried tomatoes and Italian sausage. It was London, after all, he thought, and London prices, so why not? Susan went for the cannelloni. They ordered a half-litre of red wine for the two of them. Michelle was already drinking white. She ordered linguine with clam sauce.

That done, they settled back to talk. Customers came and went, more leaving than arriving as it got close to one o'clock, and the drizzle continued to streak the window behind the slightly dirty white lace curtains.

"I'm not sure what you want from me," Michelle said. "You didn't tell me very much on the telephone."

"I'm not certain myself, Miss Chappel," said Banks. "I just hope I'll know it when I hear it."

"Call me Michelle. Please."

Banks nodded.

"You said Owen has been arrested?"

"That's right."

"On what charge?"

"You mean you don't know?"

"Well, his name's not been in the papers, and you didn't tell me over the phone. How could I know?"

"Of course not." Banks looked at Susan and nodded.

"I'm afraid it's very serious, Michelle," Susan said. "Owen's been arrested for murder. I'm sorry."

"Murder? But who ... Wait a minute ... Not that schoolgirl?"

"Deborah Harrison. Yes."

"I read about it." Michelle shook her head slowly. "Bloody hell. So he's ..." She looked back at Banks. "And what do you think I can do for you?"

"We'd like to know what you can tell us about him. He didn't seem willing to admit he knew you, or tell us who you were."

"I'll bet he didn't."

"Did something happen between you?"

Michelle frowned. "What do you know already?"

"Not much. Given the nature of the crime, we need to get some sort of grasp on what kind of person he is. We understand already that he's a bit of a loner, something of an oddball, according to some people."

"Is he? He wasn't always, you know. Not at first. He could be fun, could Owen. For a while, anyway, then ..." her eyes darkened.

"Then what?"

"Oh, just ... things change. People change. That's all."

"Well, you can see our problem, can't you?" Banks said. "He's got no close family, and no-one in Eastvale seems to know him very well. We were hoping you might be able to throw some light on his character."

"Is he going to plead insanity?"

"It's nothing like that. Why do you ask?"

"I mean, what do you want to know about him for?"

"Look, don't worry. We're not going to drag you into court or anything."

"Oh, I don't mind that."

"Then what?"

Michelle leaned forward and rested her elbows on the table. "In fact," she said, lowering her voice, "I'd be more than happy to go into court."

Banks frowned. "I don't understand, Michelle. What happened between you? All we know is that the two of you split in the summer and that Owen seemed reluctant to admit he knew you. In fact he tried to tell us the photographs were of some anonymous model."

Michelle snorted. "I'll bet he did."

"Why would he do that?"

"Why? I'll tell you why. Because he tried to kill me, too, that's why."

II

It was less than a mile from the police station to the Town Hall, and Owen would have appreciated the walk after being cooped up in a cell all weekend. But two officers escorted him straight to a van in front of the station. Before they went out of the doors, one of them threw a musty old raincoat over his head.

It was no distance from the front doors to the van, either, but on the way Owen had the awful sensation of being swallowed up by a huge mob, and he had to struggle to stop his bowels from loosening.

He could hear people shouting questions, yelling insults and cursing him. One group, all women by the sound of them, were chanting, "Hang him! Hang him!" Owen had always feared crowds, had never been able to attend a football match or a music concert in comfort. To Owen, crowds weren't really human; they were a mindless beast with the power of an elemental force. The raincoat over his head smelled of other people's fear.

Luckily the jostling didn't last. Before Owen actually lost control of his bowels and made a fool of himself, he felt himself pushed into the back of a van and heard the door slam. The shouts and chants were muffled now, and the van's engine soon drowned them out completely.

Things weren't quite as bad at the other end, where he was hustled through a smaller crowd, then taken to an antechamber. When Owen was finally able to remove the raincoat, the first person he saw was Gordon Wharton. Not the prettiest sight in the world, but a welcome one under the circumstances.

Wharton leaned back in his chair, plucked up the crease of his pinstripe trousers and crossed his legs. It was a prissy sort of gesture, Owen thought, and one that went with his supercilious expression, the pink, well-scrubbed cheeks and the way he wore his few remaining strands of oily hair combed across his gleaming skull. Though he was probably about the same age as Owen, he looked much older. It was partly the fat, Owen thought, and the baldness, and maybe the strain of overwork. Why did the only solicitor he knew turn out to be *Wharton?*

He had been the university swot, never time for a drink in the local or a film in town, and Owen had never much liked him. He sensed the feeling was mutual. The only reason they had first come into contact at all was a shared subsidiary subject in their first year, and then they had both ended up working in Eastvale and met by chance that day.

Wharton had finally arrived to see Owen on Sunday morning, having been out of town on Saturday, and had been unable to get him out on police bail.

"All right?" Wharton asked.

Owen took a few deep breaths. "I suppose so. What are they trying to do, get me torn to pieces?"

Wharton shrugged.

"What nobody seems to realize is that I'm *innocent*."

Wharton made a steeple of his fingers and looked down. "Owen, you're not the first innocent man to be arrested for some offence or other, and you won't be the last. That's why we have the law. Everyone's innocent until they're proven guilty. The police are only concerned with whether they can prove a case. It's up to the courts to decide now. Trust in justice."

Owen snorted. "The British justice system? It hasn't done me a lot of good so far, has it?"

"Carp all you may, Owen, but it *is* the best justice system in the world. In many other countries you'd be on your way to the execu-tioner already, or languishing forever in some smelly cell. Look, I suggest that you accept your situation. Complaining will do you no good at all in your present circumstances. It will only lead to self-pity. Now let us see if there's anything else we need to consider."

Pompous bastard, Owen thought. "It's all very well advising me not to complain," he said. "You're not the one who's in jail. Will I get bail at court this morning?"

Wharton shook his head. "I doubt it. Not on a charge like this one."

"Look, I'm sure if you could persuade the police to do a bit more digging around, they'll come up with the real killer."

Wharton leaned forward and rested his hands on the desk. Owen noticed the gold cufflinks flash in the light. "Owen," he said, pausing for emphasis, "you still don't seem to realize the gravity of your situation. You have been arrested for the most serious crime there is: murder. Nobody's going to let you simply walk away."

"Whose side are you on?"

Wharton held his hand up. "Let me finish. As far as the police are concerned, they have already got their man. Why would they waste their time looking for an alternative? You'll have to face up to the facts, Owen, you've been arrested for murder, you're being held, in a week or two the Crown Prosecution Service will start building a case against you, and you're going to be tried in court. I will do everything in my power to help you, including engaging the services of the best barrister I can find to represent you, but you *must* accept the situation. Do you understand me?"

Owen wasn't sure that he did, but he nodded anyway.

"Good," said Wharton.

"So what *will* happen in court? What's the point of coming here if they're only going to send me back to jail?"

"For remand. They'll either grant it or release you. As I've already said, I wouldn't depend on the latter. Then they'll set a date for the preliminary hearing."

"How long will I have to wait before that?"

"Hmm. It's hard to say. There's supposed to be a time limit of fifty-six days." Wharton gave a twisted smile. "Unfortunately, you're not the only alleged criminal in the system. We get backlogs."

Owen felt his chest tighten. "Are you saying I could be in jail until February before I even get a preliminary hearing?"

"Oh, at least. Not in Eastvale nick, though. No. Probably somewhere like Armley. And don't worry, they know well enough to keep the other prisoners away from you. Everyone knows how moral criminals get when sex crimes are involved. You'll be isolated. But don't worry about that now. Take things as they come, Owen. One day at a time. That's my advice. I'll be working for you, never fear."

Why didn't that thought comfort Owen as much as it should have? he wondered.

A clerk popped his head around the door. "Time, gentlemen."

Wharton smiled and picked up his black leather briefcase. "Come on then, Owen," he said. "Better gird up your loins."

III

The food arrived just after Michelle's remark about Owen Pierce trying to kill her, and they kept silent as the waiter passed them the hot plates and refilled the baskets of bread. It was after one o'clock now. Michelle was going to be late back for work, Banks knew, but she didn't seem to mind. She clearly wanted to tell them the worst about Owen Pierce.

Banks waited until they had all sampled their food and commented on its quality, then went on. "There was something you said earlier, about Owen being fun at first, then changing. How did he change? Was that anything to do with what happened? Did he become violent?"

"No. Well, not really *violent*. Not until the end, that is."

"The end?"

"The day I left him. The night before, rather."

"If he wasn't violent before that, then what was wrong? How did he change?"

"He was just becoming impossible, that's all. Bad-tempered. Complaining. Irrational. Jealous." She paused and took a mouthful of her linguine, following it with a sip of white wine.

"Did he have a violent temper?"

Michelle nodded. Her angel earrings danced. "He started developing one. It got worse towards the end. He just became so possessive, so jealous. He'd fly into rages over nothing."

"Is that why you left him? Fear of violence?" Susan cut in. "Were you frightened he'd hurt you?"

Michelle looked at Susan. "No," she said. "Well, not really. It was frightening, especially the last night, but ... how can I make you understand?"

"We're listening." Susan watched Banks nibble at his pizza out of the corner of her eye. "What happened? Will you tell us?"

Michelle gulped a little more wine, looked at her, then nodded. When she spoke, she looked back and forth between the two of them. "All right. Yes. I'd been out late with a friend. Owen was waiting up for me. And he'd been drinking."

"Did he usually drink much?" Banks asked.

Michelle speared some linguine and twisted it on her fork. "No, not usually, though he had been doing more lately. Especially if he was brooding about something, which he always seemed to be. Anyway, I could definitely smell the whisky on his breath that night."

Banks sipped his red wine. It tasted watery. "Had you been drinking much, too?" he asked.

"Only a couple of glasses of wine."

Banks nodded. "What happened next?"

"He started calling me terrible names and accusing me of all kinds of disgusting things and then he ... he ..."

"He what, Michelle?"

"Oh, bugger it. Get it out, Michelle." She took a deep breath and rubbed the back of her hand across her eyes. "He tried to force himself on me, that's what he did."

"He tried to rape you?"

"Yes. He tried to rape me." She wasn't crying, but her eyes glittered with anger.

"Was this the first time he had ever tried such a thing?"

"Of course it was. Do you think I'd willingly stay a moment longer than I had to with anyone who did that to me?" She hadn't finished her meal, but she pushed her plate aside and sipped some more wine.

"I don't know what your situation was," Banks said. "Sometimes people, women especially, get stuck in abusive situations. They don't know what to do."

"Yes, well, not me. I'm not like that. Oh, I'd done my best, tried to please him, given in to his ... but it was getting impossible. I was at my wits' end. His demands were getting too much for me. This was the last straw. And I was especially upset by the names he called me and the dirty things he accused me of."

"So you resisted him?"

"Yes. I thought it was awful that someone would say such horrible things to me, call me such vile names and then want to do it to me ... you know ... like animals."

"Did you struggle?"

Michelle nodded.

"Then what happened?"

"It's not very clear after that. I know he hit me at least once and then everything went dark."

"He hit you when you refused to have sex with him?"

"Yes. I just remember falling and my head hurting and everything going dark for … I don't know … maybe only a few seconds."

"What happened next?"

"I felt his hands around my neck."

"Owen was trying to strangle you?"

"Yes. He had his hands on my throat and he was pressing."

"How did you stop him?"

"I didn't. I hadn't the strength. I must have passed out again."

"Then what?"

"I woke up. It was light, early morning, and I was still on the floor, where I'd fallen. I felt all stiff and my head hurt. My clothes were torn. I had an awful headache."

"Where was Owen?"

"He was in bed asleep, or passed out. I heard him snoring and went to look."

"Had he interfered with you sexually in any way?"

"Yes. I think he'd had sex with me."

"You can't be certain?"

"No. I wasn't conscious. But I'm pretty sure he had."

"How did you know?"

She looked directly at Banks. He couldn't detect any strong emotion in her eyes now, despite the events she was relating. She wasn't exactly being cold and clinical about it all, but she wasn't overly agitated, either. The few remaining diners would never have guessed what horrors the trio near the window were talking about.

"A woman can tell about those things," she said, then she turned to Susan. "I felt sore … you know … down there."

Susan nodded and touched her arm.

Banks finished his pizza and looked around to see if anyone was smoking. Miraculously, one or two people were. The restaurant had quietened down a lot, and when Banks beckoned the waiter to bring him an ashtray, he did.

"What did you do next?" Banks asked Michelle.

"I packed up my things, what little I had, and I left."

"Where did you go?"

"I just walked and walked. I had nowhere *to* go. At least it was summer. And it wasn't raining. I remember sleeping in the sun in a park."

"And that night?"

"I tried to sleep at the railway station, but the police kept moving me on. I went in shop doorways, wherever I could find shelter. I was scared."

"And the next day?"

"I swallowed my pride, went back to my parents and faced the music. A month later I got the job down here."

"What did you tell them?" Susan asked.

"I couldn't tell them the truth, could I? I was too ashamed. I couldn't tell anyone that. I made up a story about just not, you know, being happy with Owen, and they believed it. It was what they wanted to hear. They'd only met him once and didn't like him anyway. Thought he was too old for me. All I had to do was tell them what they wanted to hear and eat enough crow. They always believed what I told them."

"Why didn't you report the incident to the police?" Banks asked.

"I told you. I was too ashamed. I'm sure Detective Constable Gay will understand that."

Susan nodded. "Yes."

"Oh, I know what I *should* have done," Michelle went on. "Especially now, after what's happened to that poor schoolgirl. In a way, I feel terribly guilty, almost responsible. But you can't really predict what a person will do, can you, how far he will go? I knew Owen was a bit unbalanced, that he could be dangerous. I should have known just *how* dangerous, and I should have reported him to the police. But I was scared." She looked at Susan again. "And I'd heard such awful things about what they do, you know, in court, to girls who make such complaints. How they make out you're the guilty one, that you're just a slut, and how they get all sorts of doctors and … I … I just didn't think I could go through with it. I mean, I *was* living with Owen, wasn't I? And I had given in to him willingly before. What would they have said about that? They'd have said I led him on, that's what."

"The courts aren't so easy on rapists these days, Michelle," said Susan. "It wouldn't have been like that."

"But how was I to know?"

"Was that the only reason you didn't report the incident?" Banks asked. "Fear of the police and the courts?"

"Well, mostly. But there was Owen, too, wasn't there? I mean, after someone's done something like that to you, something violent, you have to wonder, don't you, whether they're capable of anything. You hear about men stalking women and all the things they do to them. I was ashamed, but I was scared as well. Scared of what he might do." She looked at her watch. "My God, it's after two," she said. "Look, I really must go now. Mr Littlewood is only liberal to a degree."

"In the light of what you've just told us," Banks said, "we'd like to get a full statement from you. We can do it after you've finished work this evening, if you've got no objection."

Michelle bit her lip and thought for moment.

"No," she said. "I've got no objection. Yes. Let's do it. Let's get it over with. I finish at five-thirty."

"We'll be waiting."

They watched her go, then Banks lit another cigarette and they each ordered a cappuccino. "Well," said Banks, "it looks like we're stuck in the big city for the afternoon. Want to see the crown jewels? Maybe tour the Black Museum? Or we could always do some early Christmas shopping."

Susan laughed. "No thanks, sir. Perhaps we could give Phil Richmond a call at the Yard? He might be able to sneak away for an hour or so."

"All right," said Banks. "Why don't you phone him?"

"Yes, sir. Got a ten-pee piece?"

IV

Armley Jail loomed ahead like a medieval fortress. Owen could only see part of it through the mesh window between himself and the van's driver, but he knew the building well enough; he'd seen it many times when he was at Leeds University.

Standing on a hill to the west of the city centre, it was an enormous, sprawling Victorian edifice of black granite, complete with battlements and towers and newer sections that seemed constantly under construction. The place was practically a tourist attraction. They had kept Peter Sutcliffe, the "Yorkshire Ripper," on remand there for a while in 1981.

At least the van driver had a sense of humour. Elvis Presley belted out "Jailhouse Rock" as the van passed through the huge gates with its load of prisoners shackled in heavy cuffs. Owen wondered if he did that every trip, the way tour guides always made the same jokes.

In a low-ceilinged reception room, the cuffs were removed, and Owen found himself signed over from the police to the jailers. He might easily have been a cow or pig sold at market. Next he was given a number he made no attempt to memorize, then, after his belongings had been catalogued and placed in a box, much as in the charge room at the police station, he was taken to a cubicle and strip-searched.

After that, the governor explained that as Owen was regarded as a Category A inmate, he would spend twenty-three and a half out of twenty-four hours alone in his cell, the other half-hour being set aside for supervised exercise. He would be allowed to purchase as many cigarettes as he wanted—not that this appealed to Owen at all—and given access to writing paper and books.

The whole thing reminded Owen of the scene from Kubrick's film, *A Clockwork Orange*, where Alex is inducted into jail. This room had the same grey inhuman feel, a perfect setting for humiliation. He was now a number, no longer a man.

After a cursory medical ("Ever suffered from palpitations, shortness of breath?") no doubt required to protect the authorities should he drop dead tonight in his cell, he was ordered to take a bath in about six inches of lukewarm water. The tub was an old, Victorian model, with stained sides and claw feet. When he had dried off, he was given his prison uniform: brown trousers and a blue striped shirt that felt coarse and scratchy next to his skin.

After this, he was handed his equally rough bedding and escorted to his cell. It was in a special wing of the prison with black metal stairs and catwalks like something out of an M.C. Escher print. The walls were covered in flecked institutional-green paint, and high ceilings echoed every footstep.

His cell was slightly larger than the one in Eastvale police station, but a lot more gloomy. The whitewashed walls had turned grey with age and dirt; the floor was cold stone. The only window stood high in the wall. About as big as a handkerchief, it seemed to be made of reinforced glass. Light shone from a low wattage bulb hanging from a ceiling outlet; the shade was covered by wire mesh. Though a washstand, soap and a towel stood in the corner behind the door, there was no toilet. Looking around, Owen located a bucket beside his bed.

One added feature was the table and chair. They were so small that he could hardly get his knees underneath comfortably. The scored table was a bit rickety, but a couple of pages torn from his diary, folded and wadded beneath one of the legs, soon fixed that.

He had asked for paper and books from the prison library— science fiction if possible, to let him escape, at least in mind from his dreary surroundings. Sci-fi had been a passion during his adolescence, though he hadn't read any since. Now, curiously, he felt an urge to start reading it again. Wharton would also be bringing him his Walkman and a few cassettes as soon as possible.

He paced for a while, then tried to take approximate measure of his cell. He concluded that it was about eight feet by ten. Next he slouched on his hard, narrow mattress and stared at the cracks on the ceiling. He had expected to find days crossed off all over the walls, just like he had seen in films, but there were none. There wasn't even a trace of graffiti, a name scratched by fingernail, to show who had been here last.

Perhaps it had been the Ripper himself. Owen shivered. That was a foolish thought, he told himself. It was years ago that Sutcliffe had been held here. Dozens of people must have been in and out since then. Still ... a haunted cell, that would just about make his day.

It was time to keep his imagination in check and take stock of his situation. Certainly he was aware of what *could* happen to him, the "worst case scenario" as Wharton had put it earlier that morning, and that didn't bear thinking about.

Wharton had already been right about the Magistrates' Court; the whole thing had been over in a couple of minutes and Owen found himself on remand awaiting trial for the crime of murder. So much for truth and justice.

What worried him most now were the practical things: his job, the house, the fish, his car. Wharton had taken his keys and said he would take care of things, but still ... Had anyone let the department at college know? If so, what had the chairman done? It wouldn't be too difficult to share out his classes among his colleagues until a temporary lecturer could be brought in, but what if this thing dragged on for months? He didn't have tenure, so the college could let him go whenever they felt like it. If he lost his job because of this farce, this absurd mistake, he wondered if he could seek any kind of compensation.

The house would remain his as long as his bank account could stand the strain of the standing payment order for his mortgage, and that should be long enough. After all, he had been making fairly decent money for some time and had very little in the way of expenses. He hoped that his neighbour Ivor, who also had a key, would take good care of the fish.

The sound of footsteps disturbed his train of thought, then he heard the key turn in the lock. It was meal-time already. The warder had also brought him a felt-tipped pen, writing pad and envelopes, a surprisingly well-thumbed copy of Wordsworth's *Collected Poems* and Isaac Asimov's *Foundation* trilogy.

When he had finished his meal and the door closed again behind the warder, Owen picked up the pen and sat at the desk. He had no-one to write to, but he could certainly pass time on a journal of his experiences and impressions. Maybe someday someone would want to publish it.

Fifty-six days or longer, Wharton had said. Well, there was nothing he could do about it, was there, so he might as well just get used to it.

TEN

I

The offices of the Eastvale Crown Prosecution Service were located on the top floor of a drafty old three-storey building on North Market Street, straddling two shops between the community centre and the Town Hall. The lower floor was taken up by a clothes boutique catering to oversize people and a shop that sold imported Belgian chocolate. Somewhere else in the building, a dentist had managed to squeeze in his surgery. Sometimes you could hear the drill while discussing a case.

The chief CPS lawyer assigned to the Pierce file was Stafford Oakes, a shabby little fellow with elbow patches, greasy hair, a sharp nose and eagle eyes. Banks had worked with Oakes before on a number of occasions and had developed great respect for him.

Banks was with DI Stott, and beside Oakes sat Denise Campbell, his colleague, whose expensive and stylish designer clothes stood in stark contrast to Oakes's off-the-peg bargain items. Denise was an attractive and ambitious young lawyer with short black hair and pale skin. Banks had never once seen her smile, and she seemed far too stiff, prim and proper for her age.

In general, the police were wary of the CPS because of its negative attitude towards bringing cases to court, and indeed Banks had had more than one argument with Oakes on this subject. On the whole, though, Oakes was a fair man, and he didn't usually—like so many Crown Prosecutors—do more damage to the case than the defence did. Banks had even had a pint with him on a couple of occasions and swopped stories of life in the trenches of London, where they had both spent time.

Oakes's office was as untidy as the man himself, briefs and files all over the place. Many of them bore his trademark—linked coffee-rings, like the Olympic games symbol—for Oakes was a caffeine addict and didn't care where he rested his mug. Today it sat on top of the post-mortem report on Deborah Harrison.

It was already only a couple of weeks before Christmas, more than two weeks since they had first consulted by telephone. DNA tests had confirmed that it was, indeed, Deborah's blood on Owen's anorak and Owen's tissue under her fingernail. Banks had sent over all the witness statements and forensic test results collected in the Initial Case File. Owen Pierce's defence team would also have copies of them by now.

"I like this," Oakes was saying, tapping the foot-thick heap of files on his desk. "I particularly like this DNA analysis. Something I can really get my teeth into. No confession, you say?"

"No," Banks answered.

"Good." He slurped some coffee. "Nothing but trouble, confessions, if you ask me. You're better off without them. What do you think, Denise?"

"We've had *some* success with confessions. Limited, I'll admit. As often as not they'll retract, say the police falsified it or beat it out of them." She gave Banks a stern look. "But even scientific evidence isn't entirely problem-free. Depends very much on how it was gathered and who's presenting it."

"Oh, I know that," said Oakes, waving his hand in the air. "Remember that dithering twit in the Innes case we did in Richmond?" He looked at Banks and Stott and rolled his eyes. "Open and shut. Or should have been. Simple matter of blood-stains. By the time the defence had finished with this chap, he was a nervous wreck, not even sure any more that two and two made four. But what I mean is, a good, solid case rests on facts. Like DNA. That's what judges like and that's what juries like. Facts. Indisputable. Beautiful. Facts. Am I right, Denise?"

Denise Campbell nodded.

"Now," Oakes went on after another slug of coffee, "I trust that Mr Pierce gave his permission for the blood and hair samples to be taken?"

"Yes," said Banks. "They were taken by a registered police surgeon. You should have copies of the signed consent forms."

Oakes frowned and dug around deeper in the pile. "Ah, yes," he muttered, pulling out a few coffee-ringed sheets. "Here they are. Good. Good. And I trust his anorak was legally obtained in the first place?"

Banks looked at Stott, who said, "Yes. He gave us his permission to take it in for tests and we gave him a receipt."

"But you didn't go into his home with a search warrant?"

"No," said Stott. "At that stage in our enquiries we merely wanted to talk to Mr Pierce. Then, when I saw the orange anorak, having heard descriptions of a man in a similar orange anorak in the vicinity of the crime scene, I took the initiative and—"

Oakes flapped his hand again. "Yes, yes, yes, Inspector. All right. You're not giving evidence in court. Spare me the formalities. It's a bit flimsy, but it'll have to do."

Stott sat stiffly in his chair, red-faced, mouth tight. Banks couldn't resist a smile. It was the new lad's first taste of Stafford Oakes.

Oakes went on, thumbing through the pile on his desk. "Good stuff, most of this," he said. "DNA, hair, blood analysis. Good stuff. Can't understand a word of it myself, of course, but get the right man in the box and we'd even be able to sell it to your average *Sun* reader. That's the key, you know: plain language, without talking down." He put a thick wad of papers aside and flapped a few statements in the air. "And this," he went on. "Not so bad, either. Your vicar, what's his name ... Daniel Charters ... places our man on the bridge around the right time." He touched his index finger to the side of his nose. "Must say though, Banks, there's a hint of moral turpitude about the fellow."

"Daniel Charters was accused of making a homosexual advance to a church worker," said Banks. "A Croatian refugee called Ive Jelačić, who was also a suspect in this case, until we turned up Pierce. If it's of any interest, I don't believe Charters did it."

"Doesn't matter what *you* believe. Does it, Denise?"

"No," said Denise.

"See, my learned colleague agrees. No, what matters, Banks, is what the jury believes. Vicar with a whiff of scandal lingering around the dog-collar like a particularly virulent fart." He shook his head and tut-tutted. "Now, there, they say to themselves, goes a true hypocrite, a man who preaches the virtue of chastity, a man who belongs to a church that won't even ordain homosexual ministers, caught with his hand up the choirboy's surplice, so to speak. Well, you see what I mean? It's tabloid scandal-sheet material, that's what it is."

"The point is academic, anyway," Banks said, "as Owen Pierce openly admits to being on the bridge at the time."

"Ah-hah," said Oakes, raising a finger. "I wouldn't take too much notice of that. It's about as useful as a confession. And remember, that's what he said *before* he talked to his solicitor. A lot can change between now and the trial. Believe me, we need as much evidence as we can get."

"Charters isn't the only one who can place Pierce on the bridge around the right time. Deborah's friend Megan Preece saw him, too."

Oakes shook his head. "I've read her statement. She's not entirely *sure* it was him. Damn good thing, too. Nothing worse than children in the box. Oh, we'll use your vicar. Don't worry about that. Just playing devil's advocate. Have to anticipate all eventualities." He glanced at more statements. "The landlord of the Nag's Head places Pierce in the pub a short while before, too, I see. He's reliable, I suppose?"

Banks looked at Stott again. "Well," the latter said stiffly. "He seems a bit slow to me, but given that it wasn't a busy night and Pierce seems to have been about his only customer, I think we can rely on him, yes."

"Good. And what's this other place now ... Ah, the Peking Moon. A Chinese restaurant." He wrinkled his nose. "Chinaman, I suppose?"

"Born and bred in Whitechapel," said Stott.

"Chinaman with a cockney accent, then?"

"Yes."

Oakes shook his head. "Juries don't like Chinamen. Don't trust them. Still think of the old Fu Manchu image, you know, inscrutable, yellow peril and all that. Don't go for it myself, but you can't seem to get these racist attitudes out of people's minds as quickly as you'd like, and you certainly can't legislate them away. Still, we'll do our best. Bright fellow, is he?"

"He's very articulate," said Stott.

"Good, that'll help. Unless he seems too bright, of course. Juries don't like people who come across as being too clever. Especially foreigners. They expect it of the boffins, of course, but not of your common-or-garden sort of restaurateur. Well, can't be helped." He got up and refilled his coffee mug from the machine on the filing cabinet. "Now what really bothers me," he went on, "is this other stuff here." He reached into the pile again and pulled out more papers. "You took a statement from a woman called Michelle Chappel, an ex-girlfriend of Pierce's. It's all above board, of course, but the whole issue's dodgy." He clicked his tongue and rested his hand on the papers, as if ready to swear on the Bible. "Dodgy in the extreme."

"In what way?" asked Banks.

Oakes sat back in his chair, linked his hands behind his head and quoted at the cracked ceiling. "'A trial judge in a criminal trial has always a discretion to refuse to admit evidence if in his opinion its prejudicial effect outweighs its probative value.' Lord Diplock, Regina v. Sang, 1979."

"And do you think this is the case with Michelle Chappel's statement?" Banks asked.

"I'm saying it could be a problem. 'There should be excluded from the jury information about the accused which is likely to have an influence on their minds prejudicial to the accused which is out of proportion to the true probative value of admissible evidence conveying that information.' Same source. And it usually relates to evidence of similar fact. You're implying here, by trying to introduce the woman's statement as evidence, that Pierce was just the kind of person who would commit such a crime. Freudian mumbo-jumbo, and juries don't like it, except on television. And, more to the point, a lot of judges don't like it, either."

Banks shrugged. "I'm aware of the similar fact rule," he said, "but what we're trying to establish here is a history of violence against women. And there's a marked physical similarity between the two victims. We're trying to get at a motive."

Oakes's eyebrows shot up. "Ah, yes, that's all very well and good, Banks. But then you're an imaginative sort of chap, kind who reads a lot of fiction, aren't you? If you understand the problem of similar fact evidence, then you must see that what you're doing is saying that Pierce was the sort of person who would commit such a crime because he once acted in a way *similar* to the perpetrator of the crime under consideration. And, what's more, it's an unreported crime based purely on the evidence of a woman who no doubt despises the man for rejecting her." He tut-tutted again and drank some coffee. "Still," he mused, "stranger things have happened."

"So what's your conclusion?" Banks asked.

"My conclusion?" He slapped the stack of coffee-stained files. "Oh, we'll give it a try. Why not? At worst, her evidence can only be declared inadmissible." He chuckled. "It used to be that the definition of inadmissible evidence was anything that might help the defence. That was in the good old days. Sometimes, depending on the judge, you can get a bit of leeway on these matters, especially in a case as serious as this one. I've seen similar fact evidence admitted more than once. What the rule actually states is that the *mere fact* that the accused has previously acted in a similar way to the crime he is standing trial for is not relevant. However, if there's a *very close* similarity, something that links the two events in a convincing way as part of a whole system of actions, an emerging *pattern*, so much so that it becomes more than a matter of mere coincidence, then such evidence may be admissible. Do you follow me?"

"I think so," said Banks.

"If we attempt to show that the two assaults are part of such a pattern," Oakes continued, "then we might just be able to squeeze it in. Depending on the judge, of course. Have you got a psychologist you can consult on this? What about that young woman I've seen you with in the Queen's Arms? Pretty young thing. Redhead. Isn't she a psychologist?"

"Jenny Fuller?"

"That's the one."

"Yes. But Jenny's still teaching in America. She won't be back until after Christmas."

"That'll do fine. No hurry, dear boy, no hurry. We've got enough for committal already. Just need something to beef up the admissibility quotient, if we can."

"Are you going to prosecute, then?"

Oakes drank more coffee, looked at the papers and sniffed a few times. "Oh, I think so," he said, after what seemed like an eternity. Then he nodded. "Yes, yes, I think we've got a good case. What about you, Denise?"

Denise Campbell nodded. "Let's nail the bastard," she said. Then she blushed and put her hand over her mouth as if she had just burped.

II

Owen's committal proceeding occurred in early February. The whole affair was about as exciting as a damp squib, more reminiscent of a college faculty meeting than an affair at which grave matters were decided. Nobody was even wearing wigs and robes.

He appeared before three JPs one bitter cold morning, and on Wharton's advice, they heard the "new-style committal." That is, they read all the prosecution's statements and the defence offered no case. It was basically committal by consent. And just as Wharton had guaranteed, the JPs agreed there was *prima facie* case and Owen was bound over for trial in the Crown Court. A trial date was set for late March. There were a few spectators in court, and Owen's name was now known to the general public, but only the charges and bare details were made known to the press, not the actual evidence.

Luckily, Owen had quickly got used to the monotony of prison routine: lights on, slop out, lights out, sleep. After the first few weeks, he had lost track of time. He was allowed out of his cell only to exercise in the dreary yard for half an hour each day. He hardly saw another soul there but for his guards, and it was no pleasure walking around in circles alone.

The food reminded him of school dinners: bread-and-butter pudding, grey leathery beef, lumpy custard, Spam fritters. Usually he left most of it. Even so, he felt constipated most of the time.

The cells around him were all occupied. At night he heard voices, even crying sometimes, and one evening the person in the next cell tried to strike up a conversation, asking him what he'd done. But Owen didn't answer. What could the man possibly want to talk about? Compare notes on rape and mutilation?

Mostly, he listened to the tapes Wharton brought him and read poetry and science fiction. He had Wordsworth almost by heart after the first month.

Every few days, for some unknown reason, the prison authorities played musical cells with him. Only the smells were different. One place had a mattress acrid with spilled semen; one of the washstands seemed to breathe vomit fumes from its depths. But maybe that was his imagination. The predominating odour was of disinfectant and slops. In one cell, he discovered in the middle of the night that there was no chamber pot or bucket. He called a warder, who told him to piss on the floor. He pissed down the sink. That wasn't his imagination.

As time went on, it was the little things that began to get him down: the rough feel of his prison clothes, the lack of cooking or tea-making facilities, the lousy coffee, the dreadful food ... The more he thought about them, the less petty they seemed. These were the essential parts of the tapestry of his liberty, things he took for granted normally. Now he had no access to them, they assumed greater importance in his mind.

It was all relative, of course. For a starving child in an Ethiopian village, for example, prison food would be a luxury and freedom might simply be defined as the hour or two's relief from the agony of hunger. When people are starving, they have no true freedom. But for someone like Owen—middle-class, reasonably well-off, well-educated, living in England—freedom was made up of myriad things, some more abstract than others, but it all came down to *having a choice*.

Locked in his small, lonely cell once again, Owen actually felt relieved to be left alone at last, to be shut away from the bureaucrats, the reporters and the women who stared at him with such naked hatred in their eyes. He was protected here from the crowds outside eager for his blood, and from the policemen so anxious to rip off the surface of his life and dig their hands deep into the slimy darkness below.

His cell was the only place he felt safe now; its routine and isolation sheltered him from the malevolent absurdity of the world outside.

III

Jenny Fuller dashed into the Queen's Arms ten minutes late, shucked off her black overcoat and folded it carefully over the back of the adjacent chair. She gave her head a shake to toss back her mass of flame-coloured hair, then sat down and patted her chest. "Out of breath. Sorry I'm late. Are we on expenses?"

Dr Jennifer Fuller was a lecturer in psychology at the University of York, and over the years her focus had shifted towards criminal and deviant psychology. Now, she had even started publishing in the field and was quickly making a name for herself. Hence the summer in America. Banks had worked with her on several cases before, and an initial attraction had transformed into an enduring friendship that delighted and surprised both of them.

Banks laughed. "Afraid not."

"Pity. I was getting sort of used to that in America. Everyone's on expenses there."

"Let me buy the first one, at least."

"How kind. I'll have a small brandy please, to take the chill off."

"And to eat?"

"Chicken in a basket."

On his way to the bar, Banks recognized one or two of the local shop-owners and the manager of the NatWest Bank on his lunchbreak. Cyril had also got the coal fire going nicely. The closest table to it was already taken by a group of ramblers in hiking boots and waterproof gear, so Banks and Jenny sat off to one side, near the window. Rain spattered the red and amber diamonds and blurred the clear panes. Along with the drinks, Banks ordered Jenny's chicken and scampi and chips for himself.

Jenny rubbed her hands together and gave a mock shiver when Banks came back with the drinks, then she picked up her small glass and said, "Cheers." They clinked glasses. "Have a good Christmas?"

"The usual. My parents for Christmas Eve, Sandra's for Christmas Day and Boxing Day."

"And how is Sandra?"

"She's fine."

Jenny took another sip of brandy. "So," she said, "I see you've got your man under lock and key. Another notch in your truncheon."

Banks nodded. "It looks that way."

"I take it that's what you *do* want to pick my brains about, and this isn't just a ruse to secure the pleasure of my company?"

Banks smiled. "Yes to the first. Not that I'd be averse to the latter."

"Stop it, you sweet man. You'll make the lady blush. How can I help?"

Banks lit a cigarette. "I don't know if you can. Or if you will, rather. Just listen, first of all, and tell me if I'm going way off the tracks."

Jenny nodded. "Okay."

Banks told her what they knew about Owen Pierce and Michelle Chappel, stressing Owen's reluctance to admit to knowing Michelle, her resemblance to Deborah Harrison, and what she said Owen had done to her.

When he had finished, Jenny sat quietly for a moment, sucking her lower lip and thinking. Banks sipped some beer and said, "I've been trying to work up some sort of psychological scenario for this crime. Owen Pierce had means and opportunity, and the DNA evidence is pretty damning. I suppose I'm looking for a *motive.*"

"You should know by now that you don't always get one with crimes like this, Alan. Motiveless, stranger killings. At least not what you or I would regard as a logical or even a reasonable motive, like anger or revenge."

"True. But bear with me, Jenny. Say he's upset about the girl, Michelle, angry at her. He goes for a walk and there, out of the fog, this vision appears. Michelle. Well, maybe not exactly Michelle, but an approximation. A younger model, more innocent, perhaps more vulnerable, less threatening. So he follows her into the grave-yard, approaches her, she says something and sparks his anger. He's already been violent towards Michelle, remember, so there's a precedent. Does it make sense?"

Jenny frowned. "It could do," she said. "Sometimes, we act out, we behave towards people as if they were someone else. It's called 'displacement,' an unconscious defence mechanism where emotions or ideas are transferred from one object or person to another that seems less threatening. I think Freud defined it as one of the neuroses, but my Freud's a bit rusty at the moment. What you're asking is whether I think Owen Pierce could have displaced his feelings for Michelle to Deborah because of some vague superficial resemblance—"

"And because of his mental state at the time."

"All right, that too. And that this led him to kill her. Really he was killing Michelle."

"Yes. What do you think?"

"I think you've got a point, or the beginnings of one."

"You don't think I'm way off beam?"

"Not at all." Their food came. "How about another drink to wash this down?"

"Please. I never argue when a woman wants to buy me a drink."

Banks watched Jenny walk to the bar. She moved well and had a superb figure: long legs, narrow waist and a bum like two plums in a wet paper bag. She had a new energy and confidence in her stride, too, and it looked as if the summer in California had done her good.

She was wearing tight black jeans and a jade-green jacket, made of raw silk, over a white shirt. Judging by the cut and the material of the jacket, the way it narrowed at her waist and flared slightly over the swell of her hips, it had probably cost her a small fortune on Rodeo Drive or some such place. But Jenny always had liked nice clothes.

Banks noticed her exchange a few words with a young man who looked like a trainee bank manager while she waited for Cyril to pour the pint. Poor fellow, Banks thought; he didn't stand a chance. But Jenny was smiling. Why did he feel a pang of jealousy when he saw her flirt with another man, even to this day?

She came back with a pint of bitter for Banks and a Campari and soda for herself. He thanked her. "Making a date?" he said, nodding towards the man.

Jenny laughed. "What do you think I am, a cradle-snatcher? Besides, he's not my type." Jenny was thirty-five in December; the young man about twenty-four. As yet, Banks knew, Jenny hadn't quite figured out what her "type" was.

When Jenny smiled, her green eyes lit up and the lines around them crinkled into a map of her humour. Her tan brought out the freckles across her nose and cheeks.

"How was California?" he asked.

"All sun and surf. Just like 'Baywatch.'"

"Really?"

She wrinkled her nose. "No, not really. You'd hate it," she said. "Can't smoke anywhere."

"And they call it the Garden of Eden. Is that where you developed a taste for fried chicken?"

"Not at all. I've always had a weakness for lean, relatively fat-free meat deep-fried in batter and cholesterol. It appeases both conflicting sides of my nature." She sliced off a chunk of deep-fried chicken breast and popped it in her mouth.

Banks laughed. They finished their meals in silence, then Banks lit a cigarette and said, "Back to Pierce. Look, I know I'm putting you on the spot, Jenny, but I'd like you to work something up for the CPS."

"Like what?"

"The kind of thing we were talking about. Displacement, for example. Tell me more."

Jenny sipped her Campari and soda. Banks still had half a pint left, and he wasn't allowing himself another drink this lunch-time.

"Okay," Jenny said, "let's say that he has poor control over his anger. It's pretty much a commonplace that people often respond to frustration by getting angry, and if their anger is really intense and their inner controls are weakened even further—say by alcohol or tiredness—then it can result in physical assault, even murder. That seems to be what happened with Michelle, but what about Deborah? Had he been drinking?"

"He'd had two pints and a whisky."

"Okay. Let's say, then, that we *are* dealing with displacement, which is a coping pattern. A defence mechanism, if you like."

"Defence against what?"

"Stress, basically. If a situation really threatens your sense of adequacy, your ego, your self-esteem, then your reactions become defence-oriented, you defend your *self* from devaluation."

"How?"

"Any number of ways. Denial. Rationalization. Fantasy. Repression. Things we all do. What it basically comes down to is ridding yourself of the anxiety and the tensions that are causing the pain."

"Sexual tension?"

"Could be. But that's just one kind."

"And displacement is one of these defence mechanisms?"

"Yes. You shift the strong feelings you have from the person or object towards which they were originally intended to another person or object. Often very difficult emotions are involved, like hostility and anxiety. It's an unconscious process."

"Are you suggesting he wasn't responsible?"

"Interesting point. But I don't think so. I don't know exactly what the law is, but I'm not saying a person suffering displacement isn't responsible for his actions, especially violent ones. Just that he might not know the inner processes that are leading him to want to do what he does."

"Which you can probably say for most of us most of the time?"

"Yes. In less extreme ways."

"Okay. Go on."

"Displacement is often combined with projection, where you put the blame for your own problems on someone else, or some group."

"Women?"

"Could be. In extreme cases it leads to a form of paranoia. People become convinced that forces or groups are working against them. He *could* have formed such a projection of his anxieties and hostilities against women in general. Plenty of men do. That French-Canadian who shot all those women at the college in Montreal, for example."

"And could he also have displaced his hostile feelings for Michelle onto Deborah, given the stress of the anniversary, the effect of alcohol and the resemblance between the two women?"

"Possibly. Yes. There's a study by a psychologist called Masserman, done in 1961, where he manages to show that under sustained frustration people become more willing to accept substitute goals."

"Deborah for Michelle?"

"Yes. Look, I'm a bit rusty on this. I'll need a few days to come up with something."

"How about next week?"

Jenny smiled. "I'll see what I can do."

"If there's anything else you want to know, give me a call."

"Can you get copies of the statements to me?"

"No problem."

"Okay. Now I really must go." She stood up and reached for her raincoat. Then she leaned forward and gave Banks a quick peck on the cheek.

When she had gone, he lit another cigarette, vowing it would be his last for the day, and contemplated the remains of his pint. Another half wouldn't do any harm, he decided, so he went and got one, pouring it into the pint glass because he didn't like drinking beer from small glasses.

IV

One afternoon about three or four weeks after his committal—he was losing track of time—Owen was taken from his cell to a prison interview room, where he met for the first time the barrister Gordon Wharton had engaged to lead his defence.

In her early forties, Owen guessed, Shirley Castle, QC, was an attractive woman by any standards. She was also the first woman he had seen since his trip to the Magistrates' Court. She had glossy dark hair that fell over her shoulders and framed a pale, oval face. Her almond-shaped eyes were a peculiar shade of violet, so unusual that Owen wondered if she were wearing tinted contact lenses. She had on a grey pleated skirt and a pale pink blouse buttoned up to her chin. Her perfume smelled subtle and expensive.

Wharton sat beside her with a smug, proprietorial air about him, basking in the glory of her presence, as if to say, "Just look who I've got for you, my boy. What a treat!"

Shirley Castle took the cap off her Montblanc fountain-pen, shuffled some papers in front of her and began.

"It doesn't look very good, Owen," she said. "I don't want to give you any false hopes or illusions. We'll have an uphill struggle on our hands with this one."

"But all they've got is circumstantial evidence."

She looked at him. "The point is, that they can build a very good case on that. Look at it this way." She started to count off the points on her long fingers. "One, you had the opportunity. Two, motive in such crimes is so obscure, to say the least, that they don't really need to establish one. And, three, there's the DNA, hairs and blood."

"But I can explain it all. I have done. I never denied being in the area from the start, and I told them the girl bumped into me. Maybe that's how the hair and blood were exchanged."

"Maybe. But the police don't believe you," she said. "And quite frankly, I don't blame them, especially given that you only came up with that explanation at the eleventh hour. No, Owen, I'm afraid we're going to have to fight tooth and nail for this one."

"Are they still looking for the real murderer?"

"Why should they? They think they've already got him."

"So there's nobody out there trying to prove my innocence?"

"I'm afraid not."

"Can't you employ a private detective or someone?"

Shirley Castle laughed. It was a lighter, frothier, more vivacious sound than he would have imagined, given her overall gravity. But it was a nervous laugh, no doubt about that. "To do what?" she asked.

"Find the real murderer. Prove me innocent."

"Things don't work quite like that."

"Well, how *do* they work?"

She leaned back in her chair and frowned. "We go to court and we give them the best fight we can. There's no other way. It's only on 'Perry Mason' that the lawyer and the private eye get out on the mean streets and track down the *real* killer."

"Just let me tell them my story. I'm sure they'll believe me."

"I'm not sure yet if I'm going to put you in the witness box at all."

"Why not?"

Shirley Castle frowned. "Cross-examinations can be really tough."

"Is something bothering you?"

"Yes, as a matter of fact it is. The CPS file suggests an approach to the case that involves similar fact to try and establish a *motive* for the murder, too."

"But you said they didn't need one."

"Their case will be all that much stronger if they can come up with one."

"What are they saying?"

Shirley Castle rested her chin in her hand. "Tell me about Michelle Chappel, Owen."

Owen swallowed. His mouth felt dry. "What about her?"

"About your relationship. And why you lied to the police about the nude photographs, denied you knew her. You didn't want them to find her and talk to her, did you?"

"No, I can't say I did. Michelle ... well, let's say we parted on bad terms. She'd have nothing good to say about me."

"As I understand it, there was violence, perhaps attempted murder?"

"That's absurd! Have you talked to her?"

"No," she said. "The police have. I've just been reviewing the statement, and it's very interesting. Read for yourself." She dropped a sheaf of papers in front of him.

Owen felt rising panic as he read the transcript of the taped interview with Michelle:

Q: Miss Chappel, could you tell us how and when you first met Mr Pierce?

A: Yes. In class. He was my teacher. I was his student.

Q: How old were you at the time?

A: Seventeen.

Q: Was this at Eastvale College of Further Education?"

A: Yes.

Q: How old was Owen Pierce when you met?"

A: Thirty-two, thirty-three. I'm not exactly sure.

Q: So he was almost old enough to be your father?

A: Technically. I suppose a sixteen-year-old could be a father.

Q: Did you live at home?

A: Yes. Until I was eighteen.

Q: Where did you go then?

A: I moved in with Owen.

Q: How long did you live with him?

A: Five years.

Q: How did Mr Pierce approach you?

A: He suggested a coffee after class, one day, then he asked me out to dinner.

Q: Were your marks good?

A: Yes.

Q: Did you start seeing one another regularly?

A: Yes. We went out together a few times for dinner, to the pictures or for a drink. Sometimes he took me out for a ride in the country in his car, and we'd find a little village pub somewhere.

Q: How soon did you become lovers?

A: Very soon after we first went out.

Q: Weeks? Days?

A: Days.

Q: And the relationship went well after you moved in with him?

A: At first it did, yes. Look, I mean, you have to realize, I was very young. A bit of a misfit, too, I suppose. I wasn't very happy at home, and I didn't really have any close friends. I found most people my own age immature. I was also very shy and Owen was nice to me. I suppose I was flattered, too, by the attention. When

I talked about leaving home, he asked if I'd like to move in with him, and it seemed like a good idea. I felt safe with him.

Q: Were you still his student when you moved in with him?

A: I was in his business communications class, yes.

Q: Did you continue to do well in that course?

A: Very well.

Q: Deservedly?

A: I think so. Look, I'm not stupid, but I also admit it may have helped, sleeping with my teacher.

Q: Do you think there was a price to pay for your success?

A: What do you mean?

Q: Did Owen ever suggest or attempt to commit any unnatural acts?

A: Do you mean was he kinky?

Q: Something like that.

A: No, I wouldn't say that. I mean, he liked me to wear certain underclothes. You know, black silky things, thigh stockings, skimpy things. He liked me to keep them on when we ... you know.

Q: During intercourse?

A: Yes.

Q: Was that all?

A: All? Was what all?

Q: The skimpy clothes. Did he ever make you do anything you didn't want to?

A: He wanted to do it to me from behind, like dogs. I didn't like that.

Q: But did you do as he wished?

A: Well, I ... yes, at first I did. I wanted to please him.

Q: Because you were worried about your marks?

A: A bit, I suppose.

Q: Did he show any interest in pornography?

A: We watched a dirty video once. You know the sort of thing. I didn't really enjoy it. In fact, I thought it was dead gross, but it seemed to turn him on.

Q: How did he behave when you were watching the video?

A: Well, he was, you know, maybe a bit more ardent than usual. He wanted to try out things they were doing, you know, on the video.

Q: Against your will?"

A: No, but I thought it was a bit weird.

Q: Did he ever resort to violence for the purpose of sexual stimulation?

A: He used to like to tie me up sometimes.

Q: How did you react to this?

A: What could I do? He was stronger than me. I wanted to please him. It was uncomfortable and it frightened me a bit, but it didn't really hurt. It was just a game, really. It was something he'd seen in that silly film and it turned him on.

Q: Did he beat you at all? Flagellation?

A: No.

Q: So apart from the tying up he wasn't violent?

A: No ... not until the end. Then living with him became sort of like being in prison. Every time I went out I had to account for my movements. Some nights he wouldn't even let me go out.

Q: How did he keep you in?

A: He just made such a fuss it wasn't worth it. I felt shut in, always under observation. I couldn't breathe. I was frightened of his temper. I started rebelling in small ways, like seeing other friends and stuff, and it made him more and more possessive.

Q: Is that why you left him? Fear of violence?

A: Partly ... it was frightening, especially the last night, but ...

Q: Can you tell us about that last night, Michelle?

Michelle went on to tell about the night she claimed Owen had raped and tried to strangle her. Pale, Owen shoved the papers aside and looked at Shirley Castle.

"Well?" she asked. "What do you think of it?"

Owen shook his head slowly. "I don't know what to say."

"It's not true, then?"

"Some of it, maybe. But she even makes the truth sound different, sound bad for me, the way she slants it."

"In what way?"

"Every way. The sex, for example. She makes me sound like a pervert, but most of it was her idea. She loved it, the tying up, the talking dirty. It really got her going. And she liked the video."

"Did you hit her that last night?"

"I pushed her. I was protecting myself. She was berserk, out of control. She'd have killed me if I hadn't pushed her away."

"And she hit her head as she fell?"

"Yes."

"Knocking her unconscious?"

"Yes, but … Oh, God." Owen held his head in his hands. "I know how it sounds, but I've never hurt anyone in my life, never on purpose."

"Did you have sex with her after she'd knocked herself out?"

"No, I didn't. That's a lie. What do you take me for?"

"I'm just trying to get at the truth, Owen. Did you try to force her to have sex at any time that evening?"

"No. I mean, yes. No, I didn't try to force her, but I suggested it. I just wanted to see how she would react. It was a test. I didn't force her."

Shirley frowned. "You made advances? I'm afraid I don't understand you, Owen. You'll have to explain it to me."

How could he tell her about that night? Still vivid in his mind, it was like watching a cartoon play, the gaudy colours, the exaggerated violence, the sense of being a spectator, unable to stop the film, unable even to walk out of the cinema.

"How did it start, Owen?"

Owen tried to explain. He had grown suspicious of Michelle over the last year or so, he said, suspected that she was seeing another man, or other men. That night, when she said she was going to meet a girlfriend, he followed her into Eastvale town centre and watched her meet someone in a pub. As they talked and drank, rubbing close together, Owen sat, shielded by a frosted-glass partition and watched the shadows. At closing time, he followed them to a house not far from his own and watched outside as the bedroom light went on, then the curtains closed, and someone turned out the light.

He went home and paced and drank whisky until Michelle got in after two-thirty in the morning. Instead of challenging her immediately with what he'd found out, he made sexual advances to see how she would react.

She pushed him away and told him she was too tired, listening to her girlfriend's tales of woe till so late. He could smell the other man on her, the stale beer and smoke on her clothes, in her hair, mingled with the reek of sex. She hadn't even had the decency to take a shower afterwards.

Then he told her what he'd seen, what he had watched. She went wild, flew at him, screamed that he didn't own her and if he was no good in bed she had every damn right to find someone who was. It was like watching another person emerge from the shell of someone you thought you knew.

He called her a bitch, a whore, told her he knew she'd been at it all the time they'd been together, that she had just used him, had never really loved him. For a moment, she paused in her attack and a different look came into her eyes: hard, cold hatred. She picked up a pair of scissors from the table and lunged at him. He grabbed her hand and twisted until she dropped them.

Then she renewed the attack, kicking, scratching, flailing out wildly. He held his hands in front of his face to ward off the blows and tried to talk her down. But she wouldn't stop. Finally, out of desperation, he pushed her away, just to give himself some space to manoeuvre, and she fell over and hit her head on the chair leg.

He tried to tell Shirley Castle all this, as calmly as he could. He knew it sounded thin without the whole background of the relationship, from the early innocence to the bitter knowledge that it had all been a lie.

What he couldn't tell her, though, what he hardly dare even admit to himself, was that after Michelle had fallen on the floor, arms spread out, one leg crooked over the other, he had wanted her. Hating her even then, he had torn at her clothing, then, half-mad with jealousy and hatred, had put his hands around her throat and wanted to choke the life out of her for what she had done to him, for ruining, for defiling what he had thought was the love of a lifetime. He hated himself for wanting her, and he hated her for making him.

At that moment, the full power of his love turned to hate and overwhelmed him, and he knew that everything, her words, her gestures, her lovemaking, her promises, had all been a lie. But he let go; he couldn't kill her. He stood up, steadied himself and went to collapse on the bed. She was still breathing; there was no blood; he hadn't raped her.

In the morning he found her sulking in the spare room, nursing the bump on her head. She tried to make up to him, told him she would do anything he wanted ... *anything* ... and started squirming around under the thin sheet. It had always worked before, but this time Owen had had more than enough.

He knew that if he took her back, if he lived with her for just one more day he would lose his self-respect for ever. When he told her to go, she screamed and begged, but he threw her out in the street with only her suitcase. The next thing he knew, he got a letter with a Swiss Cottage address to send on the rest of her things. He did so.

Shirley Castle let the silence stretch after his explanation. Owen couldn't read the way she looked at him. He didn't know whether she believed him or not.

"Owen," she said finally. "Whatever the truth is, Michelle's is a very damning statement. You can imagine the case the Crown is trying to build up. A man obsessed with pornography, especially if it features young girls, capable of sexual violence against women ... You see my point?"

"But it's not true!" Owen argued. "None of it. I'm not obsessed with pornography."

Shirley held up her hand. "I'm not attacking you, Owen. I'm simply trying to demonstrate the spin the prosecution will try and put on the facts, given the chance."

Owen laid his hands on the desk and stared at the veins in his wrists. "I don't know what you must think of me," he said, his voice hardly more than a whisper, "but I want you to know that I'm not the monster they say I am. It's a distortion. If I knew only *certain* facts about your life, or anyone's, if your fantasies were laid bare for all to see ... well, I might form a picture, and it might be the wrong one. Do you know what I mean?"

He could have sworn there was an amused glint in her eyes, and perhaps a faint flush on her cheeks. "You don't need to please me, Owen," she said. "I'm here as a professional. It's not my place to make judgements about your private life, only to prove reasonable doubt. You don't need to seek my approval."

"But I want it," Owen said. "Damn it, I want it! You're not a machine, are you? You must have opinions, feelings."

Shirley Castle didn't answer. Instead, she shuffled the papers back towards her briefcase and said, "There's one more important question before I go, Owen. Why would Michelle do what she did? Why would she say all those things about you to the police if they're not true? What reason has she to want you to go to jail?"

"Don't you understand? Michelle's a user. She used me from the start, for her education, her escape from her overbearing parents, for her living-quarters, the good life. I was her passport through college. She threw me a few crumbs and I took them for love. Even now I have a hard time believing that you can live with someone for so long and not really see them for what they are, not know them at all. But it's true. Maybe I didn't *want* to see. All the time she was with me, she was going with other men, and I admit I got jealous and possessive. But she didn't care. She thought she could get away with everything, just take her clothes off for me and make it all right. At heart she's a cold, calculating monster. She has no conscience. Do you understand? Sometimes, it's only when the final piece falls into place that you see there was ever a pattern at all. That was what happened that last night. The final piece. She'd been doing it all along, lying to me, seeing other men, doing exactly what she wanted, using my home—*our* home—as a squat. I gave her all the freedom she wanted at first, before I started to suspect the truth. She was young after all. How can you keep the love of a younger woman if you try to put her in a cage? As soon as I became more vigilant, the cracks started to appear."

Shirley Castle shook her head. "I can accept all that, Owen, but it doesn't really answer my question. Why does she wish you so much harm?"

"Why? Because I found her out," Owen answered, remembering that one calm moment in the final battle, when he had seen her for what she really was. "Because I saw through her. I saw her true face. And because I rejected her. I threw her out. Though she denied me the night before, just after she'd been with her boyfriend, she offered me her body the next morning. But I wouldn't take it. She begged me to forgive her and let her stay. But I threw her out. She was like a spiteful child if she didn't get her own way. She can't forgive me for seeing the truth and having the courage to throw her out before she dumped me."

Shirley Castle nodded slowly. "Well, Owen, that's all very well," she said. "But we'd just better hope, for your sake, that she doesn't get anywhere near the witness-box."

ELEVEN

I

Wood creaked as those present in court got to their feet one rainy April day. Judge Simmonds entered, resplendent in scarlet moire and white linen. He was a wizened old man with reptilian eyes buried deep in wrinkles and folds of flesh. His face was expressionless as he looked around the courtroom before sitting.

The benches groaned as everyone in the crowded room sat down. Owen noticed that the courtroom smelled of the same lemon-scented polish his mother used to use; it made him feel sad.

"The prisoner will stand."

So this was it. Owen stood.

"Is your name Owen Pierce?" asked the Clerk of the Court.

"It is."

The clerk then read out the indictment and asked Owen how he pleaded.

"Not guilty," Owen answered, as firmly and confidently as he could manage with all eyes on him.

He scrutinized the jury as he spoke: seven men and five women, all dressed for a day at the office. A pudgy man with a slack, flabby jaw looked at him with something like awe. A pursed-lipped young woman wouldn't meet his eyes at all, but looked down at her hands folded in her lap. Most of them at least glanced at him in passing. Some were nervous; others looked as if they had already made up their minds.

It was irrational, he knew, but he decided to pick one of them to be his barometer throughout the trial, one whose expressions he would chart to tell how the case was going—for or against him. Not the frowning woman in the powder-blue suit, nor the balding chap who reminded him of his insurance agent; not the conventionally pretty girl with the pageboy cut, nor the burly wrestler-type with his brick-red neck bulging out of his tight collar. It was difficult to find someone.

At last, he decided on a woman; for some reason, it had to be a woman. She was in her late thirties, he guessed, with a moon-shaped face and short mousy hair. She had a wide red slash of a mouth and large eyes.

But it wasn't her physical appearance so much as her aura that caused him to pick her out. For some reason, he decided, this woman was good and honest. What was more, she could tell the truth from lies. At the moment, she looked puzzled and confused to find herself in such a frightening role, but she would, he knew, as soon as the trial progressed, listen carefully, weigh, judge and decide. Her decision would be the right one, and he would be able to tell from her expression what it was. Yes, he would keep a close eye on her. He would call her "Minerva."

Almost before Owen realized it, Jerome Lawrence, QC, had launched into his opening address. Lawrence was a small, dark-complexioned man with beady, restless black eyes and a perpetual five-o'clock shadow, shiny as shoe-polish on his cheeks and chin. Somehow, he seemed to fit perfectly into his robes, looking even more like a bat ready to flap its wings and take off into the night than anyone else in the room. Like Shirley Castle, he spoke with his hands a lot, and his robe swished about in a most distracting way.

"The Crown shall seek to prove," Lawrence said in his oiliest public-school voice, "that the accused is guilty of the most heinous, the most despicable, brutal, inhuman crime of all—the murder of a child, an innocent, a mere sixteen-year-old girl with her whole life before her."

And for the rest of the day, Owen could only listen, open-mouthed, to the depiction of himself as a barely human monster.

Though the parade of witnesses began dramatically enough, with Rebecca Charters tearfully recounting how she discovered Deborah Harrison's body, several things became clear to him in the first days. Probably the first and foremost of these was that you could be bored even at your own murder trial.

Witnesses came and went, people he had never met, people who didn't know him: vicars, shopkeepers, teachers, schoolgirls, policemen, pub landlords. Some of them seemed to spend hours in the box for no reason Owen could think of. Jerome Lawrence or Shirley Castle questioned most of them, but sometimes their juniors took over.

With unfailing regularity one lawyer or another would raise points of law that meant the jury had to be sent out, sometimes for hours, and all sides seemed to like nothing better than the kind of delay that meant an early adjournment for the day. Also, there were one or two days off due to illness of a jury member and another for a family bereavement. Every night, without fail, Owen was shipped back to his little cell at Armley Jail. He was becoming so used to it by now that he almost thought of it as home. He had forgotten what his real home looked like.

As far as Owen could tell, things seemed to be going quite well over the first few weeks. Shirley Castle made mincemeat of the policeman with the jug-ears for not explaining why he was visiting Owen in the first place. Detective Inspector Stott came out looking like a member of the Gestapo.

By the time Detective Chief Inspector Banks was called, Owen had lost track of the days.

II

"In the same situation, Chief Inspector, do you think you would bother to mention *everyone* you saw on the streets during a certain period?"

Banks shrugged. It was his second day giving evidence and Shirley Castle was cross-examining him. "I would hope I would do my duty and try to recall *everything* that happened around the crucial time," he answered finally.

"But you are a policeman, Chief Inspector. You have special training. Such facts and fine details are part of your job. I'm sure I wouldn't even remember most of the people I passed in the street. Nor, I imagine, would most members of the jury." And here, Shirley

Castle paused long enough to look over at the jury. Most of them seemed to agree with her, Banks thought. "Yet you expect Mr Pierce to remember every face, every detail," she went on. "I ask you again, Chief Inspector, do you really think this is reasonable?"

"Perhaps not on a busy thoroughfare at rush hour," said Banks, "but this was a foggy night in a quiet suburb. Yes, I think I would remember if I had seen a particular person. And Mr Pierce remembered as soon as—"

"That's enough, Chief Inspector. You have answered my question."

Banks couldn't help but allow himself a slight feeling of satisfaction when he saw Shirley Castle reel from his answer. She had made a small mistake; she hadn't already known the answer to the question she asked.

She hurried on. "Now, as Mr Sung, proprietor of the Peking Moon restaurant, has already testified, and as my learned friend brought out during his examination-in-chief, Mr Pierce used his credit card to pay for his meal there. If the timing of events is correct—and I stress *if*—this would have occurred shortly *after* the murder of Deborah Harrison, would it not?"

"Yes."

"Now, in your professional experience, Chief Inspector, would you not say that a criminal, someone who has just committed an attack of the most vile and brutal kind, would be a little more careful to cover his tracks?"

"Most criminals aren't that clever," said Banks. "That's why they get caught."

The members of the gallery laughed.

"But my client is *not* stupid," she went on, ignoring the interruption. "It is hardly likely that he would go and eat Chinese food and pay for it with a credit card after murdering someone, now, is it? Not to mention do it all wearing a bright orange anorak. Why would he be so foolish as to draw attention to himself in such an obvious way if he had committed the crime of which he is accused?"

"Perhaps he was distraught," Banks answered. "Not thinking clearly. Mr Sung did say he was talking to—"

"'Not thinking clearly,'" she repeated, with exactly the right tone of disdain. "Is it not a fact, Chief Inspector, that perpetrators of such random crimes are usually, in fact, thinking very clearly indeed? That they rarely get caught, unless by accident? That they take great care to avoid discovery?"

Banks fiddled with his tie. He hated having it fastened up and could only bear it if he kept the top button of his shirt undone. "There are certain schools would say that, yes. But a criminal's behaviour is not easily predictable. If it were, we'd have an easier job on our hands." He smiled at the jury; one or two of them smiled back.

"Come on, Chief Inspector Banks, you can't have it both ways. Either they're stupid and easy to catch, as you said earlier, or they're unpredictable and impossible to catch. Which is it?"

"Some are stupid; some are not. As I said before, murderers don't always act rationally. This wasn't a rational crime. There's no way of predicting what the killer would do, or why he did things the way he did."

"But aren't you in the business of reconstructing crimes, Chief Inspector?"

"Nowadays we leave that to 'Crimewatch.'"

Laughter rose up from the gallery. Judge Simmonds admonished Banks for his flippancy.

"My point is," Shirley Castle went on without cracking a smile, "that you seem to know so very little of what went on in St Mary's graveyard, or indeed, of what kind of criminal you're dealing with. Isn't that true?"

"We know that Deborah Harrison was strangled with the strap of her school satchel and that her clothing was rearranged."

"But isn't it true that you simply picked on the first person seen in the area whom you thought fit the bill, that Owen Pierce was unfortunate enough to be in the wrong place at the wrong time?"

"I'd say it was Deborah Harrison who was in the wrong place at the wrong time."

"Were there not certain elements of the crime scene that struck you as odd?"

"What elements?"

Shirley Castle consulted her notes. "As I understand it," she said, "the victim's school satchel was *open*. Doesn't that strike you as odd?"

"It could have come open during the struggle."

"Hardly," scoffed Shirley Castle. "It was fastened by two good-quality buckles. We've tested it, believe me, and it won't open unless someone *deliberately* unfastens it."

"Perhaps the murderer wanted something from her."

"Like what, Chief Inspector? Surely you're not suggesting robbery? From a schoolgirl's satchel?"

"It's possible. But I—"

"But what money could a schoolgirl have worth stealing? I understand Deborah Harrison had six pounds in her purse when she was found. If robbery were the motive, why not take that too? And wouldn't it make more sense to take the entire satchel? Why hang around the crime scene any longer than necessary?"

"Which question do you want me to answer first?"

Shirley Castle scowled. "Why would Deborah Harrison's killer remain at the scene and go through her satchel rather than take it with him?"

"I don't know. Perhaps he was looking for a trophy of some kind. Something personal to the victim."

"But was anything missing?"

"We don't know. No-one knew exact—"

"You don't know. We have heard a great deal of evidence," she went on, "placing Mr Pierce in the vicinity of St Mary's at the time of the crime, but let me ask you this, Chief Inspector: did anyone actually *see* Mr Pierce enter St Mary's graveyard?"

"He was seen—"

"A simple yes or no will suffice."

Banks was silent a moment, then said, "No."

"Is it not also possible, Chief Inspector, that Deborah went somewhere else first and returned to the graveyard later, after Mr Pierce had gone to the Peking Moon?"

"It's possible. But—"

"And that Deborah Harrison was murdered by someone she knew, perhaps because of something she was carrying in her satchel?"

Exactly what I thought at first, Banks agreed. "I think that's a rather far-fetched explanation," he said.

"More far-fetched than charging Mr Pierce here with murder?" She pointed at Pierce theatrically. "While you were busy harassing my client, did you pursue the investigation in other directions?"

"We continued with our enquiries. And we didn't har—"

She sniffed. "You continued with your enquiries. What does that mean?"

"We tried to find out as much about the victim and her movements as possible. We tried to discover, through talking to friends and family, if she had any enemies, anyone who would want to kill her. We collected all the trace evidence we could find and had it analyzed as quickly as possible. We found nothing concrete until we came up with Mr Pierce."

"And after Mr Pierce's name came up?"

Banks knew that most investigations tend to wind down once the police think they've got their man. And much as he would have liked to pursue other possibilities, there was other work to do, and there was also Chief Constable Riddle. "I continued other lines of enquiry until it became app—"

"You continued other lines of enquiry? As soon as you first interviewed him, you decided on Mr Pierce's guilt, didn't you?"

"Objection!"

"Sustained. Ms Castle, please stop insulting the witness."

Shirley Castle bowed. "My apologies, Your Honour, Chief Inspector Banks. Let me rephrase the question: what was your attitude to Mr Pierce from the start?"

"We decided he was a definite suspect, and in the absence of any evidence to the contrary, we proceeded to build up our case against him in the usual, accepted manner."

"Thank you, Chief Inspector," Shirley Castle said, sitting down and trying to look bored. "No further questions."

"Then I suggest," said Judge Simmonds, "that we adjourn for the weekend. Court will be in session again at ten-thirty Monday morning."

III

On Monday morning, it happened: exactly what Owen had been fearing.

When he tried to reconstruct the sequence of events later, back in his cell, he couldn't be sure whether Jerome Lawrence had actually managed to call out Michelle's name before Shirley Castle jumped to her feet. Either way, Judge Simmonds listened patiently to the objection, then he dismissed the jury for yet another *voir dire*.

What followed was a legal wrangle that Owen, educated as he was, could only half follow, so mired was it in tortured English and in citing of precedents. As far as he could gather, though, both sides put their points of view to the judge. Jerome Lawrence argued that Michelle's evidence was relevant because it established a *pattern* of violent behaviour that had its natural outcome in Deborah Harrison's murder, and Shirley Castle countered that the proposed evidence was nothing but vindictive fantasy from an unreliable witness, that it proved nothing, and that its prejudicial effect by far outweighed any probative value it might have.

Owen held his breath as Judge Simmonds paused to consider the arguments; he knew that his entire future might be hanging in the balance here. His mouth felt dry; his jaw clenched; his stomach churned. If Simmonds disallowed the evidence, Owen knew, there could be no reporting of what had gone on in the jury's absence. Only a very few people would ever know about what had happened between him and Michelle. If Simmonds admitted it, though, the whole world would know. And the jury. He crossed his fingers so tightly they turned white.

Finally, Simmonds puckered his lips, frowned, and declared the evidence inadmissible.

Owen let out his breath. The blood roared in his ears, and he felt his whole body relax: jaw, stomach, fingers. He thought he was going to faint.

Shirley Castle flashed him a discreet thumbs-up sign and a quick smile of victory. The jury was brought back in, and Jerome Lawrence called his next witness.

Dr Charles Stewart Glendenning made an imposing figure. Tall, with a full head of white hair and a nicotine-stained moustache, the Home Office pathologist carried himself erectly and had just the right amount of Scottish burr in his accent to make him come across as a no-nonsense sort of person. The serious expression on his face, which had etched its lines over the years, added to the look of the consummate expert witness.

He entered the witness-box as if it were his second home and spoke the oath. Owen noticed that he didn't rest his hand on a copy of the New Testament and that the wording was slightly different from everyone else's. An atheist, then? Not surprising, Owen thought, given the evidence of man's inhumanity to man he must have seen over the years.

After spending what remained of the morning establishing Dr Glendenning's credentials and responsibilities, Jerome Lawrence finally began his examination-in-chief after lunch.

"Rebecca Charters has already described finding the body and calling the police," he said. "Could you please describe, Doctor, the condition of the body at the scene?"

"The victim lay on her back. Her blouse was open, her brassiere torn and her breasts exposed. Her skirt had been lifted above her waist, exposing the pubic region, in the manner typical of a sex murder. Her underwear was missing. I understand it was later found nearby. On closer examination of the face, I noticed a reddish-purple colour and traces of bleeding from the nose, consistent with death by asphyxia. There was also a small, fresh scratch by her left eye."

"Could you tell us what you discovered at the post-mortem?"

"The girl was—had been—in good general health, to be expected in a girl of sixteen. There were no signs of toxicity in her organs. On further examination, I concluded as I had earlier, that death was caused by asphyxia due to strangulation."

"Would you care to elaborate on asphyxia for the members of the jury, Doctor?" Jerome Lawrence went on.

Glendenning nodded briefly. "Some strangulation victims die from vagal inhibition, which means heart stoppage caused by pressure on the carotid arteries in the neck." He touched the spot beside his jaw. "The victim in this case, however, died because of obstruction to the veins in her neck and the forcing of the tongue against the back of throat, cutting off her air intake. There are certain tell-tale signs. People who die from vagal inhibition are pale, those who die from asphyxia have reddish-purple colouring. There are also petechial haemorrhages, little pinpricks of blood in the whites of the eyes, eyelids, facial skin. Contrary to popular fiction, the tongue does not protrude."

Owen glanced over at Sir Geoffrey and Lady Harrison, the victim's parents, who had attended almost every day. Lady Harrison turned to her husband and let her head touch his shoulder for a moment. Both were pale.

Owen felt he glimpsed, at that moment, the cold-blooded logic of the prosecution's strategy, like the dramatic structure of a play or a novel, and it sent a chill up his spine.

After hearing Rebecca Charters's emotional account of finding the body and then Banks's solid, professional testimony about the police investigation, if things had gone according to plan the jury would next have heard Michelle's testimony. They would have seen only a sweet, innocent young girl in the witness box and heard how this monster in the dock had attempted to strangle her. (He was certain she would have touched her long, tapered fingers to her throat as she described the attack). *Then* they would have heard the gruesome medical details of the effects of strangulation. And what would they have thought of Owen after all that?

"Thank you, Doctor," Lawrence went on. "Could you tell, in this case, how the victim was strangled?"

"Yes. With a ligature. A satchel strap, in fact."

"And was this found close to the scene?"

"Yes. It was still attached to the victim's satchel."

"In your expert opinion, do you have any reason to doubt it was used as the murder weapon?"

"None at all. We carried out a number of tests. The satchel strap matched the indentations in the victim's throat perfectly. It was angled slightly upwards, cutting into the skin at the bottom part, indicating that she had been strangled from behind and that her attacker was taller than her. There was also blood around the edge of the strap."

"How much taller was the killer?" asked Jerome Lawrence.

"The victim was five foot six, so I would put the attacker at least six inches taller, perhaps more."

"And the accused is six foot two, as has already been established?"

"So I believe, yes."

"Would it have required a great deal of strength?"

"A certain amount, yes. But nothing superhuman."

"Would the manner of attack make it difficult for the victim to fight off her attacker?"

"Almost impossible. There wouldn't be much she could do. She might manage a wild scratch, of course, or a backwards kick to the shins with her heel."

"You mentioned a 'wild scratch.' Would this be possible if she were strangled from behind?"

"Oh, yes. It's quite conceivable she might reach behind and scratch her assailant."

"Was it possible to tell whether she had been killed in St Mary's churchyard or elsewhere?"

"Yes, by the extent of post-mortem lividity, such as it was. This—" he turned to explain to the jury without Lawrence's prompting, "means that when the heart stops, the blood simply obeys the force of gravity and sinks to the lowest part of the body. It gathers and stains at points where the flesh is not in contact with the ground. Parts of the body that do remain in contact with the ground will remain white, of course, because the pressure will not allow the blood to settle in the capillaries. In this case, the staining at the back of the neck, small of the back and backs of the legs indicated that the deceased had been lying in the same position since her death. Also, as lividity was in its early stages, she couldn't have been there for very long. It generally begins about thirty minutes to one hour after death, develops fully between three and four hours and becomes fixed between eight and ten hours. The lividity was still faint, and blanching still occurred."

"Could you explain blanching for the benefit of the court?"

"Certainly. Before the blood coagulates in the vessels, if you touch an area of lividity it will turn white. When you remove your fingertip, it will resume its lividity. After four or five hours the discolouration hardens, becomes clotted, and pressure will not cause blanching."

"And what does this tell you?"

"Amongst other things, it helps determine time of death. As I said, lividity had only just started and there was no sign of rigor mortis, which usually begins in the eyelids about two or three hours after death. I also took temperature readings, and based on a math-ematical calculation, I came up with time of death somewhere between five o'clock and when she was discovered."

"No earlier?"

"In my opinion, that would be very unlikely indeed."

"And as the victim's friend Megan Preece reports parting with Deborah near the bridge at six o'clock, and the evidence of Daniel Charters places Owen—"

"Objection!"

"Sustained." Judge Simmonds pointed with a bony finger. "Mr Lawrence, behave yourself. You ought to know better."

Lawrence bowed. "Your Honour. Thank you, Dr Glendenning. I have no further questions."

Shirley Castle stood up to cross-examine. "I only have a couple of questions, Doctor," she said briskly. "Minor points, really. I shan't keep you long."

Dr Glendenning inclined his head and smiled at her in a gentle-manly way.

"I assume you supervised the collection of oral, vaginal and anal swabs at the crime scene?" Shirley Castle began.

"I did."

"And did you find any traces of semen?"

"None."

"None at all?"

"That is correct."

"In your post-mortem examination, did you discover any signs of forcible intercourse?"

"I found no signs of any intercourse at all, forcible or otherwise."

Shirley Castle frowned. "Yet you referred to this as a 'sex crime' in your earlier testimony. Does that absence of evidence not strike you as unusual in such a crime?"

"Not really. There are many kinds of sex crimes. The way the clothing was disturbed was reminiscent, in my experience, of a sex-crime scene."

"And we have already heard your enviable credentials as an expert on such matters, Doctor. How accurate is your estimate of time of death?"

"It's always an approximate business," Glendenning admitted. "There are so many variables."

"Could you give the court an example of how you might determine time of death?"

"Certainly. As I have already indicated, there are a number of factors, such as rigor mortis, lividity and stomach contents, but body temperature is often the most accurate. If the temperature at the time of death is normal—thirty-seven degrees centigrade—and it takes the body twenty-four to thirty-six hours after death to fall to the temperature of the environment, then one can make a back-calculation to the time of death."

"Twenty-four to thirty-six hours," said Shirley Castle, frowning towards the jury. "That's between a day and a day and a half. That's a rather broad margin for error, isn't it?"

Glendenning smiled. "I did say it was an approximate business."

"Yes, but you didn't say how wildly inaccurate it was."

"Objection."

"Sustained, Mr Lawrence."

Shirley Castle bowed. "My apologies. Doctor, how long would it have taken Deborah Harrison's body temperature to reach that of the environment?"

"Well, again it's hard to say precisely. She was healthy, normal, slim, partially unclothed, and it was a moist evening, with a temperature of ten degrees centigrade. I'd say quicker rather than later."

"Say twenty-eight hours? Twenty-six?"

"Around there."

"Around there. Very well. Does the body cool at an even, steady rate?"

"As a matter of fact, no. It falls in a sigmoid curve."

"And how do you arrive at time of death from temperature?"

"Glaister's formula. In this case the victim's temperature was thirty-five point five degrees centigrade. One subtracts this from the normal temperature of thirty-seven degrees and multiplies by one point one. The answer, in this case, is one point six-five hours. Taking the temperature of the environment into account, that becomes between one and two hours before I arrived on the scene."

"What might affect the rate at which temperature falls?"

"It's hard to say exactly. A number of factors."

Shirley Castle took a deep breath and leaned forward. "But it is *not* hard to say, is it Dr Glendenning, that thin people cool *quicker* than fat ones, and Deborah Harrison was thin. On the other hand, healthy people cool *more slowly* than weak ones, and Deborah Harrison was healthy. Naked bodies cool quicker than clothed ones, yet Deborah Harrison was only *partially* clothed. Bodies cool quicker in water than in air, yet in the humidity of the fog Deborah Harrison was subject to both. Am I right?"

"These are all relevant factors," admitted Glendenning.

"According to evidence already given," Shirley Castle went on, "Deborah was last seen alive at six o'clock, which rules out her being murdered earlier, wouldn't you say?"

Glendenning raised his eyebrows. "I would say so, yes."

"But the body was discovered by Rebecca Charters at six forty-five. Is that correct?"

"I understand so."

"And the first police officers arrived at six fifty-nine?"

"Objection."

"Yes, Mr Lawrence?" Judge Simmonds asked.

"I'd like to know where Ms Castle is going with this line of questioning, Your Honour."

"The defence requests Your Honour's indulgence. This will become clear in a short while."

"Make it fast, Ms Castle."

"Yes, Your Honour. Deborah Harrison was last seen at about six o'clock, and her body was discovered in St Mary's graveyard at six forty-five. That leaves forty-five minutes during which she could have been murdered. Now according to your evidence as regards time of death, Doctor, she *could* have been murdered later than six-thirty, couldn't she?"

Glendenning nodded. "Yes, she *could* have been."

"In fact, death *could* have occurred even as late as six-forty, couldn't it?"

"Yes. But I believe Rebecca Charters heard—"

"Please, Doctor. You should know better than that. Rebecca Charters has already admitted that what she heard could easily have been some animal or another. Now, given that nobody actually saw Owen Pierce enter St Mary's graveyard, and given that time of death could have occurred as late as six-forty, when Mr Pierce was already in the Peking Moon, there is no direct evidence placing him at the exact scene of the crime at the exact time the crime was committed, is there, Doctor?"

"This is not—"

"And as no-one saw either Deborah Harrison *or* Owen Pierce enter the graveyard," Shirley Castle charged on before anyone could stop her, "then it follows that Deborah could have gone somewhere else first, couldn't she?"

"It's not my place to speculate on such matters," said Glendenning. "I'm here to testify on matters of medical fact."

"Ah, yes," said Shirley Castle. "Facts such as time of death. It's a lot of leeway to give the definition of a fact, isn't it, Doctor?"

"Objection."

"Sustained. Will you get on with it, Ms Castle?"

"I have no further questions, Your Honour," she said, and sat down.

Very clever, thought Owen, then he turned to watch the juror who looked like a wrestler try to scratch an egg stain off his club tie.

IV

A week later, after more legal arguments and a succession of dull, minor scientific witnesses, from the fingerprint man to the officer responsible for keeping track of the forensic exhibits, Owen watched

Shirley Castle intimidate the hair expert, who ended up retreating into scientific jargon and admitting that it was virtually impossible to prove beyond a shadow of a doubt that hair found on a victim's or suspect's clothing could be positively matched to its source.

The final prosecution witness was Dr Tasker, biologist and DNA expert, a thin-faced, thin-haired academic of about forty, Owen guessed. He seemed to know his stuff, but there was a tentativeness about his delivery that threw Jerome Lawrence off kilter occasionally.

Owen wondered if the jury were as bored as he was by the interminable descriptions of autorads and enzyme scissors, by the testimony as to the scientific validity of polymerase chain reactions and the meaning of short tandem repeats, by the seeming hours spent describing the extreme care taken against the possibility of contamination of laboratory samples.

When Shirley Castle stood up to cross-examine the next after-noon, Tasker seemed a little in awe of her, and if Owen were not mistaken, perhaps a mite smitten, too. Maybe she realized this. Her tone, as she began, was relaxed, friendly, a little flirtatious even.

"Dr Tasker," she said with a smile, "I'm sure the court was most impressed yesterday with your account of DNA analysis. You would seem to have proved, without blinding us all with science, that the DNA derived from the bloodstain on Mr Pierce's anorak was indeed the DNA of Deborah Harrison. Is this true?"

Tasker nodded. "The DNA extracted from the dried bloodstain on Mr Pierce's anorak was fifty million times *more likely to be hers* than anyone else's, and the DNA taken from the tissue sample discovered under the victim's fingernail was fifty million times more likely to be Owen Pierce's than anyone else's. All we can say is how rare such a result is compared to the rest of the population."

"Still," smiled Shirley Castle. "Those are impressive odds, aren't they?"

"Oh, yes." Tasker beamed. "I certainly wouldn't bet against them."

"Almost beyond a shadow of a doubt," Shirley Castle said, "And that is, after all, what this is all about, isn't it? However, Dr Tasker, there are one or two points you might be able to clarify for me."

Owen swore that Tasker almost flushed with pleasure. "Of course. It would be a pleasure."

Shirley Castle acknowledged the compliment with a slight tilt of her head. "How much of Deborah Harrison's blood did you find on my client's anorak?"

"A small amount."

"Could you please give the court some sense of how much that might be?"

Tasker smiled. "Well, not a great deal. But enough for polymerase chain reaction analysis, as I described earlier."

"Yes, but how much? A thimble full?"

"Oh, good heavens, no, not that much."

"As much, then, as might smear from a small cut or scratch?"

"Mmm. About that, yes."

"A pinprick?"

"Possibly."

"In other words, a spot of blood about the size of a pinhead. Am I right?"

"Perhaps a little bigger than—"

"*Approximately* the size of a pinhead?"

"I suppose so. About that, yes. But, as I said—"

"Now the court has already heard Dr Glendenning testify that there was a small scratch beside Deborah Harrison's left eye. Is this the kind of wound that might produce a similar amount of blood if some fabric brushed against it?"

Tasker shifted in his seat. "Well, I didn't see the scratch so I can't say for certain, but it *was* a small amount, definitely commensurate with a minor injury such as the one you describe."

"Where did you find this blood?"

"On the accused's anorak."

"Where on the accused's anorak?"

"On the left arm. Near the shoulder."

"Now we have already heard that Deborah Harrison was five foot six inches tall and Owen Pierce is six foot two. Would this put Deborah Harrison's left eye in the region of his upper arm?"

Tasker shrugged. "I suppose so. I couldn't say exactly."

"If Your Honour would allow me," Shirley Castle addressed Judge Simmonds, "I would like the opportunity to demonstrate to the court that this is, in fact, so."

Owen could see her holding her breath. Most judges, she had told him, hate anything that smacks overly of theatrics. She must, however, have convinced him that she was following an important line of questioning, because he granted his permission after hardly any hesitation at all.

It was a simple enough thing to do. A man and a young girl were brought in—where Shirley had found them, Owen had no idea— the girl markedly shorter than the man. They were officially measured at five foot six and six foot two, then stood side by side. The girl's eye came level with the upper part of the man's arm. Shirley Castle thanked them and continued.

"Was that the only blood you discovered on my client's clothing?"

"Yes."

Shirley Castle called for Owen's anorak to be shown to the jury. One feature, she pointed out, was the zippered pocket at the outside top of the sleeve. "Did you, Dr Tasker, find any of the girl's blood on or around this zip?"

"Yes. In the vicinity."

"Could you elaborate?"

"It was right at the end of the zip, actually."

"Would you point to the spot on the exhibit, please?"

Tasker did so.

"The edge of the metal teeth is fairly sharp there," Shirley Castle went on. "Does that not indicate to you that the girl may have scraped her cheek on the zip when she collided with Mr Pierce after running backwards in the fog?"

"It could have got there in any number of ways."

"But it could have got there in the way I suggest?"

"Yes, but—"

"And that was *all* the blood you found?"

"I've already said that. I—"

"Not very much, is it?"

"As I said, it was enough for PCR analysis."

"Ah, yes: PCR, STR, DNA, 'genetic fingerprinting.' Magic words, these days. And what does that prove, Dr Tasker?"

"That the blood on the defendant's anorak is fifty million times—"

"Yes, yes. We've already been through all that, haven't we? But the defence has *never denied* that it is Deborah Harrison's blood. She bumped into my client and scratched herself on the zip of his anorak. Would you admit that the *amount* and *location* of the blood you found bear out that explanation?"

"I suppose so."

"You suppose so. Did you find any traces of blood on the cuffs of the anorak?"

"No."

"Wouldn't you expect to if the victim were bleeding from the nose as the accused strangled her?"

"Perhaps."

"So he might be expected to get blood on his cuff if he did indeed strangle her from behind with the satchel strap?"

"Well, it's possible, yes, but—"

"And did you find any blood lower down his sleeve?"

"No. But she could have twisted side—"

"Thank you, Dr Tasker. You have answered my question. Now, given the life-and-death struggle that must have taken place, it would have been difficult to avoid *some* close contact, wouldn't it?"

"Presumably."

"And did you test the rest of anorak for blood?"

"Yes. We carried out a thorough examination."

"But you found no blood other than this infinitesimal amount high on the sleeve, at the edge of the metal teeth on the zip?"

"No."

The infatuation seemed to be on the wane, Owen noticed. Tasker didn't even want to look Shirley Castle in the eye now. Owen glanced over at "Minerva," who was regarding the doctor sternly. No more would she believe the "scientific tests have proved" commercials, if, indeed, she ever had.

"Dr Tasker, do you know where Deborah Harrison's hairs—what we have since learned only *might* in fact be Deborah Harrison's hairs—were found on Mr Pierce's anorak?"

"No, that's not my—"

"Then let me tell you. They were found on the upper left arm and on the upper left arm *only*. In fact, all three of her hairs were found in the teeth of Mr Pierce's zip, by the pinpoint bloodstain. What do you have to say to that?"

"I don't know. It's not my field."

"Not your field? But would you not say it's consistent with the scenario I just outlined for you? A minor collision?"

"I have already agreed that is a *possible* explanation."

"How much blood and skin did you find under the victim's fingernail?"

"A small amount. But enough for—"

"Consistent with what might be deposited from a light scratch?"

"Yes."

"If Deborah Harrison had been fighting for her life, wouldn't you have expected to find more, in your professional judgement?"

"Possibly. But again, it's not my—"

"I understand that, Dr Tasker. But we can't have it both ways, can we? Either she did get the opportunity to defend herself by scratching, in which case she came away with a pitiful amount of skin, or she didn't. Which is it to be, in your opinion?"

Owen saw Lawrence on the verge of an objection, but he seemed to think better of it and sank down again.

"It could have been just a lucky strike," said Tasker. "I don't know."

"You don't know. Very well. Would you at least agree that the presence of a small amount of Mr Pierce's skin under one of her fingernails could have got there during a minor collision, if she put out her hand to steady herself?"

"Yes."

"Then would you also agree that it is possible that Deborah Harrison's killer could have been someone other than my client?"

"Objection!"

"Overruled, Mr Lawrence. Witness will please answer the question."

Tasker fiddled with his tie. "Well, theoretically, yes. Of course," he gave a nervous titter. "I mean, theoretically, anything's possible. I wasn't there, I can't tell you exactly what happened. The DNA was a good match to the defendant's, so he can't be excluded."

"I submit that the DNA match is irrelevant. Is your answer to my question yes?"

"I suppose so."

"Is it?"

"Yes."

Shirley Castle turned to the judge and threw her hands in the air. "Your Honour," she said, "I find myself exasperated that the prosecution's case is based on so little and such flimsy evidence. No further questions."

For the first time, Jerome Lawrence stood up to re-examine. It must be because it's his last witness, Owen thought. He wants to leave a positive impression.

"Just two questions, Dr Tasker," he said. "You are fully aware of the nature of the crime, the nature of the victim's injuries. Would you say, in your expert opinion, that the amounts of the victim's blood left on the accused's clothing were in any way *too little* for him to have committed such a crime?"

"No, I wouldn't," said Tasker.

"And could the exchange of blood and tissue have taken place during a struggle for her life?"

"Indeed it could."

Jerome Lawrence gave an oily bow. "Thank you very much, Dr Tasker."

TWELVE

I

Nothing could have prepared Owen for the shock of seeing Michelle sitting in the gallery when he glanced nervously around the courtroom before going into the witness-box.

His heart thudded against his ribcage. He felt as if a large bird had somehow found its way inside him and was scratching and plucking at his chest and throat, beating its wings, trying to get out. She was still beautiful; she still had the power to make his heart ache and yearn.

If anything, Owen thought, Michelle looked even younger than she had when they had been together: about fifteen or sixteen. She wore no make-up to mar her delicate, alabaster complexion, a maroon blazer and a simple white blouse, very much like the St Mary's school uniform.

Her blonde hair—the same colour and length as Deborah Harrison's—hung over her shoulders in exactly the same way Deborah's had in the newspaper photographs. Her lips, the colour of the inside of a strawberry, were fixed in a childish pout. And the implication of innocence and immaturity permeated her entire bearing. Owen wondered if people knew who she was. She was sitting next to a man he had seen there often before: a reporter, Owen thought.

He tried to avoid looking at her. Why was she here? Had the Crown lured her in to upset him? He had already realized that he was participating in a drama, a theatrical event more than anything else, and that the awards would be handed out in a few days' time. Did Michelle have a part to play, too? She wasn't going into the box—Shirley Castle had taken care of that—so what was she doing in court?

He was so distracted by her presence that he didn't hear Shirley Castle calling him to give evidence at first, then the judge called him to the box.

Shirley Castle spent more than a day taking him through the events of that fateful Monday in November, as smoothly as she had before in the interview room near his cell. He felt calm as he spoke, and he hoped the jury wouldn't interpret this as lack of emotion.

"Minerva," as far as he could tell, listened to him objectively, a slight furrow of concentration in her brow. Most of the others, he noticed, appeared to be paying attention too, but a couple had disbelieving sneers etched around their lips—that "come on, tell us another one" look he had become so adept at perceiving of late. Occasionally, he sneaked a glance at Michelle. Once in a while she turned and spoke behind her hand to the reporter next to her.

The next day, after Shirley Castle had finished eliciting a reasonable and believable account of events from Owen, or so he thought, Jerome Lawrence dragged himself to his feet. "There hardly seems any point," Lawrence's weary, long-suffering movements seemed to be saying, "in bothering with this, as you and I know he's guilty, ladies and gentlemen of the jury, but duty demands we go through the motions." Owen looked at the gallery and saw Michelle was in court again.

Lawrence asked what seemed a lot of dull questions for most of the morning, and after lunch he finally began to zoom in on the crime. "Mr Pierce," he said, "you have told the jury that between the hours of about six and six-thirty on 6 November last year, you simply walked around the area of St Mary's, Eastvale, in the fog, and stood on the bridge for some time. Is this so?"

"Yes."

"Were you intoxicated, Mr Pierce?"

"Not at all."

"You drank, let me see, two pints of beer and a double Scotch at the Nag's Head, is that right?"

Owen shrugged. "I think so."

"And you weren't intoxicated?"

"I'm not saying I didn't feel the effects at all, just that I was perfectly in control. And I was walking, not driving."

"You had more to drink later, didn't you, at the Peking Moon?"

"Yes. With a large meal."

"Indeed. And can you tell the court why you spent so long standing on the bridge before a fine view that you *couldn't possibly see* because of the thick fog?"

"I don't know, really. It was just what I felt like doing. I had one or two problems to mull over and I find fog helps contemplation."

"What problems were these?"

Owen saw Shirley Castle making discreet warning signals. He looked Michelle in the eye. "Personal matters. Of no relevance."

"I see. And was it this same *personal matter* that led you to drink so much?"

"I didn't drink a lot. I've already told you, I wasn't drunk."

"And led you to hide yourself away in the corner of a restaurant and mutter to yourself?"

Owen felt himself flush with embarrassment. "That's just a habit, like when I'm adding up. I've always done it. Sometimes a thought just comes out loud, that's all. I forget that there are people around. It doesn't make me a maniac. Or a murderer."

"Are you sure you weren't muttering in the Peking Moon about what you'd just done? Murdered Deborah Harrison?"

"Of course not. That's totally absurd. I was just reasoning with myself, to calm down."

"*Calm down?*" There was no missing the verbal underlining in that repetition. "Why did you feel the need to calm down, Mr Pierce? What made you so agitated in the first place."

"I wasn't agitated. There's a difference between being a little melancholy and being agitated, isn't there? I mean—"

"Would you please stick to answering my questions?" Lawrence butted in. "If I need lessons in the English language, believe me, I shall ask for them."

"I'm the one in the dock, aren't I? Why shouldn't my opinion count? You've asked everyone else's, haven't you? Why should I let you get away with distorting the meaning—"

"Mr Pierce," Judge Simmonds grumbled. "Please answer Mr Lawrence's questions as directly and as clearly as you can."

"I'm sorry, Your Honour," said Owen. He turned back to Lawrence. "The answer is no. I wasn't agitated; I was melancholy."

"Is it not true that you were upset and dejected about your
break-up with a young lady some—"

"Objection!"

"Sustained. Mr Lawrence!"

"I apologize, Your Honour."

What the hell was that little skirmish about? Owen wondered,
his heart jumping. He glanced at Michelle again. Lawrence was
trying it on; he knew damn well that evidence had been ruled inadmissible. The bastard was trying to slip it in regardless. He thanked
his lucky stars Shirley Castle was so quick. Still, something had
been lodged with the jury, no matter how much the judge might
tell them to disregard it. He looked at "Minerva." She seemed
puzzled. Owen's breath came a little quicker.

"Let us, then, move on to the scientific evidence," Lawrence
continued. "You don't deny that Deborah Harrison's hair and blood
were found on your clothing?"

"It's not for me to accept or deny," Owen said. "I'm not a scientist.
If your experts have identified these things, that's their business."

"And when faced with this fact by Detective Chief Inspector
Banks, you gave him some story about bumping into the girl. Is this
true?"

It was plain enough that Lawrence intended "cock and bull" to
come before "story."

"I didn't bump into her," Owen said. "She bumped into me as
I was turning from the wall."

"Answer the question."

"I would answer it if it were correctly posed."

Lawrence sighed and made a long-suffering gesture to the jury.
"Very well, then, Mr Pierce. You told the police that the girl
bumped into you. Is this correct?"

"I told them exactly what happened."

"Why didn't you tell them earlier?"

"It didn't seem important."

"Come on, Mr Pierce, the police had already told you how
important everything that happened that day was the second time

they interviewed you. You knew you were in a serious situation. Why didn't you tell them earlier?"

"I've already told you. I didn't tell them about the time I had to bend down and refasten my left shoelace, either, or about stopping at the newsagent's for an evening paper, which, by the way, they didn't have. It just *didn't seem important*."

"Yet you remembered it well enough later. In fact, as soon as you were challenged with evidence of your physical contact with the victim, you suddenly came up with an explanation." Lawrence laughed and flapped like a bat. "As if by magic. Really, Mr Pierce. Do you expect the court to believe that?"

"Objection."

"Sustained. The witness's opinion on such matters of what the court should or should not believe is not required, as you well know, Mr Lawrence."

"I am sorry, Your Honour. I submit to you, Mr Pierce, that you saw Deborah Harrison part from her companion, that you followed her into the graveyard, and that you—"

"No! I did nothing of the kind," Owen cut in.

"And that you strangled Deborah Harrison with her own school satchel strap!"

Owen clenched his fists and kept them out of sight. "I did not," he said quietly, with as much dignity as he could muster.

Lawrence held him with his black, beady eyes, then breathed, "No more questions," and sat down looking pleased with himself.

It was Friday afternoon, so Judge Simmonds adjourned for the weekend and Owen was escorted back to his cell.

II

Back in the dock on Monday, Owen tried to keep his eyes off Michelle and concentrate on Jerome Lawrence's final address to the jury. From what he heard, it wasn't much different from the opening remarks: Owen was a monster, hardly even human, who had brutally murdered a pure and innocent young girl. Most of the time he found himself looking towards Michelle.

He sensed she knew he was staring at her, but she wouldn't catch his eye.

Lawrence went on for the best part of the day, piling atrocity on atrocity, outrage upon outrage, and it wasn't until Tuesday morning that Shirley Castle got to make her closing speech. Again, Owen found himself watching Michelle most of the time, and the next thing he knew, Shirley Castle was wrapping up.

"And, above all, remember the phrase *beyond reasonable doubt*," she said. "It is the very foundation upon which our justice system is built. The burden of proof lies with the Crown. Ask yourselves, has the Crown proven its case *beyond reasonable doubt*? Are you yourselves sure, beyond reasonable doubt, that this man before you is anything other than an innocent victim? Do you not harbour doubts yourselves? I think you will find that you do, and that you can honestly do no other than agree with me, and say *no*, the Crown has *not* proven its case. For you see in front of you a man who was in the wrong place at the wrong time, a man confused, worried and anxious by a police investigation he could not understand and which was not explained to him. But more than anything, you see in front of you an *innocent* man who has already been punished more than enough for a crime he did not commit. Look into your hearts, ladies and gentlemen, and I'm sure you will find there the certain knowledge that my client is innocent of all charges laid against him. Thank you."

After this carefully impassioned finale, Judge Simmonds's summing up seemed perfunctory to Owen. At least he was fair, Owen had to admit. In a detached monologue, the judge reiterated the main points of the case, careful not to indicate any bias. As the old man talked, Owen kept switching his gaze between Michelle and "Minerva."

"Minerva" was clearly listening, but Owen could not help getting the impression that this final speech was superfluous to her, that she had already made up her mind. Once, she caught him looking at her for a second and turned away quickly, blushing. He could have sworn, though, that her eyes held no trace of accusation, of condemnation. When Michelle finally decided to return Owen's gaze, she smiled, and he couldn't mistake the cold, malicious glint in her eyes; it made him shiver.

III

While the jury was out, Owen sat in a cheerless room below the court with Shirley Castle and his guards drinking bitter coffee until his stomach hurt.

He had experienced anxious waiting before—after a job interview, for example, or those long nights at the window watching for Michelle to come home—but nothing as gut-wrenching as this. His stomach clenched and growled; he bit his nails; he jumped at every sound. He tried to imagine what it must have been like when the death penalty existed, but couldn't. Shirley Castle tried to make conversation but soon stopped after his terse and jumbled responses.

Hours, it seemed, went by. At last, someone came and said the jury hadn't reached a verdict yet, and as it was late, Owen was to spend the night back in his cell. He asked Shirley Castle about the jury taking so long, and she said it was a good sign.

That night, he hardly slept at all. Fear gnawed at him; the cell walls closed in. In that nether world between sleep and waking, where memories take on the aspect of dreams, he actually watched himself strangle Deborah Harrison in a foggy graveyard. Or was it Michelle? He had been told so often that he had done it that his subconscious mind had actually been tricked into believing it. He thought he screamed out in the night, but nobody came rushing to see what was wrong. When he woke from the dream, he noticed he had an erection and felt ashamed.

Morning came: slopping out, the stink of piss and shit that seemed to permeate the place, the supervised shave, breakfast. Then Owen sat around in his suit waiting to go back to the court and face the verdict. Still nothing. By mid-morning on Wednesday, he wasn't sure how much longer he could last without going mad. Just before lunch, his cell door opened and the warder said, "Come on, lad. It looks like they're back."

In court, Owen gripped the front of the dock until his knuckles turned white. The gallery was full: Michelle leaning forward, thumbnail between her front teeth, as she often did during thrillers or when she was concentrating hard; the Harrisons; two of the detectives, Stott and Banks; the vicar, Daniel Charters and his attractive wife, Rebecca; reporters; morbid members of the public. They were all there.

The jury filed back in. Owen looked at "Minerva." She didn't glance in his direction. He didn't know what to make of that.

After the hush came the legal rigmarole about charges, then the question everyone had been waiting for: "Do you find the defendant Owen Pierce guilty or not guilty as charged?"

The split-second pause between question and answer seemed an eternity for Owen. His ears roared and he felt his head swimming. Then the spokesman, a drab-looking man Owen had guessed to be a banker, spoke the words: "We find the defendant not guilty, Your Honour."

There was more talk after that, but most of it was lost in the hubbub that raced through the courtroom like an explosive blast. Reporters dashed for phones. Owen swayed and clutched the dock for dear life. He couldn't seem to stop the ringing in his ears. He heard a woman yell, "It's a travesty!" Then everything went white and he fainted.

Owen came to in a room below the court, a cool, damp cloth pressed to his brow, with Shirley Castle and Gordon Wharton standing over him. As he recovered, he felt the stirrings of joy, like the first, tentative shoots of a new plant in spring, overtake the gnawing anxiety that had burdened him before. He was *free!* Surely it would sink in soon. Shirley Castle was talking to someone, but when she stopped and walked towards him, he could feel the muscles in his face form a smile for the first time in what seemed like years.

She smiled back, curled her fist and thumped the air triumphantly. "We did it!"

"You did it," Owen said. "I don't know how to thank you."

"Winning is thanks enough." She held out her hand. "Congratulations, Owen. And good luck."

He shook it, the first time he'd touched a woman in months, and he was conscious of the soft warmth under the firm grip. He felt her give a little tug and released her, embarrassed to realize he had held on too long. He wanted to kiss her. And not only because she had won his case. Instead, he turned to Wharton.

"What now?" he asked.

"What? Oh." The solicitor glanced away from the disappearing figure. "Wonderful woman, isn't she? I told you if anyone could do it, Shirley Castle could. It was a majority verdict, you know. Ten to two. That's what took them so long. What now? Well, you're free, that's what."

"But ... what do I do? I mean, my stuff and ..."

"Tell you what." Wharton looked at his watch. "I'll drive you back over to the prison, if you like, and you can pick your stuff up, then I'll take you back to Eastvale."

Owen nodded. "Thanks. How do we ... I mean, do we just walk out of here?"

Wharton laughed. "Yes," he said. "Yes, that's exactly what we do. Hard to get used to, eh? But I think there'll be a bit of a mob out front, we'd better leave by the back way."

"A mob?"

Wharton frowned. "Yes. Well, you've seen the papers. Those sly innuendos about the 'evidence they couldn't present in court.' That not-guilty verdict won't have sunk in with them yet, will it? People lose all sense of proportion when they get carried away by chants and whatnot. Come on."

In a daze, Owen followed Wharton through the corridors to the back exit. The sun was shining on the narrow backstreet; opposite was a refurbished Victorian pub, all black trim and etched, smoked-glass windows; under his feet, the worn paving-stones looked gold in the midday light. Freedom.

Owen breathed the air deeply; a warm, still day. When he thought about it, he realized the trial had lasted almost two months, and it was now May, the most glorious month in the Dales. Back up near Eastvale, the woods, fields and hillsides would be a ablaze with wildflowers: bluebells, wild garlic, celandines, cowslips, violets and primroses; and here and there would be the fields of bright yellow rape-seed.

As they walked towards Wharton's car, Owen could vaguely hear the crowd outside the front of the courthouse: women's voices mostly, he thought, chanting, "Guilty! Guilty! Guilty!"

IV

"Fuck it," said Barry Stott loudly. Then he said it again, banging his fist on the arm of the bench for emphasis. *"Fuck it."* A couple standing by the pub door gave him a dirty look. "Sorry," he said to Banks, blushing right up to the tips of his jug-ears. "I just had to let it out."

Banks nodded in sympathy. It was the first time he had ever heard Barry Stott swear, and he had to admit he didn't blame him.

They were sitting on the long bench outside Whitelock's in the narrow alley called Turk's Head Yard, drinks and food propped on the upturned barrel that served as a table. Along with his pint of Younger's bitter, Banks had a Cornish pasty with chips and gravy, and Stott had a Scotch egg with HP Sauce, with a half of shandy to wash it down. They had just left Leeds Crown Court after the Owen Pierce verdict.

It was a beautiful May day; the pub had lured students from their studies and encouraged office workers to linger over their lunch-hours. Not much light penetrated Turk's Head Yard because of the high walls of the buildings on both sides, but the air was warm and full of the promise of summer. Men sat with their jackets off and shirtsleeves rolled up, while bare-legged women opened an extra button or two on their blouses.

Banks took a sip of beer before tucking into the pasty. He watched Stott pick at the Scotch egg, dip little pieces in the sauce, chew and swallow, too distracted to taste the food. It was obvious that he had no appetite. He had only eaten half when he pushed his plate away. Banks finished his own lunch quickly and lit a cigarette.

"I can't believe he got off," Stott said. "I just can't believe it."

"I'm just as pissed off as you are, Barry, but it happens," said Banks. "You get used to it. Don't take it personally."

"But I do. It was me who cottoned on to him, me who tracked him down. We build a solid case, and he just walks away."

Banks didn't bother reminding him how it was teamwork and hard procedural slog that had led them to Owen Pierce. "The case obviously wasn't solid enough," he said. "Dr Tasker wasn't very good, for a start. Even Glendenning wasn't up to his usual form. Who knows? Maybe they were right?"

"Who?"

"The jury."

Stott shook his head. His ears seemed to flap with the motion. "No. I can't accept that. He did it. I know he did. I feel it in my bones. He murdered that poor girl, and he got away with it. You know, if we'd got the evidence from Michelle Chappel in, then we'd have got a conviction for certain. The judge made a hell of a mistake there."

"Perhaps. Did you see her there, by the way?"

"Where? Who?"

"Michelle Chappel. In court. I don't know if she's been there all along but she was in the public gallery for the verdict. She'd let her hair grow since last November, too. Looked more like Deborah Harrison than ever. She was even wearing a maroon blazer. She was talking to that reporter from the *News of the World*."

"See what I mean," said Stott. "If we'd been able to bring out that connection, her evidence of what he did to her, there's no jury in the country wouldn't have convicted Pierce."

"Maybe so, but that's not the point, Barry."

Stott flushed. "Excuse me, but I think it is. A guilty man has just walked out of that courtroom after committing one of the most horrible murders I have ever investigated, and you tell me that's not the point. I'm sorry, but—"

"I mean it's not the point I'm trying to make."

Stott frowned. "I don't follow."

"Why is Michelle Chappel so keen to stick the knife in Pierce?"

"Oh, I see. Well, maybe because he beat her up. Or perhaps because he tried to strangle her? Or could being raped by him after he knocked her out have upset her just a little bit?"

Banks sipped some more beer. "All right, Barry, give it a rest. I catch your drift. Perhaps you're right. But why hang around after her evidence was declared inadmissible? Just to watch him suffer? Why take time off work?"

Stott frowned. "What makes you think there's a connection?"

"It's just odd, that's all." Banks stubbed out his cigarette and drank some more beer. "Her hair was short when we talked to her."

"Women's hair," said Stott with a shrug. "Who knows anything about that?"

Banks smiled. "Good point. Another pint? Half, rather?"

"Should we?"

"Yes, we damn well should. Jimmy Riddle's going to be out for our blood. Might as well put off the inevitable as long as possible."

"Oh, all right. I'll have another half of shandy. Then I'll have to be off."

Banks edged through the crowd to the bar, looking at his reflection in the antique mirror at the back while he waited. Not too bad for his early forties, he thought, still slim and trim, despite the pints and the poor diet; a few lines around the eyes, maybe, and a touch a grey at the temples, but that was all. Besides, they added character, Sandra said.

He intended to part company with Stott after the next drink and visit an old friend while he was in Leeds: Pamela Jeffreys, a violist with the English Northern Philharmonic orchestra. About a year ago, she had been badly hurt in an attack for which Banks still blamed himself. She wasn't back in the orchestra yet, but she was working hard and getting there fast, and this afternoon, she was playing a chamber concert at the university's music department. It might go some small way towards making up for the disappointment in court this morning.

He might also, while he was so close, drop in at the Classical Record Shop and see about the Samuel Barber song collection he had been wanting for a while. Listening to Dawn Upshaw singing "Knoxville: Summer of 1915" on the drive down had made him think about it.

On the other hand, the not-guilty verdict changed things. While he was in Leeds, he would also phone DI Ken Blackstone and see about having a chat with one of Jelačić's card-playing cronies. He might even have another word with Jelačić himself.

Though the Crown would probably appeal the verdict, as far as Banks was concerned it was back to the drawing-board for the time being, a drawing-board he was beginning to feel he should never have left in the first place. And Ive Jelačić was certainly high on his list of loose ends.

"Damn that judge," said Stott when he had thanked Banks for the drink. "Just thinking about it makes my blood boil."

"I'm not convinced Michelle Chappel's testimony would have helped as much as you think, Barry," Banks said.

"Why not? At least it proves he had homicidal tendencies towards young women of Deborah Harrison's physical type."

"It proves nothing of the kind," said Banks. "Okay, I'll admit, I was as excited about the psychological possibilities it opened up as you were. And, yes, I was bloody annoyed that Simmonds excluded it. But now I think about it, looking at her in court, I'm not so sure."

Stott scratched the back of his left ear and frowned. "Why not?"

"Because I think that defence lawyer, Shirley Castle, would have made mincemeat of her, that's why. In the final analysis, she'd have had the jury believing that Michelle Chappel was lying, that she did what she did out of pure vindictiveness towards Pierce, for revenge, because she harboured a grudge for the way he treated her."

"And rightly so, after what he did to her."

"But don't you see how it would discredit her testimony, Barry, make her seem like a lying bitch? Especially with such criticisms coming from another woman. That could be pretty damning. She's good is Ms Castle. I've been up against her before. She'd have made sure that Pierce convinced them with his version of that night's events. And if they believed that he had simply been warding off the frenzied attack of a hysterical woman, then he could have gained their sympathy."

Stott took off his glasses and polished them with a spotless handkerchief. "I still think it would have helped us get a conviction."

"Well there's no way of knowing now, is there?"

"I suppose not," Stott said glumly. "What do we do now?"

"There's not much more we can do."

"Reopen the investigation?"

Banks sipped some beer. "Oh, yes. I think so, don't you? After all, Barry, someone out there killed Deborah Harrison, and according to all the hallmarks, it looks very much like someone who might do it again."

THIRTEEN

I

Vjeko Batorac was out when Banks called in the afternoon, and a neighbour said he usually came home from work at about five-thirty. Ken Blackstone, who said Batorac was probably the most believable of Jelačić's three card-playing cronies, had given Banks the address.

Grateful for the free time, Banks played truant; he went up to the university and spent a delightful hour listening to Vaughan Williams's *String Quartet No. 2*.

And he was glad he did. As he watched and listened, all the stress and disappointment of the verdict, all his fears of having persecuted the wrong man in the first place, seemed to become as insubstantial as air, at least for a while.

As he watched Pamela Jeffreys play in the bright room, prisms of light all around, her glossy raven hair dancing, skin like burnished gold, the diamond stud in her right nostril flashing in the sun, he thought not for the first time that there was something intensely, spiritually erotic about a beautiful woman playing music.

It seemed, as he watched, that Pamela first projected her spirit and emotions into her instrument, the bow an extension of her arm, fingers and strings inseparable, then she became the music, flowing and soaring with its rhythms and melodies, dipping and swooping, eyes closed, oblivious to the world outside.

Or so it seemed. Though he had taken a few hesitant steps towards learning the piano, Banks couldn't actually play an instrument, so he was willing to admit he might be romanticizing. Maybe she was thinking about her pay-cheque.

Erotic fantasies aside, it was all perfectly innocent. They had coffee and a chat afterwards, then Banks headed back to Batorac's house.

Vjeko Batorac lived in a small pre-war terrace house in Sheepscar, near the junction of Roseville Road and Roundhay Road, less than a mile from Jelačić's Burmantofts flat. There was no garden; the front door, which looked as if it had been freshly painted, opened directly onto the pavement. This time, a few minutes before six o'clock, Banks's knock was answered by a slight, hollow-cheeked young man with fair hair, wearing oil-stained jeans and a clean white T-shirt.

"*Molim?*" said Batorac, frowning.

"Mr Batorac?" Banks asked, showing his warrant card. "I wonder if I might have a word? Do you speak English?"

Batorac nodded, looking puzzled. "What is it about?"

"Ive Jelačić."

Batorac rolled his eyes and opened the door wider. "You'd better come in."

The living-room was sunny and clean, and just a hint of baby smells mingled with those of cabbage and garlic from the kitchen. What surprised Banks most of all was the bookcase that took up most of one wall, crammed with English classics and foreign titles he couldn't read. Serbo-Croatian, he guessed. The "Six O'Clock News" was on Radio 4 in the background.

"That's quite a library you've got."

Batorac beamed. "*Hvala lipo.* Thank you very much. Yes, I love books. In my own country I was a school-teacher. I taught English, so I have studied your language for many years. I also write poetry."

"What do you do here?"

Batorac smiled ironically. "I am a garage mechanic. Fortunately for me, in Croatia you had to be good at fixing your own car." He shrugged. "It's a good job. Not much pay, but my boss treats me well."

A baby started crying. Batorac excused himself for a moment and went upstairs. Banks examined the titles in more detail as he waited: Dickens, Hardy, Keats, Austen, Balzac, Flaubert, Coleridge, Tolstoy, Dostoevsky, Milton, Kafka ... Many he had read, but many were books he had promised himself to read and never got around to. The baby fell silent and Batorac came back.

"Sorry," he said. "We have a friend takes care of little Jelena during the day, while we work. When she comes home she ... how do you say this ... she misses her mother and father?"

Banks smiled. "Yes, that's right. She has missed you."

"*Has* missed. Yes. Sometimes I get the tenses wrong. What is it you wanted to see me about? Sit down, please."

Banks sat. This didn't look or smell like the kind of house where one could smoke, especially with the baby around, so he resigned himself to refrain. It would no doubt do him good. "Remember," he asked, "a few months ago when the local police asked you about an evening you said you played cards with Ive Jelačić?"

Batorac nodded. "Yes. It was true. Every Monday we play cards. Dragica, my wife, she is very indulgent. But on Mondays only." He smiled. "Tuesday I do not have to go to work, so sometimes we talk and play until late."

"And drink?"

"Yes. I do not drink much because I drive home. The streets are not safe at night. But I drink some, yes. A little."

"And are you *absolutely* certain on that Monday, the sixth of November, you were playing cards with Stipe Pavič and Ive Jelačić at Mile Pavelič's house?"

"Yes. I swear on the Bible. I do not lie, Inspector."

"No offence. Please understand we have to be very thorough about these things. Was Jelačić there the whole time?"

"Yes."

"He said that he walked to Mr Pavelič's house and back. Did he usually do that?"

"Yes. He only lives about five hundred metres away, over the waste ground."

"I'm curious, Mr Batorac—"

"Call me Vjeko, please."

"Very well, Vjeko. I'm curious as to how the four of you got together. If you don't mind my saying so, you and Ive Jelačić seem very different kinds of people."

Vjeko smiled. "There are not many of my countrymen here in Leeds," he said. "We have clubs and societies where we meet to get news from home and talk about politics. What you English call a very good grapevine. Ive knew Mile from the old country. They are both from Split. I met Stipe here, in Leeds. He is from Zagreb and I am from Dubrovnik, long way apart. Have you ever visited Dubrovnik, Chief Inspector?"

Banks shook his head,

"It is a very beautiful city. Very much history, ancient architecture. Many English tourists came before the war. You have missed much. Perhaps forever."

"When did you come here?"

"In 1991, after the siege. I could not bear to see my home destroyed." He tapped his chest. "I am a poet, not a soldier, Chief Inspector. And my health is not strong. I have only one lung." Vjeko shrugged. "When Ive came from Eastvale, he came into contact with us. He told us his parents were both killed in the fighting. Many of us have lost friends and relatives in the war. I lost my sister two years ago. Raped and butchered by Serb soldiers. It gives us a common bond. The kind of bond that transcends—is that right? Yes?—that transcends personality. After that, we just started meeting to talk and play cards." He smiled. "Not for money, you understand. My Dragica would not be so indulgent about that."

Almost on cue, the front door opened, and a pretty, petite young woman with dark hair and sparkling eyes walked in. "What would your Dragica not be so indulgent about?" she asked with a smile, going over and kissing Vjeko affectionately before turning to glance curiously at Banks.

Vjeko told her who Banks was and why he was there. "I said you would not be indulgent if I played cards for money."

Dragica thumped him playfully on the shoulder and perched on the arm of the sofa. "Sometimes," she said, "I ask myself why you must stay up most of the night playing cards with those people instead of keeping your wife warm in bed and getting up when little Jelena cries. Ive Jelačić, particularly, is nothing but a useless *pijanac*."

"*Pijanac?*" Banks repeated. "What is that?"

"Drunk," said Vjeko. "Yes, Ive is ... he does drink too much. He is not a pleasant man in many ways, Inspector. You must not judge my fellow countrymen by Ive's example. And I do not put forward the tragedy in his life as an excuse for his behaviour. He lies. He boasts. Most of all, he is greedy. He often suggests that we play cards for money, and I know he cheats. With women he is bad, too. Dragica cannot bear him near her."

"That is true," Dragica told Banks, shuddering at the thought and hugging her slight frame. "He undresses you with his eyes."

Banks remembered Susan Gay's reaction to Jelačić's ogling and nodded.

"Please excuse me," Dragica said. "I must attend to Jelena." And she went upstairs.

"He is rude, too," Vjeko went on. "Ill-mannered. And I have seen him behave violently in pubs, picking fights when he is drunk." He laughed. "When I put it like that, I wonder why I do spend time with him. It is a mystery to me. But one thing I can tell you is that Ive wouldn't kill a young girl that way. Never. Perhaps in a fight, in a pub, he could kill, but not like that, not someone weaker than himself. It is a joke with us that Ive always picks on people bigger than himself, and he usually comes off worst."

"Do you know why Mr Jelačić left Eastvale?" Banks asked.

"He told us that a svečenik, a man of God, made homosexual advances towards him."

"You said he was a liar. Do you believe his story?"

Vjeko shook his head. "No. I do not think it is true. I have listened to him talk about it, and I think he did what he did to get revenge for losing his job."

"If that's so," said Banks, "then he's caused Daniel Charters an awful lot of grief."

Vjeko spread his hands. "But what can anyone do? I did not know Ive back in Eastvale, when all this happened, and I do not know this Father Daniel Charters. Perhaps he is a good man; perhaps he is not. But I do think that Ive is tired with his revenge. He has had enough. The problem is that he is mixed up with lawyers and human-rights campaigners among our own people. It is not so easy for him to turn around and say to them it was all a lie, a mistake or a joke. He would lose face."

"And face is important to him?"

"Yes."

Dragica returned carrying a sleeping Jelena in her arms and said something in Croatian; Vjeko nodded, and she went into the kitchen.

"Dragica asked if dinner is nearly ready," he said. "I told her yes."

Banks stood up. "Then I won't use up any more of your time. You've been very helpful." He stuck out his hand.

"Why don't you stay for dinner?" Vjeko asked. "It is not very much, just *sarma*. Cabbage rolls. But we would be happy if you would share with us."

Banks paused at the door. It was almost six-thirty and he hadn't had anything since lunch at Whitelock's. He would have to eat some-time. "All right," he said. "Thanks very much. Yes, I'd love to stay."

II

Instead of continuing along Roundhay Road towards Wetherby and the A1, Banks cut back down Roseville Road and Regent Street, then headed for Burmantofts. He had dined well with the Batoracs, and conversation had ranged from books and teaching to the Balkan war and crime. After their goodbyes, it was a quarter to eight on a fine May evening, and dusk was slowly gathering when Banks pulled up near Jelačić's flat. In the failing, honeyed light, the shabby concrete tower blocks looked as eerie as a landscape on Mars.

There were plenty of people around in the recreation areas between the buildings, mostly teenagers congregated in little knots here and there, some of them playing on swings and roundabouts.

Banks managed to climb the six flights of graffiti-scarred concrete without incident, apart from a little shortness of breath, and rapped on Jelačić's door.

He could already hear the television blaring "Coronation Street" through the paper-thin walls, so when no-one answered the first time, he knocked even harder. Finally Jelačić answered the door, grubby shirt hanging out of his jeans, and scowled when he recognized Banks.

"You," he said. "*Šupak*. Why you come here? You already have killer."

"Things change, Ive," said Banks, gently shouldering his way inside. The place was as he remembered, tidy but overlaid with a patina of stale booze and cigarette smoke. Here he could light up with impunity. He turned down the sound on one of Jack and Vera Duckworth's loud public arguments.

Jelačić didn't complain. He picked up a glass of clear liquid—probably vodka, Banks guessed—from the table and flopped down on the settee. It creaked under his weight. Jelačić had put on quite a few pounds since they had last met, most of it on his gut. He looked about eight months pregnant.

"You'll be glad to hear," Banks said, "that your alibi still seems to hold water."

Jelačić frowned. "Water? Hold water? What you mean?"

"I mean we believe you were playing cards at Mile Pavelič's house at the time Deborah Harrison was killed."

"I already tell you that. So why you come here?"

"To ask you some questions."

Jelačić grunted.

"First of all, when exactly did you come here from Eastvale?"

"Was last year. September."

"So the St Mary's girls would have been back at school for a while before you left?"

"Yes. Two weeks."

Banks leaned forward and flicked his ash into an overflowing tin ashtray, which looked as if it had been stolen from a pub. "Now the last time we talked," he said, "you swore blind you'd never seen Deborah Harrison, or at most that you might just have *seen* her once or twice, in passing."

"Is true."

"Now I'm asking you to rethink. I'm giving you another chance to tell the truth, Ive. There's no blame attached to this now. You're not a suspect. But you might be a witness."

"I saw nothing."

Banks nodded towards the TV set. "I don't suppose you watch the news," he said. "But for your information Owen Pierce was found not guilty and released earlier today."

"He is free?" Jelačić stared open-mouthed, then began to laugh.

"Then you failed. You let the guilty man go free. Always that happens here." He shook his head. "Such a crazy country."

"Yes, well at least we don't shoot them first and ask questions later. But that's beside the point. He may or may not have committed the crime, but officially he didn't and we're reopening the case. Which is why I'm here. Now why is trying to get the tiniest scrap of help from you like getting blood out of a stone, Ive? Can you tell me that?"

Jelačić shrugged. "I know nothing."

"Don't you care what happened to Deborah Harrison?"

"Deborah Harrison. Deborah Harrison. Silly little English rich girl. Why I care? More girls killed in my homeland. Who cares about them? My father and mother die. My girlfriend is killed. But to you that means nothing. Nobody cares."

"'Any man's death diminishes me.' John Donne wrote that. Have you never heard it, Ive? Have you never heard of the concept that we're all in this together, all part of mankind?"

Jelačić just looked at Banks, incomprehension written on his features.

"Why don't you answer my questions?" Banks went on. "You saw the girl, you've admitted as much. You must have seen her quite often when you were working outside."

"I work inside and out. Clean church. Cut grass ..."

"Right. So you liked to watch the St Mary's girls—we know you did—and you must have noticed Deborah. She was very striking and she complained about your making lewd gestures towards her."

"I never—"

"Ive, spare me the bullshit, please. I've heard enough of it to last a lifetime. Nobody's going to arrest you or deport you for this. Bloody hell, they might even give you a medal if you tell us anything that leads to the killer."

Jelačić's eyes lit up. "Medal? You mean there is reward?"

"It was a joke, Ive," said Banks. "No, there isn't a reward. We just expect you to do your duty like any other decent, law-abiding citizen."

"I see nothing."

"Did you ever notice anyone hanging around the graveyard looking suspicious?"

"No."

"Did you ever see Deborah Harrison meet anyone in St Mary's churchyard?"

He shook his head.

"Did she ever linger around there, as if she was going to meet someone, or was up to something?"

Again, he shook his head, but not before Banks noticed something flicker behind his eyes, some memory, some sign of recognition.

"What is it?" Banks asked.

"What is what? Is nothing."

"You remembered something?"

But it was gone. "No," said Jelačić. "Like I say, I only see her when she walk home sometimes. She never stay, never meet anyone. That is all."

He was lying about something, Banks was certain. But he was equally certain Jelačić was too stubborn to part with whatever he had remembered right now. Banks would have to find more leverage. Sometimes he wished he had the freedom and power of certain other police forces in certain other countries—the freedom and power to torture and beat the truth out of Jelačić, for example—but only sometimes.

There was no point going on. Banks said goodbye and opened the door to leave. Before he had got ten feet away from the flat, he heard the sound on Jelačić's television shoot up loud again.

III

It was late that Wednesday evening when Owen finally got home. After he had picked up his belongings from the prison, he decided he didn't want to spend even one or two hours of such a beautiful day—his first moments of freedom in over six months—trapped in a car with Gordon Wharton. So he begged off, walked into town and just wandered aimlessly for a while, savouring his liberty. Late in the afternoon, he went into a pub on Boar Lane and had a pint of bitter and a roast beef sandwich, which almost made him gag after months of prison food. Then he walked over to the bus station, and by a circuitous route and a surprising number of changes, he managed to get himself back to Eastvale.

When Owen finally put his key in the lock, the door swung open by itself. He stood in the silence for a moment but could hear nothing. That seemed wrong. He knew there should have been a familiar sound, even if he couldn't, right now, remember what it was. His house had never been in such complete silence. No place ever is. And there was an odd smell. Dust he had expected, after so long away, perhaps mildew, too. He couldn't expect Ivor or Siobhan next door to do his cleaning for him. But this was something else. He stayed by the door listening for a while, then went into the living-room.

It looked like the aftermath of a jumble sale. Someone had pulled the books from the shelves, then ripped out pages and tossed them on the floor. Some of the torn pages had curled up, as if they had been wet and had dried out. Compact disc cases lay strewn, shattered and cracked, along with them. The discs themselves were mostly at the other side of the room, where marks on the wall showed that they had probably been flipped like Frisbees. The TV screen had been smashed. Scrawled on the wall beside the door, in giant, spidery red letters, were the words "JAILS TOO GOOD FOR FILTHY FUCKING PERVERTS LIKE YOU!"

Owen sagged against the wall and let his bag drop to the floor. Just for a moment, he longed for the stark simplicity of his prison cell again, the intractable order of prison life. This was too much. He didn't feel he could cope.

Taking a deep breath, he stepped over the debris and went into the study. His photos and negs lay ripped and snipped up all over the carpet. None of them looked salvageable, not even the inoffensive landscapes. His cameras lay beside them, lenses cracked in spider-web patterns. His art books had also been taken from their shelves and pages of reproductions ripped out by the handful: Gauguin, Cézanne, Renoir, Titian, Van Gogh, Vermeer, Monet, Caravaggio, Rubens, everything. That was bad enough—all or any of that was bad enough—but the thing he hadn't dared look at until last, the thing he had sensed as soon as he entered but hadn't quite grasped, was the worst of all.

The aquarium stood in darkness and silence, lights, pumps and filters switched off. The fish floated on the water's surface—danios, guppies, angelfish, jewelfish, zebrafish—their once-bright colours faded in death. It looked as if the intruder had simply switched off their life-support and left them to die. For Owen, this was the last straw. Misguided vindictiveness against himself he could understand, but such cruelty directed against the harmless, helpless fish was beyond his ken.

Owen leaned against the tank and sobbed until he couldn't get his breath, then he ran to the bathroom and rinsed his face in cold water. After that, he stood gripping the cool sides of the sink until he stopped shaking. In his bedroom, most of his clothes had been ripped or cut up with scissors and scattered over his bed.

In the kitchen, the contents of the fridge and cupboards had been dumped on the lino and smeared in the manner of a Jackson Pollock canvas. The resultant gooey mess of old marmalade, eggs, baked beans, instant coffee, sour milk, cheese slices, sugar, tea bags, butter, rice, treacle, corn flakes and a whole rack of herbs and spices looked like a special effect from a horror film and smelt worse than the yeast factory he had once worked in as a student. Right in the middle, on top of it all, sat what looked like a curled, dried turd.

He knew he should call the police, if only for insurance purposes, but the last people on earth he felt like dealing with right now were the bloody police.

And he couldn't face cleaning up.

Instead, he decided to give up on his first day of freedom. It was only about nine o'clock, just after dark, but Owen swept the torn and snipped-up clothes from his bed, burrowed under the sheets and pulled the covers over his head.

FOURTEEN

I

Like Canute holding back the tide, or the Greeks fighting off the Trojans, Banks could only postpone the inevitable, not avoid it altogether. In fact, the inevitable was waiting for him at eight o'clock on Thursday morning when he got to his office—coffee in hand, listening to Barber's setting of "Dover Beach" on his Walkman—in the strutting, fretting form of Chief Constable Jeremiah Riddle.

"Banks, take those bloody things out of your ears. And where the hell do you think you were yesterday?"

Banks told him about talking to Batorac and Jelačić while he was in Leeds, but omitted Pamela's chamber music concert and his quick visit to the Classical Record Shop.

Riddle's presence called for a cigarette, he thought. He was trying to cut out the early morning smokes, but under the circumstances, lighting up now might achieve the double purpose of both soothing his nerves and aggravating Riddle into a cardiac arrest. He lit up. Riddle coughed and waved his hand about, but he wasn't about to be distracted, or to die.

"What have you got to say about that fiasco in court yesterday?" the chief constable asked.

Banks shrugged. "There's nothing much *to* say, sir," he replied. "The jury found Pierce not guilty."

"I know that. Bloody idiots."

"That may well be, sir," said Banks, "but there's still nothing we can do about it. I thought we had a strong case. I'm certain the Crown will appeal. I'll be talking to Stafford Oakes about it when the fuss dies down."

"Hmph. We're going to look like real idiots over this one, Banks, as if we haven't got enough problems already." Riddle ran his hand over his red, shiny head. "Anyway, I want you to know that I've asked Detective Superintendent Gristhorpe to have a look over the case files. Maybe he can bring a fresh viewpoint. Either you get more evidence on Pierce or, if he really didn't do it, you damn well find out who did. I've decided I'm going to give you a week to redeem yourself on this before we hand it over to a team of independent investigators. I don't want to do that, I know how bad it looks, an admission of failure, but we've no bloody choice if we don't get results fast. I need hardly remind you of the impact a negative result might have on your future career, need I?"

"No, sir."

"And go easy on the Harrisons. They're bound to be upset by Pierce getting off, after everything they've been through. Tread softly. Understand?"

"I'll tread softly, sir."

Stupid pillock, Banks cursed after Riddle had left the office. A whole bloody week. And how, he wondered, could he do his job with one hand tied behind his back, and tied because of bloody privilege, class and wealth, not by compassion for a bereaved family? Again, he had the feeling he would soon be walking on very thin ice indeed if he were to get to the bottom of things.

He walked over to the window, pulled up the venetian blind and opened the sash a couple of inches. It was too early for tourists, but the market square was busy with Eastvalers starting their day, heels clicking on the cobbles as bank cashiers, dentists and estate agents went to work in the warren of offices around the town centre. The shops were opening and the smell of fresh-baked bread spilled in with sunlight.

Looking to his right, Banks could see south along Market Street, with its teashops, boutiques, and specialty shops, and out front was the square itself, with the NatWest bank, an estate agent, the El Toro coffee bar and Joplin's newsagent's at the opposite side. Over the shops were solicitors' offices, dentists' and doctors' surgeries.

With a sigh, Banks walked over to his filing cabinet, where he kept his own records of the salient points of the Harrison case.

The tons of paperwork and electromagnetic traces that a murder case generated couldn't possibly be stored in one detective's office, but most detectives had their own ways of summarizing and keeping track of the cases they worked on. Banks was no exception.

His filing cabinet contained his own notes on all the major cases he had been involved with since coming to Eastvale, plus a few he had brought with him from the Met. The notes might not mean much to anyone else, but with the use of his keen memory, Banks was able to fill in all the gaps his shorthand left out. His own notes also contained the hunches and accounts of off-the-record conversations that didn't make their way into the official files and statements.

It was time, he thought, to clear his mind of Owen Pierce for the moment and go back to basics. Two possibilities remained: either Deborah Harrison had been murdered by someone she knew, or a stranger other than Owen Pierce had killed her. Putting the second possibility aside, Banks picked up the names and strands of the first. Before the Pierce business, he had believed that Deborah might have arranged to meet someone on her way home from the chess club. He would spend the morning reading his notes and thinking, he decided, then after lunch he would go back to where it all started: St Mary's graveyard.

II

"Siobhan would bloody well kill me if she knew I was here with you now," Ivor said. "You don't understand what it's been like, mate. She's still convinced you did it."

They were standing at the bar of the Queen's Arms on Thursday lunch-time, after Owen had spent the entire morning cleaning up his house.

"That's ridiculous," said Owen. "I know she never really liked me, but I thought she had more sense than that. Is that why you didn't report the break-in?"

"I told you, it only happened the other day. You don't know what it's been like for us."

"Tell me."

Ivor sighed and took a swig from his pint. "You should have seen some of the things you got through your letter-box, for a start."

"What things?"

"Shit, hate-letters, used johnnies, death threats, something that looked like a lump of kidney or liver. I had to go in and clean it all up, didn't I?"

"I'm sorry. Did you report it to the police?"

"Of course I did. They sent a man round, but he didn't do anything. What can you expect?"

"The police thought I was guilty. They still do." Along with the rest of the world, he thought.

"Still," Ivor said, "you weren't living next door. You didn't have to put up with it all."

"Right. I was safely locked up in prison, all nice and comfortable in my little cell. Fucking luxury."

"You don't have to be so sarcastic, Owen. I'm just trying to explain what it was like on the outside, so you can understand people's attitudes."

"Like Siobhan's?"

"Yes."

"And yours?"

Ivor shrugged.

"What exactly is your attitude?" Owen asked.

"What's it matter? You're out now."

"Not just out, Ivor, but not guilty. Remember?"

"Well," he mumbled, "you know what people say."

"No, I don't. Tell me what people say."

"You know, guilty people get off all the time because the system's biased in their favour. We bend over backwards to help criminals and don't give a damn for their victims."

"I'm the victim here, Ivor." Owen thrust his thumb at his own chest. "Me. I even found a letter from the college waiting for me. That bastard Kemp has fired me, and he did it *before* the jury even went out."

Ivor looked away. "Yeah, well. I'm just saying what people think, in general, that's all."

"And what do *you* think, Ivor?"

"Look, I really don't want to get into this. All I'm saying, Owen, is that shit sticks."

"Meaning?"

"Oh, come on! For Christ's sake, you're supposed to be the English teacher. Meaning exactly what it says. All those rumours that went around during the trial, the stuff they couldn't bring in as evidence? Do you think nobody knew about it? Hell, I found out from one of the students in the local library."

Owen felt a shiver run up his spine. "Found out about what?"

"Everything. Your sex life, your photographic pursuits, your taste for dirty books and magazines, the porn video, how you screwed your students."

Owen toyed with a damp beer-mat. "You already knew that Michelle had been one of my students, I don't think even you would call *Lady Chatterly's Lover* a dirty book these days, and, don't forget, you watched part of one of those videos with me. I'm no worse than anyone else."

"Oh, grow up. You may not be, but the whole country doesn't know everything about anyone else, does it? You know how rumours get exaggerated. As far as they're concerned, you're the one who beats up women when they won't let you fuck them. You're the one who spends his days ogling innocent young school-girls and your nights dreaming about defiling and strangling virgins while you're watching video nasties."

Owen felt himself flush. "They're all bloody hypocrites."

"Maybe so, but that doesn't help you, does it?"

"And what does help me?"

"I don't know. I was thinking, maybe you should go away some-where ... ?"

"Run away? That's great advice. Thanks a lot, mate."

Owen ordered a couple more pints. At least the barmaid didn't seem to have recognized him. She actually *smiled* as she put down the drinks. A woman smiling, something he hadn't seen in ages, apart from Shirley Castle in her moment of victory. Either she didn't watch telly or read the papers, or prison had changed his appearance enough to fool some people. Not everyone, of course, but some people.

"Look," he went on, "get this into your thick skull. I haven't done anything. I never beat up anyone, and I certainly never raped and murdered anyone. I've been a victim of the system. They owe me something. It's doubtful they'll pay, but they owe me. In the meantime, I've lost a few months out of my life and my reputation's taken a bit of a bashing. I've got to put things in order again, and I'm damned if I'm going to start by running away. How do you think that'll look?"

Ivor paused and scratched his beard before answering. "It's not a bad idea, you know. It's not really like running away. New life somewhere else. Fresh start. You could even go live and teach English on the continent somewhere. France maybe. Your French is pretty good, as I remember. Or Japan."

Owen sniffed. "I can't believe what I'm hearing. You think that's the solution to my problems? Go live in obscurity in a foreign country? A sort of self-imposed exile. I'm telling you for the last time, Ivor, *I haven't done anything.*"

Ivor paused a little before saying, "You might find it more difficult than you think—putting things in order."

"What do you mean?"

"Nothing specific. I'm just pointing out that Siobhan's attitude isn't unique. There's probably a few others feel the same way. Locally, like. Feelings can get pretty strong."

"Are you telling me I'm in danger? A lynch mob or something?"

"All I'm saying is that when people get frightened they lash out."

"And what do you feel, Ivor? You never really answered my original question, you know. You're my neighbour. You're also supposed to be my friend. Do you think I'm a pervert?"

"What can I say? How do I know? I watched part of that video with you, like you said, didn't I? I don't think doing that turned me into a pervert. Mind you, I can't say it did a lot for me, but I watched it. More of a laugh than anything, if—"

"Fuck off, Ivor."

"What? Look—"

"Just fuck off and leave me alone."

Ivor banged his pint down on the bar; the barmaid glanced over anxiously. "All right, if that's the way you want it, mate. Just don't expect any more help from me."

Owen snorted. "Believe me, Ivor, you've earned my undying gratitude for what you've done for me already. Now just fuck off."

Ivor stormed out, red-faced above his beard, and the barmaid gave Owen an odd look, perhaps of recognition, of disapproval. Then the landlord, Cyril, he of the Popeye forearms, appeared from the back.

"What's all the noise about?" he said. He seemed to recognize Owen and started walking towards him.

"Well, you can fuck off, too!" Owen slammed his glass down on the bar so hard it broke and beer swilled over the counter.

"Here!" yelled Cyril, making for the hinged flap. But Owen shot out of the door and down the street, the base of his thumb stinging and bleeding from where a sliver of glass had pierced it.

He hurried along North Market Street, head down and hands thrust deep in his pockets, fists clenched. Ivor. That slimy, back-pedalling little turd. And Michelle? Just what was she trying to do to him?

But perhaps Ivor was right about moving. The thought wasn't quite as upsetting as it might have been a year or so earlier; somehow, the mess he had found on his release from prison had soured the house for him anyway. There were also, he realized, still too many memories of Michelle there. And moving would be a project, something to do, start looking for a new place, perhaps somewhere a little cheaper in a different part of the country. Not abroad, but in Devon, maybe, or Cornwall. He had always liked the south-west.

As he walked down the street, head bowed, Owen felt like an outsider, as if the rest of the world were swimming happily together in a huge tank and he was knocking on the glass unable to find a way in. One or two people gave him strange looks as he passed, and he realized he must have been mumbling to himself. Or maybe they recognized him. *Shit sticks*, Ivor had said. People would see him the way the rumours had depicted him, and would perhaps move aside and whisper to one another, "Here comes the Eastvale Strangler. You know, the one that got off."

When he finally looked up to see where he was, he saw he was in St Mary's. Despite all his resolutions, he had walked there, as if by instinct.

He stood at the church gate, uncertain what to do, then on an impulse he decided to go in. It was a beautiful day, and the few hawthorn trees scattered among the yews bore white, yellow or pink blossoms. Wildflowers pushed their way through the grass around some of the plots. Thriving on decomposing remains, Owen thought fancifully, before he noticed that most of the graves were from the eighteenth and nineteenth centuries. There were some recent ones, but not many.

The graveyard was peaceful; the muffled sounds of traffic on North Market Street and Kendal Road formed only a distant backdrop to the birdsongs.

Owen followed the tarmac path where it curved past the church and arrived at the Kendal Road exit. There, he walked up to the bridge and stared down at the swirling water, the colour of a pint of bitter, from the peat it picked up on its way through the dale. Ahead, facing south, he could see the formal gardens, the riverside willows and the castle high on its hill, dominating the town. It seemed so long ago he had stood here that foggy November night. No, he would not think about that again.

He took the river path home, and as he passed by the vicarage, he saw, over the garden gate, a woman hanging up washing on the line and stopped to watch her.

The plain white T-shirt she was wearing stretched taut against her heavy round breasts as she reached to peg up a sheet. Owen fancied he could see the dark nipples harden at the wind's caress.

Then she looked his way. He recognized her; he had seen her in court. She was the woman who had found the body, the one whose husband had been accused of molesting a church worker.

For a moment, she seemed about to smile and say hello, then she frowned, her jaw dropped, and she backed away inside the house, shutting the door behind her. Owen could hear the sound of a chain being fastened. She hadn't hung the sheet properly on the washing-line, and at the first light gust of wind it filled like a sail then broke free and fluttered onto the flower-bed like a shroud.

III

Banks saw the curtain in the bay window twitch just after he rang the vicarage bell, and a few moments later a nervous and jumpy looking Rebecca Charters answered the door. She looked relieved to see him and ushered him down the hall into the living-room.

It was a lot more cosy than on his previous visits, he noticed immediately, and it felt much more like a family home than a temporary encampment. The whole place had been redecorated: new wallpaper, cream with rose patterns; a new three-piece suite in a matching floral design; and three vases of flowers placed around the room. Ezekiel, the mound of brown-and-white fur, was in his usual place by the empty fireplace.

"How about some tea?" Rebecca asked. "Freshly brewed. Well, ten minutes ago."

"That'll be fine," said Banks. "No milk or sugar, thanks."

Rebecca went into the kitchen and returned seconds later with two mugs of tea. Today, she wore her hair tied back, fixed in place by a tooled-leather slide and a broad wooden pin. The style made her olive-complexioned face seem to bulge forward a little, emphasizing the slightly long nose, weak chin and curved brow, like a photograph through a fish-eye lens, but she still looked attractive, especially the dark eyes and full lips.

"I noticed you were in court for the verdict," Banks began.

Rebecca cradled her mug in her hands. "Yes," she said. "I can hardly believe it. He was here earlier. That was why I was a bit nervous when you rang."

"Owen Pierce was here? Why?"

"Not actually *here*, but he walked past on the river path. I was in the garden. I saw him."

"It's a free country, I suppose," Banks said. "And he's a free man."

"But isn't he dangerous? I mean, people still think he did it, even if he did get off."

"They're free to believe what they want. I don't think you have anything to worry about, though."

"Easy for you to say."

"Perhaps. Keep your doors and windows locked if it makes you feel better."

"I'm sorry," Rebecca said. "I don't mean to be sharp. I ..."

"It's all right," said Banks. "You're worried. You think there's a killer been set free and he's got his eyes on you. The quicker we find out whether he did it or not, the sooner you'll feel safe again."

"Do you think he did it?"

Banks scratched the little scar beside his right eye. "Right now, I don't know," he admitted. "There were times when I did, certainly, but the more I look at some of the things that struck me as odd before we latched onto Pierce, the more I start to wonder. The courts set innocent people free as well as guilty ones, sometimes, and if anyone knows the truth, he's a lucky man."

"What brought you back here?"

"I'm not really sure, except that this is where it all started."

"Yes," said Rebecca. "I remember." She gave a small shudder and fingered the neck of her dress. "And I'd like to apologize."

"For what?"

"For the last time we met. In the Queen's Arms. I seem to remember I was very rude to you. I seem to be making a habit of it."

"Don't worry," Banks said. "You get used to it in my job."

"But you shouldn't have to. I mean, I shouldn't have behaved the way I did." She put her mug down on the table. "I'm not that kind of person. Rude ... I ... Look, I don't know why I'm telling you this, except that your coming here again brings it all back."

"Brings what back? Finding the body?"

"That, yes, certainly. But it was a terrible time for me all round. The charges against Daniel, all the turmoil they caused." She took a deep breath. "You see, Chief Inspector, you didn't know the half of it. Of course you didn't, it wasn't relevant, not to your enquiries, but I lost a baby about three months before that business with Jelačić, and the doctor said it would be dangerous for me to try for another. Daniel and I hadn't talked about it as much as we should, and we had started drifting apart. We had just made some tentative inquiries about adoption when Jelačić brought the charges. Of course, everything fell through. It was worse than it was before. I'm afraid I withdrew. I blamed Daniel. There was even a time when I thought he was guilty. Since I lost the baby, we hadn't been ... well, you know ... and I thought he'd lost interest in me. It was easier to explain that by assuming he was really interested in men. What can I say? I started to drink too much. Then there was Patrick." She laughed nervously. "I don't know why I'm telling you all this. Except that you witnessed the final scene."

Banks smiled. "You'd be surprised the things people tell us, Mrs Charters. Anyway, I hope life has improved since then."

She beamed. "Yes. Yes, it has. Daniel and I are stronger than we've ever been. There are still ... well, a few problems ... but at least we're working together now."

"How's the Jelačić problem progressing?"

"It drags on. We've not heard anything for over a month now, but I believe he's got some human-rights lawyer working on it."

"And the drink?"

"Six months without."

"Patrick Metcalfe?"

"Not since that time you were here, when he caused all that fuss."

"Has he pestered you at all since then?"

She smiled. "No. I think he realized pretty quickly how carried away with himself he was getting. And I think your interest in him helped keep him at bay, too. I should thank you for that. You don't still suspect him, do you?"

"He's not off the hook yet," Banks said. "Anyway, that's not why I came. Actually, I was hoping for another look at the area where the body was found."

"Surely you don't have to ask my permission to do that?"

"No, but it's partly a matter of courtesy. And you know the area better than I do. Will you come with me?"

"Certainly."

To retrace Deborah's steps, they walked first along the riverside path from the vicarage towards the Kendal Road bridge, where worn stone steps led up to the pavement. It was another beautiful day, and over the road in St Mary's Park, lovers lay entwined, students sat reading in the shade of the trees, and children played with balls and Frisbees.

"This was where she would enter," said Rebecca, holding the wooden gate open for Banks. It was a lych-gate, with a small wooden roof, where the coffin would await the arrival of the clergyman in days gone by. "Seventeenth century," Rebecca said. "Isn't it superb?"

Banks agreed that it was.

"This is the main path we're on now," Rebecca explained.

It was about a yard and a half wide and had a pitted tarmac surface. Ahead, it curved around slightly in front of the church, separated from the doors only by a swath of grass, across which led a narrow flagstone path.

"It leads to North Market Street," Rebecca said, "near the zebra crossing where Deborah would cross to go home. And this path," she said, taking Banks by the elbow and diverting him to the right, where the entrance to the path was almost obscured by shrubbery, "is the path that leads to the Inchcliffe Mausoleum."

It was the gravel path Banks remembered from last November. After a couple of yards, the shrubbery gave way to yews and lichen-stained graves. Warm sunlight filtered through the greenery and flying insects buzzed around the dandelions and forget-me-nots.

Some of the graves were above-ground tombs with heavy lids and flowery religious epitaphs. By far the most impressive and baroque was the Inchcliffe Mausoleum, to the right.

"Now," said Banks, "we were assuming that Deborah reached the junction between the main path and this one when someone either grabbed her and dragged her up here or persuaded her to go with him of her own free will."

"But why couldn't she have come this way herself?" Rebecca asked.

"Why should she? It's out of her way."

"She had done before. I noticed her do it once or twice."

Banks raised his eyebrows. "You never mentioned this before."

Rebecca shrugged. "You never asked. And it didn't seem relevant."

"But didn't it strike you as odd?"

"No. I'm sorry. It wasn't something I was paying a lot of attention to. I suppose I assumed that she liked graveyards, as I do. And this is where the most interesting old tombs are, and the Inchcliffe Mausoleum, of course." She blushed. "Maybe she went to talk to the angel, like I did."

"When did she start using the path?"

"I've no idea. I don't remember *noticing* her go that way before last September, when school started up, but that doesn't mean she never did."

"Did you ever see anyone else with her? Or anyone going along the path before or after her?"

"No. You did ask me about that before, and I would have told you if I'd seen her meeting anyone. I would have noticed something like that. Do you think it's important that she took this path?"

Banks paused. "From the start," he explained, "I'd been working on the theory that if Owen Pierce or someone else hadn't followed Deborah into the graveyard, dragged her off the main path and killed her, then she might have been meeting the person who did. Now you're telling me you've seen her take this path before, I'm wondering if this is where she arranged the meeting. By the mausoleum. Her friend Megan Preece said Deborah had a morbid streak, that she liked spooky things. A rendezvous in the depths of a foggy graveyard beside an old mausoleum might have appealed to her."

"To meet someone she knew?"

"Yes. A lover, perhaps. Or someone else. We know that Deborah had a secret. It did cross my mind that she might have arranged to meet the person involved to discuss it, what to do about it."

"But what could she have possibly known that was so important?"

"If we knew that, then we'd probably know who the killer is."

"And do you still believe that she was meeting someone?"

"I think it's a strong possibility. She didn't tell Megan, but perhaps she wanted to be really secretive. Ive Jelačić told me he never saw her meeting anyone, but he's a pathological liar. On the other hand, you just told me yourself that you never saw anyone else around."

"It doesn't mean that there couldn't have been someone," Rebecca said. "The woods are quite deep here. And it was a foggy night. I just wish I could be of more help."

Banks stood and looked around. Rebecca was right. You could just about see the church through the trees to the south, but to the north, between the Inchcliffe Mausoleum and Kendal Road, it was a different matter. There, the yews were thicker, the undergrowth denser. It would be an ideal place for a secret meeting. And if he had learned anything from returning to the scene, it was that Deborah might have taken the gravel path of her accord, and that she had done so before.

He looked up at the Inchcliffe Mausoleum. It could have been the angle he was viewing it from, or perhaps a trick of the light, but he could have sworn the marble angel with the chipped wings was smiling.

FIFTEEN

I

"Let's assume Pierce didn't do it, just for the moment," said Banks. "That'll make things easier."

It was the first Friday in June, and the rays of late morning sunlight flooded the market square. Banks sat in Gristhorpe's office trying to get a fresh perspective on the Deborah Harrison murder.

Gristhorpe, a bulky man with a pock-marked face and bushy eyebrows, sat sideways at his large teak desk, one leg stretched out and propped up on a footstool. He insisted that the broken leg had healed perfectly, but he still got the odd twinge now and then. Given that it was same leg he had also been shot in not so long ago, that wasn't surprising, Banks thought.

Banks took a sip of coffee. "On the generous side, I'd say we've got maybe five or six suspects. If Deborah didn't have a lover we don't know about—and I don't think she did—then the key to it all might lie in the secret she had. And if Deborah knew something about someone, she might easily have misjudged the importance of what she knew, underestimated the desperation of that person. Adults can have some pretty nasty secrets. The Pierce trial redirected all our time and energy towards proving that the killer *didn't* know her, that she was a random victim, or became a victim because she had the misfortune of resembling Pierce's ex-girlfriend Michelle Chappel."

"What's happening with that now?"

"I talked to Stafford Oakes about an hour ago," Banks said, "and he's ninety-nine per cent certain the Crown will appeal the verdict on the basis of the similar fact evidence being declared inadmissible. If they get a judge who allows it in, another trial could be disastrous for Pierce, whether he did it or not."

Gristhorpe scratched his chin. "As you know, Alan," he said, "I've been able to keep an open mind on this because I wasn't part of the original investigation. I'd just like to say in the first place that I think you did good detective work. You shouldn't flagellate yourself over the result. It may still turn out that Pierce didn't do it. But I agree we should put that aside for a moment. From what I've read so far, Barry Stott seemed particularly sold on Pierce. Any idea why?"

"It was *his* lead," Banks said. "Or so he thought. Actually, if it hadn't been for Jim Hatchley stopping for a pint in the Nag's Head, he might never have turned it up. But Barry's ambitious. And tenacious. And let's not forget, Jimmy Riddle was dead set on Pierce, too."

"He's a friend of the family," Gristhorpe said. "I should imagine he just wanted an early conclusion, no matter who went down for it."

Banks nodded.

"Now," Gristhorpe went on, "the two things we have to ask ourselves are what possible secret Deborah Harrison could have learned that was important enough to kill for, and who, given the opportunity, could have killed her because of it."

Banks told him about his visit to Rebecca Charters and what he had learned about Deborah's occasional detours from the main path.

"You think she had arranged to meet her killer?" Gristhorpe asked.

"Rebecca never actually saw her meet anyone, but it's one possibility."

"Blackmail?"

"Perhaps. Though I'm not sure from what I know of Deborah that she was the type to do that. I suppose it is possible. After all, her satchel was open when we found her, and that has always bothered me. Perhaps she had some sort of hard evidence and the killer took it. On the other hand, maybe she just wanted to let whoever it was know that she knew the secret, or how she had found out. Perhaps she just wanted to flaunt her knowledge a little. Her friends say she could be a bit of a show-off. Anyway, let's say she didn't know the power or the value of what she was playing with."

"Which takes us to my questions: why and who?"

"Yes." Banks counted them on his fingers, one by one. "For a start, there's John Spinks. He was Deborah's boyfriend for part of the summer, and he's a nasty piece of work. They parted on very bad terms and I think he's the type to bear a grudge. He also has an alibi that doesn't hold much water. Ive Jelačić has a solid alibi, I'd say, in Vjeko Batorac, but I'm still certain he's involved, he knows something."

"Any idea what?"

"I'd guess he might have seen Deborah meeting someone."

"Why not tell us who, then?"

"That's not Jelačić's style. If you ask me, I'd say he's trying to work out what might be in it for him first. For crying out loud, he even asked me if there was a reward."

"What do we do, beat it out of him?"

"Believe me, that thought's crossed my mind. But no. We'll get him one way or another, don't worry about that. I'm not finished with Mr Jelačić yet."

"Who else have we got? What about that schoolteacher?"

"Patrick Metcalfe? Another possibility. Though I doubt very much that he's got the bottle, we have to consider him. He was Deborah's history teacher and he was having an affair with Rebecca Charters, the vicar's wife. One might reasonably assume that's a poor career move for a male teacher at an Anglican girls' school. If Deborah knew about the affair—and she could easily have seen Metcalfe entering or leaving the vicarage on occasion—then it could have cost Metcalfe not only his job, but his entire teaching career."

"And as I recall from the statement," Gristhorpe said, "he says he stayed home alone in his flat after Daniel Charters left."

Banks nodded. "And we've no way of confirming or denying that unless someone saw him, which no-one has admitted to so far."

"What about the vicar?"

"I've been wondering about him, too," Banks said. "In general I've been pretty sympathetic towards him, but looking at things objectively, he could be our man. He certainly has no alibi, and he's both tall and strong enough."

"Motive?"

"We know that Ive Jelačić accused him of abusing his position by making homosexual advances. Given Jelačić's character, this is probably pure fabrication—Vjeko Batorac certainly thinks it is—but let's say it's true, or it approximates the truth. And let's say Deborah saw something that could confirm it, either involving Charters and Jelačić or Charters and someone else. If it got out, he also stood to lose everything. That might give him a powerful enough motive."

"Or his wife?" Gristhorpe suggested.

"Yes. It *could* have been a woman," Banks agreed. "After all, there was no evidence of rape, and the body could have been arranged to make it look like a sex murder. Rebecca Charters is probably tall and strong enough."

"And she could have had either of two motives," Gristhorpe added. "To protect the knowledge of her affair with Metcalfe, or to protect her husband from certain dismissal." He shook his head. "It's a real *Peyton Place* we've unearthed here, Alan. Who'd think such goings on occurred in a nice little Yorkshire town like Eastvale?"

Banks smiled. "'It is my belief, Watson, founded upon my experience, that the lowest and vilest alleys in London do not present a more dreadful record of sin than does the smiling and beautiful countryside.'"

Gristhorpe smiled back. "And what about Jimmy Riddle's mates?" he said.

"Certainly not out of the question. I was beginning to think that Michael Clayton might have been having an affair with Sylvie Harrison, unlikely as it sounds. Sir Geoffrey and Michael Clayton have been close friends since university. If Clayton *were* having an affair with his wife, and if Deborah knew about that, it could have had a devastating effect. Think of how much money and prestige were at stake there."

"As I understand it, none of them have alibis either."

"That's right. And they all knew Deborah went to the chess club on a Monday, and what time she usually came home. And by what route. But even if we accept the horrible possibility that she was *capable* of such a crime, Sylvie Harrison is neither tall nor strong enough to have killed her daughter. Rebecca Charters is the only woman in this case who could remotely have done it."

"Clayton, then?"

"Possible. Certainly he's the more likely of the two. Though, again, he was the child's *godfather*."

"Let's also not forget," Gristhorpe added, "that HarClay Industries had a lot of MoD contracts. They do a lot of hush-hush work. If Deborah found out about any hanky-panky going on there, contracts with foreign governments and the like ..."

"Or even something our own government didn't want the general public to know?"

"I wouldn't put it past them," Gristhorpe agreed. "According to your notes, at the time of his daughter's murder, Sir Geoffrey Harrison was in a private meeting with a man from the government called Oliver Jackson. I happen to know Oliver Jackson, and he's not exactly from the government, he's Special Branch."

"Aren't we getting a bit far-fetched here?" Banks said. "Maybe it's just someone else with the same name?"

Gristhorpe shook his head. "I checked with the York CID. It was the same Oliver Jackson all right. They knew he was in town, but they weren't told why. It's just another aspect to consider. Any other angles?"

Banks sighed. "Not that I can think of," he said. "Unless Deborah stumbled on something illegal going on in the school— something to do with sex or drugs, perhaps—but we couldn't dig anything up there."

"It's still plenty to be going on with for the moment."

Banks stood up and walked to the door, already reaching in his pocket for his Silk Cuts.

"By the way," Gristhorpe asked, "how is DI Stott doing?"

Banks paused at door. "He's been walking around looking like death warmed up ever since Pierce got off. I'm getting a bit worried about him."

"Maybe he'll be better after a weekend's rest?"

"Maybe."

As he walked back to his own office, Banks heard raised voices down the corridor and went to see what was happening. There, at the bottom of the staircase, stood John Spinks and DC Susan Gay.

II

"The problem is not with your teaching ability, Owen. You have demonstrated that to us quite clearly over the years."

"Then I don't understand," Owen said. "Why can't I have my job back?" He was sitting in the chairman's book-lined office. Peter Kemp, with his rolled-up shirtsleeves, his freckles and ginger hair like tufts on a coconut, sat behind the untidy desk. "Kemp the Unkempt," the staff members had nicknamed him. To one side, a computer hummed, white cursor blinking in anticipation on an empty blue screen.

Kemp leaned back in his chair and linked his hands behind his head. Owen could see a dark patch of sweat under each arm. "Technically, Owen," Kemp said, "you can't demand back a job you never had. Remember, you were employed purely on a term-to-term basis, no guarantees. We simply can't use you next term."

As he spoke, Kemp looked at Owen down his nose, under the tortoiseshell rims of his glasses, as an entomologist might regard an especially interesting but ugly new bug. The office smelled of Polo mints and fresh paint. Owen longed to let in some air, but he knew from experience that none of the windows opened.

"I was depending on you," Owen said. "You've always renewed my contract before."

Kemp sat forward and rested his hairy forearms on the desk. "Ah, yes. But this time you left us in a bit of a mess, didn't you? We had to bring in someone to finish your classes. She did a good job, a very good job, under the circumstances. We can't very well chuck her out without so much as a by-your-leave, can we?"

"I don't see why not. You seem to be doing it to me, and at least I've got seniority. Besides, it was hardly my fault I got arrested."

Kemp sniggered. "Well, it *certainly* wasn't mine. But that's irrelevant. There's no such thing as seniority in temporary appointments, Owen. You know that. I'm sorry, but my hands are tied." And he held them together, linking his fingers as if to demonstrate.

"What about next January? I can just about get by until then."

Kemp pursed his lips and shook his head. "I can't see any vacancies opening up. Budgets are tight these days. Very tight."

"Look," Owen said, sitting forward. "I'm getting fed up with this. Ever since I've been in your office—and I had to wait long enough before I got to see you, by the way—I've heard nothing but flannel. You know damn well that you could find courses for me if you wanted to, but you won't. If it's nothing to do with my teaching abilities, then maybe you'd better tell me what really is the problem." Owen had a good idea what he would hear—he had read the letter, after all—but he wanted to put Kemp through the embarrassment of having to say it.

"I've told you—"

"You've told me bugger-all. Is it the trial? Is that it?"

"Well, you could hardly imagine something like that would endear you to the board, could you? But we all understand that you were mistakenly accused, and we deeply regret any hardship you suffered."

Owen laughed. "Mistakenly accused? I like that. That's a nice way of putting it."

Kemp pursed his lips. "Owen, we know how you suffered, believe me."

"Do you?" Owen felt himself redden with anger. He gripped the sides of the chair. "Do you also believe in my innocence?"

"One must put faith in the justice system, Owen, abide by the verdict of the jury."

"So you *do* believe they were right?"

"The court found you not guilty."

"That's not the same thing."

"But what else are we to base our judgements on?"

"What else? On your knowledge of the person, on character. On *trust*, damn it. After all, I've worked here for eight years."

Kemp shrugged. "But I can hardly say I *know* you, can I? Ours has always been a professional relationship, a work relationship, if you like."

"And my work has always been of the highest quality. So what about my job, then? If you believe I've done nothing wrong and you have faith in my teaching ability, why don't I get my job back?"

"You're making this very difficult for me, Owen."

Owen thumped the desk. "Oh, am I? I'm really sorry about that. Maybe it just hasn't occurred to you how fucking difficult this is for me."

Kemp backed away slowly on his wheeled office-chair. "Owen, you're not helping yourself at all by behaving in this manner."

"Don't give me that. You've already made it clear what my position is. I want you to admit why. And please don't tell me how bloody difficult it is for you."

Kemp stopped edging back and leaned forward on the desk, making a steeple of his fingers. "All right," he said. "If that's the way you want it. The college has expressed its unwillingness to employ an instructor who has a reputation for bedding his female students and photographing them in the nude. It's bad for our image. It'll make parents keep their daughters away. And seeing as we depend on the students for our livelihood, and a good percentage of them are females of an impressionable age, it was felt that your presence would be detrimental to our survival. And besides that, the college also takes a dim view of its lecturers giving marks for sexual favours rather than for academic excellence." He took a deep breath. "There, Owen, does that suit you better?"

Owen grinned at him. "It'll do. It certainly beats the bullshit you were giving out earlier. But none of what you say has been proven. It's all hearsay."

Kemp looked at the blinking cursor. "You know how rumours spread, what damage they can do. And people here were aware of your ... er ... relationship with Ms Chappel. Even at the time."

"You did nothing then. Why now?"

"Circumstances have changed."

"So I lost my job because circumstances have changed?"

"No smoke without fire."

"You smug bastard."

"Goodbye, Owen." Kemp stood up. He didn't hold out his hand.

Michelle, again. Owen felt like picking up the computer monitor and hurling it through the window, then punching Kemp on the nose. But he restrained himself. His teaching career was over here, perhaps everywhere. People would know about him wherever he applied. The academic community is small enough; word gets around quickly.

Instead of hitting Kemp, Owen contented himself with slamming the door. Striding down the corridor, he almost bumped into Chris Lorimer.

"Owen." Chris had a pile of essays under his arm and seemed to be struggling to hold onto them. "I ... it's ..."

"Kemp won't take me back."

"Hmm ... well. I suppose you can understand his position." Lorimer shifted from one foot to the other as if he desperately wanted to go to the toilet.

"Can you? Look, Chris, it's noon, the sun's over the yard-arm, as they used to say, and I'm a bit cheesed off. It's been a bad day, so far. How about a pint and a spot of lunch over the road? My treat."

Lorimer contorted to glance at his watch. "I'd like to, Owen, I really would, but I have to dash." And he really was dashing as he spoke, edging away down the corridor as if Owen had some infectious disease. "Maybe some other time, perhaps?" he called over his shoulder, before disappearing round a corner.

Sure, Owen thought, some other time. Fuck you, too, Chris Lorimer. You and the horse you rode in on.

III

"Well, well, well," said Banks, standing at the top of the stairs overlooking the open-plan ground floor. "Speak of the devil. Just the fellow I've been wanting to see. I've been looking over your file. And guess who's turned eighteen since we last met?"

Spinks looked at him. "Uh?"

"No more youth court." Banks glanced towards Susan and raised an eyebrow.

"Taking and driving away, sir," she said. "Under the influence."

"Influence of what, I wonder?" said Banks. "And so early in the day."

Spinks struggled, but Susan managed to hold onto him. "Not to mention crashing it through the window of Henry's fish and chip shop on Elmet Street," she said through gritted teeth.

Banks smiled and opened the door of the nearest interview room. "Be my guest," he said to Spinks, stretching an arm out through the open door. "Take a pew."

"I need a doctor," Spinks moaned. "The fucking steering was fucked. I hurt my head. I got whiplash. I could've been killed."

"Shut up and sit down," Banks said with enough authority that Spinks paused and obeyed. "I suppose you'll be suing the owner next?"

Spinks licked his lips. "Maybe I will."

There was a small cut just above his right eye. It was nothing serious, but Banks knew that if they didn't get him medical attention they'd be breaking a PACE directive and Spinks would probably succeed in getting his case dismissed.

"See if you can get Dr Burns, will you, Susan?" Banks asked, indicating by a private gesture that she should take her time.

Susan nodded, straightened her dress and left.

"What are you on?" Banks asked.

Spinks looked away. "I don't know what you mean."

Banks grabbed Spinks's chin with one hand and held his head up, staring at the pinpoint pupils. "Crack, is it, John? Or solvent? Maybe heroin?"

"I don't do drugs."

"Like hell you don't. You know taking and driving away is an arrestable offence, don't you, John?"

Spinks said nothing.

"Do you know what that means?"

Spinks gave a lopsided grin. A little drool had formed at the side of his mouth. "It means you can arrest me for it." He giggled.

"Good," said Banks, patting his shoulder gently. "Very good, John. Now, you might not know this, but to put it nice and simply that also means we can detain you for up to twenty-four hours, longer if the superintendent authorizes it. Which he will. But wait a minute. Do you know what day it is, John?"

"What do you mean? Course I know. It's Friday."

"That's right." Banks looked at his watch. "Pity for you, John. See, a day like this, the magistrates will all be on the golf course by now. And they don't sit on Saturday or Sunday, so you'll have to stay with us until Monday morning."

"So what?"

"Your arrest also gives us powers of search, John. We don't need a warrant. That means there'll be coppers all over your mum's place, if there aren't already. Bound to turn up something. Your mum will love you for that, won't she?"

"She doesn't give a fuck."

Banks turned the free chair around and sat with his arms resting on the back. "Anyway," he said, "I'm not interested in petty stuff like car theft and drug abuse. You don't think a detective chief inspector concerns himself with run-of-the-mill stuff like that, do you?"

Spinks sniffed. "Can't say I care one way or another."

"No. Course not. I don't suppose you do. Well, I'm not doing this by the book, John. I want you to know that. Like I said, I'm not really interested in some gormless pill-popping pillock who steals a car and can't even drive it straight."

Spinks bristled. "I can fucking drive! I told you, the steering was fucked. Fucking owner ought to be locked up."

"Know what they say about a poor workman, John? He always blames his tools."

"Fuck off."

"Look, I'm getting sick and tired of your severely limited vocabulary. Know what I think we ought to do with people like you instead of community service or jail? I think we ought to have compulsory education for gobshites like you who spent so much time blitzed on model airplane glue that they never set foot in school more than a couple of weeks a year. Know what I'd do? I'd make you read the dictionary, for a start. At least ten new words a day. And spelling tests. Every morning, first thing after slopping out. A dozen lashes for every word you get wrong. Literature, too. Lots of it. Austen, Hardy, Dickens, Trollope, George Eliot. Long books. Poetry, as well—Wordsworth, Shelley, Dryden, Milton. And Shakespeare, John. Tons and tons of Shakespeare. Memorizing poems and long, lovely speeches. Analyzing the imagery in *Macbeth* and *Othello*. Sound like fun?"

"I'd rather be in fucking jail."

Banks sighed. "You will be, John. You will be. It's just a fantasy of mine. Now I'd like you to travel back in time through that addled, worm-eaten brain of yours. I'd like you, if you can negotiate through that lump of Swiss cheese you call a mind, to go back to last summer. Specifically, to last August. Can you do that?"

Spinks frowned. "Is this about that bird what got snuffed?"

"Yes," said Banks. "This, as you so eloquently put it, is 'about that bird what got snuffed.' Remember her name, John? Deborah Harrison."

"That's right. Yeah, Debbie."

"Good. Now something happened, didn't it? Something nasty?"

"Don't know what you mean."

"Her mother and her godfather warned you off, didn't they?"

"Oh, right. Stuck-up motherfuckers. Look, what's this got to do with—"

"I told you, John. I'm not doing this by the book. This is unofficial, off the record. Okay?"

Spinks nodded, a look of suspicion forming in his glazed eyes.

"One day you went around to ask Lady Sylvie Harrison to give you money to leave her daughter alone. Right?"

"So? There's no law against it. They'd got plenty. I didn't see why I shouldn't get some compensation. Bird wasn't much of a fuck, really. More like a sack of potatoes. But—"

Banks gripped the back of the chair so hard his knuckles turned white. "Spare me your erotic memoirs, John," he said. "They might make me do something I'll regret. You might not realize it, but I'm exercising great restraint as it is."

Spinks laughed. A little more drool dripped down his chin. Banks felt so much like clocking him one that he had to look away. "Who was in the house that day?"

"What?"

"You heard. Who else was there as well as you?"

"Oh. Didn't I already tell you that? I seem to remember—"

"Humour me. Tell me again."

"Right. There was Debbie's mother, the blonde bitch. And that stuck-up prick Clayton. Fucking snobs."

"And Deborah wasn't there?"

"I already told you. No." Spinks's head started to roll from side to side. The drugs, whatever they were, wearing off. Either that or he had sustained more than superficial damage in the car crash. Just as well they had sent for Dr Burns.

"When you went to the house and found Michael Clayton there," Banks asked, "did you get the feeling that there was anything going on?"

Spinks closed his eyes. His head stopped lolling. "Don't know what you mean."

"Did you interrupt anything?"

"Interrupt?"

"Stop behaving like a parrot. Did you get the feeling there was anything going on between them?"

Spinks frowned and wiped the drool from his mouth with the back of his hand. His eyes opened again and seemed to keep shifting in and out of focus. "Going on?" he repeated. "You mean was he fucking her? You mean do I think Clayton was fucking the wicked witch?" He laughed out loud.

Banks waited patiently until he had stopped. "Well," he said. "Do you?"

"You've got a dirty mind. Do you know that?"

"Do you?"

Spinks shrugged. "Could've been, for all I know."

"But you didn't notice anything special about them, the way they behaved towards one another?"

"No."

"Were they both fully dressed?"

"Course they were."

"Did they look dishevelled at all?"

"Come again. Dish what?"

"See what I mean about the need for compulsory education? It means messed up, ruffled, untidy."

"Oh. No. I don't think so. Can't really remember, though."

"Did Deborah ever say anything about them?"

He shook his head, stopped abruptly and opened his mouth as if to say something, then carried on shaking it. "No."

Banks leaned forward on the chair back. The two front legs raised off the floor. "What were you going to tell me, John?"

"Nothing. She never said nothing." He coughed and a mouthful of yellow vomit dribbled down his chin onto his T-shirt. The smell was terrible: booze, cheese-and-onion crisps and tacos. Banks stood up and stepped back.

At that moment, there was a knock on the door and Susan Gay came in, followed by Dr Burns, the police surgeon, whose surgery was just across the market square.

"Sorry, sir," Susan said, "but the doctor's here."

"Right," said Banks, shaking hands with Burns. "He's all yours. I've had enough. Take good care of him, Nick. I might want to talk to him again."

And as he walked back to his own office, he had the strange feeling that not only had Spinks been holding back, hiding something, but that he, himself, hadn't even been asking the right questions. Something was eluding him, and he knew from experience that it would drive him around the bend until he thought of it.

SIXTEEN

I

Banks took a deep breath outside Michael Clayton's house on Saturday morning, then he got out of his car and walked up the garden path. If Chief Constable Riddle found out about this, Banks's life probably wouldn't be worth living.

Clayton's house wasn't quite as large as the Harrisons', but it was an impressive enough construction, solidly built of redbrick and sandstone, detached and surrounded by an unkempt garden. The lawn looked as if it hadn't been trimmed yet this year, and weeds choked the flower-beds.

After he rang the doorbell the first time, Banks heard nothing but silence and began to suspect that Clayton was out. He tried again. About thirty seconds later, just as he was about to head off down the path, the door opened and Clayton stuck his head out.

"Yes, what is it?" he asked crossly. "Oh, it's you, Chief Inspector." He moved aside and opened the door fully. "You'd better come in. Sorry about the mess."

Banks followed him through a door from the hallway into a room full of computer equipment. At least three computers, state-of-the-art, by the look of them, sat on their desks, two of them displaying similar graphic images. These were incomprehensible to Banks, and looked like a cross between circuit diagrams and the molecular structures he remembered from school chemistry. They were all multi-coloured, and some of the nodes and pathways between them flashed, different on each screen. The third VDU showed a deck of cards set out in what Banks recognized as the solitaire "pyramid" fashion.

"I always have a game going when I'm working," Clayton said, smiling. "It helps me concentrate. Don't ask me why."

The floor was a mass of snaking cables and Banks trod carefully not to trip over any of them.

He could almost feel the room vibrating with the electrical hum running through them.

Clayton cleared a stack of computer magazines from a hard-backed chair. Banks almost asked him what the diagrams on the screens were, but he knew that either Clayton wouldn't tell him or he wouldn't understand anyway. Best not start off looking like an ignoramus.

Sheets of paper hissed as they slid out of a laser printer. One of the computers started to emit a loud, pulsating beep. Clayton excused himself while he went over and hit a few keys.

"Diagnostic programmes," he said when he got back.

Well, that was clear enough, Banks thought. Even he knew what diagnostic programmes were. Though what they were supposed to diagnose was another matter entirely.

"Computers," Clayton went on. "They've changed the world, Chief Inspector. Nothing is the same as when you and I were children. And they're still changing it. Believe me, in the not-too-distant future, nothing will be the same as it is now. But I don't suppose you came here to talk technology with me, did you? Are you coming to apologize?"

"What for?"

"For letting the bastard who killed Deborah slip through the cracks. I was there, you know, in court with Geoff and Sylvie. They're devastated. And I've hardly been able to concentrate on my work since then. How could you let it happen?"

Banks shrugged. "I've seen it happen more often than you have. We're not living in a perfect world."

"You can say that again. I don't know what the procedure is now, but if I can help in any way ..." Clayton scratched his smooth chin. "Look, I've heard one or two disturbing rumours about this Pierce fellow beating up young girls and raping them. Is that true?"

"I can't comment on that," said Banks.

"But there *is* some evidence that wasn't admissible, isn't there? Something that might have got him convicted if it had been heard in the trial?"

"The judge rules on matters of law," Banks said. "So there might be a strong basis for the appeal. That's really all I can tell you at the moment."

Clayton paused and glanced quickly around at the computer screens. "Well, Chief Inspector, thank you for bringing me up to date. Can I help in any way?"

Banks leaned forward. "As a matter of fact, there is something. One of the results of the court's decision is that we have decided to reopen the case and examine some of the other angles again."

Clayton frowned. "I don't understand. Did you get the right man or didn't you?"

"The jury thinks we didn't."

"But what about *you*. You know more about him than you're ever allowed to tell the jury. What do *you* think?"

Banks was getting sick of that question. Now he knew what defence barristers felt when people kept asking them how they could possibly defend people they knew must be guilty. "I didn't see him do it," he said, "so there's always room for doubt."

Clayton snorted. "So just because the justice system fouls up yet again, you're going to run around reopening old wounds."

"I hoped you might look at it as co-operation," Banks said.

"About what?"

"John Spinks, for a start."

"That moron who caused all the trouble last summer?"

"That's the one."

"Sylvie told you about him?"

"Yes. And I talked to him again yesterday."

"You surely don't think *he* could have done it?"

"It's possible," Banks said.

"He doesn't have either the guts or the brains."

"Since when did it take brains to murder someone? Outside a detective novel, that is."

"It takes brains to do it and get away with it."

"Brains or luck."

Clayton shrugged. "No point in arguing. Look at it that way and anything's possible. He was certainly angry at her about what happened. I imagine anger is a familiar enough part of his limited emotional range. I suppose he could have lain in wait for her and lost his temper."

"Did he know she attended the chess club?"

"How should I know?"

"Somehow, I doubt it," said Banks. "Not if he hadn't been seeing her *after* term started. Anyway, that's beside the point. As you say, he would know the route she took and he could have simply lain in wait in the foggy graveyard ever since school came out. Now, as I understand it, Spinks came to Sir Geoffrey's house to extort money from Lady Sylvie Harrison, is that right?"

"Yes."

"And you hit him."

"No more than a little cuff. You're not going to arrest me for assault and battery are you?"

Banks smiled. "No. Believe me, sir, I've felt like doing the same thing myself on more than one occasion."

"Then you understand my feelings about him."

"Entirely. You hit him, and later you paid him off?"

"Yes. It seemed the easiest way."

"How much did you give him?"

"A hundred pounds."

"That was all?"

"Yes."

"He didn't come back for more?"

"No."

"Why?"

Clayton leaned forward and rested his hands on his knees. "Because I told him that if he did, I would certainly inform Sir Geoffrey, who would at the very least have him horsewhipped, no matter what vile threats he made." Clayton frowned and sat back. "You say you talked to Spinks again? Why? Was this in connection with reopening the case?"

"Not really. No, it was coincidence. He stole a car and crashed it."

"Pity he didn't break his neck. Serves the little bastard right."

"I suppose so," Banks said. He paused, feeling his heartbeat speed up. "What were you doing here when Spinks came?"

"What do you mean?"

"I got the impression that you're here an awful lot. Especially when Sir Geoffrey is out and his wife is at home."

Clayton's mouth dropped open and he started shaking his head very slowly. "My God, you've got a mind like a sewer," he said. "I don't believe it. On the basis of that you're suggesting ..." He put his fingertips to his temple. "Let me get this clear ... Your theory is that Sylvie and I were having a torrid affair and Deborah found out and threatened to tell her father. Instead of allowing that to happen, I waited for Deborah, my own goddaughter, in the graveyard after her school chess club one day and strangled her. Is that your theory?"

"I hadn't thought it out that far," Banks said. "I was just trying to get the lie of the land, that's all. But I must admit you've got a way of reducing things to their essentials. Thank you for putting it so succinctly."

Clayton stood up. His face was red. "This is insane, Banks. You're clutching at straws. I think you'd better leave now."

"I was just on my way. But I do have one more question."

Clayton gritted his teeth. "Very well."

"About the kind of work HarClay Industries does. Some of it is highly secret, isn't it, MoD stuff?"

"Yes. So?"

"Is there any chance that Deborah might have stumbled across something she shouldn't have, say in her father's papers?"

Clayton shook his head. "First you practically accuse me of murder, then you bring up all this James Bond stuff. No, Chief Inspector, Deborah *couldn't* have stumbled across any government secrets that got her killed. I think you already had the killer and you let him get off. Now you're casting about wildly for some sort of scapegoat."

Banks stood up to leave. "Maybe," he admitted.

"And for your information," Clayton went on, "I've known Geoff and Sylvie for years. I was there when they met. I was at university with Geoff. I have never had, nor am I having now, any other sort

of relationship with Sylvie Harrison than that of a close friend. Am
I making myself clear?"

Banks turned and met his gaze. "Perfectly."

"And just for this one time I'm willing to forget that this meeting
ever took place. But if you ever dare come here again with your—"

Banks held his hand up. "I get the message, sir. If I ask any more
questions, you'll go tell the chief constable. Fair enough."

When Banks got outside and back into his car, his hands were
shaking as he lit his first cigarette of the day.

II

Rebecca Charters hadn't known what to do at first when Owen
Pierce surprised her in the garden on Thursday. She had been
scared, as she told Chief Inspector Banks, and her instinct had been
to run inside, bolt the door and put the chain on. He hadn't tried
anything after that, even though he must have known she was
alone in the house, but she had looked through the window and
watched him stand by the garden gate for a moment before walking
off. Her heart had beat fast.

After Banks had left, she rationalized her fear away. Pierce
hadn't *done* anything, after all, or even said or threatened anything.
Perhaps she was overreacting. Pierce might not be guilty of
anything. Certainly Inspector Banks had his doubts, and his idea
of Deborah having *arranged* to meet the person who ultimately
turned out to be her murderer made sense.

But when Owen Pierce came and knocked at her door on
Saturday afternoon, while Daniel was out visiting the terminally
ill patients in Eastvale General Infirmary, she felt afraid all over
again.

Because it was a warm day and she liked the way the scents of
the flowers drifted into the living-room, Rebecca had opened the
bay window. Before moving to shut it and lock it, she shouted, "Go
away or I'll call the police."

"Please," he said. "Please listen to me. I'm not going to hurt you.
I've never hurt anyone. I just want to talk to you."

She left the window open but put her hands on top of the frame, ready to slam it down if he made any suspicious moves. "What about?" she asked.

"Just talk, that's all. Please. I need someone to talk to."

There was something in his tone that touched Rebecca, but not enough to open the door to him.

"Why me?" she asked. "You don't even know me."

"But I know *about* you. I know what you've been through. You're the vicar's wife. I've read about the accusations and everything. I just felt ... I'm not trying to say I'm especially religious or anything. I don't want to lie to you about that. Please, will you just let me come in and talk? Will someone just treat me like a human being. Please."

Rebecca could see tears in his eyes. She still didn't know why he had come. She couldn't let him in, but nor did she feel she could turn him away. After all, she was a Christian, *and* a minister's wife.

"Stay there," she said. "I'll come out." She would feel safe outside in the garden, with the constant flow of people on the river path.

Why was she doing it? she asked herself as she went outside. She knew part of the answer. Not too long ago, she had allowed herself to doubt Daniel, her own husband. Instead of offering him her unqualified support and devotion, she had turned to liquor and carnality to escape her obligations. More than that. It wasn't just her obligations she was running away from, but the horrible realization that she *had* doubted Daniel, she *had* believed him guilty. And now, here was this pathetic man, found not guilty by a jury and presumed guilty by the rest of the world. Call it pity, compassion, Christian charity or mere folly, but she *couldn't* turn him away.

Daniel had put out a couple of folding chairs in the garden. When the weather was nice, he liked to sit and watch the river as he composed his sermon. There was also a beautiful view of St Mary's Hill, the fine old houses above the gentle slope of grass and trees. Here I am, Rebecca thought, sitting in the garden with a possible murderer on a warm June afternoon.

"I still don't understand why you're here," she said.

"I told you. I want—I *need*—a friend. Or friends. Everywhere I go people turn their backs. I'm lonely and I'm scared. I heard some-where about what your husband's been going through. But you have obviously stood by him however hard it's been. I've got nobody."

Rebecca almost laughed out loud at the irony of it. Instead she said, "Yes. It has been hard. But the court found you innocent. You're free now."

Owen sniffed. "Not innocent. Just *not guilty* as charged. It's a different thing. Anyway, it doesn't matter. I'm not really free. Everyone believes I'm guilty."

"Are you?"

"Will you believe me if I promise to answer truthfully?"

Rebecca felt her heart speed up. It was such a simple question, but it seemed to her that so much depended on it. Not just Owen Pierce, here and now, but her whole moral reality, her sense of trust and, even, her faith itself. She became aware of Pierce looking at her and realized that she had probably been holding her breath. Finally, she let it out and took the leap.

"Yes," she said. "I'll believe you."

Pierce looked her in the eye. "No," he said. "No, I didn't do it."

Somehow, Rebecca felt great relief. "What can we do for you?" she asked.

Almost as if he didn't believe his good fortune, Pierce remained speechless for a while. His eyes filled with tears and Rebecca felt, for a moment, like taking his hand. But she didn't.

Finally, in a cracking voice, he said, "I need help. I have to put my life back together again and I can't do it alone." As he spoke, he regained his composure and wiped the tears away briskly. "It may seem cold, calculated," he said, "but it isn't. When I found out who you were, I remembered you from court and I was drawn to you because I thought you'd understand, you know, about being thought guilty when you're innocent, about all the hypocrisy they talk about truth and justice. I'm sure your husband didn't do what he's been accused of. No more than I did."

"But I thought you would be angry with us. My husband gave evidence against you."

Owen shook his head. "All he did was tell the truth. It didn't make any difference to the case. It *was* me on the bridge. I never denied that. And it must have been terrible for you finding the

body. No, I hold nothing against you or your husband. Look, I
have no friends, Mrs Charters. Everyone's deserted me. I have no
close family. Even strangers treat me like some sort of monster if
they recognize me. I need support, public support. I need it to be
seen that decent, intelligent people don't think I'm a monster. I
need you on my side. You and your husband."

"You might have come to the wrong place," Rebecca said. "You
wouldn't want to join a losing cause. Remember, my husband is
still under suspicion."

"Yes, but he has carried on in the face of it all. And I know you
believe in him. You've stuck by him. So have a lot of other members
of the congregation, I'm sure. Don't you see, Mrs Charters, we're
both victims, your husband and I?"

Rebecca thought for a moment, remembering the hypocrisy of
some parishioners. "All right, then," she said. "I can't guarantee
anything, but I'll talk to my husband."

"Thank you," breathed Owen.

"But will you do one thing for me?"

"Of course."

"Will you come to church tomorrow morning? I'm not trying to
convert you or anything, but it would be good if you could be *seen*
there. The people who still come to St Mary's have, for the most
part, stuck up for Daniel and believed in his innocence, as you say.
If we take you into the congregation, they might do the same for
you. I know it might sound hypocritical, the way people judge by
appearances, but they do, you know, and perhaps if ... Why are
you laughing?"

"I'm sorry, Mrs Charters, I really am. I just can't help it. Of
course I'll come to church. Believe me, it seems a very small price
to pay."

III

It was just after two o'clock in the morning and Banks kept waking
up from disturbing dreams. He and Sandra had been out to a folk
night in the Dog and Gun, in Helmthorpe, with some old friends,

Harriet Slade and her husband, David. The star of the evening was Penny Cartwright, a local singer who had given up fame and fortune to settle back in Helmthorpe a few years ago. Banks had first met her while investigating the murder of Harold Steadman, a local historian, and he had seen her once or twice in the intervening years. They chatted amicably enough when they met, but there was always a tension between them, and Banks was glad when the chit-chat was over.

Her singing was something to be relished, though. Alto, husky on the low notes but pure and clear in the higher range, her voice also carried the controlled emotion of a survivor. She sang a mix of traditional and contemporary—from Anon to Zimmerman—and her version of the latter's "I Dreamed I Saw St Augustine" had made Banks's spine tingle and his eyes prickle with tears.

But now, after a little too much port and Stilton back at Harriet and David's, Banks was suffering the consequences. He had often thought that the blue bits in Stilton, being mould, had mild hallucinogenic properties and actually gave rise to restless dreams. It didn't matter that he hadn't yet found a scientist to agree with him; he was sure of it. Because every time he ate Stilton, it happened.

These weren't satisfying dreams, the kind you need to make you feel you've had a good night's sleep, but abrupt and disturbing transformations just below the threshold of consciousness: computer games turned into reality; cars crashed through monitor screens; and the ghost of a young woman walked through a foggy graveyard. In one, he had terminal cancer and couldn't remember what his children looked like. All the while, voices whispered about demon lovers, and crows picked bodies clean to the bone.

Thus Banks was not altogether upset when the phone rang. Puzzled, but relieved in a way to be rescued from the pit of dreams. At the same time, apprehension gripped his chest when he turned over and picked up the receiver. Sandra stirred beside him and he tried to keep his voice down.

"Sir?"

"Yes," Banks mumbled. It was a woman's voice.

"This is DC Gay, sir. I'm calling from the station."

"What are you doing there? What's happened?"

"I'm sorry to bother you, sir, but it looks like there's been another one."

"Another what?"

"Another girl disappeared, sir. Name's Ellen Gilchrist. She went to a school dance at Eastvale Comprehensive tonight and never arrived home. Her mum and dad are climbing up the walls."

Banks sat up and swung his legs from under the covers. Sandra turned over. "Where are they?" he asked.

"They're here, sir, at the station. I couldn't keep them away. I said we're doing all we can, but ..."

"Have you called her friends, boyfriends?"

"Yes, sir. That's all been done. Everyone her mum and dad and her friends from the dance could think of. We've woken up half the town already. As far as I can gather, she left the dance alone just after eleven o'clock. Had a headache. Her parents only live on the Leaview Estate, so it's not more than a quarter of a mile down King Street. They got worried when she hadn't turned up by midnight, her curfew. Called us at twelve-thirty. Sir?"

"Yes?"

"They said normally they'd have given her till one, more likely, then give her a good talking to and pack her off to bed. But they said they'd heard about that killer who got off. Owen Pierce. That's why they called us so soon."

Sitting on the edge of the bed, Banks rubbed his eyes, trying once and for all to rid himself of the Stilton dreams. He sighed. From one nightmare to another. "All right," he said. "Get someone to put on a strong pot of coffee, will you, Susan? I'll be right over."

SEVENTEEN

I

An early rambler from Middlesborough set off from a bed and breakfast in Skield and found the girl's body tucked away in a fold of Witch Fell, above the village, at eight o'clock on Sunday morning. An hour later, the detectives from Eastvale and the Scene-of-Crime Officers began to dribble in, closely followed by Dr Glendenning, who was out of breath by the time he had climbed up to where the body was.

Banks stood at the edge of the terrace, which he suspected was a lynchet, an ancient Anglian ploughing strip levelled on a hillside. Such lyncheted hills went up in a series of steps, of which this was the first. The strip was about ten yards wide and dipped a little in the middle.

The girl's body lay spread-eagled in the central depression, as if cupped in the petals of a flower. The little meadow was full of buttercups and daisies; flies and more delicate winged insects buzzed in the air, some pausing to light on the girl's pale, unyielding skin for a moment.

Several buttercups and daisies had been twined in her long blonde hair, which lay spread out on the bright green grass around her head like the halo in a Russian icon. Her blouse had been torn open and her bra pulled up, revealing small, pale breasts, and her short skirt was up around her thighs, her discarded panties on the grass beside her. As Banks got closer, he noticed the discolouration around her neck, and the open shoulder-bag by her arm, some of its contents spilled on the grass: lipstick, a purse, compact, nail-file, chewing gum, perfume, keys, address book, earrings, hairbrush.

The similarities to the Deborah Harrison scene were too close to be ignored. And Banks had just convinced himself that Deborah had been murdered by someone she knew for some sort of logical reason. Now it looked as if they were dealing with a sexual psychopath—one who had murdered two young girls in the area.

Banks stood back as Peter Darby took photographs and then watched Dr Glendenning perform the on-scene examination. By then, Superintendent Gristhorpe had arrived and Jimmy Riddle was rumoured to be pacing at the bottom of the hill trying to decide whether to attempt the short climb or wait until the others came down to him.

Banks sniffed the air. It was another fine morning. A couple of sheep stood facing the drystone wall as if just wishing it would all go away. Well, it wouldn't, Banks knew. No more than the tightness in his gut, which felt like a clenched fist, would go away before tomorrow.

"Well?" he asked, after the doctor had finished his examination.

"As we're not in court, laddie," said Glendenning, with a crooked grin, "I can tell you that she probably died between ten o'clock last night and one or two o'clock in the morning."

"Do you think she was killed here?"

"Looks like it from the lividity on her back and thighs."

"So he brought her here alive all the way from Eastvale?"

Banks made a mental calculation. The girl, Ellen Gilchrist, had disappeared on her way home shortly after eleven o'clock last night. By car, it was about thirty miles from Eastvale to Skield, but some of that journey was on bad moorland roads where you couldn't drive very fast, especially at night. For one thing, the sheep were inclined to wander, and as anyone it has happened to will tell you, running into a sheep on a dark road is a very nasty experience indeed. Especially for the sheep.

It would probably have taken the killer an hour, Banks estimated, particularly if he took an indirect route to avoid being seen. Why bother? Why not just dump her in Eastvale somewhere? Was location important to him, part of his profile? Did he hope the body would remain undiscovered for longer here? Not much hope of that, Banks thought. Skield and Witch Fell were popular spots for ramblers, especially with the good weather.

"There's a nasty gash behind her left ear," Glendenning said, "which means she was probably unconscious when he brought her here, before he strangled her. It looks like it could have been caused by a hammer or some such heavy object. Cause of death, off the record, of course, is ligature strangulation, just like the last one. Shoulder-bag strap this time, instead of a satchel."

"And the bag's open, also like last time," Banks mused.

"Aye," said Glendenning. "Well, you can have the body sent to the mortuary now." And he walked off.

Banks tried to run the scenario in his mind as if it were a film: girl leaves friends at end of School Lane, walks onto King Street, busy during tourist hours but quiet at night, apart from the odd pub or two. Some street-lamps, but not an especially well-lit area. Most kids are still at the dance, but Ellen's going home ahead of her curfew because she has a headache, or so her friend said. She walks alone down the hill towards the Leaview Estate, not more than ten minutes at the most. Car pulls up. Or is it already waiting down the road, lights turned off, knowing there's a school dance, hoping someone will be careless enough to walk home alone?

He's standing by the car, looking harmless enough. He can't believe his luck. Another blonde, just like Deborah Harrison, and about the same age. Or did he know who he wanted? Had he been watching her? Did he *know* her?

As she passes, he grabs her and drags her into the passenger seat before she knows what's happening. She tries to scream, perhaps, but he puts his hand over her mouth to muffle her. He knocks her out. Now she's in the passenger seat, unconscious, bleeding behind her ear. He straps her in with the safety belt and sets off. Maybe someone saw the car, someone else leaving the dance? He has to get her to an isolated spot before he's seen.

All the way to Skield, he savours what he's going to do to her. The anticipation is almost as thrilling as the act itself, maybe even more so. He anticipates it, and later he relives it, replays it over and over in his mind.

He parks off the road, out of the way, car hidden behind a clump of trees, perhaps, and drags her up the hillside. It's not very far or very steep, the first lynchet, but he's sweating with the effort, and maybe she's coming round now, trying to struggle, beginning to realize that something terrible is about to happen to her. They get to the lynchet, and he lays her down on the grass and does ... whatever he does.

"Alan?"

"What? Oh, sorry, sir. Lost in thought."

Superintendent Gristhorpe and DC Gay had come to stand beside him as uniformed officers searched the area.

"We'd better get back to the station and get things moving," said Gristhorpe. "We can start by questioning all the friends who were at the dance with her again, and then do a house-to-house along King Street, check out the pubs, too. I'll get someone to ask around Skield as well. You never know. Someone might have been suffering from insomnia."

"Sir?"

Both Banks and Gristhorpe looked around to see PC Weaver, one of the searchers, approach with something hooked over the end of a pencil. When he got closer, Banks could see that it was one of those transparent plastic containers that 35mm films come in. Living with Sandra, he had seen plenty of those.

"Found this in the grass near the body, sir," he said.

"Near the shoulder-bag?" Gristhorpe asked.

"No, sir, that's why I thought it was odd. It was on the other side of her, a couple of yards away. Do you think it could be the killer's?"

"It could be anyone's, lad," Gristhorpe said. "A tourist's, maybe. But we'd better check it for prints as quickly as we can." He turned to Banks. "Maybe we've got one who likes to photograph his victims?"

"Possible," Banks agreed. "And we already know one keen amateur photographer, don't we? I'll get Vic Manson on it right away. He should be able to do a comparison before the morning's over."

Just at that moment, a red bald head, shiny with perspiration, appeared over the rim of the meadow. "What's going on?" grunted Chief Constable Riddle.

"Oh, we've just finished here, sir," said Banks, smiling cheekily as he walked past Riddle and headed down the slope.

II

The church was hot and smelled like dust burning on the element of an electric fire. Owen remembered hearing somewhere that most household dust was just dead skin. Which meant the church smelled like dead bits of people burning. Hell? All flesh is grass. The heaps of dead, dry grass burning in allotments, or autumn stubble burning in the country fields, vast, rolling carpets of fire spread out in the distance, palls of smoke hanging and twisting in the still twilight air.

Owen took off his jacket and loosened his tie. He had never been comfortable in churches. His parents were both dyed-in-the-wool atheists, and the only times he had really been in church were for weddings and funerals. So he always wore a suit and tie.

Of course, it was all right when you were a tourist checking out the Saxon fonts and Gothic arches, but a different story altogether when there was a vicar up front prattling on about loving thy neighbour. Owen had always distrusted overly churchy types before, feeling that the church offered a public aura of respectability to many who pursued their perversions in private. But the vicar in this case was Daniel Charters, now one of the few allies Owen had in the entire world.

Today it was the hoary old chestnut about how you get nothing but bad news in the papers and how that can make you cynical about the world, but really there are wonders and miracles going on all around you all the time.

That morning, Owen could certainly relate to the first part of the sermon, if not the uplifting bit. Just before he had set off for church, he had screwed up the *News of the World* in a ball and tossed it across the room.

Judging by the looks he got when he walked into St Mary's, and by the way so many members of the congregation leaned towards one another and whispered behind cupped hands, even the upmarket clientele of St Mary's had had a butcher's at the *News of the World* over their cappuccino and croissants.

And there it was, blazoned across the front page in thick black letters: THE STORY THEY COULDN'T TELL IN COURT. Obviously Michelle's journalist friend had probed her thoroughly. There was a reference to Owen's *liking to take photographs*, phrased in such a way that it sounded downright sinister, and a mention of his love of *kinky positions*. He also, it appeared, liked his sex rough and, as far as partners were concerned, the younger the better. Michelle came out of it sounding more like a victim than a willing lover. Which, Owen supposed, was the intention.

There was also an old, slightly blurred, photograph of the two of them and a scrap of a letter Owen had written Michelle once when he was away at a conference. The letter was a perfectly innocuous can't-wait-to-see-you again sort of thing, but in this context, of course, it took on a far more disturbing aspect.

He recalled the day the photograph was taken. Shortly after Michelle had moved in with him, they had taken a holiday in Dorset, visiting various sites associated with Thomas Hardy's novels. In the small graveyard at Stinsford, where Hardy's heart was buried, they had asked an American tourist to take a photograph of them with Owen's camera. It turned out a little blurred because the tourist hadn't quite mastered the art of manual focusing.

Somehow, seeing the photograph and handwriting reproduced in a Sunday tabloid angered Owen even more than the innuendos in the article. Michelle had obviously handed them over to the reporter. It was a violation, a deeper betrayal even than what she said about him. He was quickly beginning to wish that he *had* killed Michelle.

The whole article screamed out his guilt, of course, protested a miscarriage of justice, though the writer never said as much, not in so many words. Mostly, he just posed questions. Owen wondered if he should consider suing for libel. They were clever, though, these newspaper editors; they vetted everything before they printed it; they could afford a team of lawyers and they had the money put aside to finance large law suits. Still, it was worth considering.

The pew in front of Owen creaked and brought him back to the present. He realized he was sweating, *really* sweating, and begin-

ning to feel dizzy and nauseated, too. Churches weren't supposed
to be this hot. He hoped it wouldn't go on much longer; he especially hoped that Daniel wouldn't say anything about him.

They sang a hymn he remembered hearing once at a wedding,
then there were more readings, prayers. It seemed to be going on
forever. Owen wanted to go to the toilet now, too, and he shifted
uncomfortably in his seat.

One of the readers mentioned seeing something "as in a mirror,
dimly" and it took Owen a moment or two to realize this was the
approved modern version of "through a glass, darkly," which he
thought pretty much described his life. How could they, the
English teacher in him wondered, utterly destroy one of the most
resonant lines in the Bible, even if people did have trouble understanding what it meant. Since when had religion been about clear,
literal, logical meaning anyway?

Finally, it was over. People relaxed, stood, chatted, ambled
towards the doors. Many of them glanced at him as they passed.
One or two managed brief, flickering smiles. Some pointedly
turned away, and others whispered to one another.

Owen waited until most of them had gone. It had cooled down
a little now, with the doors open and most people gone home. He
still needed to go to the toilet, but not so urgently; he could wait
now until he got to the vicarage. That was the plan: tea at the
vicarage. He could hardly believe it.

When there were only one or two stragglers left, Owen got up
and walked to the door. Daniel and Rebecca stood there chatting
with a parishioner. Rebecca put her hand on his arm to stop him
going immediately outside, and smiled. Daniel shook his hand and
introduced him to the old woman. She looked down at her sensible
shoes, muttered some greeting or other, and scurried off. This
would obviously take time.

"Well," said Daniel, taking out a handkerchief and wiping his
moist brow. "I suppose we should be grateful Sir Geoffrey and his
wife weren't here."

Owen hadn't even thought of that. If he had considered the
mere possibility of bumping into Deborah Harrison's parents, he
wouldn't have gone near the place.

Daniel obviously saw the alarm in Owen's expression because he reached out and touched his shoulder. "I'm sorry," he said. "It was insensitive of me to say that. It's just that they used to attend. Anyway, come on, let's go."

Owen walked outside with Daniel and Rebecca, pleased to be in the breeze again and glad to know he wasn't entirely alone against the world. Then he saw four policemen hurrying down the tarmac path from the North Market Street gate. He told himself to run, but like Daniel and Rebecca, he simply froze to the spot.

III

"So, we meet again, Owen," said Banks later that Sunday in an interview room at Eastvale Divisional Headquarters. "Nice of you to assist us with our enquiries."

Pierce shrugged. "I don't think I have a lot of choice. Just for the record, I'm innocent this time, too. But I don't suppose that matters to you, does it? You won't believe me if it's not what you want to hear. You didn't last time."

Very little light filtered through the barred, grimy window and the bare bulb hanging from the ceiling was only thirty watts. There were three people in the room: Banks, Susan Gay and Owen Pierce.

One of the public-spirited parishioners at St Mary's had heard about the Ellen Gilchrist murder on the news driving home after the morning service, and he had wasted no time in using his carphone to inform the police that the man they wanted had been at St Mary's Church that very morning, and might still be there if they hurried. They did. And he was.

In the distance, Banks could hear the mob chanting and shouting slogans outside the station. They were after Pierce's blood. Word had leaked out that he had been taken in for questioning over the Ellen Gilchrist murder, and the public were very quick when it came to adding two and two and coming up with whatever number they wanted.

People had started arriving shortly after the police delivered

Pierce to the station, and the crowd had been growing ever since. Growing uglier, too. Banks feared he now had a lynch mob, and if Pierce took one step outside he'd be ripped to pieces. They would have to keep him in, if for no other reason than his own safety.

Already a few spots of blood dotted the front of his white shirt, a result of his "resisting arrest," according to the officers present; there was also a bruise forming just below his right eye.

Banks started the tape recorders, issued the caution and gave the details of the interview time and those present.

"They hit me, you know," Pierce said, as soon as the tape was running. "The policemen who brought me here. As soon as they got me alone in the car they hit me. You can see the blood on my shirt."

"Do you want to press charges?"

"No. What good would it do? I just want you to know, that's all. I just want it on record."

"All right. Last night, Owen, about eleven o'clock, where were you?"

"At home watching television."

"What were you watching?"

"An old film on BBC."

"What film?"

"Educating Rita."

"What time did it start?"

"About half past ten."

"Until?"

"I don't know. I was tired. I fell asleep before the end."

"Do you usually do that? Start watching something and leave before the end?"

"If I'm tired. As a matter of fact I fell asleep on the sofa, in front of the television. When I woke up there was nothing on the screen but snow."

"You didn't check the time?"

"No. Why should I? I wasn't going anywhere. It must have been after two, though. The BBC usually closes down then."

His voice was flat, Banks noticed, responses automatic, almost as if he didn't care what happened. But still the light burned deep in his eyes. Innocence? Or madness?

"You see, Owen," Banks went on steadily, "there was another young girl killed last night. A seventeen-year-old schoolgirl from Eastvale Comprehensive. It's almost certain she was killed by the same person who killed Deborah Harrison—same method, same ritual elements—and we think you are that person."

"Ridiculous. I was watching television."

"Alone?"

"I'm always alone these days. You've seen to that."

"So, can you see our problem, Owen? You were home, alone, watching an old film on television. Anyone could say that."

"But I'm not just anyone, am I?"

"How's the photography going, Owen?"

"What?"

"You're a keen photographer, aren't you? I was just asking how it was going."

"It isn't. My house was broken into while I was on trial and the bastard who broke in killed my fish and smashed my cameras."

Banks paused. "I'm sorry to hear that."

"I'll bet you are."

Banks took out the plastic film container and held it up for Owen to see. "Know what that is?"

"Of course I do."

"Is it yours?"

"How would I know. There are millions of them around."

"Thing is, Owen, we found this close to the body, and we found your fingerprints on it."

Owen seemed to turn rigid, as if all his muscles tightened at once. The blood drained from his face. "What?"

"We found your fingerprints on it, Owen. Can you explain to us how they got there."

"I ... I ..." he started shaking his head slowly from side to side. "It must be mine."

"Speak up, Owen. What did you say?"

"It must be mine."

"Any idea how it got out in the country near Skield?"

"Skield?"

"That's right."

He shook his head. "I went up there the other day for a walk."

"We know," said Susan Gay, speaking up for the first time. "We asked around the pub and the village, and several people told us they saw you in the area on Friday. They recognized you."

"Not surprising. Didn't you know, I'm notorious?"

"What were you doing, Owen?" Banks asked. "Reconnoitring? Checking out the location? Do you do a lot of advance preparation? Is that part of the fun?"

"I don't know what you're talking about. I admit I was there. I went for a walk. But that's the only time I've been."

"Is it, Owen? I'm trying to believe you, honest I am. I want to believe you. Ever since you got off, I've been telling people that maybe you didn't do it, maybe the jury was right. But this looks bad. You've disappointed me."

"Well, excuse me."

Banks shifted position. These hard chairs made his back ache. "What is this thing you have for rummaging around in girls' handbags or satchels?"

"I don't know what you mean."

"Do you like to take souvenirs?"

"Of what?"

"Something to focus on, help you replay what you did?"

"What did I do?"

"What did you do, Owen? You tell me how you get your thrills."

Pierce said nothing. He seemed to shrink in his chair, his mouth clamped shut.

"You can tell me, Owen," Banks went on. "I want to know. I want to understand. But you have to help me. Do you masturbate afterwards, reliving what you've done? Or can't you contain yourself? Do you come in your trousers while you're strangling them? Help me, Owen. I want to know."

Still Pierce kept quiet. Banks shifted again. The chair creaked.

"Why am I here?" Pierce asked.

"You know that."

"It's because you think I did it before, isn't it?"

"Did you, Owen?"

"I got off."

"Yes, you did."

"So I'd be a fool to admit it, wouldn't I? Even if I had done it."

"Did you do it? Did you kill Deborah Harrison?"

"No."

"Did you kill Ellen Gilchrist?"

"No."

Banks sighed. "You're not making it easy for us, Owen."

"I'm telling you the truth."

"I don't think so."

"I am."

"Owen, you're lying to us. You picked up Ellen Gilchrist on King Street last night. First you knocked her unconscious, then you drove her to Skield, where you dragged her a short distance up Witch Fell and strangled her with the strap of her handbag. Why won't you tell me about it?"

Pierce seemed agitated by the description of his crime, Banks noticed. Guilty conscience?

"What was it like, Owen?" he pressed on. "Did she resist or did she just passively accept her fate. Know what I think? I think you're a coward, Owen. First you strangled her from behind, so you didn't have to look her in the eye. Then you lay her down on the grass and tore her clothes away. You imagined she was Michelle Chappel, didn't you, and you were getting your own back, giving her what for. She didn't have a chance. She was beyond resistance. But even then you couldn't get it up, could you? You're a coward, Owen. A coward and a pervert."

"No!" The suddenness with which Pierce shot forward and slammed his fist into the desk startled Banks. He saw Susan Gay stand and make towards the door for help, but waved her down.

"Tell me, Owen," he said. "Tell me how it happened."

Pierce flopped back in his chair again, as if the energy of his outburst had depleted his reserves. "I want my lawyer," he said tiredly. "I want Wharton. I'm not saying another word. You people are destroying me. Get me Wharton. And either arrest me or I'm leaving right now."

Banks turned to Susan and raised his eyebrows, then sighed. "Very well, Owen," he said. "If that's the way you want it."

EIGHTEEN

I

By late Sunday evening, it was clear that the crowd wasn't going to storm the Bastille of Eastvale Divisional HQ, and by early Monday morning, there were only a few diehards left.

Banks turned his Walkman up loud as he passed the reporters by the front doors; Maria Callas drowned out all their questions. He said hello to Sergeant Rowe at the front desk, grabbed a coffee and headed upstairs. When he got to the CID offices, he took the earphones out and walked on tiptoe, listening for that snorting-bull sound that usually indicated the presence of Chief Constable Riddle.

Silence—except for Susan Gay's voice on the telephone, muffled behind her closed door.

Dr Glendenning's post-mortem report on Ellen Gilchrist was waiting in Banks's pigeon hole, along with a preliminary report from the forensic lab, who had put a rush on this one.

In the office, Banks closed his door and pulled up the venetian blinds on yet another fine day. Much more of this and life would start to get boring, he reflected. Still, there was a bit of cloud gathering to the south, and the weather forecast threatened rain, even the possibility of a thunderstorm.

He opened the window a couple of inches and watched the shopkeepers open their doors and roll down their awnings against the sunshine. Then he stretched until he felt something crack pleasantly in his back, and sat down to study the report. He tuned the portable radio he kept in his office to Radio 4 and listened to "Today" as he read.

Glendenning had narrowed the time of death to between eleven and one, confirmed that the victim had been killed in the place where she was found, and matched the strap of her shoulder-bag to the weal in her throat.

The wound behind her ear was round and smooth, he also confirmed, about an inch in diameter, and most likely delivered by a metal hammer-head.

This time, unfortunately, there was no scratched tissue beneath her fingernails. In fact, her fingernails were so badly chewed they had been treated with some vile-tasting chemical to discourage her from biting them.

According to the lab, though there was no blood other than the deceased's at the scene, there were several hairs on her clothing that didn't come from her body. That was understandable, given that she had been at a crowded dance. What was damning, though, was that four of the hairs matched those found on Deborah Harrison's school blazer—the ones that had already also been tested against the sample Owen Pierce had given almost eight months ago.

Hairs could be dodgy evidence, as Pierce's trial had shown. Banks read through a fair bit of jargon about melanin and fragmented medullas, then considered the neutron activation analysis printout specifying the concentration of various elements in the hair, such as antimony, bromine, lanthanum, strontium and zinc.

The lab would need another sample of the suspect's hair, the report said, because the ratios of these elements could have changed slightly since the last sample was taken, but even at this point, it was 4500 to one *against* the hair originating from anyone but Pierce.

Unfortunately, none of the hairs had follicular tissue adhering to their roots; in fact, there were no roots, so it was impossible to identify blood factors or carry out DNA analysis.

As in the Deborah Harrison murder, the swabs showed no signs of semen in the mouth, vagina or anus, and there was no other evidence of sexual activity.

But the hairs and the fingerprints Vic Manson had identified on the plastic film container would probably secure a conviction, Banks guessed. Pierce wasn't going to slip through the cracks this time.

In a way, Banks felt sad. He had almost convinced himself that Pierce had been an innocent victim of the system and that Deborah's killer was closer to home; now it looked as if he were wrong again.

He tuned in to Radio 3—where "Composer of the Week" featured Gerald Finzi—and started making notes for the meeting he would soon be having with Stafford Oakes.

Things started to get noisy at around eleven-thirty, with Pierce on his way to court for his remand hearing, the phone ringing off the hook and reporters pressing their faces at every window in the building. Banks decided it was time to sneak out by the side exit and take an early lunch.

He opened the door and popped his head out to scan the corridor. Plenty of activity, but nobody was really paying him much attention. Instead of going the regular way, down to the front door, he tiptoed towards the fire exit, which came out on a narrow street opposite the Golden Grill, called Skinner's Yard.

He had hardly got to the end of the corridor, when he heard someone call out behind him. His heart lurched.

"Chief Inspector?"

Thank God it wasn't Jimmy Riddle. He turned. It was DI Barry Stott, and he was looking troubled. "Barry. What is it? What can I do for you?"

"Can I have a word? In private."

Banks glanced around to see if anyone else was watching them. No. The coast was clear. "Of course," he said, putting his hand on Stott's shoulder and guiding him towards the fire door. "Let's go for a drink, shall we, and get away from the mêlée."

II

It was a long time since Rebecca had been to talk to the angel, but that Monday she felt the need again. And this time she wasn't drunk.

As she turned off the tarmac path onto the gravel, she wondered how she could have been so wrong about Owen Pierce. She remembered how scared she was when she first saw him after his release, then how like a little boy lost he had been when he came to talk to her. When she had asked him the all-important question and he had said he would answer truthfully, she had believed him. Now it looked as if he had lied to her. How could she be sure of anything any more? Of anyone? Even Daniel?

The air around the Inchcliffe Mausoleum was warm and still, the only sounds the drone of insects and the occasional car along Kendal Road or North Market Street. The angel continued to gaze heaven-ward. Rebecca wished she knew what he could see there.

Sober, this time, and feeling a little self-conscious, she couldn't quite bring herself to speak out loud. But her thoughts flowed and shaped themselves as she stood there feeling silly. She wondered what the policeman, Chief Inspector Banks, would think of her.

The police had claimed that Owen Pierce had killed *another* girl. That meant they also believed he had killed Deborah Harrison. There could be no way out for him now, Rebecca thought, not with public feeling as strong as it was against him.

But he had visited her at the vicarage only that Saturday after-noon, full of talk about his innocence, the need for support and understanding. She couldn't get over that, how *convinced* she had been. Was that the behaviour of someone who was intending to go out later that night, pick up a teenage girl and murder her? Rebecca didn't think so. But what did she know? Experts had done studies on these kinds of people—serial murderers, they called them—though she didn't know if having killed only two people qualified Owen for that designation.

She had, however, seen enough television programmes about psychopaths to know that some could *appear* perfectly charming, live quite normal lives outside their need to kill. Ted Bundy, for example, had been a handsome and intelligent man who had killed God knew how many young women in America. Watch out for the nice, friendly, polite boy next door, the message seemed to be, not the raggedy man with the cruel eyes muttering to himself in a corner.

A fly settled on her bare forearm and she stared at its shiny blue and green carapace for a moment before brushing it off. Then she looked up at the angel again. If only he could make things clear for her.

Perhaps the police had arrested Owen only because they still believed he had killed Deborah Harrison. Maybe they had no real evidence that he had killed the other girl. She didn't know why she should care so much. After all, Owen was still practically a stranger to her—and for a long time she had *believed* him to be a killer. Why should she be so upset when it turned out that he really was? She still couldn't help feeling that he had let her down somehow, silly as the idea was.

"Why?" she asked, surprised to find herself speaking out loud at last, face turned up to look at the angel. "Can you tell me why I care?"

But she got no answer.

She already knew part of the answer. Talking to Owen, taking him under her wing, had been a test for her. In a way, his presence had challenged her faith, her Christian feelings. For when it came to Christianity, Rebecca was a humanist, not one of these cold-fish theologians like some of the ministers she had met. Perhaps a better existence did await us in heaven, but to Rebecca, Christianity was useless if it forgot people and the here and now. Faith and belief, she felt, were no use without charity, love and compassion; religion was nothing if it focused entirely on the afterlife. Daniel had agreed. That was why they had done so well together. Up to last year.

"Why am I telling you this?" she asked the angel. "What do you know of life on earth? What is it I want from you? Can you tell me?"

Still the angel gazed fixedly heaven-wards. His expression looked stern to Rebecca, but she put that down to a trick of the light.

"Am I to be a cynic now?" she asked. "After I put so much faith in Owen and he turns out to be a killer after all?"

Again, she didn't hear any answer, but she did hear a movement coming from deeper in the woods. The area behind the Inchcliffe Mausoleum was the most overgrown in the entire graveyard, all the way back to the wall at Kendal Road. The oldest yews grew there, and the wild shrubbery was so dense in places you couldn't even walk through it easily. If there were any graves, nobody had visited them for a long time.

It must have been a small animal of some kind, Rebecca decided. Then she remembered that she had told the police and the court that the cry she heard that November evening could have come from an animal. When she really thought about it, she knew it never could have. She had simply refused to acknowledge, either to herself or to anyone else that the scream she heard was the last cry for help of a girl about to be murdered. This sound, too, was too loud to be a dog, a cat or a bird. And there were no horses or sheep in the graveyard.

She took a step towards the back of the mausoleum, aware as she did so that this was where Deborah's body had been found. "Is anybody there?" she called out.

No answer.

Then she heard another rustling sound, this time closer to the North Market Street wall.

Rebecca turned and wandered thigh-deep into the tangled undergrowth. She felt nettles sting her legs as she walked. "Is anyone there?" she called again.

Still no answer.

She paused and listened for a moment. All she could hear was her heart beating.

Suddenly to her left, through the trees, she saw a dark figure break into a run. It looked like a man dressed in brown and green, but she couldn't be certain because of the way the colours blended in with the background. Whoever it was, he couldn't get over the high wall before she caught up with him. His only alternative was to head along the wall to the North Market Street gate. If she hurried, perhaps she could catch a glimpse of him before he got away.

She turned back towards the back of the Inchcliffe Mausoleum and the gravel path. He was to her right now. She could hear him running towards the gate.

Before she could get out of the wooded area, something snagged at her ankle and she tripped, scratching her knees and hands on thorns. It only delayed her a few seconds, but when she got to her feet and ran past the mausoleum along the gravel path into the open area, all she saw was the wooden gate slam shut. She stood there and cursed whoever it was. When she looked down, she saw she had blood on her hands.

III

Avoiding the Queen's Arms, which everyone knew was the Eastvale CID local, Banks spirited Stott along Skinner's Yard, down to the Duck and Drake on one of the winding alleys off King Street. The cobbled streets were chock-a-block with antique shops, antiquarian booksellers and food specialists, all with mullioned windows and creaky wooden floors.

The Duck and Drake was a small, black-fronted Sam Smith's house with etched, smoked-glass windows and a couple of tatty hanging baskets over the door. Inside, the entrance to the snug was so low that Banks felt as if he were crawling under a particularly tight overhang in Ingleborough Cave.

The snug was also tiny, with dark wood beams and white-washed walls hung with hunting prints and brass ornaments. They were the only two people in the place. The bench creaked as Banks sat down opposite Stott with his pint of Old Brewery Bitter and his ham and cheese sandwich. Stott hadn't wanted anything at all, not even a glass of water.

"What is it, Barry?" Banks asked, chomping on his sandwich. "Off your food? You look bloody awful."

"Thanks."

"Don't mention it."

Stott was pale, with dark bags under his eyes and a two-day stubble around his chin and cheeks. His eyes themselves, behind the glasses, were dull, distant and haunted. Banks had never seen him like this before. Normally, you could depend on Barry Stott to look bright-eyed and alert at all times. Not to mention well groomed. But his suit was creased, as if he had slept in it, his tie was not properly fastened, and his hair was uncombed. He looked so miserable that even his ears seemed to droop.

"You ill?"

"As a matter, of fact," said Stott, "I *haven't* been sleeping well. Not well at all."

"Something on your mind?"

"Yes."

Banks finished his sandwich, took a sip of beer and lit a cigarette. "Out with it, then."

Stott just pursed his lips and frowned in concentration.

"Barry, are you sure it's something you want to talk to me about?"

"I *have* to," Stott replied. "By all rights, I should go to the super, or even the CC. God knows, it's bound to get that far eventually, but I wanted to tell you first. I don't know why. Respect, perhaps. It's just so difficult. I've been up wrestling with it all night, and I can't see any other way out."

Banks sat back. He had never seen Barry Stott so upset, so *consumed* by anything before, except that day when Pierce was found not guilty. Stott was a private person, and Banks wasn't sure how to handle him on a personal level, outside the job.

Was this a private, intimate matter, perhaps? Was Stott going to admit he was homosexual? Not that it mattered. Banks knew for a fact that two of the uniformed officers at Eastvale were gay. So did everyone else. They came in for a bit of baiting now and then from the more macho among their colleagues, who weren't entirely sure of their own sexuality, and for a certain amount of righteous moral disapproval from the one or two Christian fundamentalists in uniform. But Barry Stott? Banks realized he didn't even know whether Stott was married, divorced or single.

"Is this off the record, Barry?" Banks asked. "I mean, is it something personal?"

"Partly. But not really." He shook his head. "I can't understand it myself. I was so sure. So damn *certain*." He banged the table. Banks's beer-glass jumped. "Sorry."

"I think you'd better just tell me."

Stott paused. He took a handkerchief from his pocket and cleaned the lenses of his glasses. In the background Banks could hear the radio playing Jim Reeves singing "Welcome to My World."

Finally, Stott put his glasses back on, nodded and took a deep breath. "All right," he said. "I suppose the most important thing is that Owen Pierce is innocent, at least of Ellen Gilchrist's murder. We have to let him go."

Banks's jaw dropped. "What are you talking about, Barry?"

"I was *there*," Stott said. "I *know*."

Christ, what was this? A murder confession? Banks held his hand up. "Hold on, Barry. Take it easy. Go slowly. And be very careful what you say." He almost felt as if he were giving Stott a formal caution. "Where were you? King Street? Skield?"

Stott shook his head and licked his lips. "No. Not either of those places. I was outside Owen Pierce's house."

"Doing what?"

"Watching him. I've been doing it ever since he got off."

"So that's why you're looking so washed out?"

Stott rubbed his hand over his stubble. "Haven't had any sleep in a week. Soon as I finish at the station, I grab a sandwich, then head for his street and park. If he goes out, I follow him."

"All night?"

"Most of it. At least till it looks like he's settled. Sometimes as late as three or four in the morning. He doesn't go out much. Most nights he gets drunk and passes out in front of the telly."

"And he hasn't spotted you?"

"I don't know. I haven't taken any great pains to hide myself, but he hasn't said anything."

"But *why*, Barry?"

Stott smoothed down his hair with his hand, then shrugged. "I don't know. I got obsessed, I suppose. I just couldn't stop myself. I was so *sure* of his guilt, so certain he'd beaten the system ... And I knew he'd do it again. It was that kind of crime. I could feel it. I wanted to make sure he didn't kill another girl. I thought if I watched him, kept an eye on him, then either I'd catch him, stop him or, if he knew I was onto him, he wouldn't be able to do it again and the tension would get unbearable. Then maybe he'd confess or something. I wasn't thinking clearly."

Banks stubbed out his cigarette. "But why, Barry? You're a good copper. Brainy, diligent, logical. You passed all your exams. You've got a bloody university degree, for Christ's sake. You're on acceler-ated promotion. You ought to know better."

Stott shrugged. "I know. I know. I can't explain it. Something just ... went in me. Like I said, I thought if I watched him long enough I'd catch him one way or another."

Banks shook his head. "Okay. Let's get this straight. You were parked outside Owen Pierce's house on Saturday night?"

"Yes."

"What time?"

"From about five o'clock on."

"Until?"

"About two-thirty in the morning, when he turned the lights off. He didn't go out at all except to buy a bottle of something at the off-licence around nine o'clock."

"You're absolutely certain?"

"Positive. The curtains weren't quite closed. I could see him clearly whenever he got up. He was watching telly in the front room, but every now and then he'd get up to go to the toilet, or pour a drink, whatever."

"And you're certain he was there all the time? He didn't sneak out the back and come back?"

Stott shook his head. "He was there, sir. Between the crucial times. Definitely. I saw him get up and cross the room twice between eleven o'clock and midnight."

"Are you sure it couldn't have been anyone else?"

"Certain. Besides, his car was parked in front of the house the whole time."

That didn't mean much. Pierce could have stolen a car to commit the crime, and then returned it, rather than risk using his own and having his licence number taken down. When that thought had passed through his mind, Banks had experienced another irritating sense of *déjà vu*. He had felt the same thing the other day while going over the case files. It couldn't really be *déjà vu*, because it wasn't something he had already experienced, but it came with the same sort of frisson.

"What happened then?" he asked.

"He must have fallen asleep in front of the telly, as usual. I could see the light from the screen. It changed to snow at one fifty-five, when the programmes ended, but Pierce didn't move again until two-thirty. Then he drew the curtains fully, turned out the lights and went upstairs to bed. That's all."

"That's *all*. Jesus Christ, Barry, do you have any idea what you've done?"

"Of course I have. But I had to speak out. I've been struggling with my conscience all night. I could have spoken up yesterday and saved Pierce another night in jail, but I didn't. I didn't dare. That's my cross to bear. I was worried about the consequences to my career, partly, I'll admit that, but I was also trying to convince myself that I *could* have been wrong, that he *could* have done it. But there's no way. He's innocent, just like he says."

Banks shook his head. "I don't see how we can cover this up, Barry. I'm not sure what's going to happen."

Stott sat bolt upright. "I don't want you to cover it up. As I said, I grappled with my conscience all night. I prayed for an answer, an easy way out. There isn't one. I'll speak up for Pierce. I'm his alibi. I've abused my position." He reached in his inside pocket and brought out a white, business-size envelope, which he placed on the table in front of Banks. "This is my resignation."

IV

Owen was confused. The Magistrates' Court had bound him over without bail, as he had expected, but instead of being en route to Armley Jail, he was back in the cell at Eastvale. And nobody would tell him anything. Wharton had received a message from one of the uniformed policemen just as they returned to the van after the court session, and he seemed to have been running around like a blue-arsed fly ever since. Something was going on, and as far as Owen was concerned, it could only be bad.

He ate a lunch of greasy fish and chips, ironically wrapped in Sunday's *News of the World*, washed it down with a mug of strong sweet tea, and paced his cell until, shortly after one o'clock, Wharton appeared in the doorway, waistcoat buttons straining over his belly, a scarlet crescent grin splitting his bluish jowls.

"You're free to go," he announced, thumbs hooked in his waist-coat pockets.

Owen flopped on the bed. "Don't joke," he said. "What do you want?"

"I told you." Wharton came close to what looked like dancing a little jig like Scrooge on Christmas morning. "You're free. Free. Free to go."

Had he gone mad? Owen wondered. Had this new arrest been the straw that broke the camel's back? By all rights, it should be *Owen* going mad, not his solicitor, but there was no accounting for events these days. "Please," Owen said putting his fists to his temples in an attempt to stop the clamour rising inside his head. "Please stop tormenting me."

"He's right, Owen," said a new voice from behind Wharton in the doorway.

Owen looked up through the tears in his eyes and saw Detective Chief Inspector Banks leaning against the jamb, tie loose, hands in his pockets. So it wasn't a dream; it wasn't a lie? Owen hardly dared believe. He didn't know how he felt now. Choked, certainly, his head spinning, a whooshing sound in his ears. Mostly, he was still confused. That and tearful. He felt very tearful. "You *believe* me?" he asked Banks.

Banks nodded. "Yes. I believe you."

"Thank God." Owen let his head fall in his hands and gave in to the tears. He cried loud and long, wet and shamelessly, and it wasn't until he had finished and started to wipe his nose and eyes with a tissue that he noticed the two men had left him alone, but that the cell door was still open.

Gingerly, he walked towards it and poked his head out, afraid that it would slam on him. Nothing happened. He walked along the tiled corridor towards the other locked door that led, he knew, upstairs, then out to the world beyond, worried that it wouldn't be opened for him. But it was.

Banks and Wharton stood outside, in the custody suite, and Owen now feared he would be rearrested for something else, still anxious that it was all some sort of ruse.

When Banks approached him, he backed away in apprehension.

"No," said Banks, holding his hands out, palms open. "I meant it, Owen. No tricks. It's over. You're a free man. You're completely exonerated. But I'd really appreciate it if you would come to my office with me for a chat. You might be able help us find out who really did commit these murders."

"*Murders?* You believe I'm innocent of both?"

"They're too similar, Owen. Had to be the same person. And that person couldn't have been you. Please, come with me, will you? I'll explain."

As Owen preceded Banks up the stairs, he felt as if he were walking in a dream and half-expected his feet to disappear right through the steps. On the open-plan ground floor, everyone fell silent as he passed, watching him, and he felt as if he were floating, weightless in space. His vision blurred and his head started to spin, as if he had had too much to drink, but before he stumbled and fell, he felt Banks's strong hand grasp his elbow and direct him towards the stairs.

"It's all right, Owen," Banks said. "We'll have some strong coffee and a chat. You've nothing to worry about now."

Instead of taking him into a dim, smelly interview room, as Owen had been half-expecting, Banks led him into what must be his own office. It was hardly palatial, but it had a metal desk, some matching filing cabinets and two comfortable chairs.

On the wall was a *Dalesman* calendar set at June and showing a photograph of a couple of ramblers with heavy rucksacks on their backs approaching Gordale Scar, near Malham. Oddly, Owen found himself thinking he could have done a better job of the photograph himself. The venetian blinds were up, and before he sat down Owen glimpsed the cobbled market square, full of parked cars. Freedom. He sat down. God, he felt tired.

"What happened?" he asked.

"You were under surveillance," said Banks.

"What? So there was ... I mean, it was you?"

"Not me, exactly, but someone. Did you know there was someone watching you?"

"I had a funny feeling once or twice. But no, I can't honestly say I knew." Owen started to laugh.

"What is it?" Banks asked.

Owen wiped his arm over his eyes. "Oh, nothing. Just the irony of it, that's all. I was under surveillance because you thought I'd commit a crime, but as it turns out the surveillance gives me an alibi. Don't you think that's funny?"

Banks smiled. "Ironic, yes. But a young girl did get killed, Owen. Horribly. Just like Deborah Harrison."

"I know. I wasn't laughing at that. And I didn't have anything to do with it. I don't know how I can help you."

"I think you do. I don't believe you haven't considered the problem over the past couple of days."

"What problem?"

Banks sat forward and rested his palms on the blotter. "You want me to spell it out? Okay. The reason we arrested you, Owen, was partly because you had been accused of a very similar crime before, and partly because we found strong physical evidence against you at the scene. It still looks very much as if the same person killed both of those girls, and we found evidence against you at both scenes."

"The fingerprints and the hairs? Yes. And you're right: I have been thinking about how they could have got there."

"Any ideas?"

Owen shook his head. "I *did* go up Skield way, and I probably walked past the spot where ... you know. I suppose I could have dropped such a film container, but I don't think I had one with me. I told you about my camera. I didn't have it with me. As for the hairs, I suppose I must have shed a few during my walk, but I can't explain how they got on the victim's clothes. Unless ... "

"Yes?"

The coffee arrived. Banks poured. Owen blew into his cup first, then took a sip. "This is good. Thank you. Unless," he went on, "and I know this sounds crazy, paranoid even, but I can't see how any of it could have happened unless someone, the real killer, had decided to capitalize on my bad reputation, blame it on me, the way he knew everyone else would. It doesn't make sense unless someone tried to *frame* me for Ellen Gilchrist's murder."

Banks started tapping a pencil against his blotter. "Go on," he said.

"Well, if you accept that premise, then whoever it was must have broken into my house while I was in jail and wrecked the place to cover up his true intentions. Or he could have walked in easily *after* the place had been done over. The front door was unlocked when I got back. The lock was broken, in fact. This person must have thought there was a good chance I'd get off, and he wanted some insurance in case that happened and suspicion turned back on him. He must have found the empty film container in the waste-paper bin and guessed it would have my fingerprints on it. I mean, if it were empty, and I'd opened it ... Then he must have picked up some hairs from the pillow in the bedroom. That would have been easy enough to do."

Banks nodded. "Why not choose something more *obvious* to link you to the crime?"

"Failing my blood, which he couldn't get hold of, I can't think of anything more obvious than my hair and fingerprints, can you?"

Banks smiled. "I meant something with your name on, perhaps. So there could be no mistake. After all, the prints on the film container might have been blurred. He couldn't be *certain* they'd lead us to you."

"But if you think about it," Owen said, looking pointedly at Banks, "he didn't need very much, did he? You all believed I'd murdered Deborah Harrison, so it was easy to convince you I'd also killed Ellen Gilchrist. There was no point risking anything more obvious, like something with my name or photograph on it, because that would only draw suspicion. No, all he needed were my prints and hair. He knew my reputation would do the rest. Even without the prints he could have been fairly certain you'd pick on me. I'll bet the minute you saw the film container you thought of me because you knew I was an amateur photographer."

"That still leaves us one important question to answer," Banks said. "Who? Of course, it might be that the murderer was simply using you as a convenient scapegoat—that it was nothing personal—but it *could* have been someone who really wanted you to suffer. Have you any idea who would want to do that to you?"

"I've racked my brains about it. But no. The only person who hates me that much is Michelle. *Could* it have been a woman?"

"I don't think Michelle is tall enough," Banks said. "But, yes, it *could* have been a woman."

Owen shook his head. "I'm sorry. I wish I could help. Like you said, it was probably nothing personal. I mean, whoever did it just wanted *someone else* to blame. It didn't matter who."

"You're probably right. But if you think of anyone ..."

"Of course. One of the neighbours might have seen someone, you know. They wouldn't speak out before because they all thought I was guilty and deserved having my house wrecked, but now ... ? I don't know. It's worth asking them, anyway. You might start with that prick Ivor and his wife, Siobhan, next door."

"We'll do that," said Banks, standing up to indicate the interview was at an end.

Owen finished his coffee, stood awkwardly and moved towards the door. He could still hardly believe that freedom was just a few steps away again.

"What now?" Banks asked him.

He shrugged. "I don't know. I've got a lot to think about. Maybe I'll go away for a while, just get lost, like everyone suggested I should do in the first place."

Banks shook his head. "No need to run away," he said. "We know you didn't do it now. The press will fall all over themselves to support your cause, and they'll crucify us for getting the wrong man. Police incompetence."

Owen forced a smile. "Maybe. Eventually. And I can't say I'll be sorry. You deserve it. I remember what you've put me through. I remember all the terrible things you accused me of only yesterday. Perversion. Cowardice. Not to mention murder. But I can't see me getting my job or my friends back, can you? And I imagine there'll be a lot of people around these parts slow to change their minds, no matter what. Shit sticks, Chief Inspector. That's one thing I've learned from all this."

Banks nodded. "Perhaps. For a while."

Owen paused at the door. "Look," he said, "I don't expect an apology or anything, but could you just tell me again that you believe I'm innocent? Not just not guilty but *innocent*. Will you say it. I need to hear it."

"You're innocent, Owen. It's true. You're free to go."

"Thank you." Owen turned and started to pull the door shut behind him.

"Owen?" Banks called after him.

Owen felt a little shiver of panic. He turned. "Yes?"

"I *am* sorry. Good luck to you."

Owen nodded, shut the door and left the building as fast as he could.

NINETEEN

I

It wasn't until late Tuesday afternoon that a number of things clicked into place for Banks, and what had been eluding him, niggling him for days, suddenly became clear.

So far, there were no leads on the Ellen Gilchrist murder. Several cars had been spotted on King Street that night—big, small, light, dark, Japanese, French—but no-one had any reason to take down licence numbers or detailed descriptions. If the killer had used his own car, Banks reflected, then he may have parked out of sight, just around the corner on one of the sidestreets.

A couple of tourists unable to sleep on a lumpy mattress at a Gratly B & B said they heard a car pass shortly after eleven-thirty, which would have been about the right time, but they hadn't seen anything. So far, no-one in Skield had been disturbed by Saturday night's events, but that didn't surprise Banks. If the killer were clever, which he apparently was, then he would have parked off the road, well out of the hamlet itself.

Under Superintendent Gristhorpe's co-ordination, Susan Gay and Jim Hatchley were still out checking the victim's friends and acquaintances to see if she could have been killed by someone who knew her, or if anyone knew more than he or she was telling. The more he thought about it, though, the more Banks was convinced that the solution to Ellen Gilchrist's murder lay in Deborah Harrison's.

Also, when Banks arrived at the office that morning, he found a telephone message in his pigeon-hole from Rebecca Charters, dated the previous afternoon, asking him to phone her. When he rang Rebecca, she told him about surprising someone in St Mary's graveyard the previous afternoon. No, she hadn't seen who it was, couldn't even give a description. She laughed at her fears now, apologized for bothering him and said she'd been a bit jumpy lately. Yesterday, she hadn't hesitated to call, but now she had had time to think about it. Probably just a kid, she decided. Banks wasn't too sure, but he put it on the back burner for the moment.

Since Stott's revelation, after the inevitable bollocking from Jimmy Riddle and a reminder that he was close to the end of his allotted week, Banks and Superintendent Gristhorpe had also been engaged in damage control.

So far, they had managed to keep Stott's illegal surveillance from the press. And Owen Pierce certainly wasn't interested in blowing the whistle. As far as the media were concerned, Pierce had an unimpeachable alibi. All that had happened was that another innocent person had spent a night in the cells because of police incompetence. Nothing new about that. Eastvale CID came out of it looking only like prize berks, not like a combination of the Gestapo and the KGB.

As for Barry Stott, he hadn't resigned, but he had taken some of the leave due to him. God knew where he was. Wrestling with his conscience somewhere, Banks guessed. As far as Banks was concerned, though, Stott was overreacting. So, he had let himself get a bit obsessed with Pierce's guilt. So what? Things like that happened sometimes, and they rarely had dire consequences. After all, Stott had only *watched* Pierce; he hadn't beat him up or assassinated him.

Despite the hours of work a murder enquiry consumed, routine work still went on at Eastvale Divisional HQ, and routine papers still found their way to Banks's desk. On that Tuesday afternoon, when he was distracted by thoughts of Ellen Gilchrist, Deborah Harrison, Barry Stott and Owen Pierce, a proposal requiring every patrol car be fitted with a dashboard computer passed over his desk for perusal after a report on the increase of car theft in North Yorkshire.

Because Banks wasn't thinking about it, because the words simply floated into that chaotic, intuitive and creative part of his mind rather than engaging his sense of reason and logic, he was struck with that rare feeling of epiphany as a missing piece fell into place. It felt like the simultaneous telescoping and expansion of a chain of unrelated words into one inevitable conclusion: each element rolled firmly into place like the balls with the winning lottery numbers: Car. Computer. Theft. *Spinks*.

It wasn't really intuition, but a perfectly logical process, taking a number of facts and relating them in a way that made sense. It only felt like a sudden revelation.

On Friday, when Banks had questioned John Spinks about Michael Clayton and Sylvie Harrison, it had been staring him in the face. But he hadn't seen it. On Saturday, after his talk with Clayton, he had felt close to something. But he hadn't known what. Now he did. He still had some dates to check, but as he pushed the proposal aside, he was certain that John Spinks had stolen Michael Clayton's car and computer in August of last year. Whether that actually meant anything remained to be seen.

Excited by the theory, Banks checked the dates and dashed into Gristhorpe's office, where he found the superintendent immersed in the statement of Ellen Gilchrist's best friend. Gristhorpe stretched and rubbed his bushy eyebrows with his fingertips when Banks entered. After he'd done, they looked like birds' nests.

"Alan. What can I do for you?"

Banks explained about his chain of reasoning. Gristhorpe nodded here and there, and when Banks had finished, put his forefinger to his lips and furrowed his brow.

"So Lady Sylvie Harrison and Michael Clayton found Spinks and Deborah drinking wine in the back garden on 17 August, right?" he said.

Banks nodded.

"And Clayton reported his car stolen on 20 August. I remember it because when he came to inquire about our progress, he thought he was so important he had to see the top man on the totem pole. About a bloody stolen car. I ask you."

"I'm surprised he didn't go directly to Jimmy Riddle."

"Oh, he did. First off. But Riddle's in Northallerton and that was too far for Clayton to go every day. So Riddle told him to keep checking with me. I put Barry and Susan on it. Clayton was like a cat on a hot tin roof. Not over the car, though."

"The computer?"

"Got it in one."

"Yes. That's what Susan said," Banks mused. "When Clayton recognized her that time we went to talk to the Harrisons. I should have realized at the time."

Gristhorpe smiled indulgently. "I think you can be forgiven that, Alan," he said. "Wasn't it about the same time the lead on Pierce came up?"

"Yes. But—"

"Anyway, let's assume that Spinks stole Clayton's car on 20 August," Gristhorpe went on. "He did some damage, but not much. It was the missing notebook computer that really had Clayton dancing on hot coals. We know it was a very expensive one, with all the bells and whistles, but Clayton's a rich man. He could afford a new one easily. It was what was *on* the computer that he was worried about. As I recollect, it turned up on the market a couple of weeks later, no worse for wear."

"From what I've seen," Banks went on, "Spinks would have about as much chance of operating Clayton's computer as an orangoutang. But the point is that he was still seeing Deborah at that time. There's a chance she knew what he'd done. She wouldn't necessarily tell Clayton or her parents what happened, not when she was right in the middle of being rebellious, slumming it. And Deborah was bright, good at sciences. That computer would have probably been child's play to her."

"So what if she found out something from it?" Gristhorpe suggested. "Something important."

"Maybe it wasn't that Clayton was having an affair with Lady Harrison, after all," Banks said. "That's what I thought earlier. But maybe they were involved in some scam. Perhaps Clayton had been cheating Sir Geoffrey or something."

"You don't even need to go that far," Gristhorpe said. "Remember, HarClay Industries is big in the defence business. Big enough that Sir Geoffrey met in private with Oliver Jackson, of Special Branch, on the day his daughter was murdered."

"And you think there's a connection?"

"I'm saying there *could* be. Micro-electronics, computers, microchips, weapons circuits, that sort of thing. They're not only big money, but they have a strong political dimension, too. If Deborah came across something she shouldn't have seen ... If Clayton was working for someone he shouldn't have been ... selling weapons systems to enemy governments, for example ..."

"Then either Clayton or his bosses could have had Deborah killed if she threatened to blow the whistle?"

"Yes."

"And whoever killed Ellen Gilchrist simply chose a random victim to implicate Pierce?"

Gristhorpe shrugged. "Nothing simpler. Not to people like that."

"But they didn't bargain on Barry Stott's ego."

"'The best laid plans ...'"

"Why wait so long?" Banks asked. "That's what I don't understand. Deborah cracked the computer around 20 August—if indeed that's what happened—and she wasn't killed until 6 November. That's nearly three months."

Gristhorpe scratched his stubbly chin. "You've got me there," he said. "But there could be an explanation. Maybe it took her that long to fathom out what she'd got. Or maybe it took Clayton that long to figure out someone had been tampering. You know how quickly things change, Alan. Maybe the information she got didn't actually *mean* anything until three months later, when other things happened."

Banks nodded. "It's possible. But I'm not sure even Deborah was bright enough to understand Clayton's electronic schematics. I know I'm not. I saw some of them the other day and they left me dizzy."

"Well, you know what a Luddite I am when it comes to computers," Gristhorpe said. "But it could have been something obvious to her. She didn't have to understand it fully, just recognize a reference, a name or something. Perhaps someone else she knew was involved?"

"Okay," said Banks. "But we're letting our imaginations run away with us. Would Clayton even be likely to enter such important information in his notebook? Anyway, I've got a simple suggestion: why don't we bring Spinks in? See if we can't get the truth out of him?"

"Good idea," said Gristhorpe.

"And this time," Banks added, "I think we might even have something to bargain with."

II

Where was he? Swiss Cottage, that was it. London. The cash register rang and the swell of small-talk and laughter rolled up and down. He thought he could hear the distant rumble of thunder from outside, feel the tension before the storm, that electrical smell in the air, like burning dust in church.

After the police set him free he had gone back home, pushed through the throng of reporters, then got in his car and driven off, leaving everything behind. He hadn't known where he was heading, at least not consciously. Mostly, he was still in a daze over what had happened: not only his release, but the fact that someone must have deliberately set out to frame him.

And, as he told the police, the only person who hated him that much was Michelle.

They didn't seem to suspect her—they were sure it was a man, for a start—but Owen knew her better. He wouldn't put it past her. If she hadn't done it herself she might have enlisted someone, used her sex to manipulate some poor, sick bastard, the way she did so well.

So with these thoughts half-formed, one moment seeming utterly fantastic and absurd and the next feeling so real they had to be true, he had found himself heading for London, and now he was drinking in Swiss Cottage, trying to pluck up courage to go and challenge Michelle directly.

He was interested to find out what she would have to say if he turned up on her doorstep. Even if she hadn't engineered the murders to discredit him, she had slandered him in the newspapers. He knew that *for a fact*. Oh, yes. He was looking forward to hearing what she had to say for herself.

"Are you all right, mate?"

"Pardon?" It was the man next to him. He had turned his head in Owen's direction.

"I said are you all right?"

"Yes, yes ... fine." Owen realized he must have been muttering to himself. The man gave him a suspicious look and turned away.

Time to go. It was nine o'clock. What day of the week? Tuesday? Wednesday? Did it really matter? There was a good chance she'd be in. People who work nine-to-five usually stay in on weeknights, or at least get home early.

He found the telephone and the well-thumbed directory hanging beside it. Some of the pages had been torn out or defaced with felt-tipped pens, but not the one that counted. He slid his finger down until he came to her name: Chappel. No first name, just the initials, M.E. Michelle Elizabeth. There was her number.

Owen's chest tightened as he searched his pockets for a coin. He felt dizzy and had to lean against the wall a moment before dialling. Two men passed on their way out and gave him funny looks. When they had gone, he took four deep breaths to steady himself, picked up the phone, put the coin in and dialled. He let it ring once, twice, three times, four, and on the fifth ring a woman's voice said, rather testily, "Yes, who is it?"

It was *her* voice. No doubt about it. Owen would recognize that reedy quality with its little-girlish hint of a lisp anywhere.

He held the phone away and heard her repeat the question more loudly—"Look, who is it?"

After he still said nothing, she said, "Pervert," and hung up on him.

Owen looked at the receiver for a moment, then he smiled and walked out into the gathering storm.

III

John Spinks didn't seem particularly surprised to find himself back at Eastvale nick shortly after dark that evening. As predicted, he had been at the Swainsdale Centre bragging to his mates about how he spent the weekend in jail and gone up before the magistrate. The arrival of two large uniformed officers only added more credibility to his tales, and he got quite a laugh, the officers told

Banks, when he stuck out his hands for the cuffs, just like he'd seen people do on television.

He did look surprised, however, to find himself in Banks's office rather than a smelly interview room. And he looked even more surprised when Banks offered unlimited coffee, cigarettes and biscuits.

Gristhorpe and Banks had decided to tackle him together, to attempt a good-cop bad-cop approach. Spinks already knew Banks, but the superintendent was an unknown quantity, and though his baby blue eyes had instilled fear into more villains than a set of thumbscrews, Gristhorpe could appear the very model of benevolence. He also outranked Banks, which was another card to play. They had Stafford Oakes waiting in Gristhorpe's own office, should their plan be successful.

"Right, John," said Banks, "I won't beat about the bush. You're in trouble, a lot of trouble."

Spinks sniffed as if trouble were his business. "Yeah, right."

"Not only have we got you on taking and driving away," Banks went on, "but when our men searched your house, they found sufficient quantities of crack cocaine, Ecstasy and LSD for us to bring some serious drug-dealing charges against you."

"I told you, that stuff wasn't mine."

"Whose was it, then?"

"I don't know her name. Just some slag spent the night there. She must've forgotten it."

"You expect me to believe that someone would leave a fortune in drugs behind? In *your* bedroom? Come off it, John, that stuff's yours until someone else claims it, and it'll be a cold day in hell before that happens."

Spinks bit on his lower lip. He was starting to look less like a Hollywood dream-boy and more like a frightened teenager. A lock of hair slid over his eye; he started chewing his fingernails. Bravado could only take someone so far, Banks thought, but he knew it would be a mistake to act as if he were shooting fish in a barrel. Stupidity, along with stubbornness, can be valuable resources when all the big guns are turned on you. And they had served Spinks well for eighteen years.

"Got anything to say?" Banks asked.

Spinks shrugged. "I told you. It's not mine. You can't prove it is."

"We can prove whatever we want," Banks said. "A judge or a jury has only to take one look at you to throw away the key."

"My brief says—"

"These legal-aid briefs are about as useful as a sieve in a flood, John. You ought to know that. Overworked and underpaid."

"Yeah, well, my brief says you can't pin it on me. The drugs."

Banks raised his eyebrows. "She did? That's really bad news, John," he said, shaking his head. "I thought things were pretty bad, but I didn't realize that lawyers were setting up in practice before they even finished their degrees these days."

"Ha fucking ha."

The other chair creaked as Gristhorpe leaned forward. "My chief inspector might be acting a little harshly towards you, son," he said. "See, it's personal with him. He lost a son to drugs."

Spinks squinted at Banks. "Tracy never said nothing about that."

"She doesn't like to talk about it," said Banks quickly. They had decided to improvise according to responses and circumstances, but Gristhorpe had thrown him a spinner here. He smiled to himself. Why not? Play the game. As far as he knew, Brian was alive and well and still studying architecture in Portsmouth, but there was no reason for Spinks to know that.

"Like everyone his age," Banks went on, "he thought he was immortal, indestructible. He thought it couldn't happen to him. Anyone else, sure. But not him." He leaned forward and clasped his hands. "Now, I don't give a tinker's whether you smoke so much crack your brains blow out of your arsehole, but I *do* care very much that you're selling to others, especially to a crowd that at one time included my daughter. Do we understand one another?"

Spinks shifted in his chair. "What's this all about? What you after? A confession? I'm not saying anything. My brief—"

"Fuck your brief," said Banks, thumping the rickety metal desk. "And fuck *you*! Do you understand what I'm saying?"

Spinks looked rattled. Gristhorpe cut in again and said to Banks, "I don't think it's really appropriate to talk that way to Mr Spinks, Chief Inspector," he said. "I'm sure he understands you perfectly well."

"Sorry, sir," said Banks, wiping his brow with the back of his hand. "Got a bit carried away." He fumbled for a cigarette and lit it.

"You his boss?" Spinks asked, turning, wide-eyed, to look at Gristhorpe. "He called you 'sir.'"

"I thought I'd already made that clear," Gristhorpe said, then he winked. "Don't worry, son. I won't let him off his leash."

He looked back at Banks, who had removed his jacket and was loosening his tie. "He ought to be locked up, that one," Spinks went on, emboldened. "And his mate. The fat one. Hit me once, he did. Bounced my nose off a fucking table."

"Aye, well, people get carried away sometimes," said Gristhorpe. "Stress of the job. The thing is, though, that he's right in a way. You *are* in a lot of trouble. Right now, we're about the only friends you've got."

"Friends?"

"Yes," said Banks, catching his attention again. "Believe it or not, John, I'm going to do you the biggest favour anyone's ever done you in your life."

Spinks narrowed his eyes. "Oh yeah? Why should I believe you?"

"You should. In years to come you might even thank me for it. You're eighteen now, John, there's no getting around that. With the kind of charges you're looking at, you'll go to jail, no doubt about it. Hard time. Now I know you're a big boy, a tough guy and all the rest, but think about it. *Think.* It's not only a matter of getting buggered morning, afternoon and evening, of giving blow-jobs at knife-point, maybe catching AIDS, but it's a life of total deprivation, John. The food's lousy, the plumbing stinks and there's no-one to complain to. And when you get out—if you get out—however many years later, you'll have lost a good part of your youth. All you'll know is prison life. And you know what, John? You'll be back in there like a flash. It's called *recidivism.* Look it up, John. Call it a sort of death wish, but someone like you gets institutionalized and he can't survive on the outside. He gets to need jail. And as for the blow-jobs and the buggery ..." Banks shrugged. "Well, I'm sure you'd even get to like that after a while."

Banks's monologue produced no discernible effect on Spinks, as he had suspected it wouldn't. It was intended only to soften him to the point of accepting a deal. Banks knew that Spinks was already doomed to exactly the kind of existence he had just laid out for him, but that he couldn't, wouldn't, recognize the fact, and wasn't capable of making the changes necessary to avoid it.

No. What they were about to offer was simple, temporary relief, the chance for Spinks to walk free and keep on doing exactly what he was doing until the next time he got caught, if he didn't kill himself or someone else first. A sprat to catch a mackerel. Very sad, but very true.

"So what is this big favour you're going to do me?"

"First," said Banks, "you're going to tell us the truth about what happened last August. You're going to tell us how you stole Michael Clayton's car and his computer and *exactly* what happened after that."

Spinks paled a little but stood his ground. "Why would I want to do something like that?"

"To avoid jail."

"You mean confess to one crime and get off on another one?"

"Something like that."

"Christ, you're worse than the bloody criminals, you lot are." He turned to Gristhorpe. "Can he do that?" he asked. "Has he got the authority?"

"I have," said Gristhorpe softly. "I'm a superintendent, remember?"

"Don't we need a lawyer or something?"

"What's wrong, John?" said Banks. "Don't trust us?"

"I don't trust *you*. Anyway, why talk to the monkey when the organ-grinder's here?"

Banks smiled. It was working. And he hadn't denied stealing Clayton's car yet.

"There's a Crown attorney in the building," said Gristhorpe, "and he can deal with the particulars about the charges and likely sentences, if you want to talk to him."

Spinks squinted. "Maybe I'll do that. What's the deal?"

"You tell us what we want to know," said Gristhorpe, "and we'll see you stay out of jail. Dealing becomes simple possession."

"That's not enough. I want all charges dropped."

Gristhorpe shook his head. "Sorry, son. We can't do that. You see, the paperwork's already in the system."

"You can lose it."

"Maybe the odd sheet or two," said Gristhorpe. "But not all of it. The lawyer will explain it."

Spinks sat silently, brow furrowed in thought.

Banks stood up. "I've had enough of this," he said to Gristhorpe. "I told you it was no use. His brain's so addled he doesn't even recognize a piece of good fortune when he trips over it. Besides, it makes me puke sitting with a drug-dealing moron like him. Let him go to jail. He belongs there. Let him catch AIDS. See if I care." And he headed towards the door.

"Wait, just a minute," said Spinks, holding his hand up. "Hold your horses. I haven't said anything yet."

"That's the problem," said Gristhorpe. "You'd better make your mind up quickly, sonny. You don't get chances like this every day. We can probably get it down to probation, maybe a bit of community service, but you can't just walk away from it."

Spinks glared at Banks, who stood scowling with his hand on the doorknob, then looked back at Gristhorpe, all benevolence and forgiveness. Then he put his feet on Banks's desk. "All right," he said. "All right. You've got a deal. Get the brief in."

IV

Large raindrops blotched the pavement when Owen left the pub. Lightning flickered in the north and the thunder grumbled like God's empty stomach. The drinkers out on the muggy street hurried inside before the deluge arrived.

Owen felt light-headed after all the drinks, and he knew he wasn't thinking clearly. Booze had made him just brave and foolhardy enough to face Michelle.

He walked along the main road past pubs and shops open late, head bowed, jacket collar turned up in a futile attempt to keep dry. Shop-lights and street-lights smeared the pavement and gutter.

Hair that had been damp with sweat before was now plastered to his skull by rain.

He had forgotten exactly where he parked his car, but it didn't matter. Michelle's place couldn't be far.

He stopped a young couple coming out of a pub and asked them where her street was. They gave him directions as they fiddled with their umbrella. As he suspected, it was only a couple of hundred yards up the road, then left, short right and left again. He thanked them and walked on, aware of them standing watching him from behind.

Now he knew he was going to see her, his mind shot off in all directions. She wouldn't want to let him in, of course, not after what she had tried to do to him, not after what she had said about him.

Did he feel reckless enough to break in? Maybe. He didn't know. Given the address, her flat would probably be in one of those three- or four-storey London houses. Perhaps if he waited outside for her to go out, approached her in the street … She might have to go to the shop or go out to meet someone. But it was a bit late in the evening for that. Maybe if he waited until one of the other tenants went in, he could get to the door before it locked and at least gain entry to the building.

A white sports car honked as he crossed a sidestreet against a red light. He flicked the driver the V sign, then caught his foot on the kerb and stumbled, bumping into an elderly man walking his dog in the rain. The man gave him a dirty look, adjusted his spectacles and walked on.

He turned left where the couple had told him to and found himself the only pedestrian in quiet backstreets. The houses were all about three storeys high, divided into flats, with a buzzer and intercom by the front door. It wouldn't be easy.

Many rooms were lit, some without curtains, and as he walked he looked in the windows and saw fragments of blue wall, the top corner of a bookshelf, a framed Dali print, an ornate chandelier, flickering television pictures, two people talking, a cat sitting on the window-sill watching the rain—a panorama of life.

The walk had taken some of the steam out of Owen, but he still wanted to see Michelle face to face, if only to watch her squirm as he accused her of her crimes.

He climbed the steps and looked at the list by the door. M.E. Chappel, Flat 4. Would that be on the first or second floor? He didn't know. He crossed the street and looked up. Both second-floor windows were in darkness, as were those on the ground floor. On the first floor, bluish light filtered through the curtains of one, and the other was open to reveal a William Morris wall-paper design. That wasn't Michelle at all. The blue room was more like her.

He stood in the shadows wondering what to do. Rain drummed down, an oily sheen on the street. He didn't feel as brave now as he had on leaving the pub. The booze had worn off, and he had a headache. He needed another drink, but it was close to eleven; the pubs would be closing. Besides, Michelle would probably be going to bed soon. Now he was here, he couldn't wait until tomorrow.

A man and a woman huddled together under an umbrella approached the house, turned up the path and climbed the steps. The way they walked, Owen guessed they were a little tipsy. Probably unemployed and didn't have to go to work in the morning. He shrank back into the shadows. The man said some-thing, and the woman laughed. She shook out her umbrella over the steps. It wasn't Michelle.

When she turned back to the door, Owen hurried across the street behind them. It was a hell of a long shot, but it might just work. They had their backs turned, the street wasn't well lit, and they couldn't hear him because of the rain and the rumbles of thunder. Adrenalin pumped him up and seemed to rekindle some of the earlier bravado. He was close now. It all depended on how slowly the door closed on its spring behind them.

As soon as they were both inside and the man let go of the door, Owen dashed on tiptoe up the steps and put his hand out. He stopped the door just before it had completely swung back and relatched.

He looked around at the houses across the street. As far as he could make out, nobody was watching him. He heard another door open and close inside the building, and the lights went on in one of the ground floor flats.

Softly, Owen pushed the front door open and slipped inside.

V

Stafford Oakes quickly assured Spinks that the charges against him could be reduced to a manageable level—the drugs, especially. Add that he had no prior record, that he had been upset over a missed job opportunity and any number of other mitigating circumstances that affected his stress-level when he stole and crashed the car, and he'd probably get a few month's community service. Lucky community.

"So," Banks asked him when Oakes had left. "Why don't you tell us about it? Then we'll get the Crown to put the lesser charges in writing. More coffee? Cigarette."

Spinks shrugged. "Why not."

Banks poured from the carafe he had had sent up. "Off the record," he asked, "did you steal Michael Clayton's car on 20 August last year?"

Spinks snapped the filter off the cigarette and lit it. "I don't remember the exact date, but it was around then. And I didn't *steal* it. Just borrowed it for a quick spin, that's all."

"Why?"

"What do you mean, why? Because he treated me like shit, that's why. Fucking snob. Like I wasn't good enough to wipe his precious goddaughter's nose with."

"This was just after he and Lady Harrison found you and Deborah drinking wine in the back garden?"

"Yeah. We weren't doing no harm. Just having a barbie and a drop or two of the old vino. He acted like it was too good for the likes of me. It was only a fucking bottle of wine, for Christ's sake. He'd no call to be so rude to me, calling me an idle lout and a thickie and all that. It's not my fault I can't get a job, is it?"

"And you did some damage to the car, for revenge?"

"No. It was an accident. I was still learning, wasn't I? That car's got a very sensitive accelerator."

From what Banks had heard of Spinks's driving history so far, it might be a good idea if the court could somehow prevent him from ever getting a licence. Not that it seemed to have stopped him so far.

"Did you also take a notebook computer out of the car?"

"It was in the back seat under a coat."

"Did you take it?"

Spinks looked at Gristhorpe. "It's all right, sonny," the superintendent said, "you can answer any question Chief Inspector Banks asks you with complete impunity."

"Uh? Come again."

"No blame attached. It's all off the record. None of it is being recorded or written down. Remember what the solicitor told you. Relax. Feel free."

Spinks drank some coffee. "Yes," he said. "I thought it might be worth something."

"And was it?"

He shrugged. "Piss all. Bloke on the market offered me seventy-five measly quid."

And the market vendor was reselling it for a hundred and fifty, Banks remembered. A hundred and fifty quid for a six-thousand-pound computer. "So you sold it to him?"

"That's right."

"Before you sold it, did you use it at all?"

"Me? No. Don't know how to work those things, do I?"

"What about Deborah?"

"What about her?"

"She was a bright girl. Studied computers at school. She'd know how to get it going."

"Yeah, well ..."

"You *were* still seeing Deborah at that time, weren't you?"

"Yeah."

"And did she ever visit your house?"

"Yeah. Once or twice. Turned her nose up, though. Said it smelled and it was dirty." He laughed. "Wouldn't use the toilet, no matter how much she wanted to go."

"Right," said Banks. "Now what I'd like to know, John, is did Deborah have a go with the computer?"

"Yeah, well, she did, as a matter of fact." He turned to Gristhorpe, as if for confirmation that he could continue with impunity. Gristhorpe nodded like a priest. Spinks went on, "Yeah. Deb, she was with me, like, when I ... you know ... went for a ride."

"Deborah was with you when you stole Michael Clayton's car?"

"Yeah, that's what I said. Only don't use that word 'stole.' I don't like it. See, it was even more in the family with her being there wasn't it? Just like borrowing the family car, really."

"Did you ever tell him it was the two of you who'd 'borrowed' his car?"

"Course not. You think I'm stupid or something?"

"Go on."

"Anyway, she didn't like the idea at first. No bottle, hadn't Deb. But soon as I got us inside, quiet as could be, like, and got that Swedish engine purring, she took to it like a duck to water, didn't she? It was Deb noticed the computer. Said she was surprised Clayton let it out of his sight given as how he was the kind of bloke couldn't even jot down a dental appointment without putting it on his computer. I said let's just leave it. But she said no, she wanted to have a go on it."

"So what did you do?"

"After we'd finished with the car we went back to my house. My mum was out, as usual, and I was feeling a bit randy by then, after a nice fast drive. I fancied a bit of the other, but she went all funny, like she did sometimes, and after a while I didn't even want it any more. She had a way like that, you know. She could be really off-putting, really cold."

"The computer, John?"

"Yeah, well once Deb got it going I couldn't drag her away from it."

"What about the password?"

"Whatever it was, if there was one, it didn't take her very long. I will say this, though, she seemed a bit surprised at how easy it was."

"The password?"

"Whatever it took to get the bloody thing going."

"What did she say?"

"'Well, bugger me!' Not exactly those words, mind you, but that was the feeling. She didn't like to swear didn't Deb. More like gosh or golly or something."

"And then?"

Spinks shrugged. "Then she just played around with it for a while. I got bored and went upstairs for a lie-down."

"Was she still playing with it when you went back down?"

"Just finishing. It looked like she was taking something out of it. One of those little square things, what do you call them?"

"A diskette?"

"That's right."

"Where did she get it from?"

"I don't know. The computer was in a carrying case and there were a whole bunch them there, in little pockets, like. I suppose that's where she got it from."

"What did she do with it?"

"Put it in her pocket."

"Any idea what was on it?"

"No. I asked her what she was up to but she told me to mind my own business."

"Did she do anything else with computer?"

"Yeah. She tapped a few keys, watched the screen for a while, smiled to herself, funny like, then turned it off."

"And then?"

"She told me I could sell it if I wanted and keep the money." He looked towards Gristhorpe. "I mean, she practically gave it to me, right? And it was in the family. Well, he was her godfather, anyway. That has to count, doesn't it."

"It's all right," Gristhorpe assured him. "You're doing fine. Just keep on answering the questions as fully and as honestly as you can."

Spinks nodded.

"Did she tell you at any time what she'd found on the computer?"

"No. I mean, I didn't pester her about it. I could tell she didn't want to say anything. If you ask me she found out he'd been fiddling the books or something."

"What makes you say that?"

"Stands to reason, doesn't it?"

"Did she ever refer to the incident again?"

"No. Well, it wasn't much more than a week or so later when her mother caught us in bed. Then it was cards for me. On your bike, mate."

"Do you know if Michael Clayton ever found out that you took it, or that Deborah used it?"

"I certainly didn't tell him. Maybe Deb did, but neither of them ever said anything to me about it."

"And you got your seventy-five quid?"

"Right."

"Is there anything else?"

"No, that's everything. I've told you everything." He looked at Gristhorpe. "Can I go now?"

"Alan?"

Banks nodded.

"Aye, lad," said Gristhorpe. "Off you go."

"You won't forget our deal, will you?"

Gristhorpe shook his head. Spinks cast a triumphant grin at Banks and left.

"Christ," said Banks. "I need a drink to get the taste of shit out of my mouth after that."

Gristhorpe laughed. "Worth it, though, wasn't it. Come on, I'll buy. We've got a bit of thinking to do before we decide on our next move."

But they hadn't got further than the stairs when Banks heard his telephone ring. He looked at his watch. Almost ten-thirty.

"I'd better take it," he said. "Why don't you go ahead. I'll meet you over there."

"I'll wait," said Gristhorpe. "It might be important." They went into the office and Banks picked up the phone.

"Chief Inspector Banks?"

"Yes."

"It's Vjeko. Vjeko Batorac." The voice sounded a little muffled and hoarse.

"Vjeko. What is it? Is something wrong?"

"I thought I should tell you that Ive Jelačić was just here. We fought. He hit me."

"What happened, Vjeko? Start from the beginning."

Vjeko took a deep breath. "Ive came here about a half an hour ago and he was a carrying a book of some kind. A notebook, I thought. It was a diary, bound in good leather, written in English.

He said he thought it would make him rich. He couldn't read English so he brought it to me to tell him what it said. He said he would give me money." Vjeko paused. "That girl, the one who was killed, her name was Deborah Harrison, wasn't it?"

"Yes." Banks felt his grip tighten on the receiver. "Go on, Vjeko."

"It was *her* diary. I asked him where he got it, but he wouldn't tell me. He wanted me to translate for him."

"Did you?"

"I looked at it. Then I told him it was nothing important, not worth anything, and he should leave it with me. I'd throw it away."

"What happened then?"

"He became suspicious. He thought I'd found out something and wanted to cheat him out of his money. I think he was hoping to find someone he could blackmail. He said he'd take it to Mile. Mile can read some English, too. I said it was worthless and there was no point. He tried to snatch it from my hand. I held on and we struggled. He is stronger than me, Chief Inspector. He hit me. Dragica was screaming and little Jelena started crying. It was terrible."

"What happened?"

"Ive ran away with the diary."

"You said you read it?"

"Some of it."

"What did it say?"

"If I am right, Chief Inspector, that girl was in terrible trouble. I think you should send someone to get it right away before Ive does something crazy with it."

"Thanks, Vjeko," Banks said, already reaching out to cut the call off. "Stay where you are. I'm calling West Yorkshire CID right now. Jelačić was heading for Mile Pavelič's house, you said?"

VI

Owen walked up the carpeted stairs in the dark to the first-floor landing. There, he found a timer-switch on the wall and turned the light on. He knocked on the door of Flat 4, noticing it didn't have a peep-hole, and held his breath. The odds were that, if she had friends in the building, especially friends who were in the habit of dropping by to borrow a carton of milk or to have a chat, she would open it. After all, nobody had buzzed her, and not just anyone could walk in from the street.

He heard the floor creak behind the door and saw the knob begin to turn. What if it was on a chain? What if she were living with someone? His heart beat fast. Slowly the door opened.

"Yes?" Michelle said.

No chain.

Owen pushed. Michelle fell back into the room and the door swung fully open. He shut it behind him and leaned back on it. Michelle had stumbled into her sofa. She was wearing a dark-blue robe, silky in texture, and it had come open at the front. Quickly, she wrapped it around herself and looked at him.

"You. What the hell do you want?" There was more anger than fear in her voice.

"That's a good question, that is, after what you've done to me."

"You've been drinking. You're drunk."

"So what?"

"I'm going to call the police."

Michelle lunged for the telephone but Owen got there first and knocked it off its stand. This wasn't going the way he had hoped. He had just wanted to talk, find out why she had it in for him, but she was making it difficult.

They faced each other like hunter and prey for a few seconds, completely still, breathing hard, muscles tense, then she ran for the door. Owen got there first and pushed her away. This time she tipped backwards over the arm of the sofa. Owen walked towards her. Her robe had risen up high over her thighs and split open at her loins to show the triangle of curly golden hair. Owen stopped in his tracks. Michelle gave him a cool, scornful look, covered herself up and sat down.

"Well, then," she said, pushing her hair back behind her ears. "So you're here. I must admit I'm a bit surprised, but maybe I shouldn't be." She reached for a cigarette and lit it with a heavy table-lighter, blowing the smoke out through her nose. He remembered the mingled taste of tobacco and toothpaste on her mouth in bed after lovemaking. "Why don't you sit down?" she said.

"Aren't you frightened?"

Michelle laughed and put her little pink tongue between her teeth. "Should I be?"

Her blue eyes looked cool, in control. Her long, smooth neck rose out of the gown, elegant and graceful. Even at twenty-four she still looked like a teenager. It was partly the flawless, marble complexion, the delicately chiselled nose and lips whose fine lines any sculptor would be proud of.

But it was mostly in her character, Owen realized, not her looks. She was the cruel teenager who called others names, the leader of the gang who suggested new cruelties, new kicks, with not a care in the world for the feelings of the ones she bullied and taunted.

"If you really believe I murdered those women, then you should be scared," he said. "They looked like you, you know."

"You were killing me by proxy. Is that what you're saying?"

"Can you give me one good reason why I shouldn't? You're not afraid because you know I didn't do it. Am I right?"

"Well," Michelle said, "I really found it hard to believe you had the guts, I'll admit. But then I was mistaken enough to think it takes guts to strangle a woman."

"And you found out different?"

She frowned. "What do you mean?"

"You did it, didn't you, Michelle? I'm not sure about the first one, about Deborah Harrison, but you did the second, didn't you? You killed her to frame me. Or you got someone to do it."

Michelle laughed and glanced towards the door again. "You're mad," she said. "Paranoid. If you think I'd do something like that, go to all that trouble, you're insane." She stood up and walked over to the cocktail cabinet. Her legs swished against the robe. Owen stayed close to her. "I'd offer you a drink," she said, "but I think you've had too much already."

"Why did you do it, Michelle? For God's sake why?"

She raised her eyebrows. "Why did I do what?"

"You know what I mean. Kill that girl to implicate me. You broke into my house, stole the film container with my fingerprints on it and took hairs from my pillow. Then you messed the place up to make it look like a hate-crime."

Michelle shook her head "You're crazy." She poured neat Scotch into a crystal glass. Owen could see her hand was shaking.

"And what you said to the police about us," he pressed on. "That stuff in the newspapers. Why did you tell those lies about me?"

"They paid well." She laughed. "Not the police, the newspapers. And I didn't kill anyone. Don't be an idiot, Owen. I couldn't do anything like that. Besides, I didn't tell any lies."

"You *know* it didn't happen like that."

"It's all versions, Owen. That's how it happened from my perspective. I'm willing to admit yours might be different. I'm sorry. I know I shouldn't sound so ungrateful. You did help me through college. You helped me financially, you gave me somewhere to live, and you certainly helped with my marks. It was fun for a while … But you'd no right to start spying on me, following me everywhere I went. You didn't own me. And you had no right to throw me out in the street like that. Nobody ever treats me like that." Her eyes blazed like ice.

"Fun … for a while? Michelle, I was in love with you. We were going to … I can't believe you'd say that, make it all sound so meaningless. Why do you hate me so much?"

She shrugged. "I don't hate you. I just don't give a damn about you one way or another."

"You bitch."

Owen stepped towards her. She stood her ground by the cabinet and sipped her drink. Then she jerked her head back to toss her hair over her shoulders again. It was a gesture he remembered. She looked at him down her nose, lips curled in a sneer of contempt.

"Oh, come on, Owen," she said, twisting the belt of her robe around one finger. "You can do better than that. Or can't you? Do you have to murder schoolgirls these days to get your rocks off?" The smile tormented him: a little crooked, icy in the eyes and wholly malevolent. "I'm glad you've found something that turns you on at last. What are you going to do, Owen? Kill me, too? Do you know what? I don't think you can do it. That's why you have to do it to the schoolgirls and pretend it's me. Isn't that true, Owen?"

Owen snatched the tumbler from her hand and tossed it back in one.

"More Dutch courage? Is that what you need? I still don't believe—"

He didn't know how it happened. One moment he was looking at his own reflection in her pupils, and the next he had his hands around her throat. He shoved her back against the cabinet, knocking bottles and glasses over. She clawed at his eyes, but her arms weren't long enough. She scratched and pulled at his wrists, making gurgling sounds deep in her throat, back bent over the cabinet, feet off the ground, kicking him.

He was throttling her for everything she'd ever done to him: for being a faithless whore and spreading her legs for anyone who took her out for an expensive dinner; for telling the whole country he was a sick pervert who would be in jail if there were any real sting in the justice system; for framing him.

And he was strangling her for everything else, too: his arrest; the humiliation and indignity of jail; the loss of his friends, his job. The whole edifice that had been his life exploded in a red cloud and his veins swelled with rage. For all that, and for treating him like a fool, like someone she could keep on a string and order around. Someone she didn't even believe had the courage to kill her.

He pressed his fingers deep into her throat. One of her wild kicks found his groin. He flinched in pain but held on, shoving her hard up against the wall. She was sitting on the top of the cabinet among the broken crystal and spilled liquor, her legs wrapped around him in a parody of the sex act. He could smell gin and whisky. The robe under her thighs was sodden with blood and booze, as if she had wet herself.

Michelle continued to flail around, knocking over more bottles, making rasping sounds. Once she pushed forward far enough that her nails raked his cheek, just missing his eyes.

But just as suddenly as it had started, it was over. Owen loosened his grip on her throat and she slid off the cabinet onto the floor, leaning back against it, not moving.

Someone hammered on the door and yelled, "Michelle! Are you all right?"

Owen stood for a moment trying to catch his breath and grasp the enormity of what he had done, then he opened the door and rushed past the puzzled neighbour back down to the street.

VII

"I think Deborah Harrison lied to her mother about losing her diary," Banks said to Gristhorpe as they waited for Ken Blackstone's call. It was well after closing-time. No hope of a pint now. "I think she kept it hidden."

"So it would seem," Gristhorpe agreed. "The question is, how did it get into Jelačić's hands? We already know he couldn't have been in Eastvale the evening she was killed. Even if the diary had been in her satchel, Jelačić couldn't have taken it."

"I think I know the answer to that," Banks said. "Rebecca Charters surprised someone in the graveyard yesterday, in the wooded area behind the Inchcliffe Mausoleum. I thought nothing of it at the time—she didn't get a good look at whoever it was— but now it seems too much of a coincidence. I'll bet you a pound to a penny it was Jelačić."

"It was hidden there?"

Banks nodded. "And he knew where. He'd seen her hide it. When Pierce was released, and I went to question Jelačić again last week, he must have remembered it and thought there might be some profit in getting hold of it. It's ironic, really. That open satchel always bothered me. When I first saw it, I thought the killer might have taken something incriminating and most likely got rid of it. But Lady Harrison told me Deborah had lost her diary. I saw no reason why either of them would lie about that."

"Unless there were secrets in it that Deborah didn't want anyone to stumble across?"

"Or Lady Harrison. If you think about it, either of them could have lied. Sir Geoffrey had already told me that Deborah *did have* a diary, so his wife could hardly deny its existence."

"But she *could* say Deborah had told her she lost it, and we'd have no way of checking."

"Yes. And we probably wouldn't even bother looking for it. Which we didn't."

"Didn't the SOCOs search the graveyard the day after Deborah's murder?"

"They did a ground search. We weren't looking for a murder weapon, just Deborah's knickers and anything the killer might have dropped in the graveyard. All we found were a few empty fag packets and some butts. Most of those were down to Jelačić, who we knew had worked in the graveyard anyway. We put the rest down to St Mary's girls sneaking out for a smoke. Besides, it's only in books that murderers stand around smoking in the fog while they wait for their victims. Especially now everyone knows we've a good chance of getting DNA from saliva."

"What about the Inchcliffe Mausoleum? Deborah could have gained access to that, couldn't she?"

"Yes. But we searched that, too, after we found the empty bottles. At least—"

The phone rang. Banks grabbed the receiver.

"Alan, it's Ken Blackstone. Sorry it took so long."

"Any luck?"

"We've got him."

"Great. Did he give you any trouble?"

"He picked up a bruise or two in the struggle. Turns out he'd just left Pavelić's house when our lads arrived. They followed him across the waste ground. He saw them coming and made a bolt for it, right across York Road and down into Richmond Hill. When they finally caught up with him he didn't have the diary."

Banks's spirits dropped. "Didn't have it? But, Ken—"

"Hold your horses, mate. Seems he dumped it when he realized he was being chased. Didn't want to be caught with any incriminating evidence on him. Anyway, our lads went back over the route he'd taken and we found it in a rubbish bin on York Road."

Banks breathed a sigh of relief.

"What do you want us to do with him?" Blackstone asked. "It's midnight now. It'll be going on for two in the morning by the time we get him to Eastvale."

"You can sit on him overnight," Banks said. "Nobody in this case is going anywhere in a hurry. Have him brought up in the morning. But, Ken—"

"Yes, it is Deborah Harrison's diary."

"Have you read it?"

"Enough."

"And?"

"If it means what I think it does, Alan, it's dynamite."

"Tell me about it."

And Blackstone told him.

TWENTY

I

At ten o'clock the next morning, with Jelačić cooling his heels in a cell downstairs, Banks sat at his desk, coffee in hand, lit a cigarette and opened Deborah Harrison's diary. Ken Blackstone had given him the gist of it over the phone the previous evening—and he had not slept well in consequence—but he wanted to read it for himself before making his next move.

Like the inside of the satchel flap, it was inscribed with her name and address in gradually broadening circles, from "Deborah Catherine Harrison" to "The Universe."

First he checked the section for names, addresses and telephone numbers, but found nothing out of the ordinary, only family and school friends. Then he started to flip the pages.

He soon found that many of her entries were factual, with little attempt at analysis or poetic description. Some days she had left completely blank. And it wasn't until summer, when she had supposedly "lost" it, that the diary got really interesting:

5 August

Yawn. This must be the most boring summer there has ever been in my entire existence. Went shopping today in the Swainsdale Centre, just for something to do. What a grim place. Absolutely no decent shoes there at all and full of local yokels and horrible scruffy women dragging around even more horrible dirty children. I must work hard on mummy and persuade her to take me shopping to Paris again soon or I swear I shall just die from the boredom of this terrible provincial town. In the shopping centre, I met that common little tart Tiffy Huxtable from dressage. She was with some friends and asked if I'd like to hang around with them. They didn't look very interesting. They were all just sitting around the fountain looking scruffy and stupid, but there was one fit lad there so I said I might drop by one day. Life is so (yawn) boring that I really might do. Oh, how I do so need an adventure.

There were no entries for the next few days, then came this:

9 *August*

Tiffy's crowd are a bunch of silly, common bores, just as I thought. All they can talk about is television and football and sex and pop music. I mean, really, darling, who gives a damn? I'm sure not one of them has read a book in years. Quite frankly, I'd rather stay at home and watch videos. Tracy Banks seems quite intelligent, but it turns out that she's a policeman's daughter, of all things. One boy looks a bit like that really cool actor from "Neighbours" and wears a great leather jacket. He really does have very nice eyes, too, with long lashes.

After that, things started to move quickly:

12 *August*

John (Oh, such disappointment! What a terribly common, dull and ordinary name, like "Tracy"!) stole a car tonight and took me for a joy-ride. Me!! Little miss goody-two-shoes. It was brill! If Daddy knew about it he would have apoplexy. It wasn't much of a car, just a poky little Astra, but he drove it really fast out past Helmthorpe and parked in a field. It was so exciting even though I was a bit frightened we'd get caught by the police. When we parked he was like an octopus! I told him I'm not the kind of girl who does it the first time you go out, even if he did steal a car for me. Lads! I ask you. He asked me what he could do the first time, and I told him we could just kiss. I really didn't mind when he put his tongue in my mouth but I wouldn't let him touch my breasts. I didn't tell him I had never done it before. Though I came close with Pierre at Montclair last year, and if he hadn't been too much in a hurry and had that little accident first we might have done it.

Then, three days later, she wrote:

15 August

Tonight, in another "borrowed" car, as John calls them, we actually did
it for the first time! I made him take a van this time, because it's cramped
in a little Astra, and we went in the back. I wasn't going to go all the
way at first but things just got out of control. It didn't hurt, like they
say it does. I don't know if I like it or not. I did feel excited and sinful
and wicked but I don't think I had an orgasm. I don't really know,
because I don't know what they feel like, but the earth didn't move or
anything like that, and I didn't hear bells ringing, just a funny feeling
between my legs and I felt a bit sore after. I wonder if I will ever have
multiple orgasms? Charlene Gregory at school told me she can have
orgasms just from the vibrations of the engine when she's on a bus, but
I don't believe her. And Kirsty McCracken says she can get them from
rubbing against her bicycle saddle while she's riding. Maybe that's true.
I sometimes feel a bit funny when I'm horse-riding. Anyway, when he
finished, it was really disgusting the way he just tied a knot in the
condom and threw it out of the window into the field, and then he didn't
even seem to want to talk to me all the way back. Is this what happens
when you give in to lads and let them have what they want? That's
what Mummy would say, even though she is French and they're
supposed to be so sexy and all.

17 August

John came to the house today. Mummy was out and he wanted us to go
and do it upstairs but I was too frightened we'd get caught. Anyway,
we barbecued some hot dogs on the back patio and I took a bottle of
Father's special wine from the cellar and we drank that. Of course,
Mother came home! She was very nice about it, really, but I could tell
she didn't like John. Uncle Michael was there, too, and I could tell he
really hated John on sight. John says nobody ever gives him a chance.

20 August

They all went to Leeds today—Mummy and Daddy and Uncle
Michael—to some naff cocktail party or other, so I told John he could
come over to the house again. This time I knew they'd be gone a long
time so we did it in my bed! How sinful! How wickedly, deliciously
sinful! I don't know if I had an orgasm or not, but I certainly tingled a

bit, and I didn't feel at all sore. John wants me to do it without a condom, but I told him not to be stupid. I wouldn't even think of it. I don't want to get pregnant with his baby or get some sexual disease. That hurt him, that I thought he would have some disease to pass on to me. He can be so childish at times. Childish and boring.

But it wasn't until a later entry that Banks found out for himself what Ken Blackstone meant when he said the diary might be "dynamite."

21 August

I can hardly believe it, Uncle Michael is in love with me! He says he has loved me since I was twelve, and has even spied on me getting undressed at Montclair. He says I look like Botticelli's Venus! Which is stretching it a bit, if you ask me. I remember seeing it in the Uffizi when Mummy and I went to Florence last year, and I don't look a bit like her. My hair's not as long, for a start, and it's a different colour. I never thought Uncle Michael knew literature and art at all. Some of what he wrote sounds very poetic. And it's all about me!! I don't know what I shall do. For the moment, it will be my little secret. He's not really my uncle of course, just my dad's friend, so I suppose it is all right for him to be in love with me, it's not incest. It feels funny, though, because I've known him forever. Oops, I forgot to say how I know. Last night John and me stole Uncle Michael's car because he was so beastly to him last week at the barbecue (now I know why: Uncle Michael must have been jealous!!). Well, Uncle Michael had left his computer in the back seat. We took it to John's house (and thank the lord his horrible smelly mother was out—she really gives me the creeps)—and I couldn't get into all his technical stuff but it only took me about fifteen minutes to get the password to his word-processing directories: it's MONT-CLAIR, of course. After that, it was easy. Uncle Michael puts every-thing on his computer, even his shopping-lists! When I'd finished, I reformatted his hard drive. That'll show him!

Banks put the diary aside and walked to the window. Mid-morning on a hot and humid June day, cobbled market square already full of cars and coaches. He wondered if this summer was going to be as hot as the last one. He hoped not. Naturally, there was no air-conditioning in Eastvale Divisional HQ, or in the whole of Eastvale, as far as he knew. You just had to make do with open windows and fans—not a lot of use when there's no breeze and the air is hot.

The diary wasn't evidence, of course. Deborah Harrison had read some of Michael Clayton's private files and discovered that he was sexually infatuated with her; it didn't mean that he had killed her. But as Banks sat down again and read on, it became increasingly clear that Clayton, in all likelihood, *had* killed Deborah.

The telephone rang. Banks picked it up and Sergeant Rowe told him there was a Detective Sergeant Leaside calling from Swiss Cottage.

Banks frowned; he didn't recognize the name. "Better put him on."

Leaside came on. "It's about a woman called Michelle Chappel," he said. "I understand from the PNC that she was part of a case you've been involved in recently up there?"

Banks gripped the receiver tightly. "Yes. Why? What's happened?"

"She's been assaulted, sir. Quite badly. Lacerations and bruises, attempted strangulation."

"Rape?"

"No, sir. I was wondering ... We got a description of the suspect from a neighbour ..." He read the description.

"Yes," Banks said when he'd finished. "Dammit, yes. That sounds like Owen Pierce. All right, thanks Sergeant. We'll keep an eye open for him."

II

Ive Jelačić was surly after his night in the cells. Banks had him brought up to an interview room and left him alone there for almost an hour before he and Superintendent Gristhorpe went in to ask their questions. They didn't turn the tape recorder on.

"Well, Ive," said Banks, "you're in a lot of trouble now, you know that?"

"What trouble? I do nothing."

"Where did you get that diary?"

"What diary? I never see that before. You policeman put it on me."

Banks sighed and rubbed his forehead. He could see it was going to be one of those days. "Ive," he said patiently, "both Mile Pavelič and Vjeko Batorac have seen you with the diary. You asked them to read it for you. You even hit Vjeko when he tried to hang onto it."

"I remember nothing of this. I do nothing wrong. Vjeko and I, we quarrel. Is not big deal."

"Come on, lad," said Gristhorpe, "help us out here."

"I know nothing."

Gristhorpe gestured for Banks to follow him out of the room. He did so, and they stood silently in the corridor for a few minutes before going back inside. It seemed to work; Jelačić was certainly more nervous than he had been before.

"Where you go?" he asked. "What you do?"

"Listen to me, Ive," said Banks. "I'm only going to say this once, and I'll say it slowly so that you understand every word. If it hadn't been for you, an innocent man might not have spent over six months in jail, suffered the indignity of a trial and incurred the wrath of the populace. In other words, you put Owen Pierce through hell, and even though he's free now, a lot of people still think he really killed the girls."

Jelačić shrugged. "Maybe he did. Maybe court was wrong."

"But more important even than Owen Pierce's suffering is Ellen Gilchrist's life. If it hadn't been for you, Ive Jelačić, that girl might not have had to die."

"I tell you before. In my country, many people die. Nobody ca—"

Banks slammed his fist on the flimsy table. "Shut up! I don't want to hear any more of your whining self-justification and self-pity, you snivelling little turd. Do you understand me?"

Jelačić's eyes were wide open now. He nodded and glanced over at Gristhorpe for reassurance he wasn't going to be left alone with this madman. Gristhorpe remained expressionless.

"Because of you, an innocent girl was brutally murdered. Now, I might not be able to charge you with murder, as I would like to do, but I'll certainly get something on you that'll put you away for a long, long time. Understand me?"

"I want lawyer."

"Shut up. You'll get a lawyer when we're good and ready to let you. For the moment, listen. Now, I don't think we'll have much trouble getting Daniel and Rebecca Charters to testify that you tried to extort money from them in order to alter the story you told against Daniel Charters. That's extortion, for a start. And we'll also get you for tampering with evidence, wasting police time and charges too numerous to mention. And do you know what will happen, Ive? We'll get you sent back to Croatia is what."

"No! You cannot do that. I am British citizen."

Banks looked at Gristhorpe and the two of them laughed. "Well, maybe that's true," Banks said. "But you do know who Deborah Harrison's father is, don't you? He's *Sir* Geoffrey Harrison. A very powerful and influential man when it comes to government affairs. Even you must know something of the way this country's run, Ive. What would you say for your chances now?"

Jelačić turned pale and started chewing his thumbnail.

"Are you going to co-operate?"

"I know nothing."

Banks leaned forward and rested his elbows on the table. "Ive. I'll say this once more and then it's bye-bye. If you don't tell us what you know and where you found the diary, then I'll personally see to it that you're parachuted right into the middle of the war zone. Clear?"

Jelačić sulked for a moment, then nodded.

"Good. I'm glad we understand one another. And just because you've behaved like a total pillock, there's one more condition."

Jelačić's eyes narrowed.

"You drop all charges against Daniel Charters and make a public apology."

Jelačić bristled at this, but after huffing and puffing for a minute or two, agreed that he had, in fact, misinterpreted the minister's gesture.

Banks stood up and took Jelačić's arm. "Right, let's go."

They drove him to St Mary's, and he led them along the tarmac path, onto the gravel one and into the thick woods behind the

Inchcliffe Mausoleum. A good way in, he paused in front of a tree and said, "Here."

Banks looked at the tree but could see nothing out of the ordinary, no obvious hiding-place. Then Jelačić reached his hand up and seemed to insert it right into the solid wood itself. It was then that Banks noticed something very odd about the yew trees. Not very tall, but often quite wide in circumference, they were hard, strong and enduring. Some of the older ones must have been thirty feet around and had so many clustered columns they looked like a fluted pillar. The one they stood before had probably been around since the seventeenth century. The columns were actually shoots pushing out from the lower part of the bole, growing upwards and appearing to coalesce with the older wood, making the tree look as if it had several trunks all grafted together. It also, he realized, provided innumerable nooks and crannies to hide things. What Deborah had sought out for a hiding-place, and Jelačić had seen her use, was a knot-hole in this old yew, angled in such a way that it was invisible when you looked at it straight on.

Banks moved Jelačić aside and reached his hand inside the tree. All he felt was a bed of leaves and strips of bark that had blown in over the years. But then, when he started to dig down and sweep some of this detritus aside, he was sure his fingers brushed something smooth and hard. Quickly, he reached deeper, estimating that Deborah could have easily done the same with her long arms. At last, he grasped the package and drew it out. Gristhorpe and Jelačić stood beside him, watching.

"Looks like you missed the jackpot, Ive," Banks said.

It was a small square object wrapped in black bin-liner, folded over several times for good insulation. When Banks unfolded it, he brought out what he had hoped for: a computer diskette.

III

Back at the station, Banks handed the floppy disk to Susan Gay and asked her if she could get a printout of its contents. He hoped it had survived winter in the knot-hole of the yew. It should have done; it had been wrapped in plastic and buried under old leaves, wood chips and scraps of bark, which would have helped preserve it, and the winter hadn't been very cold.

Ten minutes later, Susan knocked sharply on Banks's office door and marched in brandishing a sheaf of paper. Her hand was shaking, and she looked pale. "I think you'd better have a look at this, sir."

"Let's swop." Banks pushed the diary towards her and picked up the printout.

De-bo-rah. De-bo-rah. How the syllables of your name trip off my tongue like poetry. When was it I first knew that I loved you? I ask myself, can I pinpoint the exact moment in time and space where that magical transformation took place and I no longer looked at a mere young girl but a shining girl-child upon whose every movement I fed hungrily. When, when did it happen?

Oh, Deborah, my sweet torturer, why did I ever, ever have to see you pass that moment from childhood to the flush of womanhood? Had you remained a mere child I could never have loved you this way. I could never have entertained such thoughts about your straight and hairless child's body as I do about your woman's body.

I seek you out; yet I fly from you. On the surface, all appears normal, but if people could see and hear inside me the moment you come into a room or sit beside me, they would see my heart pulling at the reins and hear my blood roaring through my veins. That day you won the dressage and walked towards me in your riding-gear, that moist film of sweat glistening on the exquisite curve of your upper lip ... and you kissed me on the cheek and put your arm around me ... I felt your small breast press softly against my side and it was all I could do to remain standing let alone furnish the required and conventional praise ... well done ... well done ... wonderful ... well done, my love, my Deborah.

The first time I saw you naked as a woman you were standing in the old bath-tub at Montclair looking like Botticelli's Birth of Venus. Remember, my love, there were no locks on the doors at Montclair. One simply knew when private rooms were engaged and refrained from entering. Mistakes were made, of course, but honest mistakes. Besides, it was family. They aren't prudes about such things, the French, Sylvie's people. I hoped only for a brief glimpse of your nakedness as you bathed. I knew I couldn't linger, that I must apologize and dash out as if I had a made a mistake before you even realized I had seen you. So fast, so fleeting a glimpse. And even now I wonder what would have happened had I not witnessed you in your full glory.

For you were standing up, reaching for the towel, and your loveliness was on display just for me. Steam hung in the air and the sunlight that slanted through the high window cast rainbows all about you. Droplets of moisture had beaded on your flushed skin; your wet hair clung to your neck and shoulders, long strands pasted over the swellings of your new breasts, where the nipples, pink as opening rosebuds stood erect. Even that early in womanhood your waist curved in and swelled out at the narrow hips. Between your legs a tiny triangle of hair like spun gold lay on the mound of Venus; the paradise I dream of; drops of water had caught among the fine, curled hairs, forming tiny prisms in the sunlight; some just seemed to glitter in clear light like diamonds . . .

I have other images locked away inside me: the thin black bra strap against your bare shoulder, the insides of your thighs when you cross your legs . . .

And so it went on. Again, it wasn't solid evidence, but it was all they had. Banks had no choice but to act on it.

IV

Owen gazed out of the train window into the darkness. Rain streaked the dirty glass and all he could see was reflections of the lights behind him in the carriage. He wished he could get another drink, but he was on the local train now, not the InterCity, and there was no bar service.

As the train rattled through a closed village station on the last leg of his journey, Owen thought again of how he had walked the

London streets all night in the rain after killing Michelle, half-hoping the police would pick him up and get it over with, half-afraid of going back to prison, this time forever.

He had covered the whole urban landscape, or so it seemed; the west end, where the bright neons were reflected in the puddles and the nightclubs were open, occasional drunks and prostitutes shouting or laughing out loud; rainswept wastelands of demolished houses, where he had to pick his way carefully over the piles of bricks with weeds growing between them; clusters of tower blocks surrounded by burned-out cars, playgrounds with broken swings; and broad tree-lined streets, large houses set well back from the road. He had walked through areas he wouldn't have gone near if he had cared what happened to him, and if he hadn't been mugged or beaten up it wasn't for lack of carelessness.

But nothing had happened. He had seen plenty of dangerous-looking people, some hiding furtively in shop doorways or hanging around in groups smoking crack in the shadows of tower-block stairwells, but no-one had approached him. Police cars had passed him as he walked along Finchley Road or Whitechapel High Street, but none had stopped to ask him who he was. If he hadn't known different, he would have said he was leading a charmed life.

At one point, close to morning, he had stood on a bridge watching the rain pit the river's surface and felt the life of the city around him, restful perhaps, but never quite sleeping, that hum of energy always there, always running through it like the river did. He didn't think it was Westminster Bridge, but still Wordsworth's lines sprung into his mind, words he had read and memorized in prison:

This City now doth, like a garment, wear
The beauty of the morning; silent, bare,
Ships, towers, domes, theatres, and temples lie
Open unto the fields, and to the sky;
All bright and glittering in the smokeless air.

Well, perhaps the air wasn't exactly "smokeless," Owen thought, but one has to make allowances for time.

Owen felt tired and empty. So tired and so empty.

Eastvale Station was in the north-eastern part of the town, on Kendal Road a couple of miles east of North Market Street. It was only a short taxi-ride to the town centre. But Owen didn't want to go to the centre, or, tired as he was, home.

He was surprised the police weren't waiting for him at the station, as they probably would be at his house. He didn't want to walk right into their arms, and however empty he felt, however *final* every second of continued freedom seemed, he still didn't want to give it up just yet. Perhaps, he thought, he was like the cancer patient who knows there's no hope but clings onto life through all the pain, hoping for a miracle, hoping that the disease will just go away, that it was all a bad dream. Besides, he wanted another drink.

Whatever his reasons, he found himself walking along Kendal Road. The day had been so hot and humid that the cooler evening air brought a mist that hung in the air like fog. At the bridge, he looked along the tree-lined banks towards town and saw the high three-quarter moon and the floodlit castle on its hill reflected in the water, all blurry in the haze of the summer mist.

Walking on, he came to the crossroads and saw the Nag's Head. Well, he thought, with a smile, it would do as well as anywhere. He had come full circle.

V

By the time Banks and Gristhorpe got Chief Constable Riddle's permission to bring Michael Clayton in for questioning, which wasn't easy, it was already dark. One of the conditions was that Riddle himself be present at the interview.

Banks was pleased to see that Clayton, as expected, was at least mildly intimidated by the sparse and dreary interview room, with its faded institutional-green walls, flyblown window, table and chairs bolted to the floor, and that mingled smell of urine and old cigarette smoke.

Clayton made the expected fuss about being dragged away from his home, like a common criminal, to the police station, but his confidence had lost a bit of its edge. He was wearing sharp-creased grey trousers and a white short-sleeved shirt; his glasses hung on a chain around his neck.

"Are you charging me with something?" Clayton asked, folding his arms and crossing his legs.

"No," said Gristhorpe. "At least not yet. Chief Inspector Banks has a few questions he wants to ask you, that's all."

Jimmy Riddle sat behind Clayton in the far corner by the window, so the suspect couldn't constantly look to him for comfort and reassurance. Riddle seemed folded in on himself, legs and arms tightly crossed. He had promised not to interfere, but Banks didn't believe it for a moment.

"About what?" Clayton asked.

"About the murder of your goddaughter, Deborah Harrison."

"I thought you'd finished with all that?"

"Not quite."

He looked at his watch. "Well, you'd better tell him to get on with it, then. I've got important work to do."

Banks turned on the tape recorders, made a note of the time and who was present, then gave Clayton the new caution, the same one he had given Owen Pierce eight months ago. Formalities done, he shuffled some papers on the desk in front of him and asked, "Remember when we talked before, Mr Clayton, and I asked you if you had been having an affair with Sylvie Harrison?"

Clayton looked from Gristhorpe to Banks. "Yes," he said to the latter. "I told you it was absurd then, and it's still absurd now."

"I know."

Clayton swallowed. "What?"

"I said I know it's absurd."

He shook his head. "So you're not still trying to accuse me of that? Then why ... ?"

"And remember I suggested that Deborah might have gained access to some sensitive business material, or some government secret?"

"Yes. Again, ridiculous."

"You're absolutely right. You weren't having an affair with Sylvie Harrison," Banks said slowly, "and Deborah didn't gain access to any important government secrets. We know that now. I got it all wrong. You were in love with your goddaughter, with Deborah. That's why you killed her."

Clayton paled. "This ... this is ludicrous." He twisted around in his chair to look at Riddle. "Look, Jerry, I don't know what they're talking about. You're their superior. Can't you do something?"

Riddle, who had read both the diary and the computer journal, shook his head slowly. "Best answer the questions truthfully, Michael. That's best for all of us."

While Clayton was staring open-mouthed at Riddle's betrayal, Superintendent Gristhorpe dropped the printed computer journal on the table in front of him. Clayton first glanced at it, then put his glasses on, picked it up and read a few paragraphs. Then he pushed it aside. "What on earth is that?" he asked Banks.

"The product of a sick mind, I'd say," Banks answered.

"I hope you're not suggesting it has anything to do with me."

Banks leaned forward suddenly, snatched back the pages and slapped them down on the table. "Oh, stop mucking us about. It came from *your* computer. The one John Spinks stole that day he took your car. He's already told us all about that, about how he saw Deborah make a copy of the files onto a diskette. You didn't know about that, did you?"

"I ... where ... ?"

"She kept it well hidden. Look, you know it's your journal. Don't deny it."

Even in his shock, Clayton managed a thin smile and rallied his defences. "Deny it? I most certainly do. And I'm afraid you'll have a hard job proving a wild accusation like that. Your suggestions are outrageous." He glanced back at Riddle. "And Jerry knows it, too. There's absolutely nothing to link that printout with me. It could have been written by anyone."

"I don't think so," said Banks. "Oh, I know that Deborah reformatted your hard drive well beyond anything an 'unerase' or 'undelete' command could bring back to life, but you must admit the contents of the journal, the circumstances, all point to you. Very damning."

"Fiction," said Clayton. "Pure fiction and fantasy. Just some poor lovestruck fool making things up. There's nothing illegal in that. There's no law against fantasies; at least not yet."

"Maybe not," said Banks. "We never checked Deborah's clothing for *your* hairs, you know."

"So?"

"You might not have left any blood or tissue, but I'm willing to bet that if we went over the hair samples again now, we'd find a positive match. That wouldn't be fantasy, would it?"

Clayton shrugged. "So what? It wouldn't surprise me. Deborah was my goddaughter, after all. We spent a lot of time together—as a family. Besides, I was in court for the so-called expert's testimony. Hairs hardly prove a thing scientifically."

"What about Ellen Gilchrist?"

"Never heard of—wait a minute, isn't that the other girl who was killed?"

"Yes. What if we found *your* hairs on her clothing, too, and hers on yours? Was she family, a friend?"

Clayton licked his lips. "I never saw her in my life. Look, I don't know what grounds you've got for assuming this, but—"

Banks dropped a photocopy of Deborah's diary in front of him. "Read this," he said.

Clayton read.

His hands were shaking when he put the diary down. "Fantasy," he said, straining to keep his voice steady. "That's not very much to go on, is it? It could be anyone."

"Come on, Michael," said Banks. "It's all over. Admit it. You know what happened. You've just read her account. Deborah read your journal and found out you'd been secretly lusting after her since she was twelve. She was both shocked and excited by the idea. But only by the idea. She was flattered, but still too much of a kid to know how serious it all was to you. And she had a bit of a crush on you anyway. So she teased you, made up a bit of romance, flirted a little, the way young girls sometimes do to tease boys they know fancy them. Didn't she, Michael?"

"This is absurd. You're not only insulting me you're also besmirching my goddaughter's memory." He looked around at Riddle again. "Sir Geoff—"

But Banks cut him off. "Besmirching? That's a good word, Michael. I like that. *Besmirching*. Sounds naughty. Very public school. So let's talk about *besmirching*. Eventually, when it became clear you wouldn't leave her alone, Deborah threatened to tell her father. You knew that if Sir Geoffrey found out he would probably kill you. At the very least it would mean the end of your business relationship. That meant a lot to you, didn't it, Michael? The two old Oxford boys, still together after all these years. Sir Geoffrey's friendship meant a lot to you, too, but it didn't stop you lusting after his twelve-year-old daughter, a girl who wasn't even born when the two of you first met."

Clayton glared, the colour drained from his face. "You'll regret this," he said, glancing at both Gristhorpe and Riddle. "All of you will, if you don't stop this right now." Banks could almost hear Clayton's teeth grinding together. Gristhorpe said nothing. Riddle polished his buttons with a virgin white handkerchief.

"You waited for Deborah in St Mary's graveyard," Banks continued calmly, "in the shrubbery that foggy Monday evening when you knew she would be walking home alone from the chess club. You were going to grab her and drag her into the bushes, but when you saw her take the gravel path, you followed her towards the Inchcliffe Mausoleum, where you snatched her satchel and strangled her with the strap. Maybe she knew it was you, and maybe she didn't. Maybe you talked first, tried to persuade her not to say anything, or maybe you didn't. But that's what happened, isn't it, Michael?"

"I'm saying nothing."

"You didn't know she was going to pick up the diary she'd been keeping and hiding ever since summer, did you? Oh, Michael, but if you'd only been patient, given her a few more seconds, she would have led you straight to it and you probably wouldn't be here now. Isn't that how it happened?"

"I won't even dignify your accusation with a response."

"When she told you she'd read your computer journal, Deborah didn't tell you that she'd copied the file about her onto a diskette, did she? But you knew she had a diary at one time. You bought it for her. That's another irony, isn't it, Michael? You knew she'd told

Sylvie she lost it, but I wouldn't be at all surprised if you had a good look around her room after you killed her. After all, you had your own key to Sir Geoffrey's house, and he and Lady Harrison were out. Even if they came back and found you there, it wouldn't have surprised them. And you opened Deborah's school satchel, too, didn't you, to see if she kept anything incriminating in there. Just in case. The only place you couldn't really get access to was her school desk, but you reasoned she'd be unlikely to keep anything important or private there."

Clayton put his hands over his ears. "This is ridiculous," he said. "I don't have to listen to this. You'll never be able to prove anything. I want—"

"Now, I'm only guessing," Banks went on, "so stop me if I'm wrong, but I also think, as you murdered Deborah, that you found out you liked it. It stimulated you. Maybe you even had an orgasm as you tightened the strap around her neck. I know you were far too clever to actually rape her because you know about DNA and all that, don't you? But you did mess around with her clothing after you killed her—partly for pure pleasure, I'd guess, and partly to make it look like a genuine sex murder.

"It was the same with Ellen Gilchrist, wasn't it? You'd been over and over it in your mind all week, planning how you'd kill again, anticipating the intimacy of it all, and when you did it, when you felt the strap tightening, pulling her back against you, feeling her soft flesh rubbing against you, that excited you, didn't it?"

"Really, Banks," Chief Constable Riddle cut in from behind. "Don't you think this is getting a little out of hand?"

Clayton turned and looked at Riddle, a cruel smile on his thin lips. "Well, thank you, Jerry, for all your support. You're absolutely right. He's talking rubbish, of course. I'd never even met the girl."

"That doesn't matter," Banks went on, mentally kicking Riddle and trying to ignore his interruption. "Unlike Deborah, Ellen Gilchrist was a random victim. Wrong place, wrong time. You got lucky when Owen Pierce was arrested for the murder of Deborah Harrison, didn't you? You thought he would get convicted, sentenced and that would be an end to it. But when the trial was nearing its close, you started to worry that he might get off. The defence was good, the prosecution had only circumstantial evidence, and you'd heard rumours about evidence that would have convicted Pierce for certain had it been admissible. But you saw it all slipping away, and the focus perhaps shifting back towards you. So you went to Owen Pierce's house while the jury was deliberating, and you either found the door open from a previous break-in, or you broke in yourself and made it look like vandals. It doesn't really matter which. You took some hairs from Owen's pillow, and you stole an open film container which you guessed would have his fingerprints on it. You set out to deliberately frame Owen Pierce for the murder of Ellen Gilchrist, knowing we'd also put Deborah's murder down to him, too, and close the file on both of them. But, you know what? I think you also *enjoyed* it. Just the way you did with Deborah. And I think there would have been more if we hadn't caught you, wouldn't there? You've developed a taste for it."

"This is insane," Clayton said. "And you can't prove a thing."

"Oh, I think we can," Banks went on. "Look what we proved against Owen Pierce, and he didn't even do anything."

Clayton smiled. "Ah, but he got off, didn't he?"

Banks paused. "Yes. Yes, he did. But maybe you should talk to him about that. I'm sure he'd be very interested to meet you. Getting off isn't all it's cracked up to be in some cases. See, maybe you're right, Michael. Maybe we won't be able to convince a jury that a fine, upstanding citizen like yourself murdered two young girls. Perhaps even with the evidence of the journal and the diary and the hairs, if we find they match, we won't be able to prove it to them. But you know who *will* believe us, don't you, Michael? You know who knows quite well who 'Uncle Michael' is, who knows what Montclair is and that there are no locks on the bathroom doors there. You know exactly who *will* know who is the writer and who's the subject. Sir Geoffrey will know. And you'll have gained nothing. In some ways, I think I'd rather take my chances with a jury, or even go to jail, than incur the wrath of Sir Geoffrey over such a matter as the murder of his only daughter by the man he's trusted for more than twenty years, don't you?"

Clayton said nothing for a moment, then he croaked, "I want

my solicitor. Now. Get my solicitor, right now. I'm not saying another word."

Bloody hell, thought Banks, here we go again. He called in the constable from outside the interview room. "Take him down to the custody suite, will you, Wigmore. And make sure you let him call his lawyer."

VI

Owen sat in the Nag's Head nursing his second pint and Scotch chaser, trying to pluck up the courage to go over the road and see Rebecca and Daniel. The problem was, he felt ashamed to face them. They had believed in his innocence, and he had let them down badly. He knew that if there were to be any sort of salvation or reclamation in this business at all, he would have to tell them the whole truth, including what he had done to Michelle. And he didn't know if he could do that right now. He could hardly even admit to himself that he had become exactly what everyone thought he was: a murderer.

He looked around at the uninspiring decor of the pub and wondered what the hell he was doing here again. It had seemed a nice irony when he saw the sign over the bridge—full circle—but now it didn't seem like such a good idea.

The Nag's Head was boisterous, with the landlord entertaining a group of cronies with dirty jokes around the bar and tables full of couples laughing and groups of underage kids who'd had a bit too much.

He didn't know what he was going to do after he finished his drinks: either go home and meet the police, or have another and go face Rebecca and Daniel. More drink wouldn't help with that, though, he realized. He would feel less like facing them if he were drunk. Best drink up and turn himself in, then, return to the custody suite, where he should feel quite at home by now.

"What did you say?"

Owen looked up at the sound of the voice. There was a lull in the conversation and laughter. The landlord was collecting empty glasses. He stood over Owen's table. "Sorry mate," he said. "I thought I heard you say something."

Owen shook his head. He realized he must have been muttering to himself. He turned away from the landlord's scrutiny. He could still feel the man looking at him, though, recognition struggling to come to the surface. He had a couple of days' growth, a few more pounds around the waist from lack of exercise and a prison pallor, but other than that he didn't look too different from the person who had sat alone in that same pub one foggy night last November.

Best finish his drinks and leave, he decided, tossing back the Scotch in one and washing it down with beer.

Then, all of a sudden, the landlord said, "Bloody hell, it *is* him! I don't bloody believe it. The nerve."

The men at the bar turned as one to look at Owen.

"It's him," the landlord repeated. "The one who was in here that night. The one who murdered those two young lasses."

Owen wiped his mouth with the back of his hand and stood up, edging towards the door.

"Nay, they let him off," someone said.

"Aye, but just because they hadn't got enough evidence," another said. "Don't you read t'papers?"

"It was a bloody cover-up."

"Bleeding shame, more like. Poor wee lasses."

"A travesty of justice."

By the time Owen actually got to the door, a journey that felt like a hundred miles, bar-stools were scraping against the stone floor and he was aware of a crowd surging towards him.

No time to sneak out surreptitiously now. He dashed through the door and ran across Kendal Road. Luckily, the traffic lights were in his favour. When he got to the other side of the road, he saw about five or six people standing outside the pub doors. For a moment, he thought they were going to give chase, but someone shouted something he didn't hear and they went back inside.

Owen still ran as if he were being chased. There was only one place he could go now. He dashed across North Market Street towards St Mary's Church. When he was through the gate, running down the tarmac path, he could see, even in the mist, that the kitchen light was on in the vicarage.

VII

Alone in his office at last, Banks went to close the blinds and looked out for a moment on the quiet cobbled market square and the welcoming lights of the Queen's Arms. Maybe he'd have a quick one there before going home. Still time. Finally, he closed the blinds, turned on the shaded table-lamp and lit a cigarette. Then he sifted through his tapes and decided on Britten's third string quartet.

For a long time he just sat there smoking, staring at the wall and letting Britten's meditative quartet wash over him. He thought about the Clayton interview, and especially about the new coldness in Chief Constable Riddle's manner towards his old lodge pal. Maybe Riddle wasn't so bad, after all; at least he had an open enough mind to change his opinions when the facts started to weigh heavily against them.

Then, when his cigarette was finished, Banks turned to Deborah's diary again, striving once more to understand what had happened between her and Clayton over the two months leading up to her death.

24 August

Disaster has struck! Mummy caught John and me in bed this after-noon. She was supposed to be at one of her charity meetings but she wasn't feeling well and came home early. It was a terrible scene with Mummy and John shouting at one another and I didn't like to see John at all behaving like that. I thought he was going to hit Mummy in the end but he broke a vase on the wall and a piece of pottery cut Mummy's face. Then when he'd gone Mummy said I absolutely must not see him again or she would tell Daddy. Then she cried and put her arms around me and I felt sorry for her. John said such terrible things, called her such horrible names and said he would do things to her I won't repeat even here in my private diary. I don't care if I never see him again. I

*hate him. He's gross. He even stole things from our house. He's just a
common thief. A thief and a thickie. What could I ever have seen in
him?*

27 August

*Michael came to the house today while Mummy and Daddy were out.
He was absolutely livid about the other day with John. I didn't know
Mummy had told him. He called me names and I thought at one point
he was going to hit me. It was then I told him. I couldn't help it. I told
him I'd read his journal about me and called him a dirty old man. He
went so white I thought he was going to faint. Then he asked me what
I was going to do. I said I didn't know. I'd just have to wait and see.
Wait for what? he asked me. To see what happens, says I.*

28 August

*Michael really is rather handsome. And much more intelligent and
sophisticated than John. Mary Taylor at school told me last term she
had an affair with a married man, a friend of her father's, who was 38
years old! And she says he was wonderful and considerate at sex and
bought her presents and all sorts of things. I think Uncle Michael might
be even older than 38 but he's not fat and ugly or anything like most
old people.*

1 September

*Michael came for dinner tonight. Mummy and Daddy were there, of
course. I wore a tight black jumper and a short skirt. Out of the corner
of my eye I could see him looking at my thighs and breasts when he
thought I wasn't watching. It really is amazing how he can seem so
normal and ordinary when we're all together, but when there's just him
and me he's so passionate and can hardly control himself!*

3 September

*Michael came again today when everyone was out. He told me he felt
such powerful desire for me he didn't know if he could control himself.
That was the word he used: desire. I don't think that anyone has ever
desired me before. It feels rather exciting. Of course, he wanted to do it,
and when I said no he got all upset and said if I let a no-good lout like*

John Spinks do it to me why wouldn't I let him? I must admit I don't know the answer to that. Except that he's Uncle Michael and I've known him all my life.

8

This is getting to be quite an adventure! Saw Michael again today and let him kiss me again. It made him happy for a while, then he said he wanted to kiss my breasts. I wouldn't let him do that but I let him touch them over my jumper. While he was doing it he took my hand and held it to the front of his trousers so I could feel he was really hard. I started to feel a bit scared because his grip was so strong and then I felt him go all wet and he gasped as if somebody had hit him just the way John used to do. Gross. I can't explain why I felt it then, but I started to panic a bit because I'd just been teasing really and this was UNCLE MICHAEL, and even if he isn't really my uncle I've still known him since I was a little girl. I just couldn't let him do it to me. It wouldn't be right. After he'd finished he went all quiet so I left.

8 September

School again. Sad, sad, sad. Saw Mucky Metcalfe in the corridor. Wonder if he knows I know he's been doing it with the vicar's wife?

There were no more entries until October, and Banks assumed that Deborah had been getting settled in at St Mary's again in the interim. But even by late October, Michael Clayton still hadn't got the message.

24 October

Can't Uncle Michael understand that whatever it was we had is over now? I've told him I don't love him, but it doesn't do any good. He keeps coming to the house when he knows I'm here alone. Now he says he just wants to see me naked, that he won't even touch me if I just take my clothes off in front of him and stand there the way I did in the bath at Montclair. I suppose it's flattering in a way to have a sophisticated older man in love with you, but to be honest he doesn't seem very sophisticated when he keeps wanting me to touch that hard thing in his pants.

I don't want to play any more. I suppose he must still be living in hope,
but doesn't he understand that summer's over and I'm back at school
now?

Obviously he didn't, thought Banks. It hadn't been just a
summer romance for Michael Clayton; it had been a dark, powerful obsession. And beneath all the veneer of sophistication and
experience, Deborah had simply been a naïve teenager misreading
the depth of an older man's passion; she was just a girl who thought
she was a woman.

But even as Deborah grew worried by Clayton's persistence, she
always kept her secret, always lived in hope that he would simply
give up and stop pestering her. She clearly knew what dreadful
consequences would occur if she told her parents, and she wanted
to avoid that if she could. But Clayton wouldn't give up and go
away. He couldn't; he was too far gone. Her final entry, dated the
day before she died, read,

> *5 November (Bonfire Night)*
> *Yesterday Uncle Michael grabbed me and held my arm until it hurt and*
> *told me I had stolen his soul and all sorts of other rubbish. I know it*
> *was cruel of me to tease him, and to let him kiss me and stuff, but it was*
> *just a game at first and he wouldn't let me stop it. I want him to stop it*
> *now because I'm getting frightened, the way he looks at me. You still*
> *wouldn't believe it if you saw him with other people around, but he*
> *really does change when he's only with me. It's like he has a split*
> *personality or something. I told him if he doesn't promise to leave me*
> *alone I'll tell Daddy when I get home from school tomorrow. I don't*
> *know if I will. I don't really want to tell Daddy because I know what*
> *he gets like and what trouble it will cause. The house won't be worth*
> *living in. Anyway, we'll see what happens tomorrow.*

Banks pushed the diary aside and lit another cigarette. The gas-
lights around the market square glowed through the gaps in the
blinds. The quartet was reaching the end of its final movement
now, the moving, introspective passacaglia, written when Britten
was approaching death.

Why do we feel compelled to record our thoughts and feelings in diaries and on tape, Banks wondered, and our acts on video and in photographs? Perhaps, he thought, we need to read about ourselves or watch ourselves to know we are truly alive. Time after time, it leads to nothing but trouble, but still the politicians keep their diaries, ticking away like time bombs, and the sexual deviants keep their visual records. And thank the Lord they do. Without such evidence, many a case might not even get to court.

When the music finished, Banks sat in silence for a while, then stubbed out his cigarette. Just as he was about to get up and go for that pint before last orders, the telephone rang. He cursed and contemplated leaving it, but his policeman's sense of duty and his even deeper-rooted curiosity wouldn't let him.

"Banks here."

"Sergeant Rowe, sir. We've just had a report that Owen Pierce is at St Mary's vicarage."

"Who called it in?"

"Rebecca Charters, sir. The vicar's wife. She says Pierce is ready to turn himself in for the murder of Michelle Chappel."

"But she's not dead."

"I suppose he doesn't know that."

"All right," said Banks. "I'll be right there."

He sighed, picked up his sports jacket and hurried out into the hazy darkness.

FINAL ACCOUNT

For Sheila

Dry bones that dream are bitter.
They dream and darken our sun.

W.B. Yeats
The Dreaming of the Bones

ACKNOWLEDGMENTS

My thanks are long overdue to Cynthia Good, my editor from the beginning of the series. I must also thank my agent, Dominick Abel, for his advice and encouragement. This book in particular could not have been completed without the help of many people, all generous with their time and expertise. My thanks go especially to Keith Wright of Nottingham CID, both detective and novelist; Douglas Lucas, Director of the Centre for Forensic Sciences, Toronto; Mario Possamai for his book *Money on the Run*; Ken McFarland, Chartered Accountant; John Picton, journalist; and to Rick Blechta for putting me right about violists. Any errors are entirely my own and were made purely in the interests of dramatic fiction.

ONE

I

The uniformed constable lifted the tape and waved Detective Chief Inspector Banks through the gate at two forty-seven in the morning.

Banks's headlights danced over the scene as he drove into the bumpy farmyard and came to a halt. To his left stood the squat, solid house itself, with its walls of thick limestone and mossy, flagstone roof. Lights shone in both the upstairs and downstairs windows. To his right, a high stone wall buttressed a copse that straggled up the daleside, where the trees became lost in darkness. Straight ahead stood the barn.

A group of officers had gathered around the open doors, inside which a ball of light seemed to be moving. They looked like the cast of a fifties sci-fi film gazing in awe on an alien spaceship or life-form.

When Banks arrived, they parted in silence to let him through. As he entered, he noticed one young PC leaning against the outside wall dribbling vomit on his size twelves. Inside, the scene looked like a film set.

Peter Darby, the police photographer, was busy videotaping, and the source of the light was attached to the top of his camera. It created an eerie chiaroscuro and sudden, sickening illuminations as it swept around the barn's interior. All he needed, Banks thought, was for someone to yell "Action!" and the place would suddenly be full of sound and motion.

But no amount of yelling would breathe life back into the grotesque shape on the floor, by which a whey-faced young police surgeon, Dr Burns, squatted with a black notebook in his hand.

At first, the position of the body reminded Banks of a parody of Moslem prayer: the kneeling man bent forward from the waist, arms stretched out in front, bum in the air, forehead touching the ground, perhaps facing Mecca. His fists were clenched in the dirt, and Banks noticed the glint of a gold cufflink, initialled "KAR," as Darby's light flashed on it.

But there was no forehead to touch the ground. Above the charcoal suit jacket, the blood-soaked collar of the man's shirt protruded about an inch, and after that came nothing but a dark, coagulated mass of bone and tissue spread out on the dirt like an oil stain: a shotgun wound, by the look of it. Patches of blood, bone and brain matter stuck to the whitewashed stone walls in abstract-expressionist patterns. Darby's roving light caught what looked like a fragment of skull sprouting a tuft of fair hair beside a rusty hoe.

Banks felt the bile rise in his throat. He could still smell the gunpowder, reminiscent of a childhood bonfire night, mixed with the stink of urine and faeces and the rancid raw meat smell of sudden violent death.

"What time did the call come in?" he asked the PC beside him.

"One thirty-eight, sir. PC Carstairs from Relton was first on the scene. He's still puking up out front."

Banks nodded. "Do we know who the victim was?"

"DC Gay checked his wallet, sir. Name's Keith Rothwell. That's the name of the bloke who lived here, all right." He pointed over to the house. "Arkbeck Farm, it's called."

"A farmer?"

"Nay, sir. Accountant. Some sort of businessman, anyroad."

One of the constables found a light switch and turned on the bare bulb, which became a foundation for the brighter light of Darby's video camera. Most regions didn't use video because it was hard to get good enough quality, but Peter Darby was a hardware junkie, forever experimenting.

Banks turned his attention back to the scene. The place looked as if it had once been a large stone Yorkshire barn, with double doors and a hayloft, called a "field house" in those parts. Originally, it would have been used to keep the cows inside between

November and May, and to store fodder, but Rothwell seemed to have converted it into a garage.

To Banks's right, a silver-grey BMW, parked at a slight angle, took up about half the space. Beyond the car, against the far wall, a number of metal shelf units held all the tools and potions one would associate with car care: anti-freeze, wax polish, oily rags, screwdrivers, spanners. Rothwell had retained the rural look in the other half of the garage. He had even hung old farm implements on the whitewashed stone wall: a mucking rake, a hay knife, a draining scoop and a Tom spade, among others, all suitably rusted.

As he stood there, Banks tried to picture what might have happened. The victim had clearly been kneeling, perhaps praying or pleading for his life. It certainly didn't look as if he had tried to escape. Why had he submitted so easily? Not much choice, probably, Banks thought. You usually don't argue when someone is pointing a shotgun at you. But still ... would a man simply kneel there, brace himself and wait for his executioner to pull the trigger?

Banks turned and left the barn. Outside, he met Detective Sergeant Philip Richmond and Detective Constable Susan Gay coming from around the back.

"Nothing there, sir, far as I can tell," said Richmond, a large torch in his hand. Susan, beside him, looked pale in the glow from the barn entrance.

"All right?" Banks asked her.

"I'm okay now, sir. I was sick, though."

Richmond looked the same as ever. His sang-froid was legendary around the place, so much so that Banks sometimes wondered if he had any feelings at all or whether he had come to resemble one of those computers he spent most of his time with.

"Anyone know what happened?" Banks asked.

"PC Carstairs had a quick word with the victim's wife when he first got here," said Susan. "All she could tell him was that a couple of men were waiting when she got home and they took her husband outside and shot him." She shrugged. "Then she became hysterical. I believe she's under sedation now, sir. I fished his wallet from his pocket, anyway," she went on, holding up a plastic bag. "Says his name's—"

"Yes, I know," said Banks. "Have we got an Exhibits Officer yet?"

"No, sir," Susan answered, then both she and Phil Richmond looked away. Exhibits Officer was one of the least popular jobs in an investigation. It meant keeping track of every piece of possible evidence and preserving a record of continuity. It usually went to whoever was in the doghouse at the time.

"Get young Farnley on the job, then," Banks said. PC Farnley hadn't offended anyone or cocked up a case, but he lacked imagination and had a general reputation around the station as a crashing golf bore.

Clearly relieved, Richmond and Susan wandered off towards the Scene-of-Crime team, who had just pulled into the farmyard in a large van. As they piled out in their white boiler suits, they looked like a team of government scientists sent to examine the alien landing-spot. Pretty soon, Banks thought, if they weren't all careful, there would be a giant spider or a huge gooey blob rolling around the Yorkshire Dales gobbling up everyone in sight.

The night was cool and still, the air moist, tinged with a hint of manure. Banks still felt half-asleep, despite the shock of what he had seen in the garage. Maybe he was dreaming. No. He thought of Sandra, warm at home in bed, and sighed.

Detective Superintendent Gristhorpe's arrival at about three-thirty brought him out of his reverie. Gristhorpe limped over from his car. He wore an old donkey-jacket over his shirt, and he clearly hadn't bothered to shave or comb his unruly thatch of grey hair.

"Bloody hell, Alan," he said by way of greeting, "tha looks like Columbo."

There's the pot calling the kettle black, Banks thought. Still, the super was right. He had thrown on an old raincoat over his shirt and trousers because he knew the night would be chilly.

After Banks had explained what he had found out so far, Gristhorpe took a quick look in the barn, questioned PC Carstairs, the first officer at the scene, then rejoined Banks, his usually ruddy, pock-marked face a little paler. "Let's go in the house, shall we, Alan?" he said. "I hear PC Weaver's brewing up. He should be able to give us some background."

They walked across the dirt yard. Above them, the stars shone cold and bright like chips of ice on black velvet.

The farmhouse was cosy and warm inside, a welcome change from the cool night and the gruesome scene in the barn. It had been renovated according to the yuppie idea of the real rustic look, with exposed beams and rough stone walls in an open, split-level living-room, all earthy browns and greens. The remains of a log fire glowed in the stone hearth, and beside it stood a pair of antique andirons and a matching rack holding poker and tongs.

In front of the fire, Banks noticed two hard-backed chairs facing one another. One of them had fallen over, or had been pushed on its side. Beside both of them lay coils of rope. One of the chair seats looked wet.

Banks and Gristhorpe walked through into the ultra-modern kitchen, which looked like something from a colour supplement, where PC Weaver was pouring boiling water into a large red teapot.

"Nearly ready, sir," he said when he saw the CID officers. "I'll just let it mash a couple of minutes."

The kitchen walls were done in bright red and white patterned tiles, and every available inch of space had been used to wedge fitted microwave, oven, fridge, dishwasher, cupboards and the like. It also boasted a central island unit, complete with tall pine stools. Banks and Gristhorpe sat down.

"How's his wife?" Gristhorpe asked.

"There's a wife and daughter here, sir," said Weaver. "The doctor's seen them. They're both unharmed, but they're suffering from shock. Hardly surprising when you consider they found the body. They're upstairs with WPC Smithies. Apparently there's also a son rambling around America somewhere."

"Who was this Rothwell bloke?" Banks asked. "He must have had a bob or two. Anything missing?"

"We don't know yet, sir," Weaver said. He looked around the bright kitchen. "But I see what you mean. He was some sort of financial whiz-kid, I think. These new-fangled kitchens don't come cheap, I can tell you. The wife's got in the habit of leaving the *Mail on Sunday* supplement open at some design or another. Her way of dropping hints, like, and about as subtle as a blow on the head with a hammer. The price of them makes me cringe. I tell her the one we've got is perfectly all right, but she—"

As he talked, Weaver began to pour the tea into the row of cups and mugs he had arranged. But after filling the second one, he stopped and stared at the door. Banks and Gristhorpe followed his gaze and saw a young girl standing there, her slight figure framed in the doorway. She rubbed her eyes and stretched.

"Hello," she said. "Are you the detectives? I'd like to talk to you. My name's Alison Rothwell and someone just killed my father."

II

She was about fifteen, Banks guessed, but she made no attempt to make herself look older, as many teenagers do. She wore a baggy, grey sweatshirt advertising an American football team, and a blue tracksuit bottom with a white stripe down each side. Apart from the bruiselike pouches under her light blue eyes, her complexion was pale. Her mousy blonde hair was parted in the centre and hung in uncombed strands over her shoulders. Her mouth, with its pale, thin lips, was too small for her oval face.

"Can I have some tea, please?" she asked. Banks noticed she had a slight lisp.

PC Weaver looked for direction. "Go ahead, lad," Gristhorpe told him. "Give the lass some tea." Then he turned to Alison Rothwell. "Are you sure you wouldn't rather be upstairs with your mum, love?"

Alison shook her head. "Mum'll be all right. She's asleep and there's a policewoman sitting by her. I can't sleep. It keeps going round in my mind, what happened. I want to tell you about it now. Can I?"

"Of course." Gristhorpe asked PC Weaver to stay and take notes. He introduced Banks and himself, then pulled out a stool for her. Alison gave them a sad, shy smile and sat down, holding the mug of tea to her chest with both hands as if she needed its heat. Gristhorpe indicated subtly that Banks should do the questioning.

"Are you sure you feel up to this?" Banks asked her first.

Alison nodded. "I think so."

"Would you like to tell us what happened, then?"

Alison took a deep breath. Her eyes focused on something Banks couldn't see.

"It was just after dark," she began. "About ten o'clock, quarter past or thereabouts. I was reading. I thought I heard a sound out in the yard."

"What kind of sound?" Banks asked.

"I ... I don't know. Just as if someone was out there. A thud, like someone bumping into something or something falling on the ground."

"Carry on."

Alison hugged her cup even closer. "At first I didn't pay it any mind. I carried on reading, then I heard another sound, a sort of scraping, maybe ten minutes later."

"Then what did you do?" Banks asked.

"I turned the yard light on and looked out of the window, but I couldn't see anything."

"Did you have the television on, some music?"

"No. That's why I could hear the sounds outside so clearly. Usually it's so quiet and peaceful up here. All you can hear at night is the wind through the trees, and sometimes a lost sheep baa-ing, or a curlew up on the moors."

"Weren't you scared being by yourself?"

"No. I like it. Even when I heard the noise I just thought it might be a stray dog or a sheep or something."

"Where were your parents at this time?"

"They were out. It's their wedding anniversary. Their twenty-first. They went out to dinner in Eastvale."

"You didn't want to go with them?"

"No. Well ... I mean, it was *their* anniversary, wasn't it?" She turned up her nose. "Besides, I don't like fancy restaurants. And I don't like Italian food. Anyway, it's not as if it was *Home Alone* or something. I *am* nearly sixteen, you know. And it was my choice. I'd rather stay home and read. I don't mind being by myself."

Perhaps, Banks guessed, they hadn't invited her. "Carry on," he said. "After you turned the yard light on, what did you do?"

"When I couldn't see anything, I just sort of brushed it off. Then I heard another noise, like a stone or something, hitting the wall. I was fed up of being disturbed by then, so I decided to go out and see what it was."

"You still weren't frightened?"

"A bit, maybe, by then. But not *really* scared. I still thought it was probably an animal or something like that, maybe a fox. We get them sometimes."

"Then what happened?"

"I opened the front door, and as soon as I stepped out, someone grabbed me and dragged me back inside and tied me to the chair. Then they put a rag in my mouth and put tape over it. I couldn't swallow properly. It was all dry and it tasted of salt and oil."

Banks noticed her knuckles had turned white around the mug. He worried she would crush it. "How many of them were there, Alison?" he asked.

"Two."

"Do you remember anything about them?"

She shook her head. "They were both dressed all in black, except one of them had white trainers on. The other had some sort of suede slip-ons, brown I think."

"You didn't see their faces?"

Alison hooked her feet over the crossbar. "No, they had bala-clavas on, black ones. But they weren't like the ones you'd buy to keep you warm. They were just made of cotton or some other thin material. They had little slits for the eyes and slits just under the nose so they could breathe."

Banks noticed that she had turned paler. "Are you all right, Alison?" he asked. "Do you want to stop now and rest?"

Alison shook her head. Her teeth were clenched. "No. I'll be all right. Just let me ..." She sipped some tea and seemed to relax a little.

"How tall were they?" Banks asked.

"One was about as big as you." She looked at Banks, who at only five foot nine was quite small for a policeman—just over regulation height, in fact. "But he was fatter. Not really fat, but just not, you know, wiry ... like you. The other was a few inches taller, maybe six foot, and quite thin."

"You're doing really well, Alison," Banks said. "Was there anything else about them?"

"No. I can't remember."

"Did either of them speak?"

"When he dragged me back inside, the smaller one said, 'Keep quiet and do as you're told and we won't hurt you.'"

"Did you notice his accent?"

"Not really. It sounded ordinary. I mean, not foreign or anything."

"Local?"

"Yorkshire, yes. But not Dales. Maybe Leeds or something. You know how it sounds different, more citified?"

"Good. You're doing just fine. What happened next?"

"They tied me to the chair with some rope and just sat and watched television. First the news was on, then some horrible American film about a psycho slashing women. They seemed to like that. One of them kept laughing when a woman got killed, as if it was funny."

"You heard them laugh?"

"Just one of them, the tall one. The other one told him to shut up. He sounded like he was in charge."

"The smaller one?"

"Yes."

"That's all he said: 'Shut up'?"

"Yes."

"Was there anything unusual about the taller man's laugh?"

"I ... I don't ... I can't remember." Alison wiped a tear from her eye with the sleeve of her sweatshirt. "It was just a laugh, that's all."

"It's all right. Don't worry about it. Did they harm you in any way?"

Alison reddened and looked down into her half-empty mug. "The smaller one came over to me when I was tied up, and he put his hand on my breast. But the other one made him stop. It was the only time he said anything."

"How did he make him stop? What did he do?"

"He just said not to, that it wasn't part of the deal."

"Did he use those exact words, Alison? Did he say, 'It's not part of the deal'?"

"Yes. I think so. I mean, I'm not completely sure, but it was something like that. The smaller man didn't seem to like it, being told what to do by the other, but he left me alone after that."

"Did you see any kind of weapon?" Banks asked.

"Yes. The kind of gun that farmers have, with two barrels. A shotgun."

"Who had it?"

"The smaller man, the one in charge."

"Did you hear a car at any time?"

"No. Only when Mum and Dad came home. I mean, I heard cars go by on the road sometimes, you know, the one that goes through Relton and right over the moors into the next dale. But I didn't hear anyone coming or going along our driveway."

"What happened when your parents came home?"

Alison paused and swirled the tea in the bottom of her mug as if she were trying to see into her future. "It must have been about half past eleven or later. The men waited behind the door and the tall one grabbed Mum while the other put his gun to Dad's neck. I tried to scream and warn them, honest I did, but the rag in my mouth ... I just couldn't make a sound ..." She ran her sleeve across her eyes again and sniffled. Banks gestured to PC Weaver, who found a box of tissues on the window-sill and brought them over.

"Thank you," Alison said. "I'm sorry."

"You don't have to go on if you don't want," Banks said. "It can wait till tomorrow."

"No. I've started. I want to. Besides, there's not much more to tell. They tied Mum up the same as me and we sat there facing each other. Then they went outside with Dad. Then we heard the bang."

"How long between the time they went out and the shot?"

Alison shook her head dreamily. She held the mug up close to her throat. The sleeves of her sweatshirt had slipped down, and Banks could see the raw, red lines where the rope had cut into her flesh. "I don't know. It seemed like a long time. But all I can remember is we just sat looking at each other, Mum and me, and we didn't know what was happening. I remember a night-bird calling somewhere. Not a curlew. I don't know what it was. And it seemed like forever, like time just stretched out and Mum and I got really scared now looking at one another not knowing what was going on. Then we heard the explosion and ... and it was like it all snapped and I saw something die in Mum's eyes, it was so, so ..." Alison dropped

the mug, which clipped the corner of the table then fell and spilled
without breaking on the floor. The sobs seemed to start deep inside
her, then she began to shake and wail.

Banks went over and put his arms around her, and she clung
onto him for dear life, sobbing against his chest.

III

"It looks like his office," Banks said, when Gristhorpe turned on the
light in the last upstairs room.

Two large desks formed an L-shape. On one of them stood a
computer and a laser printer, and on a small table next to them
stood a fax machine with a basket attached at the front for collecting the cut-off sheets. At the back of the computer desk, a hutch
stood against the wall. The compartments were full of boxes of
disks and software manuals, mostly for word-processing, spread-
sheets and accounting programmes, along with some for standard
utilities.

The other desk stood in front of the window, which framed a
view of the farmyard. Scene-of-Crime officers were still going
about their business down there: taking samples of just about everything in sight, measuring distances, trying to get casts of footprints,
sifting soil. In the barn, their bright arc lamps had replaced Darby's
roving light.

This was the desk where Rothwell dealt with handwritten correspondence and phone calls, Banks guessed. There was a blotter,
which looked new—no handy wrong-way-around clues scrawled
there—a jam-jar full of pens and pencils, a blank scratch-pad, an
electronic adding machine of the kind that produces a printed tape
of its calculations and an appointment calendar open at the day of
the murder, 12th May.

The only things written there were "Dr Hunter" beside the
10:00 A.M. slot, "Make dinner reservation: Mario's, 8:30 P.M." Below
that, and written in capitals all across the afternoon, "FLOWERS?"
Banks had noticed a vase full of fresh flowers in the living-room. An
anniversary present? Sad when touching gestures like that outlive

the giver. He thought of Sandra again, and suddenly he wanted very much to be near her, to bridge the distance that had grown between them, to hold her and feel her warmth. He shivered.

"All right, Alan?" Gristhorpe asked.

"Fine. Someone just walked over my grave."

"Look at all this." Gristhorpe pointed to the two metal filing cabinets and the heavy-duty shelves that took up the room's only long, unbroken wall. "Business records, by the looks of it. Someone's going to have to sift through it." He looked towards the computer and grimaced. "We'd better get Phil to have a look at this lot tomorrow," he said. "I wouldn't trust myself to turn the bloody thing on without blowing it up."

Banks grinned. He was aware of Gristhorpe's Luddite attitude towards computers. He quite liked them, himself. Of course, he had only the most rudimentary skills and never seemed to be able to do anything right, but Phil Richmond, "Phil the Hacker" as he was known around the station, ought to be able to tell them a thing or two about Rothwell's system.

Finding nothing else of immediate interest in the office, they walked out to the rear of the house, which faced north, and stood in the back garden, the hems of their trousers damp with dew. It was after five now, close to dawn. A pale sun was slowly rising in the east behind a veil of thin cloud that had appeared over the last couple of hours, mauve on the horizon, but giving the rest of the sky a light grey wash and the landscape the look of a water-colour. A few birds sang, and occasionally the sound of a farm vehicle starting up broke the silence. The air smelled moist and fresh.

It was certainly a *garden* they stood in, and not just a backyard. Someone—Rothwell? His wife?—had planted rows of vege-tables—beans, cabbage, lettuce, all neatly marked—a small area of herbs and a strawberry patch. At the far end, beyond a dry-stone wall, the land fell away steeply to a beck that coursed down the daleside until it fed into the River Swain at Fortford.

The village of Fortford, about a mile down the hillside, was just waking up. Below the exposed foundations of the Roman fort on its knoll to the east, the cottages with their flagstone roofs huddled around the green and the square-towered church. Already, smoke drifted from some of the chimneys as farm labourers and shop-keepers prepared themselves for the coming day. Country folk were early risers.

The whitewashed front of the sixteenth-century Rose and Crown glowed pink in the early light. Even in there, someone would soon be in the kitchen, making bacon and eggs for the paying guests, especially for the ramblers, who liked to be off early. At the thought of food, his stomach rumbled. He knew Ian Falkland, the landlord of the Rose and Crown, and thought it might not be a bad idea to have a chat with him about Keith Rothwell. Though he was an expatriate Londoner, like Banks, Ian knew most of the local dalesfolk, and, given his line of work, he picked up a fair amount of gossip.

Finally, Banks turned to Gristhorpe and broke the silence. "They certainly seemed to know what was what, didn't they?" he said. "I don't imagine it was a lucky guess that the girl was in the house alone."

"You're thinking along the same lines as I am, aren't you, Alan?" said Gristhorpe. "An execution. A hit. Call it what you will."

Banks nodded. "I can't see any other lines to think along yet. Everything points to it. The way they came in and waited, the position of the body, the coolness, the professionalism of it all. Even the way one of them said touching the girl wasn't part of the deal. It was all planned. Yes, I think it was an execution. It certainly wasn't a robbery or a random killing. They hadn't been through the house, as far as we could tell. Everything seems in order. And if it was a robbery, they'd no need to kill him, especially that way. The question is why? Why should anyone want to execute an accountant?"

"Hmm," said Gristhorpe. "Unhappy client, maybe? Someone he turned in to the Inland Revenue?" Nearby, a peewit sensed their closeness to its ground nest and started buzzing them, piping its high-pitched call. "One of the things we have to do is find out how *honest* an accountant our Mr Rothwell was," Gristhorpe went on. "But let's not speculate too much yet, Alan. We don't know if there's anything missing, for a start. Rothwell might have had a million in gold bullion hidden away in his garage for all we know. But you're right about the execution angle. And that means we could be dealing with something very big, big enough to contract a murder for."

"Sir?"

At that moment, one of the SOC officers came into the garden through the back door.

Gristhorpe turned. "Yes?"

"We've found something, sir. In the garage. I think you'd both better come and have a look for yourselves."

IV

They followed the officer back to the brightly lit garage. Rothwell's body had, mercifully, been taken to the morgue, where Dr Glendenning, the Home Office pathologist, would get to work on it as soon as he could. Two men from the SOC team stood by the barn door. One was holding something with a pair of tweezers and the other was peering at it closely.

"What is it?" Banks asked.

"It's wadding, sir. From the shotgun," said the SOCO with the tweezers. "You see, sir, you can buy commercially made shotgun cartridges, but you can also reload the shells at home. Plenty of farmers and recreational shooters do it. Saves money."

"Is that what this bloke did?" Banks asked.

"Looks like it, sir."

"To save money? Typical Yorkshireman. Like a Scotsman stripped of his generosity."

"Cheeky southern bastard," said Gristhorpe, then turned to the SOCO. "Go on, lad."

"Well, sir, I don't know how much you know about shotguns, but they take cartridges, not bullets."

Banks knew that much, at least, and he suspected that Gristhorpe, from Dales farming stock, knew a heck of a lot more. But they usually found it best to let the SOCOs show off a bit.

"We're listening," said Gristhorpe.

Emboldened by that, the officer went on. "A shotgun shell's made up of a primer, a charge of gunpowder and the pellets, or shot. There's no slug and there's no rifling in the barrel, so you can't get any characteristic markings to trace back to the weapon. Except from the shell, of course, which bears the imprint of the firing and loading mechanisms. But we don't have a shell. What we do have is this." He held up the wadding. "Commercial wadding is usually made of either paper or plastic, and you can sometimes trace the shell's manufacturer through it. But this isn't commercial."

"What exactly is it?" asked Banks, reaching out.

The SOCO passed him the tweezers and said, "Don't know for certain yet, but it looks like something from a colour magazine. And luckily, it's not too badly burned inside, only charred around the edges. It's tightly packed, but we'll get it unfolded and straightened out when we get it to the lab, then maybe we'll be able to tell you the name, date and page number."

"Then all we'll have to do is check the list of subscribers," said Banks, "and it'll lead us straight to our killer. Dream on."

The SOCO laughed. "We're not miracle workers, sir."

"Has anyone got a magnifying glass?" Banks asked the assembly at large. "And I don't want any bloody cracks about Sherlock Holmes."

One of the SOCOs passed him a glass, the rectangular kind that came with the tiny-print, two-volume edition of the *Oxford English Dictionary*. Banks held up the wadding and examined it through the glass.

What he saw was an irregularly shaped wad of crumpled paper, no more than about an inch across at its widest point. At first he couldn't make out anything but the blackened edge of the wadded paper, but it certainly looked as if it were from some kind of magazine. He looked more closely, turning the wadding this way and that, holding it closer and farther, then finally the disembodied shapes coalesced into something recognizable. "Bloody hell," he muttered, letting his arm fall slowly to his side.

"What is it, Alan?" Gristhorpe asked.

Banks handed him the glass. "You'd better have a look for yourself," he said. "You won't believe me."

Banks stood back and watched Gristhorpe scrutinize the wadding, knowing that it would be only a matter of moments before he noticed, as Banks had done, part of a pink tongue licking a dribble of semen from the tip of an erect penis.

TWO

I

Traditional police wisdom has it that if a case doesn't yield leads in the first twenty-four hours, then everyone is in for a long, tough haul. In practice, of course, the period doesn't always turn out to be twenty-four hours; it can be twenty-three, nine, fourteen, or even forty-eight. That's the problem: when do you scale down your efforts? The answer, Banks reminded himself as he dragged his weary bones into the "Boardroom" of Eastvale Divisional Police Headquarters at ten o'clock that morning, is that you don't.

The Suzy Lamplugh case was a good example. It started as a missing-persons report. One lunch-time, a young woman left the estate agent's office in Fulham, where she worked, and disappeared. Only after over a year's intensive detective work, which resulted in more than six hundred sworn statements, thousands of interviews, 26,000 index cards and nobody knew how many man-hours, was the investigation wound down. Suzy Lamplugh was never found, either alive or dead.

By the time Banks arrived at the station, Superintendent Gristhorpe had appointed Phil Richmond Office Manager and asked him to set up the Murder Room, where all information regarding the Keith Rothwell case would be carefully indexed, cross-referenced and filed. At first, Gristhorpe thought it should be established in Fortford or Relton, close to the scene, but later decided that they had better facilities at the Eastvale station. It was only about seven miles from Fortford, anyway.

Richmond was also the only one among them who had training in the use of the HOLMES computer system—acronym for the Home Office Major Enquiry System, with a superfluous "L" for effect. HOLMES wasn't without its problems, especially as not all the country's police forces used the same computer languages. Still, if no developments occurred before long, Richmond's skill might prove useful.

Gristhorpe had also given a brief press conference first thing in the morning. The sooner photographs of Keith Rothwell and descriptions of the killers, balaclavas and all, were sitting beside the public's breakfast plates or flashing on their TV screens, the sooner information would start to come in. The news was too late for that morning's papers, but it would make local radio and television, the *Yorkshire Evening Post* and tomorrow's national dailies.

Of course, Gristhorpe had given hardly any details about the murder itself. At first, he had even resisted the idea of releasing Rothwell's name. After all, there had been no formal identification, and they didn't have his fingerprints on file for comparison. On the other hand, there was little doubt as to what had happened, and they were hardly going to drag Alison or her mother along to the mortuary to identify the remains.

Gristhorpe had also been in touch with the anti-terrorist squad at Scotland Yard. Yorkshire was far from a stranger to IRA action. People still remembered the M62 bomb in 1974, when a coach carrying British servicemen and their families was blown up, killing eleven and wounding fourteen. Many even claimed to have heard the explosion from as far away as Leeds and Bradford. More recently, two policemen had been shot by IRA members during a routine traffic check on the A1.

The anti-terrorist squad would be able to tell Gristhorpe whether Rothwell had any connections, however tenuous, that would make him a target. As an accountant, he could, for example, have been handling money for a terrorist group. In addition, forensic information and details of the *modus operandi* would be made known to the squad, who would see if the information matched anything on file.

While Gristhorpe handled the news media and Richmond set up the Murder Room, Banks and Susan Gay had conducted a breakfast-time house-to-house of Relton and Fortford—including a visit to the Rose and Crown and a generous breakfast from Ian Falkland—

trying to find out a bit about Rothwell, and whether anyone had seen or heard anything unusual on the night of the murder.

Gristhorpe, Richmond and Susan Gay were already in the room when Banks arrived and poured himself a large black coffee. The conference room was nicknamed the "Boardroom" because of its well-polished, heavy oval table and ten stiff-backed chairs, not to mention the coarse-textured burgundy wallpaper, which gave the room a constant aura of semi-darkness, and the large oil painting (in ornate gilt frame) of one of Eastvale's most successful nineteenth-century wool merchants, looking decidedly sober and stiff in his tight-fitting suit and starched collar.

"Right," said Gristhorpe, "time to get up to date. Alan?"

Banks slipped a few sheets of paper from his briefcase and rubbed his eyes. "Not much so far, I'm afraid. Rothwell was trained as an accountant. At least we've got that much confirmed. Some of the locals in Relton and Fortford knew him, but not well. Apparently, he was a quiet sort of bloke. Kept himself to himself."

"Who did he work for?"

"Self-employed. We got this from Ian Falkland, landlord of the Rose and Crown in Fortford. He said Rothwell used to drop by now and then for a quick jar before dinner. Never had more than a couple of halves. Well-liked, quiet, decent sort of chap. Anyway, he used to work for Hatchard and Pratt, the Eastvale firm, until he started his own business. Falkland used him for the pub's accounts. I gather Rothwell saved him a bob or two from the Inland Revenue." Banks scratched the small scar by his right eye. "There's a bit more to it than that, though," he went on. "Falkland got the impression that Rothwell owned a few businesses as well, and that accountancy was becoming more of a sideline for him. We couldn't get any more than that, but we'll be having a close look at his office today."

Gristhorpe nodded.

"And that's about it," Banks said. "The Rothwell family had been living at Arkbeck Farm for almost five years. They used to live in Eastvale." He looked at his watch. "I'm going out to Arkbeck Farm again after this meeting. I'm hoping Mrs Rothwell will have recovered enough to tell us something about what happened."

"Good. Any leads on the two men?"

"Not yet, but Susan spoke to someone who thinks he saw a car."

Gristhorpe looked at Susan.

"That's right, sir," she said. "It was around sunset last night, before it got completely dark. A retired schoolteacher from Fortford was coming back home after visiting his daughter in Pateley Bridge. He said he liked to take the lonely roads over the moors."

"Where did he see this car?"

"At the edge of the moors above Relton, sir. It was parked in a turn-off, just a dip by the side of the road. I think it used to be an old drover's track, but it's not used any more, and only the bit by the road is clear. The rest has been taken over by moorland. Anyway, sir, the thing is that the way the road curves in a wide semi-circle around the farm, this spot would only be about a quarter of a mile away on foot. Remember that copse opposite the farmhouse? Well, it's the same one that straggles up the daleside as far as this turn-off. It would provide excellent cover if someone wanted to get to the farm without being seen, and Alison wouldn't have heard the car approaching if it had been parked way up on the road."

"Sounds promising," said Gristhorpe. "Did the witness notice anything about the car?"

"Yes, sir. He said it looked like an old Escort. It was a light colour. For some reason he thought pale blue. And there was either rust or mud or grass around the lower chassis."

"It's hardly the bloody stretch-limousine you associate with hit men, is it?" Gristhorpe said.

"More of a Yorkshire version," said Banks.

Gristhorpe laughed. "Aye. Better follow it up, then, Susan. Get a description of the car out. I don't suppose your retired school-teacher happened to see two men dressed in black carrying a shotgun, did he?"

Susan grinned. "No, sir."

"Rothwell didn't do any farming himself, did he?" Gristhorpe asked Banks.

"No. Only that vegetable patch we saw at the back. He rented out the rest of his land to neighbouring farmers. There's a fellow

I know farms up near Relton I want to talk to. Pat Clifford. He should know if there were any problems in that area."

"Good," said Gristhorpe. "As you know, a lot of locals don't like newcomers buying up empty farms and not using them properly."

Gristhorpe, Banks knew, had lived in the farmhouse above Lyndgarth all his life. Perhaps he had even been born there. He had sold off most of the land after his parents died and kept only enough for a small garden and for his chief off-duty indulgence, a dry-stone wall he worked on periodically, which went nowhere and fenced nothing in.

"Anyway," Gristhorpe went on, "there's been some bad feeling. I can't see a local farmer hiring a couple of killers—people like to take care of their own around these parts—but stranger things have happened. And remember: shotguns are common as cow-clap around farms. Anything on that wadding yet?"

Banks shook his head. "The lab's still working on it. I've already asked West Yorkshire to make a few enquiries at the kind of places that sell that sort of magazine. I talked to Ken Blackstone at Millgarth in Leeds. He's a DI there and an old mate."

"Good," said Gristhorpe, then turned to Richmond. "Phil, why don't you go up to Arkbeck Farm with Alan and have a look at Rothwell's computer before you get bogged down managing the office?"

"Yes, sir. Do you think we should have it brought in after I've had a quick look?"

Gristhorpe nodded. "Aye, good idea." He scratched his pock-marked cheek. "Look, Phil, I know you're supposed to be leaving us for the Yard at the end of the week, but—"

"It's all right, sir," Richmond said. "I understand. I'll stick around as long as you need me."

"Good lad. Susan, did you find anything interesting in the appointment book?"

Susan Gay shook her head. "Not yet, sir. He had a doctor's appointment for yesterday morning with Dr Hunter. I called the office and it appears he kept it. Routine physical. No problems. I'm working my way through. He didn't write much down—or maybe he kept it on computer—but there's a few names to check out, mostly local businesses. I must say, though, sir, he didn't exactly have a full appointment book. There are plenty of empty days."

"Maybe he didn't need the money. Maybe he could afford to pick and choose. Have a word with someone at his old firm, Hatchard and Pratt. They're just on Market Street. They might be able to tell us something about his background." Gristhorpe looked at his watch. "Okay, we've all got plenty to do, better get to it."

II

"I'm afraid my mother's still in bed," Alison told Banks at Arkbeck Farm. "I told her you were here …" She shrugged.

That was odd, Banks thought. Surely a mother would want to comfort her daughter and protect her from prying policemen? "Have you remembered anything else?" he asked.

Alison Rothwell looked worn out and worried to death. She wore her hair, unwashed and a little greasy, tied back, emphasizing her broad forehead, a plain white T-shirt and stonewashed designer jeans. She sat with her legs tucked under her, and as she talked, she fiddled with a ring on the little finger of her right hand. "I don't know," she said. The lisp made her sound like a little girl.

They sat in a small, cheerful room at the back of the house with ivory-painted walls and Wedgwood blue upholstery. A bookcase stood against one wall, mostly full of paperbacks, their spines a riot of orange, green and black. Against the wall opposite stood an upright piano with a highly lacquered cherry-wood finish. On top of it stood an untidy pile of sheet music. WPC Smithies, who had stayed with the Rothwells, sat discreetly in a corner, notebook open. Phil Richmond was upstairs in Keith Rothwell's study, clicking away on the computer.

The large bay window, open about a foot to let in the birdsongs and fresh air, looked out over Fortford and the dale beyond. It was a familiar enough view to Banks. He had seen it from "Maggie's Farm" on the other side of Relton, and from the house of a man called Adam Harkness on the valley bottom. The sight never failed to impress, though, even on a dull day like today, with the grey-brown ruins of Devraulx Abbey poking through the trees of its grounds, the village of Lyndgarth clustered around its lopsided green and, towering over the patchwork of pale green fields and dry-stone walls that rose steeply to the heights, the forbidding line of Aldington Edge, a long limestone scar streaked with fissures from top to bottom like gleaming skeleton's teeth.

"I know it's painful to remember," Banks went on, "but we need all the help we can get if we're to catch these men."

"I know. I'm sorry."

"Do you remember hearing any sounds between the time they went outside and when you heard the bang?"

Alison frowned. "I don't think so."

"No sounds of a struggle, or screaming?"

"No. It was all so quiet. That's what I remember."

"No talking?"

"I didn't hear any."

"And you don't know how long they were out there before the explosion?"

"No. I was scared and I was worried. Mum was sitting facing me. I could see how frightened she was, but I couldn't do anything. I just felt so powerless."

"When it was all over, did you hear any sounds then?"

"I don't think so."

"Try to remember. Did you hear what direction they went off in?"

"No."

"Any sounds of a car?"

She paused. "I think I heard a car door shut, but I can't be sure. I mean, I didn't hear it drive it away, but I think I kept sort of drifting in and out. I think I heard a sound like the slam of a car door in the distance."

"Do you know which direction it came from?"

"Farther up the daleside, I think. Relton way."

"Good. Now, can you remember anything else about the men?"

"One of them, the one who touched me. I've been thinking about it. He had big brown eyes, a sort of light hazel colour, and watery. There's a word for it. Like a dog."

"Spaniel?"

"Yes. That's it. Spaniel eyes. Or puppy dog. He had puppy-dog eyes. But they're usually ... you know, they usually make you feel sorry for the person, but these didn't. They were cruel."

"Did either of the men say anything else?"

"No."

"Did they go anywhere else in the house? Any other rooms?"

"No."

"Did you see them take anything at all?"

Alison shook her head.

"When your father saw them and later went outside with them, how did he seem?"

"What do you mean?"

"Was he surprised?"

"When he first came in and they grabbed him, yes."

"But after?"

"I ... I don't know. He didn't do anything or say anything. He just stood there."

"Do you think he recognized the men?"

"How could he? They were all covered up."

"Did he seem surprised after the immediate shock had worn off?"

"I don't think he did, no. Just ... resigned."

"Was he expecting them?"

"I ... I don't know. I don't think so."

"Do you think he knew them, knew why they were there?"

"How could he?"

She spoke with such disbelief that Banks wondered if she had noticed that her father really *wasn't* so shocked or surprised and it confused her. "Do you think he knew what was happening?" he pressed. "Why it was happening?"

"Maybe. No. I don't know. He couldn't possibly, could he?" She screwed up her eyes. "I can't see it that clearly. I don't want to see it clearly."

"All right, Alison. It's all right. I'm sorry, but I have to ask."

"I know. I don't mean to be a cry-baby." She rubbed her bare arm over her eyes.

"You're being very brave. Just one more question about what happened and then we'll move on. Okay?"

"Okay."

"Did your father go quietly or did they have to force him?"

"No, he just walked out with them. He didn't say anything."

"Did he look frightened?"

"He didn't look anything." She reddened. "And he didn't *do* anything. He just left Mum and me all tied up and let them take him and … and kill him like an animal."

"All right, Alison, calm down. How did you get free from the chair after they'd gone?"

Alison sniffled and blew her nose. "It was a long time," she said finally. "Hours maybe. Some of the time I just sat there, but not really there, if you know what I mean. I think Mum had fainted. They'd really tied us tight and I couldn't feel my hands properly."

As she spoke, she rubbed at her wrists, still ringed by the burn-marks. "In the end, I tipped my chair and crawled over near the table where my mother's sewing basket was. I knew there were scissors in there. I had to rub my hands for a long time, so they could feel properly, and I don't know how … but in the end I cut the rope, then I untied Mum." She shifted her position. "I'm worried about Mum. She's not herself. She doesn't want to eat. What's going to happen to her?"

"I'm all right, Alison, dear. There's no need to worry."

The voice came from the doorway, and Banks turned for his first glance of Mrs Rothwell. She was a tall woman with short grey hair and fine-boned, angular features, the small nose perhaps just a little too sharply chiselled. There seemed an unusually wide space, Banks thought, between her nose and her thin upper lip, which gave her tilted head a haughty, imperious aspect. Banks could see where Alison got her small mouth from.

Her chestnut-brown eyes looked dull. Tranquillizers prescribed by Dr Burns, Banks guessed. They would help to explain her listless movements, too. Her skin was pale, as if drained of blood, though Banks could tell she had put some make-up on. In fact, she had made a great effort to look her best. She wore black silk slacks over her thin, boyish hips, and a cable-knit jumper in a rainbow pattern, which looked to Banks's untutored eye like an exclusive design. At least he had never seen one like it before. Even in her sedated grief, there was something controlled, commanding and attention-demanding about her, a kind of tightly reined-in power.

She sat down in the other armchair, crossed her legs and clasped her hands on her lap. Banks noticed the chunky rings on her fingers: diamond clusters, a large ruby and a broad gold wedding band.

Banks introduced himself and expressed his condolences. She inclined her head slightly in acceptance.

"I'm afraid I have some difficult questions for you, Mrs Rothwell," he said.

"Not about last night," she said, one bejewelled hand going to her throat. "I can't talk about it. I feel faint, my voice goes and I just can't talk."

"Mummy," said Alison. "I've told him about ... about that. Haven't I?" And she looked at Banks as if daring him to disagree.

"Yes," he said. "Actually, it wasn't that I wanted to ask about specifically. It's just that we need more information on your husband's movements and activities. Can you help?"

She nodded. "I'm sorry, Chief Inspector. I'm not usually such a mess." She touched her hair. "I must look dreadful."

Banks murmured a compliment. "Did your husband have any enemies that you knew of?" he asked.

"No. None at all. But then he didn't bore me with the details of his business. I really had no idea what kind of people he dealt with." Her accent, Banks noticed, was Eastvale filtered through elocution lessons. *Elocution lessons.* He hadn't thought people took those in this day and age.

"So he never brought his business home, so to speak?"

"No."

"Did he travel much?"

"Do you mean abroad?"

"Anywhere."

"Well, he did go abroad now and then, on business, and of course, we'd holiday in Mexico, Hawaii or Bermuda. He also travelled a lot locally in the course of business. He was away a lot."

"Where did he go?"

"Oh, all over. Leeds, Manchester, Liverpool, Birmingham, Bristol. Sometimes to London, Europe. He had a very important job. He was a brilliant financial analyst, much in demand. He could pick and choose his clients, could Keith, he didn't have to take just any old thing that came along."

"You mentioned financial analysis. What exactly did he do?"

She picked at the wool on her sleeve with long, bony fingers. "As I said, he didn't tell me much about work, not about the details, anyway. He qualified as a chartered accountant, of course, but that was only part of it. He had a genius for figures. He advised people what to do with their money, helped businesses out of difficulties. I suppose he was a kind of trouble-shooter, if you like. A very exclusive one. He didn't need any new clients and people only found out about him by word of mouth."

That all sounded sufficiently vague to be suspicious to Banks. On the other hand, what did *he* do? Investigate crimes, yes. But to do so, he chatted with locals over a pint, interviewed bereaved relatives, pored over fingerprints and blood samples. It would all sound rather nebulous and aimless to an outsider.

"And you never met any of his business associates?"

"We had people for dinner occasionally, but we never talked business."

"Maybe, if you have a moment later, you could make a list of those you entertained most frequently?"

She raised her eyebrows. "If you want."

"Now, Mrs Rothwell," Banks said, wishing he could have a cigarette in what was obviously a non-smoking household, "this next question may strike you as rather indelicate, but were there any problems in the family?"

"Of course not. We're a happy family. Aren't we, Alison?"

Alison looked at Banks. "Yes, Mother," she said.

Banks turned back to Mrs Rothwell. "Had your husband been behaving at all unusually recently?" he asked. "Had you noticed any changes in him?"

She frowned. "He *had* been a bit edgy, tense, a bit more preoccupied and secretive than usual. I mean, he was always quiet, but he'd been even more so."

"For how long?"

She shrugged. "Two or three weeks."

"But he never told you what was wrong?"

"No."

"Did you ask?"

"My husband didn't appreciate people prying into his private business affairs, Chief Inspector."

"Not even his wife?"

"I assumed that if and when he wanted to tell me, he would do so."

"What did you talk about over dinner yesterday?"

She shrugged. "Just the usual things. The children, the house extension we wanted to have done ... I don't know, really. What do *you* talk about when you're out for dinner with *your* wife?"

Good question, Banks thought. It had been so long since he and Sandra had gone out to dinner together that he couldn't remember what they talked about. "Did you have any idea what he might have been worried about?" he asked.

"No. I suppose it was one of the usual business problems. Keith really cared about his clients."

"What business problems? I thought he didn't talk to you about business."

"He didn't, Chief Inspector. Please don't twist what I say. He just made the occasional offhand comment. You know, maybe he'd read something in the *Financial Times* or something and make a comment. I never understood what he meant. Anyway, I think one of the companies he was trying to help was sinking fast. Things like that always upset him."

"Do you know which company?"

"No. It'll be on his computer. He put everything on that computer." Suddenly, Mrs Rothwell put the back of one ringed hand to her forehead in what seemed to Banks a gesture from a nineteenth-century melodrama. Her forehead looked clammy. "I'm afraid I can't talk any more," she whispered. "I feel a bit faint and dizzy. I ... Alison."

Alison helped her up and they left the room. Banks glanced over at WPC Smithies. "Have you picked up anything at all from them?" he asked.

"Sorry, sir," she said. "Nothing. I'll tell you one thing, though, they're a weird pair. It's an odd family. I think they're both retreating from reality, in their own ways, trying to deny what happened, or *how* it happened. But you can see that for yourself."

"Yes."

Banks listened to a clock tick on the mantelpiece. It was one of those timepieces with all its brass and silver innards showing inside a glass dome.

A couple of minutes later, Alison came back. "I'm sorry," she said. "Mummy's still weak and in shock. The doctor gave her some pills."

"That's understandable, Alison," said Banks. "I'd almost finished, anyway. Just one last question. Do you know where your brother is? We'll have to get in touch with him."

Alison picked up a postcard from the top of the piano, gave it to Banks and sat down again.

The card showed the San Francisco Golden Gate Bridge, which looked orange to Banks. He flipped it over. Postmarked two weeks ago, it read,

> *Dear Ali,*
> *Love California, and San Francisco is a* <u>*great*</u> *city, but it's time to move on. I'm even getting used to driving on the wrong side of the road! This sightseeing's a tiring business so I'm off to Florida for a couple of weeks just lying in the sun. Ah, what bliss! Also to check out the motion picture conservatory in Sarasota. I'm driving down the coast highway and flying to Tampa from LA on Sunday. More news when I get there. Love to Mum,*
>
> *Tom*

"How long has he been gone?"

"Six weeks. Just over. He left on March 31st."

"What does he do? What was that about a motion picture conservatory?"

Alison gave a brief smile. "He wants to work in films. He worked in a video shop and saved up. He's hoping to go to film college in America and learn how to become a director."

"How old is he?"

"Twenty-one."

Banks stood up. "All right, Alison," he said. "Thanks very much for all your help. WPC Smithies will be staying here for a while, so if you need anyone … And I'll ask the doctor to pay your mother another visit."

"Thank you. Please don't worry about us."

Banks looked in on Richmond, who sat bathed in the bluish glow of Rothwell's monitor, oblivious to the world, then went out to his car and lit a cigarette. He rolled the window down and listened to the birds as he smoked. Birds aside, it was bloody quiet up here. How, he wondered, could a teenager like Alison stand the isolation? As WPC Smithies had said, the Rothwells were an odd family.

As he drove along the bumpy track to the Relton road, he slipped in a tape of Dr John playing solo New Orleans piano music. He had developed a craving for piano music—*any* kind of piano music—recently. He was even thinking of taking piano lessons; he wanted to learn how to play *everything*—classical, jazz, blues. The only thing that held him back was that he felt too old to embark on such a venture. His forty-first birthday was coming up in a couple of weeks.

In Relton, a couple of old ladies holding shopping baskets stood chatting outside the butcher's shop, probably about the murder.

Banks thought again about Alison Rothwell and her mother as he pulled up outside the Black Sheep. What were they holding back? And what was it that bothered him? No matter what Mrs Rothwell and Alison had said, there was something wrong in that family, and he had a hunch that Tom Rothwell might know what it was. The sooner they contacted him the better.

III

Laurence Pratt delved deep in his bottom drawer and pulled out a bottle of Courvoisier VSOP and two snifters.

"I'm sorry," he apologized to DC Susan Gay, who sat opposite him at the broad teak desk. "It's not that I'm a secret tippler. I keep it for emergencies, and I'm afraid what you've just told me most definitely constitutes one. You'll join me?"

"No, thank you."

"Not on duty?"

"Sometimes," Susan said. "But not today."

"Very well." He poured himself a generous measure, swirled it and took a sip. A little colour came back to his cheeks. "Ah ... that's better."

"If we could get back to Mr Rothwell, sir?"

"Yes. Yes, of course. But you must understand Miss, Miss ... ?"

"Gay, sir. DC Gay."

She saw the inadvertent smile flash across his face. People often smiled like that when she introduced herself. "Gay" had been a perfectly good name when she was a kid—her nickname for a while had been "Happy" Gay—but now its meaning was no longer the same. One clever bugger had actually asked, "Did you say AC or DC Gay?" She comforted herself with the thought that he was doing three to five in Strangeways, thanks largely to her court evidence.

"Yes," he went on, a frown quickly displacing the smile. "I'd heard about Keith's death, of course, on the radio this lunch-time, but they didn't say *how* it happened. That's a bit of a shock, to be honest. You see, I knew Keith quite well. I'm only about three years older than he, and we worked here together for some years."

"He left the firm five years ago, is that right?"

"About right. A big move like that takes quite a bit of planning, quite a bit of organizing. There were client files to be transferred, that sort of thing. And he had the house to think of, too."

"He was a partner?"

"Yes. My father, Jeremiah Pratt, was one of the founders of the firm. He's retired now."

"I understand the family used to live in Eastvale, is that right?"

"Yes. Quite a nice house out towards the York roundabout. Catterick Street."

"Why did they move?"

"Mary always fancied living in the country. I don't know why. She wasn't any kind of nature girl. I think perhaps she wanted to play Lady of the Manor."

"Oh? Why's that?"

Pratt shrugged. "Just her nature."

"What about her husband?"

"Keith didn't mind. I should imagine he liked the solitude. I don't mean he was exactly anti-social, but he was never a great mixer, not lately, anyway. He travelled a lot, too."

Pratt was in his mid-forties, Susan guessed, which did indeed make him just a few years older than Keith Rothwell. Quite good-looking, with a strong jaw and grey eyes, he wore his white shirt with the sleeves rolled up and his mauve and green tie clipped with what looked like a silver American dollar sign. His hairline was receding and what hair remained was grey at the temples. He wore black-framed glasses, which sat about halfway down his nose.

"Did you ever visit him there?"

"Yes. My wife and I dined with the Rothwells on several occasions."

"Were you friends?"

Pratt took another sip of cognac, put his hand out and waggled it from side to side. "Hmm. Somewhere between friends and colleagues, I'd say."

"Why did he leave Hatchard and Pratt?"

Pratt broke eye contact and looked into the liquid he swirled in his snifter. "Ambition, maybe? Straightforward accountancy bored him. He was fond of abstractions, very good with figures. He certainly had a flair for financial management. Very creative."

"Does that imply fraudulent?"

Pratt looked up at her. She couldn't read his expression. "I resent that implication," he said.

"Was there any bad feeling?"

"I don't know what you mean."

"When he left the firm. Had there been any arguments, any problems?"

"Good lord, this was five years ago!"

"Even so."

Pratt adopted a stiffer tone. "No, of course there hadn't. Everything was perfectly amicable. We were sorry to lose him, of course, but ..."

"He wasn't fired or anything?"

"No."

"Did he take any clients with him?"

Pratt shuffled in his chair. "There will always be clients who feel they owe their loyalty to an individual member of the firm rather than to the firm as a whole."

"Are you sure this didn't cause bad feeling?"

"No, of course not. While it's unprofessional to solicit clients and woo them away, most firms *do* accept that they will lose some business whenever a popular member leaves to set up on his own. Say, for example, you visit a particular dentist in a group practice. You feel comfortable with him. He understands how you feel about dentists, you feel safe with him. If he left and set up on his own, would you go with him or stay and take your chances?"

Susan smiled. "I see what you mean. Do you think you could provide me with a list of names of the clients he took?"

Pratt chewed his lower lip for a moment, as if debating the ethics of such a request, then said, "I don't see why not. You could find out from his records anyway."

"Thank you. He must have made a fair bit of money somehow," Susan said. "How did he do it?"

Pratt, who if truth be told, Susan thought, suppressing a giggle, might not be entirely happy about *his* name, either, made a steeple of his hairy hands. "The same way we all do, I assume," he said. "Hard work. Good investments. Excellent service. Arkbeck Farm was in pretty poor shape when they bought it, you know. It didn't cost a fortune, and he'd no trouble arranging a fair mortgage. He put a lot into that house over the years."

Susan looked at her notes and frowned as if she were having trouble reading or understanding them. "I understand Mr Rothwell actually owned a number of businesses. Do you know anything about this?"

Pratt shook his head. "Not really. I understand he was interested in property development. As I said, Keith was an astute businessman."

"Did Mrs Rothwell work?"

"Mary? Good heavens, no! Well, not in the sense that she went out and made money. Mary was a housewife all the way. Well, perhaps 'house manager' or 'lady of leisure' would be a more appropriate term, as she didn't actually do the work herself. Except for the garden. You must have seen Arkbeck, how clean it is, how well appointed?"

"I'm afraid I had other things on my mind when I was there, sir," Susan said, "but I know what you mean."

Pratt nodded. "For Mary," he went on, "everything centred around the home, the family and the immediate community. Everything had to be just so, to look just right, and it had to be *seen* to look that way. I imagine she was a hard taskmaster, or should that be taskmistress? Of course, she didn't spend *all* her time in the house. There were the Women's Institute, the Church committees, the good works and the charities. Mary kept very busy, I can assure you."

"Good works? Charities?" There was something positively Victorian about this. Susan pictured an earnest woman striding from hovel to hovel in a flurry of garments, long dress trailing in the mud, distributing alms to the peasants and preaching self-improvement.

"Yes. She collected for a number of good causes. You know, the RSPCA, NSPCC, cancer, heart foundation and the like. Nothing political—I mean, no ban the bomb or anything—and nothing controversial, like AIDS research. Just the basics. She was the boss's daughter, after all. She had certain Conservative standards to keep up."

"The boss's daughter?"

"Yes, didn't you know? Her maiden name was Mary Hatchard. She was old man Hatchard's daughter. He's dead now, of course."

"So Keith Rothwell married the boss's daughter," Susan mused aloud. "I don't suppose that did his career any harm?"

"No, it didn't. But that was more good luck than good management, if you ask me. Keith didn't just marry the boss's daughter, he got her pregnant first, with Tom, as it turns out, *then* he married her."

"How did that go over?"

Pratt paused and picked up a paper-clip. "Not very well at first. Old man Hatchard was mad as hell. He kept the lid on it pretty well, of course, and after he'd had time to consider it, I think he was glad to get her off his hands. He could hardly have her married to a mere junior, though, so Keith came up pretty quickly through the ranks to full partner."

Pratt twisted the paper-clip. He seemed to be enjoying this game, Susan thought. He was holding back, toying with her. She had a sense that if she didn't ask exactly the right questions, she wouldn't get the answers she needed. The problem was, she didn't know what the right questions were.

They sat in his office over Winston's Tobacconists, looking out on north Market Street, and Susan could hear the muted traffic sounds through the double-glazing. "Look," Pratt went on, "I realize I'm the one being questioned, but could you tell me how Mary is? And Alison? I do regard myself as something of a friend of the family, and if there's anything I can do ..."

"Thank you, sir. I'll make sure they know. Can you think of any reason anyone might have for killing Mr Rothwell?"

"No, I can't. Not in the way you described."

"What do you mean?"

"Well, I suppose I could imagine a burglar, say, perhaps killing someone who got in the way. You read about it in the papers, especially these days. Or an accident, some kids joy-riding. But this ...? It sounds like an assassination to me."

"When was the last time you saw him?"

"About a month ago. No, earlier. In March, I think. Shortly after St Patrick's Day. The wife and I went for dinner. Mary's a splendid cook."

"Did they entertain frequently?"

"Not that I know of. They had occasional small dinner parties, maximum six people. Keith didn't like socializing much, but Mary loved to show off the house, especially if she'd acquired a new piece of furniture or something. So they compromised. Last time it was the kitchen we had to admire. They used to have a country-style one, Aga and all, but someone started poking fun at 'Aga-louts' in the papers, so Mary got annoyed and went for the modern look."

"I see. What about the son, Tom? What do you know of him?"

"Tom? He's travelling in America, I understand. Good for him. Nothing like travel when you're young, before you get too tied down. Tom was always a cheerful and polite kid as far as I was concerned."

"No trouble?"

"Not in any real sense, no. I mean, he wasn't into drugs or any of that weird stuff. At worst I'd say he was a bit uncertain about what he wanted to do with his life, and his father was perhaps just a little impatient."

"In what way?"

"He wanted Tom to go into business or law. Something solid and respectable like that."

"And Tom?"

"Tom's the artsy type. But he's a bright lad. With his personality he could go almost anywhere. He just doesn't know where yet. After he left school, he drifted a bit. Still is doing, it seems."

"Would you say there was friction between them?"

"You can't be suggesting—"

"I'm not suggesting anything." Susan leaned back in the chair. "Look, Mr Pratt, as far as we know Tom Rothwell is somewhere in the USA. We're trying to find him, but it could take time. The reason I'm asking you all these questions is because we need to know *everything* about Keith Rothwell."

"Yes, of course. I'm sorry. But what with the shock of Keith's death and you asking about Tom ..."

Susan leaned forward again. "Is there any reason," she asked, "why you should think I was putting forward Tom as a suspect?"

"Stop trying to read between the lines. There's nothing written there. It was just the way you were asking about him, that's all. Tom and his father had the usual father-son arguments, but nothing more."

"Where did Tom get the money for a trip to America?"

"What? I don't know. Saved up, I suppose."

"You say you last saw Keith Rothwell in March?"

"Yes."

"Have you spoken with him at all since then?"

"No."

"Did he seem in any way different from usual then? Worried about anything? Nervous?"

"No, not that I can remember. It was a perfectly normal evening. Mary cooked duck à l'orange. Tom dropped in briefly, all excited about his trip. Alison stayed in her room."

"Did she usually do that?"

"Alison's a sweet child, but she's a real loner, very secretive. Takes after her father. She's a bit of a bookworm, too."

"What did you talk about that evening?"

"Oh, I can't remember. The usual stuff. Politics. Europe. The economy. Holiday plans."

"Who else was there?"

"Just us, this time."

"And Mr Rothwell said nothing that caused you any concern?"

"No. He was quiet."

"Unusually so?"

"He was usually quiet."

"Secretive?"

Pratt swivelled his chair and gazed out of the window at the upper storey of the Victorian community centre. Susan followed his gaze. She was surprised to see a number of gargoyles there she had never noticed before.

When he spoke again, Pratt still didn't look at Susan. She could see him only in profile. "I've always felt that about him, yes," he said. "That's why I hesitated to call him a *close* friend. There was always something in reserve." He turned to face Susan again and placed his hands, palms down, on the desk. "Oh, years ago we'd let loose once in a while, go get blind drunk and not give a damn. Sometimes we'd go fishing together. But over time, Keith sort of reined himself in, cut himself off. I don't really know how to explain this. It was just a feeling. Keith was a very private person ... well, lots of people are ... But the thing was, I had no idea what he lived for."

"Did he suffer from depression? Did you think—"

Pratt waved a hand. "No. No, you're getting me wrong. He wasn't suicidal. That's not what I meant."

"Can you try and explain?"

"I'll try. It's hard, though. I mean, I'd be hard pushed to say what I live for, too. There's the wife and kids, of course, my pride and joy. And we like to go hang-gliding over Semerwater on suitable weekends. I collect antiques, I love cricket and we like to explore new places on our holidays. See what I mean? None of that's what I actually *live for*, but it's all part of it." He took off his glasses and rubbed the back of his hand over his eyes and the bridge of his nose, then put them back on again. "I know, I'm getting too philosophical. But I told you it was hard to explain."

Susan smiled. "I'm still listening."

"Well, all those are just *things*, aren't they? Possessions or activities. Things we do, things we care about. But there's something behind them all that ties them all together into *my* life, who I am, what I am. With Keith, you never knew. He was a cipher. For example, I'm sure he loved his family, but he never really showed it or spoke much about it. I don't know what really *mattered* to him. He never talked about hobbies or anything like that. I don't know what he did in his spare time. It's more than being private or secretive, it's as if there was a dimension *missing*, a man with a hole in the middle." He scratched his temple. "This is ridiculous. Please forgive me. Keith was a perfectly nice bloke. Wouldn't hurt a fly. But you never really knew what gripped him about life, what his *dream* was. I mean, mine's a villa in Portugal, but a dream doesn't have to be a thing, does it? I don't know ... maybe he valued abstractions too much."

He paused, as if he had run out of breath and ideas. Susan didn't really know what to jot down, but she finally settled for "dimension missing ... interests and concerns elusive." It would do. She had a good memory for conversations and could recount verbatim most of what Pratt had said, if Banks wished to hear it.

"Let's get back to Mr Rothwell's work with your firm. Is there anything you can tell me about his ... style ... shall we say, his business practices?"

"You want to know if Keith was a crook, don't you?"

She did, of course, though that wasn't why she was asking. Still, she thought, never look a gift horse in the mouth. She gave him a "you caught me at it" smile. "Well, was he?"

"Of course not."

"Oh, come on, Mr Pratt. Surely in your business you must sail a little close to the wind at times?"

"I resent that remark, especially coming from a policeman."

Susan let that one slip by. *"Touché,"* she said. Pratt seemed pleased enough with himself. Let him feel he's winning, she thought, then he'll tell you anyway, just to show he holds the power to do so. She was still sure he was holding something back. "But seriously, Mr Pratt," she went on, "I'm not just playing games, bandying insults. If there was anything at all unusual in Mr Rothwell's business dealings, I hardly need tell you it could have a bearing on his murder."

"Hmm." Pratt swirled the rest of the brandy and tossed it back. He put the snifter in his "Out" tray, no doubt for the secretary to take and wash. "I stand by what I said," he went on. "Keith Rothwell never did anything truly *illegal* that I knew of. Certainly nothing that could be relevant to his death."

"But ... ?"

He sighed. "Well, maybe I wasn't *entirely* truthful earlier. I suppose I'd better tell you about it, hadn't I? You're bound to find out somehow."

Susan turned her page. "I'm listening," she said.

THREE

I

The Black Sheep was the closest Swainsdale had to a well-kept secret. Most tourists were put off by the pub's external shabbiness. Those who prided themselves on not judging a book by its cover would, more often than not, pop their heads around the door, see the even shabbier interior and leave.

The renowned surliness of the landlord, Larry Grafton, kept them away in droves, too. There was a rumour that Larry had once refused to serve an American tourist with a Glenmorangie and ginger, objecting to the utter lack of taste that led her to ask for such a concoction. Banks believed it.

Larry was Dales born and bred, not one of the new landlords up from London. So many were recent immigrants these days, like Ian Falkland in the Rose and Crown. That was a tourist pub if ever there was one, Banks thought, probably selling more lager and lime, pork scratchings and microwaved curries than anything else.

The Black Sheep didn't advertise its pub grub, but anyone who knew about it could get as thick and fresh a ham and piccalilli sandwich as ever they'd want from Elsie, Larry's wife. And on some days, if her arthritis hadn't been bothering her too much and she felt like cooking, she could do you a fry-up so good you could feel your arteries hardening as you ate.

As usual, the public bar was empty apart from one table of old men playing dominoes and a couple of young farm-hands reading the sports news in the *Daily Mirror*.

As Banks had expected, Pat Clifford also stood propping up the bar. Pat was a hard, stout man with a round head, stubble for hair and a rough, red face burned by the sun and whipped by the wind and rain for fifty years.

"Hello, stranger," said Pat, as Banks stood next to him. "Long time, no see."

Banks apologized for his absence and brought up the subject of Keith Rothwell.

"So tha only comes when tha wants summat, is that it?" Pat said. But he said it with a smile, and over the years Banks had learned that Yorkshire folk often take the sting out of their criticisms that way. They put a sting *in* their compliments, too, on those rare occasions they get around to giving any.

In this case, Banks guessed that Pat wasn't mortally offended at his protracted absence; he only wanted to make a point of it, let Banks know his feelings, and then get on with things. Banks acknowledged his culpability with a mild protest about the pressures of work, as expected, then listened to a minute or so of Pat's complaining about how the elderly and isolated were neglected by all and sundry.

When Pat's glass was empty, an event which occurred with alarming immediacy at the end of the diatribe, Banks's offer to buy him another was grudgingly accepted. Pat took a couple of sips, put the glass down on the bar and wiped his lips with the back of his grimy hand.

"He came in once or twice, did Mr Rothwell. Local, like. Nobody objected."

"How often?"

"Once a week, mebbe. Sometimes twice. Larry—?" And he asked the landlord the same question. Larry, who hardly had a charabanc full of thirsty customers to serve, came over and stood with them. He still treated Banks with a certain amount of disdain—after all, Banks was a southerner *and* a copper—but he showed respect, too.

Banks had never tried *too* hard to fit in, to pretend he was one of the crowd like some of the other incomers. He knew there was nothing that annoyed a Dalesman so much as pretentiousness, airs and graces, and that there was nothing more contemptible or condescending than a southerner appropriating Dales speech and ways, playing the expert on a place he had only just come to. Banks kept his distance, kept his counsel, and in return he was accorded that particular Yorkshire brand of grudging acceptance.

"Just at lunch-times, like," Larry said. "Never saw him of an evening. He'd come in for one of Elsie's sandwiches and always drink half a pint. Just one half, mind you."

"Did he talk much?"

Larry drifted off to dry some glasses and Pat picked up the threads. "Nay. He weren't much of chatterbox, weren't Mr Rothwell. Bit of a dry stick, if you ask me."

"What do you mean? Was he stuck-up?"

"No-o. Just had nowt to talk abaht, that's all." He tapped the side of his nose. "If you listen as much as I do," he said, "you soon find out what interests people. There's not much when it comes down to it, tha knows." He started counting on the stubby fingers that stuck out of his cut-off gloves. "Telly, that's number one. Sport—number two. And sex. That's number three. After that there's nobbut money and weather left."

Banks smiled. "What about politics?" he asked.

Pat pulled a face. "Only when them daft buggers in t'Common Market 'ave been up to summat with their Common Agricultural Policy." Then he grinned, showing stained, crooked teeth. "Aye, I suppose that's often enough these days," he admitted, counting it off. "Politics. Number four."

"And what did Mr Rothwell talk about when he was here?" Banks asked.

"Nowt. That's what I'm telling thee, lad. Oh, I s'pose seeing as he was an accountant, he was interested in money, but he kept that to himself. He'd be standing there, all right, just where you are, munching on his sandwich, supping his half-pint, and nodding in all the right places, but he never had owt to say. It seemed to me as if he were really somewhere else. And he didn't know 'Neighbours' from 'Coronation Street,' if you ask me—or Leeds United from Northampton."

"There's not a lot of difference as far as their performances go over the last few weeks, if you ask me, Pat."

Pat grunted.

"So you didn't really know Keith Rothwell?" Banks asked.

"No. Nobody did."

"That's right, Mr Banks," added Larry as he stood by them to pull a pint. "He said he came for the company, what with working alone at home and all that, but I reckon as he came to get away from that there wife of his." Then he was gone, bearing the pint.

Banks turned to Pat. "What did he mean?"

"Ah, take no notice of him," Pat said with a dismissive wave in Grafton's direction. "Mebbe he was a bit henpecked, at that. It must be hard working at home when the wife's around all the time. Never get a minute's peace, you wouldn't. But Larry's lass, Cathy, did for Mrs Rothwell now and again, like, and she says she were a bit of an interfering mistress, if you know what I mean. Standing over young Cathy while she worked and saying that weren't done right, or that needed a bit more elbow grease. I nobbut met Mrs Rothwell once or twice, but my Grace speaks well of her, and that's enough for me."

Banks thought he might have a word with Larry's lass, Cathy. He noticed Pat's empty glass. "Another?"

"Oh, aye. Thank you very much." Banks bought him a pint, but decided to forgo a second himself, much as the idea appealed. "There were one time, when I comes to think on it," Pat said, "that Mr Rothwell seemed a bit odd."

"When was this?"

"Abaht two or three weeks ago. He came in one lunch-time, as usual, like, but he must have had a couple of pints, not 'alves. Anyroad, he got quite chatty, told a couple of jokes and we all had a good chuckle, didn't we, Larry?"

"Aye," shouted Larry from down the bar.

That sounded odd to Banks. According to Mrs Rothwell, her husband had been tense and edgy over the past three weeks. If he could chat and laugh at the Black Sheep, then maybe the problem had been at home. "Is that all?" he asked.

"*All?* Well, it were summat for us to see him enjoying himself for once. I'd say that were enough, wouldn't you?"

"Did he say anything unusual?"

"No. He just acted like an ordinary person. An ordinary *happy* person."

"As if he'd received some good news or something?"

"He didn't say owt about that."

Banks gave up and moved on. "I know there's been a bit of ill feeling among the hill-farmers about incomers lately," he said. "Did any of it spill over to Mr Rothwell?"

Pat sniffed. "You wouldn't understand, Mr Banks," he said softly, offering an unfiltered cigarette. Banks refused it and lit a Silk Cut. "It's not that there's any ill feeling, as such. We just don't know where we stand, how to plan for the future. One day the government says this, the next day it's something else. Agricultural Policy ... Europe ... grugh." He spat on the floor to show his feelings. Either nobody noticed or the practice was perfectly welcome in the Black Sheep, another reason why people stayed away. "It needs years of experience to do it right, does hill-farming," Pat went on. "Continuity, passed on from father to son. When too many farms fall to weekenders and holiday-makers, pasture gets abused, walls get neglected. Live and let live, that's what I say. But we want some respect and some under- standing. And right now we're not getting any."

"But what about the incomers?"

"Aye, hold thy horses, lad, I'm getting to them. We're not bloody park-keepers, tha knows. We don't graft for hours on end in all t'weather God sends keeping stone walls in good repair because we think they look picturesque, tha knows. They're to keep old Harry Cobb's sheep off my pasture and to make sure there's no hanky-panky between his breed and mine."

Banks nodded. "Fair enough, Pat. But how deep did the feeling go? Keith Rothwell bought that farm five years ago, or thereabouts. I've seen what he's done to it, and it's not a farm any more."

"Aye, well at least Mr Rothwell's a Swainsdale lad, even if he did come from Eastvale. Nay, there were no problems. He sold off his land—I got some of it, and so did Frank Rowbottom. If you're thinking me or Frank did it, then ..."

"No, nothing like that," Banks said. "I just wanted to get a sense of how Rothwell fitted in with the local scene, if he did."

"Well, he did and he didn't," said Pat. "He was here and he wasn't, and that's all I can tell thee. He could tell a joke well enough when he put his mind to it, though." Pat chuckled at the memory.

As puzzled as he was before, Banks said goodbye and went outside. On the way back, he slipped in a cassette of Busoni's Bach transcriptions. The precise, ordered music had no influence on the chaos of his thoughts.

II

Back in his office, Banks first glanced at Dr Glendenning's post-mortem notes. Generally, there was no such thing as a *preliminary* post-mortem report, but Dr Glendenning usually condescended to send over the main points in layman's language as quickly as possible. He also liked to appear at the scene, but this time he had been staying overnight with friends in Harrogate.

There was nothing in the notes that Banks hadn't expected. Rothwell hadn't been poisoned before he was shot; the stomach contents revealed only pasta and red wine. Dr Glendenning gave cause of death as a shotgun wound to the occipital region, the back of head, most likely a contact wound given the massive damage to bone and tissue. He also noted that it was lucky they already knew who the victim was, as there wasn't enough connected bone or tissue left to reconstruct the face, and though the tooth fragments could probably be collected and analyzed, it would take a bloody long time. The blood group was "O," which matched that supplied by Rothwell's doctor, as well as that of about half the population.

Rothwell had most likely been killed in the place and position they found him, Dr Glendenning pointed out, because what blood remained had collected as purplish hypostasis around the upper chest and the ragged edges of the neck. He estimated time of death between eleven and one the previous night.

A cadaveric spasm had caused Rothwell to grab and hold onto a handful of dust at the moment of death, and Banks thought of the T.S. Eliot quotation, "I will show you fear in a handful of dust," which he had come across as the title of an Evelyn Waugh novel.

Rothwell had been in generally good shape, Dr Glendenning said, and the only evidence of any ill health was an appendix scar.

Rothwell's doctor, Dr Hunter, was able to verify that Rothwell had had his appendix removed just over three years ago.

When Banks had finished, he phoned Sandra to say he didn't know when he would be home. She said that didn't surprise her. Then he went over to the window and looked down on the cobbled market square, most of which was covered by parked cars. The gold hands against the blue face of the church clock stood at a quarter to four.

Banks lit a cigarette and watched the local merchants taking deliveries and the tourists snapping pictures of the ancient market cross and the Norman church front. It was fine enough weather out there, sports jacket warm, but the grey wash that had come at dawn still obscured the sunshine. On Banks's *Dalesman* calendar, the May photograph showed a field of brilliant pink and purple flowers below Great Shunner Fell in Swaledale. So far, the real May had been struggling against showers and cool temperatures.

Sitting at his rattly metal desk, Banks next opened the envelope of Rothwell's pocket contents and spread them out in front of him.

There were a few business cards in a leather slip-case, describing Rothwell as a "Financial Consultant." In his wallet were three credit cards, including an American Express Gold; the receipt from Mario's on the night of his anniversary dinner; receipts from Austick's bookshop, a computer supplies shop and two restaurants, all from Leeds, and all dated the previous week; and photos of Alison and Mary Rothwell. Happy families indeed. In cash, Rothwell had a hundred and five pounds in his wallet, in new twenties and one crumpled old fiver.

Other pockets revealed a handkerchief, good quality silk and monogrammed "KAR," like the cufflinks on the body, BMW keys, house keys, a small pack of Rennies, two buttons, a gold Cross fountain pen, an empty leather-bound notebook and—horror of horrors—a packet of ten Benson and Hedges, six of which had been smoked.

Banks felt a surge of respect for the late Keith Rothwell. But perhaps the cigarettes helped to explain something, too. Banks was certain that Mary Rothwell would never have permitted her husband to pollute the house with his filthy habit. Smoking, then, could be the main reason he liked to sneak off to the Black Sheep or the Rose and Crown every now and then. It certainly wasn't drinking. A secret smoker, then? Or did she know? He found no gold lighter, only a sulphurous old box of Pilot matches; and Rothwell was the kind of person who put his spent matches back in the box facing the opposite direction from the live ones.

It was almost six when the phone rang: Vic Manson calling from the forensic lab. Vic spent almost as much time with the Scene-of-Crime team from North Yorkshire Headquarters, in Northallerton, as he did at the lab, and though Banks knew Vic was a fingerprints expert, he sometimes wasn't sure exactly what he did or where he really worked.

"What have you got for us?" Banks asked.

"Hold your horses."

"Social call, is it, then?"

"Not exactly."

"Then what?"

"The wadding, for a start."

"What about it?"

"We managed to get some more of the paper unfolded. It wasn't too badly burned inside. Anyway, the document analysts say it's good magazine quality, probably German. No prints. Nothing but blurs. It's not your common-or-garden girlie magazine, but it's not hard-core perversion either. The fullest picture we could get seemed to be a shaved vagina with a finger touching the clitoris. Bright red nail varnish. The fingernail, that is."

"That must be the other side of what I saw," said Banks. "Does it help?"

"It might do. Apparently there are people who have a fetish about shaved vaginas. It's something to go on, anyway."

Banks sighed. "Or maybe our killer's just got a warped sense of humour. We can check with the PNC, anyway, see if there's been any similar incidents. What about the weapon?"

"Twelve-gauge, double-barrel. Judging by the amount of shot we've collected, the bastard who did it must have used both of them."

"Anything from the house?"

"No prints, if that's what you mean. They wore gloves. And there was nothing special about the rope they used to tie up the wife and daughter, either. By the way, remember one of the chairs was wet, the one overturned by the table?"

"Yes."

"It was urine. The poor lass must have been so scared she pissed herself."

Banks swallowed. That was Alison's chair. She was the one who had eventually made her way to the sewing basket and toppled her chair. "Any footprints?" he asked.

"We're still working on it, but don't hold your breath. The ground had pretty much dried out after last week's rain."

"Okay, Vic, thanks for calling. Keep at it and keep me informed, okay?"

"Will do."

After he had hung up, Banks lit another cigarette and walked over to the window again. Most of the tourists were getting in their cars, removing the crook-locks and driving home. The cobbles, cross and church front looked slate grey in the dull afternoon light. At the far side of the square, the El Toro coffee bar and Joplin's newsagent's seemed to be doing good business.

Banks thought of Alison, who had shown so much courage in telling them about what had happened at Arkbeck Farm. Someone had scared her so much she had sat in her own urine, probably for hours. The idea of her indignity and humiliation made him angry. He vowed he would find whoever was responsible for doing that to her and make damn sure they suffered.

III

The Queen's Arms was always busy at six o'clock on a Friday, and it was only through good luck and quick reflexes that Banks and Susan Gay managed to grab a copper-topped table by the window when a party of cashiers from the NatWest Bank gathered their things and left.

As happened so often in the Dales, the weather had changed dramatically over a very short period. A light breeze had sprung up and blown away the clouds. Now, the early evening sunlight glowed through the red and amber panes and shot bright rays though the clear ones, lighting on a foaming glass of ale and high-lighting the smoke swirling in the air.

The sunlight and smoke reminded Banks of the effect the projection camera created at the cinema when smoking was allowed there. As kids, he and his friends used to put their money together for a packet of five Woodbines, then go to the morning matinee at the Palace: a Three Stooges short, a Buck Rogers or Flash Gordon serial and a black-and-white western, maybe a Hopalong Cassidy. Slumped down in their seats, they would smoke "wild woodies" until they felt sick. He smiled at the memory and reached for a Silk Cut.

Conversation and laughter ebbed and flowed all around them, and the general mood was ebullient. After all, it was the weekend. For most people in the pub, there would be no work until Monday morning. They could go off shopping to York or Leeds, wallpaper the bedroom, visit Aunt Maisie in Skipton or just lounge around and watch football or racing on telly. It was Cup Final day tomorrow, Banks remembered. Fat chance he'd get of watching it.

The best he could hope was that he would get home before too late tonight and spend some time with Sandra. It was the ideal opportunity for a bit of bridge-building. Tracy was away in France on a school exchange, and Brian was at Portsmouth Polytechnic, so they had the house to themselves for once. He would be too late for a shared dinner, but maybe a nice bottle of claret, a few Chopin "Nocturnes," candlelight ... then, who knew what might follow?

It was a nice fantasy. But right now he was waiting for Gristhorpe and Richmond, here to combine the pleasure of a pint and a steak-and-kidney pud with the business of swopping notes and fishing for leads at an informal meeting.

Once in a while, through the laughter and the arguments, Banks heard the Rothwell case mentioned. "Did you hear about that terri-ble murder up near Relton ... ?" "Hear about that bloke got shot out in the dale? I heard they blew his head right off his shoulders ..." By now, of course, everyone had had a chance to read the *Yorkshire Evening Post*, and people were only too willing to embroider on the scant details the newspaper gave. Rumour and fantasy were rife. What Gristhorpe hadn't told the media so far was that Rothwell had been executed "gangland" style, and that the weapon used was a shotgun.

The best the press could manage so far was "LOCAL BUSI-NESSMAN MURDERED ... Not more than a mile above the peaceful Swainsdale village of Fortford, a mild-mannered account-ant was shot to death in his own garage in the early hours of this morning ..." There followed an appeal for information about "two men in black" and a photograph of Keith Rothwell, looking exactly like a mild-mannered accountant, with his thinning fair hair combed back, showing the slight widow's peak, his high forehead, slightly prissy lips and the wire-rimmed glasses. The glasses, Banks knew, had been found shattered to pieces along with the other wreckage of Rothwell's skull.

Banks waved to Gristhorpe and Richmond, who nudged their way through the crowd to join them at the table. While he was on his feet, Richmond went to get a round of drinks and put in the food orders.

"At least we don't have to worry about civilians overhearing classified information," Gristhorpe said as he sat down and scraped his stool forward along the worn stone flagging. "I can hardly even hear myself think."

When Richmond got back with the tray of drinks, Gristhorpe said, "Right, Phil, tell us what you found."

They huddled close around the table. Richmond took a sip of his St Clements. "There are several items that have been either encrypted or assigned passwords," he said. "Some are complete directories, and one's just a document file in a directory. He's called it 'LETTER.'"

"Can you get access?" Gristhorpe asked.

"Not easily, no, sir. Not unless you type the password at the prompt. Believe me, I've tried every trick and all I've got for my pains is gibberish."

"All right." Gristhorpe coughed and waved away Banks's smoke with an exaggerated gesture. "Let's assume he had some special reason for keeping these items secret. That means we're definitely interested. You said you couldn't gain access easily, but is there a way?"

Richmond cleared his throat. "Well, yes there is. Actually, there are two ways."

"Come on, then, lad. Don't keep us in suspense."

"We could bring in an expert. I mean a *real* expert, like someone who writes the programmes."

"Aye, and the other option?"

"Well, it's not much known, for obvious reasons, but I went to a seminar once and the lecturer told me something that struck me as very odd."

"What?"

"Well, there's a company that sells by-pass programmes for various software security systems."

"That would probably be cheaper and quicker, wouldn't it?" said Gristhorpe. "Can you get hold of a copy?"

"Yes, sir. But it's not cheap. Actually, it's quite expensive."

"How much?"

"About two hundred quid."

Gristhorpe whistled between his teeth, then he said, "We don't have a lot of choice, do we? Go ahead, order one."

"I already have done, sir."

"And?"

"They're based in Akron, Ohio, but they told me there's a distributor in Taunton, Devon, who has some in stock. It could take a while to get it up here."

"Tell the buggers to send it by courier, then. We might as well be hung for a sheep as a lamb. Lord knows what the DCC will have to say come accounting time."

"Maybe if it helps us solve the case," Banks chipped in, "he'll increase our budget."

Gristhorpe laughed. "In a pig's arse, he will. Go on, Phil."

"That's all, really," said Richmond. "In the meantime, I'll keep trying and see what I can do. People sometimes write their passwords down in case they forget them. If Rothwell did, the only problem is finding out *where* and in what form."

"Interesting," Banks said. "I've got one of those plastic cards, the ones you use to get money at the hole in the wall. I keep the number written in my address book disguised as part of a telephone number in case I forget it."

"Exactly," said Richmond.

"Short of trying every name and number in Rothwell's address book," Gristhorpe said, "is there any quick way of doing this?"

"I don't think so, sir," Richmond said. "But often the password is a name the user has strong affinities with."

"'Rosebud'?" Banks suggested.

"Right," said Richmond. "That sort of thing. Maybe something from his childhood."

"'Woodbines,'" said Banks. "Sorry, Phil, just thinking out loud."

"But it could be anything. The name of a family member, for example. Or a random arrangement of letters, spaces, numbers and punctuation marks. It doesn't have to make any sense at all."

"Bloody hell." Gristhorpe ran his hand through his unruly thatch of grey hair.

"All I can say is leave it with me, sir. I'll do what I can. And I'll ask the software distributor to put a rush on it."

"All right. Susan? Anything from Hatchard and Pratt?"

Susan leaned forward to make herself heard. Just as she was about to start, Cyril called out their food number, and Richmond and Banks went through to bring back the trays. After a few mouthfuls, Susan started again. "Yes," she said, dabbing at the side of her mouth with a napkin. "As it turns out, Rothwell was asked to leave the firm."

"Asked to leave?" Gristhorpe echoed. "Does that mean fired?"

"Not exactly, sir. He was a partner. You can't just fire partners. He was also married to the boss's daughter. Mary Rothwell's maiden name is Hatchard. He was asked to resign. They didn't want a fuss."

"Interesting," said Gristhorpe. "What was it all about, then?"

Susan ate another mouthful of her Cornish pasty, then washed it down with a sip of Britvic orange and pushed her plate aside. "Laurence Pratt was reluctant to tell me about it," she said, "but I think he knew he'd be in more trouble if we found out some other way. It seems Rothwell was caught padding the time sheets. It's not a rare fiddle, according to Pratt. And he doesn't regard it as strictly illegal, but it *is* unethical, and it's bad luck for anyone who gets caught. Rothwell got off lucky."

"What happened?" asked Gristhorpe.

"This was about five years ago. Rothwell was doing a lot of work for a large company. Pratt wouldn't tell me who it was, but I don't think that really matters. The point is that Pratt's father was looking over the billings and noticed that Rothwell had doubled up on his hours here and there, at times he couldn't have been working on their account because he'd been on another job, or out of town."

"What did he do? Isn't there some regulatory board he should have been reported to?"

"Yes, sir, there is. But, remember, Rothwell was married to Hatchard's daughter, Mary. They'd been together nearly sixteen years by then, had two kids. Old man Hatchard would hardly want his son-in-law struck off and his family name dragged through the mud, which is probably what would have happened if Rothwell had been reported. I also got the impression that it might have been Mary's demands that set Rothwell padding his accounts in the first place. Nothing was directly stated, you understand, sir, just hinted. Imagine the headlines: 'Accountant fired for padding books to keep boss's daughter in the manner to which she was accustomed.' Hardly bears thinking about, does it? Anyway, Laurence Pratt and Rothwell were quite close friends then, so Pratt interceded and stuck up for him. Rothwell was lucky. He had a lot going for him. And there's another reason they didn't want a hue and cry."

"Which is?"

"Confidence and confidentiality, sir. If it got out to the large company that Rothwell was fiddling, then it would put the partnership in an awkward position. Much better they don't find out and Rothwell simply decides to move on. Keep it in the family. They'd never question the bills, or miss the money."

"I see." Gristhorpe rubbed his whiskery chin.

"It's something that could have led to a motive, isn't it, sir? Greed, dishonesty."

"Aye," said Gristhorpe. "It is that. Which makes me think even more that these secret files might prove interesting reading." He tapped the table-top. "Good work, Susan. Let's make Rothwell's business affairs a major line of enquiry. I'll get in touch with the Fraud Squad. I've heard from the anti-terrorist squad, by the way, and they've come up with nothing so far. They want to be kept up to date, of course, but I think we can rule out Rothwell dealing arms or money to the IRA. Anything to add, Alan?"

"I think we should follow up on the wadding. There could be a porn connection."

"Rothwell in the porn business?"

"It's possible. After all, he had plenty of money, didn't he? He must have got it from somewhere. I'm not suggesting he was a front player, one who got his hands dirty. Maybe he just made some investments or handled finances. Take the lid off that can of worms—video nasties, prostitution and the like—and it wouldn't surprise me to find murder. Perhaps the wadding was a kind of signature, a symbol."

"It sounds a bit too fanciful to me," said Gristhorpe, "but I take your point. It's all tied together, anyway, isn't it? If he was in the porn business, then that makes porn part of his business affairs. We'll follow up on it."

"DS Hatchley's coming back on Monday," said Banks. "I think he'd be a good man for the job. Remember he spent a while working on the Vice Squad for West Yorkshire? Besides, he'd enjoy it."

Gristhorpe snorted. "I suppose he would. But keep him on a tight leash. He's like a bloody bull in a china shop."

Banks grinned. He knew that Gristhorpe and Hatchley didn't get along. Jim Hatchley was a big, bluff, burly, boozy, roast-beef sort of Yorkshireman, a rugby prop forward until cigarettes and drink took their toll. More at home playing darts in the public bar than chatting in the lounge, he was the kind of person everyone underestimated, and that often worked to the advantage of the Eastvale CID. And he also had a valuable, county-wide network of low-life, quasi-criminal informers that nobody had been able to penetrate.

"The Rothwells are an interesting family," Banks went on after a sip of Theakston's. "Mrs Rothwell assured me everything was fine and dandy on the domestic front, but methought the lady did protest too much. I wonder how much communication there really was between them all. It's nothing I can put my finger on, but there's something bothering me. I think the son, Tom, might have something to do with it."

"I got that impression, too," said Susan. "It all looks fine on the surface, but I'd like to know what life at Arkbeck Farm was like. After I'd talked to Laurence Pratt, I got to thinking that if Tom was the reason Keith and Mary Rothwell had to get married, and Rothwell was unhappy in his marriage, then he might blame Tom. Irrational, of course, but things happen like that."

"I'd leave the psychology to Jenny Fuller," said Gristhorpe.

Susan reddened.

"Susan's right," said Banks. "The sooner we find Tom Rothwell, the better."

Gristhorpe shrugged. "It's up to the Florida police now. We've passed on all the information we've got. Come on, Alan, surely you don't think the wife and daughter had anything to do with it?"

"It would be hard to believe, wouldn't it? On the other hand, we've only *their* word for what happened. Nobody else saw the two men in black. What if Alison and her mother *did* want rid of Rothwell for some reason?"

"Next you'll be telling me the wife and daughter were making porno films for Rothwell. You talked to Alison. You could see the lass was upset."

"Alison might not have had anything to do with it."

"You mean Mrs Rothwell? Wasn't she in shock?"

"So I'm told. I didn't get to see her until late this morning. That gave her plenty of time to compose herself, work up an act."

"But the SOC team went through the place as thoroughly as they usually do, hayloft and all. They couldn't find any traces of a weapon."

"I'm not saying she shot him."

"What then? She hired a couple of killers to do it for her?"

"I don't know. She could certainly afford it. I suppose I'm playing devil's advocate, trying to look at it from all angles. I still maintain they're an odd family. Alison was genuinely terrified, I know that.

But there's something not quite right about them all, and I'd like to know what that is. I knew when I drove away from Arkbeck Farm that something I'd seen there was bothering me, nagging away, but I didn't know what it was until a short while ago."

"And?" asked Gristhorpe.

"It was Tom's postcard from California. It was addressed to Alison—he called her Ali—and at the end he wrote, 'Love to Mum.' There was no mention of his father."

"Hmm," said Gristhorpe. "It doesn't have to mean anything."

"Maybe not. But that's not all. When I looked through Rothwell's wallet a while back, I found photos of Mary and Alison, but none of Tom. Not one."

FOUR

I

A good night's sleep is supposed to refresh you, not make you feel as if you're recovering from a bloody anaesthetic, thought Banks miserably on Saturday morning.

Never a morning person at the best of times, he sat over his second cup of black coffee and a slice of wholewheat toast and Seville marmalade, newspaper propped up in front of him, trying to muster enough energy to get going. As a background to the radio traffic reports, he could hear Sandra having a shower upstairs. Banks hated the contraption—he always seemed to get a lukewarm dribble rather than a hot shower—but Sandra and Tracy swore by it. Banks preferred a long, hot bath with a little quiet background music and a good book.

After catching up with paperwork, he hadn't got home until almost eleven the previous night. He wished Sandra had been angry that they'd had to miss the claret, the Chopin and the candlelight, but she hadn't seemed to care. He didn't know whether she was pretending or she *really* didn't care. In fact, she said she'd just got back from a reception at the community centre herself. It was getting to be par for the course. They had seen so little of one another lately that they were fast becoming strangers. It seemed to Banks that what had been a strength in their relationship—their natural independence—was quickly becoming a threat.

And while Sandra had slept like a log, Banks had tossed and turned all night beside her, worried about the Rothwell case, with only brief, fitful periods of sleep full of shifting images: the pornographic wadding, the headless corpse. Now it was eight-thirty the next morning, and his eyes felt like sandpaper, his brain stuffed with cotton wool.

The national dailies and radio news carried stories on the Keith Rothwell killing—sandwiched between a bloodthirsty put-down of riots on a Caribbean island, where another dictator was nearing the end of his reign of terror, and a male Member of Parliament caught *in flagrante delicto* with a sixteen-year-old rent-boy on Clapham Common. It probably wouldn't have even made the papers if it had happened somewhere a bit more up-market, like Hampstead Heath, Banks thought.

The Rothwell murder would be on television too, no doubt, amidst all the speculation on that afternoon's Cup Final, but Banks had never been able to bring himself to turn the thing on during daylight hours.

Now, hints were appearing in the media that the killing was more than a run-of-the-mill domestic disagreement or a burglary gone wrong. According to the radio, Scotland Yard, Interpol and the FBI had been called in. That, Banks reflected, was a slight exaggeration. The Americans had been asked to help trace Tom Rothwell, though as far as Banks knew it was the Florida State Police, not the FBI. Interpol was something the reporters always threw in for good measure, these days, and Scotland Yard was an outright lie.

Banks scanned the *Yorkshire Post* and *The Independent* reports to see if either newspaper knew more than the police. Sometimes they did, and it could be damned embarrassing all round. Not this time, though. To them, Rothwell was as much the "quiet, unassuming local accountant and businessman" as he was to the rest of the world.

"More coffee?"

Banks looked up to see Sandra standing at the machine in her navy-blue bathrobe, wet hair hanging over the terry-cloth at her shoulders. He hadn't heard her come down.

"Please." He held his cup out.

Sandra poured, then put some bread in the toaster and picked up the *Yorkshire Post*. After she had read about Rothwell, she whistled. "Is this what kept you out so late last night?"

"Hmm," murmured Banks.

The toast popped up. Sandra put the paper down and went to see to it. "I've met her a couple of times, you know," she said over her shoulder, buttering toast.

Banks folded *The Independent* and looked at Sandra's profile. When it was wet, her hair looked darker, of course, but one of the things Banks found attractive about her was the contrast between her blonde hair and black eyebrows. This time, when he looked at her, he felt an ache deep inside. "Who?" he asked.

"Mrs Rothwell. Mary Rothwell."

"How on earth did you come across her?"

"At the gallery."

Sandra ran the local gallery in the Eastvale community centre, where she organized art and photography exhibitions.

"I didn't know she was the artistic type."

"She's not really. I think for her it was just the thing to do. Women's Institute sort of stuff, you know, organize cultural outings." Sandra sat down with her toast and wrinkled her nose.

Banks laughed, sensing a definite thaw in the cold war. "Snob."

"What! Me?" She hit him lightly with the folded newspaper.

"Anyway," Banks said, "the poor woman's on tranquillizers. Both she and her daughter saw Rothwell's body before they called us, and you can take my word for it, that's enough to give anyone the heebie-jeebies."

"How's the daughter?"

"Alison? Not quite so bad, at least not on the surface." Banks shrugged. "More resilient, maybe, or she could just be repressing it more. Tina Smithies says she's worried they're both losing touch." He looked at his watch. "I'd better go."

Sandra followed him to the door and leaned against the bannister. She nibbled her toast as she watched him put on his light grey sports jacket and pick up his briefcase. "I can't say I know her well enough to get any kind of impression," she said, holding her dressing-gown at the collar when Banks opened the door, "but I did sense that she's the kind who ... well, she puts on a few airs and graces. Not so much as to be a complete pseud, but you can tell there's a touch of the Lady Muck about her. Imperious. And she likes people to know she's not short of a bob or two. You know, she flashes her rings, jewellery, stuff like that. She also struck me as being a very *cold* woman, I don't know why. All sharp edges, like a drawer full of kitchen knives."

Banks leaned against the door jamb. "It's a bloody strange family altogether," he said.

Sandra shrugged. "Just thought I'd put in my two penn'orth. I don't suppose you know when you'll be back?"

"No. Sorry, got to dash." Banks risked a quick kiss on the lips. They tasted of strawberry jam.

"Can you leave me the car, today?" Sandra called after him. "There's a water-colour exhibition I want to see in Ripon. One of our locals is exhibiting. I don't know when I'll be back, either."

"Okay," said Banks, wincing at the barb. He could always sign a car out of the pool if he needed one. It wouldn't have a cassette deck, but then this was hardly the best of all possible worlds, was it? At least it should have a radio. He set off determined, after a miserable night, not to let things get him down.

It was a beautiful morning. Calendar weather. May, as he knew it, had finally arrived. The sky was a cloudless blue, apart from a few high milky swirls, and even this early in the morning the temperature seemed to have risen a few notches since yesterday. Banks wouldn't be surprised if it were shirtsleeves weather before the day was out.

As he walked, he plugged in his earphones and switched on the Walkman in his briefcase. The tape started at the jazzy "Forlane" section of Ravel's *Le Tombeau de Couperin*. Not bad for a walk to work on a fine spring morning.

It was only about a mile to the station along Market Street, and Banks liked the way the townscape changed almost yard by yard as he walked. At his end of town, the road was broad, and the area was much like the outer part of any town centre: the main road with its garage, supermarket, school, zebra crossings and roundabouts, surrounded by residential streets of tall Victorian houses, most of them converted to student flats, all with names like Mafeking Avenue, Sebastopol Terrace, Crimea Close and Waterloo Road, and a strong smell of petrol and diesel fumes pervading the air.

But the closer Market Street got to the actual market-place, the more it narrowed and turned into a tourist attraction with its overhanging first-floor bays, where people could almost shake hands with someone across the street; the magnifying-glass windows of twee souvenir shops; an expensive walkers' gear shop with orange Gore-tex clothing hanging by the doorway and a stand of walking-sticks out on the pavement; a Waterstone's Bookshop, the street's most recent addition; the mingled aromas from Hambleton's Tea and Coffee Emporium and Farleigh's bakery across the street; an Oddbins wine shop; the Golden Grill café; and a newsagent's with a rack of newspapers out front, some of them folded over at Rothwell's grainy photograph, and a display of local guides and Ordnance Survey maps in the window. This narrow part of Market Street was always jammed with honking traffic, too—mostly visitors and delivery vans.

Halfway through the "Menuet" section, Banks arrived at the station, a three-storey, Tudor-fronted building facing the market square. First he called in at the Murder Room and talked to Phil Richmond. The Florida State Police had tracked down the car rental company Tom Rothwell had used at Tampa airport. At least it was a start. Now the police had a licence number to look for among the millions of cars parked at the thousands of Florida hotels, motels and beach clubs.

The PNC reported nothing doing on the use of pornographic wadding at other crime scenes.

Gristhorpe was in a meeting with Inspector Macmillan of the Fraud Squad, and Susan Gay was in her hutch phoning around the list of Rothwell's clients Laurence Pratt had given her. Banks poured a coffee and went to his office.

He opened his window and sniffed the air, then lit a cigarette and stood looking down on the early tourists in their bright anoraks and cagoules milling about the cobbled square. It was ten past nine on a Saturday morning, market-day in Eastvale, and the vendors at their canvas-covered stalls, like the old wild-west wagon trains, hawked everything from flat caps and multi-pocketed fishing jackets to burglar alarms, spark plugs and non-stick ovenware. The cheese van was there, as usual, and Banks thought he might nip out and buy a wedge of Coverdale or Wensleydale Blue if he got the chance. If.

Banks mulled over what Sandra had told him about Mary Rothwell. So far, he had an impression of her as an ostentatious and overbearing woman who put too much value on appearances, and of Keith Rothwell as an unassuming, yet sly and greedy, man, easily prey to temptation. Greed, as Susan Gay had remarked, is often a way of making dangerous enemies, and a habit of secrecy is a damn good way of making things difficult for the police. But did the greed originate in Rothwell himself, or had he felt pushed into it by the demands of his wife?

There had certainly been hints in what both Ian Falkland and Larry Grafton had said that Rothwell had been something of a henpecked husband, escaping to the pub for a half-pint and a quiet smoke whenever he could.

In Banks's experience, such people often developed rich and secret fantasy lives, which sometimes imposed on reality with messy and unpredictable results. Keith Rothwell had supplied his wife and children with all the conveniences and many of the luxuries they wanted. What did he get out of it? What did he have going for himself? Nobody seemed to know or care what made him tick.

Banks moved away from the window and stubbed out his cigarette. There was at least one thing he could do right now, he thought, reaching for a pen and notepad. "WANTED," he wrote, "male Caucasian, about five feet nine, slight paunch, large wet brown eyes, commonly described as 'spaniel' or 'puppy dog' eyes, fondness for shotguns, can't keep his hands off young girls and probably has a taste for pornography of the shaved pussy variety." He could just imagine the laughter and the nudge-nudges in police stations around the country as that went out over the PNC.

Just as he was about to start working on a revised version, the phone rang and Sergeant Rowe put him through to a distraught woman asking for the ubiquitous "someone in charge."

"Can I help you?" Banks asked her.

"They said they'd put me through to someone in charge. Are you in charge?"

"Depends what you mean," said Banks. "In charge of what? What's it about?"

"The man in the paper this morning, the one who was killed."

Suddenly Banks pricked up his ears. Was he mistaken, or was she sobbing as she spoke? "Yes," he said. "Go on."

"I knew him."

"You knew Keith Rothwell?"

"No, no—" She sobbed again then came back on the line. "You've got it wrong. That's not his name. His name is Robert. Robert Calvert. That's who he is. You've got it all wrong. Is Robert really dead?"

The back of his neck tingling, Banks gripped his pen tight between his fingers. "I think we'd better have a talk, love," he said. "The sooner, the better. Would you like to give me your name and address?"

II

Susan Gay drove the unmarked police Fiesta to Leeds, with Banks beside her tapping his fingers on his knees. It wasn't because of her driving. Ordinarily, he would enjoy such a trip and take his time if there were no rush, but today he was anxious to interview the woman who had phoned, Pamela Jeffreys.

He wasn't smoking, either, and that also made him jittery. He refrained in deference to Susan, though she magnanimously said it was okay if he opened the windows. There wasn't much worse, in his experience, than trying to enjoy a cigarette in a car next to a non-smoker with a force nine gale blowing all around you, no matter how good the weather.

As Banks had hoped, though the car had no cassette player, it did have a radio, and he was able to lose himself in a Poulenc chamber concert on Radio Three as he considered the implications of what he had just heard.

"How are we going to play this, sir?" Susan asked as she turned onto the Inner Ring Road and went into the yellow-lit tunnel.

Banks dragged himself out of a passage in the "Sextet" where a sense of sadness seemed to pervade the levity of the woodwinds. "By ear," he said.

They had already called DI Ken Blackstone, out of courtesy for intruding on his patch, and Ken had found nothing on Pamela Jeffreys in records. Hardly surprising, Banks thought, as there was no reason to suppose she was a criminal. He glanced out of the window and saw they were crossing the bridge over the River Aire and the Leeds-Liverpool Canal. The dirty, sluggish water looked especially vile in the bright sunlight.

"Do we tell her anything?" Susan asked.

"If she's read the papers, she'll know almost as much about Keith Rothwell's life as we do. Whether she'll believe it or not is another matter."

"What do you think it's all about?"

"I haven't a clue. We'll soon find out."

Susan negotiated the large roundabout on Wellington Road. Above them, the dark, medieval fortress of Armley Jail loomed on its hill. Susan veered right at the junction with Tong Road, passed the disused Crown bingo hall, the medical centre and the New Wortley Cemetery and headed towards Armley. It was an area of waste ground and boarded-up shopfronts, with the high black spire of St Bartholomew's visible above the decay. She slowed to look at the street names, found Wesley Road, turned right, then right again and looked for the address Pamela Jeffreys had given.

"This is it, sir," she said finally, pulling into a street of terraced back-to-backs, nicely done up, each with a postage-stamp lawn behind a privet hedge, some with new frosted-glass or wood-panel doors and dormer windows. "Number twenty, twenty-four ... Here it is." She pulled up outside number twenty-eight.

The row of houses stood across the street from some allotments behind a low stone wall, where a number of retired or unemployed men worked their patches, stopping now and then to chat. Someone had rested a transistor radio on the wall, and Banks could hear the preamble to the Cup Final commentary. Not far down the street was an old chapel which, according to the sign, had been converted into a Sikh temple. They walked down the path to number twenty-eight and rang the doorbell.

The woman who opened the door had clearly been crying, but it didn't mar her looks one bit, Banks thought. Perhaps the whites of her almond eyes were a little too red and the glossy blue-black hair could have done with a good brushing, but there was no denying that she was a woman of exceptional beauty.

Northern Indian, Banks guessed, or perhaps from Bangladesh or Pakistan, she had skin the colour of burnished gold, with high cheekbones, full, finely drawn lips and a figure that wouldn't be out of place in *Playboy*, revealed to great advantage by skin-tight ice-blue jeans and a jade-green T-shirt tucked in at her narrow waist. Around her neck, she wore a necklace of many-coloured glass beads. She also wore a gold stud in her left nostril. She looked to be in her mid-twenties.

Her fingers, Banks noticed as she raised her hand to push the door shut, were long and tapered, with clear nails cut very short. A spiral gold bracelet slipped down her slim wrist over her forearm. On the other wrist, she wore a simple Timex with a black plastic strap. She had only one ring, and that was a gold band on the middle finger of her right hand. Light down covered her bare brown arms.

The living-room was arranged for comfort. A small three-piece suite with burgundy velour upholstery formed a semi-circle around a thick glass coffee-table in front of the fireplace, which may once have housed a real coal fire but now was given over to an electric one with three elements and a fake flaming-coals effect. On the coffee-table, the new Mary Wesley paperback lay open, face down beside a copy of the *Radio Times* and an earthenware mug half full of milky tea.

A few family photographs in gilt frames stood on the mantel-piece. On the wall above the fire hung a print of Ganesh, the elephant god, in a brightly coloured, primitive style. In the corner by the front window stood a television with a video on a shelf underneath. The only other furniture in the room was a mini stereo system and several racks of compact discs, a glass-fronted cabinet of crystalware and a small bookcase mostly full of modern fiction and books about music.

But it was the far end of the room that caught Banks's interest, for there stood a music stand, with some sheet music on it, and beside that, on a chair, lay what he first took to be an oversized violin, but quickly recognized as a viola.

The woman sat on the sofa, curling her legs up beside her, and Banks and Susan took the armchairs.

"Are you a musician?" Banks asked.

"Yes," she said.

"Professional?"

"Uh-huh. I'm with the Northern Philharmonia, and I do a bit of chamber work on the side. Why?"

"Just curious." Banks was impressed. The English Northern Philharmonia played for Opera North, among other things, and was widely regarded as one of the best opera orchestras in the country. He had been to see Opera North's superb production of *La Bohème* recently and must have heard Pamela Jeffreys play.

"Ms Jeffreys," he began, after a brief silence. "I must admit that your phone call has us a bit confused."

"Not half as much as that rubbish in the newspaper has *me* confused." She had no Indian accent at all, just West Yorkshire with a cultured, university edge.

Banks slipped a recent good-quality photograph of Keith Rothwell from his briefcase and passed it to her. "Is this the man we're talking about?"

"Yes. I think this is Robert, though he looks a bit stiff here." She handed it back. "There's a mistake, isn't there? It must be someone who looks just like him, that's it."

"What exactly was your relationship?"

She fiddled with her necklace. "We're friends. Maybe we were more than that, at one time, but now we're just friends."

"Were you lovers?"

"Yes. For a while."

"For how long?"

"Three or four months."

"Until when?"

"Six months ago."

"So you've known him for about ten months altogether?"

"Yes."

"How did you meet?"

"In a pub. The Boulevard, on Westgate, actually. I was with some friends. Robert was by himself. We just got talking, like you do."

"Have you seen him since you stopped being lovers?"

"Yes. I told you. We remained friends. We don't see each other as often, of course, but we still go out every now and then, purely Platonic. I like Robert. He's good fun to be with, even when we stopped being lovers. Look, what's all this in—"

"When did you last see him, Ms Jeffreys?"

"Pamela. Please call me Pamela. Let me see ... it must have been a month or more ago. Look, is this some mistake, or what?"

"We don't know yet, Pamela," Susan Gay said. "We really don't, love. You'll help us best get it sorted out if you answer Chief Inspector Banks's questions."

Pamela nodded.

"Was there anything unusual about Mr ... about Robert the last time you saw him?" Banks asked.

"No."

"He didn't say anything, tell you about anything that was worrying him?"

"No. Robert never seemed to worry about anything. Except he hated being called Bob."

"So there was nothing at all different about him?"

"Well, I wouldn't say that."

"Oh?"

"It's just a guess, like."

"What was it?"

"I think he'd met someone else. Another woman. I think he was in love."

Banks swallowed, hardly able to believe what he was hearing. This couldn't be dull, dry, mild-mannered Keith Rothwell. Surely Rothwell wasn't the kind of man to have a wife and children in Swainsdale and a beautiful girlfriend like Pamela Jeffreys in Leeds, whom he could simply dump for yet *another* woman?

"Don't get me wrong," Pamela went on. "I'm not bitter or anything. We had a good time, and it was never anything more.

We didn't lie to each other. Neither of us wanted to get too involved. And one thing Robert doesn't do is mess you around. That's why we can still be friends. But he made it clear it was over between us—at least in *that* way—and I got the impression it was because he'd found someone else."

"Did you ever see this woman?"

"No."

"Did he ever speak of her?"

"No. I just *knew*. A woman can tell about these things, that's all."

"Did you ask him about her?"

"I broached the subject once or twice."

"What happened?"

"He changed it." She smiled. "He has a way."

"How often did you see each other?"

"When we were going out?"

"Yes."

"Just once or twice a week. Mostly late in the week, weekends sometimes. He travels a lot on business. Anyway, he's usually at home every week at some time, at least for a day or two."

"What's his business?"

"Dunno. That's another thing he never said much about. I can't say I was really that interested, either. I mean, it's boring, isn't it, talking about business. I liked going out with Robert because he was fun. He could leave his work at home."

"Did he smoke?"

"What an odd question. Yes, as a matter of fact. Not much, though."

"What brand?"

"Benson and Hedges. I don't mind people smoking."

Encouraged, Banks slipped his Silk Cut out of his pocket. Pamela smiled and brought him a glass ashtray. "What was he like?" Banks asked. "What kind of things did you used to do together?"

Pamela looked at Banks with a glint of naughty humour in her eyes and raised her eyebrows. Banks felt himself flush. "I mean where did you used to go?" he said quickly.

"Yeah, I know. Hmmm ... Well, we'd go out for dinner about once a week. Brasserie 44—you know, down by the river—or La

Grillade, until it moved. He likes good food. Let's see … sometimes we'd go to concerts at the Town Hall, if I wasn't playing, of course, but he's not very fond of classical music, to be honest. Prefers that dreadful trad jazz. And sometimes we'd just stay in, order a pizza or a curry and watch telly if there was something good on. Or rent a video. He likes oldies. *Casablanca, The Maltese Falcon,* that kind of thing. So do I. Let me see … we'd go to Napoleon's every once in a while—"

"Napoleon's?"

"Yeah. You know, the casino. And he took me to the races a couple of times—once at Pontefract and once at Doncaster. That's about it, really. Oh, and we went dancing now and then. Quite fleet on his feet is Robert."

Banks coughed and stubbed out his cigarette. "Dancing? The casino?"

"Yes. He loves a flutter, does Robert. It worried me sometimes the way he'd go through a hundred or more some nights." She shrugged. "But it wasn't my place to say, was it? I mean it wasn't as if we were *married* or anything, or even living together. And he seemed to have plenty of money. Not that that's what interested me about him." She pulled at her necklace again. "Can't you tell me what's going on, Chief Inspector? It's not the same person that was murdered, is it? I was so upset when I saw the paper this morning. Tell me it's a case of mistaken identity."

Banks shook his head. "I don't know. Maybe he had a double. Did he ever say anything about being married?"

"No, never."

"Did he have an appendix scar?"

This time, Pamela blushed. "Yes," she said. "Yes, he did. But so do lots of other people. I had mine out when I was sixteen."

"When you spent time together," Banks said, "did he always come here, to your house? Didn't you ever visit him at his hotel?"

She frowned. "Hotel? What hotel?"

"The one he stayed at when he was in town, I assume. Did you always meet here?"

"Of course not. Sometimes he came here, certainly. I've nothing to be ashamed of, and I don't care what the neighbours say. Bloody racists, some of them. You know, my mum and dad came over to Shipley to work in the woollen mills in 1952. *Nineteen fifty-two.* They even changed their name from Jaffrey to Jeffreys because it sounded more English. Can you believe it? I was born here, brought up here, went to school and university here and some of them still call me a bleeding Paki." She shrugged. "What can you do? Anyway, you were saying?"

"I was asking why you never saw him at his hotel."

"Oh, that's easy. I don't know what you're talking about. You see, it *can't* be the same person, can it? That proves it." She leaned forward quickly and clapped her hands. The bracelet spiralled. "You see, Robert didn't stay at any hotel. Sometimes he came here, yes, but not always. Other times I went to his place. His flat. He's got a flat in Headingley."

III

Banks turned the Yale key in the lock and the three of them stood on the threshold of Robert Calvert's Headingley flat. It was in the nice part of Headingley, more West Park, Banks noted, not the scruffy part around Hyde Park that was honeycombed with student bedsits.

It hadn't been easy getting in. Pamela Jeffreys didn't have a key, so they had to ask one of the tenants in the building to direct them to the agency that handled rentals. Naturally, it was closed at four o'clock on a Saturday afternoon, so then they had to get hold of one of the staff at home and arrange for her to come in, grumbling all the way, open up the office and give them a spare key.

And no, she told them, she had never met Robert Calvert. The man was a model tenant; he paid his rent on time, and that was all that mattered. One of the secretaries probably handed him the key, but he'd had the place about eighteen months and turnover in secretaries was pretty high. However, if Banks wanted to come back on Monday morning ... Still, Banks reflected as they stood at the front door, all in all it had taken only about an hour and a half from the first time they had heard of the place, so that wasn't bad going.

"Better not touch anything," Banks said as they stood in the hallway. "Which is the living-room?" he asked Pamela.

"That one, on the left."

The door was ajar and Banks nudged it open with his elbow. The bottom of the door rubbed over the fitted beige carpet. Susan Gay and Pamela walked in behind him.

"There's only this room, a bedroom, kitchen and bathroom," Pamela said. "It's not very big, but it's cosy."

The living-room was certainly not the kind of place Banks could imagine Mary Rothwell caring much for. Equipped with all the usual stuff—TV, video, stereo, a few jazz compact discs, books, armchairs, gas fireplace—it smelled of stale smoke and had that comfortable, lived-in feel Banks had never sensed at Arkbeck Farm. Perhaps it was something to do with the old magazines—mostly jazz and racing—strewn over the scratched coffee-table, the overflowing ashtray, the worn upholstery on the armchair by the fire or the framed photographs of a younger-looking Rothwell on the mantelpiece. On the wall hung a framed print of Monet's "Waterloo Bridge, Grey Day."

They went into the bedroom and found the same mess. The bed was unmade, and discarded socks, underpants and shirts lay on the floor beside it.

There was also a small desk against one wall, on which stood a jar of pens and pencils, a roll of Sellotape and a stapler, in addition to several sheets of paper, some of them scrawled all over with numbers. "Is this the kind of thing you're looking for?" Pamela asked.

Carefully, Banks opened the drawer and found a wallet. Without disturbing anything, he could see, through the transparent plastic holder inside, credit cards in the name of Robert Calvert. He put it back.

A couple of suits hung in the wardrobe, along with shirts, ties, casual jackets and trousers. Banks felt in the pockets and found nothing but pennies, sales slips, a couple of felt-tip pens, matches, betting slips and some fluff.

As wood doesn't usually yield fingerprints, he didn't have to be too careful opening cupboards and drawers. Calvert's dresser contained the usual jumble of jeans, jumpers, socks and underwear. A packet of condoms lay forlornly next to a passport and a selection of Dutch, French, Greek and Swiss small change in the drawer of the bedside table. The passport was in the name of Robert Calvert. There were no entry or exit stamps, but then there wouldn't be if he did most of his travelling in Europe, as the coins seemed to indicate. On the bedside table was a shaded reading lamp and a copy of *The Economist*.

The kitchen was certainly compact, and by the sparsity of the fridge's contents, it looked as if Calvert did most of his eating out. A small wine-rack stood on the counter. Banks checked the contents: a white Burgundy, Veuve Clicquot Champagne, a Rioja.

Calvert's bathroom was clean and tidy. His medicine cabinet revealed only the barest of essentials: paracetamol tablets, Aspro, Milk of Magnesia, Alka Seltzer, Fisherman's Friend, Elastoplast, cotton swabs, hydrogen peroxide, Old Spice deodorant and shaving cream, a packet of orange disposable razors, toothbrush and a half-used tube of Colgate. Calvert had squeezed it in the middle, Banks noticed, not from bottom to top. Could this be the same man who returned his used matches to the box?

"Come on," Banks said. "We'd better use a call-box. I don't want to risk smudging any prints there may be on the telephone."

"What's going on?" Pamela asked as they walked down the street.

"I'm sorry," Susan said to her. "We really don't know. We're not just putting you off. We're as confused as you are. If we can find some of Robert's fingerprints in the flat, then we can check them against our files and find out once and for all if it's the same man."

"But it just *can't* be," Pamela said. "I'm sure of it."

A pub on the main road advertised a beer garden at the back, and as they were all thirsty, Banks suggested he might as well make the call from there.

He phoned the station and Phil Richmond said he would arrange to get Vic Manson to the flat as soon as possible.

That done, he ordered the drinks and discovered from the barman that Arsenal had won the FA Cup. Good for them, Banks thought. When he had lived in London, he had been an Arsenal supporter, though he always had a soft spot for Peterborough United, his home-town team, struggling as they were near the bottom of the First Division.

The beer garden was quiet. They sat at a heavy wooden bench beside a bowling green and sipped their drinks. Two old men in white were playing on the green, and occasionally the clack of the bowls disturbed the silence. Banks and Susan shared salted roast peanuts and cheese-and-onion crisps, as neither had eaten since breakfast. The sun felt warm on the back of Banks's neck.

"You can go home whenever you want," Banks told Pamela as she took off the tan suede jacket she had put on to go out. "We have to stay here, but we'll pay for a taxi. I'm sorry we had to ruin your day for you."

Pamela squinted in the sun, reached into her bag and pulled out a pair of large pink-rimmed sunglasses. "It's all right," she said, picking up her gin and tonic. "I know it wasn't Robert they were talking about in the paper. Who was this man, this Keith Rothwell?"

"He was an accountant who got murdered," Banks told her. "We can't really say much more than that. Did you ever hear the name before?"

Pamela shook her head. "The papers said he was married."

"Yes."

"Robert didn't act like a married man."

"What do you mean?"

"Guilt. Secrecy. Fleeting visits. Furtive phone calls. The usual stuff. There was none of that with Robert. We went about quite openly. He wasn't tied down. He was a dreamer. Besides, you just *know*." She took her glasses off and squinted at Banks. "I'll bet you're married, aren't you?"

"Yes," said Banks, and saw, he hoped, a hint of disappointment in her eyes.

"Told you." She put her sunglasses on again.

Banks noticed Susan grinning behind her glass of lemonade. He gave her a dirty look. A clack of bowls came from the green and one of the old men did a little dance of victory.

"So, you see," Pamela went on. "It can't be the same man. If I'm sure of one thing, it's that Robert Calvert definitely wasn't a married man with a family."

Banks picked up his pint and raised it in a toast. "I hope you're right," he said, looking at her brave smile and remembering the scene in Rothwell's garage only two nights ago. "I sincerely hope you're right."

FIVE

I

There was always something sad about an empty farmyard, Banks thought as he got out of the car in front of Arkbeck Farm again. There should be chickens squawking all over the place, the occasional wandering cow, maybe a barking sheepdog or two.

He thought of the nest egg he had held at his Uncle Len's farm in Gloucestershire on childhood family visits. They used it to encourage hens to lay, he remembered, and when his Aunt Chloe had handed it to him in the coop, it had still felt warm. Banks also remembered the smells of hay and cow dung, the shiny metal milk churns sitting by the roadside waiting to be picked up.

As he rang the doorbell, he doubted that the Rothwells felt the same way about empty farmyards. The place seemed to suit Alison's introspective nature; her father had no doubt appreciated the seclusion and the protection from prying eyes and questions it offered; and Mary Rothwell ... well, Banks could hardly imagine her mucking out the byre or feeding the pigs. He couldn't imagine her handing a child a warm porcelain egg, either.

"Do come in," Mary Rothwell said, opening the door. Banks followed her to the split-level living-room. Today she wore a white shirt that buttoned on the "man's" side and a loose grey skirt that reached her ankles. Alison lay sprawled on the sofa reading.

On the way to Arkbeck Farm, he had considered what to say to them regarding his talk with Pamela Jeffreys in Leeds, but he hadn't come up with any clear plan. Vic Manson hadn't got back to him yet about the prints, so he still couldn't be absolutely certain that Robert Calvert and Keith Rothwell were the same person. Best play it by ear, he decided.

"How are you doing?" he asked Mary Rothwell.

"Could be worse," she replied. He noticed her eyes were baggy under the make-up. "I haven't been sleeping well, despite the pills, and I'm a mass of nerves, but if I keep myself busy, time passes. I have the funeral to organize. Please, sit down."

Banks had come partly to explain that a van was on its way to pick up Keith Rothwell's computer disks and business files and spirit them off to the Fraud Squad's headquarters in Northallerton, where a team of suits would pore over them for months, maybe years, costing the taxpayers millions. He didn't put it like that, of course. Just as he had finished explaining, he heard the van pull up out front.

He went to the front door and directed the men to Rothwell's office, then returned to the living-room, shutting the door firmly behind him. It was dark in the room, and a little chilly, despite the fine weather outside. "They shouldn't bother us," he said. "Perhaps a little music?"

Mary Rothwell nodded and turned on the radio. Engelbert Humperdinck came on, singing "Release Me." Banks often regretted that humans hadn't been born with the capacity to close their ears as they did their eyes. He did his best, anyway, and reflected that it was all in a good cause, blanking out the sounds of Keith Rothwell's office being dismantled and carried away.

"Have you found Tom?" Mary Rothwell said, sitting down. She sat at the edge of the armchair, Banks noticed, and twisted her hands in her lap, a mass of gold and precious stones. She seemed so stiff he wished someone would give her a massage. Her skin, he felt, would be brittle as lacquered hair to the touch.

Banks explained that they had tracked down the car rental agency he had used and that it wouldn't be long before someone spotted the car.

"He should be home," she said. "We need him. There's the funeral ... all the arrangements ..."

"We're doing our best, Mrs Rothwell."

"Of course. I didn't mean to imply anything."

"It's all right. Are you up to answering a few more questions?"

"I suppose so. As long as you don't want to talk about what I went through the other night. I couldn't bear that." Her eyes moved in the direction of the garage and Banks could see the fear and horror flood into them.

"No, not that." She would have to talk about it sometime, Banks almost told her, but not now, not yet. "It's Mr Rothwell I want to talk about. We need a better idea of how he spent his time."

"Well, it's hard to say, really," she began. "When he was here, he was up in his office most of the time. I could hear him clicking away on the computer."

"Did you ever hear him on the phone?"

"He had his own line up there. I didn't listen in, if that's what you mean."

"No, I didn't mean that. But sometimes you just can't help over-hearing something, anything."

"No. He always kept the door shut. I could hear his voice, like I could hear the keyboard, but it was muffled, even if I was passing by the office."

"So you never knew who he was talking to or what he was saying?"

"No."

"Did he have many calls in the days leading up to his death?"

"Not so much as I noticed. No more than usual. I could always hear it ring, you see, even from downstairs." She stood up. "Would you like a cup of tea? I can—"

"Not at the moment, thank you," Banks said. He didn't want her crossing the path of the removal team. For one thing, it would upset and distract her, and for another she would start telling them off about trailing dirt in and out.

She walked over to the fireplace, straightened a porcelain figurine, then came and sat down in the same position. Alison went on reading her book. It was *Villette*, by Charlotte Brontë, Banks noticed. Surely a bit heavy for a fifteen-year-old?

"I understand your husband would drop in at the Black Sheep or the Rose and Crown now and then?" Banks asked.

"Yes. He wasn't much of a drinker, but he liked to get out of the house for an hour or so. You do when you work at home, don't you? You get to feel all cooped up. He'd usually walk there and back. It was good exercise. Businessmen often don't exercise enough, do they, living such sedentary lives, but Keith believed in keeping in good shape. He swam regularly, too, in Eastvale, and he would sometimes go for long runs." She started picking pieces of imaginary lint from her skirt. Banks heard a thud from the staircase, and this time he couldn't stop her from dashing to the door and yanking it open.

"Watch what you're doing, you clumsy little man!" she said. "Just look at this. You've gouged a hole in my wall. The plaster's fallen off. You'll have to pay for that, you know. I'll be talking to your superior." She popped her head back around the door and said, "I'll make that tea now, shall I?" then disappeared into the kitchen.

Banks, still sitting, noticed Alison look up and raise her eyes. "She's been like this since yesterday," she said. "Can't sit still. It's even worse than usual."

"She's upset," Banks said. "It's her way of dealing with it."

"Or *not* dealing with it. I saw him too, you know. Do you think I can forget so easily?"

"You've got to talk to each other," Banks said. He noticed the book was shaking in her hands and she was making an effort to keep it still.

"If Tom doesn't come home soon, I'm going to run away," she said. "I can't stand it any longer. She's always going on about something or other and running about like a headless chi—" She put her hand to her mouth. "My God, what a thing to say. I'm awful, aren't I? Oh, I hope Tom comes back soon. He must or I'll go mad. We'll both go mad."

A bit melodramatic, Banks thought, but perhaps to be expected from a young girl on a steady diet of Charlotte Brontë.

Mary Rothwell came in bearing a tea tray and wearing a brave smile. Alison picked up her book again and lapsed into moody silence while her mother poured the tea into delicate china cups with hand-painted roses on the sides and gold around the rims. Banks always felt clumsy and nervous drinking from such fine china; he was afraid he would drop the cup or break off the flimsy handle while lifting it to his mouth.

"Why are they taking all Keith's files anyway?" Mary Rothwell asked.

"We're beginning to think that your husband might have been involved in some shady financial dealings," Banks explained. "And they could have something to do with his murder."

"Shady?" She said it as Lady Bracknell said, "A handbag?"

"He might not have known what he was involved in," Banks lied. "It's just a line of enquiry we have to follow."

"I can assure you that my husband was as honest as the day is long."

"Mrs Rothwell, can you tell me *anything* about what your husband did when he was travelling on business?"

"How would I know? I wasn't there."

"Which hotels did he stay in? You must have phoned him."

"No. He phoned me occasionally. He told me it was better that way for his tax expenses." She shrugged. "Well, *he* was the businessman. I've already told you he travelled all over the place."

"You never went with him?"

"No, of course not. I have an aversion to lengthy car rides. Besides, they were business trips. One doesn't take one's spouse on business trips."

"So you've no idea what he got up to in Leeds or wherever?"

She put down her cup. "Are you implying something, Chief Inspector? Keith didn't 'get up to' anything."

Banks was dying for a cigarette. He finished the weak tea and put his cup and saucer down gently on the coffee-table. "Do you know if your husband was much of a gambler?" he asked.

"Gambler?" She laughed. "Good heavens, no. Keith never even bet on the Grand National, and most people do that, don't they? No, money for my husband was too hard earned to be frittered away like that. Keith had a poor childhood, you know, and one learns the value of money quite early on."

"What sort of childhood?"

"His father was a small shopkeeper, and they suffered terribly when the supermarkets started to become popular. He eventually went bankrupt. Keith didn't like to talk about it."

Banks remembered the cigarettes he had found among the contents of Rothwell's pockets. "Did you know that your husband smoked?" he asked.

"One minor weakness," Mary Rothwell said, turning up her nose. "It's a smelly and unpleasant habit, as well as a possibly fatal one. I certainly wouldn't let him do it in the house, and I was always trying to persuade him to stop."

I'll bet you were, Banks thought. "Have you ever heard of a woman called Pamela Jeffreys?" he asked.

Mary Rothwell frowned. For the first time, she sat back in the chair and gripped its arms with both hands. "No. Why?" Banks saw suspicion and apprehension in her eyes.

Outside, the van door closed and the engine revved up. Banks noticed Mrs Rothwell glance towards the window. "They're finished," he said. "What about Robert Calvert? Does the name mean anything to you?"

She shook her head. "No, nothing. Look, what's this all about? Are these the people you think killed Keith? Are these the ones who got him involved in this criminal scheme you were talking about?"

Banks sighed. "I don't know," he said. "Maybe, but I don't know."

"Why don't you go and arrest *them* instead of bothering us?"

Banks didn't think he was likely to get anything else out of Mary Rothwell, or out of Alison. He stood up. "I'm sorry we had to bother you," he said. "We'll be in touch as soon as we track down your son. And please let us know if you hear from him first. Don't worry, I'll see myself out." And he left.

Maybe she hadn't heard of Pamela Jeffreys, he thought as he got in the car, but he was certain that she suspected her husband might have been seeing another woman. It was there in her eyes, in the whiteness of her knuckles.

He slipped a Thelonious Monk tape in the deck and set off for his next appointment. As the edgy, repetitive figure at the opening of "Raise Four" almost pushed his ears to the limits of endurance, he wondered how long Mary Rothwell would be able to maintain her thinly-lacquered surface before the cracks started to show.

II

"Well, now, if it ain't Mr Banks again," said Larry Grafton when Banks walked into the Black Sheep that lunch-time with *The Sunday Times* folded under his arm. "Twice in one week. We are honoured. What can we do for you this time?"

"You could start with a pint of best bitter and follow it with a plate of your Elsie's delightful roast beef and Yorkshire pud. And you could cut the bloody sarcasm."

Grafton laughed and started pulling. Elsie's Sunday lunches were another well-kept secret, and only a privileged few got to taste them. Banks didn't fool himself that he was an accepted member of the élite; he knew damn well that publicans liked to keep on the good side of the law.

"And," he said, when Larry handed him his pint, "I'd like a word with your Cathy, if I might."

"About the Rothwells, is it?"

"Yes."

"Aye. Well she's just having her dinner. I'll send her through when she's done."

"Thanks."

Banks took his drink and sat by the tiled fireplace. Before he sat, he glanced at the collection of butterflies pinned to a board in a glass case on the wall. The pub wasn't as busy as most on a Sunday lunch-time. Of course, there was no sandwich-board outside advertising "Traditional Sunday Lunch."

Banks's roast beef and Yorkshires came, as good as ever. Not for the first time, he reflected that Elsie's was the only roast beef in Yorkshire, apart from Sandra's, that was pink in the middle. As he ate, he propped the paper against a bottle of HP sauce and began to read an analysis of the growing political unrest on an obscure Caribbean island, feeling an irrational rage grow in him as he read. Christ, how he loathed these tinpot dictators, the ones who stuffed their maws with the best of everything while their subjects starved, who tortured and murdered anyone who dared to complain.

Just as he had picked up the books supplement, he noticed a tourist couple walk in and look around. They went to the bar and the man asked Larry Grafton what food he offered.

"Nowt," said Grafton. "We don't do food."

The man looked towards Banks. "But he's got some."

"Last plate."

The man looked at his watch. "But it's only twelve-thirty."

Grafton shrugged.

"Besides, you said you don't do food. You're contradicting your-self. You heard him, didn't you, darling?"

His wife said nothing; she just stood there looking embarrassed. He had the kind of upper-class accent that expects immediate subservience, but he obviously didn't know there could be nothing more calculated to get right up a Yorkshireman's nose.

"Look," said Grafton, "does tha want a drink or doesn't tha?"

"We want food," the man said.

His wife tugged at his sleeve. "Come on, darling," she whis-pered just in Banks's range of hearing. "Don't cause a fuss. Let's go. There are plenty of other pubs."

"But I—" The man glared petulantly at Grafton, who stared back stone-faced, then followed his wife's advice.

"Really," Banks heard him say on his way out, "you'd think these people didn't want to make an honest living. They're supposed to be in the service industry."

Larry Grafton winked at Banks and ambled off to serve one of the locals. Banks reflected that maybe the tourist was right. What the hell was wrong with Larry Grafton? Nowt so queer as folk, he decided, and went back to his roast beef. A couple of minutes later, when he had just finished, Cathy Grafton came from the back and joined him. He folded up his newspaper, pushed his empty plate aside and lit a cigarette.

Cathy was a plump girl of about sixteen with a fringe and a blotchy complexion, as if she had been sitting too close to the fire too long. She also had the longest, curliest and most beautiful eyelashes Banks had ever seen.

"Dad says you want to talk to me," she said, wedging herself into a chair. Her accent was thick, and Banks had to listen closely to understand everything she said, even though he had been in Swainsdale for four years.

"You helped Mary Rothwell do the housework at Arkbeck Farm, didn't you?"

"Aye. I do for a few folk around here. I know I should be paying more mind to school, like, but Mum says we need t'money."

Banks smiled. Not surprising, given the way Grafton scared

business away. "What was it like, working at Arkbeck?" he asked.

Cathy frowned. "What do you mean?"

"Did you like working there?"

"It were all reet."

"How about Mary Rothwell? Did you get along well with her?"

Cathy wouldn't meet his eyes. She shifted in her chair and looked down at the scored table.

"Cathy?"

"I heard. It's just I was always told not to speak ill."

"Of the dead? Mary Rothwell isn't dead."

"No. Of me employer."

"Am I to take it that you *didn't* get along, then?"

"Take it as you will, Mr Banks."

"Cathy, this could be very important. Mr Rothwell was killed, you know."

"Aye, I know. It's got nowt to do with *her*, though, does it?"

"We still need to know all we can about the family."

Cathy contemplated the table for a while longer. More locals came in. One or two looked in Banks's direction, nudged their friends and raised their eyebrows.

"She were just bossy, that's all," Cathy said at last.

"Mary Rothwell was?"

"Aye. She'd stand over you while you were working, with her arms folded, like this, and tell you you'd missed a bit or you weren't polishing hard enough. I used to hate doing for her. Will I still have to, do you think?"

"I don't know," Banks said. "What about Alison?"

"What about her?"

"You're about the same age, surely you must have had things in common, things to talk about. Pop stars and the like."

Cathy emitted a loud snort. "Little Miss La-di-da," she sneered, then shook her head. "No, I can't say as we did. She always had her nose stuck in a book."

"You never chatted with her?"

"No. Every time she saw me she turned up her nose. Stuck-up little madam."

"How did the family members get along with one another?"

"I weren't there often enough to notice. Not when they was all together, like."

"But you must have some idea, from your observations?"

"They didn't say much. It were a quiet house. He were in his office, when he were at home, like, and I were never allowed up there."

"Who cleaned it?"

"Dunno. Maybe he did it himself. I know he didn't like people to go in. Look, Mr Banks, I've got to get back and help me mum. Is there anything else?"

"Did you notice any changes in the family recently. Did they behave any differently?"

"Not so far as I could tell."

"What about Tom, the son? Did you know him?"

"He were t'best of the lot," Cathy said without hesitation. "Always had a smile and a good-morning for you." She blushed.

"He's been away for a while now. Did you notice any changes before he left?"

"They used to argue."

"Who did?"

"Him and his father."

"What about?"

"How would I know? I didn't listen. Sometimes you couldn't help but hear."

"Hear what?"

"Just their voices, when they were shouting, like."

"Did you ever hear what they were arguing about?"

"Once t'door were open a bit, and I heard his dad mention a name then say something like, 'I'm disappointed in you.' He said 'shame,' too."

"What was a shame?"

"No. Just the word. I just heard the word 'shame,' that's all. I could tell Mr Rothwell were very angry, but he sounded cold, you know."

"Did he say why he was disappointed?"

She shook her head.

"What was the name he mentioned?"

"Sounded like Aston or Afton or summat like that."

"Did you hear what Tom said back?"

"He said, 'You're a right one to talk about being disappointed in *me*.'"

"Did you hear anything more?"

"No." The chair scraped along the stone flags as she stood up. "I've got to go, really. Me mum'll kill me." And she hurried back behind the bar with surprising agility.

III

"Vic Manson matched prints from the Calvert flat with the ones from the body," Gristhorpe explained back at the station later that afternoon. "There were a couple of other sets, too, mostly smudged, not on file."

It was hot, and Banks was standing by the open window of his office. Gristhorpe sat with his feet up on the desk.

"So Rothwell was Calvert and Calvert was Rothwell," Banks said.

"It certainly looks that way, aye."

Banks leaned against the window frame and shook his head. "I still can't believe it. All right, so we know Rothwell had a secretive side to his nature, and he was greedy, or desperate for cash, to the point of dishonesty once. But this Calvert sounds to me like some sort of playboy. If you could have heard Pamela Jeffreys. Casinos, races, dancing … bloody hell. And you should have seen her, the one he chucked over."

"So you've told me already, two or three times at least," Gristhorpe said with a smile. "A proper bobby-dazzler by the sound of her. I'll take your word for it."

"Well, she dazzled this bobby, anyway," said Banks, sitting opposite Gristhorpe. He sighed. "I suppose we just have to accept it: Rothwell led a double life. Like Alec Guinness in that film about the ship's captain."

"*The Captain's Paradise?*"

"That's the one. The question we have to ask ourselves now is what, if anything, does that fact have to do with his murder?"

"Has the girlfriend dazzled you so much you haven't considered she might have a part to play?"

"The thought's crossed my mind once or twice, yes. I just can't see how. Apparently Roth … Calvert found *another* woman five or six months ago. Pamela Jeffreys seemed to think he'd fallen in love. It's her we need to find, but she hasn't come forward yet."

"There's always jealousy as a motive, then."

"I don't think so. It's *possible*, though. Maybe Mary Rothwell found out about him and arranged a hit."

"I was thinking more about this Pamela Jeffreys."

"Couldn't afford it. She's a classical musician. Besides, she didn't really strike me as the jealous type. She said Calvert was just fun to be with. They never made any commitments."

"She could be lying."

"I suppose so."

"And don't forget the possible porn connection. If Rothwell was mixed up with beautiful women, even under another identity, who knows?"

Banks couldn't believe it, but he didn't bother protesting to Gristhorpe. "I'll have to talk to her again anyway," he said.

"Poor you."

"What did the Fraud Squad have to say?"

Gristhorpe scratched his hooked nose. "Funny lot, aren't they?" he said. "I spent a good part of this morning with DI Macmillan. Used to be in banking. Boring little bugger, but you should have seen his eyes light up when he heard about the locked files. Anyway, they've had a quick look at the stuff from Arkbeck Farm, and Macmillan and I had another chat about an hour ago. They haven't much to go on, yet, of course, and they're as anxious as young Phil for that by-pass software, but Macmillan's even more excited now."

"Where has the software got to, by the way?"

"On its way, according to Phil. Apparently they were out of stock but they managed to scrounge around."

"Sorry. What did Macmillan have to say?"

"Well, he said he won't know anything for certain until they manage to open some of those locked directories. He thinks that's where the really interesting stuff is. But even some of the written documents in the filing cabinets gave him enough to suspect Rothwell was heavily into money-laundering or abetting tax evasion. Apparently, there was a fair bit of cryptic correspondence with foreign banks: Liechtenstein, Netherlands Antilles, Jersey, Switzerland, the Cayman Islands, among others. Dead giveaway, Macmillan said."

"Tax havens," said Banks. "Isn't that what they are?"

Gristhorpe held up a finger. "Aha! That was my first thought, too. But they're only tax havens because they have strict secrecy policies and a very flexible attitude towards whom they take on as their clients."

"In other words," offered Banks, "if you want to deposit a lot of money with them, they'll take it, no questions asked?"

"That's about it, aye. Within the law, of course. They do insist that they verify the money's source is legal. When it comes down to it, though, banks are basically run on greed, aren't they?"

"I won't argue with that. So Keith Rothwell was putting a lot of money in foreign banks?"

"Macmillan thought he might have been acting for a third party. He could hardly have made that much money himself. It's a very complicated business. As I said, either he was involved in aiding and abetting some pretty serious tax evasion, or he was part of a money-laundering scheme. There are still more questions than answers."

"Did Macmillan tell you how this money-laundering business works?" Banks asked.

"Aye, a bit. According to him, it's basically simple. It's only in the application it gets complicated. What happens is that some-body gets hold of a lot of money illegally, and he wants it to look legal so he can live off it without raising any suspicions." Gristhorpe paused.

"Go on," Banks urged.

Gristhorpe ran his hand through his hair. "Well, that's about it, really. I told you it was basically simple. Macmillan said it would take forever to explain all the technicalities of doing it. As far as legal money is concerned, he said, you can either earn it, borrow it or receive it as a gift. When you've laundered your dirty money, it has to look like it came to you one of those ways."

"I assume we're talking about drug money here," Banks said. "Or the profits from some sort of organized crime—prostitution, pornography, loan sharks?"

Gristhorpe nodded. "You know as well as I do, Alan, that the top cats in the drug trade pull in enormous wads of cash every day. You can't just walk into a showroom and buy a Rolls in cash without raising a few eyebrows, and the last thing you want is any attention from the police or the Inland Revenue."

Banks walked over to the window again and lit a cigarette. Most of the cars were gone from the cobbled square now and the hush of an early Sunday evening had fallen over the town. A young woman in jeans and a red T-shirt struck a pose by the ancient market cross as her male companion took a photograph, then they got into a blue Nissan Micra and drove off.

"What's in it for the launderer?" Banks asked.

"According to Macmillan, he'd get maybe four per cent for laundering the safer sort of funds and up to ten per cent for seriously dirty money."

"Per cent of what?"

"Depends," said Gristhorpe. "On a cursory glance, Macmillan estimated about between four and six million quid. He said that was conservative."

"Over how long?"

"That's four to six a year, Alan."

"Jesus Christ!"

"Money worth murdering for, isn't it? In addition to Rothwell's legitimate earnings as a financial consultant, if he were in this money-laundering racket he also stood to earn, let's say five per cent of five million a year, to make it easy. How much is that?"

"Quarter of a million quid."

"Aye, my arithmetic was never among the best. Well, no wonder the bugger could afford a BMW and a new kitchen." He rubbed his hands together. "And that's about it. Macmillan said they'll start putting a financial profile together first thing in the morning: bank accounts, credit cards, building societies, Inland Revenue, loans, investments, the lot. He said they shouldn't have any trouble getting a warrant from the judge, given the circumstances. He's also getting in touch with the Yard. This is big, Alan."

"What about Calvert?" Banks asked.

"Well, they'll have to cover him too, now, won't they?"

A sharp knock at the door was immediately followed by Phil Richmond holding a small package. "I've got it," he said, an excited light in his eyes. "The by-pass software. Give me a few minutes to study the manual and we'll see what we can do."

They all followed him to the computer room, once a cupboard for storing cleaning materials, and stood around tensely in the cramped space while he booted up and consulted the instructions. All Rothwell's computer gear and records were with the Fraud Squad, but Richmond had made back-up disks of the relevant files.

Susan Gay popped her head around the door and, finding no room left inside, stood in the doorway. Banks watched as Richmond went through a series of commands. Dialogue boxes appeared and disappeared; drive lights flashed on and off; the machine buzzed and hummed. Banks noticed Gristhorpe chewing on his thumbnail.

"Got it," Richmond said. Then a locked file called SUMMARY.924 came to the screen:

Halcyon Props.	16/9/92	82062	C.I.		Ibk.	GCA
Mercury Exps.	18/9/92	49876	Jsy.Cbk	PA		
Jupiter Pds.	23/9/92	47650	Lst.		Zbk	SA
Marryat Dvpts.	4/10/92	76980	N.A. Kbk	PA		
	(end 1st shpt)					
Neptune Hlds	6/11/92	65734	Jsy. Cbk	SPA		
City Ents	13/11/92	32450	Sw.		Nbk	LRA
Harbour Trst.	21/11/92	23443	BVI. Hbk	DTFA		
Sunland Props	29/11/92	85443	B.		Gbk	RDA

"What the hell is all that about?" Banks asked.

"It looks like financial records for the last quarter of 1992," Gristhorpe said. "Companies, banks, dates, maybe numbered accounts. Keep going, Phil. Try that 'LETTER' file you mentioned."

Richmond highlighted the locked file, tapped at the keyboard again, and the file appeared unscrambled, for all to see.

It was a letter, dated 1st May and addressed to a Mr Daniel Clegg, Solicitor, of Park Square, Leeds, and on first glance, it seemed innocuous enough:

Dear Mr Clegg,
In the light of certain information that has recently come to my
attention, I regret that we must terminate our association.

Yours faithfully,
Keith Rothwell

"That's it?" Gristhorpe asked. "Are you sure you didn't lose anything?"

Richmond returned to the keyboard to check, then shook his head. "No, sir. That's it."

Banks backed towards the door. "Interesting," he said. "I wonder what 'information' that was?" He looked at Gristhorpe, who said, "Get it printed out, will you, Phil, before it disappears into the bloody ether."

SIX

I

In Park Square on that fine Monday morning in May, with the pink and white blossom still on the trees, Banks could easily have imagined himself a Regency dandy out for a stroll while composing a satire upon the Prince's latest folly.

Opposite the Town Hall and the Court Centre, but hidden behind Westgate, Park Square is one of the few examples of elegant, late eighteenth-century Leeds remaining. Unlike most of the fashionable West End squares, it survived Benjamin Gott's Bean Ing Mills, an enormous steam-powered woollen factory which literally smoked out the middle-classes and sent them scurrying north to the fresher air of Headingley, Chapel Allerton and Roundhay, away from the soot and smoke carried over the town on the prevailing westerly winds.

Banks faced the terrace of nicely restored two- and three-storey Georgian houses, built of red brick and yellow sandstone, with their black iron railings, Queen Anne pediments and classical-style doorways with columns and entablatures. Very impressive, he thought, finding the right house. As expected, it was just the kind of place to have several polished brass nameplates beside the door, one of which read "Daniel Clegg, Solicitor."

A list on the wall inside the open front door told him that the office he wanted was on the first floor. He walked up, saw the name on the frosted-glass door, then knocked and entered.

He found himself in a dim anteroom that smelled vaguely of paint, where a woman sat behind a desk sorting through a stack of letters. When he came in, he noticed a look of fear flash through her eyes, quickly replaced by one of suspicion. "Can I help you?" she asked, as if she didn't really want to.

She was about thirty, Banks guessed, with curly brown hair, a thin, olive-complexioned face and a rather long nose. Her pale green eyes were pink around the rims. She wore a loose fawn cardigan over her white blouse, despite the heat. Banks introduced himself and showed his card. "I'd like to see Mr Clegg," he said. "Is he around?"

"He's not here."

"Do you know when he'll be back?"

"No." It sounded like "dough."

"Do you know where he is?"

"No."

"What's your name?"

"Elizabeth. Elizabeth Moorhead. I'm Mr Clegg's secretary. Everyone calls me Betty." She took a crumpled paper tissue from the sleeve of her cardigan and blew her nose. "Cold," she said. "Godda cold. In May. Can you believe it? I hate summer colds."

"I'd like to see Mr Clegg, Betty," Banks said again. "Is there a problem?"

"I should say so."

"Can I help?"

She drew back a bit, as if still deciding whether to trust him. "What do you want him for?"

Banks hesitated for a moment, then told her. At least he would get some kind of reaction. "I wanted to ask a few questions about Keith Rothwell."

Her brow wrinkled in a frown. "Mr Rothwell? Yes, of course. Poor Mr Rothwell. He and Mr Clegg had some business together now and then. I read about him in the papers. It was terrible what happened."

"Did you know him well?"

"Mr Rothwell? No, not at all, not really. But he'd been here, in this office. I mean, I knew him to say hello to."

"When did you see him last?"

"Just last week, it was. Tuesday or Wednesday, I think. He was standing right there where you are now. Isn't it terrible?"

Banks agreed that it was. "Can you try and remember which day it was? It could be important."

She muttered to herself about appointments and flipped through a heavy book on her desk. Finally, she said, "It was Wednesday, just before I finished for the day at five. Mr Rothwell didn't have an appointment, but I remember because it was just after Mr Hoskins left, a client. Mr Rothwell had to wait out here a few moments and we chatted about how lovely the gardens are at this time of year."

"That's all you talked about?"

"Yes."

"Then what?"

"Then Mr Clegg came out and they went off."

"Do you know where?"

"No, but I think they went for a drink. They had business to discuss."

So Rothwell had visited Clegg in Leeds the day before his murder, almost two weeks after the letter ending their association. Why? It certainly hadn't been noted in his appointment book. "How did Mr Rothwell seem?" he asked.

"No different from usual."

"And Mr Clegg?"

"Fine. Why are you asking?"

"Did you notice any tension between them?"

"No."

"Has anything odd been happening around here lately? Has Mr Clegg received any strange messages, for example?"

"No-o." Some hesitation there. He would get back to it later.

Banks glanced around the small, tidy anteroom. "Does everything go through you? Mail, phone calls?"

"Most things, yes. But Mr Clegg has a private line, too."

"I see. How did he react to the news of Mr Rothwell's death?"

She studied Banks closely, then appeared to decide to trust him. She sighed and rested her hands on the desk, palms down. "That's just the problem," she said. "I don't know. I haven't seen him since. He's not here. I mean, he's not just out of the office right now, but he's disappeared. Into thin air."

"Disappeared? Have you told the local police?"

She shook her head. "I wouldn't want to look a fool."

"Has he done anything like this before?"

"No. Never. But if he *has* just gone off ... you know. With a woman or something ... I mean he *could* have, couldn't he?"

"When did you last see him?"

"Last Thursday. He left the office about half past five and that was the last I saw of him. He didn't come in to work on Friday morning."

"Have you tried to call him at home?"

"Yes, but all I got was the answering machine."

"Did he say anything about a business trip?" Banks asked.

"No. And he usually tells me if he's going to be away for any length of time."

"Do you know what kind of business relationship Mr Clegg had with Keith Rothwell?"

"No. I'm only his secretary. Mr Clegg didn't take me into his confidence. All I know is that Mr Rothwell came to the office now and then and sometimes they'd go out to lunch together, or for drinks after work. I knew Mr Rothwell was an accountant, so I supposed it would be something to do with tax. Mr Clegg special-izes in tax law, you see. I'm sorry I can't be of more help."

"Maybe you can be. It seems a bit of a coincidence, doesn't it, Mr Rothwell getting killed and Mr Clegg disappearing around the same time?"

She shrugged. "I didn't hear about Mr Rothwell's death until Saturday. I just never thought ..."

"Have you ever heard of someone called Robert Calvert?"

"No."

"Are you sure? Did Mr Clegg never mention the name?"

"No. He wasn't a client. I'm sure I'd remember."

"Why didn't you get in touch with the police when you realized Mr Clegg had disappeared and you heard about Mr Rothwell's murder?"

"Why should I? Mr Clegg had a lot of clients. He knew a lot of businessmen."

"But they don't usually get murdered."

She sneezed. "No. As I said, it's tragic what happened, but I don't see how as it connects with Mr Clegg."

"Maybe it does, and maybe it doesn't," Banks said. "But don't you think that's for us to decide?"

"I don't know what you mean." She reached for the tissue again. This time it disintegrated when she blew her nose. She dropped it in the waste-paper bin and took a fresh one from the box on her desk.

Banks regarded her closely. He didn't think she was lying or evading the issue; she simply didn't understand what he was getting at. He sometimes expected everyone to view the world with the same suspicious mind and jaundiced eye as he did. Besides, she didn't know about the letter Rothwell had left in the locked file.

He sat on the edge of the desk. "Right, Betty, let's go back a bit. When I came in, you were frightened. Why?"

She paused for a moment, then said, "I thought you might be one of them again."

"One of whom?"

"On Saturday morning I was here doing some filing and two men came in and started asking questions about Mr Clegg. They weren't very nice."

"Is that what you were thinking of when I asked you earlier if anything odd had been going on?"

"Yes."

"Why didn't you tell me then?"

"It ... I ... I didn't connect it. You've got me all confused."

"All right, Betty, take it easy. Did they hurt you?"

"Of course not. Or I certainly *would* have called the police. You see, sometimes in this business you get people who are ... well, less than polite. They get upset about money and sometimes they don't care who they take it out on."

"And these men were just rude?"

"Yes. Well, just a bit brusque, really. Nothing unusual. I mean, I'm only a secretary, right? I'm not important. They can afford to be short with me."

"So what bothered you? Why does it stick in your mind? Why were you frightened? Did they threaten you?"

"Not in so many words. But I got the impression that they were testing me to see what I knew. I think they realized early on that I didn't know anything. If they'd thought differently, I'm sure they would have hurt me. Don't ask me how I know. I could just feel it. There was something about them, some sort of coldness in their eyes, as if they'd done terrible things, or witnessed terrible things." She shivered. "I don't know. I can't explain. They were the kind of people you look away from when they make eye contact."

"What did they want to know about?"

"Where Mr Clegg was."

"That's all?"

"Yes. I asked them why they wanted to know, but they just said they had important business with him. I'd never seen them before, and I'm sure I'd know if they were new clients."

"Did they leave their names?"

"No."

"What did they look like?"

"Just ordinary businessmen, really. One was black and the other white. They both wore dark suits, white shirts, ties. I can't remember what colours."

"What about their height?"

"Both about the same. Around six foot, I'd say. But the white one was burly. You know, he had thick shoulders and a round chest, like a wrestler or something. He had very fair hair, but he was going bald on top. He tried to disguise it by growing the hair at the side longer and combing it right over, but I just think that looks silly, don't you? The black man was thin and fit looking. More like a runner than a wrestler. He did most of the talking."

Banks got her to describe them in as much detail as she could and took notes. They certainly didn't match Alison Rothwell's description of the two men in black who had tied her up and killed her father. "What about their accents?" he asked.

"Not local. The black one sounded a bit cultured, well educated, and the other didn't speak much. I think he had a slight foreign accent, though I couldn't swear to it and I can't tell you where from."

"You've done fine, Betty."

"I have?"

Banks nodded.

"There's something else," she said. "When I came in this morning, I got the impression that someone had been in the place since then. Again, I can't say why, and I certainly couldn't prove it, but in this job you develop a feel for the way things should be— you know, files, documents, that sort of thing—and you can just tell if something's out of place without knowing what it really is, if you follow my drift."

"Were there any signs of forced entry?"

"No. Nothing obvious, nothing like that. Not that it would be difficult to get in here. It's hardly the Tower of London. I locked myself out once when Mr Clegg was away on business and I just slipped my Visa card in the door and opened it." She put her hand to her mouth. "Oops. I don't suppose I should be telling you that, should I?"

Banks smiled. "It's all right, Betty. I've had to get into my car with a coat-hanger more than once. Was anything missing?"

"Not so far as I can tell. It's pretty secure inside. There's a good, strong safe and it doesn't look as if anyone tried to tamper with it."

"Could it have been Mr Clegg?"

"I suppose so. He sometimes comes in on a Sunday if there's something important in progress." Then she shook her head. "But no. If it had been Mr Clegg I'd have known. Things would have looked different. They looked the same, but not quite the same, if you know what I mean."

"As if someone had messed things up and tried to restore them to the way they were originally?"

"Yes."

"Do you employ a cleaning lady?"

"Yes, but she comes Thursday evenings. It can't have been her."

"Did she arrive as usual last Thursday?"

"Yes."

"May I have a look in the office?"

Betty got up, took a key from her drawer and opened Clegg's door for him. He stood on the threshold and saw a small office with shelves of law books, box files and filing cabinets. Clegg also had a computer and stacks of disks on a desk at right angles to the one on which he did his other paperwork. The window, closed and locked,

Banks noticed, looked out over the central square with its neatly cut grass, shady trees and people sitting on benches. The office was hot and stuffy.

Certainly nothing *looked* out of the ordinary. Banks was careful not to disturb anything. Soon, the Fraud Squad would be here to pore over the books and look for whatever the link was between Rothwell and Clegg.

"Better keep it locked," he told Betty on his way out. "There'll be more police here this afternoon, most likely. May I use the phone?"

Betty nodded.

Banks phoned Ken Blackstone at Millgarth and told him briefly what the situation was. Ken said he'd send a car over right away. Next he phoned Superintendent Gristhorpe in Eastvale and reported his findings. Gristhorpe said he'd get in touch with the Fraud Squad and see if they could co-ordinate with West Yorkshire.

He turned back to Betty. "You'll be all right here," he said. "I'll wait until the locals arrive. They'll need you to answer more questions. Just tell them everything you told me. What's your address, in case I need to get in touch?"

She gave him the address of her flat in Burmantofts. "What do you think has happened?" she asked, reaching for her tissue again.

Banks shook his head.

"You don't think anything's happened to him, do you?"

"It's probably nothing," Banks said, without conviction. "Don't worry, we'll get to the bottom of it."

"It's just that Melissa will be so upset."

"Who's Melissa?"

"Oh, didn't you know? It's Mrs Clegg. His wife."

II

After a hurried bowl of vegetable soup in the Golden Grill, Susan Gay walked out into the street, with its familiar smells and noises: petrol fumes, of course; car horns; fresh coffee; bread from the bakery; a busker playing a flute by the church doors.

In the cobbled market square, she noticed an impromptu evangelist set up his soapbox and start rabbiting on about judgment and sin. It made her feel vaguely guilty just hearing him, and as she went into the station, she contemplated asking one of the uniforms to go out and move him on. There must be a law against it somewhere on the books. Disturbing the peace of an overworked DC?

Charity prevailed, and she went up to her office. It faced the car park out back, so she wouldn't have to listen to him there.

First, she took out the blue file cards she liked to make notes on and pinned them to the cork-board over her desk. It was the same board, she remembered, that Sergeant Hatchley had used for his pin-ups of page-three girls with vacuous smiles and enormous breasts. Now Hatchley was due back any moment. What a thought.

Then, after she had made another appointment to talk to Laurence Pratt, she luxuriated in the empty office, stretching like a cat, feeling as if she were in a deep, warm bubble-bath. Out of the window she could see the maintenance men with their shirtsleeves rolled up washing the patrol cars in the large car park. Sun glinted on their rings and watch-straps and on the shiny chrome they polished; it spread rainbows of oily sheen on the bright windscreens.

One of the men, in particular, caught her eye: well-muscled, but not overbearingly so, with a lock of blond hair that slipped over his eye and bounced as he rubbed the bonnet in long, slow strokes. The telephone broke into her fantasy. She picked it up. "Hello. Eastvale CID. Can I help you?"

"To whom am I speaking?"

"Detective Constable Susan Gay."

"Is the superintendent there?"

"I'm afraid not."

"And Chief Inspector Banks?"

"Out of the office. Can I help you? What's this about?"

"I suppose you'll have to do. My name is Mary Rothwell. I've just had a call from my son, Tom."

"You have? Where is he?"

"He's still in Florida. A hotel in Lido Key, wherever that is. Apparently the British newspapers are a couple of days late over

there, and he's just read about his father's murder. It's only eight in
the morning there. He can't get a flight back until this evening.
Anyway, he said he should get into Manchester at about seven
o'clock tomorrow morning. I'm going to meet him at the airport
and bring him home."

"That's good news, Mrs Rothwell," Susan said. "You do know
we'd like to talk to him?"

"Yes. Though I can't imagine why. You'll pass the message on to
the Chief Inspector, will you?"

"Yes."

"Good. And by the way, I've made funeral arrangements for
Wednesday. That *is* still all right, isn't it?"

"Of course."

"Very well."

"Is there anything else, Mrs Rothwell?"

"No."

"Goodbye, then. We'll be in touch."

Susan hung up and stared into space for a moment, thinking
what an odd woman Mary Rothwell was. Imperious, highly strung
and businesslike. Probably a real Tartar to live with. But was she a
murderess?

Though it would take the Fraud Squad a long time to work out
exactly how much Rothwell was worth—and to separate the legal
from the illegal money—it was bound to be a fortune. Money
worth killing for. The problem was, though Susan could imagine
Mary Rothwell being cold-blooded enough to have her husband
killed, she could not imagine her having it done in such a bloody,
dramatic way.

The image of the kneeling, headless corpse came back to her and
she tasted the vegetable soup rise in her throat. No, she thought, if
the wife were responsible, Rothwell would have been disposed of in
a neat, sanitary way—poison, perhaps—and he certainly wouldn't
have made such a mess on the garage floor. What was the phrase?
You don't shit on your own doorstep. It was too close to home for Mary; it
would probably taint Arkbeck Farm for her forever.

Still, there was a lot of money involved. Susan had seen
Rothwell's solicitor that morning, and, according to him, Rothwell

had owned, or part-owned, about fifteen businesses, from a ship-
ping company registered in the Bahamas to a dry cleaner's in
Wigan, not to mention various properties dotted around England,
Spain, Portugal and France. Of course, the solicitor assured her,
they were all legitimate. She suspected, however, that some had
served as fronts for Rothwell's illegal activities.

As Susan was wondering if Robert Calvert's money would now
simply get lumped in with Keith Rothwell's, she became aware of a
large shadow cast over her desk by a figure in the doorway.

She looked up, startled, right into the smiling face of Detective
Sergeant Jim Hatchley. So soon? she thought, with a sinking
feeling in the pit of her stomach. Now she knew there really was no
God.

"Hello, love," said Hatchley, lighting a cigarette. "I see you've
taken my pin-ups down. We'll have to do something about that
now I'm back to stay."

III

At one-thirty, the hot, smoky pub was still packed with local clerks
and shopkeepers on their lunch break. When Banks had phoned
Pamela Jeffreys before leaving for Leeds that morning, she had
suggested they meet in the pub across from the hall in West Leeds,
where she was rehearsing with a string quartet. There was no beer
garden, she said, but the curry of the day was usually excellent.
Though he had to admit to feeling excitement at the thought of
seeing Pamela again, this wasn't a meeting Banks was looking
forward to.

She hadn't arrived yet, so Banks got himself a pint of shandy at
the bar—just the thing for a hot day—and managed to grab a small
table in the corner by the dartboard, fortunately not in use. There,
he mulled over Daniel Clegg's disappearance and the mysterious
goons Betty Moorhead had seen.

There was no end of trouble a lawyer could get himself into,
Banks speculated. Especially if he were a bit crooked to start with.
So maybe there was no connection between Clegg's disappearance

and Rothwell's murder. But there were too many coincidences—the letter, the timing, the shady accounts—and Banks didn't like coincidences. Which meant that there were two sets of goons on the loose: the ones who killed Rothwell, and the ones who scared Clegg's secretary. But did they work for the same person?

He was saved from bashing his head against a brick wall any longer by the arrival of Pamela Jeffreys, looking gorgeous in black leggings and a long white T-shirt with the Opera North logo on front. She had her hair tied back and wore black-rimmed glasses. As she sat down, she smiled at him. "The professional musician's look," she said. "Keeps my hair out of my eyes so I can read the music."

"Would you like a drink?" Banks asked.

"Just a grapefruit juice with an ice-cube, please, if they've got any. I have to play through 'Death and the Maiden' again this afternoon."

While he was at the bar, Banks also ordered two curries of the day.

"What's been happening?" Pamela asked when he got back.

"Plenty," said Banks, hoping to avoid the issue of Calvert's identity for as long as possible. "But I've no idea how it all adds up. First off, have you ever heard of a man called Daniel Clegg?"

She shook her head. "No, I can't say as I have."

"He's a solicitor."

"He's not mine. Actually, I don't have one."

"Are you sure Robert never mentioned him?"

"No, and I think I'd remember. But I already told you, he never talked about his work, and I never asked. What do I know or care about business?" She looked at him over the top of her glass as she sipped her grapefruit juice, thin black eyebrows raised.

"Did you ever introduce Robert to any of your friends?"

"No. He never seemed really interested in going to parties or having dinner with people or anything, so I never pushed it. They probably wouldn't have got on very well anyway. Most of my friends are young and artsy. Robert's more mature. Why?"

"Did you ever meet anyone he knew when you were out together, say in a restaurant or at the casino?"

"No, not that I can recall."

"So you didn't have much of a social life together?"

"No, we didn't. Just a bit of gambling, the occasional day at the races, then it was mostly concerts or a video and a pizza. That was a bit of a problem, really. Robert was a lot of fun, but he didn't like crowds. I'm a bit more of a social butterfly, myself."

"I don't mean to embarrass you," Banks said slowly, "but did Robert show any interest in pornography? Did he like to take photographs, make videos? Anything like that?"

She looked at him open-mouthed, then burst out laughing. "Sorry, sorry," she said, patting her chest. "You know, most girls might be insulted if you suggested they moonlighted in video nasties, but it's so absurd I can't help but laugh."

"So the answer's no?"

"Don't look so embarrassed. Of course it's no, you silly man. The very thought of it ..." She laughed again and Banks felt himself blush.

Their curries came and they tucked in. They were, as Pamela had said, delicious: delicately spiced rather than hot, with plenty of chunks of tender beef. They exchanged small talk over the food, edging away from the embarrassing topic Banks had brought up earlier. When they had finished, Pamela went for more drinks and Banks lit a cigarette. Was she going to ask now, he wondered, or was he going to have to bring it up? Maybe she was avoiding the moment, too.

Finally, she asked. "Did you find out anything? You know, about Robert and this Rothwell fellow." Very casual, but Banks could sense the apprehension in her voice.

He scraped the end of his cigarette on the rim of the red metal ashtray and avoided her eyes. A group at the next table burst into laughter at a joke one of them had told.

"Well?"

He looked up. "It looks very much as if Robert Calvert and Keith Rothwell were the same person," he said. "We found fingerprints that matched. I'm sorry."

For a while she said nothing. Banks could see her beautiful almond eyes fill slowly with tears. "Shit," she said, shaking her head and reaching in her bag for a tissue. "Sorry, this is stupid of me. I don't know why I'm crying. We were just friends really. Can we ... I mean ..." She gestured around.

"Of course." Banks took her arm and they left the pub. Fifty yards along the main road was a park. Pamela looked at her watch and said, "I've still got a while yet, if you don't mind walking a bit."

"Not at all."

They walked past a playground where children screamed with delight as the swings went higher and higher and the roundabout spun faster and faster. A small wading-pool had been filled with water because of the warm weather and more children played there, splashing one another, squealing and shouting, all under their mother's or father's watchful eyes. Nobody let their kids play out alone these days, as they used to do when he was a child, Banks noticed. Being in his job, knowing what he knew, he didn't blame them.

Pamela seemed lost in her silent grief, head bowed, walking slowly. "It's crazy," she said at last. "I hardly knew Robert and things had cooled off between us anyway, and here I am behaving like this."

Banks could think of nothing to say. He was aware of the warmth of her arm in his and of her scent: jasmine, he thought. What the hell did he think he was doing, walking arm in arm in the park with a beautiful suspect? What if someone saw him? But what could he do? The contact seemed to form an important link between Pamela and something real, something she could hold onto while the rest of her world shifted under her feet like fine sand. And he couldn't deny that the touch of her skin meant something to him, too.

"I was wrong about him, wasn't I?" she went on. "Dead wrong. He was married, you say? Kids?"

"A son and a daughter."

"I should know. I read it in the paper but it didn't sink in because I was so *sure* it couldn't have been him. Robert seemed so ... such a free spirit."

"Maybe he was."

She glanced sideways at him. "What do you mean?"

They stopped at an ice-cream van and Banks bought two cornets. "It was a different life he lived with you," he said. "I can't begin to understand a man like that. It's not that he had a split personality or anything, just that he was capable of existing in very different ways."

"What ways?" Pamela stuck out her pink tongue and licked the ice-cream.

"The people in Swainsdale knew him as a quiet, unassuming sort of bloke. Bit of a dry stick really."

"Robert?" she gasped. "A dry stick?"

"Not Robert. Keith Rothwell. The hard-working, clean-living accountant. The man who put his spent matches back in the box in the opposite direction to the unused ones."

"But Robert was so alive. He was fun to be with. We laughed a lot. We dreamed. We danced."

Banks smiled sadly. "There you are, then. Keith Rothwell probably had two left feet."

"Are you saying it *wasn't* the same man?"

"I don't know what I'm saying. Just that your memories of Robert Calvert won't change, shouldn't change. He's who he was to you, what he meant to you. Don't let this poison it for you. On the other hand, I need to know who killed Keith Rothwell, and it looks as if there might be a connection."

She put her arm in his again and they walked on. There was hardly any breeze at all, but they passed a boy trying to fly a red-and-green kite. He couldn't seem to get it more than about twenty feet off the ground before it came flopping down again.

"What do you mean, a connection?" Pamela asked, shifting her gaze from the kite back to Banks.

"Maybe something in his life as Robert Calvert spilled over into his life as Keith Rothwell. Are you sure you didn't know he was married, you didn't suspect it?"

She shook her head. "No. I've been a right bloody fool, haven't I? Muggins again."

"But you were sure he'd found a new girlfriend?"

"Ninety-nine per cent certain, yes."

"How did you feel about that?"

"What?"

"His new girlfriend. How did you feel about her? On the one hand you tell me you shouldn't be so upset, you hardly knew Robert Calvert, and your relationship had cooled off anyway. On the other hand, it seems to me from what you say and the way you behave that you were extremely fond of him. Maybe in love with him. What's the truth? How did you really feel when someone else came along and stole him from you? Surely you must have felt hurt, angry, jealous?"

Pamela pulled back her arm and stepped aside from him, an expression of pain and anger shadowing her face. She dropped her ice-cream. It splattered on the tarmac path. "What's that got to do with anything? What are you saying? What are you getting at? First you imply that I'm some kind of porn actress, and now you're implying that *I* killed Robert out of jealousy?"

"No," said Banks quickly. "No, nothing like that."

But she was already backing away from him, hands held up, palms out, as if to ward him off.

"Yes, you are. How could you even ...? I thought you ..."

Banks stepped towards her. "That's not what I mean, Pamela. I'm just—"

But she turned and started to run away.

"Wait!" Banks called after her. "Please, stop."

One or two people gave him suspicious looks. As he set off walking quickly after her, a child's coloured ball rolled in front of him, and he had to pull up sharply to avoid knocking into its diminutive owner, whose large father, fast approaching from the nearest bench, didn't seem at all happy about things.

Pamela reached the park exit and dashed across the road, dodging her way through the traffic, back towards the hall. Banks stood there looking after her, the sweat beading on his brow. The remains of his ice-cream had started to melt and drip over the flesh between his thumb and first finger.

"Shit," he cursed under his breath. Then louder, "Shit!"

The little boy looked up, puzzled, and his father loomed closer.

SEVEN

I

The Merrion Centre was one of the first indoor shopping malls in Britain. Built on the northern edge of Leeds city centre in 1964, it now seems something of an antique, a monument to the heady sixties' days of slum clearance, tower blocks and council estates.

Covered on top, but open to the wind at the sides, it also suffers competition from a number of more recent, fully enclosed, central shopping centres, such as the St John's Centre, directly across Merrion Street, and the plush dark green and brass luxury of the Schofields Centre, right on The Headrow.

Still, the Merrion Centre does have a large Morrison's super-market, Le Phonographique discothèque—the longest surviving disco in Leeds—a number of small specialty shops, a couple of pubs, a flea market and the Classical Record Shop, which is how Banks had come to know the place quite well. And on a warm, windless May afternoon it can be pleasant enough.

Banks found Clegg's Wines and Spirits easily enough. He had phoned Melissa Clegg an hour or so earlier, still smarting over his acrimonious parting with Pamela Jeffreys in the park, and she had told him she could spare a little time to talk. It was odd, he thought, that she hadn't seemed overly curious about his call. He had said that it concerned her husband, yet she had asked for no details.

He opened the door and found himself in a small shop cluttered with bottles and cases. There were a couple of bins of specials on the floor by the door—mostly Bulgarian, Romanian and South African varietals, and some yellow "marked down" cards on a few of the racks that lined the walls to his right and left, including a Rioja, a Côtes du Rhône and a claret.

Banks looked at the racks and thought he might take something home for dinner, assuming that he and Sandra ever got the chance to sit down to dinner together again, and assuming that she wanted to. Perhaps they could have that wine, candlelight and Chopin evening he had had to cancel when the Rothwell enquiry got in the way.

Behind the counter ranged the bottles of single malt Scotch: Knockando, Blair Athol, Talisker, Glendronach. Evocative names, but he mustn't look too closely. He had a weakness for single malt that Sandra said hit them too hard in the pocket. Besides, he still had a drop of Laphroaig left at home.

The spotty young man behind the counter smiled. "Can I help you, sir?" He wore a candy-striped shirt with the sleeves rolled up and his tie loose at the neck, the way Banks always wore his own when he could get away with it. His black hair had so much gel or mousse on that it looked like an oil slick.

"Boss around?" Banks asked, showing his card.

"In the back." He lifted up the counter flap and Banks went through. Stepping over and around cases of wine, he walked along a narrow corridor, then saw on his left a tiny office with the door open. A woman sat at the desk talking on the phone. It sounded to Banks as if she were complaining over non-delivery of several cases of Hungarian Pinot Noir.

When she saw him, she waved him in and pointed to a chair piled high with papers. Banks moved them to the edge of the desk and she grinned at him over the mouthpiece. There were no windows, and it was stuffy in the back room, despite the whirring fan. The office smelled of freshly cut wood. Banks took his jacket off and hung it over the back of the chair. He could feel the steady draught of the fan on the left side of his face.

Finally, she put the phone down and rolled her eyes. "Some suppliers ..."

She was wearing a yellow sun-dress with thin straps that left most of her nicely tanned and freckled shoulders and throat bare. About forty, Banks guessed, she looked as if she watched what she ate and exercised regularly, tennis probably. Her straight blonde hair, parted in the middle, hung just above her shoulders, framing a heart-shaped face with high cheekbones. It was a cheerful face, one to which a smile was no stranger, and the youthful, uneven fringe suited her. But Banks also noticed marks of stress and strain in the wrinkles under her blue-grey eyes and around her slightly puckered mouth. A pair of no-nonsense glasses with tortoiseshell frames dangled on a cord around her neck.

"Your phone call piqued my curiosity," she said, leaning back in her chair and linking her hands behind her head. Banks noticed the shadow of stubble under her arms. "What has Danny-boy been up to now?"

"I'm sorry?" said Banks. "I don't follow."

"Didn't Betty tell you?"

"Tell me what?"

"Oh, God, that woman. Gormless. About Danny and me. We're separated. Have been for about two years now. It was all perfectly amicable, of course."

Of course, Banks thought. How often had he heard that? If it was all so bloody amicable, he wondered, then why aren't you still together? "I didn't know," he said.

"Then I'm sorry you're probably on a wild goose chase." She changed her position, resting her hands on the desk and playing with a rubber band. There were no rings on her fingers. "Anyway, I'm still intrigued," she said. "I *am* still fond of Danny. I would be concerned if I thought anything had happened to him. It hasn't, has it?"

"Do you still see one another?"

"From time to time."

"When did you last see him?"

"Hmm ..." She pursed her lips and thought. "A couple of months ago. We had lunch together at Whitelocks."

"How did he seem?"

"Fine." She stretched the rubber band tight. "Look, you've got me worried. All this interest in Danny all of a sudden. First those clients of his. Now you."

Banks pricked up his ears. "What clients?"

"On Saturday. Saturday afternoon. Just a couple of businessmen wondering if I knew where he was."

"Did they know you were separated?"

"Yes. They said it was a long shot and they were sorry to bother me but they'd had an appointment scheduled with him that morning and he hadn't shown up. He'd mentioned me and the shop at some time or other, of course. He often does, by way of sending me business. What a sweetheart. Anyway, they asked if I had any idea where he was, if he'd suddenly decided to go away for the weekend. As if I'd know. It all seemed innocent enough. Is something wrong?"

"What did they look like?"

She described the same two men who had visited Betty Moorhead. It wouldn't have been difficult for them to find out about Melissa's shop—perhaps even Betty had told them—and if they were looking for Clegg, it was reasonable to assume that his ex-wife might know where he was. She must have convinced them quickly that she neither knew nor cared.

The rubber band snapped. "Look," she said, "I've a right to know if something's happened to Danny, haven't I?"

"We don't know if anything has happened to him," Banks said. "He's just gone missing."

She breathed a sigh of relief. "So that's all."

Banks frowned. "His secretary seems worried enough. She says it's unusual."

"Oh, Betty's a nice enough girl, but she is a bit of an alarmist. Danny always did have an eye for the ladies. That's one reason we're no longer together. I should imagine if he's gone missing, then something came up, so to speak." She grinned, showing slightly overlapping front teeth.

"Wouldn't he at least let his secretary know where he was?"

"I'll admit that is a bit unusual. While Danny was never exactly tied to his desk, he didn't like to be too far from the action. You know the type, always on his car phone to the office. Who knows? Maybe he's having a mid-life crisis. Maybe he and his bit of crumpet have gone somewhere where there are no telephones. He's such a romantic, is Danny."

The phone rang and Mrs Clegg excused herself for a moment. Banks caught her half of the conversation about an order of *méthode champenoise.* A couple of minutes later she put the phone down. "Sorry. Where were we?"

"Mrs Clegg, we think your husband might have been mixed up in some shady dealings and that might have had something to do with his disappearance."

She laughed. "Shady dealings? That hardly surprises me."

"Do you know anything about his business activities?"

"No. But dishonest in love ..." She let the thought trail, then shrugged. "Danny never was one of the most ethical, or faithful, of people. Careful, usually, yes, but hardly ethical."

"Would you say he was the type to get mixed up in something illegal?"

She thought for a moment, frowning, then answered. "Yes. Yes, I think so. If he thought the returns were high enough."

"Is he a greedy man?"

"No-o. Not in so many words, no. I wouldn't call him greedy. He just likes to get what he wants. Women. Money. Whatever. It's more a matter of power, manipulation. He just likes to win."

"What about the risk?"

She tipped her head to one side. "There's always *some* risk, isn't there, Chief Inspector? If something's worth having. Danny's not a coward, if that's what you mean."

"Did you know Keith Rothwell?"

"Yes. Not well, but I had met him. Poor man. I read about him in the paper. Terrible. You're not suggesting there's any link between his murder and Danny's disappearance, are you?"

She's quicker on the ball than Betty Moorhead, Banks thought. "We don't know. I don't suppose you'd be in a position to enlighten us about their business dealings?"

"Sorry. No. I haven't seen Keith since Danny and I split up. Even then I'd just bump into him at the office now and then, or when he helped with my taxes."

"So you've no idea what kinds of dealings they were involved in?"

"No. As I said, Keith Rothwell did my accounts a couple of times—you know, the wine business—when Dan and I were together, before things became awkward and our personal life got in the way. He was a damn good accountant. He saved me a lot of money from the Inland Revenue—all above board. Now, it doesn't take a Sherlock Holmes to figure out that if the two of them were in business together it probably involved tax havens of one kind or another, and that they both probably did quite well from it."

"Have you ever heard of a man called Robert Calvert?"

"Calvert? No. I can't say I have. Should I have? Look, I'm really sorry I can't help you, Chief Inspector. And I certainly didn't mean to sound callous at all. But knowing Danny, I'm sure he's popped off to Paris for the weekend with some floozie or other and just got too over-excited to remember to let anyone know. He'll turn up."

Banks stood up. "I hope you're right, Mrs Clegg. And if he gets in touch, please let us know." He gave her his card. She stood up as he left the office. He turned in the doorway and smiled. "One more thing."

"Yes."

"Could you recommend a decent claret for dinner, not too pricey?"

"Of course. If you're not absolutely stuck on Bordeaux, try a bottle of the Chateau de la Liquière. It's from Faugères, in Languedoc. Very popular region these days. Lots of character." She smiled. "And you can even afford it on a policeman's salary."

After Banks thanked her, he made his way back down the corridor, dodging the wine cases, and bought the bottle she had suggested. Not an entirely wasted visit, he thought. At least he'd got a decent bottle of wine out of it. And then there was the Classical Record Shop just around the corner. He couldn't pass so closely without going in. Besides, he needed balm for his wounds. He was still feeling annoyed with himself after the way he had messed things up with Pamela Jeffreys. The new CD of the Khachaturian Piano Concerto, if they had it, might just help make him feel better.

As he walked outside with his bottle of wine, he felt a large hand clap down on his shoulder.

"Well, if it isn't my old mate, Banksy," a voice said in his ear.

Banks spun round and saw the source of the voice: Detective Superintendent Richard "Dirty Dick" Burgess, from Scotland Yard. What the hell was he doing here?

"I hope you haven't been accepting bribes," Burgess said, pointing to the wine. Then he put his arm around Banks's shoulders. "Come on," he said. "We need to go somewhere and have a little chat."

II

Laurence Pratt was waiting in his office, again with his shirtsleeves rolled up, black-framed glasses about halfway down his nose, fingers forming a steeple on the neat desk in front of him. His white shirt was more dazzling than any Susan had seen in a detergent advert. Susan felt stifled. The temperature outside was in the twenties, and the window was closed.

Pratt seemed less easy in his manner this time, Susan observed, and she guessed it was because he had given too much away on her last visit. This was going to be a tough one, she thought, taking her notebook and pen out of her handbag. They had discovered a lot more about Keith Rothwell since Friday, and this time, *she* didn't want to give too much away.

Susan opened her notebook, resisting the impulse to fan her face with it, and unclipped her pen. "The last time I talked to you, Mr Pratt," she began, "you told me you saw the Rothwells for the last time in March."

"That's right. Carla and I were out to Arkbeck for dinner. Duck *à l'orange*, if I remember correctly."

"And the new kitchen."

"Ah, yes. We all admired the new kitchen."

"Can you be a bit more precise about the date?"

Pratt frowned and pulled at his lower lip. "Not exactly. It was just after St Patrick's Day, I think. Hang on a sec." He fished in his briefcase by the side of the desk and pulled out a Filofax. "Be lost without it," he grinned. "Even in the computer age. I mean, you don't want to turn the computer on every time you need an address, do you?" As he talked, he flipped through the pages. "Ah, there it is." He held up the open page for Susan to see. "19th March. Dinner with Keith and Mary."

"And you said Tom dropped in to talk about his trip?"

"Yes."

"From where?"

"What? Oh, I see. From his room, I suppose. At least I think he'd been up there. He just came in to say hello while we were having cocktails. Is he back from America, by the way?"

No harm in telling a family friend that, Susan thought. "He's on his way," she said. "What was the atmosphere like between Tom and his father that night?"

"They didn't talk, as I remember."

"Did you notice any antagonism or tension between them?"

"I wouldn't say that, no. I told you before that their relationship was strained because Tom drifted off the course his father had set for him."

"Was anything said about that on the night you were there?"

"No, I'm certain of it. They didn't talk to one another at all. Tom was excited about going to America. I think he'd been upstairs poring over a map, planning his route."

"And Keith Rothwell said nothing during your little chat?"

"No. He just sat there rather po-faced. Now you mention it, that *was* a bit odd. I mean, you'd hardly call old Keith a live wire these days, but he'd usually take a bit more interest than he did that night. Especially as his son was off on a big adventure."

"So his behaviour *was* strange?"

"A little unusual, on reflection, yes."

"What about Tom? Did he say anything to or about his father?"

Pratt shook his head slowly. Susan noticed a few beads of sweat around his temples where his hairline was receding. She could feel her own sweat tickling her ribs as it slid down her side. So much for the expensive extra-dry, long-lasting anti-perspirant she had put on after her morning shower. This didn't happen to the high-powered women executives and airline pilots in the television adverts. On the other hand, *they* didn't have to deal with the return of Sergeant Hatchley. It had taken her a good five minutes to stop shaking after he had left the office.

She asked Pratt to open the window. He complied, but it didn't do much good. The air outside was still and hot. Even the gargoyles on the upper walls of the community centre looked grumpy and sweaty.

"Did Mr Rothwell ever express any interest in pornography?"

Pratt raised his eyebrows. "Good lord. How do you mean? As a business venture or for personal consumption?"

"Either."

"Not in my presence. As I said, I don't know about the extent of his business interests, but he always struck me as rather ... say ... sexless. When we were younger, of course, we'd chase the lasses, but since his marriage ..."

"Have you ever met a solicitor called Daniel Clegg?"

"No. The name doesn't sound familiar. Are you sure he practises in Eastvale?"

"You've never met him?"

"I told you, I've never even heard of him. Why do you ask? Is there some—"

"Did Mr Rothwell ever mention him?"

"Is there some connection?"

"Did Mr Rothwell ever mention him?"

Pratt stared at Susan for about fifteen long seconds, then said, "No, not that I recall."

Susan ran the back of her hand across her moist brow. She was beginning to feel a little dizzy. "What about Robert Calvert?"

"Never heard of him, either. Is this another business colleague of Keith's? I told you we never talked about his business. He played his cards close to his chest."

"Did he ever mention a woman called Pamela Jeffreys?"

Pratt raised an eyebrow. "A woman? Keith? Another woman? Good lord, no. I told you he didn't strike me as the type. Not these days, anyway. Besides, Mary would have killed him. Oh, my God ..."

"It's all right, Mr Pratt," Susan said. "Slip of the tongue. Jealous type, is she?"

He pushed his glasses back up to the bridge of his nose. "Mary? Well, I'd guess so, yes."

"But you don't know for certain?"

"No. It's just the impression she gives. How everything centred around Keith, the house, the family. If anything came along to jeopardize that, threaten it, then she'd be a formidable enemy. Possessive, selfish, I'd say, definitely. Is that the same thing?"

Susan closed her notebook and stood up. "Thank you, Mr Pratt. Thank you very much. Again, you've been most helpful." Then she hurried out of the hot, stuffy office before she fainted.

III

They walked down to Stumps, under the museum, and made their way to the bar, where Burgess ordered a pint of McEwan's lager and Banks a pint of bitter. It wasn't Theakston's, but it would have to do.

As it was a warm day, they took their drinks outside and found a free table. There was a broad, tiled area between the museum-library complex and the buses roaring by on The Headrow, and pedestrians hurried back and forth, some heading for the Court Centre or the Town Hall and some taking short-cuts to Calverley Street and the Civic Hall. A group of people stood playing chess with oversize figures on a board drawn on the tiles. Scaffolding covered the front of one of the nineteenth-century buildings across The Headrow, Banks noticed. Another renovation.

Banks felt both puzzled and apprehensive at Burgess's arrival on the scene. The last time they had locked horns was over the killing of a policeman at an anti-government demonstration in Eastvale back in the Thatcher era.

Burgess had fitted in just fine back then. An East Ender, son of a barrow boy, he had fought his way up from the bottom with a fierce mixture of ego, ambition, cunning and a total disregard for the rules most people played by. He also felt no sympathy for those who had been unable to do likewise. Now, at about Banks's age, he was a Detective Superintendent working for a Scotland Yard department that was not quite Special Branch and not quite MI5, but close enough to both to give Banks the willies.

In a period when a fully functioning human heart was regarded as a severe disability, he had been one of the new, golden breed of working-class Conservatives, up there in the firmament of the new Britain alongside the bright young things in the City, the insider traders and their like. Cops and criminals: it didn't seem to make a lot of difference, as long as you were successful. But then, it never did to some people.

Nobody could gainsay Burgess's abilities—intelligence and physical courage being foremost among them—but "The end justifies the means" could have been written just for him. The "end" was some vague sort of loyalty to whatever the people in power wanted done for the preservation of order, as long as the people in power weren't liberals or socialists, of course; and as for the "means," the sky was the limit.

Maybe he had changed, Banks wondered. After all the recent inquiries and commissions, a policeman could surely no longer walk into a pub, pick up the first group of Irish people he saw and throw them in jail as terrorists, could he? Or walk down Brixton Road and arrest the first black person he saw running? According to the public-relations people, today's policeman was a cross between Santa Claus and a hotel manager.

On the other hand, perhaps that was only according to the PR people: truth in advertising, *caveat emptor* and the rest. Besides, if there was one thing not likely to make the slightest impression on Burgess's obsidian consciousness, it was political correctness.

Banks lit a cigarette and held out his lighter as Burgess fired up one of his Tom Thumb cigars. He was still in good shape, though filling out a bit around the belly. He had a square jaw and slightly crooked teeth. His black, slicked-back hair was turning silver at the temples and sideboards, and the bags under his seen-it-all grey eyes looked as if they had taken on a bit more weight since Banks had last seen him. About six feet tall, casually dressed in a black leather jacket, open-neck shirt and grey cords, he was still handsome enough to turn the heads of a few thirtyish women, and had a reputation as something of a rake. It wasn't entirely unfounded, Banks had discovered the last time they worked together.

Banks reached for his pint. "To what do I owe the honour?" he asked. He had never dignified Burgess with the "sir" his rank demanded, and he was damned if he was about to start now.

Burgess swigged some lager, swished it around his mouth and swallowed.

"Well?" said Banks. "Enough bloody theatrics, for Christ's sake."

"I don't suppose you'd believe me if I said I'd missed you?"

"Get on with it."

"Right. Thought not. Ever heard of a place called St Corona?"

"Of course. It's a Caribbean island, been in the news a bit lately."

"Clever boy. That's the one. Population about four point eight million. Area about seven thousand square miles. Chief resources: bauxite, limestone, aluminium, sugar cane, plus various fruits and spices, fish and a bit of gold, silver and nickel. A lot of tourism, too, or there used to be."

"So you've been studying *Whitaker's Almanac*," said Banks. "Now what the bloody hell is this all about?"

A tipsy youth bumped into the table and spilled some of Burgess's lager. The youth stopped to apologize, but the look Burgess gave him sent him stumbling off into the bright afternoon sunlight before he could get the words out.

"Fucking lager lout," Burgess muttered, wiping the beer off the table-top with a handkerchief. "Gone to the dogs, this country. Where was I? Oh, yes. St Corona. Imports just about everything you need to live, including the machinery to make it. Lots of television sets, radios, fridges, washing machines." He paused and whistled between his teeth as a young redhead in a mini-skirt walked by. "Now *that's* not bad," he said. "Which reminds me, have you rogered that young redhead in Eastvale yet? You know, the psychologist." He flicked the stub of his cigar towards the gutter; it hit the wall just above with a shower of sparks.

Burgess meant Jenny Fuller, as he knew damn well. Banks managed a smile, remembering what happened the last time those two met. "St Corona," he said. "You were saying?"

Burgess pouted. "You're no fun. Know who the president is?"

"What is this, bloody 'Mastermind'? Martin Churchill. Now, if you've got something to tell me, get it off your chest and let me go home. It's been a long day."

"Back to that lovely wife of yours, eh? Sandra, isn't it? All right, all right. St Corona is a republic, and you're right, Martin Churchill is president for life. Good name for the job, don't you think?"

"I've read about him."

"Yes, well, the poor sod's a bit beleaguered these days, what with the opposition parties raking up the muck and the independence and liberation movements going from strength to strength." He sighed. "I don't know. It seems people just don't believe in a good old benevolent dictatorship any more."

"Benevolent, my arse," said Banks. "He's been bleeding the country dry for ten years and now they're closing in on him. What am I supposed to do, cry?"

Burgess glared at Banks through squinting eyes. "Still the bloody pinko, huh? Still the limp-wristed, knee-jerking liberal?" He sighed. "Somehow, Banks, I hadn't expected you to change. That's partly why I'm here. Anyway, whatever you or I might think about it, the powers that be decided it was a good idea to have a stable government in that part of the world, someone we could trust. Of course, it doesn't seem quite so important now, with the Russkies swapping their rusty old atomic warheads for turnips, but other threats exist. Anyway, Britain, France, Canada, the States and a few others pumped millions into St Corona over the years, so you can estimate how important it is to us."

Banks listened intently. There could be no rushing Burgess; he would get where he was going in his own sweet time.

"Churchill's finished," Burgess went on with a sweeping hand gesture. "It's just a matter of time. Weeks ... months. He knows it. We know it. The only thing now is for him to get out alive with his family while he still can and take up life in exile."

"And he wants to come here?"

Burgess looked around at the chess players and The Headrow. "Well, I don't think he's got the north of England in mind specifically, but you're on the right track. Maybe a nice little retirement villa in Devon or Cornwall, the English Riviera. Somewhere where the weather's nice. Cultivate his herbaceous borders. Live out his days in the contemplation of nature. Prepare himself for the life hereafter. Make his peace with the Almighty. That kind of thing. Somewhere he won't do any more harm."

Burgess lit another little cigar and spat out a flake of loose tobacco. "The Yanks have said no, but then they've got a good record of turning their backs on their mates. The French are dithering and jabbering and waving their arms about, as usual. They'd probably sneak him in the back door like the good little hypocrites they are, if they had any real incentive left. And the Canadians ... well, they're just too fucking moral for their own good. The bottom line, Banks, is that there's a lot of pressure on our government to take him in, as quietly as possible, of course."

"Sneak him in the back door, you mean, like the hypocritical French?"

"If you like."

"His human rights record is appalling," Banks said. "The infant mortality rate in St Corona is over fifteen per cent, for a start. Life expectancy isn't much more than fifty for a man and sixty for a woman."

"Oh, dear, dear. You've been reading *The Guardian* again, haven't you, Banks?"

"And other papers. The story's the same."

"Well, you should know better than to believe all you read in the papers, shouldn't you?" Burgess looked around conspiratorially and lowered his voice. Nobody seemed in the least bit interested in them. Laughter and fragments of conversation filled the air. "Have you ever wondered," he said, "why women always seem to have a higher life expectancy rate than men? Don't they have as many bad habits as we do? Maybe they just don't work as hard, don't suffer as much stress? Maybe it's all that slimming and aerobics, eh? Maybe there's something in it.

"Anyway, back to Mr Churchill's predicament. And this is classified, by the way. There are some people in power who want him here, who feel we owe him, and there are some who don't, who feel he's a low-life scumbag and deserves to die as slowly and painfully as possible." As usual, Burgess liked to show off his American slang. He went to the States often, on "courses."

"Oh, come off it," said Banks. "If they want him here it's not out of any sense of duty, it's because he's got something they want, or because he's got something on them."

Burgess scratched his cheek. "Cynic," he said. "But you're partly right. He's not a nice man. As far as I can gather he's a glutton, a boor, a murderer and a rapist, sodomy preferred. But that's not the issue at all. The problem is that we educated him, made him what he is. Eton and Cambridge. He read law there. Did you know that? He went through school and university with a lot of important people, Banks. Cabinet ministers, bankers, power brokers, back-room boys. You know how people can behave indiscreetly when they're young? Do things they wouldn't want to come back and haunt them when they're in the public eye? And we're talking about people who have the power to loosen the government purse strings now and then, whenever St Corona asks for more aid. And rumour has it that he's also got quite a nice little savings account that won't do our economy any harm at all."

"Let me guess," said Banks. "Laundered money?"

Burgess raised his eyebrows. "Well, of course. Which brings me to the murder of Keith Rothwell. You are senior field investigator, I understand?"

"Yes."

"That's why I thought I'd better deal with you in person. I know you, Banks. You're still a pinko liberal, as you've proved time and time again. In fact, as soon as they told me you were on the case, I thought, 'Oh, fuck we're in trouble.' You've no respect for the venerable institutions of government, or for the necessity of secrecy in some of their workings. You've got no respect for tradi-tion and you don't give a toss about preserving the natural order of things. You probably don't even stand up for 'God Save the Queen.' In short, you're a bloody bolshie troublemaker and a menace to national security."

Banks smiled. "Thanks for the compliment," he said. "But I wouldn't go quite *that* far."

Burgess grinned. "Maybe I exaggerate. But you get my point?"

"Loud and clear."

"Good. That's why I'm going to tell you something very, very important and very, very secret, and I'm going to trust you with it. We've been keeping an eye on the St Corona situation, and anything that could possibly have to do with Martin Churchill gets flagged. Now, we just got a report from your Fraud Squad late yesterday evening that they found something on Keith Rothwell's computer that indicates he may have been laundering money for

Martin Churchill. Lots of trips to the Channel Islands and the Caribbean. Some very dodgy bank accounts. Some very dodgy banks, too, for that matter. Anyway, there's a pattern and a time period that matches exactly the sort of thing we've been looking for. We've known this was going on for some time, but until now we hadn't a clue who was doing it. There's no proof it was Rothwell, yet—the Fraud Squad still has a lot of work to do, chasing down transactions and what have you—but if I'm right, then we're talking about a lot of money. Something in the region of thirty or forty million pounds over three or four years. Mostly money that was originally provided as aid by leading western nations. It's the same kind of thing Baby Doc did in Haiti."

"And you think this might have something to do with Rothwell's murder?"

Burgess shook his head. "I don't really know, but the odds are that there's some kind of connection, don't you think? Especially considering the way he was killed. I mean, it was hardly a domestic, was it?"

"Possibly," Banks agreed. "Do you have any leads on the killers?"

"No more than you. I'm only *suggesting* that Churchill might be behind them."

"And if he is?"

"Watch your back."

Banks thought about that for a moment. He wasn't sure who constituted the greatest threat to his exposed back, Churchill or Burgess. "I must say this is pretty quick work on your part," he said.

Burgess shrugged. "Like I said, orders to flag. When I called your station, Superintendent Gristhorpe told me where you were. I missed you at the solicitor's office, but the secretary told me you were coming here."

"What's Daniel Clegg's connection with all this?"

"We don't know yet. We don't even know if there is one. I only just found out about his disappearance. It's early days yet."

"Two other men have been looking for him, too. One black, one white. Are they your lot?"

Burgess frowned. "No, they're nothing to do with me."

"Know anything about them?"

"No."

He was lying, Banks was certain. "So why are you here?" he asked. "What do you want me to do?"

"Nothing. Just carry on as normal. I simply wanted to warn you to tread very carefully, that's all, that things might be more complicated than they appear on the surface. And to let you know there's help available if you want it, of course. Naturally, if you get close to uncovering the killers' identities, I'd be interested in talking to them."

"Why?"

"Because I'm interested in everything to do with Martin Churchill, as I told you." Burgess looked at his watch. "Good lord, is that the time already?" he said, then knocked back the rest of his pint, winked and stood up. "Got to be off now. Be seeing you." And he strutted off over the square towards Park Row.

Banks lit a cigarette and brooded over the meeting as he finished his pint, wondering what the hell the bastard was up to. He didn't trust Burgess as far as he could throw him, and he was convinced that all that stuff about offering help and giving a friendly warning was rubbish. Burgess was up to something.

At a guess, he wanted to be one of the first to get to the killers so he could find a way of hushing them up. The last thing he would want was a big story about Churchill hiring assassins to murder a Yorkshire accountant splashed all over the press. Churchill might well be up to much worse things on St Corona, but this was England, after all.

Still, no matter what Burgess suspected, and whether or not Martin Churchill was behind it all, Banks still had two killers to find, locals by the sound of them, and he wasn't going to do that by sitting around in Stumps fretting about Dirty Dick Burgess.

IV

Banks didn't expect to find anything new in Calvert's Headingley flat, but for some reason he felt the need to revisit the place after he had picked up the Khachaturian compact disc.

West Yorkshire police had talked to the other tenants, who all said they knew nothing about Mr Calvert or Keith Rothwell: they never really saw much of him; he was out a lot; and, yes, now you mention it, there was a resemblance, but it was only a newspaper photo and Mr Calvert didn't look quite the same; besides, Calvert wasn't an Eastvale accountant, was he? He lived in Leeds. Couldn't argue with that. Banks headed upstairs.

The only immediate difference he noticed was the thin layer of fingerprint powder on surfaces of metal or glass: around the gas fireplace, on the glass-topped coffee-table and the TV set.

This time, Banks examined the books more closely. There weren't many, and most of them were the usual best-seller list paperbacks: Tom Clancy, Clive Cussler, Ken Follett, Robert Ludlum. There was also some espionage fiction—Len Deighton, John le Carré, Adam Hall, Ian Fleming—plus a couple of Agatha Christies and an oddly out-of-place copy of *Middlemarch*, which looked unread. Hardly surprising, Banks thought, having given up on even the television adaptation. The only other books were *Palgrave's Golden Treasury*, the first part of William Manchester's Churchill biography and a *Concise Oxford Dictionary*.

The small compact disc collection concentrated entirely on jazz, mostly Kenny Ball, Acker Bilk and a few collections of big-band music. Banks noticed some decent stuff: Louis, Bix, Johnny Dodds, Bud Powell. On the whole, though, judging from the Monet print over the fireplace, the *Palgrave* and the music, Robert Calvert had agreed with Philip Larkin about the evils of Parker, Pound and Picasso.

In the bedroom, all the papers had been removed from the desk, as had the wallet with the Calvert identification and credit card. The Fraud Squad would be working already on Calvert's financial profile, now they knew that he and Rothwell were one and the same. The magazines and coins were still there, the bed still unmade.

Why had Rothwell *needed* Calvert? Banks wondered. Simple escapism? According to what everyone said, he was a different person altogether at Arkbeck Farm and in the wider community of Swainsdale. Most people there spoke of him as a rather dull chap, maybe a bit henpecked.

Then there was Robert Calvert, the dancing, gambling, laughing, fun-loving Lothario and dreamer. The man who had attracted and bedded the beautiful Pamela Jeffreys. The man who squeezed his toothpaste tube in the middle.

So which was the real Keith Rothwell? Both or neither? In a sense, Banks guessed, he needed both worlds. Did that make him a Jekyll and Hyde figure? Did it mean he was mad? Banks didn't think so.

He remembered Susan's account of her interview with Laurence Pratt, in which Pratt had indicated that Rothwell had changed over the years, cut himself off, penned himself in. Perhaps he had once been the kind of person who liked gambling, dancing and drinking. Then he had been pushed into marriage with the boss's daughter, and marriage had changed him. It happened often enough; people settled down. But, for some reason, Rothwell had felt the need for an outlet, one that would not interfere with his family life, or with his local image as a respectable, decent citizen.

Banks could think of one good reason why it was important for Rothwell to maintain this fiction: Rothwell was a crook. He certainly didn't want to draw attention to himself by high living. As Calvert, he could relive his youth as much as he wished and enjoy the proceeds of his money-laundering. Perfect.

Did Mary Rothwell know about her husband's other life? She had probably suspected something was wrong time and time again over the last few years, but denied and repressed the suspicions in order to maintain the illusion of happy, affluent family values in the community. She probably needed to believe in the lies as much as her husband needed to live them.

But you can only maintain an illusion for so long, Banks thought, then cracks appear and the truth seeps in. You can ignore that for a long time, too, but ultimately the wound begins to fester and infect everything. That's when the bad things start to happen. Did Alison know? Or Tom? It would be interesting to meet the lad.

He looked through the wardrobe and dresser drawers again. Most of Calvert's clothes were still there, though the condoms had gone. Genuine scientific testing, Banks wondered, or a Scene-of-Crime Officer with a hot date and no time to get to the chemist's?

He looked under chairs, under the bed, on top of the wardrobe, in the cistern, and in all the usual hiding places before he realized that Vic Manson and his lads had probably already done most of that, even though the flat wasn't a crime scene *per se*, and that he didn't know what he was looking for anyway. He paused by the front window, which looked out onto a tree-lined side-street off Otley Road.

Fool, he told himself. He had been looking for Keith Rothwell in Robert Calvert's flat. But he wasn't there. He wasn't anywhere; he was just a slab of chilled meat waiting for a man with his collar on the wrong way around to chant a few meaningless words that might just ease the living's fear of death until the next time it touched too close to home for comfort.

As he glanced out of the window, he glimpsed two men in suits across the street looking up at him. They were partially obscured by trees, but he could see that one was black, the other white.

He hurried down to the street. When he got there, nobody was about except a young man washing his car three houses down.

Banks approached him and showed his identification. The man wiped the sweat off his brow and looked up at Banks, shielding his eyes from the glare. Sunlight winked on the bubbles in his bucket of soapy water.

"Did you see a couple of blokes in business suits pass by a few minutes ago?" Banks asked.

"Yeah," said the man. "Yeah, I did. I thought it was a bit odd the way they stopped and looked up at that house. To be honest, though, the way they were dressed I thought they were probably coppers."

Banks thanked him and went back to the car. So he wasn't getting paranoid. How did the saying go? Just because you think they're out there following you, it doesn't mean they aren't.

EIGHT

I

Tom Rothwell resembled his father more than his mother, Banks thought, sitting opposite him in the split-level living-room at Arkbeck Farm the following morning. Though his hair was darker and longer, he had the same thin oval face and slightly curved nose and the same grey eyes as Banks had seen in the photograph. His sulky mouth, though, owed more to early Elvis Presley, and was no doubt more a result of artifice than nature.

His light brown hair fell charmingly over one eye and hung in natural waves over his ears and the collar of his blue denim shirt. Both knees of his jeans were torn, and the unlaced white trainers on his feet were scuffed and dirty.

The best of the lot, Cathy Grafton had said, and it wasn't hard to guess why a rather plain girl like her would value a smile and a kind word from a handsome lad like Tom.

But right from the start Banks sensed something else about him, an aura of affected arrogance, as if he were condescending from a great intellectual and moral height to answer such stupid questions as those relating to his father's murder.

It was rebellious youth, in part, and Banks certainly understood that. Also, Tom seemed to exhibit that mix of vanity and over-confidence that Banks had often encountered in the wealthy. In addition there was a hell of a lot of the wariness and subterfuge that he usually associated with someone hiding a guilty secret. Tom's body language said it all: long legs stretched out, crossed at the ankles, arms folded high on his chest, eyes anywhere but on the questioner. Susan Gay sat in the background to take notes. Banks wondered what she thought about Tom.

"Did you have any problems getting a flight?" Banks asked.

"No. But I had to change at some dreary place in Carolina, and then again in New York."

"I know you must be tired. I remember from my trip to Toronto, the jet lag's much worse flying home."

"I'm all right. I slept a little on the plane."

"I can never seem to manage that."

Tom said nothing. Banks wished that Alison and Mary Rothwell weren't flanking Tom on the sofa. And again the room felt dark and cold around him. Though it had windows, they were set or angled in such a way that they didn't let in much natural light. And they were all closed.

"I imagine you're upset about your father, too," he said.

"Naturally."

"We wanted to talk to you so soon," Banks said, "because we hoped you might be able to tell us something about your father, something that might help lead us to his killers."

"How would I know anything? I've been out of the country since the end of March."

"It's possible," Banks said, weighing his words carefully, "that the roots of the crime lie farther back than that."

"That's ridiculous. You lot have far too much imagination for your own good."

"Oh? What do *you* think happened?"

Tom curled his lip and looked at the carpet. "It was clearly a robbery gone wrong. Or a kidnap attempt. Dad *was* quite well off, you know."

Banks scratched the scar beside his right eye. "Kidnapping, eh? We'd never thought of that. Can you explain?"

"Well, that's your job, isn't it? But it's hardly difficult to see how it could have been a kidnap attempt gone wrong. My father obviously wouldn't co-operate, so they had to kill him."

"Why not just knock him out and take him away?"

Tom shrugged. "Perhaps the gun went off by accident."

"Then why not take the body and pretend he was still alive till they got the money?"

"How would I know? You're supposed to be the professionals. I only said that's what it *might* have been. I also suggested a bungled robbery."

"Look, Tom, this is a pointless game we're playing. Believe me, we've covered all the possibilities, and it wasn't a kidnap attempt or a bungled burglary. I realize how difficult it is for the family to accept that a member may have been involved in something illegal, but all the evidence points that way."

"Absurd," spat Mary Rothwell. "Keith was an honest business-man, a good person. And if you persist in spreading these vicious rumours, we'll have to contact our solicitor."

"Mrs Rothwell," Banks said, "I'm trying to talk to your son. I'd appreciate it if you would keep quiet." More than once he had thought about breaking the news that her husband led another existence as Robert Calvert, but he held back. In the first place, it would be cruel, and in the second, Gristhorpe said the Chief Constable wanted it kept from the press and family, if possible, at least until they developed a few more leads on the case.

Mary Rothwell glared at him, lips pressed so tight they were white around the edges.

Banks turned back to Tom. "Were you close to your father?"

"Close enough. He wasn't ..." Tom turned up his nose. "He wasn't a clinging, emotional sort of person."

"But you were on good terms?"

"Yes, of course."

"Then you might know something that could help us."

"I still don't see how, but if I can be of any use ... Ask away."

"Did he ever mention a man called Martin Churchill?"

"Churchill? No."

"Do you know who he is?"

"That chap in the Caribbean?"

"Yes."

"Are you serious?" Tom looked puzzled. "You are, aren't you. The answer's no, of course he didn't. Why would he?"

"Did you ever see your father with two well-dressed men, both about six feet tall, one black, one white?"

Tom frowned. "No. Look, I'm sorry but I don't know what you're talking about."

"Did he ever talk to you about business?"

"No."

"Did you ever meet any of his business associates?"

"Only if they came over to dinner. And even then, I wasn't generally invited." Tom looked at his mother. "I had to find something else to do for the evening. Which usually wasn't much trouble." He glanced over at Susan, and Banks sensed a softening in his expression as he did so. He seemed interested in her presence, curious about her.

The radio had been playing a request programme quietly in the background, and Banks suddenly picked out the haunting chorus of Delibes's "Viens, Mallika … Dôme épais," popularized as the "Flower Duet" by a television advert. Even trivialization couldn't mar its beauty and clarity. After pausing for a moment, he went on.

"When did you leave for your holiday?"

"March," he said. "The thirty-first. But I don't see—"

"What about your job?"

"What job?"

"The one in the video shop in Eastvale."

"Oh, that. I packed it in."

"What kind of videos did they deal in?"

"All sorts. Why?"

"Under-the-counter stuff?"

"Oh, come off it, Chief Inspector. Suddenly my father's a crook and I'm a porn merchant? You should be writing for television." Alison looked up from her book and giggled. Tom smiled at her, obviously pleased with his insolence. "It was called Monster Videos, that place in the arcade by the bus station. Ask them if you don't believe me."

"Why did you leave?" Banks pressed on.

"Not that it's any of your business, but it was hardly a fast track to a career."

"Is that what you want?"

"I'm going to film school in the States."

"I see."

"I want to be a movie director."

"Was that what your father wanted?"

"I don't see that what *he* wanted has anything to do with it."

It was there, the rancour, Banks thought. Time to push a little harder. "It's just that I understood you had a falling out over your career choice. I gather he wanted you to become an accountant or a lawyer but he thought you preferred to be an idle, shiftless sod."

"How dare you?" Mary Rothwell jumped to her feet.

"It's all right, Mother," Tom sneered. "Sit down. It's all part of their game. They only say things like that to needle you into saying something you'll regret. Just ignore it." He looked at Susan again, as if expecting her to defend Banks, but she said nothing. He seemed disappointed.

Mary Rothwell sat down again slowly. Alison, at the other side of Tom, glanced up from *Villette* again for a couple of seconds, raised the corners of her lips in what passed for a smile, then went back to her book.

"Well?" said Banks.

"Well what?"

"What is it that I might needle you into regretting you said?"

"Clever. It was just a figure of speech."

"All right. Did you and your father have such an argument?"

"You must know as well as I do," Tom said, "that fathers and sons have their disagreements. Sure, Dad wanted me to follow in his footsteps, but I had my own ideas. He's not big on the arts, isn't Dad, except when it's good for business to get tickets for the opera or the theatre or something to impress his clients."

"Where did you travel in America?"

"All over. New York. Chicago. Los Angeles. San Francisco. Miami. Tampa."

"How did you get around?"

"Plane and car rental. Where is this—"

"Did you visit the Caribbean? St Corona?"

"No, I didn't."

"How did you finance the trip?"

"What?"

"You heard me. You were over there a month and a half, and you'd still be there now if it weren't for your father's death. All that travelling costs money. You can't have earned that much working in a video shop, especially one that only deals in legal stuff. How could you afford a lengthy trip to America?"

Tom shifted uncomfortably. "My parents helped me out."

Banks noticed a confused look flit across Mary Rothwell's face.

"Did you?" Banks asked her.

"Why, yes, of course."

He could tell from the hesitation that she knew nothing about it. "Do you mean your father helped you?" he asked Tom.

"He was the one with all the money, wasn't he?"

"So your father financed your trip. How?"

"What do you mean?"

"How did he finance it? Cash? Cheque?"

"He got me the ticket, some travellers' cheques and a supplementary card on his American Express Gold account. You can check the records, if you haven't done already."

Banks whistled between his teeth. "American Express Gold, eh? Not bad." Judging by the look on Mary Rothwell's face, it was news to her. Alison didn't seem to care. She turned a page without looking up. "Why would he do that?" Banks asked.

"I'm his son. It's the kind of thing parents do, isn't it? Why not?"

Banks had never spent so much on Brian and Tracy, but then he had never been able to afford it. "Was he usually so generous?" he asked.

"He was never mean."

Banks paused. When the silence had made Tom restless, he went on. "Just before you went away, you had an argument with your father in which he expressed great disappointment in you. Now, I know why that is. You've just told me you didn't want to follow the career he set out for you. But you also expressed disappointment in him. Why did you do that?"

"I don't remember any argument."

"Come on, Tom. You can do better than that."

Tom looked at Susan again, and Banks noticed a plea for help in his eyes. He looked left and right for support, too, but found none. His mother seemed lost in thought and Alison was still deep in her Charlotte Brontë.

"I'm telling you," Tom said, "I don't know what you're talking about."

"Why were you disappointed in your father, Tom?"

Tom reddened. "I wasn't. I don't know what you mean."

"Did you find out something incriminating about his business dealings?"

"Is *that* what you think?"

"You'd better tell me, Tom. It could help us a lot. What was he up to?"

Tom seemed to relax. "Nothing. *I* don't know. You're way off beam."

"Does the name Aston or Afton mean anything to you?"

Banks was sure he saw a flicker of recognition behind Tom's eyes. Recognition and fear. "No," Tom said. "Never heard of him."

Banks decided they would get nothing more out of this situation, not with the whole family closing ranks. It would be best to leave it for now. No doubt, when Banks and Susan left, the Rothwells would fall into an argument, for Mary Rothwell wasn't looking at all pleased with the return of her prodigal son. Tom could stew over whatever it was that confused him. Plenty of time.

It was a gorgeous morning in the dale. Banks put a Bill Evans solo piano tape in the cassette player as he drove through Fortford, gold and green in the soft, slanting light. To their left, the lush fields of the Leas were full of buttercups, and here and there the fishermen sat, still as statues, lines arcing down into the River Swain.

"What do you think?" he asked Susan.

"He's lying, sir."

"That's obvious enough. But why? What about?"

"I don't know. Everything. I just got a strange feeling."

"Me, too. Next time, I think it might be a good idea if you talked to him alone."

"Maybe I can catch him after the funeral?"

"You were thinking of going? Damn!"

Half a mile before the road widened at the outskirts of Eastvale, a farmer was moving his sheep across from one pasture to another. There was nothing to be done. They simply had to stop until the sheep had gone.

"Stupid creatures," Banks said.

"I think they're rather cute, in a silly way," Susan said. "Anyway, I thought I might go. You never know, the murderers might turn up to pay their respects, like they do in books."

Banks laughed. "Do you know that actually happened to me once?" he said.

"What?"

"It did. Honest. Down in London. There was a feud between two families, the Kinghorns and the Franklins—none of them exactly intellectual giants—been going on for years. Anyway, old man Franklin gets shot in broad daylight, and there's half a dozen witnesses say they saw Billy Kinghorn, the eldest son, do it. Only trouble is, Billy does a bunk. Until the funeral, that is. Then there he is, young Billy, black tie, armband and all, face as long as a wet Sunday, come to pay his last respects."

"What happened?"

"We nabbed him."

Susan laughed. The sheep kept wandering all over the road, despite the ministrations of an inept collie, which looked a bit too long in the tooth for such exacting work.

"I thought there had to be a reason for going," Susan said. "Anyway, I quite like funerals. My Auntie Mavis died when I was six and my mum and dad took me to the funeral. It was very impressive, the hymns, the readings. I couldn't understand a word of it at that age, of course, but it certainly sounded important. Anyway, when we got outside I asked my mum where Auntie Mavis was and she sniffled a bit then said, 'In Heaven.' I asked her where that was and she pointed up at the sky. It was a beautiful blue sky, a bit like today, and there was only one cloud in it, a fluffy white one that looked like a teddy bear. From then on I always thought when people died they became clouds in a perfect blue sky. I don't know … it made me feel happy, somehow. I mean, I know funerals are solemn occasions, but I don't seem to mind them so much after that."

The last sheep finally found the gate and scrambled through. The farmer held up his hand in thanks, as if Banks had had any option but to wait, and closed the gate behind him. Banks set off.

"Rather you than me," he said. "I can't stand them. Anyway, see if you can take young Tom aside, take him for a drink or something. I've a feeling he really wants to tell us what he knows. Did you notice the way he kept looking at you?"

"Yes."

"Think he fancies you?"

"No," Susan said, after a pause for thought. "No. Somehow, I don't think it was that at all."

II

Banks crunched the last pickled onion of his ploughman's lunch and swilled it down with a mouthful of Theakston's bitter, then he lit a cigarette. He would have to resort to a Polo mint if he found himself interviewing anyone in the afternoon. Superintendent Gristhorpe sat opposite him in the Queen's Arms, cradling a half-pint. It was the first time they had been able to get together since Banks had met Burgess.

"So," Gristhorpe said, "according to Burgess, Rothwell was laundering money for Martin Churchill?"

"Looks that way," said Banks. "He said he couldn't be certain but I don't think he'd come all the way up here if he wasn't, do you?"

"Knowing how little Burgess thinks of the north, no. But I still don't think we should overlook the possibility of Rothwell's involvement in some other kind of organized crime, most likely drugs, prostitution or porn. Even if he were laundering money for Churchill, he could have been into something else dirty too. We can't assume it was the Churchill link that got him killed until we know a hell of a lot more."

"I agree," said Banks.

"Better do as Burgess says and watch your back, though."

"Don't worry, sir, I will."

"Anyway," Gristhorpe went on, "I've just had a meeting with Inspector Macmillan, and he tells me that Daniel Clegg acted as Robert Calvert's reference for his bank account and his credit card in Leeds. The account has about twenty thousand in it. Interesting, isn't it?"

"Play money," Banks said.

"Aye. I wouldn't mind that much to play with, myself. Anyway, according to Inspector Macmillan, the bank employees didn't recognize Rothwell's picture as Calvert because they hardly saw him. He used a busy branch in the city centre, and the only person who did make the connection when Macmillan pushed it said Calvert looked and dressed so differently she wouldn't have known."

"Thank the lord for Pamela Jeffreys, then."

"Aye, or we might never have known. What does his family have to say?"

Banks sighed and put the edge of his hand to his throat. "I've had it up to here with the bloody Rothwells," he said. "They give a whole new meaning to 'dysfunctional.' There's the victim laundering illegal money and leading a double life just for a hobby. There's the daughter, who'd rather bury her face in a book than face reality now that the shock and the tiredness have worn off. There's a son with more than a few guilty secrets hidden away. And then, watching over them all, there's the Queen Bee, who just wants to keep up the usual upper-middle-class appearances and swears the sun shone out of her husband's arse."

"What do you expect her to do, Alan? Her world's fallen apart. She must be having a hell of a job just holding things together. Have a bit more bloody compassion, lad."

Banks took a drag at his cigarette and blew the smoke out slowly. "You're right," he said. "I'm sorry. I've just had it with the bloody Rothwells, that's all. What do they know? It's hard to tell. I think the wife suspects something weird was going on, but she doesn't know what and she doesn't want to know. She denies it, especially to herself."

"Could they have any involvement?"

"I've thought about it," Banks said, "and I've discussed it with Susan. In the final analysis, I don't really think so. Mary Rothwell might well hit out at anything that threatens her comfortable world, and if she thought her husband were profiting from porn, for

example, I can't just see her sitting still and accepting it." He shook
his head. "But not this way. This brings her exactly the kind of attention she *doesn't* want. I don't know how she'd deal with him—Susan
guessed poison, maybe, or an accident—but it wouldn't be like this."

"Hmm. Try this for size," said Gristhorpe. "One: let's assume
that Rothwell and Clegg are in the money-laundering business
together, for Martin Churchill or whoever."

Banks nodded. "It makes sense, Clegg being a tax specialist and
all."

"And we'll leave Robert Calvert out of it, as, say, just a personal
aberration on Rothwell's part, at least for the moment. A red
herring, right?"

"Okay."

"Something goes wrong. Rothwell finds out something that
makes him want to get out of it, so he writes to Clegg ending their
association."

"And," said Banks, "Churchill, or whoever it is they're working
for, doesn't like this at all."

"Makes sense, doesn't it?"

"So far. Keep going."

"Rothwell gets scared. Either he's been cheating on his masters,
and they've found out, or they're afraid he's getting nervous and is
going to blow the whistle. So what do they do?"

"Take out a contract."

"Right. And that's the end of Rothwell."

Gristhorpe paused as a couple of office-workers on a lunch
break brushed past them and sat down at the next table. Cyril's cash
register rang up another sale.

"He could have been cheating on them to finance his life as
Calvert," said Banks. "I know we were going to leave him out of the
equation, but it fits. He had twenty grand in the bank, you say, and
he liked to gamble, according to Pamela Jeffreys."

"True, but let's stick to the simple line. What's important is
that Rothwell has become a liability, or a threat, and his masters
want him dead. They've got enough money to be able to pay for
the privilege without getting their own hands dirty. Which brings
us to Mr Daniel Clegg. The killers had a fair bit of information

about Rothwell. They seemed to know that he and his wife would be out celebrating their wedding anniversary, for example. Clegg could probably have told them that. They knew Rothwell had a daughter, too, and that she would be at home. She wasn't 'part of the deal,' remember? And they knew where he lived, the layout, everything."

"Clegg?"

Gristhorpe nodded. "Let's put it this way. If Rothwell were laundering money for someone, there'd be as little, if any, contact between him and his masters, wouldn't there?"

"That would seem to be one point of a laundering operation," Banks agreed. "Certainly Tom Rothwell seemed genuinely puzzled when I brought up Martin Churchill."

"Right. And Clegg was the only other person we suspect was involved, and he had information about Rothwell's personal life."

"So you reckon Clegg was behind it?"

"It's a theory, isn't it? They weren't exactly friends, Alan. Not according to what you've told me. They were business colleagues. Different thing. It was a matter of you scratch my back, I'll scratch yours. Strange bedfellows, maybe. And crooked too. It's an odd thing is a professional gone bad. They talk about bent coppers, but what about bent lawyers, bent accountants, bent doctors? If push came to shove, would you expect one crooked businessman to stick up for another?"

"So you think Clegg was not just involved in the laundering business but in Rothwell's murder, too?"

"Aye. He could be our link."

"And his disappearance?"

"Scarpered. He knew what was coming, knew when. Maybe they paid him well. It doesn't matter whether he was scared of us or them, the result was the same. He took his money and ran, collected two hundred pounds when he passed go, didn't go to jail. Then his bosses couldn't get in touch with him, so they sent their two goons to find him. The timing's right."

"What about this scenario," Banks offered. "Maybe Churchill had Clegg killed, too. With Rothwell gone, Clegg might just be a nuisance who knew too much, a loose cannon on the deck. If

Churchill is planning on coming here, maybe he wanted a clean break."

Gristhorpe took a sip of his beer. "Possible, I'll grant you."

"You know, it's just struck me," said Banks, "but do we know if Clegg ever practised criminal law?"

"Seems to be the only kind he practised," replied Gristhorpe, then held up his hand and grinned as Banks groaned. "All right, all right, Alan. I promise. No more bad lawyer jokes. As far as we know he didn't. He's a solicitor, not a barrister, so he didn't represent clients in court. But people might have come to him, and he could have referred them. Why?"

"I was just wondering where a man like Clegg might meet a killer for hire."

"Local Conservative Club, probably," said Gristhorpe. "But I see what you mean. It's a loose end we've got to pursue. If we assume Clegg was involved in arranging for Rothwell's murder, then we can look through his contacts and his activities to find a link with a couple of likely assassins. We've got that and the wadding. Not very much is it?"

"No," said Banks. "What if Clegg's dead?"

"Nothing changes. West Yorkshire police keep looking for a body and we keep nosing around asking questions. We could get in touch with Interpol, see if he's holed up somewhere in Spain." He looked at his watch. "Look, Alan, I'd better get finished and be off. I've got another meeting with the Chief Constable this afternoon."

"Okay. I'll be over in a minute."

Gristhorpe nodded and left, but no sooner had Banks started to let his imagination work on Clegg meeting two hired guns in a smoky saloon than the superintendent poked his head around the door again. "They think they've found the killers' car," he said. "Abandoned near Leeds city centre. Ken Blackstone asks if you want to go and have a look."

Banks nodded. "All roads lead to Leeds," he sighed. "I might as well bloody move there." And he followed Gristhorpe out.

NINE

I

A tape of Satie's piano music, especially the "Trois Gymnopédies," kept Banks calm on his way to Leeds, even though the A1 was busy with juggernauts and commercial travellers driving too fast. He found the car park without too much difficulty; it was an old school playground surrounded by the rubble of demolished buildings just north of the city centre.

"Cheers, Alan," said Detective Inspector Ken Blackstone. "You look like a bloody villain with those sunglasses on. How's it going?"

"Can't complain." Banks shook his hand and took off the dark glasses. He had met Blackstone at a number of courses and functions, and the two of them had always got along well enough. "And how's West Yorkshire CID?"

"Overworked, as usual. Bit of a bugger, isn't it?" said Blackstone. "The weather, I mean."

Banks scratched the scar beside his right eye. Sometimes when it itched, it was trying to tell him something; other times, like this, it was just the heat. "I remember an American once told me that all we English do is complain about the weather," he said. "It's either too hot or too cold for us, too wet or too dry."

Blackstone laughed. "True. Still, the station could do with a few of those air-conditioner thingies the Yanks use. It's hotter indoors than out. Sends the crime figures up, you know, a heat wave. Natives get restless."

A light breeze had sprung up from the west, but it did nothing to quell the warmth of the sun. Banks took off his sports jacket and slung it over his shoulder as they walked across the soft tarmac to the abandoned car. His tie hung askew, as usual, and his top shirt button was open so he could breathe easily. He could feel the sweat sticking his white cotton shirt to his back. This weather was following a pattern he recognized; it would get hotter and hazier until it ended in a storm.

"What have you got?" he asked.

"You'll see in a minute." Despite the weather, Ken Blackstone looked cool as usual. He wore a lightweight navy-blue suit with a grey herringbone pattern, a crisp white shirt with a stiff collar and a garish silk tie, secured by a gold tie-clip in the shape of a pair of handcuffs. Banks was willing to bet that his top button was fastened.

Blackstone was tall and slim with light brown hair, thin on top but curly over the ears, and a pale complexion, definitely not the sun-worshipping kind. His Cupid's bow lips and wire-rimmed glasses made him look about thirty, when he was, in fact, closer to Banks's age. He had a long, dour sort of face and spoke with a local accent tempered by three years at Bath University, where he had studied art history.

Blackstone had, in fact, become something of an expert on art fraud after his degree, and he often found himself called in to help out when something of that nature happened. In addition, he was a fair landscape artist himself, and his work had been exhibited several times. Banks remembered Blackstone and Sandra getting into a long conversation about the Pre-Raphaelites at a colleague's wedding once, and remembered the stirrings of jealousy he had felt. Though he was eager to learn, read, look and listen as much as his time allowed, Banks was always aware of his working-class background and his lack of a true formal education.

They arrived at a car guarded by two hot-looking uniformed constables and Banks stood back to survey it. Ancient, but not old enough to attract attention as an antique, the light blue Ford Escort was rusted around the bottom of the chassis and had spider-leg cracks on the passenger side of the windscreen. It matched the description, as far as that went.

"How long's it been here?" Banks asked.

"Don't know," said Blackstone. "Our lads didn't notice it until last night. When they ran the number they found it was stolen."

Banks knelt by the front tire. Flat. There was plenty of soil and gravel lodged in the grooves. They could have it analyzed and at least discover if it came from around Arkbeck Farm. He looked through the grimy window. The beige upholstery was dirty, cracked and split. A McDonald's coffee cup lay crushed on the floor at the driver's side, but apart from that he could see nothing else inside.

"We've looked in the boot," said Blackstone. "Nothing. Not even a jack or a spare tire. I've arranged for it to be taken to our police garage for a thorough forensic examination, but I thought you'd like a look at it *in situ* first."

"Thanks," said Banks. "I don't expect we'll get any prints, if they were pros, but you never know. Who's the lucky owner?"

"Bloke called Ronald Hamilton."

"When did he report it missing?"

Blackstone paused before answering. "Friday morning. Said he left it in the street as usual after he got in about five or six in the evening and it was gone when he went out at ten the next morning. Thought it was maybe kids joy-riding. There's been a lot of it on the estate lately. It's not the safest place in the city. He lives on the Raynville estate in Bramley. Ring any bells?"

Banks shook his head. Pamela Jeffreys lived in Armley, which wasn't far away, and Daniel Clegg lived in Chapel Allerton, a fair distance in both miles and manners. Most likely the killers had picked it at random a good distance from where they lived. "That's four days ago, Ken," said Banks. "And nobody spotted it before last night?"

Again, Blackstone hesitated. "Hamilton's an unemployed labourer," he said finally. "He's got at least one wife and three kids that we know of, and lately he's been having a few problems with the social. He's also got a record. Dealing. Aggravated assault."

"You thought he'd arranged to have it nicked for the insurance?"

Blackstone smiled. "Something like that. I wasn't involved personally. I don't know what you lot do, but here in the big city we don't send Detective Inspectors out on routine traffic incidents."

Banks ignored the sarcasm. It was just Blackstone's manner. "So your lads didn't exactly put a rush on it?"

"That's right." Blackstone glanced towards the horizon and sighed. "Any idea, Alan, how many car crimes we've got in the city now? You yokels wouldn't believe it. So when some scurvy knave comes on with a story about a beat-up old Escort, you think he'd have to pay somebody to steal that piece of shit. So let the fucking insurance company pay. They can afford it. In the meantime we've got joy-riding kids, real villains and organized gangs of car thieves to deal with. I'm not making excuses, Alan."

"Yeah, I know." Banks leaned against a red Orion. The metal burned through his shirt, so he stood up straight again.

"Didn't you once tell me you came up from the Met for a peaceful time in rural Yorkshire?" Blackstone asked.

Banks smiled. "I did."

"Getting it?"

"I can only suppose it's got proportionately worse down there."

Blackstone laughed. "Indeed. Business is booming."

"Have you talked to Hamilton?"

"Yes. This morning. He knows nothing. Believe me, he's so scared of the police he'd sell his own mother down the tubes if he thought we were after her." Blackstone made an expression of distaste. "You know the type, Alan, belligerent one minute, yelling that you're picking on him because he's black, then arse-licking the next. Makes you want to puke."

"Where's he from?"

"Jamaica. He's legit; we checked. Been here ten years."

"What's his story?"

"Saw nothing, heard nothing, knows nothing. To tell you the truth, I got the impression he'd driven back from the pub after a skinful then settled in front of the telly with a few cans of lager while his wife fed the kiddies and put them to bed. After that he probably passed out. Whole bloody place smelled of shitty nappies and roll-ups and worse. We could probably do him for possession if it was worth our while. At ten the next morning he staggers out to go and sign on, finds his car missing and, bob's your uncle, does the outraged citizen routine on the local bobby, who's got more sense, thank the lord."

Blackstone stood, slightly hunched, with his hands in his pockets, and kicked at small stones on the tarmac. You could see your face in his shoes.

"Do me a favour, Ken, and have another go at him. You said he was done for dealing?"

"Uh-huh. Small stuff. Mostly cannabis, a little coke."

"It's probably just a coincidence that the car used belongs to a drug dealer, but pull his record and have another go at him all the same. Find out who his suppliers are. And see if he has any connections with St Corona. Friends, family, whatever. There might be a drug connection or a Caribbean connection in Rothwell's murder, and it's a remote possibility that Mr Hamilton might have done some work for the organization behind it, whoever they are."

"You mean he might have *loaned* his car?"

"It's possible. I doubt it. I think we're dealing with cleverer crooks than that, but we'd look like the rear end of a pantomime horse if we didn't check it out."

"Will do."

"Have you questioned the neighbours?"

"We're doing a house-to-house. Nothing so far. Nobody sees anything on these estates."

"So that's that?"

"Looks like it. For the moment, anyway."

"No car-park attendant?"

"No." Blackstone pointed to the rubble. "As you can see, it's just an old schoolyard with weeds growing through the tarmac. The school was knocked down months ago."

Banks looked around. To the south-west he could see the large dome of the Town Hall and the built-up city centre; to the west stood the high white obelisk of the university's Brotherton Library, and the rest of the horizon seemed circled with blocks of flats and crooked terraces of back-to-backs poking through the surrounding rubble like charred vertebrae. "I could use a break on this, Ken," Banks said.

"Aye. We'll give it our best. Hey up, the lads have come to pick up the car."

Banks watched the police tow-team tie a line to the Escort. "I'd better be off," he said. "You'll let me know?"

"Just a minute," said Blackstone. "What are your plans?"

"I'm checking into the Holiday Inn. For tonight, at least. There's a couple of people I want to talk to again in connection with Clegg and Rothwell—Clegg's secretary and his ex-wife, for a start. I'd like to get a clearer idea of their relationship now we've got a bit more to go on."

"Holiday Inn? Well, la-di-da. Isn't that a bit posh for a humble copper?"

Banks laughed. "I could do with a bit of luxury. Maybe they'll give me the sack when they see my expenses. These days we can't even afford to do half the forensic tests we need."

"Tell me about it. Anyway, if you're going to be sticking around, I'd appreciate it if we could have a chat. There seems to be a lot going on here I don't know about."

"There's a lot I don't know about, too."

"Still ... I'd appreciate it if you would fill me in."

"No problem."

Blackstone hesitated and shifted from foot to foot. "Look," he said, "I'd like to invite you over for a bit of home-cooking but Connie left a couple of months ago."

"I'm sorry to hear that," said Banks. "I didn't know."

"Yeah, well, it happens, right? Comes with the territory. Still taking care of that lovely wife of yours?"

"You wouldn't think so by the amount of time we've spent together lately."

"I know what you mean. That was one of the problems. She said we were living such separate lives we might as well make it official. Anyway, I'm not much of a cook myself. Besides, Connie got the house and I'm in a rather small bachelor flat for the moment. But there's a decent Indian restaurant on Eastgate, near the station, if you fancy it? It's called the Shabab. About half past six, seven o'clock? We might have something on Hamilton and the car by then, too."

"All right," said Banks. "You're on. Make it seven o'clock."

"And, Alan," said Blackstone as Banks walked away, "you watch yourself. Hotels give married men strange ideas sometimes. I suppose it's the anonymity and the distance from home, if you know what I mean. Anyway, there's some seem to act as if the normal vows of marriage don't apply in hotels."

Banks knew what Blackstone meant, and he felt guilty as an image of Pamela Jeffreys flashed unbidden through his mind.

II

Susan Gay heard Sergeant Hatchley burp before she had even opened the office door after more fruitless interviews with Rothwell's legitimate clients. She felt apprehension churn in her stomach like a badly digested meal. She could not work with Hatchley; she just couldn't.

Hatchley sat at his desk, smoking. The small, stifling room stank of stale beer and pickled onions. The warped window was open about as far as it would go, but that didn't help much. If this oppressive weather didn't end soon, Susan felt she would scream.

And, by God, he's repulsive, she thought. There was his sheer bulk, for a start—a rugby prop forward gone to fat. Then there was his face: brick-red complexion, white eyelashes and piggy eyes; straw hair, thinning a bit at the top; a smattering of freckles over a broad-bridged nose; fleshy lips; tobacco-stained teeth. To cap it all, he wore a shiny, wrinkled blue suit, and his red neck bulged over his tight shirt collar.

From the corner of her eye, Susan noticed the coloured picture on the cork-board: long blonde hair, exposed skin. Without even stopping to think, she walked over and pulled it down so hard the drawing-pin shot right across the room.

"Oy!" said Hatchley. "What the hell do you think you're playing at?"

"I'm not playing at anything," Susan said, waving the picture at him. "With all respect, sir, I don't care if you are my senior officer, I won't bloody well have it!"

A hint of a smile came to Hatchley's eyes. "Calm down, lass," he said. "You've got steam coming out of your ears. Maybe you're being a bit hasty?"

"No, I'm not. It's offensive. I don't see why I should have to work with this kind of thing stuck to the walls. You might think it's funny, but I don't. Sir."

"Susan. Look at it."

"No. Why—"

"Susan!"

Slowly, Susan turned the picture over and looked at it. There, in all her maternal innocence, Carol Hatchley, with her long blonde hair hanging over her shoulders, held her naked, newborn baby to her breast, which was covered well beyond the point of modesty by a flesh-tone T-shirt. Susan felt herself blush. All she had seen were the woman's face, hair and a lot of skin colour. "I ... I thought ..." She could think of nothing else to say.

"I know what you thought," said Hatchley. "You thought my daughter's head was a tit. You *could* apologize."

Susan felt such a fool she couldn't even bring herself to do that.

"All right," Hatchley said, putting his feet up on the desk, "then you can listen to me. Now, nobody's ever going to convince me that looking at a nice pair of knockers is wrong. Since time immemorial, since our ancestors scratched images on cave walls, men have enjoyed looking at women's tits. They're beautiful things, nothing dirty or pornographic about them at all."

"But they're private," Susan blurted out. "Don't you understand? They're a woman's private parts. You don't see pictures of men's privates all over the place, do you? You wouldn't like people staring at yours, would you?"

"Susan, love, if I thought it would make you happy I'd drop my trousers right now. But that's not the point. What I'm saying is it's my opinion that there's nowt wrong in admiring a nice pair of bristols. A lot of people agree with me, too. But you don't like it." He held up his large hand. "All right, now I might not be the most sensitive bloke in Christendom, and I certainly reserve my right to disagree with you, but I'm not that much of a monster that I'd use my rank to expose you to something you feel offends you day in, day out, however wrong-headed I think you are. I respect your opinion. I don't agree with you, and I never will, but I respect it. I can live without.

"And another thing. I know you're a bugger about smoking. I'll try and cut down on the cigarettes in the office, too. But don't expect miracles, and don't expect it's going to be all bloody give and no take on my part. You don't like my smoke. I don't like your perfume. It makes my nose itch and it's probably rotting my lungs as we speak. But for better or for worse, lass, we've got to work together, and we've got to do it in the same damn little cubby-hole for the time being. Mebbe one day we'll have separate offices. Myself, I can hardly wait. But for now, let's just keep the window open and make a bit of an effort to get along, all right?"

Susan nodded. She felt all the wind go out of her sails. She swallowed. "All right. Sorry, sir."

Hatchley swung his legs to the floor and rubbed his hands together. "We'll say no more, then. Now, about that wadding?"

"Yes, sir?"

Hatchley burped again and put his hamlike hand to his mouth. "Shaved pussies. Smooth and shiny as a baby's bottom."

"Yes, sir." Susan felt herself blush again and hated herself for it. Hatchley smiled at her. He seemed to be enjoying himself. Her spirits sank. She had thought for a moment that he might be getting serious about the case, but here he was simply creating another opportunity to embarrass her.

"Aye. Now, I know that's not a lot to go on, but at least we know it's not kiddie porn or the bum brigade. And we've got penetration and a clear image of 'a penis in an excited state,' as it says in the book, so this is definitely under-the-counter stuff."

"True, sir."

"And as far as I can tell," he went on, "there's no sign of dogs or cats, either."

"Sir, can you get to the point?" Susan couldn't keep the impatience out of her voice.

"Hold your horses, lass." He started to laugh. "Get that? No animals. Hold your horses? Never mind. The point is, shaved pussies aren't exactly ten a penny, though if we'd come up with something *really* kinky it would have made my job a lot easier. I mean, there aren't many people sell photos of Rottweilers bonking thirteen-year-old girls that we don't know about."

"I still don't see what you're getting at, sir," said Susan, a little calmer. She should have known that, if anyone was, Hatchley would be an expert on pornography. "Surely most of that stuff is sent through the mail from abroad, or from London?"

"Not all of it. There's a fair chance it was bought under the counter somewhere. When I did my stint on Vice with West Yorkshire a few years back, I made one or two useful contacts. Now, if we're assuming these lads were at all local, the odds are they're from the city, as there aren't that many killers-for-hire living in rural areas. Too exposed. That means Leeds, Bradford, Manchester, maybe Newcastle or Liverpool at a stretch. Now if the boss thinks this Clegg chap from Leeds was involved, then Leeds is as good a choice as any, agreed?"

Susan nodded. "Yes. The daughter, Alison, thought the man had a Leeds accent. She could be wrong about that, of course. Not everyone's accurate on voices. I don't reckon I could tell the difference. But it looks like they've found the car used for the job there. Anyway, as I've already told you, West Yorkshire's got some men asking around. Have had for days."

"Well, you know how I hate sitting idle," Hatchley said. "Guess where I've been this lunch-time."

"The Queen's Arms, sir?"

Hatchley smiled. "Not far off. We'll make a detective of you yet, lass. I've been having drinks with an old informer of mine in The Oak, that's what." He touched the side of his nose. "Lives in Eastvale now, but he used to live in Leeds. Gone straight. See, I thought I probably remembered a few purveyors of this kind of porn—if they're still around, that is—and it's odds on that some wet-behind-the-ears young pansy DC fresh from university doesn't even know they exist. There aren't as many as you think, you know, at least not selling shaved pussy porn. It *is* something of a specialist taste. Anyway, there's still plenty prefer the friendly old corner shop to the impersonal supermarket, if you get my drift. I'm not talking about sex shops—I imagine they've all been checked already—just regular newsagents that sell a bit of imported stuff from under the counter along with their *Woman's Weekly*s and gardening magazines. Harmless enough. Hardly any reason for our lads to be interested, really. So I asked my old friend."

"And?"

"Yes. They're still in business, still selling the same kind of stuff to the same old customers. Some of them, anyway. A couple have retired, some have moved on, and one's dead. Heart attack. Not business related. The point is, I knew these blokes were a bit bent, but I left them alone. In exchange, they'd pass on the odd tip if anyone came hawking really serious stuff, like kiddie porn or snuff films. Live and let live. Now, what I propose is that you and me go to Leeds and ask a few questions of our own." He looked at his watch. "Tomorrow, of course. Don't worry, I'll arrange permission from the super and from West Yorkshire CID. Are you game?"

Susan was aware of her jaw dropping. He made sense, all right, and that was the problem. She was about to go on a porn hunt with Sergeant Hatchley, she could feel it in her bones. But it could pay off. If it led to the owner of the wadding, that would be feathers in both their caps. She swallowed.

"It's a hell of a long shot," she said.

Hatchley shrugged. "Nothing ventured, nothing gained. What do you say?"

Susan thought for a moment. "All right," she said. "But *you've* got to convince Superintendent Gristhorpe."

"Right, lass," Hatchley beamed, rubbing his hands together. "You're on."

Oh my God, thought Susan, with that sinking feeling. *A porn hunt*. What have I let myself in for?

III

By the looks of it, the heat had drawn one or two refugees from the Magistrates Court over to the Park Square. Two skinheads, stripped to the waist, dozed on the grass under a tree. One, lying on his back, had tattoos up and down his arms and scars criss-crossing his abdomen, old knife wounds by the look of them; the other, on his stomach, boasted a giant butterfly tattoo between his shoulder-blades.

In Clegg's offices, Betty Moorhead was still holding the fort and fighting off her cold.

"Oh, Mr Banks," she said when he entered the anteroom. "It's nice to see a friendly face. There's been nothing but police coming and going since you were last here, and nobody will tell me anything."

Had she forgotten he was a policeman, too? he wondered. Or was it just that he had been the first to arrive and she had somehow latched onto him as a lifeline?

"Some men in suits took most of his papers," she went on, "and there's been others asking questions all day. They've got someone keeping an eye on the building as well, in case those two men come back. Then there was that man from Scotland Yard. I don't know what's what. They all had identification cards, of course, but I don't know whether I'm coming or going."

Banks smiled. "Don't worry, Betty," he said. "I know it sounds complicated, but we're all working together."

She nodded and pulled a tissue from the box in front of her and blew her nose; it looked red raw from rubbing. "Is there any news of Mr Clegg?" she asked.

"Nothing yet. We're still looking."

"Did you talk to Melissa?"

"Yes."

"How is she?"

Banks didn't really know what to say. He wasn't used to giving out information, just digging it up, but Betty Moorhead was obviously concerned. "She didn't seem unduly worried," he said. "She's sure he'll turn up."

Betty's expression brightened. "Well, then," she said. "There you are."

"Do you mind if I ask a few more questions?"

"Oh, no. I'd be happy to be of help."

"Good." Banks perched at the edge of her desk and looked around the room. "Sitting here," he said, "you'd see everyone who called on Mr Clegg, wouldn't you? Everyone who came in and out of his office."

"Yes."

"And if people phoned, you'd speak to them first?"

"Well, yes. But I did tell you Mr Clegg has a private line."

"Did he receive many calls on it?"

"I can't say, really. I heard it ring once in a while, but I was usually too busy to pay attention. I'm certain he didn't give the number out to just anyone."

"So you didn't unintentionally overhear any of the conversations?"

"I know what you're getting at," she said, "and you can stop right there. I'm not that sort of a secretary."

"What sort?"

"The sort that listens in on her boss's conversations. Besides," she added with a smile, "the walls are too thick. These are old houses, solidly built. You can't hear what's being said in Mr Clegg's office with the door shut."

"Even if two people are having a conversation in there?"

"Even then."

"Or arguing?"

"Not that it happened often, but you can only hear the raised voices, not what they're saying."

"Did you ever hear Mr Clegg arguing with Mr Rothwell?"

"I don't remember. I don't think so. I mean if they ever *did*, it would certainly have been a rarity. Normally they were all cordial and businesslike."

"Mr Clegg specializes in tax law, doesn't he?"

"Yes."

"How many clients does he have?"

"That's very hard to say. I mean, there are regular clients, and then people you just do a bit of work for now and then."

"Roughly? Fifty? A hundred?"

"Closer to a hundred, I'd say."

"Any new ones?"

"He's been too busy to take on much new work this year."

"So there's been no new clients in, say, the past three months?"

"Not really, no. He's done a bit of extra work for friends of friends here and there, but nothing major."

"What I'm getting at," Banks said, leaning forward, "is whether there's been anyone new visiting him often or phoning in the past two or three months."

"Not visiting, no. There's been a few funny phone calls, though."

"What do you mean, funny?"

"Well, abrupt. I mean, I know I told you people are sometimes rude and brusque, but usually they at least tell you what they want. Since you were here last, I've been thinking, trying to remember, you know, if there was anything odd. My head's so stuffed up I can hardly think straight, but I remembered the phone calls. I told the other policeman, too. "

"That's okay. Tell me. What did this brusque caller say?"

"I don't know if it was the same person each time, and it only happened two or three times. It was about a month ago."

"Over what time period?"

"What? Oh, just a couple of days."

"What did he say? I assume it was a *he*?"

"Yes. He'd just say, 'Clegg?' And if I said Mr Clegg was out or busy, he'd hang up."

"I see what you mean. What kind of voice did he have?"

"I couldn't say. That's all I ever heard him say. It just sounded ordinary, but clipped, impatient, in a hurry."

"And this happened two or three times over a couple of days?"

"Yes."

"You never heard the voice again?"

"I never had that sort of call again, if that's what you mean."

"Nobody visited the office who sounded like the man?"

She sneezed, then blew her nose. "No. But I told you I don't think I would recognize it."

"It wasn't anything like one of the men who came around asking questions?"

"I don't know. I don't think so. I'm sorry."

"That's all right."

"What's going on?"

"We don't know," Banks lied. He was testing Gristhorpe's theory about Clegg's involvement in Rothwell's murder, but he didn't want Betty Moorhead to realize he suspected her boss of such a crime. Certainly the odd phone calls *could* have been from someone giving him orders, or from the people he hired to do the job. The timing was about right. "Do you think Mr Clegg might have given this caller his private number?"

She nodded. "That's what must have happened. The first two times, Mr Clegg was out or with a client. The third time, I put the caller through, and he never called me again."

"And you're sure you never put a face to the voice?"

"No."

Banks stood up and walked around the small room. Well-tended potted plants stood on the shelf by the small window at the back that looked out onto narrow Park Cross Street. Clegg had obviously been careful where Betty Moorhead was concerned. If he had been mixed up with hired killers and Caribbean dictators, he had been careful to keep them at arm's length. He turned back to Betty. "Is there anything else you can tell me about Mr Clegg?"

"I don't know what you mean."

"How would you describe him as a person?"

"Well, I wouldn't know."

"You never socialized?"

She blushed. "Certainly not."

"Had he been depressed lately?"

"No."

"Did Mr Clegg have many women calling on him?"

"Not as far as I know. What are you suggesting?"

"Did you ever see or hear mention of a woman called Pamela Jeffreys? An Asian woman."

She looked puzzled. "No. She wasn't a client."

"Did he have a girlfriend?"

"I wouldn't know. He kept his private life private."

Banks decided to give up. Melissa Clegg might know a bit more about her husband's conquests, or Ken Blackstone's men would question his colleagues and perhaps come up with something. It was after five and he was tired of running around in circles. Betty Moorhead clearly didn't know anything else, or if she did she didn't realize its importance. Getting at information like that was like target practice in the dark.

Why not just accept Gristhorpe's theory that Clegg had arranged for Rothwell to be killed, and that they hadn't a hope in hell of finding either Clegg or the killers? And what could they do to Martin Churchill, if indeed he was behind it all? Banks didn't like the feeling of impotence this case was beginning to engender.

On the walk back to his hotel, Banks picked up a half-bottle of Bell's. It would be cheaper than using the minibar in his room. As he threaded his way among the office workers leaving the British

Telecom Building for their bus-stops on Wellington Street, Banks wished he could just go home and forget about the whole Clegg-Rothwell-Calvert mess.

After leaving Blackstone at the car park, he had phoned Pamela Jeffreys at home, half-hoping she might be free for a drink that evening, but he had only got her answering machine. She was probably playing with the orchestra or something. He had left a message anyway, telling her which hotel he was staying at, and now he was feeling guilty. He remembered Blackstone's warning about hotels.

On the surface, he wanted to apologize for their misunderstanding yesterday, but if truth be told, he had let himself get a bit too carried away with his fantasies. Would he do anything if he had the chance? If she agreed to come back to his hotel room for a nightcap, would he try to seduce her? Would he make love to her if she were willing? He didn't know.

He remembered his attraction to Jenny Fuller, a professor of psychology who occasionally helped with cases, and wondered what his life would be like now if he had given in to his desires then. Would he have told Sandra? Would they still be together? Would he and Jenny still be friends? No answer came.

Rather glumly, he recalled the bit at the beginning of the Trollope biography he was reading, where Trollope considers the dreary sermons persuading people to turn their backs on worldly pleasure in the hope of heaven to come and asks, if such is really the case, then "Why are women so lovely?" That set him thinking again about Pamela's shapely, golden body, her bright personality and her passion for music. Well, at least he had a curry with Ken Blackstone to look forward to, and time for a shower and a rest before that. He thought he might even check out the hotel's Health and Leisure Club, maybe have a swim, take a sauna or a whirlpool.

There were no messages. Banks went straight up to his room, took off his shoes and flopped on the bed. He phoned Sandra, who wasn't in, then called the Eastvale station again and spoke to Susan Gay. Nothing new, except that she sounded depressed.

After a brisk shower, much better than the tepid dribble at home, he poured himself a small Scotch and put the television on while he dried off and dressed. He caught the end of the international news and heard that the St Corona riots had been put down swiftly and brutally by Martin Churchill's forces. And Burgess wanted to give the man a retirement villa in Cornwall?

After that, he was only half paying attention to the local news, but at one point, he saw a house he recognized and heard the reporter say, "... when she failed to report for rehearsals today. Police are still at the scene and so far have refused to comment ..."

It was Pamela Jeffreys's house, and outside it stood two patrol cars and an ambulance. Stunned, Banks sat on the side of the bed and tossed back his Scotch, then he got his jacket out of the cupboard and left the room so fast he forgot to turn off the television.

TEN

I

It was hard to imagine that anything terrible could happen on such a fine spring evening, but the activity around the little terrace house in Armley indicated that evil made no allowances for the weather.

Three police cars were parked at angles in front of the house. Beyond the line of white tape, reporters badgered the PCs on guard duty, one of whom jotted down Banks's name and rank before he let him through. Neighbours stood on their doorsteps or by privet hedges and gazed in silence, arms folded, faces grim, and the people working their allotments stopped to watch the spectacle. A small crowd also stood gawping from the steps of the Sikh Temple down the street.

Banks stood on the threshold of the living-room. Whatever had happened here, it had been extremely violent: the glass coffee-table had been smashed in two; the three-piece suite had been slashed and the stuffing ripped out; books lay torn all over the carpet, pages reduced to confetti; the glass front of the cocktail cabinet was shattered and the crystalware itself lay in bright shards; the music stand lay on the floor with the splintered pieces and broken bow of Pamela's viola beside it; even the print of Ganesh over the fireplace had been taken from its frame and torn up. Worst of all, though, was the broad dark stain on the cream carpet. Blood.

One of the officers cracked a racist joke about Ganesh and another laughed. The elephant god was supposed to be the god of good beginnings, Banks remembered. Upstairs, someone was whistling "Lara's Theme" from *Doctor Zhivago*.

"Who the hell are you?"

Banks turned to face the plainclothes man coming out of wreck-age of the kitchen.

"Press?" he went on before Banks had time to answer. "You're not allowed in. You ought to bloody well know that. Bugger off." He grabbed Banks's arm and steered him towards the door. "What does that fucking useless PC think he's up to, letting you in? I'll have his bloody balls for Christmas tree decorations."

"Hang on." Banks finally managed to get a word in and jerk his arm free of the man's grasp. He showed his card. The man relaxed.

"Oh. Sorry, sir," he said. "Detective Sergeant Waltham. I wasn't to know." Then he frowned. "What's North Yorkshire want with this one, if you don't mind my asking?"

He was in his early thirties, perhaps a few pounds overweight, about three inches taller than Banks, with curly ginger hair. He had a prominent chin, a ruddy complexion and curious catlike green eyes. He wore a dark brown suit, white shirt and plain green tie. Behind him stood a scruffy-looking youth in a leather jacket. Probably his DC, Banks guessed.

"First things first," said Banks. "What happened to the woman who lives here?"

"Pamela Jeffreys. Know her?"

"What happened to her? Is she still alive?"

"Oh, aye, sir. Just. Someone worked her over a treat. Broken ribs, broken nose, broken fingers. Multiple lacerations, contusions. In fact, multiple just about everything. And it looks as if she broke her leg when she fell. She was in a coma when we found her. First officer on the scene thought she was dead."

Banks felt a wave of fear and anger surge through his stomach, bringing the bile to his throat. "When did it happen?" he asked.

"We're not sure, sir. There's a clock upstairs was smashed at twenty past nine, but that doesn't necessarily mean anything. A bit too Agatha Christie, if you ask me. Doc thinks last night, but we're still interviewing the neighbours."

"So you think she lay there for nearly twenty-four hours?"

"Could be, sir. The doctor said she'd have bled to death if she hadn't been a good clotter."

Banks swallowed. "Raped?"

Waltham shook his head. "Doc says no signs of sexual assault. When we found her she was fully clothed, no signs of interference. Some consolation, eh?"

"Who found her?"

"One of her musician friends got worried when she didn't show up for rehearsals this morning. Some sort of string quartet or something. Apparently she'd been a bit upset lately. He said she was usually reliable and had never missed a day before. He phoned the house several times during the day and only got her answering machine. After work he drove by and knocked. Still no answer. Then he had a butcher's through the window. After that, he phoned the local police. He's in the clear."

Banks said nothing. DS Waltham leaned against the bannister. The scruffy DC squeezed by them and went upstairs. In the front room, someone laughed out loud again.

Waltham coughed behind his hand. "Er, look, sir, is there something we should know? There'll have to be questions, of course, but we can be as discreet as anyone if we have to be. What with you showing up here and …"

"And what, Sergeant?"

"Well, I recognize your voice from her answering machine. It *was* you, wasn't it?"

Banks sighed. "Yes, yes it was. But no, there's nothing you need to be discreet about. There is probably a lot you should know. Shit." He looked at his watch. Almost seven. "Look, Sergeant, I'd clean forgot I'm supposed to be meeting DI Blackstone for dinner."

"*Our* DI Blackstone, sir?"

"Yes. Know him?"

"Yes, sir."

"Do you think you can get one of the PCs to page him or track him down. It's the Shabab on Eastgate."

Waltham smiled. "I know it. Very popular with the lads at Millgarth. I'll see to it, sir."

He went to the door and spoke to one of the uniformed constables, then came back. "He's on his way. Look, sir, PC O'Brien there just told me there's an old geezer across the street thinks he might have seen something. Want to come over?"

"Yes. Very much." Banks followed him down the path and through the small crowd. One or two reporters shouted for comments, but Waltham just waved them aside. PC O'Brien stood by the low, dark stone wall that ran by the allotments, talking to a painfully thin old man wearing a grubby, collarless shirt. Behind them, other allotment workers stood in a semi-circle, watching, some of them leaning on shovels or rakes. Very Yorkshire Gothic, Banks thought.

"Mr Judd, sir," O'Brien said, introducing Waltham, who, in turn, introduced Banks. "He was working his allotment last night just before dark." Waltham nodded and O'Brien walked off. "Keep those bloody reporters at bay, will you, please, O'Brien?" Waltham called after him.

Banks sat on the wall and took out his cigarettes. He offered them around. Waltham declined, but Mr Judd accepted one. "Might as well, lad," he croaked, tapping his chest. "Too late to worry about my health now."

He did look ill, Banks thought. Sallow flesh hung off the bones of his face above his scrawny neck with its turkey-flaps and puckered skin, like a surgery scar, around his Adam's apple. The whites of his eyes had a yellow cast, but the dark blue pupils glinted with intelligence. Mr Judd, Banks decided, was a man whose observations he could trust. He sat by and let Waltham do the questioning.

"What time were you out here?" Waltham asked.

"From seven o'clock till about half past nine," said Judd. "This time of year I always come out of an evening after tea for a bit of peace, weather permitting. The wife likes to watch telly, but I've no patience with it, myself. Nowt but daft buggers acting like daft buggers." He took a deep draw on the cigarette. Banks noticed him flinch with pain.

"Were you the only one working here?" Waltham asked.

"Aye. T'others had all gone home by then."

"Can you tell us what you saw?"

"Aye, well it must have been close to knocking-off time. It were getting dark, I remember that. And this car pulled up outside Miss Jeffreys's house. Dark and shiny, it were. Black."

"Do you know what make?"

"No, sorry, lad. I wouldn't know a Mini from an Aston Martin these days, to tell you the truth, especially since we've been getting all these foreign cars. It weren't a big one, though."

Waltham smiled. "Okay. Go on."

"Well, two men gets out and walks up the path."

"What did they look like?"

"Hard to say, really. They were both wearing suits. And one of them was a darkie, but that's nowt to write home about these days, is it?"

"One of the men was black?"

"Aye."

"What happened next?"

Judd went through a minor coughing fit and spat a ball of red-green phlegm on the earth beside him. "I packed up and went home. The wife needs a bit of help getting up the apples and pears to bed these days. She can't walk as well as she used to."

"Did you see Miss Jeffreys open the door and let the men in?"

"I can't say I was watching that closely. One minute they were on the doorstep, next they were gone. But the car was still there."

"Did you hear anything?"

"No. Too far away." He shrugged. "I thought nothing of it. Insurance men, most like. That's what they looked like. Or maybe those religious folks, Jehovah's Witnesses."

"So you didn't see them leave?"

"No. I'd gone home by then."

"Where do you live?"

Judd pointed across the street. "Over there. Number fourteen." It was five houses down from Pamela Jeffreys's. "Been there forty years or more, now. A right dump it was when we first moved in. Damp walls, no indoor toilets, no bathroom. Had it done up over the years, though, bit by bit."

Waltham paused and looked at Banks, who indicated he would like to ask one or two questions. Waltham, Banks noted, had been a patient interviewer, not pushy, rude and condescending towards the old, like some. Maybe it was because he had a DCI watching over his shoulder. And maybe that was being uncharitable.

"Did you know Miss Jeffreys at all?" Banks asked.

Judd shook his head. "Can't say as I did."

"But you knew her to say hello to?"

"Oh, aye. She was a right nice lass, if you ask me. And a bonny one, too." He winked. "Always said hello if she passed me in the street. Always carrying that violin case. I used to ask her if she were in t'mafia and had a machine-gun in it, just joking, like."

"But you never stopped and chatted?"

"Not apart from that and the odd comment about the weather. What would an old codger like me have to say to a young lass like her? Besides, people round here tend to keep themselves to themselves these days." He coughed and spat again. "It didn't used to be that way, tha knows. When Eunice and I first came here there used to be a community. We'd have bloody great big bonfires out in the street on Guy Fawkes night—it were still just cobbles, then, none of this tarmac—and everyone came out. Eunice would make parkin and treacle-toffee. We'd wrap taties in foil and put 'em in t'fire to bake. But it's all changed. People died, moved away. See that there Sikh Temple?" He pointed down the street. "It used to be a Congregationalist Chapel. Everyone went there on a Sunday morning. They had Monday whist drives, too, and a youth club, Boys' Brigade and Girl Guides for the young uns. Pantos at Christmas.

"Oh, aye, it's all changed. People coming and going. We've got indoor toilets now, but nobody talks to anyone. Not that I've owt against Pakis, like. As I said, she was a nice lass. I saw them taking her out on that stretcher an hour or so back." He shook his head slowly. "Nowadays you keep your door locked tight. Will she be all right?"

"We don't know," Banks said. "We're keeping our fingers crossed. Did she have many visitors?"

"I didn't keep a look out. I suppose you mean boyfriends?"

"Anyone. Male or female."

"I never saw any women call, not by themselves. Her mum and dad came now and then. At least, I assumed it was her mum and dad. And there was one bloke used to visit quite regularly a few months back. Used to park outside our house sometimes. And don't ask me what kind of car he drove. I can't even remember the colour. But he stopped coming. Hasn't been anyone since, not that I've noticed."

"What did this man look like?"

"Ordinary really. Fair hair, glasses, a bit taller than thee."

Keith Rothwell—or Robert Calvert, Banks thought. "Anyone else?"

Judd shook his head then smiled. "Only you and that young woman, t'other day."

Banks felt Waltham turn and stare at him. If Judd had seen Banks and Susan visit Pamela Jeffreys on Saturday, then he obviously didn't miss much—morning, afternoon or evening. Banks thanked him.

"We'll get someone to take a statement soon, Mr Judd," said Waltham.

"All right, son," said the old man, turning back to his allotment. "I won't be going anywhere except my final resting place, and that'll be a few months off, God willing. I only wish I could have been more help."

"You did fine," said Banks.

"What the bloody hell was all that about, sir?" Waltham asked as they walked away. "You didn't tell me you'd been here before."

Banks noticed Ken Blackstone getting out of a dark blue Peugeot opposite the Sikh Temple. "Didn't have time," he said to Waltham, moving away. "Later, Sergeant. I'll explain it all later."

II

Banks and Blackstone sat in an Indian restaurant near Woodhouse Moor, a short drive across the Aire valley from Pamela Jeffreys's house, drinking lager and nibbling at pakoras and onion bhaji as they waited for their main courses. Being close to the university, the place was full of students. The aroma was tantalizing—cumin, coriander, cloves, cinnamon, mingled with other spices Banks couldn't put a name to. "Not exactly the Shabab," Blackstone had said, "but not bad." A Yorkshire compliment.

In the brief time they had been there, Banks had explained as succinctly as he could what the hell was going on—at least to the extent that he understood it himself.

"So why do you think they beat up the girl?" Blackstone asked.

"They must have thought she knew where Daniel Clegg was, or that she was hiding something for him. They ripped her place up pretty thoroughly."

"And you think they're working for Martin Churchill?"

"Burgess thinks so. It's possible."

"Do you think it was the same two who visited Clegg's secretary and his ex-wife?"

"Yes. I'm certain of it."

"But they didn't beat up either of them, or search their places. Why not?"

"I don't know. Maybe they were getting desperate by the time they got to Pamela. Let's face it, they'd found out nothing so far. They must have been frustrated. They felt they'd done enough pussyfooting around and it was time for business. Either that or they phoned their boss and he told them to push harder. They also probably thought she was lying or holding out on them for some reason, maybe something in her manner. I don't know. Perhaps they're just racists."

Banks shook his head, feeling a sudden ache and rage. He couldn't seem to banish the image of Pamela Jeffreys at the hands of her torturers: her terror, her agony, the smashed viola. And would her broken fingers ever heal enough for her to play again? But he didn't know Blackstone well enough to talk openly about his feelings. "They'd been polite but pushy earlier," he said. "Maybe they just ran out of patience."

The main course arrived: a plate of steaming chapatis, chicken bhuna and goat vindaloo, along with a selection of chutneys and raita. They shared out the dishes and started to eat, using the chapatis to shovel mouthfuls of food and mop up the sauce. Blackstone ordered a couple more lagers and a jug of ice water.

"There is another explanation," Blackstone said between mouthfuls.

"What?"

"That she *did* know something. That she was involved in the double-cross, or whatever it was. From the quick look I got at her house, I'd agree there's no doubt they were looking for something. DS Waltham suggested the same thing."

"Don't think I haven't considered it," Banks said, carefully piling a heap of the hot vindaloo on a scrap of chapati. "But I'm sure she didn't even know Clegg."

"That's only what she told you, remember."

"Nobody else contradicted her, Ken. Not Melissa Clegg, not the secretary, not even Mr Judd."

"Oh, come on, Alan. The old man can't have seen everything. Nor could the secretary or the ex-wife have *known* everything. Maybe Clegg never visited her at her home. They could have had some clandestine relationship, met in secret."

"Why the need for secrecy? Neither of them was married."

"Perhaps because they were involved in some funny business— not necessarily of a sexual nature—and it wouldn't be good to be seen together. Maybe she was involved in whatever scam Clegg and Rothwell had going?"

Banks shook his head. "Clegg was a lawyer, Rothwell a financial whiz-kid and Pamela Jeffreys is a classical musician. It just doesn't fit."

"They *could* have had business interests in common, though."

"True. Anything's possible. But remember, Pamela Jeffreys knew *Robert Calvert*. She told me they met by chance in a pub. She'd never heard of Keith Rothwell until after his murder, when his photo appeared in the papers. She had no reason to lie. She was even putting herself in an awkward situation by calling us. She needn't have done so. We hadn't heard of Robert Calvert and might never have done if it weren't for her. Usually people want to stay as far away from a murder investigation as they can get. You know that, Ken. Until we find out differently, we have to assume that Calvert was a persona invented by Rothwell, with Clegg's help, solely for pleasure."

Blackstone swallowed a mouthful of bhuna. "I sometimes think I could do with one of those myself," he said.

Banks laughed. "Calvert helped Rothwell express another side of his nature, a side he couldn't indulge at home. Or perhaps it helped him be the way he used to be, relive something he'd lost. As Calvert, he'd have fun gambling and womanizing, and probably subsidizing himself with his illicit earnings from the money-laundering. And

Pamela Jeffreys wasn't his only conquest, you know. There were no doubt others before her, and she was convinced that he'd met someone else, someone he'd really fallen for."

"That would upset the apple-cart, wouldn't it?" said Blackstone.

Banks stopped chewing for a moment.

"Alan?" Blackstone said. "Alan, are you all right? I know the curry's hot, but ..."

"What? Oh, yes. It was just something you said, that's all. I'm surprised I never thought of it before."

"What?"

"If *Calvert* really did do it, you know, fall in love, the real thing, with all the bells and whistles, then what would happen to Rothwell?"

"I don't get you. It's the same person, isn't it?"

"Yes and no. What I mean is, how could he go on living his Rothwell life, the one we assumed was his *real* life, at Arkbeck Farm with Mary, Alison and Tom. Forgive me, I'm just thinking out loud, going nowhere. It doesn't matter."

"I do see what you mean," said Blackstone. "It would bugger up everything, wouldn't it?"

"Hmm." Banks finished his meal and washed away some of the spicy heat with a swig of watery lager. His lips still burned, though, and he felt prickles of sweat on his scalp. The signs of a good curry.

"Did the suspects in the Jeffreys beating know about Rothwell?" Blackstone asked.

Banks shook his head. "Don't know. They haven't been seen locally, and they certainly don't match the daughter's description of his killers."

"How old is she?"

"Alison? Fifteen."

"She didn't see their faces. Could she be wrong?"

"It's possible, but not that wrong, I don't think. Nothing matches."

"Just a thought. I mean, if Rothwell and Clegg were in the laundering business together, and whoever they were working for sent a couple of goons to find Clegg and whatever money he's made off with, you'd think they'd start with Rothwell's family, wouldn't you?"

"Perhaps. But we've been keeping too close a watch. They wouldn't dare show up within twenty miles of Arkbeck Farm."

"And another thing: if they killed Rothwell, why did they use different people to chase down Clegg? It seems a bit excessive, doesn't it?"

"Again," said Banks, "I can only guess. I think some of what's been happening took them by surprise. It's possible that they asked Clegg to get rid of Rothwell and he hired his own men. As you know, we're looking into what connections he might have had with criminal types."

Blackstone nodded. "I see," he said. "Then Clegg became a problem and they had to send their own men?"

"Something like that."

"Makes sense. Clegg was a bit of a ladies' man, you know, according to my DC who talked to his colleagues," Blackstone said.

"Yes. His estranged wife, Melissa, suggested as much. Did he have a girlfriend?"

"Yes. Apparently nothing serious since he split up with his wife. Prefers to play the field. Recently he's been seeing a receptionist from Norwich Insurance. Name of Marci Lapwing, if you can believe that. Aspiring actress. DC Gaitskill had a word with her this morning. Says she's a bit of a bimbo with obvious attractions. But he's a bit of an arsehole himself, is Gaitskill, so I'd take it with a pinch of salt. Anyway, they saw each other the Saturday before Clegg's disappearance. They went for dinner, then to a nightclub in Harehills. She spent the night with him and he took her home—that's Seacroft—after a pub lunch out at the Red Lion in Burnsall on Sunday afternoon. She hasn't seen or heard from him since."

"Is she telling the truth?"

"Gaitskill says so. I'd trust him on that."

"Okay. Thanks, Ken."

"Clegg had a reserved parking space at the back of the Court Centre. According to what we could find out, he used to eat at a little trattoria on The Headrow after work on Thursdays. The waiters there remember him, all right. Nothing odd about his behaviour. He left about six-thirty or a quarter to seven last

Thursday, heading west, towards where his car was parked, and that's the last sighting we have."

"The car?"

"Red Jag. Gone. We've put it out over the PNC along with this." Blackstone took a photograph from his briefcase and slid it over the tablecloth. It showed the head and shoulders of a man in his early forties, with determined blue eyes, a slightly crooked nose, fair hair and a mouth that had a cruel twist to its left side.

"Clegg?"

Blackstone nodded and put the photograph back in his brief-case. "We've also been through Clegg's house in Chapel Allerton. Nothing. Whatever he was up to, he kept it at the office."

"Anything on Hamilton and the other car?"

"The boffins are still working on the car. I pulled Hamilton's record myself and we had another chat with him at the station this after-noon." He shook his head. "I can't see it, Alan. The man's as thick as two short planks. I don't think he's even *heard* of St Corona, and he's strictly small fry on the drugs scene. By the time he gets his stuff to sell, it's been stepped on by just about every dealer in the city."

"It was just a thought. Thanks for giving it a try."

"No problem. We'll have another shot in a day or two, just in case. And we'll keep a discreet eye on him. Look, back to what I was saying before. How do you think the goons knew about Pamela Jeffreys if she wasn't involved?"

Banks felt the anger flare up inside him again, but he held it in check. "That's all too easy," he said. "Remember, they were also following me around yesterday. I think they started at Clegg's office first thing yesterday morning and one, or both of them, stayed on my tail until I spotted them outside Calvert's flat that evening. They didn't know who the hell I was, and the only other person I met that they hadn't talked to already was Pamela Jeffreys. They must have thought we were in it together. I met her near the hall where she was rehearsing, and either one of them hung around to follow her home, or they found out some other way who she was and where she lived.

"She must have looked like their best lead so far. They thought she had some connection with Clegg and that she knew where he was or was holding something for him. Clegg has obviously got something they want. Most likely money. If he was laundering for their boss, then it looks like he might have skipped with a bundle. Either that or he's got some sort of evidence for blackmail—books, bank account records. And that's probably what they were looking for when they tore her place apart. Back to square one. The goons worked Pamela over because they thought she knew something, or had something of theirs. She didn't. And I blame myself. I should have bloody well known I was putting her at risk."

"Come off it, Alan. How could you know?"

Banks shrugged and tapped out a cigarette. He was the only smoker in the entire restaurant and had to ask the waiter specially for an ashtray. It was getting like that these days, he noted glumly. He'd have to stop sometime soon; he knew he was only postponing the inevitable. He had thought about getting a nicotine patch, then quickly dismissed the idea. It was the feel of the cigarette between his fingers he wanted, the sharp intake of tobacco smoke into the lungs, not some slow oozing of poison through his skin into his blood. Pity about the health problems.

He felt rather like St Augustine must have felt when he wrote in his *Confessions*: "Give me chastity and continency—but not yet!"

"You know what really pisses me off?" Banks said after he had lit the cigarette. "Dirty Dick Burgess was following me around that day, too, and it wouldn't surprise me at all if he'd seen them outside Melissa Clegg's shop."

"How would he know who they are?"

"Oh, I think he knows them, all right."

"Even so, what could he have done? They hadn't broken any laws."

Banks shrugged. "I suppose not. It's too bloody late now, anyway," he said. "Let's just hope they don't go back to see Betty Moorhead and Melissa Clegg."

"Don't worry. Charlie Waltham will have them both covered by now. He's a good bloke, Alan. And he'll have descriptions of Mutt and Jeff out, too. They won't get far."

"I hope not," said Banks. "I bloody hope not. I'd like a few minutes alone with them in a quiet cell."

III

Back at the hotel, Banks felt caged. Anger burned inside him like the hot Indian spices, but it would take more than Rennies to quell it. What a bloody fool he'd been to do nothing when he realized he had been followed. He had practically signed Pamela Jeffreys's death warrant, and it was through no virtue of his that she had survived her ordeal. So far.

He poured himself a shot of Bell's and turned on the television. Nothing but a nature programme, a silly comedy, an interview with a has-been politician and an old Dirty Harry movie. He watched Clint Eastwood for a while. He had never much enjoyed cop films or cop programmes on television, but watching right here and now, he could identify with Dirty Harry tracking down the villains and dealing with them his own way. He had meant what he said to Blackstone. A few minutes alone with Pamela Jeffreys's attackers and they would know what police brutality was all about.

But he hated himself when he felt that way. Luckily, it was rare. After all, policemen are only human, he reminded himself. They have their loyalties, their lusts, their prejudices, their agonies, their tempers. The problem was that they have to keep these emotions in check to do their jobs properly.

"You go home and puke in your own time if you want to get anywhere in this job, lad," one of his early mentors had told him at a grisly crime scene. "You don't do it all over the corpse. And you go home and punch holes in your own wall, not in the child moles-ter's face."

Unable to concentrate, even on Dirty Harry, he turned off the television. He couldn't stand up, couldn't sit down, didn't know what he wanted to do. And all the time, the anger and pain churned inside him, and he couldn't find a way to get them out.

He picked up the phone and dialled the code for Eastvale, then put it down before he started dialling his own number. He wanted to talk to Sandra, but he didn't think he could explain his feelings to her right now, especially the way they'd been drifting apart of late. God knew, under normal circumstances she was an understanding wife, but this would be pushing it a bit far: a woman he had lusted after, fantasized about, gets beaten within a hair's breadth of her life, and he's whipping himself over it. No, he couldn't explain that to Sandra.

And it wasn't just a fantasy. Had things turned out differently, he would have phoned Pamela Jeffreys again and would probably be having dinner or drinks with her right now, plucking up the courage to ask her up to his hotel room, Bell's at the ready. Well, he would never know the outcome now; his virtue hadn't even been put to the test. Hadn't St Augustine said something about that, too, or was that someone else?

He phoned the hospital, and after a bit of officious rank-pulling, actually got a doctor on the line. Yes, Ms Jeffreys was stable but still in intensive care ... no, she was still unconscious ... there was no way of telling when or if she would come round ... no idea yet if there was any permanent damage. He didn't feel any better when he hung up.

It was just after nine-thirty. He knocked back the rest of the glass of Scotch, grabbed his sports jacket and went out. Maybe a walk would help, or the anonymous comfort of a crowded pub, not that he expected Leeds city centre on a Tuesday evening to be the West End.

He walked along Wellington Street past the National Express coach station and the tall Royal Mail Building to City Square, which was deserted except for the silent nymphs, who stood bearing their torches around the central statue of the Black Prince on his horse. From somewhere along Boar Lane, a drunk shouted in the night; a bottle smashed and a woman laughed loudly.

Banks crossed City Square. He walked fast, trying to burn off some of his rage, and soon found himself in the empty Bond Street Centre with only his reflection in the shop windows he passed.

His memories of Leeds's city centre were vague, but he was sure that somewhere among the jungle of refurbished Victorian arcades and modern shopping centres there were a number of pubs down the dingy back alleys that riddled the heart of the old city centre.

And he was right.

The first one he found was an old brass, mirrors and dark wood Tetleys house with a fair-sized crowd and a jukebox at tolerable volume. He ordered a pint and stood sideways at the bar, just watching people chat and laugh. It was mostly a young crowd. Only kids seemed to venture into the city centres at night these days. Perhaps that was why their parents and grandparents stayed away. The pubs in Armley and Bramley, in Headingley and Kirkstall, would be full of locals of all age groups mixed together.

As he leaned against the bar, drinking and smoking, nobody paid him any attention. Banks had always been pleased that he didn't stand out as an obvious policeman. There'd be no mistaking Hatchley or Ken Blackstone no matter how "off duty" they were, but Banks could fit in almost anywhere without attracting too much attention. Over the years, he had found it a useful quality. It wasn't only that he didn't look like a copper, whatever that meant, but for some reason his presence didn't set off the usual warning bells. At the same time, he didn't like to sit or stand with his back to the door, and he didn't miss much.

He finished his pint quickly and ordered another one, lighting up again. He was smoking too much, he realized, and he would feel it in the morning. But that was the morning. In the meantime, it gave him something to do with his hands, which, left to their own devices, curled and hardened into fists.

His second pint went down easily, too. The ebb and flow of conversation washed over him. Loudest was a group of two middle-aged couples sitting behind the engraved smoked glass and dark wood at the side of the door. The only people over twenty-five, apart from Banks and the bar staff, they had all had a bit too much to drink. The men were on pints of bitter, and the women on oddly coloured concoctions with umbrellas sticking out of them and bits of fruit floating around. By the sound of things, they were cele-brating the engagement of one couple's daughter, who wasn't present, and this brought forth all the old, blue jokes Banks had ever heard in his life.

"There's these three women," said one of the men. "The prosti-tute, the nymphomaniac and the wife. After sex, the prostitute says, 'That's it, then,' all businesslike. The nympho says, 'That's *it?*' And the wife says, 'Beige. I think the ceiling should be beige.'"

They howled with laughter. One of the women, a rather blowsy peroxide blonde, like a late-period Diana Dors, with too much make-up and unfocused eyes, looked over and winked at Banks. He winked back and she nudged her friend. They both started to laugh. A man Banks assumed to be her husband popped his head around the divide and said, "Tha's welcome to her, lad, but I'll warn thee, she'll have thee worn out in a week. Bloody insatiable, she is." She hit him playfully and they all laughed so much they had tears in their eyes. Banks laughed with them, then turned away. The barmaid raised her eyebrows and drew a finger across her throat. Banks drank up and moved on.

Outside, he noticed that the evening had turned a little cooler and dark clouds were fast covering the stars. There was an electric edge to the air that presaged a storm. As if he didn't feel tense and wound up enough already without the bloody weather conspiring against him, too.

The next pub, down another alley off Briggate, was busier. Groups of young people stood about outside, leaning against the wall or sitting on the wooden benches. The place danced with long shadows like something out of an old Orson Welles film. Banks took his pint out into the narrow, whitewashed alley and rested it on a ledge at elbow level, like a bar.

He thought of his last meeting with Pamela Jeffreys. She had run off in tears and he had stood there like an idiot in the park watching his ice-cream melt. He had wanted to apologize for treating her feelings so shoddily, but at the same time another part of him, the professional side, knew he had had to ask, and knew an apology would never be completely genuine. Still, he was only human; susceptible to beauty, he found her attractive, and he liked her warm, open personality, her enthusiasm for life and her sense of humour. Her connection with music also excited him. How much of that would she have left when she came out of hospital? If she came out.

Now, slurping his ale in a back alley in Leeds, he considered again what Blackstone had suggested about her involvement in the affair, but he didn't think Pamela Jeffreys was that good an actress. She had liked Calvert; they had had simple fun together, with no demands, no strings attached, no deep commitment. And what was wrong with that? She may have felt hurt when he found someone else—after all, nobody likes rejection—but she had liked him enough to swallow her pride and remain friends. She was young; she had energy enough to deal with a few hard knocks. If she had been jealous enough for murder, she would have killed Robert Calvert, probably in his Leeds flat, and if she had been involved in the laundering operation with Rothwell and Clegg, she wouldn't have phoned the Eastvale station and told them about Calvert.

It was close to eleven; most of the people had gone home. Banks ordered one more for the road, as he would be walking beside it, not driving on it. He was glad he had taken a little time out. The drink had helped douse his anger, or at least dampen it for a while. He was also rational enough to know that tomorrow he would be the professional again and nobody would ever know about his complex, knotted feelings of lust and guilt for Pamela Jeffreys.

He drained his glass, put his cigarettes back in his jacket pocket and set off down the alley. It was long and narrow, rough white-washed stone on both sides, and lit only by a single high bulb behind wire mesh. When he was a couple of yards from the end, two men walked in from the street and blocked the exit. One of them asked Banks for a light.

Contrary to what one sees on television, detectives rarely find themselves in situations where immediate physical violence is threatened. Banks couldn't remember the last time he had been in a fight, but he didn't stop to try to remember. A number of thoughts flashed through his mind at once, but so quickly that an observer would not have seen him hesitate for a second.

First, he knew that they underestimated him; he was neither as drunk nor as unfit as they probably believed. Secondly, he had learned an important lesson from schoolyard fights: you go in first, fast, dirty and hard. Real violence doesn't take place in slow motion, like a Sam Peckinpah film; it's usually over before anyone realizes it has begun.

Before they could make their move, Banks took a step closer, pretended to fumble for matches, then grabbed the nearest one by his shirt-front and nutted him hard on the bridge of the nose. The man put his hands over his face and went down on his knees groaning as blood dripped down his shirt-front.

The other hesitated a moment to glance down at his friend. Mistake. Banks grabbed him by the arm, whirled him around and slammed him into the wall. Before the man could get his breath back, Banks punched him in the stomach, and as he bent forward in pain, brought his knee up into the man's face. He felt cheekbone or teeth smash against his kneecap. The man fell, putting his hands to his mouth to stem the flow of blood and vomit.

His mate had clambered to his feet by now and he threw himself at Banks, knocking him hard into the wall and banging the side of his head against the rough stone. He got in a couple of close body punches, but before he could gain any further advantage, Banks pushed him back far enough to start throwing quick jabs at his already broken nose. In the sickly light of the alley, Banks could see blood smeared over his attacker's face, almost closing one eye and dripping down his chin. The man backed off and slumped against the wall.

By this time, the other was back wobbling on his feet, and Banks went for him. He aimed one sharp blow to the head after the other, splitting an eyebrow, a lip, jarring a tooth loose. The other stumbled away towards the exit. There was no fight left in either of them, but Banks couldn't stop. He kept slugging away at the man in front of him, feeling the anger in him explode and pour out. When the man tried to protect his face with his hands, Banks pummelled his exposed stomach and ribs.

The man backed away, begging Banks to stop hitting him. His friend, swaying at the alley's exit now, yelled, "Come on, Kev, run for it! He's a fucking maniac! He'll fucking kill us both!" And they both staggered off towards Commercial Street.

Banks watched them go. There was no-one else around, thank God. The whole debacle couldn't have taken more than a couple of minutes. When they were out of sight, Banks fell back against the whitewashed wall, shaking, sweating, panting. He took several deep breaths, smoothed his clothes and headed back to the hotel.

ELEVEN

I

The storm broke in the middle of the night. Banks lay in the dark in his strange hotel bed tossing and turning as lightning flashed and thunder first rumbled in the distance then cracked so loudly overhead that the windows rattled.

Once unbound, the shape of his rage was fluid; it could be as easily warped and twisted into fanciful images by sleep as it had been channelled into violence earlier. He kept waking from one nightmare and drifting back into another. Rain lashed against the windows, and in the background something hissed constantly, the way something always hisses in hotel rooms.

In the worst nightmare, the one he remembered the most clearly, he was talking on the telephone to a woman who had dialled his number by mistake. She sounded disoriented, and the longer she spoke the longer the spaces stretched between her words. Finally, silence took over completely. Banks called hello a few times, then hung up. As soon as he had done so, he was stricken by panic. The woman was committing suicide. He knew it. She had taken an overdose of pills and fallen into a coma while she was still on the line. He didn't know her name or her telephone number. If he had kept the line open and not hung up, he would have been able to trace her and save her life.

He awoke feeling guilty and depressed. And it wasn't only his soul that hurt. His head pounded from too much whisky and from the "Glasgow handshake" he had given one of his attackers, his chest felt tight from smoking, his knuckles ached and his side felt sore where he had been slammed into the wall. His mouth tasted as dry as the bottom of a budgie's cage and as sour as month-old milk.

When he got up to go to the toilet, he felt a stabbing pain shoot through his kneecap and found himself limping. He felt about ninety. He took three extra-strength Panadols from his traveller's survival kit and washed them down with two glasses of cold water.

It was four twenty-three A.M. by the red square numbers of the digital clock. Cars hissed by through the puddles in the road. Around the edges of the curtains, he could see the sickly amber glow of the street-lights and the occasional flash of distant lightning as the storm passed over to the north.

He didn't want to be awake, but he couldn't seem to get back to sleep. All he could do was lie there feeling sorry for himself, remembering what a bloody fool he had been. What had started as a simple bit of childish self-indulgence, drowning his sorrows in drink, had turned into a full-blown exhibition of idiocy, and both his skinned knuckles and the empty Scotch bottle on the bedside table were evidence enough of that.

After the fracas, he had dashed back to the hotel and hurried straight up to his room before anyone could notice his bloody knuckles or torn jacket. Once safe inside, he had poured himself a stiff drink to stop the shakes. Lying on the bed watching television until the programmes ended for the night, he had poured another, then another. Soon, the half-bottle was empty and he had fallen asleep. Now it was time to pay. He had heard once that guilt and shame contributed to the pain of hangovers, and at four thirty-two that morning, he certainly believed it.

Christ, it was so bloody easy to slide down one's thoughts into the pit of misery and self-recrimination at four thirty-two A.M. At four thirty-two, if you feel ill, you just *know* you have cancer; at four thirty-two, if you feel depressed, suicide seems the only way out. Four thirty-two is the perfect time for fear and self-loathing, the time of the dark night of the soul.

But it wouldn't do, he told himself. Feeling sorry for himself just wouldn't bloody well do. So he wasn't perfect. He had contemplated committing adultery. So what? He wasn't the first and he wouldn't be the last. He felt responsible for Pamela Jeffreys's injuries. Maybe, just *maybe*, he should have acted differently when he knew he was being followed—put a guard on everyone he had talked to—but it was a big maybe. He wasn't God almighty; he couldn't anticipate everything.

Most detective work was pissing about in the dark, anyway, waiting for the light to grow slowly, as it was doing now outside. On rare occasions, the truth hit you quick as a lightning flash. But they were very rare occasions indeed. Even then, before the lightning hit you, you had spent months looking for the right place to stand.

So last night, in the alley, he had lost it. So what? Two yobbos had tried to mug him and he had gone wild on them, plastered them all over the walls. Most of it was a blur now, but he remembered enough to embarrass him.

They had just been kids, really, early twenties at most, out looking for aggro. But one had been black and one white, like the men who had put Pamela Jeffreys in hospital. Banks knew in his mind that they weren't the same ones, but when the bubble of his anger burst and the fury unleashed itself, when the blood started to flow, they were the ones he was lashing out at. No wonder they ran away shitting bricks. There was nothing rational about it; blinded by rage, he had thought he was hurting the people he really wanted to hurt. He had taken out his anger on two unwary substitutes. They had simply been in the wrong place at the wrong time.

Still, he told himself, they bloody well deserved it, bleeding amateurs. At least he might have discouraged two apprentice muggers from their chosen career. And nobody would ever know what happened. *They* certainly wouldn't say anything. After all, he *hadn't* killed them; they had managed to run away and lick their wounds. They would survive to fight again another day, if they got back the bottle. It wasn't the worst thing he had ever done. And soon, surely, that feeling of being a total fucking idiot would go away and he could get on with his life.

He dozed briefly and woke again at five forty-one. Not quite as bad as four thirty-two, he thought, at first glance. He got up and looked outside at the grey morning. The road and pavement were still awash with puddles. Green double-decker buses were already running people to work, splashing up the water where it had collected in the gutters. Banks was on the fifth floor, and he could see the grey sky streaked with blood and milk behind the majestic dome of the Town Hall. Already, dim shadows were shuffling out of the Salvation Army shelter opposite.

Banks made a cup of instant coffee with the electric kettle and sachet provided and took it back to bed with him. He turned on the bedside light and picked up the copy of Evelyn Waugh's *Sword of Honour* trilogy he had brought with him. Guy Crouchback's misadventures should cheer him up a bit. At least he didn't have *that* much misfortune.

He would put last night behind him, he decided, sipping the weak Nescafé. A man was allowed his mistakes; he had just better not cling to them or they would drag him down to the bottom of the abyss.

II

At nine o'clock that morning, Susan Gay sat alone on the second pew from the back of the small non-denominational chapel at Eastvale Crematorium. It was cool inside, thanks to a large fan below the western stained-glass window, and the lighting was suitably dimmed. The place smelled of shoe-polish, not the usual musty hymn-books she associated with chapels.

The service went briskly enough. The rent-a-vicar said a few words about Keith Rothwell's devotion to his family and his dedication to hard work, then he read Psalm 51. Susan thought it particularly apt, all that guff about being cleansed of sin. "Bloodguiltiness" was a word she hadn't heard before, and it made her give a little shudder without knowing why. The mention of "burnt offering" brought the unwelcome image of Rothwell's corpse, the head a black mess, as if it had indeed been burned, but "Wash me; and I shall be whiter than snow" almost made her laugh out loud. It brought to mind an old television advert for detergent, then Rothwell's money-laundering.

After the vicar read a bit from "Revelation" about a new heaven and a new earth and all sorrow, pain and death disappearing, it was all over.

The Rothwells, all suitably dressed in shades of black for the occasion, sat in the front row. Throughout the ceremony, Mary sat stiffly, Alison kept glancing around her at the stained-glass and the font and Tom sat hunched over. As far as Susan could tell from behind, nobody reached for a handkerchief.

When she watched them walk out into the sunlight, she could tell she was right: dry eyes; not a tear in sight; Mary Rothwell doing her stiff-upper-lip routine, bearing her loss and grief with dignity.

Everyone ignored Susan except Tom, who approached her and said, "You're the detective who was at our house when I got back from the States, aren't you?"

"Yes. DC Susan Gay, in case you've forgotten."

"I hadn't forgotten. What are you doing here?"

"I'd like a word with you, if you can spare a few minutes."

Tom took a silver pocket-watch from his waistcoat and looked at it. Susan saw it was attached by a chain to one of his belt loops. Somehow, it seemed like a very affected gesture in one so young. Maybe it had impressed the Americans. He slipped it back in his pocket. "All right," he said. "But I can't come just now. Everyone's going back to Mr Pratt's for coffee and cake. I'll have to show up."

"Of course. How about an hour?"

"Okay."

"Look, it's a fine morning," Susan said. "How about that café by the river, the one near the pre-Roman site?"

"I know it."

Susan busied herself with paperwork back at the station for three quarters of an hour, then set off to keep her appointment.

The River Swain was flowing swiftly, still high after the spring thaw. On the grass by the bank, the owner of the small café had stuck a couple of rickety white tables and chairs. Susan bought a tin of Coke for Tom and a pot of tea for herself and they sat by the water. Two weeping willows framed the rolling farmland beyond. Right across, in the centre of the view, was a field of bright yellow rape-seed.

Flies buzzed around her head, and Susan kept fanning them away. "How was it?" she asked.

Tom shrugged. "I hate those kinds of social gatherings," he said. "And Laurence Pratt gets on my nerves."

Susan smiled. At least they had something in common. She let the silence stretch as she looked closely at the youth sitting opposite her. Wavy brown hair fell over his ears about halfway down his neck. He was tanned, slender, handsome and he looked as good now in his mourning suit as he had in torn jeans and a denim shirt. The more she let herself simply feel his presence, the more she was sure she was right about him.

He shifted in his chair. "Look," he said, "I'm sorry about the other day. I was rude, I know. But I was tired, upset."

"I understand," Susan said. "It's just that I got the impression there was something you wanted to tell me."

Tom looked away over the river. His face was scrunched up in a frown, or maybe the sun was in his eyes. "You know, don't you?" he asked. "You can tell."

"That you're homosexual? I have a strong suspicion, yes."

"Am I that obvious?"

Susan laughed. "Maybe not to everyone. Remember, I'm a detective."

Tom managed a weak smile. "Funny thing, that, isn't it?" he said. "You'd think it would be men who'd guess."

"I don't know. Women are used to responding to men in certain ways. They can tell when something's ..."

"Wrong?"

"I was going to say missing, but even that's not right."

"Different, then?"

"That'll do. Look, I'm not judging you, Tom. You mustn't think that. It's really none of my business, unless your sexual preference connects somehow with your father's murder."

"I can't see how it does."

"You're probably right. Tell me about this Aston, or Afton, then. When Chief Inspector Banks mentioned the name, you assumed it was a man. Why?"

"Because I didn't assume. I know damn well who he is. His name's Ashton. Bloody Clive Ashton. How could I forget?"

"Who is he?"

"He's the son of one of my father's clients—Lionel Ashton. We were at a party together once. I made a mistake."

"You made advances towards him?"

"Yes."

"And they weren't welcome?"

Tom gave a dry laugh. "Obviously not. He told his father."

"And?"

"And his father told my father. And my father told me I was disgusting, sick, *queer*, and that I should see about getting myself cured. That's the exact word he used, *cured*. He said it would kill Mum if she ever found out."

"And he suggested you take off to America for a while, at his expense?"

"Yes. But that came a bit later. First we let it lie while we figured out what was best."

"What did you do in the meantime?"

Tom looked at her, tilted his tin back and finished his Coke. His Adam's apple bobbed up and down. Susan turned away and watched a family of ducks drift by on the Swain. Tom wiped his lips with the back of his hand, then said, "I followed him."

She turned back towards him. "You followed your father? Why?"

"Because I thought he was up to something. He was away so often. He was always so remote, like he wasn't really with us even when he was at home. I thought he was doing damage to the family."

"He wasn't always like that?"

Tom shook his head. "No. Believe it or not, Dad used to have a bit of life about him. I'm sorry, I didn't intend to make a bad joke."

"I know. How long had he been behaving this way?"

"Hard to say. It was gradual, like. But this past couple of years it was getting worse. You could hardly talk to him." He shrugged.

"Was that the only reason you followed him, because you thought he was up to something?"

"I don't know. Maybe I wanted to get something on *him*. Revenge, I don't know. Find out what *his* guilty secret was."

"And did you?"

Tom took a deep breath, held it for a moment, then let it out loudly with a nervous laugh. "This is harder than I thought. Okay.

Here goes. Yes. I saw my father with another woman." He said it fast, staccato-style. "There, that's it. I said it."

Susan paused a moment to take the information in, then asked, "When?"

"Sometime in February."

"Where?"

"Leeds. In a pub. They were sitting together at a table in the Guildford, on The Headrow. They were holding hands. Christ." His eyes were glassy with gathering tears. He rubbed the backs of his hands over them and collected himself. "Do you know what that feels like?" he asked. "Seeing your old man with another woman. No, of course you don't. It was like a kick in the balls. Sorry."

"That's all right. Did your father see you?"

"No. I kept myself well enough hidden. Not that they had eyes for anyone but each other."

"What happened next?"

"Nothing. I left. I was so upset I just got in the van and drove around the countryside for a while. I remember stopping somewhere and walking by a river. It was very cold."

"Was the woman dark-skinned? Indian or Pakistani?"

Tom looked surprised. "No."

Susan took her notepad and pen out. "What did she look like?"

Tom closed his eyes. "I can see her now," he said, "just as clearly as I could then. She was young, much younger than Dad. Probably in her mid-twenties, I'd guess. Not much older than me. She was sitting down, so I couldn't really see her figure properly, but I'd say it was good. I mean, she didn't look fat or anything. She looked nicely proportioned. She was wearing a blouse made of some shiny white material and a scarf sort of thing, more like a shawl, really, over her shoulders, all in blues, whites and reds. It looked like one of those Liberty patterns. She had long fingers. I noticed them for some reason. Am I going too fast?"

"No," said Susan. "I've got my own kind of shorthand. Carry on."

"Long, tapered fingers. No nail varnish, but her nails looked well kept, not bitten or anything. She had blonde hair. No, that's not quite accurate. It was a kind of reddish blonde. It was piled and twisted on top with some strands falling loose over her cheeks and shoulders. You know the kind of look? Sort of messy but ordered."

Susan nodded. Hairstyles like that cost a fortune.

"She was extraordinarily good-looking," Tom went on. "Very fine, pale skin. A flawless complexion, like marble, sort of translucent. The kind where you can just about see the blue veins underneath. And her features could have been cut by a fine sculptor. High cheekbones, small, straight nose. Her eyes were an unusual shade of blue. They may have been contact lenses, but they were sort of light but very bright blue. Cobalt, I guess. Is that it?"

"It'll do. Go on."

"That's about all really. No beauty spots or anything. She was wearing long dangly earrings, too. Lapis lazuli. No rings, I don't think."

"That's a very good description, Tom. Do you think you could work with a police artist on this? I think we'd like to have a talk with this woman, and your description might help us find her."

Tom nodded. "No problem. I could paint her myself from memory if I had the talent."

"Good. We'll arrange something, then. Maybe this evening."

Tom took his watch out again. "I suppose I'd better be going home. Mum and Alison need my support."

"Did you ever challenge your father about what you saw?" Susan asked.

Tom shook his head. "I came close once, when he kept going on about how disappointed he was in me, how sick I was. I told him I was disappointed in him, too, but I wouldn't tell him why."

"What did he say?"

"Nothing. Just carried on as if I hadn't spoken."

"Does your mother know?"

He shook his head. "No. She doesn't know. I'm sure of it."

"Do you think she suspects?"

"Maybe. Who knows? She's been living in a bit of a dream world. I'm worried about her, actually. Sometimes I get the feeling that underneath all the lies she knows the truth but she just won't admit it to herself. Do you know what I mean?"

"Yes. What about Alison?"

"Alison's a sweet thing really, but she hasn't got a clue. Lives in her books. She's Brontë mad, is Alison, you know. Reads nothing but. And she's got notebooks full of her own stories, all in tiny handwriting like the Brontës did when they were kids. Made up her own world. I keep thinking she'll grow out of it, but ... I don't know ... she seems even worse since ... since Dad ..." He shook his head slowly. "No, she doesn't know. I wouldn't confide in her. I kept it all to myself. Can you imagine that? I still do. You're the first person I've told." He stood up. "Look, I really must be off."

"We'll be in touch about the artist, then."

"Yes. Okay. And ..."

"Yes?"

"Thanks," he said, then turned abruptly and hurried off.

Susan watched him go down the path, hands in pockets, shoulders slumped. She poured herself another cup of tea, stewed though it was, and looked out at the river. A beautiful insect with iridescent wings hovered a few feet above the water. Suddenly, a chaffinch shot out from one of the trees and took the insect in its beak in mid-air. Susan left her lukewarm tea and headed off to meet Sergeant Hatchley. The porn hunt awaited.

III

After Banks had gone for a swim in the hotel pool, taken a long sauna, and put away three cups of freshly brewed coffee and a plateful of bacon and eggs, courtesy of room service, he was feeling much better.

As he made a few phone calls, he tried to remember something that had been nagging away at him since the early hours, something he should do, but he failed miserably. At about the same time that Susan Gay was talking to Tom Rothwell, he went out for his first appointment, with Melissa Clegg.

The morning sun had burned off most of the rain, and the pavements had absorbed the rest, leaving them the colour of sandstone, with small puddles catching the light here and there. As wind ruffled the water's surface, golden light danced inside the puddles.

It wasn't as warm as it had been, Banks noticed. He had left his torn sports jacket at the hotel. All he wore on top was a light blue, open-neck shirt. He carried his notebook, wallet, keys and cigarettes in his briefcase.

A cool wind whispered through the streets, and there were plenty of dark, heavy clouds now lurking on the northern horizon behind the Town Hall. It looked like the region was in for some "changeable" weather, as the forecasters called it: sunny with cloudy periods, or cloudy with sunny periods.

He could drive to his appointment, he knew, but the one-way system was a nightmare. Besides, the city centre wasn't all that big, and the fresh air would help blow away the cobwebs that still clung to his brain.

Banks had grown quite fond of Leeds since he had been living in Yorkshire. It had an honest, slightly shabby charm about it that appealed to him, despite the new "Leeds-look" architecture— redbrick revival with royal blue trim—that had sprouted up everywhere, and despite the modern shopping centres and the yuppie developments down by the River Aire. Leeds was a scruff by nature; it wouldn't look comfortable in fancy dress, no matter what the price. And then there was Opera North, of course.

Avoiding City Square and the scene of the previous evening's debacle, he cut up King Street instead, walked past the recently restored Metropole Hotel, all redbrick and gold sandstone masonry, and along East Parade through the business section of banks and insurance buildings in all their jumbled glory. Here, Victorian Gothic rubbed shoulders with Georgian classicism and sixties concrete and glass. As in many cities, you had to look up, above eye level, to see the interesting details on the tops of the buildings: surprising gables where pigeons nested, gargoyles, balconies, caryatids.

As he walked along The Headrow past Stumps and the art gallery, he became aware again of the sharp pain in his knee, with which he had probably chipped a cheekbone or broken a jaw the previous evening.

He arrived at the Merrion Centre a couple of minutes early. Melissa Clegg had told him on the phone that she had a very busy day planned. She was expecting a number of important deliveries and had appointments with her suppliers. She could, however, allow him half an hour. There was a quiet coffee bar with outside tables, she told him, on the second level, up the steps over the entrance to Le Phonographique. She would meet him there at half past ten.

Banks found the coffee bar, and an empty table, with no trouble. At that time on a Wednesday morning, the Merrion Centre was practically deserted: especially the upper level, which seemed to have nothing but small offices and hairdressers.

Melissa Clegg arrived on time with all the flurry of the busy executive. When she sat down, she tucked her hair behind her ears. Today, she wore a pink dress cut square at her throat and shoulders.

The last thing on earth Banks felt he needed was another cup of coffee, but he took an espresso just to have something in front of him. Also, by the feel of his chest, he didn't need a cigarette, either, but he lit one nonetheless. The first few drags made him a bit dizzy, then it tasted fine.

"You look a bit the worse for wear," Melissa observed.

"You should have seen the other two," Banks said. He could tell by the way she laughed that she didn't believe him, just as he had expected. But he had also noticed the angry contusion high on his left cheek, just to the side of his eye, when he shaved that morning. Another result of his crash into the alley wall. He tried to keep his skinned knuckles out of sight, which made drinking coffee difficult.

"What can I do for you this time, Inspector, or Chief Inspector, is it?"

"Chief Inspector. I don't suppose you've heard anything from your husband?"

"Ex. Well, near as. No, I haven't. But he's hardly likely to get in touch with me. I still don't know why you're so worried. I'm sure he'll turn up."

"I don't think so, Mrs Clegg. Remember last time we met I asked you if you knew a Robert Calvert?"

"Yes. I said I didn't and I still don't."

"I'd appreciate it if you would keep this quiet for the moment, but we believe that Robert Calvert was also Keith Rothwell."

"I don't understand. Do you mean he had a false name, an alias?"

"Something like that. More, actually. He lived in Leeds, had a flat in the name of Robert Calvert. A whole other life. Mary Rothwell doesn't know, so—"

"Don't worry, I won't say anything. You've got me puzzled."

"We were, too. But the reason I'm telling you this is that your husband acted as a reference for Robert Calvert in the matter of his bank account and credit card. Also, ironically enough, Calvert listed his employer as Keith Rothwell."

"Curiouser and curiouser," said Melissa. "Daniel must have known about this double life, then?"

"It looks that way."

"Well, I certainly knew nothing about it. As I told you before, I haven't seen Keith Rothwell since Danny and I split up two years ago." She frowned. "I must say it surprises me that Daniel would risk doing something so obviously dishonest as that. Not that dishonesty is beneath him, but it seems too much of a risk for no return."

"We don't know what the returns were," Banks said. "How close are you and Daniel?"

"What do you mean?"

"Did he ever mention a woman called Marci Lapwing to you?"

"God, what a name. No. Who is she? His girlfriend?"

"Someone he's been seeing lately."

"Well, he wouldn't tell me about her, would he?"

"Why not?"

She shrugged. "He never does. Maybe he thinks I'd be jealous."

"Would you?"

"Look, I don't see what it has to do with anything, but no. It's over. O. V. E. R. We made our choices."

"Is there someone else?"

She blushed a little but met his gaze with steady eyes as she fingered the top of her dress over her freckled collarbone. "As a matter of fact there is. But I won't tell you anything more. I don't want him dragged into this. It's none of your business, anyway. Danny's probably run off with his bimbo."

"No. Marci Lapwing is still around. Never mind. Let's move on. How do you explain the two men who visited you?"

"I don't know. Perhaps her husband sent them?"

"Whose husband?"

"The bimbo's. Marci whatever-her-name-is."

"She's not married. Since we last talked," Banks said, lowering his voice, "things have taken several turns for the worse. We're talking about very serious matters indeed. It looks as if your husband might be implicated in murder, money-laundering, theft and fraud, and that he may be partly responsible for the savage beating of a young woman."

"My God ... I ..."

"I know. You didn't take all this seriously. Nor did you want to. Now will you?"

She began to fidget with her coffee-spoon. "Yes. Yes, of course. I assume you're talking about Keith Rothwell's murder?"

"Yes."

"And who has been beaten?"

"A friend of Mr Rothwell's. The way it looks, both Keith Rothwell and your husband were laundering money for a Mr X. We think we know his identity, but I'm afraid I can't reveal it to you. Rothwell was either stealing or threatening to talk, or both, and Mr X asked your husband to get rid of him."

She shook her head. "Danny? No. I don't believe it. He couldn't kill anyone."

"Hear me out, Mrs Clegg. He did as he was asked. Maybe his own life was threatened, we don't know. Immediately after he arranged to get rid of Keith Rothwell, he either became a threat himself, or he made off with a lot of illegal money, so Mr X sent two goons to track him down. Maybe he'd seen it coming and anticipated what they would do. At this point, there's a lot we can only speculate about."

"And that explains the two men?"

"Yes." Banks leaned forward and rested his arms on the table. "They visited your ex-husband's office, they visited you, then they visited a girl they saw me talking to. She was the one they beat up. Now tell me again, Mrs Clegg, have you ever seen or heard of a woman called Pamela Jeffreys? She was born here in Yorkshire, but her family came originally from Pakistan. She's about five foot four, slender figure, with almond eyes and long black hair that she sometimes wears tied back. She has a smooth, dark gold complexion and a gold stud through her left nostril. She's a classical musician, a violist with the Northern Philharmonia."

Banks watched Melissa's face as he described Pamela Jeffreys. When he had finished, she shook her head. "Honestly," she said, "I've never seen her, and Danny never mentioned anyone like that. She sounds impressive, but he doesn't go for that type."

"What type?"

"Bright women. Career women. It scared him to death when I started to make a success of the wine business. At first he could just look down on it as my little hobby. You said she was a classical musician?"

"Yes."

"He doesn't like classical music. All he likes is that bloody awful trad jazz. A woman like the one you describe would bore Danny to death. Besides, she sounds so gorgeous, I'm sure I'd remember her."

A gentle gust of wind blew through the centre, carrying the smells of espresso and fried bacon from the café. "Two more things," Banks said. "First, in the time you lived with your husband, did you ever come across any acquaintances, say, or clients of his whom you'd describe as shady?"

She laughed. "Oh, a tax lawyer has plenty of shady clients, Chief Inspector. That's what keeps him in business. But I assume you mean something other than that?"

"Yes. If Daniel did have anything to do with Keith Rothwell's death, he certainly didn't commit the murder himself, as you pointed out."

"That's true. The Daniel I know wouldn't have had the stomach for it."

"So he must have hired someone. You don't usually just walk into your local and say, 'Look chaps, I need a couple of killers. Do you think you could help me out?'"

Melissa smiled. "You might try it at a Law Society banquet. I'm sure you'd get a few takers. But I see what you mean."

"So he might have known someone who would consider the task, and it might have been someone he met through his practice.

I doubt very much that the two of you socialized with hit-men, but there might be someone who struck you as dangerous, perhaps?"

"Who knows who we socialized with?" Melissa said. "Who knows anything about anyone, when it comes right down to it? No-one immediately springs to mind, but I'll think about it, if I may."

"Okay." Banks passed on Alison Rothwell's vague description of the two men, especially the one with the puppy-dog eyes, the only distinguishing feature. "I'll be at the Holiday Inn here for the next day or so, or you can leave a message with Detective Inspector Blackstone at Millgarth."

"Is he the one who came over last night with my bodyguard?"

"No, that's Detective Sergeant Waltham. I don't honestly believe you're in any danger, Mrs Clegg—I think they're probably miles from here by now—but it's best to be on the safe side. Are you happy with the arrangement?"

"I didn't really understand all the fuss at first, but after what you've just told me I'll sleep easier tonight for knowing there's someone out there watching over me." She looked at her watch. "Sorry, Mr Banks. Time's pressing. You said you had two things to ask."

"Yes. The other is a bit more personal."

Melissa raised her eyebrows. "Yes?"

"I mean personal in the true sense, not necessarily embarrassing."

She frowned, still looking at him. It was a strong, attractive face with its reddish tan and freckles over the nose and upper cheeks; every little wrinkle around her grey-blue eyes looked as if it had been earned.

"We think Daniel Clegg has probably done a bunk with a lot of money," Banks began. "Enough to set him up for life, otherwise these goons wouldn't be so keen on finding him. But it's a bloody big world if you don't know where to look. The two of you shared your dreams at one stage, I suppose, like most married couples. Where do you think he would go? Where did he dream of living?"

Melissa continued to frown. "I see what you mean," she murmured. "That's an interesting question. Where's Danny's Shangri-la, his Eldorado?"

"Yes. We all have one, don't we?"

"Well, Danny wasn't much of a dreamer, to tell you the truth. He didn't have a lot of imagination. But whenever he talked of winning the pools and packing it all in, it was always Tahiti."

"Tahiti?"

"Yes. He was a big fan of *Mutiny on the Bounty*. Had every version on video. I think he liked the idea of those bare-breasted native girls serving him long, cool drinks in coconut shells." She laughed and looked at her watch again. "Look, Mr Banks, I'm sorry, but I really *do* have to go now. I've got a hell of a day ahead." She pushed her chair back and stood up.

Banks stood with her. "Of course," he said, shaking her hand.

"But if I can be any more help, I'll get in touch. I mean it. I never thought Danny was capable of real evil, but if what you say is true ..." She shrugged. "Anyway, I'll give what you said some thought. I ... just a minute."

Her brow furrowed and she turned her eyes up, as if inspecting her eyelashes. She looked at her watch again, bit her lip, then perched on the edge of the chair, knees together, clutching her briefcase to her chest. "There *was* someone. I really can't stay. I'm going to be late. I can't think of the name, but I might be able to remember if you give me a bit of time. He did have those sort of sad eyes, like a puppy, now I think of it."

Banks sat forward. "What were the circumstances?"

"I told you Danny doesn't do criminal work, but he is a solicitor, and apparently he was the only one this chap knew. According to Danny, they met in a pub, had a few drinks, got talking. You know how it is. This chap had been in the army or something, over in Northern Ireland. When he got himself arrested, Danny was the only one he knew to call on."

"What happened?"

"Danny referred him to someone else. I only remember because he came round to the house once. He wasn't too happy about the solicitor Danny passed him on to for some reason. I think it might have been the fee or something like that. They argued a bit, then Danny managed to calm him down. They had a drink, then the man left. I never saw or heard of him again. I'm sorry, I didn't really hear what was going on. Not that I'd remember now."

"How long ago was it?"

"A little over two years. Shortly before we separated."

"And you remember nothing more about this man?"

"No. Not off-hand."

"What pub did they meet in?"

"I can't remember. Isn't that odd? You mentioning about meeting a killer in a pub? What if it was him?"

"What was he arrested for?"

"It was something to do with assault, I think. A fight. I know it wasn't really serious. Certainly not murder or anything. Look, I really must go. I'll try and remember more, I promise."

"Just one thing," Banks said. "Can you remember the name of the solicitor your husband referred him to? We might be able to trace him through our records."

She compressed her lips in thought for a moment, then said, "Atkins. Of course, it would have been Harvey Atkins. He and Danny are good friends, and Harvey does a fair bit of criminal work."

"Thank you," Banks said, but she was already dashing away.

"I'll be in touch," she called over her shoulder.

Banks headed for the staircase. While he had been talking with Melissa Clegg, he had remembered what it was that had been nagging at him all morning. He decided to satisfy his curiosity before meeting Ken Blackstone. Things were moving fast.

TWELVE

I

"Take the scenic route," said Sergeant Hatchley. "We're not in a hurry."

Instead of going east to the A1 at the roundabout by the Red Lion Hotel, Susan headed south-west along the edge of the Dales through Masham, Ripon and Harrogate.

Hatchley didn't smoke at all during the journey, though he insisted she stop once at a café in Harrogate for a cup of coffee, during which he chain-smoked three cigarettes. It was very different from travelling with Banks. For a start, Banks liked to drive, and with him there was always music, sometimes tolerable, sometimes execrable. Hatchley preferred to sit with his arms crossed and look out of the window at the passing scenery, no doubt with visions of bare breasts flashing through what passed for his mind.

She wished she didn't have to work with men all the time. One crying jag or sharp response, and it was PMT; a day off for any reason meant it was "that time of the month." She had to put up with it without complaint, just take it all in her stride.

Maybe she was being unfair, though. Hatchley aside, the men she worked with were mostly okay. Phil Richmond, with whom she spent the most time, was a sweetheart. But Phil was leaving soon.

Superintendent Gristhorpe frightened her a little, perhaps because he made her think of her father, and she always felt like a silly little girl when he was around.

Banks, though, was like an older brother. And, like a brother, he teased her too much, especially about music when they were in the car. She was sure he played some terrible things just to make her uncomfortable. Right now, though, as she approached the busy

Leeds Ring Road, she would have welcomed something soothing to listen to.

Susan was building up a nice collection of classical music. Every month, she bought a magazine that gave away a free CD of bits and pieces of the works reviewed. It provided a breakdown of what to listen for at what points of time—like "6:25: The warm and sunny feeling of the spring day returns," or "4:57: Second theme emerges from interplay of brass and woodwinds." Susan found it very helpful, and if she liked the part she heard, she would buy the complete work, unless it was a lengthy and expensive opera. At the moment her favourite piece was Beethoven's "Pastoral" Symphony. She knew Banks would approve, but she was too embarrassed to tell him.

Susan went on to think about her talk with Tom Rothwell by the river, and about the agonies he must be going through. It was hard enough being homosexual anywhere, she imagined, but it would be especially tough in Yorkshire, where men prided themselves on their masculinity and women were supposed to know their place and stick to it.

There was a prime example of Yorkshire manhood sitting right next to her, she thought, all Rugby League, roast beef and pints of bitter. And she couldn't imagine what he could find offensive about her perfume. It certainly smelled pleasant enough to her, and she used it sparingly.

The traffic snarled up on the Ring Road, and Hatchley sat there with the tattered Leeds and Bradford A to Z on his lap squinting at signs. He was the kind of navigator who shouted, "Turn here!" just as you passed by the turning. After several misdirections and a couple of hair-raising U-turns, they pulled up outside candidate number one, a newsagent's shop at the edge of a rundown council estate in Gipton.

Two scruffy kids swaggered out as Susan and Hatchley went in. The girl behind the counter couldn't have been more than fifteen or sixteen. She was pale as a ghost and skinny as a rake. Her hair, brown streaked with silver, red and green, teetered untidily on top of her head, and unruly strands snaked down over her white neck and face, partly covering one over-mascaraed eye.

She looked as if she had a small, pretty mouth underneath the full and pouting one she had superimposed with brownish purple lipstick. Susan also noticed a pungent scent, which she immediately classified as cheap, not at all like her own. The girl rested her ring-laden fingers with the long crimson nails on the counter and slanted her bony shoulders towards them, head tilted to one side. She wore a baggy white T-shirt with "SCREW YOU" written in black across her flat chest.

"Mr Drake around, love?" Hatchley asked.

She moved her head a fraction; the hair danced like Medusa's snakes. "In the back," she said, without breaking the rhythm of her chewing.

He moved towards the counter and lifted the flap.

"Hey!" she said. "You can't just walk through like that."

"Can't I, love? Do you mean I have to be announced all formally, like?" Hatchley took out his identification and held it close to her eyes. She squinted as she read. "Maybe you'd like to get out your salver?" he went on. "Then I can put my calling card on it and you can take it through to Mr Drake and inform him that a gentleman wishes to call on him?"

"Sod off, clever arse," she said, slouching aside to let them pass. "You're no fucking gentleman. And don't call me love."

"Who have we got here, then?" Hatchley stopped and said. "Glenda Slagg, feminist?"

"Piss off."

They went through without further ceremony into the back room, an office of sorts, and Susan saw Mr Drake sitting at his desk.

Below the greasy black hair was the lumpiest face Susan had ever seen. He had a bulbous forehead, a potato nose and a carbuncular chin, over all of which his oily, red skin, pitted with blackheads, stretched tight, and out of which looked a pair of beady black eyes, darting about like tiny fish in an aquarium. His belly was so big he could hardly get close enough to the desk to write. A smell of burned bacon hung in the stale air, and Susan noticed a hotplate with a frying-pan on it in one corner.

When they walked in, he pushed his chair back and grunted, "Who let you in? What do you want?"

"Remember me, Jack?" said Hatchley.

Drake screwed up his eyes. They disappeared into folds of fat. "Is it ... ? Well, bugger me if it isn't Jim Hatchley."

He floundered to his feet and stuck out his hand, first wiping it on the side of his trousers. Hatchley leaned forward and shook it.

"Who's the crumpet?" Drake asked, nodding towards Susan.

"The 'crumpet,' as you so crudely put it, Jack, is Detective Constable Susan Gay. And show a bit of respect."

"Sorry, lass," said Drake, executing a little bow for Susan. She found it hard to hold back her laughter. She knew that old-fashioned sexism was alive and well and living in Yorkshire, but it felt strange to have Sergeant Hatchley defending her honour. Drake turned back to Hatchley. "Now what is it you want, Jim? You're not still working these parts, are you?"

"I am today."

Drake held his hands out, palms open. "Well, I've done nowt to be ashamed of."

"Jack, old lad," said Hatchley heavily, "you ought be ashamed of being born, but we'll leave that aside for now. Girlie magazines."

"Eh? What about 'em?"

"Still in business?"

Drake shifted from one foot to the other and cast a beady eye on Susan, guilty as the day is long. "You know I don't go in for owt illegal, Jim."

"Believe it or not, at the moment I couldn't care less. It's not you I'm after. And it's *Sergeant* Hatchley to you."

"Sorry. What's up, then?"

Hatchley asked him about the masked killer with the puppy-dog eyes. Drake was shaking his head before he had finished.

"Sure?" Hatchley asked.

"Aye. Swear on my mother's grave."

Hatchley laughed. "You'd swear night was day on your mother's grave if you thought it would get me off your back, wouldn't you, Jack? Nonetheless, I'll believe you, this time. Any ideas where we might try?"

"What have you got?"

"Shaved pussies, excited penises. Right up your alley, I'd've thought."

Drake turned up his misshapen nose in disgust. "Shaved pussies? Why, that's pretty much straight stuff. Nay, Jim, times have changed. They're all into the arse-bandit stuff or whips and chains these days."

"I'm not just talking about the local MPs, Jack."

"Ha-ha. Very funny. Even so."

Hatchley sighed. "Benny still in business?"

Drake nodded. "Far as I know. But he deals mostly in body-piercing now. Very specialized taste." He looked at Susan. "You know, love—pierced nipples, labia, foreskins, that kind of thing."

Susan repressed a shudder.

"Bert Oldham?" Hatchley went on. "Mario Nelson? Henry Talbot?"

"Aye. But you can practically sell the stuff over the counter, these days, Ji—Sergeant."

"It's the 'practically' that interests me, Jack. You know what the law says: no penetration, no oral sex and no hard-ons. Anyroad, if you get a whiff of him, phone this number." He handed Drake a card.

"I'll do that," said Drake, dropping back into his chair again. Susan thought the legs would break, but, miraculously, they held.

The girl didn't look up from her magazine as they went out. "Better give that reading a rest, love," said Hatchley. "It must be hell on your lips."

"Fuck off," she said, chewing gum at the same time.

Shit, thought Susan, it's going to be one of those days.

II

Banks was right, he saw, as he stood on the threshold of Robert Calvert's flat and surveyed the wreckage. The only difference between this and Pamela Jeffreys's flat was that there had been no human being hurt and no prized possessions utterly destroyed. Stuffing from the sofa lay strewn over the carpet, which had been partly rolled up to expose the bare floorboards. In places, wallpaper had been ripped down, and the television screen had been shattered.

So they had come back. It supported his theory. They obviously didn't know that Banks was a policeman, didn't know that Calvert's flat had already been thoroughly searched by professionals. If they had known, they would never have come here.

It was as he had suspected. They had started following him when he left Clegg's Park Square office on Monday morning. They must have seen the police arrive first, but from their point of view, the police arrived sometime *after* Banks, and he left alone, so there was no reason to make a connection, certainly none to suspect that *he* was a policeman. For all they knew, he could have been a friend of Betty Moorhead's, or a colleague of Clegg's.

Still looking for clues to Clegg's whereabouts, they had trailed him on his lunch date with Pamela and noted where she was rehearsing. One of them must have found out where she lived. They didn't know about the Calvert flat until Banks led them there, and they must have thought the place had something to do with Clegg. Finally, when Banks saw them from the window, they ran off, only to come back later and search the place when the coast was clear.

Where were they now? Already, their descriptions had been sent to other police forces, to the airports and ports. If the men had any sense, they would lie low for a while before trying to leave the country. But criminals don't always have sense, Banks knew. In fact, more often than not, they were plain stupid.

And what about Rothwell's killers? If the man Melissa Clegg remembered was involved—and it was a big if—then he was local. Was he the kind to stay put or run? And what about his partner?

No-one else was at home in the building, and there was no point looking over the rest of the flat. From the box at the corner of the street, Banks went through the motions of calling the local police to report the break-in, but he knew there was nothing they could do. He had no doubts as to *who* had done it; he just had to find them. Dirty Dick Burgess knew something, Banks believed, but he would talk only when he wanted and tell only as little as he needed.

When Banks had finished the call, he took a bus to Millgarth at the bottom of Eastgate. Over the road, on the site of the demolished Quarry Hill flats, stood the new West Yorkshire Playhouse with its "City of Drama" sign. It seemed uncannily appropriate, Banks thought, given the events of the past couple of days. Beyond the theatre, high on a hill, was Quarry House, new home of the Department of Health and Social Security, and already nicknamed "The Kremlin" by locals.

Ken Blackstone was in his office bent over a stack of paperwork. He pushed the pile aside and gestured for Banks to sit opposite him.

"No earth-shattering developments to report, before you get your hopes up," he said. "We're still no closer to finding Clegg or Rothwell's killers, but there's a couple of interesting points. First off, you might like to know that the lab boys say the dirt and gravel on the tires of Ronald Hamilton's Escort match that around Arkbeck Farm. They said a lot of other things about phosphates and sulphides or whatever, which I didn't understand, but it looks like the car the killers used. Rest of it was clean as a whistle. And airport security at Heathrow have found Clegg's red Jag in the long-stay car park."

"Surprise, surprise," said Banks.

"Indeed. Coffee?"

Banks's stomach was already grumbling from too much caffeine, so he declined. Blackstone went and poured himself a mug from a machine in the open-plan office and returned to his screened-off corner. There was a buzz of constant noise around them—telephones, computer printers, fax machines, doors opening and closing and the general banter of a section CID department—but Blackstone seemed to have carved himself a small corner of reasonably quiet calm.

Banks told him about Calvert's flat.

"Interesting," said Blackstone. "When do you think that happened?"

"I'd say before they went to Pamela's," Banks said. "Finding nothing there would put them in a fine mood for hurting someone. Is there any news from the hospital?"

Blackstone shook his head. "No change. She's stable, at least." He frowned at Banks and touched the side of his own cheek. "What about you? And I noticed you limping a bit when you came in."

"Slipped in the shower. Look, Ken, I might have a lead on one of Rothwell's killers." He went on quickly to tell Blackstone what Melissa Clegg had said about the mysterious client with the puppy-dog eyes that Clegg had passed on to Harvey Atkins.

Blackstone put the tip of a yellow pencil to his lower lip. "Hmm ..." he said. "We're already running a check on all Clegg's contacts and clients. We can certainly check the court records. At least we've got the brief's name, which helps a bit. Harvey Atkins is certainly no stranger around here. He's not a bad bloke, as lawyers go. It's a bit vague, though, isn't it? About two years ago, she says, something to do with assault, maybe? Do we know if the bloke was convicted?"

Banks shook his head. "I'm afraid we'll have to depend on the kindness of microchips."

Blackstone scowled. "Hang on a minute." He made a quick phone call and set the inquiry in motion. "They say it could take a while," he said. "It might be a long list."

Banks nodded. "What do you know about Tahiti?" he asked.

"Tahiti? That's where Captain Bligh's men deserted in the film. It's part of French Polynesia now, isn't it?"

"I think so. It's in the South Pacific at any rate. And Gauguin painted there."

"Why are you interested?"

Banks told him what Melissa Clegg had said.

"Hmm," said Blackstone. "It wouldn't do any harm to put a few inquiries in motion, check on flights, would it? Especially now we've found the car at Heathrow. A relative newcomer might stand out there. I'll see what I can do."

"Thanks. Anything else?"

"We finished the house-to-house in Pamela Jeffreys's street. Nothing really, except I think we've fixed the time. One neighbour remembered hearing some noise at about nine-fifteen Monday evening, which fits with what the doc said, and with Mr Judd's statement."

Banks nodded.

"The people on the other side were out."

"These neighbours," said Banks, "they said they just heard *some noise?*"

"Yes."

"Ken, imagine how much noise it must have made when they smashed that stuff. Imagine how Pamela Jeffreys must have screamed for help when she realized what was happening."

"I know, I know." Blackstone shook his head and sighed. "I suppose they would have gagged her."

"Still ..."

"Look, Alan, according to DC Hyatt, who talked to them, they said they thought it was the television at first. He asked them if she usually played her television set so loud, and they said no. Then they said they thought she was having a fight with her boyfriend. He asked them if that was a regular occurrence, too, and again they said no. Then they said, or implied, that dark-skinned people have odd forms of entertaining themselves and that we white folks had best leave them to it."

"They really said that?"

Blackstone nodded. "Words to that effect. They're the sort of people who wouldn't cross the street to piss on an Asian if she was on fire. And they don't want to get involved."

"And that's it?"

"Afraid so." Blackstone looked at his watch. "I don't know about you, but I'm a bit peckish. What do you say about lunch, on me?"

Banks didn't feel especially hungry, but he knew he ought to try to eat something if he were to keep going all day. "All right, you're on," he said. "But no curries."

III

The other shops were not much different from the first: usually with the windows barred or covered in mesh, and usually close to dilapidated, graffiti-scarred corporation estates or surviving pre-war terraces of back-to-backs in areas like Hunslet, Holbeck,

Beeston and Kirkstall. One moment the sun was out, the next it looked like rain. Around and around they drove, Hatchley flipping through the *A to Z*, which had now become so well-thumbed that the pages were falling out, missing turnings, looking for obscure streets. It was all depressing enough to Susan, and a far cry from the nice big semi at the top of the hill in Sheffield where she grew up.

But Hatchley, she noticed, seemed to relish the task, even though after another three visits they had got nowhere. His reputation for laziness, she was beginning to realize, might be unfounded. He certainly didn't like to waste energy, and usually took the line of least resistance, but he was hardly alone in that.

Susan had known truly lazy policemen—some of them had even made detective sergeant—but none of them were like Hatchley. They simply put in the time until the end of their shift, generally trying to stay out of the way of any situation that might generate paperwork. Hatchley was determined. When he was after something, he didn't let go until he got it.

The fifth shop was larger and more modern than the others, a kind of mini-market-cum-off-licence that sold milk, tinned foods, bread and all sorts of odds and ends as well as booze, newspapers and magazines. It was on Beeston Road, not far from Elland Road, where Leeds United played, and it was run, Hatchley said, by a man called Mario Nelson, who, as his name suggested, had an Italian mother and an English father.

It was immediately clear to Susan that Mario took after his father. She knew there were blond-haired Italians in the north of the country, but they didn't look as downright Nordic as Mario. Tall, slim, wearing a white smock, he looked far too elegant to be running a shop. In his early fifties, Susan guessed, he was handsome in a Robert Redford sort of way, and he looked as if he would be more comfortable being interviewed on a film set than unpacking a box of mushroom soup, which is what he was doing when they entered. When he saw Hatchley, a look of caution came to his ice-blue eyes. There was nobody else in the shop.

"Mario, old mate," said Hatchley. "Long time no see."

"Not long enough for me," muttered Mario, putting the box aside. "What can I do for you?"

"No need to be so surly. How's business?" Hatchley took out a cigarette and lit up.

"There's no smoking in here."

Hatchley ignored him. "I asked how's business?"

Mario stared at him for a moment, then broke off eye contact. "Fair to middling."

"Doing much special trade?"

"Don't know what you mean. Look, if you've just come to chat, I'm a busy man."

Hatchley looked exaggeratedly around the shop. "Doesn't look that way to me, Mario."

"There's more to running a shop than serving customers."

"Well, soon as you've answered our questions, you can get back to it." He described the man in the balaclava. "Ever seen anyone like that in here? Is he on your list?"

"It's a bit of a vague description."

"True, but concentrate on the eyes. They'd just about come up to your chin. Poor misguided bloke has an appetite for shaved pussy magazines, and I know you supply them."

"You've never proved that."

"Come off it! The only reason you're still in business is that you've done me a few favours over the years. Remember that. You're a filth-peddler. You know I don't like filth-peddlers, Mario. You know I rank them a bit below a dollop of dog-shit on my shoe."

Hatchley made some very interesting distinctions, Susan thought, some delicate moral judgments. Simple display of naked flesh was fine with him, obviously, but anything more was pornographic. Bit of a puritan, really, when it came down to it.

She watched Mario shift from foot to foot, and she saw something in his eyes other than wariness; she saw that he recognized Hatchley's description, or thought he did. Hatchley noticed it, too. And she saw fear.

Hatchley dropped his cigarette on the floor and ground it out. "Susan," he said, "would you go put up the 'Closed' sign, please?"

"You can't do that," said Mario, coming out from behind the counter and moving to stop Susan. Hatchley got in the way. He was about the same height and two stones heavier. Mario stopped. Susan went to the door and turned the sign over.

"Might as well drop the latch and pull the blinds down, too," said Hatchley, "seeing as it's such a quiet time."

Susan did as he said.

"Right." Hatchley turned to face Mario. "What's his name?"

"Whose name? I don't know what you're on about."

"We're not gormless, Susan and I. We're detectives. That means we detect. And I detect that you're lying. What's his name?"

Mario looked pale. Beads of sweat formed on his brow. Susan almost felt sorry for him. Almost. "Honest, Mr Hatchley, I don't know what you mean," he said. "I run an honest business here. I—"

But before he could finish, Hatchley had grabbed him by the lapels of his shop-coat and pushed him against the shelves. A jar of instant coffee fell to the floor and smashed; tins dropped and rolled all over; a packet of spaghetti noodles burst open.

"Watch what you're doing!" Mario cried. "That stuff costs money."

Hatchley pushed him up harder against the shelving, twisting the lapels. Mario's face turned red. Susan was worried he was going to have a heart attack or something. She wished she hadn't become part of this. Gristhorpe would find out, she knew, and she would be thrown off the force in shame. Outside, she heard somebody rattle the door. Do something, her inner voice screamed. "Sir," she said levelly. "Maybe Mr Nelson wants to tell us something, and he's having difficulty speaking."

Hatchley looked at Nelson and relaxed his grasp. "Is that so, Mario?"

Mario nodded as best he could under the circumstances. Hatchley let him go. A jar of pickled onions rolled off the shelf and smashed, infusing the air with the acrid smell of vinegar.

"Who is he?" asked Hatchley.

Mario massaged his throat and gasped for breath. "You ... shouldn't ... have ... done ... that," he wheezed. "Could have k-k-killed me. Weak heart. I c-c-could report you."

"But we both know you won't, don't we? Imagine trying to run an honest business with the local police breathing down your neck day and night. Come on, give us the name, Mario."

"I ... I don't know his name. J-just that he's been in occasionally."

"For your under-the-counter stuff? Shaved pussies?"

Mario nodded.

Hatchley shook his head. "I wouldn't believe it if I hadn't seen it with my own eyes," he said, "but you're lying again. After all this." He reached out for Mario's lapels.

"No!" Mario jumped back, dislodging a few more tins from the shelf. A bottle of gin fell and smashed. He put his hands out. "No!"

"Come on, then," said Hatchley. "Give."

"Jameson. Mr Jameson. That's all I know," said Mario, still rubbing his throat.

"I want his address, too. He's on one of your paper routes, isn't he? I'll bet one of your lads delivers his papers, maybe with a special colour supplement on Sundays, eh? Come on."

"No. I don't know."

"Be reasonable, Mario. It's no skin off your nose, is it? And it'll put you in good stead with the local bobbies. What's his address?"

Mario paused a moment, then went behind the counter and looked in the ledger where he kept the addresses for newspaper deliveries. "Forty-seven Bridgeport Road," he said. "But you won't find him there."

"Oh?"

"Cancelled his papers."

"How long for?"

"Three weeks."

"Since when?"

"Last Friday."

"Where's he gone?"

"I've no idea, have I? Off on his holidays, maybe."

"Don't come the clever bugger with me."

"I'm not. Honest."

"Is that all you know?" Hatchley moved forward and Mario backed off.

"I swear it. We're not mates or anything. He's just a customer. And do me a favour—when you do find him, don't tell him you found out from me."

"Scared of him?"

"He's got a bit of a reputation for scrapping, that's all. When he's had a few, like. I don't think he'd take kindly."

"Aye, all right, then," said Hatchley. "Susan, would you do the honours?"

Susan went over and unlocked the door. A red-faced old woman bustled in. "What's going on here? I've been waiting five minutes. My poor Marmaduke is going to starve to death if you—" She stopped talking, looked at the mess on the floor, then back at the three of them.

"Slight accident, Mrs Bagshot," said Mario, straightening his tie and smiling. "Nothing serious."

Hatchley bent down and grabbed a pickled onion. After a cursory check to make sure there was no broken glass clinging to it, he popped it in his mouth, smiled at Mrs Bagshot and left.

IV

After a light lunch in the police canteen with Ken Blackstone—a toasted cheese sandwich and a plastic container of orange juice—Banks set off back to the hotel. The weather was the same, fast-moving cloud on the wind, sun in and out casting shadows over the streets and buildings. He would have to do something about his jacket, he realized as he walked past the Corn Exchange. Maybe he could get it fixed this afternoon. The hotel should be able to help. Or maybe he should buy a new one.

He wasn't looking forward to explaining his adventures to Sandra, either. He hadn't phoned her last night, and she would probably be out until this evening. He could phone the gallery, he knew, but she would be busy. Besides, it would only worry her if he told her about the fight over the telephone. He might get his jacket fixed, but there would be no hiding the skinned knuckles and bruised cheekbone from Sandra, let alone the bruises that would soon show up on his side.

All he had to say was that two kids had tried to mug him, simple as that. It might not be the complete truth, but it certainly wasn't a lie. On the other hand, he wondered who he was trying to fool. If he couldn't talk to Sandra about what had happened, who could he talk to? Right now, he just didn't know.

A local train must have just come in, judging from the hordes issuing from the station and heading for the bus stops around City Square and Boar Lane. Banks picked up a *Yorkshire Evening Post* from the aged vendor, who was shouting out a headline that sounded like "TURKLE AN HONEST LIAR" but which, on reading, turned out to be "TWO KILLED IN HUNSLET FIRE." Banks refused the free packet of Old El Paso Taco Shells he was offered with his newspaper.

At the hotel, he found three messages: one to call Melissa Clegg at the wine shop; one to meet Sergeant Hatchley and Susan Gay at The Victoria, behind the Town Hall, as soon as possible; and one to call Ken Blackstone at Millgarth. First, he went to his room and phoned Melissa Clegg.

"Oh, Mr Banks," she said. "I didn't want to get your hopes up, but I've remembered his name, the man Daniel met in the pub."

"Yes?"

"Well, I knew there was something funny about it. After I left you I just couldn't get it out of my mind. Then I was filling some orders and I saw it written down. It came to me, just like that."

"Yes?"

"Irish whiskey. Funny how the mind works, isn't it?"

"Irish whiskey?"

"His name. It was Jameson. I'm sure of it."

Banks thanked her and called Ken Blackstone.

"Alan, we've got some names for you," Blackstone said. "Quite a lot, I'm afraid."

"Never mind," said Banks. "Is Jameson among them?"

Banks heard Blackstone muttering to himself as he went through the list. "Yes. Yes, there he is. Bloke called Arthur Jameson. Alan, what—"

"I can't talk now, Ken. Can you pull his file and meet me at The Victoria in about fifteen minutes? I assume you know where it is?"

"The Vic? Sure. But—"

"Fifteen minutes, then." Banks hung up.

THIRTEEN

I

It was foolish, Susan knew, but she couldn't help feeling butterflies in her stomach as she turned the corner where Courtney Terrace intersected Bridgeport Road at number thirty-five. It was mid-afternoon; there was no-one about. She felt completely alone, and the click of her heels, which seemed to echo from every building, was the only sound breaking the blanket of silence. Her instructions were simple: find out what you can about Arthur Jameson and his whereabouts.

In her blue jacket and matching skirt, carrying a briefcase and clipboard, she looked like a market researcher. A light breeze ruffled her tight blonde curls and a sudden burst of sun through the clouds dazzled her. She could smell rain in the air.

We know he's not at home, she repeated to herself. He has cancelled his papers for three weeks and gone on a long holiday on the proceeds earned from killing Keith Rothwell. He doesn't answer his telephone, and the two men observing the house over the past hour or so have seen no signs of occupation. So there's nothing to worry about.

But still she worried. She remembered Keith Rothwell kneeling there on the garage floor in his suit, his head blown to a pulp. She remembered the tattered pieces of the girlie magazine, ripped images of women's bodies, as if the killer had intended some kind of sick joke.

And she remembered what Ken Blackstone had told her about Jameson at the makeshift briefing in The Victoria. He had been kicked out of the army for rushing half-cocked, against orders, into an ambush that had killed two innocent teenage girls as well as one suspected IRA trigger-man. After that, he had drifted around Africa and South America as a mercenary. Then, back home, he had beaten an Irishman senseless in a pub because the man's Belfast accent hit a raw nerve. Since the GBH, he hadn't done much except work on building sites and, perhaps, the occasional hit, though there was no evidence of this. He had four A-levels and an incomplete degree in Engineering from the University of Birmingham.

Susan looked around her as she walked. Bridgeport Road was a drab street of dirty terrace houses with no front gardens. From each house, two small steps led right onto the worn pavement, and the tarmac road surface was in poor repair. At the back, she knew, each house had a small bricked-in backyard, complete with privy, full of weeds, and each row faced an identical row across an alley. A peculiar smell hung in the air, a mix of raw sewage and brewery malt, Susan thought, wrinkling her nose.

Outside one or two houses, lines of washing propped up by high poles hung out to dry right across the street. A woman came out of her house with a bucket and knelt on the pavement to scour her front steps. She glanced at Susan without much interest, then started scrubbing. If Jameson really is our man, Susan thought, he'll probably be looking for somewhere a bit more upmarket to live after he has laid low for a while.

There was nobody at home in the first two houses; the timid woman at number thirty-nine said she knew nothing about anyone else in the street; the man at number forty-one didn't speak English; the West Indian couple at number forty-three had just moved into the area and didn't know anyone. Number forty-five was out. Susan felt her heart beat faster as she lifted the brass lion's head knocker of number forty-seven, Jameson's house. She was sure the whole street could hear her heart and the knocker thumping in concert, echoing from the walls.

She had it all rehearsed. If the man with the puppy-dog eyes answered the door, she was going to lift up her clipboard and tell him she was doing market research on neighbourhood shopping habits: how often did he use the local supermarket, that kind of thing. Under no circumstances, Banks had said, was she to enter the house. As if she would. As her mother used to say, she wasn't as green as she was cabbage-looking.

But the heavy knocks just echoed in the silence. She listened. Nothing stirred inside. All her instincts told her the house was empty. She relaxed and moved on to number forty-nine.

"Yes?" An old lady with dry, wrinkled skin opened the door, but kept it on the chain.

Susan kept her voice down, even though she was sure Jameson wasn't home. She showed her card. "DC Susan Gay, North Yorkshire Police. I'd like to talk to you about your neighbour Mr Jameson, if I may."

"He's not at home."

"I know. Do you know where he is?"

The face looked at Susan for some time. She couldn't help but be reminded of reptile skin with slit lizard eyes peeping out of the dry folds.

The door shut, the chain rattled, and the door opened again. "Come in," the woman said.

Susan walked straight into the small living-room, which smelled of mothballs and peppermint tea. Everything was in shades of dark brown: the wallpaper, the wood around the fireplace, the three-piece suite. And in the fireplace stood an electric fire with fake coals lit by red bulbs. All three elements blazed away. There might be a chilly breeze outside, but the temperature was still in the mid-teens. The room was stifling, worse than Pratt's office. As the door closed, Susan suddenly felt claustrophobic panic, though she had never suffered from claustrophobia in her life. A heavy brown curtain hung from a brass rail at the top of the door; it swept along the floor with a long hissing sound as the door closed.

"What's Arthur been up to now?" the woman asked.

"Will you tell me your name first?"

"Gardiner. Martha Gardiner. What's he been up to? Here, sit down. Can I get you a cup of tea?"

Susan remained by the door. "No, thank you," she said. "I can't stop. It's very important we find out where Mr Jameson is."

"He's gone on his holidays, that's where. Has he done anything wrong?"

"Why do you keep asking me that, Mrs Gardiner? Would it surprise you?"

She chuckled. "Surprise me? Nowt much surprises me these days, lass. That one especially. But he's a good enough neighbour. When my lumbago plays me up he'll go to the shops for me. He keeps an eye on me, too, just in case I drop dead one of these days. It happens with us old folk, you know." She grabbed Susan's arm with a scrawny talon and hissed in her ear. "But I know he's been in jail. And I saw him with a gun once."

"A gun?"

"Oh, aye. A shotgun." She let go. "I know a shotgun when I see one, young lady. My Eric used to have one when we lived in the country, bless his soul. Young Arthur doesn't think I know about it, but I saw him cleaning it through the back window once. Still, he's always polite to me. Gives me the odd pint of milk and never asks for owt. Who am I to judge? If he likes to go off shooting God's innocent creatures, then he's no worse than many a gentleman, is he? Ducks, grouse, whatever. Even though he says he's one of that *green* lot."

"How long ago did you see him with the shotgun?"

"Couldn't say for certain. Time has a funny way of moving when you're my age. Couple of months, perhaps. Are you going to arrest him? What are you going to arrest him for? Who'll do my shopping?"

"Mrs Gardiner, first we've got to find him. Have you any idea where he went?"

"How would I know? On his holidays, that's what he said."

"Abroad?"

She snorted. "Shouldn't think so. Doesn't like foreigners, doesn't Arthur. You should hear him go on about the way this country's gone downhill since the war, all because of foreigners taking our jobs, imposing their ways. No, he's been abroad, he said, and had enough of foreigners to last him a lifetime. Hates 'em all. 'Foreigners begin at Calais, Mrs Gardiner, just you remember that.' That's what he says. As if I needed reminding. My Eric was in the war. In Burma. Never the same, after. England for the English, that's what Mr Jameson always says, and I can't say I disagree."

Susan gritted her teeth. "And all he told you was that he was going on holiday?"

"Aye, that's what he told me. Likes to drive around the English countryside. At least that's what he's done before. Sent me a post-card from the Lake District once. He wished me well and asked me to keep an eye on his place. You know, in case somebody broke in. There's a lot of that these days." She snorted. "Foreigners again, if you ask me."

"I don't suppose he left you a key, did he?"

She shook her head. "Just asked me to keep an eye out. You know, check the windows, try the door every now and then, make sure it's still locked."

"When did he leave?"

"Late Thursday afternoon."

"When did you last see him?"

"Just before he went. About four o'clock."

"Was he driving?"

"Of course he was."

"What kind of car does he drive?"

"A grey one."

"Did he take his shotgun with him?"

"I didn't see it, but he might have. I don't know. I imagine he'd want to shoot a few animals if he's on holiday, wouldn't he?"

Susan could feel the sweat itching behind her ears and under her arms. Her breathing was becoming shallow. She couldn't take much more of Mrs Gardiner's hothouse atmosphere. But there were other things she needed to know.

"What make was the car?"

"A Ford Granada. I know because he told me when he bought it."

"I don't suppose you know the number?"

"No. It's new, though. He only got it last year."

That would make it an "M" registration, Susan noted. "How was he dressed?" she asked.

"Dressed. Just casual. Jeans. A short-sleeved shirt. Green, I think it was. Or blue. I've always been a bit colour blind. One of those anoraks—red or orange, I think it was."

"And he drove off at about four o'clock on Thursday."

"Yes, I told you."

"Was he alone?"

"Aye."

"Do you have any idea where he was heading first?"

"He didn't say."

Susan needed to know about any friends Jameson might have entertained, but she knew if she stayed in the house a moment longer she would faint. She opened the door. The welcome draught of fresh air almost made her dizzy. Banks would want to question Mrs Gardiner further, anyway. They would need an official statement. Any other questions could wait. They had enough.

"Thank you, Mrs Gardiner," she said, edging out of the door. "Thank you very much. Someone else will be along to see you soon to take a statement."

And she hurried off down the street, heels clicking in the silence, to where Banks and the rest waited in their cars in the Tesco car park off the main road.

II

It took the locksmith all of forty-five seconds to open Arthur Jameson's door for Banks and Blackstone to get in. As it wasn't often that four detectives and two patrol cars appeared in Bridgeport Road, and as it was still a nice enough day, despite the occasional clouds, everyone who happened to be home at the time stood out watching, gathered on doorsteps, swapping explanations. The consensus of opinion very quickly became that Mr Jameson was a child molester, and it just went to show you should never trust anyone with eyes like a dog. And, some added, this kind of thing wouldn't happen if the authorities kept them locked up where they belonged, or fed them bromide with their cornflakes or, better still, castrated them.

Like Mrs Gardiner's, Jameson's front door opened directly into the living-room. But unlike the gloomy number forty-nine, this room had cream wallpaper patterned with poppies and cornflowers twined around a trellis. Banks opened the curtains and the daylight gave the place a cheery enough aspect. It smelled a little musty, but that was to be expected of a house that had been empty for almost six days.

Jameson's mug shot and a description of his car had already gone out to police all over the country. They had got the Granada's number quickly enough from the central Driver and Vehicle Licensing Centre in Swansea. Local police were warned *not* to approach him under any circumstances, simply to observe and report.

Hatchley and Susan Gay were taking a statement from the woman next door, whom they had managed to persuade, at Susan's insistence, to accompany them to the local station. Mrs Gardiner had, in fact, been quite thrilled to be asked to "come down to the station," just like on television, and had managed a regal wave to all the neighbours, who had whistled and whooped their encouragement as she got in the car. Things were on the move.

In the living-room, Banks and Blackstone examined a small bookcase filled with books on nature, the English heritage and the environment: rain forests, ozone layers, whaling, oil spills, seal-clubbing, the whole green spectrum. Jameson had a healthy selection on birds, flowers and wildlife in general, including Gilbert White's *Natural History of Selborne* and Kilvert's diaries. There were also a few large picture books on stately homes and listed buildings.

Blackstone whistled. "Probably a member of Greenpeace and the National Trust, as well," he said. "There'll be trouble if we arrest this one, Alan. Loves Britain's heritage, likes furry little animals and wants to save the seals. They'll be calling him the Green Killer, just you wait and see."

Banks laughed. "It's not every murderer you meet has a social conscience, is it?" he said. "I suppose we should take it as an encouraging sign. Loves animals and plants but has no regard for human life." He pulled a girlie magazine from down the side of a battered armchair. "Yes, it looks like we've got a real nature boy here."

After the living-room, they went into the kitchen. Everything was clean, neat and tidy: dishes washed, dried and put away, surfaces scrubbed clean of grease. The only sign of neglect was a piece of cheddar, well past its sell-by date, going green in the fridge. The six cans of Tetleys Bitter on the shelf above it would last for a long time yet.

As he looked in the oven, Banks remembered a story he had heard from Superintendent Gristhorpe's nephew in Toronto about a Texan who hid his loaded handgun in the oven when he went to Canada to visit his daughter and son-in-law, Canadian gun laws being much stricter than those in the USA. He forgot about it when he got back, until his wife started to heat up the oven for dinner the first night. After that, he always kept it in the fridge. Jameson didn't keep his shotgun in the oven or the fridge.

The first bedroom was practically empty except for a few cardboard boxes of small household appliances: an electric kettle, a Teasmade, a clock radio. They looked too old and well used to be stolen property. More likely things that had broken, things he hadn't got around to fixing or tossing out. There were also an ironing board and a yellow plastic laundry basket.

The other bedroom, clearly the one Jameson slept in, was untidy but basically clean. The sheets lay twisted on the bed, and a pile of clothes lay on the floor under the window. A small television stood on top of the dresser-drawers opposite the bed. All the cupboard held was clothes and shoes. Perhaps the soil expert might be able to find something on the shoes linking Jameson to Arkbeck Farm and its immediate area. After all, he had succeeded with the car. The only reading material on his bedside table was a British National Party pamphlet.

There was a small attic, reached through a hatch in the landing ceiling. Banks stood on a chair and looked around. He saw nothing but rafters and beams; it hadn't been converted for use at all.

Next, they opened the cistern and managed to get the side of the bath off, but Jameson had avoided those common hiding places.

Which left the cellar.

Banks never had liked cellars very much, or any underground places, for that matter. He always expected to find something gruesome in them, and he often had when he worked in London. At their very best, they were dark, dank, dirty and smelly places, and this one was no exception. The chill air gripped them as soon as they got down the winding steps and Banks smelled mould and damp coaldust. It must have been there for years, he thought, because the area was a smoke-free zone now, like most of the country. Thank the lord there was an electric light.

The first thing they saw was a bicycle lying in parts on the floor next to a workbench and a number of planks of wood leaning against the wall. Next to them hung a World War II gas mask and helmet.

Dark, stained brick walls enclosed a number of smaller storage areas, like the ones used for coal in the old days. Now they were empty. The only thing of interest was Jameson's workbench, complete with vice and expensive tool-box. On the bench lay a box of loose shot and a ripped and crumpled page from a magazine. When Banks rubbed his latex-covered index finger over the rough surface wood, he could feel grains of powder. He lifted up the finger and sniffed. Gunpowder.

There was a drawer under the bench and Banks pulled it open. Inside, among a random collection of screws, nails, electrical tape, fuse wire and used sandpaper, he found a half-empty box of ammunition for a 9mm handgun.

"Right, Ken," he said. "I think we've got the bastard, National Trust or not. Time to call in the SOCOs."

III

Banks cadged a lift with Blackstone back to Millgarth, where Susan and Hatchley were just about to take Mrs Gardiner home before returning to Eastvale. They had found out nothing more from her, Hatchley said as they stood at the doors ready to leave. It seemed that Jameson was a bit of a loner. He had had no frequent visitors, male or female, and she had seen no-one answering the vague description of his partner. Neither had the other neighbours, according to the results of the house-to-house.

Banks asked about Pamela Jeffreys's condition and was told there had been some improvement but that she was still in intensive care.

Christ, Banks thought, as he sat opposite Blackstone, it had been a long day. He felt shagged out, especially given his previous night's folly, which seemed light years ago now. He looked at his watch: ten to six. He wanted to go home, but knew he might not be able to make it tonight, depending on the developments of the next few hours. At least he could go back to the hotel and have a long bath, phone Sandra, listen to Classic FM and read the army and probation officer's reports on Jameson while he waited around. If nothing happened by, say, eight o'clock, then he would perhaps go back to Eastvale for the night.

He slipped the reports into his briefcase and again decided to walk back to the hotel. It was that twilight hour between the evening rush-hour and going-out-on-the-town time. The city centre was practically deserted; the shops had closed, workers had gone home, and only a few people lingered in the few cafés and restaurants still open in the arcades and pedestrian precincts off Vicar Lane and Briggate. The sun had at last won its day-long battle with cloud; it lay in proud gold pools on the dusty streets and pavements, where last night's rain was a dim memory; it cast black shadows that crept slowly up the sides of buildings; it reflected harshly in shop windows and glittered on the specks of quartz embedded in stone surfaces.

Back at the hotel, he picked up his jacket, which he had handed over to be mended before leaving for The Vic. There was one message for him: "Please come to Room 408 as soon as you get back, where you will find out some useful information." It wasn't signed.

That was odd. Informers didn't usually operate this way. They certainly didn't book rooms in hotels to pass along their information.

"Who's staying in room 408?" Banks asked, slipping his jacket on. After the obligatory refusal to give out such information on the part of the clerk, and the showing of a warrant card on the part of Banks, he discovered that the occupant of said room was a Mr Wilson. Very odd indeed. It was a common enough name, but Banks couldn't remember, offhand, any Mr Wilson.

He was tempted to ignore the message and carry on with what he planned, but curiosity got the better of him, as it always did.

When the lift stopped at the fourth floor, he poked his head through the doors first to see if there was anyone in the corridor. It was empty. He followed the arrow to room 408, took a deep breath and knocked. He debated whether to stand aside, but decided it was only in American films that people shot holes through hotel doors. Still, he found himself edging away a little, so he couldn't be seen through the peep-hole.

The door opened abruptly. Banks tensed, then let out his breath. Before him stood Dirty Dick Burgess.

"You again? What the hell?" Banks gasped. But before he could even enter the room Burgess had put on a leather jacket and taken him by the elbow.

"About bloody time, Banks," he said. "I'm sick of being cooped up in here. There's been developments. Come on, let's go get a drink."

FOURTEEN

I

Despite Burgess's protest that it would be full of commercial travellers and visiting rugby teams, Banks insisted on their drinking in the Holiday Inn's idea of a traditional English pub, the Wig and Pen. He did this because his car was nearby and he still held hopes of getting back to Eastvale that evening. As it turned out, Burgess seemed to take a shine to the place.

He sat at the table opposite Banks with his pint of McEwan's lager, lit a Tom Thumb and looked around the quiet pub. "Not bad," he said, tapping his cigar on the rim of the ashtray. "Not bad at all. I never did like those places with beams across the ceiling and bedpans on the walls."

"Bed warmers," Banks corrected him.

"Whatever. Anyway, what do you think of those two over there as a couple of potential bed warmers? Do you think they fancy us?"

Banks looked over and saw two attractive women in their late twenties or early thirties who, judging by their clothes, had dropped by for a drink after working late at one of the many Wellington Street office buildings. There was no doubt about it, the one with the short black hair and the good legs did give Burgess the eye and whisper something in her friend's ear.

"I think they do," said Burgess.

"Didn't you say something about developments?"

"What? Oh, yes." Burgess looked away from the women and leaned forward, lowering his voice. "For a start, Fraud Squad think they've found definite evidence in Daniel Clegg's books and records that Clegg and Rothwell were laundering money for Martin Churchill."

"That hardly counts as a development," Banks said. "We were already working on that assumption."

"Ah, but now it's more than an assumption, isn't it? You've got to hand it to those Fraud Squad boys, boring little fuckers that they are, they've been burning the candle at both ends on this one."

"Have you any idea why Churchill would use a couple of provincials like Rothwell and Clegg?"

"Good point," said Burgess. "As it happens, yes, I do know. Daniel Clegg and Martin Churchill were at Cambridge together, reading law. Simple as that. The old boy network. I'd reckon the one knew the other was crooked right from the start."

"Did they keep in touch over the years?"

"Obviously. Remember, Clegg's a tax lawyer. He's been using St Corona as a tax shelter for his clients for years. It must have seemed a natural step to call on him when Churchill needed expert help. You can launder money from just about anywhere, you know. Baby Doc used a Swiss lawyer and did a lot of his business in Canada. You can take it out or bring it into Heathrow or Gatwick by the suitcase-load, using couriers, or you can run it through foreign exchange, wire services, whatever. Governments keep coming up with new restrictive measures, but it's like plugging holes in a sieve. It's easy if you know how, and a tax lawyer and a financial consultant with a strong background in accounting certainly knew how."

"What made Clegg choose Rothwell as his partner?"

"How would I know? You can't expect me to do your job for you, Banks, now can you? But they clearly knew one another somehow. Clegg must have known that Rothwell was exceptionally good with finances and none too concerned about their source. Takes one to know one, as they say."

Burgess looked over at the two women, who had got another round of drinks, and smiled. The black-haired one crossed her long legs and smiled back shyly; the other put her hand over her mouth and giggled.

"My lucky night, I think," Burgess said, clapping his hands and showering cigar ash over his stomach. He had a disconcerting habit of sitting still for ages then making a sudden, jerky movement. "I'll say one thing for the north," he went on, "you've got some damned accommodating women up here. *Damned* accommodating. Look, why don't you get a couple more pints in, then I'll tell you something else that might interest you? And mine's lager, remember, not that pissy real ale stuff."

Banks thought about it. Two pints. Yes, he would be fine for driving back to Eastvale, if he got the chance. "All right," he said, and went to the bar.

"Okay," said Burgess, after his first sip. "The two men, the white one and the darkie who were following you around?"

Banks lit a cigarette. "You know who they are?"

"I've got to admit, I wasn't entirely truthful with you last time we met."

"When have you ever been?"

"Unfair."

"So you knew who they were last time we talked?"

"Suspected. Now we've got confirmation. They're Mickey Lanois and Gregory Jackson, two of Churchill's top enforcers. They came into Heathrow last Friday. The way it looks is that Churchill asked Clegg to get rid of Rothwell, and after he did it he took off with a lot of money, probably figuring that he might be next. Churchill heard about Clegg's scarpering pretty quickly and sent his goons to do some damage control. You know what their favourite torture is, Banks?"

Banks shook his head. He didn't want to know, but he knew Burgess would tell him anyway.

"They get a handful of those little glass tubes the doctors use to keep liquid in. What do you call them, phials, right? Really thin glass, anyway. And they put them in the victim's mouth, lots of them. Then they tape the mouth shut securely and beat him a bit about the face. Or her. Churchill himself thought that up. He likes to watch. Think about it."

Banks thought, swallowed and felt his throat constrict. "Been letting you practise it at the Yard, have they?" he asked.

Burgess laughed. "No, not yet. They're still running tests in Belfast. Anyway, the point is that we know who they are."

"No, that's not entirely the point," said Banks. "The point is where are they now and what are you going to do about them?"

Burgess shook his head. "That's a whole different ball game. We're talking about international politics here, politically sensitive issues. It's out of your hands, Banks. Accept that. All you need to know is that we know who they are and we're keeping tabs."

"Don't give me that politically sensitive crap," said Banks, stabbing out his cigarette so hard that sparks flew out of the ashtray. "These two men damn near killed a woman here a few days ago. You say they like to go around stuffing people's mouths full of glass, then you tell me to trust you, you're keeping tabs. Well, bollocks, that's what I say."

Burgess sighed. "Somehow, I knew you were going to be difficult, Banks, I just knew it. Can't you leave it be? They won't get away with it, don't worry."

"Do you know where they are now?"

"They won't get away with it," Burgess repeated.

Banks took a sip of his beer and held back his rage. There was something in Burgess's tone that hinted he had something up his sleeve. "What are you telling me?" Banks asked.

"That we'll get them. Or somebody will. But they'll go down quietly, no fuss, no publicity."

Banks thought for a moment. He still didn't trust Burgess. "Can I talk to them?" he asked, aware he was speaking through clenched teeth, still keeping his anger in check.

Burgess narrowed his eyes. "Got to you, did it? What they did to the girl? I've seen pictures of her, before and after. Nasty. I'll bet you fancied her, didn't you, Banks? Nice dusky piece of crumpet, touch of the tarbrush, probably knew a lot of those *Kama Sutra* tricks. Just your type. Tasty."

Banks felt his hand tighten on the pint glass. Why did he always let Burgess get to him this way? The bastard had a knack of touching on exactly the right raw nerve. Did it every time. "I'd just like to be there when you question them, that's all," he said quietly.

Burgess shrugged. "No problem. If it's possible, I'll arrange it. All I'm saying is no publicity on the Churchill matter, okay? Let your liberal humanist sentiments fuck this one up and you'll be in deep doo-doo, Banks, very deep doo-doo indeed."

"What about the press?"

"They can be dealt with. Have you ever considered that for every scandal you read about how many you don't? Do you think it's all left to chance? Don't be so bloody naïve."

"Come off it. You might be able to tape a few mouths shut, but even you can't guarantee that no hotshot investigative reporters aren't going to be all over this one like flies around shit."

Burgess shrugged. "Maybe they'll hear Churchill's been killed in a coup. Maybe they'll even see the body."

"Maybe it'd be best for everyone if he did get killed in a coup. Less embarrassing all round."

Burgess remained silent for a moment, glass in hand. Then he said, slowly, "And maybe he's got life insurance."

"Well, I suppose you'd know. Let's hope there's a good plastic surgeon on St Corona."

"Look," Burgess said, "let's stop pissing around. What I want from you is a promise that you won't talk to the press about the Churchill angle."

Banks lit another cigarette. What could he do? If Burgess were telling the truth, Mickey Lanois and Gregory Jackson would be caught and punished for their crimes. He could live with that. He would have to. Burgess certainly had a better chance of catching them than Banks did, by the sound of things. Perhaps they were even in custody already.

Also, with luck, Arthur Jameson and his accomplice would go down for the murder of Keith Rothwell. But was Burgess telling the full truth? Banks didn't know. All he knew was that he couldn't trust the bastard. It all sounded too easy. But what choice did he have?

"All right," he said.

Burgess reached over and patted his arm. "Good," he said. "Good. I knew I could depend on you to keep mum when it counts."

Banks jerked his arm away. "Don't push it. And if I find out you've been buggering me around on this one, my promise is null and void, okay?"

Burgess held up his hands in mock surrender. "Okay, okay."

"There is another thing."

"What's that?"

"Rothwell's killers. Lanois and Jackson didn't do that."

Burgess shook his head. "I'm not interested in them. They're not in my brief."

"So what happens when we catch Jameson, if we catch him?"

"Jameson?"

"Arthur Jameson. One of Rothwell's killers."

"I don't give a monkey's toss. That's up to you. I'm not interested. It's unlikely that this Jameson, whoever he is, knows anything about Churchill's part in the matter. He was probably just a hired killer working for Clegg, who has conveniently disappeared with a shitload of cash."

"Any ideas where?"

Burgess shook his head then jabbed his finger in the air close to Banks's chest. "But I can tell you one thing. Wherever he is, he won't be there for long. Churchill has the memory of an elephant, the reach of a giraffe and the tenacity of a bloody pit bull. He didn't get to bleed an entire country dry for nothing. It takes a special talent. Don't underestimate the man just because he's a butcher."

"So we write off Clegg?"

"I think he's already written himself off by double-crossing Churchill."

"And Jameson?"

"*If* he goes to trial, and *if* he talks—both big ifs, by the way—all he can say is that Clegg hired him to kill Rothwell. I doubt that Clegg would tell him the real reason. He might be a crooked lawyer, but I'm sure he still knows the value of confidentiality. He wouldn't want to let his hired killers know exactly how much money was involved, would he? It would make him too vulnerable by half. Anyway, I trust you'll have enough physical evidence to prosecute this Jameson when the time comes. If not, maybe we can fabricate some for you. Always happy to oblige." He held his hand up. "Only kidding. My little joke."

Burgess glanced over at the two women, who had got yet another round of drinks and seemed to be laughing quite tipsily. "Look," he said, "if I don't strike soon they'll be past it. Are you sure you won't join me? It'll be a laugh, and the wife need never know."

"No," said Banks. "No, thanks. I'm going home."

"Suit yourself." Burgess stretched back his shoulders and sucked in his gut. "Anything to liven up a miserable evening in Leeds," he said. "Once more unto the breach." And with that, he strutted over to their table, smiling, pint in hand. Banks watched them make room for him, then shook his head, drank up and left.

II

"What on earth happened to you?" asked Sandra when Banks walked into the living-room at about ten o'clock that evening.

"I had a slight disagreement with a couple of would-be muggers," Banks said. "Don't worry, I'm okay." And he left it at that. Sandra raised her dark eyebrows but didn't pursue it. He knew she wouldn't. She wasn't the mothering type, and she rarely gave him much sympathy when he whimpered through flu or moaned through a bad cold.

Banks walked over to the cocktail cabinet and poured a stiff shot of Laphroaig single malt whisky. Sandra said she'd have a Drambuie. A good sign. After that, he put on his new CD of Khachaturian's piano concerto and flopped onto the sofa.

As he listened to the music, he looked at Sandra's framed photograph over the fireplace: a misty sunset in Hawes, taken from the daleside above the town, all subdued grey and orange with a couple of thin streaks of vermilion. The unusual church tower, square with a turret attached to one corner, dominated the grey slate roofs, and smoke curled up from some of the chimneys. Banks sipped the peaty malt whisky and smacked his lips.

Sandra sat beside him. "What are you thinking?" she asked.

Banks told her about his meetings with Dirty Dick Burgess. "There's always some sort of hidden agenda with him," he said. "I'm not sure what he's up to this time, but there's not a hell of a lot I can do about it except wait and see. That's about all we can do now, wait."

"'They also serve ...'"

"I was thinking about the Rothwells on the drive home, too. How could a man lead an entire other life, away from his family, under another name?"

"Is that what happened?"

"Yes." Banks explained about Robert Calvert and his flat in Leeds, his fondness for gambling, women and dancing. "And Pamela Jeffreys said she was sure he wasn't a married man. She said she'd have been able to tell."

"Did she? Who's Pamela Jeffreys?"

"His girlfriend. It doesn't matter."

Sandra sipped her drink and thought it over. "It's probably not as difficult as you think for two people who live together on the surface to lead completely separate lives, one unknown to the other. Lord knows, so many couples have drifted so far apart anyway that they don't communicate any more."

Banks felt his chest tighten. "Are you talking about us?" he asked, remembering what Ken Blackstone had said about *his* marriage.

"Is that what you think?"

"I don't know."

Sandra shrugged. "I don't know, either. It was just a comment. But if the cap fits ... Think about it, Alan. The amount we see each other, talk to each other, we could both be living other lives. Mostly, we just meet in passing. Let's face it, you could be up to anything most of the time. How would I know?"

"Most of the time I'm working."

"Just like this Rothwell was?"

"That's different. He was away a lot."

"What about the last couple of nights? You didn't phone, did you?"

Banks sat forward. "Oh, come on! I tried. You weren't home."

"You could have left a message on the machine."

"You know how I hate those things. Anyway, it's not as if you didn't know where I was. You could easily have checked up on me. And it's not that often I'm away from home for a night or more."

"Secret lives don't always have to be lived at night."

"This is ridiculous."

"Is it? Probably. All I'm saying is we don't talk enough to know."

Banks slumped back and sipped his drink. "I suppose so," he said. "Is it my fault? You always seemed to handle my absences so well before. You understand the *Job* better than any other copper's wife I've met."

"I don't know," Sandra said. "Maybe it just took longer for the strain to work its way through. Or maybe it's just worse because *I'm* busy a lot now, too."

He put his arm around her. "I don't know what's been happening to us lately, either," he said, "but maybe we'll go away when this is all over."

He felt Sandra stiffen beside him. "Promises," she said. "You've been saying that for years."

"Have I?"

"You know you have. We haven't had a bloody holiday since we moved to Eastvale."

"Well, dust off your camera. I've got a bit of leave due and I might just surprise you this time."

"How long do you think the case will last?"

"Hard to say."

"There you are, then."

He stroked her shoulder. "Tell me you'll think about it."

"I'll think about it. Tracy comes back on Sunday."

"I know."

"Won't you be pleased to see her? Will you even be around to meet her at the airport?"

"Of course I will."

Sandra relaxed a little and moved closer. A very good sign. The Drambuie was clearly working. "You'd better," she said. "*She* phoned earlier tonight. She sends her love."

"How's she getting on?"

Sandra laughed. "She said it's not quite like *A Year in Provence* down there, but she likes it anyway. She hasn't bumped into John Thaw yet."

"Who?"

"John Thaw. You know, the actor who was in *A Year in Provence* on television? I liked him better as Morse."

"Who?"

She elbowed him in the ribs. "You know quite well who I'm talking about. I know you liked Morse. He used to be in *The Sweeney*, too, years ago, and you used to watch that down in London. Remember, in your old macho days? Didn't you even go drinking with him once?"

"What do you mean, 'old'?" Banks flexed his biceps.

Sandra laughed and moved closer. "I don't want to fight," she said. "Honest, I don't. Not since we've seen so little of one another."

"Me neither," said Banks.

"I just think we've got a few problems to deal with, that's all. We need to communicate better."

"And we will. How about a truce." He tightened his arm around her shoulder.

"Mmm. All right."

"I'll have to call the station and see if there's been any developments," he said.

But he didn't move. He felt too comfortable. His limbs felt pleasantly heavy and weary, and the warmth of the malt whisky flowed through his veins. The slow second movement started in its haunting, erotic way. Soon, the eerie flexatone entered and sent shivers up and down his spine. A cheap effect, perhaps, but sometimes effective if you happened to be in the right mood.

Banks drained his glass and put it on the table by the sofa. Sandra let her head rest between his shoulder and chest. Definitely a good sign. "Remember that silly film we saw on TV a while back?" he said. "The one where the couple has sex listening to Ravel's *Bolero*?"

"Hmm. It's called *10*. Dudley Moore and Bo Derek. And I don't think they were really listening. More like using it as background music."

"Well, I've never really liked *Bolero*. It's far too ordered and mechanical. It's got a kind of inevitability about it that's too predictable for my taste. I've always thought this Khachaturian piece would be a lot better to make love to. Much better. Wanders all over the place. You never really know where it's going next. Slow and dreamy at the start, with plenty of great climaxes later on."

"Sounds good to me. Have you ever tried it?"

"No."

Sandra moved her head up until she was facing him, her lips about two inches away. He swept back a strand of hair from her cheek and let his fingers rest on her cool skin. "I thought you had to call the station?" she said.

"Later," he said, stroking her cheek. "Later. Are the curtains closed?"

III

Boredom. They never told you about that down at the recruitment drives, thought PC Grant Everett as he rolled down the window of the patrol car and lit a cigarette. His partner, PC Barry Miller, was good about the smoking. He didn't indulge, himself, but he understood Grant's need to light up every now and then, especially on a quiet night like this one.

They were parked in a lay-by between Princes Risborough and High Wycombe. To the south, through the rear-view mirror, Grant could see the faint glow of the nearest town, while to the north only isolated lights twinkled from scattered farms and cottages. All around them spread the dark, rolling landscape of the Chilterns. It was an attractive spot on a nice day, especially in spring with the bluebells and cherry blossom out, but in the dark it seemed somehow forbidding, inhospitable.

A light breeze swirled the smoke out of the car. Grant inhaled deeply. It had just stopped raining and he loved the way the scent of rain seemed to blend with the tobacco and make it taste so much better. It was at moments like this when he understood why he smoked, despite all the health warnings. On the other hand, he never quite understood it when he got up after a night's chain-smoking in the pub and coughed his guts up for half an hour.

Next to him, Barry was munching on a Mars bar. Grant smiled to himself. Six foot two and sixteen stone already and the silly bugger still needed to feed his face with chocolate bars. Who am I to talk? Grant thought, sucking on his cigarette again. To each his own poison.

Grant felt sleepy and the cigarette helped keep him awake. He had never got used to shift work; his biological rhythms, or whatever they were, had never adapted. When he lay down his head in the morning as the neighbour's kids were going to school, the postman was doing his rounds and everyone else was off to work, he could never get to sleep. Especially if the sun were shining. And then there was Janet, bless her soul, doing her best, trying hard to be as quiet as she could around the house, and Sarah, only six months, crying for feeding and nappy-changing. And the bills to pay, and ... Christ, he wasn't going to think about that. At least the job got him out of the house, away from all that for a while.

A lorry rumbled by. Grant flicked the stub of his cigarette out of the window and heard it sizzle as it hit a puddle. Occasionally, voices cut through the static on the police radio, but the messages weren't for them.

"Shall we belt up and bugger off, then?" said Barry. He screwed up the wrapper of his Mars bar and put it in his pocket. Ever the careful one, Grant thought, with an affectionate smile. Wouldn't even be caught littering, wouldn't Barry.

"Might as well." Grant reached for his belt. Then they heard the squealing sound of rubber on wet tarmac. "What the fuck was that?"

On the main road, a north-bound car skidded as it turned the bend too fast, then righted itself.

"Shall we?" said Barry.

"My pleasure."

Grant loved it when the lights were flashing and the siren screaming. First he was pushed back in the seat by the force when he put his foot down, and then he felt as if he were taking off, seeming somehow to be magically freed from all the restraints of the road: not just the man-made rules, but the laws of nature. Sometimes, Grant even felt as if they were really taking off, wheels no longer on the ground.

But there was no chase to be had here; it was over before it began. The car was about two hundred yards ahead of them when its driver seemed to realize they meant business. He slowed down as they caught up and pulled over to the side of the road, spraying up water from the hedgerow. His number-plate was too muddy to read.

Grant pulled up behind him, and Barry got out to approach the car.

It wasn't likely to be much, Grant thought as he sniffed the fresh night air through the open window—maybe a drunk, maybe a few outstanding parking tickets—but at least it was *something* to relieve the boredom for a few minutes.

He could hear perfectly clearly when Barry asked the driver to turn off his ignition and present his driving documents. The driver did as he was told. Barry looked at the papers and passed them back. Next, he asked the man if he had been drinking. Grant couldn't hear the man's reply, but it seemed to satisfy Barry. Grant knew he would be listening for slurred words and sniffing for booze on the driver's breath.

After that, Barry asked the man where he had been and where he was going. Grant thought he heard the man mention Princes Risborough.

No other cars passed. The night was quiet and Grant caught a whiff of beech leaves and cherry wood on the damp air. He thought he heard some cows low in the distance and, farther still, a nightingale.

Then Barry asked the man to get out of the car and clean off his number-plate. Grant heard him explain patiently that it was an offence to drive with a number-plate that is "not easily distinguishable" and smiled to himself at the stilted, textbook phrase. But the man would get off with a caution this time; Barry seemed satisfied with his behaviour.

The man got back in the car and Grant heard Barry speak over his personal radio.

"465 to Control."

"465 go ahead."

"Ten nine vehicle check please."

The voices crackled unnaturally over the country night air.

"Pass your number."

"Mike four, three, seven, Tango Zulu Delta."

"Stand by."

Grant knew it would take three or four minutes for the operator to check the number on the computer, then, all being well, they could be on their way.

Barry and the driver seemed to be chatting amiably enough as they waited. Grant looked at the newly cleaned number-plate and reached idly for the briefing-sheet beside him. There seemed to be *something* familiar about it, something he ought to remember.

He ran his finger down the list of stolen cars. No, not there. He wouldn't remember any of those numbers; there were always too many of them. It had to be something more important: a vehicle used in a robbery, perhaps? Then he found it: M437 TZD, grey Granada.

Suddenly, he felt cold. The owner was wanted in connection with a murder in North Yorkshire. Possibly armed and dangerous. Shit. All of a sudden, Barry seemed to be taking a hell of a long time out there.

A number of thoughts passed quickly through Grant's mind, the first of which was regret that they didn't do things the American way. Get the guy out of the vehicle, hands stretched on the roof, legs apart, pat him down. "Assume the position, asshole!" Why pretend they were still living in a peaceful society where the local bobby was your best friend? Christ, how Grant wished he had a gun.

Should he go out and try get Barry to the car, use some excuse? He could say they'd been called to an emergency. Could he trust himself to walk without stumbling, to speak without stuttering? His legs felt like jelly and his throat was tight. But he felt so impotent, just watching. All he could hope was that the radio operator would understand Barry's predicament and give the guy a clean bill of health. According to the information on the sheet, the man, Arthur Jameson, didn't even *know* he was wanted.

The radio crackled back into life.

"Control to 465."

"Go ahead, over."

"Er ... Mike four, three, seven, Tango Zulu Delta ... No reports stolen. Er ... Do you require keeper details over?"

"Affirmative."

More static. Grant tensed in his seat, hand on the door-handle. Too many pauses.

"Keeper is Arthur Jameson, 47 Bridgeport Avenue, Leeds. Er ... is keeper with you over?"

"Affirmative. Any problem?"

She was blowing it, Grant sensed. Someone, probably the super, was standing over her trying to help her calmly get Barry back to the car and the driver on his way, but she was nervous, halting. It was all taking far too long, and if the suspect couldn't sense there was something wrong over the radio, then he was an idiot.

"No reports stolen."

"You already told me that, love," said Barry. "Is something wrong?"

"Sorry ... er ... 465 ... Stand by."

Grant tightened his grip on the door-handle. This was it. He wasn't going to stand around and let his partner, who had probably dozed off at the briefing and to whom the number obviously meant bugger-all, just stand there and take it.

But before he got the door half open, he saw Barry, all sixteen stone and six foot two of him, drop to the wet road clutching the side of his neck, from which a dark spray of blood fountained high and arced to the ground. Then he heard the shots, two dull cracks echoing through the dark countryside.

Left foot still in the car, right foot on the road, Grant hesitated. Mistake. His last thought was that it was so bloody unfair and pointless and miserable to die like this by a roadside outside High Wycombe. Then a bullet shattered the windscreen and took him full in the face, scattering blood, teeth and bone fragments all over the car. After its echo had faded, the Granada revved up and sped off into the night, and the nightingale sang again into the vacuum of silence the car left behind.

FIFTEEN

I

The sky was a sheet of grey shale, smeared here and there by dirty
rags of cloud fluttering over the wooded hillsides on a cool wind.
Rooks and crows gathered noisily in the roadside trees like shards
of darkness refusing to dispel. Even the green of the dense beech
forests looked black.

Banks and Sergeant Hatchley, who had driven through the
night at breakneck speed from Eastvale, stood and looked in silence
at the patrol car with the shattered windscreen and at the outline of
the body on the tarmac about six or seven feet ahead, near which dark
blood had coagulated in shallow puddles on the road surface. Close
by, Detective Superintendent Jarrell from the Thames Valley Police
paced up and down, shabby beige raincoat flapping around his legs.

The road had been cordonned off, and several patrol cars, lights
circling like demented lighthouses, guarded the edges of the scene,
where the SOCOs still worked. Local traffic had been diverted.

"It was a cock-up," Superintendent Jarrell growled, glaring at the
two men from Yorkshire the minute they got out of Banks's Cortina
and walked over to him. "A monumental cock-up."

Jarrell was clearly looking for somewhere to place the blame,
and it irritated the hell out of him that no matter how hard he tried,
it fell squarely on his own shoulders. The two PCs might have
made a mistake in not tattooing the Granada's number on their
memories, and the radio operator had certainly screwed up royally,
but in the police force, as in other hierarchical structures, when an
underling screws up, the responsibility goes to the top. You don't
blame the foot-soldiers, you blame the general, and *everybody* gets a
good bollocking, from the top down.

Banks knew that Ken Blackstone at West Yorkshire had followed correct procedure in getting a photograph, description and details about Arthur Jameson out to all divisions. And the point he had most emphasized was, "May be armed. Observe only. UNDER NO CIRCUMSTANCES ATTEMPT TO APPREHEND."

Jarrell's was one of those unfortunate faces in which the individual features fail to harmonize: long nose, small, beady eyes, bushy brows, a thin slit of a mouth, prominent cheekbones, receding chin, mottled complexion. Somehow, though, it didn't dissolve into total chaos; there was an underlying unity about the man himself that, like a magnetic field, drew it all together.

"Any update on the injured officer, sir?" Banks asked.

"What? Oh." Jarrell stopped pacing for a moment and faced Banks. He had an erect, military bearing. Suddenly the fury seemed to bleed out of him like air from a tire. "Miller was killed outright, as you know." He gestured at the outline and the surrounding, stained tarmac with his whole arm, as if indicating a cornucopia. "There's about seven pints of his blood here. Everett's still hanging on. Just. The bullet went in through his upper lip, just under the nose, and it seems to have been slowed down or deflected by cartilage and bone. Anyway, it didn't get a chance to do serious brain damage, so the doc says he's got a good chance. Bloody fool."

"If you don't mind my saying so, sir," Banks said, "it looks like they got into a situation they couldn't get out of. We had no reason to think Jameson knew we were onto him. Nor had we any reason to think he was a likely spree killer. We want him for a job he was hired to do cold-bloodedly. He must have panicked. I know it doesn't help the situation, sir, but the men *were* inexperienced. I doubt they'd handled much but traffic duty, had they?"

Jarrell ran his hand through his hair. "You're right, of course. They pulled him over on a routine traffic check. When Miller called in the vehicle number, the radio operator called the senior officer on the shift. He tried to talk her through it calmly, but ... Hell, she was new to the job. She was scared to death. It wasn't her fault."

Banks nodded and rubbed his eyes. Beside him, Hatchley's gaze seemed fixed on the bloody tarmac. When Banks had got the call close to two A.M.—his first night at home in days—he had first thought of taking Susan Gay, then, not without malice entirely, though affectionate malice, he had decided that it was time Sergeant Hatchley got his feet wet. He knew how Hatchley loved his sleep. Consequently, they hadn't said much on the way down. Banks had played Mitsuko Uchida's live versions of the Mozart piano sonatas, and Hatchley had seemed content to doze in the passenger seat, snoring occasionally.

Most chief inspectors, Banks knew, would have had someone else drive, but he was using his own car, the old Cortina, no longer produced now and practically an antique. And, damn it, he *liked* driving it himself.

"Seen enough here?" Jarrell asked.

"I think so."

"Me, too. Let's go."

Jarrell drove them down the road. "Believe it or not," he said, "this is very pretty countryside under the right circumstances."

About a mile along the road, towards Princes Risborough, Jarrell turned left onto a muddy farm track and bumped along until they got to a gate on the right, where he pulled up. A hedgerow interspersed with hawthorns shielded the field and its fence from view. Cows mooed in the next field.

The gate stood open, and as Banks and Hatchley followed Jarrell through, they both sank almost to their ankles in mud. Too late, Banks realized, he hadn't brought the right gear. He should have known to bring the wellingtons he always carried in the boot of his car. Like most policemen, he took pride in keeping his shoes well polished; now they were covered in mud and probably worse, judging by the prevalence of cows. He cursed and Jarrell laughed. Hatchley stood holding onto the gatepost trying to wipe most of it off on the few tufts of grass there. Banks looked at the muddy field dotted with cow-pats and didn't bother. They'd only get dirty again.

In the field, a group of men in white boiler suits and black wellington boots worked around a car that stood bogged down in the mud with its doors open. The air was sharp with the tang of cow-clap.

One of the men had propped a radio on a stone by the hedgerow, and it was tuned to the local breakfast show, at the moment featuring a golden oldie: Cilla Black singing "Anyone Who Had a Heart." One of the SOCOs sang along with it as he worked. The cows mooed even louder, demonstrating remarkably good taste, Banks thought. They weren't so far away after all. They were, in fact, all lying down in a group just across the field. Cows lying down. That meant it was going to rain, his mother always said. But it had rained already. Did that mean they'd been in the same position for hours? That it was going to rain again?

Giving up on folk wisdom, Banks turned instead to look at the abandoned Granada, the bottom of its chassis streaked with mud and cow-shit. It had been found, Jarrell said, just over an hour ago, while Banks and Hatchley had been in transit.

"Anything?" Jarrell shouted over to the team.

One of the men in white shook his head. "Nothing but the usual rubbish, sir," he said. "Sweet wrappers, old road maps, that sort of thing. He must have taken everything of use or value. No sign of any weapons."

Jarrell grunted and turned away.

"He'd hardly have left his guns, would he?" said Banks, "Not now he's officially on the run. I'd guess he probably had a rucksack or something with him in the car. Look, sir, you know the landscape around here better than I do. If you were him, where would you go?"

Jarrell looked up at the louring sky for a moment, as if for inspiration, then rubbed at the inside corner of his right eye with his index finger. "He has a couple of choices," he said. "Either head immediately for the nearest town, get to London and take the first boat or plane out of the country, or simply lie low." He pointed towards the hills. "A man could hide himself there for a good while, if he knew how to survive."

"We'd better cover both possibilities," Banks said. "He's spent time in the army, so he's probably been on survival courses. And if he heads for London, he'll likely know someone who can help him."

"Whatever he does, I'd say he'll most likely go across country first," said Jarrell. "He'd be smart enough to know that stealing a car or walking by the roadside would be too risky." He looked at his watch. "The shooting occurred at about half past twelve. It's half past six now. That gives him a six-hour start."

"How far could he get, do you reckon?"

"I'd give him about three miles an hour in this terrain, under these conditions," Jarrell went on. "Maybe a bit less."

"Where's the nearest station?"

"That's the problem," said Jarrell slowly. "This is close to prime commuter country. There's Princes Risborough, Saunderton and High Wycombe on the Chiltern Line, all nearby. If he heads east, he can get to the Northampton Line at Tring, Berkhamsted or Hemel Hempstead. If he heads for Amersham, he can even get on the underground, the Metropolitan Line. Unfortunately for us, there's no shortage of trains to London around here, and they start running early."

"Let's say he's managed about sixteen or seventeen miles," said Banks. "What's his best bet?"

"Probably the Chiltern Line. Plenty of trains and an easy connection with the underground. He could even be in London by now."

They started walking back to the car. "I can tell you one thing," said Banks. "Wherever he is, his shoes will be bloody muddy."

II

If. If. If. Such were Banks's thoughts as he followed Superintendent Jarrell into Jameson's rented cottage an hour or so later. *If* Everett and Miller hadn't stopped Jameson last night. *If* Jameson hadn't panicked and shot them. *If.*

In an ideal world, they would have tracked Jameson to this cottage through a cheque stub or a circled address in an accommodation guide. Quietly, they would have surrounded the place when they were certain Jameson was inside, then arrested him, perhaps as he walked out to his car, unsuspecting, without a shot being fired. For he *hadn't known.* That was the stinger; he hadn't known they were after him. Now, though, things were different. Now he was a dangerous man on the run.

As it turned out, they discovered that Jameson was renting a cottage just to the east of Princes Risborough through an Aylesbury estate agent shortly after the office opened at eight-thirty that Friday morning. Policemen were showing Jameson's photograph around and asking the same questions in every estate agent's, hotel and bed and breakfast establishment in Buckinghamshire, and the pair of DCs given the Aylesbury estate agents just happened to get lucky. Like Everett and Miller got unlucky. Swings and round-abouts. That was often the way things happened.

Jameson had simply driven off from Leeds on his holidays. Being a lover of nature, he had headed for the countryside. Why the Chilterns? It was anyone's guess. It could just as easily have been the Cotswolds or the Malverns, Banks supposed.

According to the estate agent, the man had simply dropped in one afternoon and asked after rental cottages in the area. He had paid a cash deposit and moved in. There was no need for subterfuge or secrecy. Arthur Jameson had nothing to fear from anyone. Or he wouldn't have had, were it not for a weakness for pornography, a fleeting contact with Daniel Clegg's estranged wife, Melissa, and Sergeant Hatchley's network of informers. He had either been careless about the wadding, or he thought it was a joke; they didn't know which yet. It hadn't shown up as a trademark in any other jobs over the past few years.

Last night he had probably gone into High Wycombe for a bite to eat, lingered over his dessert and coffee, maybe celebrated his new-found wealth with a large cognac, then headed back for the rented cottage, taking the bend a little too fast.

The cottage was certainly isolated. It stood just off a winding lane about two miles long, opposite a small, perfectly rounded tor. The lane carried on, passed another farmhouse about a mile further on, then meandered back to the main road.

From the mud on the floor, it looked very much as if Jameson had been there after the shooting. A bit of a risk, maybe, but the cottage wasn't far from his abandoned car. In the kitchen, yester-day's lunch dishes soaked in cold water, and breadcrumbs, cheese shavings and tiny florets of yellowed broccoli dotted the counter.

In the living-room, Jameson had left the contents of his suitcase strewn around, including a number of local wildlife guides beside a girlie magazine on the table. Hatchley picked up the magazine and flipped through it quickly, tilting the centrefold to get a better look. Then they all followed the mud trail upstairs.

At the bottom of the wardrobe, hardly hidden at all by the spare blankets Jameson had obviously used to cover them, lay a twelve-gauge shotgun wrapped in an oil-stained cloth, and a small canvas bag. Carefully, Banks leaned forward and opened the flap of the bag with the tip of a Biro. It was empty, but on the floor by the blankets lay a few used ten-pound notes. Banks visualized the hunted man hurriedly stuffing the notes into his pockets until they spilled over on the floor. The shotgun was obviously too big and awkward for him to take with him, but he was still armed with the handgun.

Banks pointed to the shotgun and the canvas bag. "Can we get this stuff to your lab?" he asked Jarrell. "That shotgun's probably evidence in a murder case."

Jarrell nodded. "No problem."

As Hatchley bent to pick up the shotgun, careful to handle only the material it was wrapped in, and as Banks reached for the canvas bag, a message for Jarrell crackled through on his personal radio.

"Jarrell here. Over."

"HQ, sir. Subject, Arthur Jameson, spotted at Aylesbury railway station at nine fifty-three A.M. Subject bought London ticket. Now standing on platform. Locals await instructions. Over."

"Has he spotted them?"

"They say not, sir."

"Tell them to keep their distance." Jarrell looked at his watch. It was ten o'clock. "When's the next train?" he asked.

"Twelve minutes past ten, sir."

"Which route?"

"Marylebone via Amersham."

"Thank you. Stand by." Jarrell turned to Banks and Hatchley. "We can pick up that train at Great Missenden or Amersham if you want," he said.

Banks looked first at Hatchley, then back at Jarrell. "Come on, then," he said. "Let's do it."

III

Banks and Hatchley boarded the train separately at Amersham at ten thirty-two. Reluctantly, Superintendent Jarrell, being the local man, had agreed to stay behind and co-ordinate the Thames Valley end of the operation.

Neither Banks nor Hatchley looked much like a policeman that morning. Waking miserably to the middle-of-the-night phone call, Banks had put on jeans, a light cotton shirt and a tan sports jacket. Over this, he had thrown on his Columbo raincoat. Even though he had done his best to clean the mud off his shoes with a damp rag, it still showed.

Sergeant Hatchley wore his shiny blue suit, white shirt and no tie; he looked as if he had been dragged through a hedge backwards, but there was nothing unusual in that.

They had been told by the Transport Police, who had spotted Jameson, that the suspect still resembled his photograph except that he had about two days' growth around his chin and cheeks. He looked like a rambler. He was wearing grey trousers of some light material tucked into walking boots at the ankles, a green open-neck shirt and an orange anorak. Nice of him, Banks thought, dressing so easy to spot. He was also carrying a heavy rucksack, which no doubt held his gun and money, amongst other things.

The train rattled out of the station. Banks managed to find a seat next to a young woman who smiled at him briefly as he sat down, then went back to reading her copy of *PC Magazine*. Banks had his battered brown leather briefcase with him, and its chief contents were his omnibus paperback copy of Waugh's *Sword of Honour* and his Walkman. He opened the book at the marker and started to read, but every so often he glanced at the man in the green short-sleeve shirt who sat about four seats down, over to his left. The rucksack and the orange anorak lay on the luggage rack above.

The train moved in a comforting rhythm, but Banks couldn't help feeling tense. He left the Walkman in his briefcase because he was too distracted to listen to music.

They could probably take Jameson right now, he thought. He and Jim Hatchley. Just approach quietly from behind like anyone

going to the toilet and grab an arm each. The gun, surely, was up
in the rucksack on the luggage rack.

But it wasn't worth the risk. Something could go wrong.
Jameson could hold the entire coach hostage. It didn't bear thinking about. This way was far safer and would, with a little patience,
skill and luck, guarantee success.

Banks and Hatchley had got on the train simply to keep an eye
on Jameson. At the station, Superintendent Jarrell had talked to the
Yard, who promised that there would be a number of plainclothes
officers waiting at Marylebone, mixed in with the crowds. These
men were experts at surveillance, and they would keep Jameson in
sight, no matter how he travelled, without being spotted, until he
arrived at his final destination, be it hotel or house.

Some were posing as taxi-drivers, and, with luck, Jameson
would get into one of their cabs. Banks had every intention of
trying to keep up with the chase, but it was comforting to know
that if he lost sight of Jameson, someone else would have him.
There were plainclothes officers at all the stops on the way, too,
in case he got off, but Jameson had bought a ticket for London
and it was almost certain that was where he was heading. Given
his past, he would likely know someone there who could help
get him out of the country. What Banks hoped—and this was
one of the main reasons for letting their quarry go to ground—
was that Jameson would lead them to his accomplice in the
Rothwell murder.

As the train rattled out of Rickmansworth, Jameson got up and
walked past Banks on his way to the toilet. Banks looked down at
his book, not registering the words his eyes passed over. While
Jameson was gone, he stared at the khaki rucksack and held himself
back. How easy it would be, he thought, just to take it, then grab
Jameson when he came back. But he had to keep thinking like a
policeman, not give in to the maverick instinct, however strong.
This way, with a little patience, the catch might be bigger.

And there was another reason. The gun might not be in the
rucksack. Jameson's trousers were of the bulky, many-pocketed kind
favoured by ramblers. Banks had glanced quickly as he went by and
hadn't been able to discern the weight or outline of a gun, but it

could be there, and there were too many civilians present to make the risk worthwhile. Best wait. He thought of how much money there might be in the rucksack and smiled at how ironic it would be if someone snatched it while Jameson was having a piss.

Jameson came back. They passed Harrow and entered a landscape of factory yards, piles of tires and orange oil drums, pallets, warehouses, schoolyards full of screaming kids, bleak housing estates, concrete overpasses. Before long, the people in the carriage were standing up to get their jackets and bags as the train rumbled slowly into Marylebone station, all anxious to be first off.

Banks spotted Hatchley ahead of him, his head above most people in the crowd that shuffled through the ticket gate. Jameson had his anorak on now and was easy to keep in sight. Banks noticed him look around and lick his lips every now and then, sad, cruel puppy-dog eyes scanning the station forecourt.

But there was nothing to see. Nothing out of the ordinary. The uniformed Transport Police went about their business as usual, people leafed through magazines at the bookstall or headed for the buffet, checked the schedule displays, ran for trains. Carts of luggage and mail threaded in and out of the crowds, announcements about forthcoming departures came over the public-address system in the usual monotone echoing from the roof, where pigeons nested. To Banks, the station smelled of diesel oil and soot, though the age of steam was long gone.

Jameson made his way through the exit and managed to get a taxi. That was their first stroke of good fortune. If things went according to plan, the driver would be a DC; if not, then a taxi crawling through London traffic was easy enough for even a one-legged septuagenarian on foot to follow.

Banks opened the door of the next taxi, Hatchley beside him now. Banks was dying to jump in and say, "Follow that taxi!" but the driver didn't want to let them in. He leaned over and tried to pull the door shut, holding up a police ID card. "Sorry, mate," he said. "Police business. There's another one behind." Just in time, Banks managed to get his own card out. "Snap," he said. "Now open the fucking door."

"Sorry, sir," said the driver, eyes on the road, following Jameson's cab through the thick traffic on Marylebone Road. "I wasn't to know. They never said to expect a DCI jumping in the cab."

"Forget it," said Banks. "I'm assuming it's one of your men driving in the taxi ahead?"

"Yes, sir. DC Formby. He's a good bloke. Don't worry, we're not going to lose the bastard."

With excruciating slowness, the taxis edged their way south towards Kensington, along the busy High Street and down a side street of five- or six-storey white buildings with black metal railings at the front. Jameson's taxi stopped outside one that announced itself a HOTEL on the smoked glass over the huge shiny black doors. Across the street came the sound of drilling where workmen stood on scaffolding renovating the building opposite. The air was dry with drifting stone dust and thick with exhaust fumes. Jameson got out, looked around quickly and went into the hotel. His taxi drove off.

"Right," said Banks. "Looks like we've run the bastard to earth. Now we wait for the reinforcements."

IV

For grey, the hotel manager could have given John Major a good run for his money. His suit was grey; his hair was grey; his voice was grey. He also had one of those faces—receding chin, goofy teeth, stick-out ears—that attract such abusive and bullying attention at school. At the moment, his face was grey, too.

He reminded Banks of Parkinson, a rather unpleasant large-nosed boy who had been the butt of ridicule and recipient of the occasional thump in the fourth form. Banks had always felt sorry for Parkinson—had even defended him once or twice—until he had met him later in life, fully transformed into a self-serving, arrogant and humourless Labour MP. Then he felt Parkinson probably hadn't been thumped enough.

The manager had obviously never seen so many rough-looking, badly dressed coppers gathered in one place since they stopped showing repeats of *The Sweeney*. Jeans abounded, as did leather jackets, anoraks, blousons, T-shirts and grubby trainers. There wasn't a uniform, a tie or a well-polished shoe in sight, and the only suit was Sergeant Hatchley's blue polyester one, which was so shiny you could see your face in it.

It was also obvious that a number of the officers were armed and that two of them wore bullet-proof vests over their T-shirts.

Short of the SAS, Police Support Units or half a dozen Armed Response Vehicles, none of which the police authorities wanted the public to see mounting a major offensive on a quiet Kensington hotel on a Thursday lunch-time, these two were probably the best you could get. Vest One, the tallest, was called Spike, probably because of his hair, and his smaller, more hirsute associate was called Shandy. Spike was doing all the talking.

"See, squire," he said to the wide-eyed hotel manager, "our boss tells us we don't want a lot of fuss about this. None of this evacuating the area bollocks you see on telly. We go in, we disarm him nice and quiet, then bob's your uncle, we're out of your hair for good. Okay? No problems for us and no bad publicity for the hotel."

The manager, clearly not used to being called "squire," swallowed, bobbing an oversize Adam's apple, and nodded.

"But what we do need to do," Spike went on, "is to clear the floor. Now, is there anyone else up there apart from this Jameson?"

The manager looked at the keys. "Only room 316," he said. "It's lunch-time. People usually go out for lunch."

"What about the chambermaids?"

"Finished."

"Good," said Spike, then turned to one of the others in trainers, jeans and leather jacket. "Smiffy, go get number 316 out quietly, okay?"

"Right, boss," said Smiffy, and headed for the stairs.

Spike tapped his long fingers on the desk and turned to Banks. "You know this bloke, this Jameson, right, sir?" he said.

Banks was surprised he had remembered the honorific. "Not personally," he said, and filled Spike in.

"He's shot a policeman, right?"

"Yes. Two of them. One's dead and the other's still in the operating room waiting to find out if he's got a brain left."

Spike slipped a stick of Wrigley's spearmint gum from its wrapper and popped it in his mouth. "What do you suggest?" he asked between chews.

Banks didn't know if Spike was being polite or deferential in asking an opinion, but he didn't get a chance to find out. As Smiffy came down the stairs with a rather dazed old dear clutching a pink dressing-gown around her throat, the phone rang at the desk. The manager answered it, turned even more grey as he listened, then said, "Yes, sir. Of course, sir. At once, sir."

"Well?" Spike asked when the manager had put the phone down. "What's put the wind up you?"

"It was *him*. The man in room 324."

"What's he want?"

"He wants a roast beef sandwich and a bottle of beer sent up to his room."

"How'd he sound?"

"Sound?"

"Yeah. You know, did he seem suspicious, nervous?"

"Oh. No, just ordinary."

"Right on," said Spike, grinning at Banks. "Opportunity knocks." He turned back to the manager. "Do the doors up there have those peep-hole things, so you can see who's knocking?"

"No."

"Chains?"

"Yes."

"No problem. Right," said Spike. "Come with me, Shandy. The rest of you stay here and make sure no-one gets in or out. We got the back covered?"

"Yes, sir," one of the blousons answered.

"Fire escape?"

"That, too, sir."

"Good." Spike looked at Banks. "I don't suppose you're armed?"

Banks shook his head. "No time."

Spike frowned. "Better stay down here then, sir. Sorry, but I can't take the responsibility. You probably know the rules better than I do."

Banks nodded. He gave Spike and Shandy a floor's start, then turned to Sergeant Hatchley. "Stay here, Jim," he said. "I don't want to lead you astray."

Without waiting for an answer, he slipped into the stairwell. One of the Yard men in the lobby noticed but made no move to stop him. At the first-floor landing, Banks heard someone wheezing behind him and turned.

"Don't worry, I'm not deaf," said Hatchley. "I just thought you might like some company anyway."

Banks grinned.

"Mind if I ask you what we're doing this for?" Hatchley whispered, as they climbed the next flight.

"To find out what happens," said Banks. "I've got a funny feeling about this. Something Spike said."

"You know what curiosity did."

They reached the third floor. Banks peeked around the stairwell and put his arm out to hold Hatchley back.

Glancing again, Banks saw Spike point at his watch and mouth something to Shandy. Shandy nodded. They drew their weapons and walked slowly along the corridor towards Jameson's room.

The worn carpet that covered the floor couldn't stop the old boards creaking with each footstep. Banks saw Spike knock on the door and heard a muffled grunt from inside.

"Room service," said Spike.

The door rattled open—on a chain, by the sound of it. Someone—Spike or Jameson—swore loudly, then Banks saw Shandy rear back like a wild horse and kick the door open. The chain snapped. Spike and Shandy charged inside and Banks heard two shots in close succession, then, after a pause of three or four seconds, another shot, not quite as loud.

Banks and Hatchley waited where they were for a minute, out of sight. Then, when Banks saw Spike come out of the room and lean against the door jamb, he and Hatchley walked into the corridor. Spike saw them coming and said, "It's all over. You can go in now, if you like. Silly bugger had to try it on, didn't he?"

They walked into the room. Banks could smell cordite from the gunfire. Jameson had fallen backwards against the wall and slid down into a perfect sitting position on the floor, legs splayed, leaving a thick red snail's trail of blood smeared on the wallpaper. His puppy-dog eyes were open. His face bore no expression. The front of his green shirt, over the heart, was a tangle of dark red rag and tissue, spreading fast, and there was a similar stain slightly above it, near his shoulder. His hands lay at his side, one of them holding his gun. Another dark wet patch spread between his legs. Urine.

Banks thought of the chair at Arkbeck Farm, where this man had scared Alison Rothwell so much that she had wet herself. "Jesus Christ," he whispered.

"We'd no choice," Spike said behind him. "He had his gun in his hand when he came to the door. You can see for yourself. He fired first."

Two shots, in close succession, followed by another, sounding slightly different. Two patches of spreading blood. "Our boss tells us we don't want a lot of fuss about this."

Banks looked at the two policemen, sighed and said, "Give my regards to Dirty Dick."

Shandy came back with a not very convincing, "Who's that?"

Spike grinned, rubbed the barrel of his gun against his upper thigh, and said, "Will do, sir."

SIXTEEN

I

Banks had always hated hospitals: the antiseptic smells, the
starched uniforms, the mysterious and unsettling pieces of shiny
equipment around every corner—things that looked like modern
sculpture or instruments of torture made of articulated chrome.
They all gave him the creeps. Worst of all, though, was the way the
doctors and nurses seemed to huddle in corridors and doorways
and whisper about death, or so he imagined.

It was Saturday afternoon, 21st May, just over a week since
Rothwell's murder and two days after Jameson's shooting, when
Banks walked into Leeds Infirmary.

He had spent Thursday night in London, then headed back to
Amersham for his car the next morning. After spending a little time
with Superintendent Jarrell, Banks and Hatchley had driven back to
Eastvale that Friday evening and arrived a little after nine.

On Saturday morning, he had to go into Leeds to consult with
Ken Blackstone and wrap things up. After their pub lunch, he had
taken a little time off to go and buy some more compact discs at the
Classical Record Shop and pay a sick visit before heading back to
Eastvale for Richmond's farewell bash. Sandra was off with the
Camera Club photographing rock formations at Brimham Rocks, so
he was left to his own devices for the day.

Banks paused and looked at the signs, then turned left. At last,
he found the right corridor. Pamela Jeffreys shared a room with one
other person, who happened to be down in X-ray when Banks
called. He pulled up a chair by the side of the bed and put down
the brown paper package he'd brought on the table. Pamela looked
at it with her one good eye. The other was covered in bandages.

"Grapes," said Banks, feeling embarrassed. "It's what you bring when you visit people in hospital, isn't it?"

Pamela smiled, then decided it hurt too much and let her face relax.

"And," Banks said, pulling a cassette from his pocket, "I made you a tape of some Mozart piano concertos. Thought they might cheer you up. Got a Walkman?"

"Wouldn't go anywhere without it," Pamela said out of the side of her mouth. "It's a bit difficult to get the headphones on with one hand, though." She directed his gaze to where her bandaged right hand lay on the sheets.

He set the cassette on the bedside table beside the grapes. "The doctor says you're going to be okay," he said.

"Hm-mm," murmured Pamela. "So they tell me." It came out muffled, but Banks could tell what she said.

"He said you'll be playing the viola again in no time."

"Hmph. It might take a bit longer than that."

"But you *will* play again."

She uttered a sound that could have been a laugh or a sob. "They broke two fingers on my right hand," she said. "My bowing hand. It's a good thing they know bugger all about musical technique. If they'd broken my wrist that might really have put an end to my career."

"People like that aren't chosen for their intelligence, as a rule," said Banks. "But the important thing is that there's no permanent damage to your fingers, or to your eye."

"I know, I know," she said. "I ought to think myself lucky."

"Well?"

"Oh, I'm okay, I suppose. Mostly just bored. There's the tapes and the radio, but you can't listen to music all day. There's nothing else to do but watch telly, and I can stomach even less of that. Reading still hurts too much with just one good eye. And the food's awful."

"I'm sorry," Banks said. "And I'm sorry about that day in the park."

She moved her head slowly from side to side. "No. My fault. You had to ask. I overreacted. Is this an official visit? Have you come about the men? The men who hurt me?"

"No. But we know who they are. They won't get away with it."

"Why have you come?"

"I ... that's a good question." Banks laughed nervously and looked away, out of the window at the swaying tree-tops. "To see you, I suppose," he said. "To bring you some grapes and some Mozart. I just happened to be in the area, you know, buying CDs."

"What did you get?"

Banks showed her: Keith Jarrett playing Shostakovitch's 24 preludes and fugues; Nobuko Imai playing Walton's viola concerto. She raised her eyebrow. "Interesting." Then she tapped the Walton. "It's beautiful if you get it right," she said. "But so difficult. She's very good."

"It says in the notes that the viola is an introvert of an instrument, a poet-philosopher. Does that describe you?"

"My teacher told me I had to be careful not to get overwhelmed by the orchestra. That tends to happen to violas, you know. But I manage to hold my own."

"How long are they going to keep you here?"

"Who knows? Another week or so. I'd get up and go home right now but I think my leg's broken."

"It is. The right one."

"Damn. The prettiest."

Banks laughed.

"Did you catch the men who killed Robert?" she asked. "Was it the same ones?"

Banks gave her the gist of what had happened with Jameson, avoiding the more lurid details.

"So one got away?" she said.

"So far."

"That's not bad going."

"Not bad," Banks agreed. "Fifty per cent success rate. It's better than the police average."

"Will you get a promotion out of it?"

He laughed. "I doubt it."

"Don't look so worried," she said, resting her bandaged hand on his. "I'll be all right. And don't blame yourself ... you know ... for what happened to me."

"Right. I'll try not to." Banks felt his eyes burn. He could see her name bracelet and the tube attached to the vein in her wrist. It made him feel squeamish, even more so than seeing Jameson's body against the wall in the hotel room. It didn't make sense: he could take a murder scene in his stride, but a simple intravenous drip in a hospital made him queasy.

Pamela was right. She would be fine. Her wounds would heal; her beauty would regenerate. In less than a year she would be as good as new. But would she ever recover fully inside? How would she handle being alone in the house? Would she ever again be able to hear someone walking up the garden path without that twinge of fear and panic? He didn't know. The psyche regenerates itself, too, sometimes. We're often a damn sight more resilient than we'd imagine.

"Will you come and see me again?" she asked. "I mean, when it's all over and I'm home. Will you come and see me?"

"Sure I will," said Banks, thinking guiltily of the feelings he had had for Pamela, not sure at all.

"Do you mean it?"

He looked into her almond eye and saw the black shape of fear at its centre. He swallowed. "Of course I mean it," he said. And he did. He leaned forward and brushed his lips against her good cheek. "I'd better go now."

II

Why was he born so beautiful?
Why was he born so tall?
He's no bloody use to anyone,
He's no bloody use at all.

Richmond took the Yorkshire compliment, delivered in shaky harmonies by Sergeant Hatchley and an assorted cat's choir of PCs, very well, Banks thought, especially for someone who listened to music that sounded like Zamfir on Valium.

"Speech! Speech!" Hatchley shouted.

Embarrassed, Richmond gave a sideways glance at Rachel, his fiancée, then stood up, cleared his throat and said, "Thank you. Thank you all very much. And thanks specially for the CD-ROM. You know I'm not much at giving speeches like this, but I'd just like to say it's been a pleasure working with you all. I know you all probably think I'm a traitor, going off down south—" Here, a chorus of boos interrupted his speech. "But as soon as I've got that lot down there sorted out," he went on, "I'll be back, and you buggers had better make sure you know a hard drive from a hole in the ground. Thank you."

He sat down again, and people went over to pat him on the back and say farewell. Everyone cheered when Susan Gay leaned forward and gave him a chaste kiss on the cheek. She blushed when Richmond responded by giving her a bear-hug.

They were in the back room of the Queen's Arms on Saturday night, and Banks leaned against the polished bar, pint of Theakston's in his hand, with Sandra on one side and Gristhorpe on the other. Someone had hung balloons from the ceiling. Cyril had hooked up the old jukebox for the occasion, and Gerry and the Pacemakers were singing "Ferry Across the Mersey."

Banks knew he should have been happier to see the end of the Rothwell case, but he just couldn't seem to get rid of a niggling feeling, like an itch he couldn't reach. Jameson had killed Rothwell. True. Now Jameson was dead. Justice had been done, after a fashion. An eye for an eye. So forget it.

But he couldn't. The two men who had beaten Pamela Jeffreys hadn't been caught yet. Along with Jameson's accomplice, that left three on the loose. Only a twenty-five per cent success rate. Not satisfactory at all.

But it wasn't just that. Somehow, it was all too neat. All too neat and ready for Martin Churchill to slip into the country one night with a new face and a clean, colossal bank account and retire quietly to Cornwall, guarding the secrets of those in power to the grave. Which might not be far off. Banks wouldn't be surprised if someone from MI6 or wherever slipped into Cornwall one night and both Mr Churchill *and* his insurance had a nasty accident.

Susan Gay walked over from Richmond's table and indicated she'd like a word. Banks excused himself from Sandra and they found a quiet corner.

"Sorry for dragging you away from the festivities, sir," Susan said, "but I haven't had a chance to talk to you since you got back. There's a couple of things you might be interested in."

"I'm listening."

Susan told him about her talk with Tom Rothwell after the funeral, about his homosexuality and what he had seen his father do that day he followed him into Leeds. "The artist came in on Wednesday evening, sir, and we managed to get the impression in the papers on Thursday, while you were down south."

"Any luck?"

"Well, yes and no."

"Come on, then. Don't keep me in suspense."

"We've found out who she is. Her name's Julia Marshall and she lives in Adel. That's in north Leeds. She's a schoolteacher. We got a couple of phone calls from colleagues. Apparently, she was a quiet person, shy and private."

"Was?"

"Well, I shouldn't say that, really, sir, but it's just that she's disappeared. That's all we know so far. I just think we should find her, that's all," she said. "Talk to her friends. I don't really know why. It's just a feeling. She might know something."

"I think you're right," said Banks. "It's a loose end I'd like to see tied up as well. There are too many bloody disappearances in this case for my liking. Is there anything else?"

"No. But it's not over yet, is it, sir?"

"No, Susan, I don't think it is. Thanks for telling me. We'll follow up on it first thing tomorrow. For now, we'd better get back to the party or Phil will think we don't love him."

Banks walked back to the bar and lit a cigarette. The music had changed; now it was the Swinging Blue Jeans doing "Hippy, Hippy Shake" and some of the younger members of the department were dancing.

Banks thought about Tom Rothwell and his father. Susan had been sharp to pick up on that. It didn't make sense, given Rothwell's *other* interests, that he should be so genuinely upset that his son didn't want to be an accountant or a lawyer. On the other hand, perhaps nothing was more of an anathema, an insult, to a confirmed heterosexual philanderer than a gay son.

"Penny for them?" Sandra said.

"What? Oh, nothing. Just thinking, that's all."

"It's over, Alan. Leave it be. It's another feather in your cap. You can't solve the whole world's problems."

"It feels more like a lead weight than a feather. I think I'll have another drink." He turned and ordered another pint. Sandra had a gin and tonic. "You're right, of course," he said, standing the drink on the bar. "We've done the best we can."

"You've done *all* you can. It's being pipped at the post by Dirty Dick that really gets your goat, isn't it?" Sandra taunted. "You two have got some kind of macho personal vendetta going, haven't you?"

"Maybe. I don't know. I won't say it's a good feeling, knowing the bastard's got his way."

"You did what you could, didn't you?"

"Yes."

"But you still think Burgess has won this time, and it pisses you off, doesn't it?"

"Maybe. Yes. Yes, it bloody well does. Sandra, the man had someone *shot*."

"A cold-blooded murderer. Besides, you don't know that."

"You mean I can't prove it. And we're not here to play vigilantes. If Burgess had Jameson shot, you can be damn sure it wasn't just an eye for an eye. He was making certain he didn't talk."

"*Men*," said Sandra, turning to her drink with a long-suffering sigh.

Gristhorpe, who had been listening from the other side, laughed and nudged Banks in the ribs. "Better listen to her," he said. "I can understand how you feel, but there's no more you can do, and there's no point making some kind of competition out of it."

"I know that. It's not that. It's ... oh, maybe Sandra's right and it is macho stuff. I don't know."

At that moment, Sergeant Rowe, who had been manning the front desk across the street, pushed through the crowd of drinkers and said to Banks, "Phone call, sir. He says it's important. Must talk to you in person."

Banks put his pint glass back on the bar. "Shit. Did he say who?"

"No."

"All right." He turned to Sandra and pointed at his pint. "Guard that drink with your life. Back in a few minutes."

He couldn't ignore the call; it might be an informer with important information. Irritated, nonetheless, he crossed Market Street and went into the Tudor-fronted police station.

"You can take it in here, sir," said Rowe, pointing to an empty ground-floor office.

Banks went in and picked up the receiver. "Hello. Banks here."

"Ah, Banks," said the familiar voice. "It's Superintendent Burgess here. Remember me? What do you want first, the good news or the bad?"

Speak of the devil. Banks felt his jaw clench and his stomach start to churn. "Just tell me," he said as calmly as he could.

"Okay. You know those two goons, the ones that beat up the tart of colour?"

"Yes. Have you got them?"

"We-ell, not exactly."

"What then?"

"They got away, slipped through our net. That's the bad news."

"Where did they go?"

"Back home, of course. St Corona. That's the good news."

"What's so good about that?"

"Seems they didn't realize they'd become *persona non grata* there, or whatever the plural of that is."

"And?"

"Well, I have it on good authority that they've both been eating glass."

"They're dead?"

"Of course they're bloody dead. I doubt they'd survive a diet like that."

"How do you know this?"

"I told you. Good authority. It's the real McCoy. No reason to doubt the source."

"Why?"

"Ours is not to reason why, Banks. Let's just say that their bungling around England drawing attention to themselves didn't help much. Things are in a delicate balance."

"Did you know in advance that they were out of favour? Did you let them slip out of the country, knowing what would happen? Did you even try to find them?"

"Oh, Banks. You disappoint me. How could you even think something like that of me?"

"Easy. The same way I think you sent Spike and Shandy down to Kensington to make damn sure Arthur Jameson didn't survive to say anything embarrassing in court."

"I told you, Jameson wasn't in my brief."

"I know what you told me. I also know what happened in that hotel room. They shot the bastard down, Burgess, and you're responsible."

"*Superintendent* Burgess, to you. And he shot first is what I heard. That's the official version, at any rate, and I don't see any reason not to believe it. As our cousins over the pond would say, it was a 'righteous shoot.'"

"Bollocks. They shot him twice then fired off a round from his gun to make it look like he fired first. Apart from the shots, do you know what gave them away?"

"No, but I'm sure you're going to tell me."

"They left the gun in his hand for me to see. Procedure is that you disarm a suspect *first thing*, whether you think he's dead or not."

"Well, hurray for you, Sherlock. Don't you think they might have got careless in the heat of the moment?"

"No. Not with their training."

"But it doesn't matter, does it? You weren't there, officially, were you? In fact you were ordered to stay on the ground floor. Anyway, I don't think we need to go into all that tiresome stuff, do we? Do you really want me to have to pull rank? Believe it or not, I *like* you, Banks. Life would be a lot duller without you. I wouldn't want to see you throw your career down the tubes over this. Take my word for it, *nobody* will take kindly to your rocking the boat. The official verdict is the only one that counts."

"Not to me."

"Leave it alone, Banks. It's over."

"Why does everyone keep telling me that?"

"Because it's true. One more thing. And don't interrupt me. We found an address book in Jameson's stuff and it led us to an old ex-army crony of his called Donald Pembroke. Ring any bells?"

"No."

"Anyway, it seems this Pembroke just inherited a lot of money, according to his neighbour. The first thing he did was buy a fast sports car, cash down according to the salesman. Two days later he lost control on a B road in Kent—doing eighty or ninety by all accounts—and ran it into a tree."

"And?"

"And he's dead, isn't he? What's more, there's no way you can put it down to me. So don't say there's no justice in the world, Banks. Goodbye. Have a good life." Burgess hung up abruptly, leaving Banks to glare into the receiver. He slammed it down so hard that Sergeant Rowe popped his head around the door. "Everything all right, sir?"

"Yes, fine," said Banks. He took a deep breath and ran his hand through his short hair. "Everything's just bloody fine and dandy." He sat in the empty office gaining control of his breathing. Susan's words echoed in his mind. *"It's not over yet, is it, sir?"* No, it bloody well wasn't.

SEVENTEEN

I

Banks sat at a *tavérna* by the quayside sipping an ice-cold Beck's and smoking a duty-free Benson and Hedges Special Mild. When he had finished his cigarette, he popped a *dolmáde* into his mouth and followed it with a black olive. One or two of the locals, mostly mustachioed and sun-leathered fishermen, occasionally glanced his way during a pause in their conversation.

It was a small island, just one village built up the central hillside, and though it got its share of tourists in season, none of the big cruise ships came. Banks had arrived half an hour ago on a regular ferry service from Piraeus and he needed a while to collect his thoughts and get his land-legs back again. He had a difficult interview ahead of him, he suspected. He had already contacted the Greek police. Help had been offered, and the legal machinery was ready to grind into action at a word. But Banks had something else he wanted to try first.

By Christ, it was hot, even in the shade. The sun beat down from a clear sky, a more intense, more saturated blue than Banks had ever seen, especially in contrast to the white houses, shops and *tavérnas* along the quayside. A couple of sailboats and a few fishing craft were moored in the small harbour, bobbing gently on the calm water. It was hard to describe the sea's colour; certainly there were shades of green and blue in it, aquamarine, ultramarine, but in places it was a kind of inky blue, too, almost purple. Maybe Homer was right when he called it "wine-dark," Banks thought, remembering his conversation with Superintendent Gristhorpe before the trip. Banks had never read *The Odyssey*, but he probably would when he got back.

He paid for his food and drink and walked out into the sun. On his way, he popped into the local police station in the square near the harbour, as promised, then set off along the dirt track up the hill.

The main street itself was narrow enough, but every few yards a side-street branched off, narrower still, all white, cubist, flat-roofed houses with painted shutters, mostly blue. Some of the houses had red pantile roofs, like the ones in Whitby. Many people had put hanging baskets of flowers out on the small balconies, a profusion of purple, pink, red and blue, and lines of washing hung over the narrow streets. By the roadside were poppies and delicate lavender flowers that looked like morning glories.

Mingled with the scents of the flowers were the smells of tobacco and wild herbs. Banks thought he recognized thyme and rosemary. Insects with red bodies and transparent wings flew around him. The sun beat relentlessly. Before Banks had walked twenty yards, his white cotton shirt stuck to his back. He wished he had worn shorts instead of jeans.

Banks looked ahead. Where the white houses ended halfway up the hillside, scrub and rocky outcrops took over. The house he wanted, he had been told, was on his right, a large one with a high-gated white wall and a shaded courtyard. It wasn't difficult to spot, now about fifty yards ahead, almost three-quarters of the length of the road.

He finally made it. The ochre gate was unlocked, and beyond it, Banks found a courtyard full of saplings, pots of herbs and hanging plants by a *krokalia* pathway of black and white pebbles winding up to the door. Expensive, definitely. The door was slightly ajar, and he could hear voices inside. By the plummy tones, it sounded like the BBC World Service news. He paused a moment for breath, then walked up to the door and knocked.

He heard a movement inside, the voices stopped, and in a few seconds someone opened the door. Banks looked into the face that he had thought for so long had been blown to smithereens.

"Mr Rothwell?" he said, slipping his card out of his wallet and holding it up. "Mr Keith Rothwell?"

II

"You've come, then?" Rothwell said simply.

"Yes."

He looked over Banks's shoulder. "Alone?"

"Yes."

"You'd better come in."

Banks followed Rothwell into a bright room where a ceiling fan spun and a light breeze blew through the open blue shutters. It was sparsely furnished. The walls were plastered white, the floor was flagged, covered here and there by rugs, and the ceiling was panelled with dark wood. Outside, he could hear birds singing; he didn't know what kind.

He sat down in the wicker chair Rothwell offered, surprised to be able to see the sea down below through the window. Now he was at the end of his journey, he felt bone weary and more than a little dizzy. It had been a long way from Eastvale and a long uphill walk in the sun. Sweat dribbled from his eyebrows into his eyes and made them sting. He wiped it away with his forearm. At least it was cooler inside the room.

Rothwell noticed his discomfort. "Hot, isn't it?" he said. "Can I get you something?"

Banks nodded. "Thanks. Anything as long as it's cold."

Rothwell went to the kitchen door and turned, with a smile, just as he opened it. "Don't worry," he said. "I won't run away."

"There's nowhere to run," replied Banks.

A minute or so later he came back with a glass of ice water and a bottle of Grolsch lager. "I'd drink the water first," he advised. "You look a bit dehydrated."

Banks drained the glass then opened the metal gizmo on the beer. It tasted good. Imported, of course. But Rothwell could afford it. Banks looked at him. The receding sandy hair, forming a slight widow's peak, had bleached in the sun. He had a good tan for such a fair-skinned person. Behind wire-rimmed glasses, his steady grey eyes looked out calmly, not giving away any indication as to his state of mind. He had a slightly prissy mouth, a girl's mouth, and his lips were pale pink. He looked nothing at all like the photo-graph of Daniel Clegg.

He wore a peach short-sleeve shirt, white shorts and brown leather sandals. His toenails need cutting. He was an inch or so taller than Banks, slim and in good shape—about all he did have in common with Clegg, apart from the colour of his hair, his blood group and the appendicitis scar. When he went to get the drinks, Banks noticed, he moved with an athlete's grace and economy. There was nothing of the sedentary pen-pusher about his bearing.

"Anyone else here?" Banks asked.

"Julia's gone to the shops," he said, glancing at his watch. "She shouldn't be long."

"I'd like to meet her."

"How did you find me?" Rothwell asked, sitting opposite, opening a tin of Pepsi. The gas hissed out and liquid frothed over the edge. Rothwell held it at arm's length until it had stopped fizzing, then wiped the tin with a tissue from a box on the table beside him.

"It wasn't that difficult," said Banks. "Once I knew who I was looking for. We found you partly through Julia." He shrugged. "After that it was a matter of routine police work, mostly boring footwork. We checked travel agents, then we contacted the local police through Interpol. It didn't take that long to get word back about two English strangers who resembled your descriptions taking a lease on a captain's house here. Did you really believe we wouldn't find you eventually?"

"I suppose I must have," said Rothwell. "Foolish of me, but there it is. There are always variables, loose ends, but I thought I'd left enough red herrings and covered my tracks pretty well. I planned it all *very* carefully."

"Do you have any idea what you've done to your family?"

Rothwell's lips tightened. "It wasn't a family. It was a sham. A lie. A façade. We played at happy families. I couldn't stand it any more. There was no love in the house. Mary and I hadn't slept together in years and Tom ... well ..."

Banks let Tom pass for the moment. "Why not get a divorce like anyone else? Why this elaborate scheme?"

"I assume, seeing as you're here, you know most of it?"

"Humour me."

Rothwell squinted at Banks. "Look," he said. "I can't see where you'd have any room to hide one, but you're not 'wired' as the Americans say, are you?"

Banks shook his head. "You have my word on that."

"This is just between you and me? Off the record?"

"For the moment. I am here officially, though."

Rothwell sipped some Pepsi then rubbed the can between his palms. "I might have asked Mary for a divorce eventually," he said, "but it was still all very new to me, the freedom, the taste of another life. I'm not even sure she would have let me go that easily. The way things turned out, though, I had to appear dead. If he thinks I'm alive, there'll be no peace, no escape anywhere."

"Martin Churchill?"

"Yes. He found out I was taking rather more than I was entitled to."

"How did you find out he knew?"

"A close source. When you play the kind of games I did, Mr Banks, it pays to have as much information as you can get. Let's say someone on the island tipped me that Churchill knew and that he was pressuring Daniel Clegg to do something about it."

"Is that how it happened?"

"Yes. And it made sense. I'd noticed that Daniel had been behaving oddly lately. He was nervous about something. Wouldn't look me in the eye. Now I had an explanation. The bastard was planning to have me executed."

"So you had him killed instead?"

Rothwell gazed out of the window at the sea and the mountainside in silence for a moment. "Yes. It was him or me. I beat him to it, that's all. Someone had to die violently, someone who could pass for me under certain circumstances. We looked enough alike."

"Without a face, you mean?"

"I ... I didn't look ... in the garage ... I couldn't."

"I'll bet you couldn't. Go on."

"We were about the same age and build, same hair colour. I knew he'd had his appendix out. I even knew his blood group was 'O,' the same as mine."

"How did you know that?"

"He told me. We were talking once about blood tainted by the HIV virus. He wondered if he had a greater chance of catching it from a transfusion because he shared his blood group with over forty per cent of the male population."

"What did you do once you had the idea of passing him off as you?"

"There was this man we'd both met in the Eagle a couple of times, down there for the Ed O'Donnell Band on a Sunday lunch-time, and he'd boasted about being a mercenary and doing anything for money. Arthur Jameson was his name. He was a walking mass of contradictions. He loved animals and nature, but he liked hunting and duck-shooting, and he didn't seem to give a damn for human life. I found him fascinating. Fascinating and a little frightening.

"It was perfect. Daniel knew him, too, of course, and he told me that Jameson had even approached him for some legal help once, shortly after we met. I thought if you found out anything, that would be it. He might have had something in his files. You know how lawyers hoard every scrap of paper. But there was nothing linking Jameson to *me*. It would only reinforce what you suspected already, that Daniel had had *me* killed instead of the other way round. You weren't to know that I was with Daniel the day we met Jameson, or that I'd chatted with Jameson on a number of subse-quent occasions."

"So you and Clegg were pals? Socialized together, did you?"

Rothwell paused. A muscle by his jaw twitched. "No. It wasn't quite like that," he said quietly. "Daniel had a hold over me, but sometimes he seemed to want to play at being boozing buddies. I didn't understand it, but at least for a while we could bury our differences and have a good time. The next day it would usually be back to cold formality. At bottom, Daniel was a terrible snob. Been to Cambridge, you know."

"How much did you pay Jameson?"

"Fifty thousand pounds and a plane ticket to Rio. I know it's a lot, but I thought the more I paid him the more likely he'd be to disappear for good with it and not get caught."

"First mistake."

"How did it happen?"

Banks told him about the wadding and about Jameson's attitude to the world beyond Calais. Rothwell laughed, then stared at the sea again. "I knew it was a risk," he said. "I suppose I should have known, the way he used to go on about the Irish and the Frogs sometimes. But if you have a dream you have to take risks for it, pay a price, don't you?"

"You needn't try to justify your actions to me," said Banks, finally feeling steady and cool enough to light a cigarette. He offered one to Rothwell, who accepted. "I was the one left to clean up your mess. And Jameson killed one policeman and seriously wounded another trying to escape." The fan drew their smoke up to it, then pushed it towards the windows.

"I'm sorry."

"I'll bet you are."

"It wasn't my fault, what Jameson did, was it? You can't blame me."

"Can't I? Let's get back to your relationship with Daniel Clegg. How did you get involved?"

"We met in the George Hotel, on Great George Street. It was about four years ago. A year or so after I left Hatchard and Pratt, anyway. Expenses were high, what with renovations to Arkbeck and everything else, and business wasn't exactly booming, though I wasn't doing too badly. They have jazz at the George on Thursdays, and as I was in Leeds on business, I thought I'd drop by rather than watch television in the hotel room. It turns out we were both jazz fans. We just got talking, that's all.

"I didn't tell him very much at first, except that I was a freelance financial consultant. He seemed interested. Anyway, we exchanged business cards and he put a bit of work my way, off-shore banking, that sort of thing. Turns out some of it was a bit shady, though I wasn't aware at the time—not that I mightn't have done it, anyway, mind you—and he brought that up later, in conversation."

"He put pressure on you?"

"Oh, yes." Rothwell paused and looked Banks in the eye. "A smooth blackmailer, was Danny-boy. I suppose you know about my bit of bad luck at Hatchard and Pratt's, don't you?"

"Yes."

"That was five years ago. We'd just moved into Arkbeck then and we couldn't really afford it. Not that the mortgage itself was so high, but the place had been neglected for so long. There was so much needed doing, and I'm no DIY expert. But Mary wanted to live there, so live there we did. The upshot was that I had to pad the expenses a little. If I hadn't been married to the boss's daughter, and if Laurence Pratt hadn't been a good friend, things could have gone very badly for me at the firm then. As it was, after I left I didn't have a lot of work at first, and Mary ... well, that's another story. Let's just say she doesn't have a forgiving nature. One night, in my cups, I hinted to Daniel about what had happened, how I had parted company with Hatchard and Pratt.

"Anyway, later, Daniel used what he knew about me as leverage to get me involved when his old college friend Martin Churchill first made enquiries about rearranging his finances. That was a little over three years back. See, he knew he couldn't handle the task by himself, that he needed my expertise. He told me he could still report me to the board, that it wasn't too late. Well, maybe they would have listened to him, and maybe they wouldn't. Who knows now? Quite frankly, I didn't care. I already knew a bit about money-laundering, and it looked to me like a licence to print money. Why wouldn't I want in? I think Daniel just enjoyed manipulating people, having power over them, so I didn't spoil his illusion. But he really wasn't terribly bright, wasn't Danny-boy, despite Cambridge."

"A bit like Frankenstein and the monster, isn't it?"

Rothwell smiled. "Yes, perhaps. And I suppose you'd have to say that the monster far outstripped his creator, though you could hardly say the good doctor himself was without sin."

"How did you arrange it all? The murder, the escape?"

Rothwell emptied his tin, put it on the table and leaned back. The chair creaked. Outside, gulls cried as they circled the harbour looking for fish. "Another Grolsch?" he asked.

There was still an inch left in the bottle. "No," said Banks. "Not yet."

Rothwell sighed. "You have to go back about eighteen months to understand, to when I first started using the Robert Calvert identity. Daniel and I were doing fine laundering Churchill's money, and he allowed us a decent percentage for doing so. I was getting rich quick. I suppose I should have been happy, but I wasn't. I don't know exactly when I first became aware of it, but life just seemed to have lost its savour, its sweetness. Things started to oppress me. I felt like I was shrivelling up inside, dying, old before my time. Call it mid-life crisis, I suppose, but I couldn't see the *point* of all that bloody money.

"All Mary wanted was her bridge club, more renovations, additions to the house, jewellery, expensive holidays. Christ, I should have known better than to marry the boss's daughter, even if I did get her pregnant. One simple mistake, that and my own bloody weakness. What was it the philosopher said about the erect penis knowing no conscience? That may be so, but it certainly understands penitence, regret, remorse. One bloody miserable, uncomfortable screw in the back of an Escort halfway up Crow Scar set me on a course straight to hell. I'm not exaggerating. Twenty-one years. After that long, my wife hated me, my children hated me, and I was beginning to hate myself."

Banks noticed that Rothwell had picked up the empty Pepsi tin and started to squeeze until it buckled in his grip.

"Then I realized I was handling millions of pounds—literally, millions—and that my job was essentially to clean it and hide it ready for future use. It wasn't difficult to find a few hiding places of my own. Small amounts at first, then, when no-one seemed to miss it, more and more. Shell companies, numbered accounts, dummy corporations, property. I liked what I was doing. The manipulation of large sums of money intrigued me and excited me like nothing else, or almost nothing else. Just for the sake of it, much of the time. Like art for art's sake.

"I began to spend more time away from home on 'business.' Nobody cared one way or another. They never asked me where I'd been. They only asked for more money for a new kitchen or a sunporch or a bloody gazebo. When I was home, I walked around like a zombie—the dull, boring accountant, I suppose—and mostly kept to my office or nipped out to the pub for a smoke and a jar occasionally. I had plenty of time to look back on my life, and though I didn't like a lot of what I saw, I remembered I hadn't always been so bloody bored or boring. I used to go dancing, believe it or not. I used to like a flutter on the horses now and then. I had friends. Once in a while, I liked to have too much to drink with the lads and stagger home singing, happy as a lark. That was before life came to resemble an accounts ledger—debits and credits, profit and loss, with far too much on the loss side." He sighed. "Are you sure you wouldn't like another beer?"

"Go on, then," Banks said. His bottle was empty now.

Rothwell brought back a Pepsi for himself and another Grolsch for Banks. His glasses had slipped down over the bridge of his nose and he pushed them back.

"So I invented Robert Calvert," Rothwell said after a sip of Pepsi.

"Where did you get the name?"

"Picked it from a magazine I was reading at the time. With a pin. *The Economist*, I believe."

"Go on."

"I rented the flat, bought new clothes, more casual. God, you've no idea how strange it felt at first. Good, but strange. There were moments when I really did believe I was going mad, turning into a split personality. It became a kind of compulsion, an addiction, like smoking. I'd go to the bookie's and put bets on, spend a day at the races, go listen to trad jazz in smoky pubs—the Adelphi, the George, the Duck and Drake—something I hadn't done since my early twenties. I'd go around in jeans and sweatshirts. And nobody back at Arkbeck Farm ever asked where I'd been, what I'd been doing, as long I turned up every now and then in my business suit and the money kept coming in for a new freezer, a first edition Brontë, a Christmas trip to Hawaii. After a while I realized I wasn't going mad, I was just becoming myself, returning to the way I was before I let life grind me down.

"And, sure enough, the money kept coming in. I had tapped into an endless supply, or so I thought. So I played the family role part of the time, and I started exploring my real self as Robert Calvert. I had no idea where it would lead, not then. I was just trying out ways of escape. I told Daniel Clegg one night when we'd had a few, and he thought it was a wild idea. I had to tell someone and I couldn't tell my family or Pratt or anyone local, so why not tell my blackmailer, my confidant? He helped me get a bank account and credit card as Calvert, which he thought gave him an even stronger hold over me. He could always claim he'd been deceived, you see."

"What about the escape?"

"You're jumping ahead a bit, but as I'd already created Robert Calvert successfully enough, it wasn't very difficult to go on from there and create a third identity: David Norcliffe. As you no doubt know, seeing as you're here. Rothwell was dead, and I couldn't go as Calvert. I had to leave him behind; that was part of the plan. So I shuffled more money into various bank accounts in various places over a period of several weeks. After all, that's what I do best. I've laundered and hidden millions for Churchill and his wife."

"How much for yourself?"

"Three or four million," he said with a shrug. "I don't know exactly. Enough, anyway, to last us our lifetime. And there was plenty left in Eastvale for my family. They're well provided for in the will and by the life insurance. I made sure of that. Believe me, they'll be better off without me."

"What about Daniel Clegg? What about Pamela Jeffreys?"

"Pamela? What about her?"

Banks told him.

He put his head in his hands. "Oh, my God," he said. "I would never have hurt Pamela ... It wasn't meant to be like that."

"How did you meet her?"

Rothwell sipped some more Pepsi and rubbed the back of his hand across his brow. "I told you the Calvert thing felt very strange at first. Mostly, I just used to walk around Leeds in my jeans and sweatshirt. I'd drop in at a pub now and then and enjoy being someone else. Occasionally, I got chatting to people, the way you do in pubs. I'll never forget how frightening and how exciting it was the first time someone asked me my name and I said 'Robert Calvert.' I knew it was still me—you have to understand that— we're not really talking about a split personality here. I was Keith Rothwell, all right, just playing a part, or trying to find himself, perhaps. It gave me an exhilarating sense of freedom.

"Anyway, as I said, I used to drop in at pubs now and then, mostly in the city centre or up in Headingley, near the flat. One night I saw Pamela in The Boulevard—you know, the tarted-up Jubilee Hotel on The Headrow. It seemed a likely place to meet women. They stay open till midnight on weekends and they've got a small dance-floor. Pamela was with some friends. They'd been doing something at the Town Hall, a Handel oratorio, or something like that. Anyway, something happened, some spark. We caught one another's eye.

"She wasn't with anyone in particular. I mean, she didn't seem to have a boyfriend with her. The next time she was at the bar, I made sure I got there, too, next to her, and we got chatting. I wasn't a great fan of classical music, but Pamela's a down-to-earth sort of person, not a highbrow snob or anything. I asked her to dance. She said yes. We just got on, that's all. We slept together now and then, but both of us knew it was just a casual relationship really. I don't mean to denigrate it by saying that. We had a wonderful time. I was astounded she fancied me. Flattered. It was the first time in my entire marriage that I'd been with another woman, and the hell of it was that I didn't feel guilty at all. She was fun to be with, and we had a great time, but we weren't in love."

"What came between you?"

"What? Well, we stayed friends, really. At least, I like to think we did. There was her work, of course. It's very demanding and between us we couldn't always be sure we could make time to get together. And Pamela was more outgoing. She wanted more of a social life. She wanted me to meet her friends, and she wanted to meet mine."

"But you didn't have any?"

"Exactly. And I didn't want to get too well known around the place. It was a risk, playing Calvert, always a risk."

"Go on. What happened next?"

"I met Julia."

"How?"

"We met on a bus, would you believe? It had been raining, one of those sudden showers, and I was out walking without an umbrella. So I jumped on a bus into town. Then the rain stopped and the sun came out. I'd been looking at her out of the corner of my eye. She was so beautiful, like a model, such delicate, fragile, sculpted features. I imagined she was probably stuck-up and wouldn't talk to the likes of me. Anyway, she left her umbrella. I saw it, grabbed it, and dashed after her. When I caught her up she seemed startled at first, then I gave it to her and she blushed. She seemed flustered, so I asked her if she wanted to go for a coffee. She said yes. She was very shy. It was hard to get her talking at first, but slowly I found out she was a teacher and she lived in Adel and she adored Greek history and literature.

"Do you believe in love at first sight, Mr Banks? Do you? Because that's what this is all about, really. It's not just about money. It's not just about leaving my old life behind and seeking novelty. I fell in love with Julia the moment I saw her, and that's the truth. It might sound foolish and sentimental to you, but I have never in my life felt that way before. Bells ringing, earth moving, all the clichés. And it's mutual. She's everything I've ever wanted. When I met Julia, nothing else mattered. I knew we had to get away, find our Eden, if you like, our paradise. I had to get a new life, a new identity. Everything was in such a mess, falling apart. No-one was supposed to get hurt."

"Except Daniel Clegg."

Rothwell banged on his chair arm with his fist. "I told you! That wasn't my fault. I had to appear to have been violently murdered. By Daniel himself, or by someone he'd hired. And that's exactly the way it would have been, too, if I hadn't been tipped off and made other plans. But Julia knew nothing of that. She's a complete innocent. She knows nothing of the things we've just been talking about."

"So you invited Clegg over to the Calvert flat to get his fingerprints there? Am I right?"

"Yes. On the Monday. I said I had some business to discuss that couldn't wait and he came over. I showed him around, had him touch things. I'd cleaned the place thoroughly. Daniel was a touchy-feely kind of person. Anything he saw, he'd pick it up and have a look: compact discs, wallet, credit cards in Calvert's name, coins, books, you name it. He'd even let his fingers rest on surfaces as if he were claiming them or something. He handled just about everything in the place. I was much more careful to make mine blurred." Rothwell laughed quietly. "He really was a fool, you know. Every time I got him to help me with something illegal, like setting up the Calvert bank account and credit card, for example, he thought *he* was getting more power over *me*."

"So you must have known we'd find out about the Calvert identity, about Pamela, about Clegg and the money-laundering?"

"Of course. As I said earlier, I had to leave Calvert behind. It was part of my plan that you should find out about him. Another dead end. But please believe me, Pamela wasn't meant to be a part of it, except maybe to confirm the Calvert identity. I mean, I thought she might get in touch with the police if she saw my picture in the papers. Or someone else might, someone who thought they recognized me. It was meant to confuse you, that's all. I left a careful trail for you. I thought it led the wrong way. I knew the police would be able to unlock and interpret the data on my computer eventually, that they would realize I'd been laundering money for Martin Churchill. I also left a letter for Daniel Clegg in a locked file. I knew you'd get at that eventually, too."

"That was one of the things that bothered me," Banks said. "In retrospect, it was all too easy. And we never found a copy of the letter among his papers. He could have destroyed it, of course, but it was just one those little niggling details. Lawyers tend to hang onto things."

"I never sent it," said Rothwell. "I just created the file so you'd get onto Daniel if you hadn't already. It was a way of telling you his name, but I couldn't make it *too* easy. Then you'd assume he'd had me killed and disappeared with the money."

"Oh, we did," said Banks. "We did."

"Then why are you here?"

"Because I'm a persistent bastard, among other things. There were too many loose ends. They worried me. Two different sets of thugs roaming the country, for a start. They could be explained, of course, but it still seemed odd. And we couldn't find any trace of Clegg, no matter how hard we tried. His ex-wife said he fancied Tahiti, but we had no luck there. We had no luck anywhere else, either. Of course we didn't. We were looking for the wrong person. But mostly, I think, it was the connection with Julia that really did you in."

"How did you find out about her?"

"Pamela Jeffreys mentioned her first. She said she thought you were in love. Just a feeling she had, you understand. Then I began to wonder how it would upset the apple-cart if you fell in love as *Robert Calvert*. How would you handle it? Then Tom came back from America for your funeral."

"Ah, Tom. My Achilles heel."

"Oh, he didn't realize the significance of it. But you made him angry. He followed you to Leeds once. He saw you have lunch with a woman. Julia Marshall. You didn't know that, did you? But Tom couldn't imagine the scale of your plans. He's just a kid who caught his father with another woman. He was already angry, mixed up and confused at the way you treated him. He was after getting his own back, but what he saw upset him so much that all he could do was keep it to himself."

"Christ," he muttered. "I didn't know that. He didn't tell Mary?"

"No. He wanted to protect her."

"My God." Rothwell ran his hand over the side of his face. "Maybe you think I reacted too harshly, Chief Inspector? I know we're living in liberal times, where anything goes. I know it's old-fashioned of me, but I still happen to believe that homosexuality is an aberration, an abomination of nature, and not just an 'alternative life-style,' as the liberals would have it. And to find out that *my* own son ..."

"So you decided it would be best to send Tom away?"

"Yes. It seemed best for both of us if he went away, a long way away. He was well provided for. As it turned out, he wanted to go travelling in America and try to get into film school there. By then I knew I had to get away, too, so it seemed best to let him go. At least he had a good chance. I might have abhorred his homosexuality, but I'm not a tyrant. He was still my son, after all."

"Tom gave us an accurate description of Julia," Banks went on. "He's a very observant young man. We ran the artist's impression in the *Yorkshire Post* and a woman called Barbara Ledward came forward, a colleague of Julia's, then Julia's family. Nobody lives in a vacuum. When we followed up on their phone calls, we found out that Julia had resigned from her teaching job suddenly and told everyone she was going away, that she had a once-in-a-lifetime opportunity abroad but couldn't divulge the details. She said she'd be in touch, then she simply disappeared about three days before your apparent murder. Her family and friends were worried about her. She didn't usually behave so irresponsibly. But they didn't report her as a missing person because she had *told* them she was going away.

"We might have been a bit slow on the uptake, but we're not stupid. All Julia's friends and colleagues mentioned how fascinated she was by the ancient Greeks. She even tried to teach the kids about the classics at school, though I'm told it didn't go down well with the head. He wanted them to study computers and car main-tenance instead. We had to assume you didn't think we'd find out about Julia. Oh, you might have suspected we'd find out there was *someone*, but you didn't think we'd try to find her, did you?"

"No," said Rothwell. "After all, why should you want to? No more than I thought you would waste time and money doing tests to see if it really was *my* body in the garage. Another risk. I was clearly dead, executed because of my involvement in international crime. What did it matter if I, or Calvert, had a girlfriend? I never thought for a moment you'd look very closely at the rest of my private life."

"Then you shouldn't have revealed the Calvert identity to us," Banks said. "If it hadn't been for that, we might have gone on think-ing you were a dull, mild-mannered accountant who just happened to get into something beyond his depth. But Calvert showed imag-ination. Calvert showed a dimension to your character I had to take into account. And I had to ask myself, what if Calvert fell in love?"

"I couldn't get rid of Calvert," said Rothwell. "You know that. I didn't have time. Too many people had seen him. I had to figure out a way to make him work to my advantage quickly. I thought he'd be a dead end."

"Your mistake. Poor judgment."

"Obviously. But I had no choice. What else could I do?"

"So how did you handle the killing?"

"Another drink?"

"Please."

Banks stared out over the pink and purple flowers in the window box at the barren hillside and the blue sea below. Rothwell's mention of the forensic tests galled him. He knew they should have tried to establish the identity of the deceased beyond doubt. Forensics should have reconstructed the teeth and checked dental records. That was an oversight. It was understandable, given the way Rothwell had apparently been assassinated, and given the state the teeth were in, but it was an oversight, nevertheless.

Of course, the lab had been as burdened with work as usual, and tests cost money. Then, when the fingerprints at Calvert's flat matched the corpse's, they didn't think they needed to look any further. After all, they had the pasta meal, the appendix scar and the right blood group, and Mary Rothwell had identified the dead man's clothing, watch and pocket contents.

A red flying insect settled on his bare arm. He brushed it off gently. When Rothwell came back with a Grolsch and a Pepsi, he was not moving with quite the same confidence and grace as he had before.

"I gave Jameson instructions to hold Alison until we got back," he began, "but *not* to harm her in any way."

"That's considerate of you. He didn't. What about his accomplice, Donald Pembroke?"

Rothwell shook his head. He held the Pepsi against his shorts. The tin was beaded with moisture and Banks watched the damp patch spread through the white cotton. "I never met him. That was Jameson's business. He said he needed someone to help and I left it to him, getting guarantees of discretion, of course. I never even knew the man's name, and that's the truth. Pembroke, you say? What happened to him?"

Banks told him.

Rothwell sighed. "I suppose fate catches up with us all in the end, doesn't it? What is it the eastern religions call it? Karma?"

"Back to the murder."

Rothwell paused a moment, then went on. "They held Alison, then when Mary and I got home, they tied her up, too, and took me out to the garage. They had instructions to pick Clegg up after dinner. I knew he didn't like to cook for himself and on Thursdays he always dropped by a trattoria near the office for a quick pasta before going home. That's why I chose that day. I knew Mary and I would be going out for the annual anniversary dinner, and I arranged for us to eat at Mario's. You see, I thought of everything. Even the stomach contents would match.

"They'd already knocked Clegg out and secured him earlier. I even made sure to tell Jameson to use loose handcuffs to avoid rope burns on Clegg's wrists. We got him into my clothes as quickly as possible. He was starting to come round. He was on his hands and knees, I remember, shaking his head as if he was groggy, just waking up, then Jameson put the shotgun to the back of his head. I … I turned away. There was a terrible explosion and a smell. Then we went through the woods and they drove me to Leeds. I drove Clegg's Jaguar to Heathrow, wearing gloves, of course. Then I left the country as David Norcliffe. I already had a passport and bank accounts set up in that name. I joined Julia here. It was all pre-arranged. It had to be so elaborate because I was supposed to be murdered. I'd read about a similar murder in the papers a while back and it seemed one worth imitating."

"Well, you know what the poet said. 'The best laid plans …'"

"But you can't prove anything," said Rothwell.

"Don't be an idiot. Of course we can. We can prove that you're alive and Daniel Clegg was murdered in your garage."

"But you can't prove I was there. It's only your word against mine. I could say they were taking me out to kill both of us. I managed to get away and I ran and hid here. They killed Daniel, but I escaped."

"They killed him in *your* clothes?" Banks shook his head slowly. "It won't wash, Keith."

"But it's all circumstantial. Jameson and Pembroke are both dead. A good lawyer could get me off, and you know it."

"You're dreaming. Say you do beat the murder conspiracy charge, which I think is unlikely, there's still the money-laundering and the rest."

Rothwell looked around the room, mouth set firmly. "I'm not going back," he said. "You can't make me. I know there are European extradition treaties. Procedures to follow. They take time. You can't just take me in like some bounty hunter."

"Of course I can't," said Banks. "That was never my intention." He heard the gate open and walked over to the window.

A pale, beautiful woman in a yellow sun-dress, red-blonde hair piled and knotted high on her head, had walked into the courtyard and paused to check on the flowers and potted plants. She carried a basket of fresh bread and other foodstuffs in the crook of her arm. She put out her free hand and bent to hold a purple blossom gently between her fingers for a moment, then inspected the herbs. The sun brought out the blonde highlights in her hair. "It looks like Julia's back," Banks said. "Doesn't tan well, does she?"

Rothwell jumped up and looked out. "Julia knows nothing," he said quickly, speaking quietly so she couldn't hear him. "You have to believe that. I told her I had business problems, that I had to burn a lot of bridges if we were to be together, that we'd be well set up for life but we couldn't go back. Ever. She agreed. I don't know if you can understand this or not, but *I love her*, Banks, more than anyone or anything I've ever loved in my life. I mean it. It's the first time I've ever … I already told you. I love her. She knows nothing. You can do what you want with me, but leave her alone."

Banks kept quiet.

"You'll never be able to prove anything," Rothwell added.

"Maybe I don't even want to take that risk," said Banks. By now they could both see Julia and hear her humming softly as she rubbed the leaves on a pot of basil and sniffed her fingers. "Maybe I'd rather you made a clean breast of it," he went on, keeping his voice low. "A confession. It might even go in your favour, you never know. Especially the love bit. Juries love lovers."

Julia stood up. Some of her piled tresses had come loose and trailed over her cheeks. She was flushed from the walk and some of the hairs stuck to her face, dampened with sweat.

"You must be mad if you think I'd give all this up willingly," Rothwell said.

"You can't buy paradise with blood, Keith," said Banks. "Come on home. Tell us everything about Martin Churchill's finances, every-thing you know about the bastard. Let's go public, make plenty of noise, sing louder than a male-voice choir. We can make sure he never sets foot in the country even if he turns up looking like Mr Bean. We could offer you protection, then perhaps another identity, another new life. You'd do some time, of course, but I'm willing to bet that by the time you got out, Martin Churchill would be just another of history's unpleasant footnotes, and Julia would be still waiting."

"You're insane, do you know that? I'd kill you before I'd do what you're suggesting."

"No, you wouldn't, Keith. Besides, there'd be others after me."

Rothwell paused on his way to the door and stared at Banks, eyes wide open and wild, no longer calm and steady. "Do you know what will happen if I go home?"

"It might not be half as bad as what will happen if I let Churchill know you're still alive," said Banks. "They say he has a long reach and a nasty line in revenge." Julia had almost reached the door. "It wouldn't stop at you," Banks said.

Rothwell froze. "You wouldn't. No. Not even *you* would do a thing like that."

At that moment, Banks hated himself probably more than at any other time in his life. He felt sorry for Rothwell, and he found himself on the verge of relenting.

Then he remembered Mary Rothwell, living in a haze of tran-quillizers; Alison, burying her head deep in her books and fast losing touch with the real world; and Tom, flailing around in his own private mire of guilt and confusion. Rothwell could have helped these people. Then he thought of Pamela Jeffreys, just out of hospital, physically okay, but still afraid of every knock at her door and unsure whether she would get back the confidence to play her viola again.

For this man's gamble on paradise, Daniel Clegg lay in his grave with his head blown off, Barry Miller had died on a wet road at midnight and Grant Everett might have to spend the next few years of his life relearning how to walk and talk. Even Arthur Jameson and Donald Pembroke were Rothwell's victims, in a way.

And, much farther away but no less implicated, was a dictator who got fat while his people starved, a man who liked to watch people eat glass, a man who, now, if Banks could help it, would never enjoy a peaceful retirement in the English countryside, no matter what he had on some powerful members of the establishment.

And the more Banks thought about these people, victims and predators alike, the less able he was to feel sorry for the fallen lovers.

"Try me," he said.

Rothwell glared at him, then all the life seemed to drain out of him until he resembled nothing more than a tired, middle-aged accountant. Banks still felt dirty and miserable, and despite his resolve, he wasn't certain he could go through with his threat. But Rothwell believed him now, and that was all that mattered. This bastard had caused enough trouble already. There was no more room for pity. Banks felt his pulse race, his jaw clench. Then the door opened and Julia drifted in, all blonde and yellow, with a big smile for Rothwell.

"Hello, darling! Oh," she said, noticing Banks. "We've got company. How nice."

DEAD RIGHT

For my Canadian family:
Gord & Shirley, John, Lynn & Bob,
Kate, Sarah, Pat & Brian, Alex,
Elizabeth, Brian & Amy

ONE

I

The boy's body sat propped against the graffiti-scarred wall in a ginnel off Market Street, head lolling forward, chin on chest, hands clutching his stomach. A bib of blood had spilled down the front of his white shirt.

Detective Chief Inspector Alan Banks stood in the rain and watched Peter Darby finish photographing the scene, bursts of electronic flash freezing the raindrops in mid-air as they fell. Banks was irritated. By rights, he shouldn't be there. Not in the rain at half past one on a Saturday night.

As if he didn't have enough problems already.

Banks had got the call the minute he walked in the door after an evening alone in Leeds at Opera North's *The Pearl Fishers*. Alone because his wife, Sandra, had realized on Wednesday that the benefit gala she was supposed to host for the Eastvale community centre clashed with their season tickets. They had argued—Sandra expecting Banks to forego the opera in favour of her gala—so, stubbornly, Banks had gone alone. This sort of thing had been happening a lot lately—going their own ways—to such an extent that Banks could hardly remember the last time they had done anything together.

The limpid melody of the "Au fond du temple saint" duet still echoed around his mind as he watched Dr Burns, the young police surgeon, start his *in situ* examination under the canvas tent the Scene-of-Crime officers had erected over the body.

PC Ford had come across the scene at eleven forty-seven while walking his beat, community policing being a big thing in Eastvale these days. At first, he said, he thought the victim was just a drunk too legless to get all the way home after the pubs closed. After all, there was a broken beer bottle on the ground beside the lad, he seemed to be holding his stomach, and in the light of Ford's torch, the dark blood could easily have passed for vomit.

Ford told Banks he didn't know quite what it was that finally alerted him this was no drunk sleeping it off; perhaps it was the unnatural stillness of the body. Or the silence: there was no snoring, no twitching or muttering, the way drunks often did, just silence inside the hiss and patter of the rain. When he knelt and looked more closely, well, of course, then he knew.

The ginnel was a passage no more than six feet wide between two blocks of terrace houses on Carlaw Place. It was often used as a short cut between Market Street and the western area of Eastvale. Now, onlookers gathered at its mouth, behind the police tape, most of them huddled under umbrellas, pyjama bottoms sticking out from under raincoats. Lights had come on in many houses along the street, despite the lateness of the hour. Several uniformed officers were circulating in the crowd and knocking on doors, seeking anyone who had seen or heard anything.

The ginnel walls offered some protection from the rain, but not much. Banks could feel the cold water trickling down the back of his neck. He pulled up his collar. It was mid-October, the time of year when the weather veered sharply between warm, misty, mellow days straight out of Keats and piercing gale-force winds that drove stinging rain into your face like the showers of Blefuscuan arrows fired at Gulliver.

Banks watched Dr Burns turn the victim on his side, ease down his trousers and take the rectal temperature. He had already had a glance at the body, himself, and it looked as if someone had beaten or kicked the kid to death. The features were too severely damaged to reveal much except that he was a young white male. His wallet was missing, along with whatever keys and loose change he might have been carrying, and there was nothing else in his pockets to indicate who he was.

It had probably started as a pub fight, Banks guessed, or perhaps the victim had been flashing his money about. As he watched Dr Burns examine the boy's broken features, Banks imagined the scene as it might have happened. The kid scared, running perhaps, realizing that whatever had started innocently enough was quickly getting out of control. How many of them were after him? Two, probably, at least. Maybe three or four. He runs through the dark, deserted streets in the rain, splashing through puddles, oblivious to his wet feet. Does he know they're going to kill him? Or is he just afraid of taking a beating?

Either way, he sees the ginnel, thinks he can make it, slip away, get home free, but it's too late. Something hits him or trips him, knocks him down, and suddenly his face is crushed down against the rainy stone, the cigarette ends and chocolate wrappers. He can taste blood, grit, leaves, probe a broken tooth with his tongue. And then he feels a sharp pain in his side, another in his back, his stomach, his groin, then they're kicking his head as if it were a football. He's trying to speak, beg, plead, but he can't get the words out, his mouth is too full of blood. And finally he just slips away. No more pain. No more fear. No more anything.

Well, maybe it had happened like that. Or they could have been already lying in wait for him, blocking the ginnel at each end, trapping him inside. Some of Banks's bosses had said he had too much imagination for his own good, though he found it had always come in useful. People would be surprised if they knew how much of what they believed to be painstaking, logical police work actually came down to a guess, a hunch or a sudden intuition.

Banks shrugged off the line of thought and got back to the business at hand. Dr Burns was still kneeling, shining a pen-light inside the boy's mouth. It looked like a pound of raw minced meat to Banks. He turned away.

A pub fight, then? Though they didn't usually end in death, fights were common enough on a Saturday night in Eastvale, especially when some of the lads came in from the outlying villages eager to demonstrate their physical superiority over the arrogant townies.

They would come early to watch Eastvale United or the rugby team in the afternoon, and by pub chucking-out time they were usually three sheets to the wind, jostling each other in the fish-and-chip-shop queues, slagging everyone in sight, just looking for trouble. It was a familiar pattern: "What are you looking at?" "Nothing." "You calling *me* nothing!" Get out of that if you can.

By midnight, though, most of the boozers had usually gone home, unless they had moved on to one of Eastvale's two night-clubs, where for a modest entrance fee you got membership, an inedible battered beefburger, a constant supply of ear-splitting music and, most important of all, the chance to swill back watery lager until three in the morning.

It wasn't that Banks had no sympathy for the victim—after all, the boy was *somebody's* son—but solving this case, he thought, would simply be a matter of canvassing the local pubs and finding out where mi-laddo had been drinking, whom he'd been upsetting. A job for Detective Sergeant Hatchley, perhaps; certainly not one for a wet Detective Chief Inspector with Bizet's melodies still caressing his inner ear; one whose only wish was to crawl into a nice warm bed beside a wife who probably still wasn't speaking to him.

Dr Burns finished his examination and walked over. He looked far too young and innocent for the job—in fact, he looked more like a farmer, with his round face, pleasant, rustic features and mop of chestnut hair—but he was quickly becoming conversant with the number of ways in which man could dispatch his fellow man to the hereafter.

"Well, it certainly looks like a boot job," he said, putting his black notebook back in his pocket. "I can't swear to it, of course—that'll be for Dr Glendenning to determine at the post-mortem—but it looks that way. From what I can make out on first examination, one eye's practically hanging out of its socket, the nose is pulped and there are several skull fractures. In some places the bone frag-ments might possibly have punctured the brain." Burns sighed. "In a way, the poor bugger's lucky he's dead. If he'd survived, he'd have been a one-eyed vegetable for the rest of his days."

"No sign of any other injuries?"

"A few broken ribs. And I'd expect some severe damage to the internal organs. Other than that ..." Burns glanced back at the body and shrugged. "I'd guess he was kicked to death by someone wearing heavy shoes or boots. But don't quote me on that. It also looks as if he was hit on the back of the head—maybe by that bottle."

"Just one person?"

Burns ran his hand over his wet hair and rubbed it dry on the side of his trousers. "I'm sorry, I didn't mean to imply that. It was more likely two or three. A gang, perhaps."

"But one person *could* have done it?"

"As soon as the victim was down on the ground, yes. Thing is, though, he looks pretty strong. It might have taken more than one person to *get* him down. Unless, of course, that was what the bottle was used for."

"Any idea how long he's been there?"

"Not long." Burns looked at his watch. "Allowing for the weather conditions, I'd say maybe two hours. Two and a half at the outside."

Banks made a quick back-calculation. It was twenty to two now. That meant the kid had probably been killed between ten past eleven and eleven forty-seven, when PC Ford found the body. A little over half an hour. And a half-hour that happened to coincide with pub closing time. His theory was still looking good.

"Anyone know who he is?" Banks asked.

Dr Burns shook his head.

"Any chance of cleaning him up enough for an artist's impression?"

"Might be worth a try. But as I said, the nose is pulped, one eye's practically—"

"Yes. Yes, thank you, doctor."

Burns nodded briskly and walked off.

The Coroner's Officer directed two ambulance attendants to bag the body and take it to the mortuary, Peter Darby took more photographs and the SOCOs went on with their search. The rain kept falling.

Banks leaned back against the damp wall and lit a cigarette. It might help concentrate his mind. Besides, he liked the way cigarettes tasted in the rain.

There were things to be done, procedures to be set in motion. First of all, they had to find out who the victim was, where he had come from, where he belonged, and what he had been doing on the day of his death. Surely, Banks thought, someone, somewhere, must be missing him. Or was he a stranger in town, far from home?

Once they knew something about the victim, then it would simply be a matter of legwork. Eventually, they would track down the bastards who had done this. They would probably be kids, certainly no older than their victim, and they would, by turn, be contrite and arrogant. In the end, if they were old enough, they would probably get charged with manslaughter. Nine years, out in five.

Sometimes, it was all so bloody predictable, Banks thought, as he flicked his tab-end into the gutter and walked to his car, splashing through puddles that reflected the revolving lights of the police cars. And at that point, he could hardly be blamed for not knowing how wrong he was.

II

The telephone call at eight o'clock on Sunday morning woke Detective Constable Susan Gay from a pleasant dream about visiting Egypt with her father. They had never done anything of the kind, of course—her father was a cool, remote man who had never taken her anywhere—but the dream seemed real enough.

Eyes still closed, Susan groped until her fingers touched the smooth plastic on her bedside table, then she juggled the receiver beside her on the pillow.

"Mmm?" she mumbled.

"Susan?"

"Sir?" She recognized Banks's voice and tried to drag herself out of the arms of Morpheus. But she couldn't get very far. She frowned and rubbed sleep from her eyes. Waking up had always been a slow process for Susan, ever since she was a little girl.

"Sorry to wake you so early on a Sunday," Banks said, "but we got a suspicious death after closing time last night."

"Yes, sir." Susan raised herself from the sheets and propped herself against the pillows. *Suspicious death*. She knew what that meant. Work. Now. The thin bedsheet slipped from her shoulders and left her breasts bare. Her nipples were hard from the morning chill in the bedroom. For a moment, she felt exposed talking to

Banks while she was sitting up naked in bed. But he couldn't see her. She told herself not to be so daft.

"We've got scant little to go on," Banks went on. "We don't even know the victim's name yet. I need you down here as soon as you can make it."

"Yes, sir. I'll be right there."

Susan replaced the receiver, ran her fingers through her hair and got out of bed. She stood on her tiptoes and stretched her arms towards the ceiling until she felt the knots in her muscles crack, then she padded to the living-room, pausing to note the thickness of her waist and thighs in the wardrobe mirror on her way. She would have to start that diet again soon. Before she went to take a shower, she started the coffee-maker and put some old Rod Stewart on the CD player to help her wake up.

As the hot water played over her skin, she thought of last night's date with Gavin Richards, a DC from Regional Headquarters. He had taken her to the Georgian Theatre in Richmond to see an Alan Bennett play, and after that they had found a cosy pub just off Richmond market square, where she had eaten cheese-and-onion crisps and drunk a half-pint of cider.

Walking to her car, both of them huddled under her umbrella because it was raining fast and, like a typical man, Gavin hadn't bothered to carry one, she had felt his warmth, felt herself responding to it, and when he had asked her back to his house for a coffee she had almost said yes. Almost. But she wasn't ready yet. She wanted to. Oh, she wanted to. Especially when they kissed good night by her car. It had been too long. But they had only been out together three times, and that was too soon for Susan. She might have sacrificed her personal life for her career over the last few years, but she wasn't about to hop into bed with the first tasty bloke who happened to come along.

When she noticed she had been standing in the shower so long that her skin had started to glow, she got out, dried herself off briskly and threw on a pair of black jeans and a polo-neck jumper that matched her eyes. She was lucky that her curly blonde hair needed hardly any attention at all. She added a little gel to give it lustre, then she was ready to go. Rod Stewart sang "Maggie Mae" as she sipped the last of her black, sugarless coffee and munched a slice of dry toast.

Still eating, she grabbed a light jacket from the hook and dashed out the door. It was only a five-minute drive to the station, and on another occasion she might have walked for the exercise. Especially this morning. It was a perfect autumn day: scrubbed blue skies and only the slightest chill in the air. The recent winds had already blown some early lemon and russet leaves from the trees, and they squished under her feet as she walked to her car.

But today Susan paused only briefly to sniff the crisp air, then she got in her car and turned the key in the ignition. Her red Golf started on the first try. An auspicious beginning.

III

Banks leaned by his office window, his favourite spot, blew on the surface of his coffee and watched the steam rise as he looked out over the quiet market square. He was thinking about Sandra, about their marriage and the way it all seemed to be going wrong. Not so much wrong, just nowhere. She still hadn't spoken to him since the opera. Not that she'd had much chance, really, with him being out so late at the crime scene. And this morning she had barely been conscious by the time he left. But still, there was a discernible chill in the house.

Last night's rain had washed the excesses of Saturday night from the cobbles, just as the station cleaning-staff disinfected and mopped out the cells after the overnight drunk-and-disorderlies had been discharged. The square and the buildings around it glowed pale grey-gold in the early light.

Banks had his window open a couple of inches, and the sound of the church congregation singing "We plough the fields, and scatter" drifted in. It took him back to the Harvest Festivals of his childhood, when his mum would give him a couple of apples and oranges to put in the church basket along with everyone else's. He often wondered what happened to all the fruit after the festival was over.

The *Dalesman* calendar on his wall showed Healaugh Church, near York, through a farm gate. It wasn't a particularly autumnal shot, Banks was thinking, as he heard the tap on his door.

It was Susan Gay, first to arrive after Detective Superintendent Gristhorpe, who was already busy co-ordinating with Regional HQ and arranging for local media coverage.

As usual, Susan looked fresh as a daisy, Banks thought. Just the right amount of make-up, blonde curls still glistening from the shower. While no-one would describe Susan Gay as an oil painting, with her small button nose and her serious, guarded expression, her clear, blue-grey eyes were intriguing, and she had a beautiful, smooth complexion.

Not for Susan, Banks thought, the wild, boozy Saturday nights favoured by Jim Hatchley, who followed hot on her heels looking like death warmed over, eyes bleary and bloodshot, lips dry and cracked, a shred of toilet paper stuck over a shaving cut, thinning straw hair unwashed and uncombed for a couple of days.

After the two of them had sat down, both nursing cups of coffee, Banks explained how the boy had been killed, then he walked over to the map of Eastvale on the wall by his filing cabinet and pointed to the ginnel where the body had been discovered.

"This is where PC Ford found him," he began. "There are no through roads leading west nearby, so people tend to cut through the residential streets, then take the Carlaw Place ginnel over the recreation ground to King Street and the Leaview Estate. Thing is, it works both ways, so he could have been heading in either direction. We don't know."

"Sir," said Susan, "you told me on the telephone that he'd probably been killed shortly after closing time. If he'd been out drinking, isn't it more likely that he was heading *from* Market Street? I mean, that's quite a popular spot for young people on a Saturday night. There's a fair number of pubs, and some of them have live bands or karaoke."

Karaoke. Banks felt himself shudder at the thought. The only other words that had similar effect on him were *country-and-western music.* An oxymoron if ever there was one.

"Good point," he said. "So let's concentrate our survey on the Market Street pubs and the Leaview Estate to start with. If we draw a blank there, we can extend the area."

"How much *do* we know, sir?" Sergeant Hatchley asked.

"Precious little. I've already had a look at the overnight logs, and there are no reports of any major shindigs. We've talked to the occupants of the terrace houses on both sides of the ginnel, as well as the people across the street. The only one with anything to say was watching television, so he didn't hear anything too clearly, but he was sure he did hear a fight or something outside during the Liverpool–Newcastle game on 'Match of the Day.'"

"What exactly did he hear, sir?" Susan asked.

"Just some scuffling and grunting, then the sound of people running away. He thought more than one, but he couldn't say how many. Or which direction. He thought it was just the usual drunken yobs, and he certainly had no intention of going outside and finding out for himself."

"You can hardly blame him, these days, can you?" said Sergeant Hatchley, picking gingerly at the tissue over his shaving cut. It started to bleed again. "Some of these yobs'd kill you as soon as look at you. Besides, it were a bloody good match."

"Anyway," Banks went on, "you'd better check with Traffic, too. We don't know for certain whether the attackers ran home or drove off. Maybe they got a parking ticket or got stopped for speeding."

"We should be so lucky," muttered Hatchley.

Banks pulled two sheets of paper from a folder on his desk and passed one each to Susan and Hatchley. It showed an artist's impression of a young man, probably in his early twenties, with thin lips and a long, narrow nose. His hair was cut short and combed neatly back. Despite his youth, it seemed to be receding at the temples and looked very thin on top. There was nothing particularly distinctive about him, but Banks thought he could perceive a hint of arrogance in the expression. Of course, that was probably just artistic licence.

"The night-shift attendant at the mortuary came up with this," he said. "A few months back, he got bored with having no-one to talk to on the job, so he started sketching corpses as a way of passing the time. *Still lifes*, he calls them. Obviously a man of hidden talents. Anyway, he told us this was mostly speculation, especially the nose, which had been badly broken. The cheekbones had been fractured, too, so he was guessing about how high and how prominent they might have been. But the hair's right, he says, and the general shape of the head. It'll have to do for now. The only things we know for certain are that the victim was a little over six foot tall, weighed eleven stone, was in fine physical shape—an athlete, perhaps—and he had blue eyes and blond hair. No birthmarks, scars, tattoos or other distinguishing features." He tapped the folder. "We'll try to get this on the local TV news today and in the papers tomorrow morning. For now, you can start with the house-to-house, then after opening time you can canvass the pubs. Uniform branch has detailed four officers to help. Our first priority is to find out who the poor bugger was, and the second is to discover who he was last seen with before he was killed. Okay?"

They both nodded and stood up to leave.

"And take your mobiles or personal radios and stay in touch with one another. I want the right hand to know what the left hand's doing. All right?"

"Yes, sir," said Susan.

"As for me," said Banks with a grim smile, "Dr Glendenning has kindly offered to come in and do the post-mortem this morning, so I think one of us should pay him the courtesy of being present. Don't you?"

IV

A lot of detectives complained about house-to-house enquiries, much preferring to spend their time in scummy pubs with low-life informers, getting the *real* feel of the Job, or so they thought. But Susan Gay had always enjoyed a good house-to-house. At the very least it was a good exercise in patience.

Of course, you got the occasional nutter, the boor, and the lecherous creep with his Hound of the Baskervilles straining at the end of its chain. Once, even, a naked child had toddled out to see what was happening and peed all over Susan's new shoes. The mother had thought it hilarious.

Then there were those endless hours in the rain, wind and snow, knocking at door after door, your feet aching, the damp and chill fast seeping right into the marrow of your bones, wishing you'd chosen some other career, thinking even marriage and kids would be better than this.

And, needless to say, every now and then some clever-arse pillock would tell her she was too pretty to be a police*man*, or would suggest she could put her handcuffs on him any time she wanted, *ha-ha-ha*. But that was all part of the game, and she didn't mind as much as she sometimes pretended she did to annoy Sergeant Hatchley. As far as Susan was concerned, the human race would always contain a large number of clever-arse pillocks, no matter what you thought. And the greatest percentage of them, in her experience, were likely to be men.

But on a fine morning like this, the valley sides beyond the town's western edge criss-crossed with limestone walls, slopes still lush green after the late-summer rains, and the purple heather coming into bloom up high where the wild moorland began, it was as good a way as any to be earning your daily crust. And there was nothing like a house-to-house for getting to know your patch.

The morning chill had quickly given way to warmth, and Susan guessed Eastvale might hit seventy before the day was over. Indian summer, indeed. She took her jacket off and slung it over her shoulder. At that time of year in the Dales, any good day was a bonus not to be wasted. Tomorrow might come rain, flood and famine, so seize the moment. Children played football in the streets, or rode around on bicycles and skateboards; men with their shirtsleeves rolled up flung buckets of soapy water over their cars, then waxed them to perfection; groups of teenagers stood around street corners smoking, trying to look sullen and menacing, and failing on both counts; doors and windows stood open; some people even sat on their doorsteps reading the Sunday papers and drinking tea.

As Susan walked, she could smell meat roasting and cakes baking. She also heard snatches of just about every kind of music, from Crispian St Peters singing "You Were on My Mind" to the opening of Elgar's cello concerto, which she only recognized because it was the same excerpt as the one on the CD she got free with her classical music magazine last month.

The Leaview Estate had been built just after the war. The houses, a mix of bungalows, semis and terraces, were solid, their style and materials in harmony with the rest of Swainsdale's limestone and gritstone architecture. No ugly maisonettes or blocks of flats spoiled the skyline the way they did across town on the newer East Side Estate. And on the Leaview Estate, many of the streets were named after flowers.

It was almost noon, and Susan had already covered the Primroses, the Laburnums and the Roses without any luck. Now she was about to move on to the Daffodils and Buttercups. She carried a clipboard with her, carefully ticking off all the houses she visited, putting question marks and notes beside any responses she found suspicious, keeping a keen eye open for bruised knuckles and any other signs of recent pugilism. If someone weren't home, she would circle the house number. After every street, she used her personal radio to report back to the station. If Hatchley or any of the uniformed officers got results first, then the communications centre would inform her.

A boy came speeding around the corner of Daffodil Rise on Rollerblades, and Susan managed to jump out of the way in the nick of time. He didn't stop. She held her hand to her chest until her heartbeat slowed to normal and thought about arresting him on a traffic offence. Then the adrenalin ebbed away and she got her breath back. She rang the bell of number two.

The woman who answered was probably in her late fifties, Susan guessed. Nicely turned out: hair recently permed, only a touch of lipstick, face-powder. Maybe just back from church. She wore a beige cardigan, despite the heat. As she spoke, she held it closed over her pale pink blouse.

"Yes, dearie?" she said.

Susan showed her warrant card and held out the mortuary attendant's sketch. "We're trying to find out who this boy is," she said. "We think he might live locally, so we're asking around to find out if anyone knows him."

The woman stared at the drawing, then tilted her head and scratched her chin.

"Well," she said. "It *could* be Jason Fox."

"Jason Fox?" It sounded like a pop star's name to Susan.

"Yes. Mr and Mrs Fox's young lad."

Well, Susan thought, tapping her pen against her clipboard, that's enlightening. "Do they live around here?"

"Aye. Just over the street." She pointed. "Number seven. But I only said it *might* be. It's not a good likeness, you know, love. You ought to get a proper artist working for you. Like my lad, Laurence. Now there's an artist for you. He sells his prints at the craft centre in town, you know. I'm sure he—"

"Yes, Mrs ... ?"

"Ingram's the name. Laurence Ingram."

"I'll bear him in mind, Mrs Ingram. Now, is there anything you can tell me about Jason Fox?"

"The nose isn't right. That's the main thing. Very good with noses, is my Laurence. Did Curly Watts from 'Coronation Street' down to a tee, and that's not an easy one. Did you know he'd done Curly Watts? Right popular with the celebrities is my Laurence. Oh, yes, very—"

Susan took a deep breath, then went on. "Mrs Ingram, could you tell me if you've seen Jason Fox around lately?"

"Not since yesterday. But then he's never around much. Lives in Leeds, I think."

"How old is he?"

"I couldn't say for certain. He's left school, though. I know that."

"Any trouble?"

"Jason? No. Quiet as a mouse. As I said, you hardly ever see him around. But it *does* look like him except for the nose. And it's easy to get noses wrong, as my Laurence says."

"Thank you, Mrs Ingram," said Susan, glancing over at number seven. "Thank you very much." And she hurried down the path.

"Wait a minute," Mrs Ingram called after her. "Aren't you going to tell me what's happened? After all the help I've given you. Has summat happened to young Jason? Has he been up to summat?"

If Jason's the one we're looking for, Susan thought, then you'll find out soon enough. As yet, he was only a "possible," but she knew she had better inform Banks before barging in on her own. She went back to the corner of the street and spoke into her personal radio.

V

Banks walked quickly through the narrow streets of tourist shops behind the police station, then down King Street towards Daffodil Rise. Beyond the Leaview Estate, the town gradually dissolved into countryside, the sides of the valley narrowing and growing steeper the further west they went.

Near Eastvale, Swainsdale was a broad valley, with plenty of room for villages and meadows, and for the River Swain to meander this way and that. But twenty or thirty miles in, around Swainshead, it was an area of high fells, much narrower and less hospitable to human settlements. One or two places, like Swainshead itself, and the remote Skield, managed to eke out an existence in the wild landscape around Witch Fell and Adam's Fell, but only just.

The last row of old cottages, Gallows View, pointed west like a crooked finger into the dale. Banks's first case in Eastvale had centred around those cottages, he remembered as he hurried on towards Daffodil Rise.

Graham Sharp, who had been an important figure in the case, had died of a heart attack over the summer, Banks had heard. He had sold his shop a few years ago, and it had been run since by the Mahmoods, whom Banks knew slightly through his son, Brian. He had seen them down at the station, too, recently; according to Susan, someone had lobbed a brick through their window a couple of weeks ago.

In what used to be empty fields around Gallows View, a new housing estate was under construction, scheduled for completion in a year's time. Banks could see the half-dug foundations scattered with puddles, the piles of bricks and boards, sun glinting on idle cranes and concrete-mixers. One or two streets had been partially built, but none of the houses had roofs yet.

Number seven Daffodil Rise really stood out from the rest of the houses on the street. Not only had the owners put up a little white fence around the garden and installed a panelled, natural-pine-look door, complete with a stained-glass window-pane (lunacy, Banks thought, so easy to break and enter), they also had one of the few gardens in the street that lived up to the flower motif. And because it had been a long summer, many of the flowers usually gone by the end of September were still in bloom. Bees droned around the red and yellow roses that clung to their thorny bushes just under the front window, and the garden beds were a riot of chrysanthemums, dahlias, begonias and gladioli.

The front door was ajar. Banks tapped softly before walking in. He had told Susan Gay over the radio that she should talk to the parents and try to confirm whether the drawing might be of their son before he arrived, but not to tell them anything until he got there.

When Banks walked in, Mrs Fox was just bringing a tea-tray through from the kitchen into the bright, airy living-room. Cut flowers in crystal vases adorned the dining-table and the polished wood top of the fake-coal electric fire. Roses climbed trellises on the cream wallpaper. Over the fireplace hung a framed antique map of Yorkshire, the kind you can buy in tourist shops for a couple of quid. Along the narrowest wall stood floor-to-ceiling wooden shelving that seemed to be full of long-playing records.

Mrs Fox was about forty, Banks guessed. Sandra's age. She wore a loose white top and black leggings that outlined her finely tapered legs, with well-toned calves and shapely thighs—the kind you only got at that age from regular exercise. She had a narrow face, and her features seemed cramped just a little too close together. Her hair was simply parted in the middle and hung down as far as her shoulders on each side, curling under just a little at the bottom. The roots were only a slightly darker shade of blonde.

Mr Fox stood up to shake hands with Banks. Bald except for a couple of black chevrons above his ears, with a thin, bony face, he wore black-rimmed glasses, jeans and a green sweatshirt. He was exceptionally skinny, which made him appear tall, and he looked as if he had the kind of metabolism that allowed him to eat as much as he wanted without putting on a pound. Banks wasn't quite as skinny himself, but he never seemed to put on much weight either, despite the ale and the junk food.

Tea poured, Mrs Fox sat down on the sofa with her husband and crossed her long legs. Husband and wife left enough space for another person to sit between them, but Banks took a chair from the dining-table, turned it around and sat, resting his arms on the back.

"Mr and Mrs Fox were just telling me," Susan Gay said, getting her notebook out, "that Jason looks like the lad in the drawing, and he didn't sleep here last night."

"She won't tell us anything." Mrs Fox appealed to Banks with her small, glittering eyes. "Is our Jason in any trouble?"

"Has he ever been in trouble before?" Banks asked.

She shook her head. "Never. He's a good boy. He never caused us any problems, has he, Steven? That's why I can't understand you coming here. We've never had the police here before."

"Weren't you worried when Jason didn't sleep here last night?"

Mrs Fox looked surprised. "No. Why should I be?"

"Weren't you expecting him?"

"Look, what's happened? What's going on?"

"Jason lives in Leeds, Chief Inspector," Steven Fox cut in. "He just uses our house when it suits him, a bit like a hotel."

"Oh, come on, Steven," his wife said. "You know that's not fair. Jason's grown up. He's got his own life to live. But he's still our son."

"When it suits him."

"What does he do in Leeds?" Banks cut in.

"He's got a good job," said Steven Fox. "And there's not many as can say that these days. An office job at a factory out in Stourton."

"I assume he's also got a flat or a house in Leeds, too?"

"Yes. A flat.".

"Can you give DC Gay the address, please? And the name and address of the factory?"

"Of course." Steven Fox gave Susan the information.

"Do either of you know where Jason was last night?" Banks asked. "Or who he was with?"

Mrs Fox answered. "No," she said. "Look, Chief Inspector, can't you please tell us what's going on? I'm worried. Is my Jason in trouble? Has something happened to him?"

"I understand that you're worried," Banks said, "and I'll do everything I can to hurry things up. Please bear with me, though, and answer just a few more short questions. Just a few more minutes. Okay?"

They both nodded reluctantly.

"Do you have a recent photograph of Jason?"

Mrs Fox got up and brought a small framed photo from the sideboard. "Only this," she said. "He was seventeen when it was taken."

The boy in the photo looked similar to the victim, but it was impossible to make a positive identification. Teenagers can change a lot in three or four years, and heavy boots do a great deal of damage to facial features.

"Do you know what Jason did yesterday? Where he went?"

Mrs Fox bit her lip. "Yesterday," she said. "He got home about twelve o'clock. We had sandwiches for lunch, then he went off to play football, like he usually does."

"Where?"

"He plays for Eastvale United," Steven Fox said.

Banks knew the team; they were only amateur players, but he'd taken Brian to see them once or twice, and they had demonstrated the triumph of enthusiasm over talent. Their matches had become quite popular with the locals, and they sometimes managed to draw two or three hundred to their bumpy field on a few acres of waste ground between York Road and Market Street.

"He's a striker," said Mrs Fox, with pride. "Top goal scorer in North Yorkshire last season. Amateur leagues, that is."

"Impressive," said Banks. "Did you see him after the game?"

"Yes. He came home for his tea after he'd had a quick drink with his mates from the team, then he went out about seven o'clock, didn't he, Steven?"

Mr Fox nodded.

"Did he say whether he'd be back?"

"No."

"Does he normally stop here on weekends?"

"Sometimes," Mrs Fox answered. "But not always. Sometimes he drives back to Leeds. And sometimes he doesn't come up at all."

"Does he have his own key?"

Mrs Fox nodded.

"What kind of car does he drive?"

"Oh, my God, it's not a car crash, is it?" Mrs Fox put her hands to her face. "Oh, please don't tell me our Jason's been killed in a car crash."

At least Banks could assure her of that honestly.

"It's one of those little Renaults," said Steven Fox. "A Clio. Bloody awful colour, it is, too. Shiny green, like the back of some sort of insect."

"Where does he park when he's here?"

Mr Fox jerked his head. "There's a double garage round the back. He usually parks it there, next to ours."

"Have you looked to see if the car's still there?"

"No. I'd no call to."

"Did you hear it last night?"

He shook his head. "No. We usually go to bed early. Before Jason gets back, if he's stopping the night. He tries to be quiet, and we're both pretty heavy sleepers."

"Would you be kind enough to show DC Gay where the garage is?" Banks asked Steven Fox. "And, Susan, if the car's there, see if he left the keys in it."

Steven Fox led Susan out through the back door.

"Does Jason have a girlfriend?" Banks asked Mrs Fox while they were gone.

She shook her head. "I don't think so. He might have someone in Leeds, I suppose, but ..."

"He never mentioned her or brought her here?"

"No. I don't think he had anyone steady."

"Do you think he would have told you if he had?"

"I can't see any reason why he wouldn't."

"How do you and Jason get along?"

She turned away. "We get along just fine."

Susan and Steven Fox came back from the garage. "It's there all right," Susan said. "A green Clio. I took the number. And no keys."

"What is it?" Mrs Fox asked. "If Jason wasn't in a car crash, did he hit someone? Was there an accident?"

"No," said Banks. "He didn't hit anyone." He sighed and looked at the map over the fireplace. He couldn't really hold back telling them any longer. The best he could do was play up the uncertainty aspect. "I don't want to alarm you," he said, "but a boy was killed last night, probably in a fight. DC Gay showed you the artist's impression, and someone suggested it might resemble Jason. That's why we need to know his movements and whereabouts."

Banks waited for the outburst, but it didn't come. Instead, Mrs Fox shook her head and said, "It *can't* be our Jason. He wouldn't get into fights or anything like that. And you can't really tell from the picture, can you?"

Banks agreed. "I'm sure you're right," he said. "He's probably gone off somewhere with his mates for the weekend without telling you. Kids. No consideration sometimes, have they? Would Jason do something like that?"

Mrs Fox nodded. "Oh, yes. Never tells us owt, our Jason, does he, Steven?"

"That's right," Mr Fox agreed. But Banks could tell from his tone that he wasn't quite as convinced as his wife about Jason's not being the victim. In his experience, mothers often held more illusions about their sons than fathers did.

"Does Jason have any friends on the estate he might have gone out with?" Banks asked. "Anyone local?"

Mrs Fox looked at her husband before answering. "No," she said. "See, we've only been living in Eastvale for three years. Since we moved from Halifax. Besides, Jason doesn't drink. Well, not hardly."

"When did he get this job in Leeds?"

"Just before we moved."

"I see," said Banks. "So he hasn't really spent much time here, had time to settle in and make friends?"

"That's right," said Mrs Fox.

"Does he have any other relations in the area he might have gone to visit? An uncle, perhaps, someone like that?"

"Only my dad," said Mrs Fox. "That's why we moved here, really, to be nearer my dad. My mam died two years ago, and he's not getting any younger."

"Where does he live?"

"Up in Lyndgarth, so he's not far away, in case of emergencies, like. Eastvale was the closest town Steven could get a transfer."

"What kind of work do you do, Mr Fox?"

"Building society. Abbey National. That big branch on York Road, just north of the market square."

Banks nodded. "I know the one. Look, it's just a thought, but does Jason spend much time with his grandfather? Might he be stopping with him?"

Mrs Fox shook her head. "He'd have let us know, Dad would. He's got a telephone. Didn't want one, but we insisted. Besides, Jason would've needed the car."

"Would your father know anything more about Jason's friends and his habits?"

"I don't think so," said Mrs Fox, fidgeting with her wedding ring. "They used to be close when Jason were a young lad, but you know what it's like when kids grow up." She shrugged.

Banks did. He well remembered preferring the company of his grandparents to that of his mother and father when he was young. They were more indulgent with him, for a start, and would often give him a tanner for sweets—which he'd usually spend on sherbet, gobstoppers and a threepenny lucky bag. He also liked his grandfather's pipe-rack, the smell of tobacco around the dark-panelled house, the tarnished silver cigarette case with the dint where a German bullet had hit it, saving his grandfather's life—or so his grandfather had told him. He had loved the stories about the war—not the second, but the first— and his grandfather had even let him wear his old gas mask, which smelled of rubber and dust. They had spent days walking by the River Nene, standing by the railway tracks to watch the sleek, streamlined *Flying Scotsman* go by. But all that had changed when Banks entered his teens, and he felt especially guilty about not seeing his granddad for a whole year before the old man died, while Banks was at college in London.

"Are there any other family members?" he asked. "Brothers or sisters?"

"Only Maureen, my daughter. She's just turned eighteen."

"Where is she?"

"Nurses' training school, up in Newcastle."

"Would she be able to help us with any of Jason's friends?"

"No. They're not particularly close. Never were. Different as chalk and cheese."

Banks glanced over at Susan and indicated she should put her notebook away. "Would you mind if we had a quick look at Jason's room?" he asked. "Just to see if there's anything there that might help us find out what he was doing last night?"

Steven Fox stood up and walked towards the stairs. "I'll show you."

The tidiness of the room surprised Banks. He didn't know why—stereotyping, no doubt—but he'd been expecting the typical teenager's room, like that of his son, Brian, which usually looked as if it had just been hit by a tornado. But Jason's bed was made, sheets so tightly stretched across the mattress you could bounce a coin on them, and if he had dirty washing lying around, as Brian always had, then Banks couldn't see it.

Against one of the walls stood shelving similar to that downstairs, also stacked with long-playing records and several rows of 45s.

"Jason likes music, I see," Banks said.

"Actually, they're mine," said Steven Fox, walking over and running his long fingers over a row of LPs. "My collection. Jason says it's okay to use the wall space because he's not here that often. It's mostly sixties stuff. I started collecting in 1962, when 'Love Me Do' came out. I've got everything The Beatles ever recorded, all originals, all in mint condition. And not only The Beatles. I've got all The Rolling Stones, Grateful Dead, Doors, Cream, Jimi Hendrix, The Searchers... If you can get it on vinyl, I've got it. But I don't suppose you're interested in all that."

Banks *was* interested in Mr Fox's record collection, and on another occasion he would have been more than happy to look over the titles. Just because he loved opera and classical music in general didn't mean he looked down on rock, jazz or blues—only on country-and-western and brass bands. This latter opinion was regarded as a serious lapse of taste in Yorkshire, Banks was well aware, but he felt that anyone who had had to endure an evening of brass-band renditions of Mozart arias, as he once had, was more than entitled to it.

Apart from Steven Fox's record collection, the room was strangely Spartan, almost an ascetic's cell, and even on such a warm day it seemed to emanate the chill of a cloister. There was only one framed print on the wall, and it showed a group of three naked women. According to the title, they were supposed to be Norse goddesses, but they looked more like bored housewives to Banks. There was no television or video, no stereo and no books. Maybe he kept most of his things in his flat in Leeds.

Steven Fox stood in the doorway as Banks and Susan started poking around the spotless corners. The dresser drawers were full of underclothes and casual wear—jeans, sweatshirts, T-shirts. By the side of the bed lay a set of weights. Banks could just about lift them, but he didn't fancy doing fifty bench-presses.

In the wardrobe, he found Jason's football strip, a couple of very conservative suits, both navy blue, and some white dress shirts and sober ties. And that was it. So much for any clues about Jason Fox's life and friends.

Back downstairs, Mrs Fox was pacing the living-room, gnawing at her knuckles. Banks could tell she was no longer able to keep at bay the terrible realization that something bad might have happened to her son. After all, Jason hadn't come home, his car was still in the garage, and now the police were in her house. A part of him hoped, for her sake, that the victim wasn't Jason. But there was only one way to find out for certain.

TWO

I

Frank Hepplethwaite reached for his inhaler, aimed it at the back of his throat and let off a blast of nitro. Within seconds the pain in his chest began to abate, along with that suffocating sense of panic that always came with it.

Frank sat completely still in his favourite armchair, the one that Edna had been constantly nagging him to get rid of. True, the seat-cushion was worn, and it bulged like a hernia through the support slats underneath; and true, the frayed upholstery had long since lost whatever pattern it might have had and faded to a sort of dull brown with a worn, greasy spot where he had rested the back of his head year after year. But he had never found anywhere else quite so comfortable to sit and read in all his seventy-six years—and though he was seventy-six, his eyes were as good as they'd ever been. Well, almost, if he put his reading glasses on. Better than his teeth and his heart, at any rate.

When he felt steady enough again, he rested his palms on the threadbare patches of fabric and pushed himself up, slowly, to standing position. Five foot ten in his stockinged feet, and he still weighed no more than ten stone.

Face it, though, Frank, he told himself as he wrapped his scarf around his neck and reached for his tweed jacket on the hook behind the door, you won't be able to go on like this by yourself much longer. Even now, Mrs Weston came in once or twice a week to tidy up and make his meals. And his daughter, Josie, came over from Eastvale to do his washing and to vacuum.

He could still manage the little domestic tasks, like boiling an egg, washing what few dishes he used, and making his bed in a morning—but he couldn't change the sheets, and any sort of elaborate meal was well beyond him. Not that he lacked the ability—he had been a passable cook in his time—he merely lacked the stamina. And for how much longer would he be able to manage even the little necessities? How long would it be before a simple visit to the toilet was beyond him, a bowel movement too much of a strain on his heart?

Best not think about that, he told himself, sensing the abyss that awaited him. Beyond this point be monsters. At least Edna had gone first, bless her soul, and while he missed her every minute he continued to live, at least he wouldn't have to worry about her coping after he'd gone.

Frank went into the hall and paused at the front door. He rarely got any letters these days, so he was surprised to see one lying on the carpet. It must have arrived yesterday, Saturday. He hadn't been out since Friday, hadn't even had cause to go into the hall, so it was no wonder he hadn't noticed it. Bending carefully, knees creaking, he picked it up and slipped it into his inside pocket. It could wait. It wasn't a bill. At least, it didn't look official; it didn't have one of those windows.

He opened the door, sniffed the air and smiled. Well, well, another taste of summer, with just a hint of peat smoke from the village. What strange weather the dale had been having these past few years. Global warming, the papers said, damage to the ozone layer, greenhouse effect. Whatever all that was. Bloody grand, anyway.

He decided to be devil-may-care today and took off his scarf, then he walked down the road towards the green, pausing by the whitewashed façade of The Swainsdale Heifer to watch out for traffic hurtling across the blind corner, the way it did despite the warning signs. Then he walked on the broad cobbled area in front of the gift shop, the small Barclay's Bank branch and the estate agent's office, past The King's Head to the third pub in the village, The Black Bull.

It would have to be the bloody farthest pub from his house, he always grumbled to himself, but The Black Bull had been his local for over forty years, and he was damned if he was going to change it now, even if the walk did sometimes put him out of breath. And even if the new landlord didn't seem to give a toss for anyone but tourists with plenty of readies to flash around.

Frank had seen a dozen landlords come and go. He was all right in his way, was old Jacob—a London Jew born of one of the few families lucky enough to escape to England from Germany just before the war—and he had his living to make, but he was a tight old skinflint. A drink or two on the house now and then would make an old man's pension go a lot further. The last landlord had understood that. Not Jacob. He was as close with his brass as old Len Metcalfe had been over ten years back.

Frank pushed the heavy door, which creaked as it opened, and walked across the worn stone flagging to the bar. "Double Bell's, please," he said.

"Hello, there, Frank," said Jacob. "How are you today?"

Frank touched his chest. "Just a twinge or two, Jacob," he said. "Just a twinge. Other than that I'm right as rain."

He took his drink and wandered over to his usual small table to the left of the bar, where he could see down the corridor to the machines and the billiard table on the raised area at the far end. As usual, he said hello to Mike and Ken, who were sitting on stools at the bar agonizing over a crossword puzzle, and to that poncy southern windbag, Clive, who was sitting a stool or two down from them puffing on his bloody pipe and pontificating about sheep breeding, as if he knew a bloody thing about it. A few of the other tables were occupied by tourists, some of them kitted out for a day's walking or climbing. It was Sunday, after all. And a fine one, at that.

Frank took a sip of Bell's, winced at the sharpness and hoped the burning he felt as it went down was just the whisky, not the final heart attack. Then he remembered the letter he had put in his pocket. He put on his reading glasses, reached his hand in and slipped it out.

The address was handwritten, and there was no indication of who had sent it. He didn't recognize the writing, but then he hardly ever saw handwriting these days. Everything you got was typed or done on computers. He couldn't make out the postmark clearly, either, but it looked like Brighouse, or maybe Bradford. It could even be Brighton or Bristol, for all he knew. Posted on Thursday.

Carefully, he tore the envelope open and slid out the single sheet of paper. It had type on both sides, in columns, and a large bold heading across the top. At first he thought it was a flyer for a jumble sale or something, but as he read, he realized how wrong he was.

Confused at first, then angry, he read the printed words. Long before he had finished, tears came to his eyes. He told himself they were Scotch tears, just the burning of the whisky, but he knew they weren't. He also knew who had sent him the flyer. And why.

II

Some of the more modern mortuaries were equipped with video cameras and monitor screens to make it easier for relatives to identify accident or murder victims from a comfortable distance. Not in Eastvale, though. There, the attendant still slid the body out of the refrigerated unit and slipped back the sheet from the face.

Which was odd, Banks thought, as the mortuary was certainly the most recently renovated part of that draughty old pile of stone known as Eastvale General Infirmary.

Steven and Josie Fox had been unwilling at first to come and view the body. Banks could see their point. If it *were* Jason, they would have to face up to his death; and if it *weren't*, then they would have gone through all the unpleasantness of looking at a badly beaten corpse for nothing.

Reluctantly, though, they had agreed, but refused Banks's offer of a police car and chose to walk instead. Susan Gay had returned to the station.

Because the hospital was small, old and too close to the tourist shops, another, much larger, establishment was under construction on the northern edge of the town. But, for now, Eastvale General was all there was. Every time he walked up the front steps, Banks shuddered. There was something about the dark, rough stone, even on a fine day, that made him think of operations without anaesthetic, of unsterilized surgical instruments, of plague and death.

He led the Foxes through the maze of high corridors and down the stairs to the basement, where the mortuary was. Banks identified himself to one of the attendants, who nodded, checked his files and touched Mrs Fox lightly on the arm. "Please, follow me," he said.

They did. Along a white-tiled corridor into a chilled room. There, the attendant checked his papers again before sliding out the tray on which the body lay.

Banks watched the Foxes. They weren't touching one another at all, not holding hands or clutching arms the way many couples did when faced with such a situation. Could there really be such distance between them that even the possibility of seeing their son dead at any second couldn't bridge it? It was remarkable, Banks had often thought, how people who no longer have any feelings for one another can keep on going through the motions, afraid of change, of loneliness, of rejection. He thought of Sandra, then pushed the thought aside. He and Sandra were nothing like the Foxes. They weren't so much separate as *independent*; they gave one another space. Besides, they had too much in common, had shared too much joy and pain over the years to simply go through the motions of a failed marriage, hadn't they?

The attendant pulled back the white sheet to reveal the corpse's face. Josie Fox put her hand to her mouth and started to sob. Steven Fox, pale as the sheet that covered his son, simply nodded and said, "It's him. It's our Jason."

Banks was surprised at what a good job the mortuary had done on the boy's face. While it was clear that he had been severely beaten, the nose was straight, the cheekbones aligned, the mouth shut tight to cover the shattered teeth. The only wrong note was the way that one eye stared straight up at the ceiling and the other a little to the left, at Mr and Mrs Fox.

Banks could never get over the strange effect looking at dead people had on him. Not bodies at the crime scene, so much. They sometimes churned his guts, especially if the injuries were severe, but they were essentially *work* to him; they were human beings robbed of something precious, an insult to the sanctity of life.

On the other hand, when he saw bodies laid out in the mortuary or in a funeral parlour, they had a sort of calming effect on him. He couldn't explain it, but as he looked down at the shell of what had once been Jason Fox, he knew there was nobody home. The pale corpse resembled nothing more than a fragile eggshell, and if you tapped it hard enough, it would crack open revealing nothing but darkness inside. Somehow, the effect of all this was to relieve him, just for a few welcome moments, of his own growing fear of death.

Banks led the dazed Foxes out into the open air. They stood on the steps of the hospital for a moment, silently watching the people come out of the small congregationalist church.

Banks lit a cigarette. "Is there anything I can do?" he asked.

After a few moments, Steven Fox looked at him. "What? Oh, sorry," he said. Then he shook his head. "No, there's nothing. I'll take Josie home now. Make her a nice cup of tea."

His wife said nothing.

They walked down King Street, still not touching. Banks sighed and turned up towards the station. At least he knew who the victim was now; first, he would let his team know, and then they could begin the investigation proper.

III

Detective Sergeant Jim Hatchley would normally have enjoyed nothing more than a pub-crawl any day of the week, any hour of the day or night, but that Sunday, all he wanted to do as he walked into his fifth pub, The Jubilee, at the corner of Market Street and Waterloo Road, was go home, crawl into bed and sleep for a week, a month, nay, a bloody year.

For the past two weeks, his daughter, April, named after the month she was born because neither Hatchley nor his wife, Carol, could agree on any other name, had kept him awake all night, every night, as those bloody inconvenient lumps of calcium called teeth bored their way through the tender flesh of her gums with flagrant disregard for the wee bairn's comfort. Or for his. And he hadn't been well enough prepared for it. In fact, he hadn't been prepared for it at all.

The first year and a bit of April's life, you would never have known she was there, so quiet was she. At worst, she'd cry out a couple of times when she was hungry, but as soon as Carol's tit was in her mouth she was happy as a pig in clover. And why not, thought Hatchley, who felt exactly the same way about Carol's tit himself, not that he'd been getting much of *that* lately, either.

But now April had suddenly turned into a raging monster and put paid to his sleep. He knew he looked like he'd been on the piss every morning he went into work—he could see the way they were all looking at him—but if truth be told, he hadn't had a drink in weeks. A real drink in a pub, that was.

He remembered some story, an old wives' tale probably, about rubbing whisky on a teething baby's gums to quieten it down. Well, Carol wouldn't let him do that—she said she had enough on her plate with one boozer in the family—so he had rubbed it on his own gums, so to speak, or rather let it caress them briefly and gently on its way down to his stomach. Sometimes that helped him get a ten-minute nap between screaming sessions. But he never had more than two or three glasses a night. He hadn't had a hangover in so long that not only had he almost forgotten what they felt like, he was actually beginning to miss them.

So it was with both a sense of nostalgia and a feeling that he'd rather be anywhere else, especially asleep in bed, that Sergeant Hatchley entered The Jubilee that Sunday lunch-time.

Contrary to rumours around the station, Hatchley didn't know the landlord of every pub in Eastvale. Apart from The Queen's Arms, the station's local, he tended to avoid the pubs near the town centre, especially those on Market Street, which always seemed to be full of yobs. If there were trouble on a Saturday night, which there often was these days, you could bet it would be on York Road or Market Street.

The Jubilee was also a chain pub: all fruit machines, theme nights, trivia and overpriced food. Overpriced ale, too. Rock bands played there on Friday and Saturday nights, and it had a reputation for getting some of the best up-and-coming bands in Yorkshire. Not that Hatchley gave a toss about rock music, being a brass-band man himself. The Jubilee was also reputed to be a fertile hunting ground for birds and drugs.

On Sunday lunch-times, though, it became a family pub, and each family seemed to have about six children in tow. All of them screaming at once.

Hatchley leaned over the bar and presented his warrant card to the barmaid as she pulled someone a pint.

"Any trouble here Saturday night, love?" he asked.

She jerked her head without looking up at him. "Better ask His Nibs over there. I weren't working."

Hatchley edged down the bar and shoved his way through the drinkers standing there, getting a few dirty looks on the way. He finally caught the barman's attention and asked for a word. "Can't you see I'm rushed off my feet?" the man protested. "What is it you want?" Like everyone else behind the bar, he wore black trousers and a blue-and-white striped shirt with THE JUBILEE stitched across the left breast.

When Hatchley showed his card, the man stopped protesting that he was too busy and called one of the other bar staff to stand in for him. Then he gestured Hatchley down to the far end of the bar, where it was quiet.

"Sorry about that," he said. "I hate bloody Sunday lunch-times, especially after working a Saturday night." He scratched his thinning hair and a shower of dandruff fell on his shoulders. How bloody hygienic, Hatchley thought. "My name's Ted, by the way."

"Aye well, Ted, lad," Hatchley said slowly, "I'm sorry to disturb you, but we all have our crosses to bear. First off, was there any trouble in here on Saturday night?"

"What do you mean, trouble?"

"Fights, barneys, slanging matches, hair-pulling, that sort of thing."

Ted frowned. "Nowt out of the ordinary," he said. "I mean, we were busy as buggery, so there was no way I could see what were going on everywhere at once, especially with the bloody racket that band were making."

"I appreciate that," said Hatchley, who had had the same conversation five times already that morning and was getting steadily sick of it. He slipped the sketch from his briefcase. "Recognize him?" he asked.

The barman squinted at the drawing then passed it back to Hatchley. "Could be any number of people, couldn't it?"

Hatchley wasn't sure why, but he felt the back of his scalp prickle. Always a sign something wasn't quite right. "Aye, but it's not," he said. "It's an amateur artist's reconstruction of a lad's face, a face that were booted to a bloody pulp after closing time last night. So any help you could give us would be much appreciated, Ted."

Ted turned pale and averted his eyes before answering. "Well, seeing as you put it like that … But I'm telling you the truth. Nothing happened."

Hatchley shook his head. "Why don't I find myself believing you, Ted? Can you answer me that?"

"Look." Ted held his hand up, palm out. "I don't want any trouble."

Hatchley smiled, showing stained and crooked teeth. "And I'm not here to give you any."

"It's just …"

"Frightened of something?"

"No. It's not that." Ted licked his lips. "I mean, I wouldn't want to swear to owt, but there were a lad looked a bit like that in last night. It could've been him."

"What was he doing?"

"Having a drink with a mate."

"What did this mate look like?"

"About my height. That's five foot six. Stocky build. Tough-looking customer, you know, like he lifted weights or summat. Short fair hair, almost skinhead, but not quite. And an earring. One of them loops, like pirates used to have in old films."

"Had you seen them before?"

"Only the one in the drawing, if it is him. Sometimes comes in on a weekend after a match, like, just for a quick one with the lads. Plays for United."

"Aye, so I've heard. Troublemaker?"

"No. Not at all. Not even much of a boozer. He's usually gone early. It's just …" Ted scratched his head again, sending more flakes of dandruff onto the polished bar. "There was a bit of a scuffle Saturday night, that's all."

"No punches?"

He shook his head. "Far as I can tell, the lad in the picture bumped into another lad and spilled some of his drink. The other lad said something and this one replied, like, and gave him a bit of a shove for good measure. That's all that happened. Honest. Pushing and shoving. It were all over before it began. Nobody got beat up."

"Could it have continued outside?"

"I suppose it could have. As I said, though, it seemed like summat and nowt to me."

"This other lad, the one whose drink got spilled, did he have any mates with him?"

"There were three of them."

Hatchley pointed to the sketch again. "Did you see this lad and his mate leave?"

"Aye. I remember them because I had to remind them more than once to drink up."

"Were they drunk?"

"Mebbe. A bit. They weren't arse over tit, if that's what you mean. They could still walk in a straight line and speak without slurring. Like I said, I'd seen the one in the picture a few times before, and he weren't much of a drinker. He might have had a jar more than usual, but who hasn't had by closing time on a Saturday night?"

"And it wasn't till after eleven o'clock that you got rid of them, right?"

"Aye. About quarter past. I know some places are a bit lax, but there's no extension of drinking-up time in The Jubilee. The manager makes that clear."

"What about the other three?"

"They'd gone by then."

"Were they drunk, too?"

"No. At least they didn't act it."

"Anything else you can tell me about them?"

Ted looked away.

"Why do I get the impression you're still holding something back, Ted?"

"I don't know, do I?"

"I think you do. Is it drugs? Worried we'll close the place down and you'll lose your job?"

"No way. Look, like I said ... I don't want to cause any bother."

"What makes you think you'd be causing bother by telling me the truth, Ted? All right. Let me guess. If it's not drugs, then you're probably frightened these three hooligans are going to come back and wreck your pub if they find out you ratted on them. Is that it?"

"Partly, I suppose. But they weren't hooligans."

"Oh? Who were they, then? Did you recognize them?"

"Aye. I recognized them. Two of them, anyroad."

"Names?"

"I don't know their names, but one of them's that lad from the shop off Cardigan Road. You know, the one opposite the bottom of the Leaview Estate. And the other one's dad owns that new restaurant in the market square. The Himalaya."

Hatchley raised his eyebrows.

"See what I mean?" Ted went on. "See what I'm worried about, now? I don't want to get stuck in the middle of some bloody racial incident, do I? The lad in your picture called one of them a 'Paki bastard' and told him to get out of the fucking way. That's what happened."

IV

Gallows View, *déjà vu*, Banks thought, as he pulled up outside the Mahmoods' shop. Of course, the street had changed a lot in six years, and the wire mesh that covered the display windows was one of the changes. Inside, the smell of cumin and coriander was another.

The Mahmoods were one of three Asian families in Eastvale. In these parts of Yorkshire north of Leeds and Bradford you saw very few visible minorities, even in the larger cities like York and Harrogate.

Mahmood had enlarged the shop, Banks noticed. Originally, it had occupied the ground floor of only one cottage, and the Sharps had used the other as their living-room. But now the shop had been extended to take up the frontage of both cottages, complete with extra plate-glass window and a new freezer section. The Mahmoods sold a whole range of products, from bread, eggs, cigarettes, milk and beer to washing-up liquid, tights, magazines, lipstick, stationery and toothpaste. They also rented out videos.

Pretty soon, when the new estate was finished, the shop would be a little gold mine.

Unlike most people the racist bigots refer to as "Pakis," Charles Mahmood actually did hail from Pakistan. Or rather, his father, Wasim Mahmood, did. Wasim and family emigrated to England in 1948, shortly after partition. Charles was born in Bradford in 1953, around the time of Queen Elizabeth's coronation, and he was, naturally, given the name of her only male child because the Mahmoods were proud of their new country and its royal heritage.

Unfortunately for Charles, when his own son was born in 1976, the Prince of Wales had yet to marry and produce offspring. To name his child, Charles had to take the devious route of stealing one of the prince's middle names. He chose George. Why he didn't choose Philip, which might have been easier on the lad at school, nobody knew. As for George himself, he said he was only glad his dad hadn't called him Arthur, which would have seemed even more old-fashioned than George to his classmates.

Banks knew all this because George had been a contemporary of his own son, Brian, at Eastvale Comprehensive, and the two had become good friends during their last couple of years there. George had spent quite a bit of time at the Banks household, and Banks remembered his love of music, his instinctive curiosity about things and his sense of humour. They had all laughed at the story of the family names, for example.

Now the kids seemed to have lost touch, drifted apart as people do, and Banks hadn't seen George for a while. Brian had just started his third year at college in Portsmouth, and George was still in Eastvale, pretty much unemployed, as far as Banks knew, apart from helping his dad out at the shop. Even though they hadn't seen one another in a while, Banks still felt a little uneasy about interviewing George in connection with a criminal matter.

Charles Mahmood greeted Banks with a smile of recognition; his wife, Shazia, waved from the other side of the shop, where she was stacking shelves with jars of instant coffee.

"Is it about that brick-chucking?" asked Charles in his broad West Yorkshire accent.

Banks told him it wasn't, but assured him that the matter was still under investigation.

"What's up, then?" Charles asked.

"George in?"

"George?" He flicked his head. "Upstairs. Why, what's happened?" Banks didn't think she could have heard, but Shazia Mahmood had stopped putting jars on shelves and seemed to be trying to eavesdrop.

"We don't know yet," Banks said. "There's nothing to worry about. I'd just like to talk to him. Okay?"

Charles Mahmood shrugged. "Fine with me."

"How's he doing these days?"

Charles nodded towards the stairs. "You'd better ask him. See for yourself. He's in his room."

"Problems?"

"Not really. Just a phase he's going through. Another seven-day wonder."

Banks smiled, remembering the way his father used to say that about every hobby he took up, from Meccano to stamp-collecting. He'd been right, too. Banks still felt that he lurched restlessly from interest to interest. "What particular phase is this one?" he asked.

"You'll find out soon enough."

"I'd better go talk to him, then," said Banks. "The curiosity's killing me."

He walked upstairs, aware of Shazia Mahmood's eyes drilling into his back, and didn't realize until he got to the top that he didn't know *which* room was George's. But it didn't matter by then. At the end of the hallway, beside the bathroom, a door stood slightly ajar and from inside the room, Banks could smell sandal-wood incense and hear piano music.

It was jazz, certainly, but not Monk, Bill Evans or Bud Powell. No-one like that. It didn't even resemble the wild flights of Cecil Taylor, one of whose records Banks had made the mistake of buying years ago on the strength of a review from a usually reliable critic. This music was repetitive and rhythmic, a sort of catchy, jangling melodic riff played over and over again with very few changes. It was vaguely familiar.

He tapped on the door and George Mahmood opened it. George was a good-looking boy with thick black hair, long eyelashes and loam-brown eyes. He looked at Banks for a moment, then said, "You're Brian's dad, aren't you? The copper."

It wasn't exactly the warm welcome Banks had hoped for; he had thought George might have remembered him with more affection. Still, attitudes change a lot in three years, especially when you're young. He smiled. "Right. That's me. The copper. Mind if I come in?"

"Is this a social call?"

"Not exactly."

"I didn't think so." George stood aside. "Better come in, anyway. I don't suppose I could stop you even if I wanted to."

Banks entered the bedroom and sat on a hardback chair at the desk. George slouched in an armchair. But not before he turned down the music a couple of notches. He was wearing baggy black trousers and a white top with a Nehru collar.

"Who is that playing?" Banks asked.

"Why?"

"I like it."

"It's Abdullah Ibrahim. He's a South African pianist."

Now that George mentioned the name, Banks realized he had heard of Ibrahim and his music before. "Didn't he used to be called Dollar Brand?" he asked.

"That's right. Just like Muhammad Ali used to be called Cassius Clay."

Banks hadn't heard of Cassius Clay in years, and he was surprised that someone as young as George had ever heard Ali's old name at all. They made a little uneasy small talk about Brian, then Banks got quickly to the point he had come for. "George," he said, "I've come to ask you about Saturday night."

"What about it?" George looked away towards the window. "And my name's not George any more. That's a stupid name, just my father's post-colonial genuflection. My name's Mohammed Mahmood."

As he spoke, George turned to look at Banks again and his eyes shone with defiant pride. Now Banks saw what Charles Mahmood meant. Now it made sense: Dollar Brand/Abdullah Ibrahim, the

Koran lying on the bedside table. George was exploring his Islamic roots.

Well, Banks told himself, be tolerant. Not all Muslims support death threats against writers. He didn't know much about the religion, but he supposed there must be as many forms of Islam as there are of Christianity, which runs a pretty broad spectrum if you include the Sandemanians, the Methodists, the Quakers and the Spanish Inquisition.

Why, then, did he feel so uncomfortable, as if he had lost someone he had known? Not a close friend, certainly, but a person he had liked and had shared things with. Now he was excluded—he could see it in George's eyes—he was the enemy. There would be no more music, laughter or understanding. Ideology had come between them, and it would rewrite history and deny that the music, laughter and understanding had ever happened in the first place. Banks had been through it once before with an old school friend who had become a born-again Christian. They no longer spoke to one another. Or, more accurately, Banks no longer spoke to *him*.

"Okay, Mohammed," he said, "did you go to The Jubilee with a couple of mates on Saturday night?"

"What if I did?"

"I thought Muslims weren't supposed to drink?"

Banks could swear he saw George blush. "I don't," he answered. "Well, not much. I'm stopping."

"Who were you with?"

"Why?"

"Is there any reason you don't want to tell me?"

George shrugged. "No. It doesn't matter. I was with Asim and Kobir."

"Are they from around here?"

"Asim is. Asim Nazur. His dad owns the Himalaya. They live in the flat above it."

"I know the place," said Banks, who had eaten there on more than one occasion. He also knew that Asim Nazur's father was some sort of bigwig in the Yorkshire Muslim community. "And the other lad?"

"Kobir. He's Asim's cousin from Bradford. He was just visiting, so we took him out to listen to some music, that's all. Look, why are—"

"What time did you leave the pub?"

"I wasn't looking at my watch."

"Before closing time?"

"Yes."

"Where did you go?"

"We bought some fish and chips at Sweaty Betty's, just down Market Street, then we ate them in a shop doorway because it were pissing down. After that we went home. Why?"

"You went your separate ways?"

"Course we went separate ways. You'd have to do, wouldn't you, if you lived in opposite directions?"

"Which way did you walk home?"

"Same way I always do from up there. Cut through the Carlaw Place ginnel over the rec."

"What time would this be?"

"I'm not sure. Probably elevenish by then."

"Not later?"

"No. A bit before, if anything. The pubs hadn't come out."

"Mum and dad still up?"

"No, they were asleep when I got back. They close the shop at ten on a Saturday. They'd been up since before dawn."

"Did you see anyone on your way?"

"Not that I remember."

"Doesn't it worry you, walking alone across the rec at night?"

"Not particularly. I can handle myself."

"Against how many?"

"I've been taking lessons. Martial arts."

"Since when?"

"Since some bastard chucked a brick through our window and cut me mum. *They* might accept what's going on, but I won't."

"What do you mean, 'what's going on'?"

There was scorn in his voice. "Racism. Pure and simple. We live in a racist society. It doesn't matter that I was born here, and my mum and dad before me, it's the colour of your skin people judge you on."

"Not everyone."

"Shows how much you know. The police are part of it, anyway."

"Geor—Sorry, Mohammed, I didn't come here to argue the politics of racism with you. I came to find out about your movements on Saturday."

"So what's happened? Why are you picking on me?"

"I understand there was an altercation in The Jubilee?"

"Altercation?"

"Yes. A disagreement."

"I know what it means. I'm not just some ignorant wog just got off the boat, you know. I'm trying to remember. Do you mean that stupid pillock who bumped into me and called me a Paki bastard?"

"That's right."

"So what?"

"What do you mean, 'so what'? You're telling me you just let it go at that? You? With all your martial-arts training?"

George puffed up his chest. "Well, I was all for doing the pair of them over, but Asim and Kobir didn't want any trouble."

"So you just let it go by, a racial slur like that?"

"When you look like I do, you get used to it."

"But you were angry?"

George leaned forward and rested his palms on his knees. "Of course I were bloody angry. Every time you hear something like that said about you, you just get filled with anger and indignation. You feel dehumanized." He shrugged. "It's not something you'd understand."

"Because I'm white?"

George slumped back in his chair. "You said it."

"But you listened to your friends this time?"

"Yes. Besides, we were in a crowded pub. Just about everyone else in the place was white, apart from a couple of Rastas selling drugs. And the last thing those bastards would do was come to our aid if anything happened. They'd probably join in with the whiteys."

"What made you think they were selling drugs?"

"That's what they do, isn't it?"

Talk about racism, Banks thought. He moved on. "Did you know the lad who insulted you?"

"I've seen him around once or twice. Arrogant-looking pillock, always looked down his nose at me. Lives on the Leaview Estate, I think. Why? You going to arrest him for racism?"

"Not exactly," said Banks. "He's dead."

George's jaw dropped. "He's wha … ?"

"He's dead, Mohammed. His name was Jason Fox. Someone unknown, or several someones unknown, kicked seven shades of shit out of him in the Carlaw Place ginnel sometime after eleven o'clock last night."

"Well it wasn't me."

"Are you sure? Are you sure you weren't so upset by what Jason called you that you and your friends waited in the ginnel? You just admitted you knew Jason lived on the Leaview Estate, so it would be a pretty good guess that he'd take the same short cut home as you, wouldn't it? You waited there, the three of you, and when Jason came along, you gave him what for. I'm not saying you intended to kill him, just teach him a lesson. But he *is* dead, George, and there's no remedy for that."

George looked so stunned he didn't even bother correcting Banks over his name. "I'm not saying owt more," he said. "I want a solicitor. This is a fit-up."

"Come on, George. It doesn't have to be like this."

"Like hell it doesn't. If you're accusing me and my mates of killing someone, then you'd better arrest us. *And* get us a lawyer. And I told you, my name's Mohammed, not George."

"Look, Mohammed, if I do what you're asking, I'll have to take you down to the station. And your mates."

George stood up. "Do it then. I'm not afraid. If you think I'm a killer you'd be taking me anyway, wouldn't you?"

Oh, bloody hell, Banks thought. He didn't want to do this, but the silly bugger had left him no choice. He stood up. "Come on, then," he said. "And we'd better take the shoes and clothes you wore last night along with us too."

THREE

I

The crosswinds on the A1 just south of Aberford almost blew Banks off the road. He felt relieved at last when he was able to edge out from between the two juggernauts that had him sandwiched and exit onto Wakefield Road.

It was another of those changeable days, with gale-force winds blowing a series of storms from the west. Between the bouts of rain, the sky would brighten, and Banks had even seen a double rainbow near the Ripon turn-off.

Even though Wakefield Road was busy, Banks still felt able to relax a little after the ordeal of the A1. He had been playing a Clifford Brown tape, finding the sound of the trumpet suited the weather, but he had hardly been able to listen for concentrating on the road. "The Ride of the Valkyries" would have been more apt for his drive so far, with the big vans and lorries spraying up dirty rain all over his windscreen. Now, however, he found "Gertrude's Bounce" a fine accompaniment for the wind blowing the leaves off the distant trees.

It was Monday morning, and Banks was on his way to Leeds to talk to Jason Fox's employer. George Mahmood and his friends were in custody at Eastvale station, where they could be kept for another six or seven hours. They all claimed racial discrimination and refused to say anything.

Though Banks felt sorry for them, especially for George, he was also bloody irritated by their attitude. And it was Jason Fox who deserved his pity, he reminded himself, not the cowardly bastards who had booted him to death. *If* they had done it. Banks couldn't see George Mahmood as a killer, but then he had to admit he was prejudiced. And George had changed. Nevertheless, he was willing to keep an open mind until an eyewitness or forensic evidence tipped the balance one way or the other. In the meantime, he needed to know more about Jason Fox's life, starting with where he worked and where he lived. He could have phoned the factory, but he really wanted a face-to-face chat with someone who knew something about Jason.

Banks entered the industrial landscape of south-east Leeds. He turned down Clifford Brown and concentrated on traffic lights and directions as he headed towards Stourton.

Just off Pontefract Road, he found the long, fenced laneway that led to the plastics factory where Jason had worked. Ahead, the horizon was a jumble of factory buildings and warehouses. A row of power-station cooling towers, the hour-glass shape of which always reminded Banks of old corsets adverts, spewed out grey smoke into the already grey air. Between the factories and the power station ran the sluggish River Aire, delivering its load of industrial effluent to the Humber estuary and the North Sea beyond.

Banks identified himself to the guard at the gate and asked where he could find the Personnel Department. "Human Resources," the guard told him, pointing. "Over there."

He should have known. Everyone used to call it Personnel a few years back, but now even the North Yorkshire police had their Human Resources Department. Why the change? Had "personnel" suddenly become insulting to some pressure group or other, and therefore exiled to the icy wastes of the politically incorrect?

A hundred yards or so farther on, Banks pulled up in front of the three-storey office block.

The Human Resources office was much like any other—untidy desks, computers, filing cabinets and constantly ringing telephones. A dark-haired young woman looked up and smiled as Banks walked in.

"Can I help you?" she asked.

"Hope so." Banks showed her his card.

If she was surprised, she didn't show it. "What is it?" she asked. "My name's Mary, by the way. Mary Mason."

"I've come about one of your employees. A lad called Jason Fox. I'd like to speak to his boss and workmates, if I can."

Mary Mason frowned. "I don't believe I know the name. Still, there's a lot of people work here, and I'm quite new to the job." She smiled. "Do you know what department he's in?"

The Foxes hadn't been that specific, Banks remembered. All he knew was that Jason worked in an office.

"Well," Mary said, "at least that lets out the shop floor, doesn't it? Just a minute." She tapped away at her computer. A few moments later, she swivelled away from the screen and said, "No. It's not just me. We don't have a Jason Fox working here."

Banks raised his eyebrows in disbelief. "Are you sure?"

"According to payroll records."

"Computers make mistakes sometimes."

Mary laughed. "Don't I know it. Every once in a while my mouse starts running wild, all over the place. Nobody's managed to work out why yet, but they call it 'mad mouse disease.' In this case, though, I'd tend to believe the computer. Are you sure he was on the clerical staff?"

Banks scratched the scar beside his right eye. He wasn't sure of anything now. "That's what I was told. Would it be too difficult to check all your employees?"

Mary shook her head. "No. It'll take just a little longer. One of the benefits of computers. They do things fast, then you can spend the rest of your time varnishing your fingernails."

"I'll bet."

Mary tapped a few keys and did the Ouija-board thing with her mouse, which wasn't running wild today as far as Banks could tell, then clicked the buttons a few times and squinted at the screen.

"Nope," she said, shaking her head. "No Jason Fox anywhere in the company. Maybe he worked for another branch?"

"You have other branches?"

"Rochdale. Coventry. Middlesbrough."

"No. His parents definitely said he lived and worked in Leeds. Look, are there any back records you can check, just in case?" It was probably pointless, but it was worth a look while he was here.

"I can search the files for the past few years, if you've got a bit of patience left."

Banks smiled. "If you would, please. I've got plenty of patience."

Mary returned to her computer. Banks found himself tapping his foot on the floor as he waited. He wanted a cigarette. No chance in here; you just had to sniff the air.

Finally, with a frown creasing her brow, Mary whistled and said, "Well, what do you know ... ?"

"You've found him?"

"I have indeed."

"And?"

"Jason Fox. Can't be two, I don't suppose?"

"I doubt it."

"Well, according to our records, he left the company two years ago after working for us for only one year."

Now it was Banks's turn to frown. "He left? I don't understand. Why?"

Mary stared at the screen and pressed her lips together in thought, then she looked at Banks with her warm, dark eyes, smiled and said, "Look, I appreciate that you're a policeman, and a pretty senior one at that. I also appreciate this might be important, even though you haven't told me a thing. But personnel records are private. I'm afraid I can't just go around giving people any information they want at the drop of a hat, or a warrant card. I'm sure you could get a court order, if you really want to know. But I'm only doing my job. I'm sorry. I couldn't tell you any more, even if I knew."

"I appreciate that," said Banks. "Can you tell me anything at all about his time here, about his friends?"

She shook her head. "As I said, it was before my time. I've never heard of him." She turned to face the others in the office. "Anyone remember a Jason Fox used to work here?"

All she got in return was blank stares and shaking heads. Apart from one woman, who said, "The name sounds familiar."

"You're thinking of Jason Donovan," someone else said, and they laughed.

"Can you at least tell me what department he worked in?" Banks asked.

"That I can tell you," Mary said. "He was in sales. Domestic. You'll find them in the old office building, across the yard. And," she said, smiling, "you should also find some of the people he worked with are still there. Try David Wayne first. He's one of the regional sales managers now."

"Just a minute," came the voice from the back of the office. "Jason Fox, you said? Now I remember. It was a couple of years back. I'd just started here. There was some trouble, some sort of scandal. Something hushed up."

II

The sound of the car pulling up woke Frank from his afternoon nap. Slowly, he groped his way back to consciousness—it seemed to take longer every time, as if consciousness itself were slowly moving farther and farther away from him—and walked over to the window. There they were: the three of them, struggling up the path against the wind. Well, he supposed they would have to come some time; Josie had already telephoned and told him what had happened to Jason.

He answered the knock, let them in and told them to make themselves comfortable while he went to put the kettle on. The good old English custom of a nice cup of tea, he thought, had helped people avoid many an embarrassing moment. Not that they should be embarrassed about what had happened, of course, but Yorkshire folk, especially, often fell short of words when it came to strong emotions.

Josie gave him a silent hug when he came through from the kitchen, then she sat down. Grief suited her in a way, he thought; she had always looked a bit pinched to him. These days, she had also started to look more like mutton dressed as lamb, too, with that make-up, her roots showing and those figure-hugging outfits she wore. At her age. Her mother would have been ashamed of her.

Steven looked as lacklustre as ever. Couldn't Josie, he wished again, have chosen someone with a bit of spunk in him?

Then there was Maureen. Good-natured, bustling, hard-working, no-nonsense Maureen. The best of the lot of them, in his book. A proper bonny lass, too; she'd break a few hearts in her time, with her laughing eyes and smiling lips and hair like spun gold all the way down to her waist. Well, not today. But that was how he remembered her. She had cut her hair short just after she started nurses' training. A real shame, that, he thought.

"When's the funeral?" he asked.

"Thursday," Josie answered. "Oh, you should have seen what they'd done to him, Dad." She sniffled. "Our poor Jason."

Frank nodded. "Nay, lass ... Police getting anywhere?"

"Even if they were," Josie sniffed, "they wouldn't tell us, would they?"

The kettle boiled. Frank moved to rise, but Maureen sprang to her feet. "I'll get it, Granddad. Stay where you are."

"Thanks, lass," he said gratefully, and sank back into his armchair. "What *have* they told you?"

"They've got some lads helping them with their enquiries," Josie said. "Pakistanis." She sniffed. "They think it might have started as an argument in a pub, and that these lads followed our Jason, or waited for him in the ginnel and beat him up. The police think they probably didn't mean to kill him."

"What do *you* think?" Frank asked.

Maureen came back with the teapot and raised her eyebrows at the question. "We haven't really had much time to think about it at all yet, Granddad," she said. "But I'm sure the police know their business."

"Aye."

"What is it?" Steven Fox said, speaking for the first time. "You don't think they'll do a good job?"

"I wouldn't know about that," Frank said.

"Well what is it, then?" Josie Fox repeated her husband's question. Maureen started pouring milk and tea into mugs, spooning in sugar.

"Nowt," said Frank. He fingered the folded, creased sheet of paper in his top shirt pocket and pulled it out.

"What's that, Granddad?" Maureen asked.

"Just something I got in the post."

Maureen frowned. "But what ... I don't ..."

"Oh, for crying out loud," said Frank, his patience with them finally snapping. "Don't you know what happened? Don't you know anything? Did you all turn your bloody backs?" He turned towards Maureen. "What about you?" he snapped. "I'd have expected more of you."

Maureen started to cry. Frank felt the familiar pain, almost an old friend now, grip his chest. Hand shaking, he tossed the sheet towards Josie. "Go on," he said. "Read it."

III

Banks crossed the factory yard, dodging puddles rainbowed with oil. Crates and chunks of old machinery were stacked up by the sides of long, one-storey buildings with rusty corrugated iron roofs. Machine noises buzzed and roared from inside. Forklifts beetled back and forth across the uneven yard, carrying boxes on pallets. The place smelled of diesel oil and burnt plastic.

He soon found the old office building, which had probably been adequate in the early days, before the company grew. There was no receptionist, just a large open area with desks, computers, telephones and people. Filing cabinets stood against the walls. At the far end of the room, several small offices had been partitioned off, their lower parts wood and the upper parts, above waist height, glass.

A woman dashed by Banks on her way to the door, a couple of file folders stuffed under her arm. When he asked her if David Wayne was around, she nodded and pointed to the middle office. Banks walked between the rows of desks, attracting no attention at all, then knocked on the door that bore the nameplate "David C. Wayne."

The man who invited him in was younger than Banks had expected. Late twenties, early thirties at the most. He wore a white shirt with a garish tie, wavy brown hair falling over his collar. He had one of those high foreheads with little shiny red bumps at each side that made his hairline seem to be prematurely receding, and he smelled of Old Spice. A dark sports jacket hung over the back of his chair.

He frowned as he studied Banks's warrant card, then gestured to the spare chair and said, "How can I help you?"

Banks sat down. "I'm making enquiries about Jason Fox," he said. "I understand he used to work here?"

Wayne's frown deepened. "That's going back a bit."

"But you *do* remember him?"

"Oh, yes. I remember Jason all right." Wayne leaned back in his chair and put his feet on the desk. The telephone rang; he ignored it. In the background, Banks could hear the hubbub of the office through the flimsy partition. "Why do you want to know?" Wayne asked.

Much as Banks hated parting with information, it would do no harm in this case, he thought, and it might get Wayne to open up more quickly. He could already sense that something was not quite right, and the woman in the Human Resources Department had implied some sort of cover-up. So he told Wayne that Jason had been found dead, and that his parents had said he was working for this company.

"After all this time." Wayne shook his head slowly. "Amazing."

"Why did he leave?"

"He didn't leave. Not exactly."

"He was fired?"

"No."

"Made redundant?"

"No."

Banks sighed and shifted position. "Look, Mr Wayne," he said, "I didn't come here to play a guessing game. I came to get information that might be important in a serious police investigation."

"I'm sorry," said Wayne, scratching his head. "It's all still a bit embarrassing, you see."

"Embarrassing? In what way?"

"I wasn't in management back then. I was just one of Jason's co-workers. I had more experience, though. In fact, I was the one who trained him."

"Was he a poor worker?"

"On the contrary. He was very good at his job. Bright, energetic, quick to learn. Showed an extraordinary aptitude for computers, considering he'd had no formal training in that area. Still, that's often the case."

"Then what—"

"The job isn't everything, Chief Inspector," Wayne went on quickly. "Oh, it's important, I'll grant you that. You can put up with a lot of idiosyncrasies if someone's as good as Jason was. We've had our share of arseholes in our time and, by and large, if they're competent, hard-working arseholes, you just tend to put up with them."

"But it was different with Jason?"

"Yes."

"In what way?"

"It was his *attitude*," Wayne explained. "I suppose you'd call it his political beliefs."

"Which were?"

"To put it in a nutshell, Jason was a racist. White power and all that. And it didn't take a lot to get him on his hobby-horse. Just some item in the newspaper, some new opinion poll or crime statistics."

"What exactly did he say?"

"You name it. Asians and West Indians were his chief targets. According to Jason, if something wasn't done soon the immigrants would take over the country and run it into the ground. Anarchy would follow. Chaos. The law of the jungle. He said you only had to look around you to see what damage they'd done already. AIDS. Drugs. Unemployment. He put them all down to immigrants." Wayne shook his head again. "It was disgusting, really sick, some of the things he came out with."

"Is that why he left?"

Wayne nodded. "As I said, he didn't exactly leave. It was more of a mutual parting of the ways, maybe a little more desired on our side than his. But the company paid him off adequately and got rid of him. No blemish on his references, either. I suppose whoever employed him next found out what the bugger was like soon enough. I mean, it's all very well to crack the odd ... you know ... off-colour joke, have a bit of a laugh. We all do that, don't we? But Jason was serious. He didn't have a sense of humour about these things. Just hatred. A palpable hatred. You could feel it burning out of him when he spoke, see it in his eyes." Wayne gave a little shudder.

"Do you know where he got it from?"

"No idea. Where *do* people get these things from? Are they born like that? Do we blame the parents? Peers at school? The recession? Society?" He shrugged. "I don't know. Probably a bit of everything. But I do know that it was always there with Jason, always just beneath the surface, if it wasn't actually showing. And, of course, we have a number of Asian and West Indian employees here."

"Did he ever insult anyone to their face?"

Wayne rubbed his forehead and glanced away from Banks, out at the bustling business activity through his window. "Mostly he just made them feel uncomfortable," he said, "but once he went too far. That was enough. One of the secretaries. Milly. Nice woman. From Barbados. Jason usually kept her at arm's length. Anyway, she got pregnant, and at some point—so she said—when it started to show, Jason made some remark to her about all her kind could do was procreate, and there were too many of them already. Milly was upset, understandably, and she threatened to report him to the Race Relations Board. Well, the directors didn't want that ... you know ... the whole operation under the microscope, racism in the workplace and all that ... so they asked Jason to leave."

"They offered him money?"

"A fair settlement. Just what he would have got if he'd been made redundant."

"And he went quietly?"

Wayne nodded.

"Could I speak to Milly?"

"She's no longer with the company."

"Do you have her address?"

"I suppose I can tell you. I shouldn't, but given the circumstances." He got up, pulled out a file from one of the cabinets against his wall, and told Banks the address. Then he sat down again.

"Do you know where Jason went after he left here?" Banks asked.

Wayne shook his head. "Not a clue. He never got in touch again, and I can't say I was exactly eager to seek him out."

"So when he left here he disappeared from your life?"

"Yes."

"Did he have any close friends here?"

"Not really. I wasn't even particularly close to him myself. He was a bit of a loner. Never talked about his outside interests, family, girlfriends, that sort of thing. He had no patience with the usual office chit-chat. Except football. He loved to talk about football. Mad about it. On a Monday morning he'd talk about the weekend games for so long it was sometimes hard to get him working at all."

"People listened, then? The same ones who were sickened by his racism?"

Wayne spread his hands. "What can I say? There's nothing like an enthusiasm for sports to make a person seem more human. And we seem able to overlook an awful lot in our sports heroes, don't we? I mean, look at Gazza. The bugger beats up his wife and he's still a national hero."

"What about enemies?"

Wayne raised his eyebrows. "Probably just about every immigrant in the country. At least the ones who knew what he was."

"Anyone in particular?"

"Not that I can think of."

"What was he like as a person? How would you describe him?"

Wayne put a pencil against his lips and thought for a moment, then he said, "Jason was one of those people who can frighten you with their intensity. I mean, mostly he was withdrawn, quiet, in his own world. On first impression, he seemed rather shy, but when he did come out, whether to talk about a football game or comment on some political article in the paper, then he became very passionate, very fervent. He had charisma. You could imagine him speaking to groups, swaying their opinions."

"A budding Hitler, then? Interesting." Banks closed his notebook and stood up. He could think of nothing more to ask. "Thanks for your time," he said, holding out his hand. "I might want to talk to you about this again."

Wayne shook hands and nodded. "I'll be here."

And Banks walked through the busy office, back out into the bleak factory yard, the oil smell, the machinery noise, overflowing skips, the rainbowed puddles. Just as he got to the car, his mobile beeped.

IV

"No, Gavin, I can't possibly go out for a drink with you tonight. We're very busy."

"The boy wonder got you working overtime, then?"

"I wish you wouldn't call him that."

Susan heard Gavin chuckle over the line. "Who's he got pegged for this one, then? Our local MP? Leader of the hunt?" He laughed again.

Susan felt herself flush. "That's not very funny." She hated it when Gavin made fun of Banks.

"How about Saturday? We can go—"

"Maybe," Susan said. "Maybe Saturday. I'll have to see. Got to go now, Gavin. Work to do."

"Okay. See you Saturday."

"I said *maybe*. Just a minute ... What's that?" Susan could hear sounds of shouting and scuffling, and they seemed to be coming from downstairs. "Got to go, Gavin," she said. "I'll ring you back."

"Susan, what's—"

Susan dropped the receiver on its cradle and walked to the top of the stairs. The scene below was utter chaos. Every Asian in Eastvale— all nine or ten of them—seemed to be pushing through the front doors: George Mahmood's parents, Ibrahim Nazur, owner of the Himalaya, and a handful of students from Eastvale College. A number of uniformed officers were holding them back, but they wanted to see the detectives, and Susan was the only CID officer in the station.

"Would you *please* not all shout at once!" Susan yelled from halfway down the stairs.

"What are you going to do about our children?" asked an angry Charles Mahmood. "You can't just lock them up for nothing. This is racism, pure and simple. We're British citizens, you know."

"Please believe me, Mr Mahmood," said Susan, advancing down the stairs. "We're only keeping them until we get—"

"No!" yelled Ibrahim Nazur. "It's not fair. One law for whites and another law for us."

That met a chorus of agreement and they surged forward again.

Suddenly, the front doors opened and a loud voice bellowed,

"What in God's name is going on here?" It had enough authority to command silence. Then Susan saw over the crowd the shiny, bald head of Chief Constable Jeremiah "Jimmy" Riddle, and for the first time ever, she was grateful for the sight.

"Sergeant Rowe," she heard Riddle say, "would you please order your officers to remove these people from the police station? Tell them if they'll kindly wait outside we'll have some news for them in just a few minutes." Then Riddle made his way through the silent crowd, cutting a swath rather like Moses parting the Red Sea.

Behind him, Sergeant Rowe muttered, "Yes, sir," and ordered three constables to usher the group out onto the street. They went without putting up a fight.

"That's better," said Riddle, approaching Susan. "It's DC Gay, isn't it?"

"Yes, sir."

"Where's DCI Banks?"

"Leeds, sir. Pursuing enquiries."

"'Pursuing enquiries,' is he? Shopping, more bloody like. That Classical Record Shop of his. Anyone else here?"

"No, sir. Just me."

Riddle jerked his head. "Right, you. Upstairs."

Susan turned and started walking up the stairs, feeling, she imagined, somewhat like a prisoner being sent down by the judge.

It could hardly be a worse time to piss off Jimmy Riddle.

Susan had passed the first parts of her sergeant's exam, the written, almost a year ago. But police promotion is a long-drawn-out process. The last stage consisted of an appearance before the promotion board—presided over by an Assistant Chief Constable and a Chief Superintendent from Regional HQ.

That was six months ago now, but Susan still broke into a cold sweat every time she remembered the day of her board.

She had spent weeks reading up on policy, national guidelines and equal opportunities, but none of it prepared her for what lay behind the door. Of course, they kept her waiting in the corridor for about half an hour, just to make her extra nervous, then the Chief Superintendent came out, shook her hand and led her in. She could have sworn there was a smirk on his face.

First they asked her a few personal questions to get some idea of her overall bearing, confidence and articulateness. She thought she managed to answer clearly, without mumbling or stuttering, except when they asked what her parents thought of her choice of career. She was sure that she flushed, but rather than flounder around trying to explain, she simply paused to collect herself and said, "They didn't approve, sir."

Next came the scenarios. And her interviewers added complications, changed circumstances and generally did everything they could to confuse her or get her to change her mind.

"One of the men on your shift is regularly late in the morning," the ACC began, "putting extra pressure on his mates. What do you do?"

"Have a private word with him, sir, ask him why he's being late all the time."

The ACC nodded. "His mother's dying and she needs expensive care. He can't afford it on a copper's salary, so he's playing in a jazz band until the wee hours to make a bit extra."

"Then I'd tell him he needs permission to work outside the force and advise him to get help and support from our Welfare Department, sir."

"He thanks you for your concern, but he keeps on playing with the band and turning up late."

"Then I'd think some disciplinary action would be in order, sir."

The ACC raised his eyebrows. "Really? But his mother is dying of cancer. He *needs* the extra income. Surely this is a reasonable way of earning it? After all, it's not as if he's taking bribes or engaging in other criminal acts."

Susan stuck to her guns. "He's causing problems for his fellow officers on the shift, sir, and he's disobeying police regulations. I think disciplinary action is called for if all other avenues have been exhausted."

And she passed. Now she was due to go up before the chief next week for her *official* promotion. And that "Chief," of course, was Chief Constable Riddle.

Still, she reminded herself as she walked into the small office she shared with Sergeant Hatchley, there was nothing Riddle could do now to block her promotion. She had already earned it, and the next step was purely a formality, a bit of pomp and circumstance. Unless, of course, she *really* screwed up. Then, she supposed, he could do whatever he wanted. He was, after all, the chief constable. And, if nothing else, he could certainly make her life uncomfortable.

The office seemed crowded with Riddle in it. The man's restless, pent-up energy consumed space and burned up the oxygen like a blazing fire. Susan sat in her chair and Riddle perched on the edge of Hatchley's desk. He was a tall man, and he seemed to tower over her.

"Who authorized the arrest?" he asked.

"They're not exactly under arrest, sir," Susan said. "Just detained for questioning."

"Very well. Who authorized their detention?"

Susan paused, then said softly, "I think it was DCI Banks, sir."

"Banks. I knew it." Riddle got up and started to pace, until he found out there was not enough room to do so, then he sat down again, his pate a little redder. Banks always said you could tell how angry Riddle was by the shade of his bald head, and Susan found herself stifling a giggle as she thought she could see it glow. It was like one of those mood rings that were a fad when she was a child, only Riddle's mood never softened to a peaceful green or calm, cool blue.

"On what evidence?" Riddle continued.

"There'd been some trouble earlier in the pub, sir. The Jubilee. It involved the Mahmood boy and the victim, Jason Fox. When DCI Banks questioned George Mahmood about it, he refused to co-operate. So did his friends. They asked for a lawyer."

"And did they get one?"

"No, sir. Well, not until this morning. It was Sunday."

"Any rough stuff?"

"No, sir."

Riddle slid his hand across his head. "Well, let's at least be thankful for small mercies. Have you any idea who Ibrahim Nazur *is*?"

"Owner of the Himalaya, sir."

"More than that. He owns a whole bloody chain of restaurants, all over Yorkshire, and the Himalaya's just the latest. He's also a highly respected member of the Muslim community and one of the prime movers in that new mosque project down Bradford way."

"Ah," said Susan.

"'Ah,' indeed. Anything from forensics?"

"Nothing conclusive, sir. Not yet."

"Witnesses?"

"None, sir. Not so far. We're still looking."

Riddle stood up. "Right. I want the three of them out of here. Now. Do you understand?"

Susan stood too. "Yes, sir," she said.

"And tell Banks I'll be seeing him very soon."

Susan nodded. "Yes, sir."

And with that, Jimmy Riddle straightened his uniform and marched downstairs to face his public.

V

Late that afternoon, Banks walked up to the bar of The Black Bull in Lyndgarth and ordered a double Bell's for Frank Hepplethwaite and a half of Theakston's XB for himself.

According to Susan, who had phoned Banks earlier, Hepplethwaite was Jason Fox's granddad, and he said he had some information about Jason. He insisted on talking to the "man in charge." Banks had phoned Frank and, finding out that he didn't own a car, agreed to meet him in The Black Bull.

Before setting off back for Swainsdale, though, Banks had called at the Leeds address Jason Fox's parents had given him and found that Jason hadn't lived there for at least eighteen months. The flat was now occupied by a student called Jackie Kitson, and she had never heard of Jason Fox. There, the trail ended.

The barman of The Black Bull was a skinny, hunched, crooked-shouldered fellow in a moth-eaten, ill-fitting pullover. His greasy black hair and beard obscured most of his face, except the eyes that stared out in a way reminiscent of photos of Charles Manson. He served the drinks without a word, then took down Banks's order for one chicken-and-mushroom pie and one Old Peculier casserole.

The Black Bull was one of those rare exceptions to the no-food-after-two-o'clock rule that blights most pubs.

Banks took the drinks and joined Frank at a round table by the door. At the bar, one man started telling the barman how much more cosy it was now most of the tourists had gone. He had a whiny, southern accent, and actually lowered his voice when he said "tourists." The barman, who clearly knew it was the tourist business that kept the place going, grunted "Aye" without looking up from the glass he was drying.

Two other bar-stool regulars working at a crossword puzzle seemed overjoyed to discover that "episcopal" was an anagram of "Pepsi-Cola." To the left, down the far end where the billiard tables were, two American couples were stuffing coins into the fruit machine, shifting occasionally to the video trivia game opposite.

"You must know Mr Gristhorpe, young lad?" said Frank after thanking Banks for the drink.

Banks nodded. "He's my boss."

"Lives here in Lyndgarth, he does. Well, I suppose you know that. Can't say I know him well, mind you. I'm a fair bit older, myself, and he's been away a lot. Good family, though, the Gristhorpes. Got a good reputation around these parts, anyroad." He nodded to himself and sipped his Bell's.

Frank Hepplethwaite was a compact man with a thin, lined face, all the lines running vertically, and a fine head of grey hair. His skin was pale and his eyes a dull bottle-green. He looked as if he had once had quite a bit more flesh on his bones but had recently lost weight due to illness.

"Anyway," he said, "thank you for coming all the way out here. I don't get around so well these days." He tapped his chest. "Angina."

Banks nodded. "I'm sorry. No problem, Mr Hepplethwaite."

"Call me Frank. Of course," he went on, tapping his glass, "I shouldn't be indulging in this." He pulled a face. "But there's limits to what a sick man will put up with." He glanced at the table, where Banks had unconsciously rested his cigarettes and lighter. "Smoke if you like, lad. I like the smell of tobacco. And second-hand smoke be buggered."

Banks smiled and lit up.

"Nice state of affairs, isn't it," said Hepplethwaite, "when a man has to indulge his vices by proxy."

Banks raised his eyebrows. The words sounded familiar, but he couldn't place them.

"Raymond Chandler," said Hepplethwaite with a sly grin. "General Sternwood at the beginning of *The Big Sleep*. One of my favourite films. Bogey as Philip Marlowe. Must have seen it about twenty times. Know it by heart."

So that was it. Banks had seen the film on television just a few months ago, but he had never read the book. Ah well, another one for the lengthening list. As a rule, he didn't read detective fiction, apart from Sherlock Holmes, but he'd heard that Chandler was good. "I'm sorry about what happened to your grandson," he said.

The old man's eyes misted over. "Aye, well ... nobody deserves to die like that. He must have suffered like hell." He took a folded sheet of paper from his pocket and passed it to Banks. "This is why I asked you to come."

Banks nodded. He took the sheet, opened it and spread it on the table in front of him. It looked professionally printed, but most things did these days, with all the laser printers and desktop publishing packages around. Banks could remember the time—not so long ago—when all the copying in a police station was done from "spirit masters" on one of those old machines that made your fingers all purple. Even now, as he remembered it, he fancied he could smell the acrid spirit again.

The masthead, in very large, bold capitals, read THE ALBION LEAGUE and underneath that, it said in italics, *"Fighting the good fight for you and your country."*

Banks drew on his Silk Cut and started to read.

Friends, have you ever looked around you at the state of our once-great nation today and wondered just how such terrible degradation could have come about? Can you believe this nation was once called *Great* Britain? And what are we now? Our weak politicians have allowed this once-great land to be overrun by parasites. You see them everywhere—

in the schools, in the factories and even in the government, sapping our strength, undermining the fabric of our society. How could this be allowed to happen? Many years ago, Enoch Powell foresaw the signs, saw the rivers of blood in our future. But did anyone listen? No …

And so it went on, column-inch after column-inch of racist drivel. It ended,

And so we ask you, the true English people, heirs to King Arthur and St George, to join us in our struggle, to help us rid this great land of the parasite immigrant who crawls and breeds his filth in the bellies of our cities, of the vile and trai-torous Jew who uses our economy for his own purposes, of the homosexual deviants who seek to corrupt our children, and of the deformed and the insane who have no place in the new order of the Strong and the Righteous. To purify our race and reestablish the new Albion in the land that is rightfully ours and make it truly our "homeland" once again.

Banks put it down. Even a long draught of Theakston's couldn't get the vile taste out of his mouth. Reluctantly, he turned back to the pamphlet, but he could find no sign of an address, no mention of a meeting-place. Obviously, whoever wanted to join the Albion League would first have to find it. At the bottom of the pamphlet, however, in tiny print in the far right-hand corner, he could make out the letters *http://www.alblgue.com/index.html*. A Web-site address. Everyone had them these days. Next, he examined the envelope and saw that it had been posted in Bradford last Thursday.

Their food arrived and they continued to speak between mouthfuls.

"What makes you think Jason sent you this?" Banks asked.

Frank Hepplethwaite turned away to face the dark wood parti-tion between their table and the door. One of the Americans complained loudly that too many of the trivia questions dealt with English sports. "I mean, how the hell am I supposed to know which player transferred from Tottenham Hotspurs to Sheffield

Wednesday in 1976? What game do they play, anyway? And what kinda name is that for a sports team? Sheffield *Wednesday*." He shook his head. "These Brits."

Frank turned back to Banks and said, "Because it arrived only a couple of days after I let something slip. For which may God forgive me."

"What did you let slip?"

"First you have to understand," Frank went on, "that when Jason was just a wee lad, we were very close. They used to come up here for summer holidays sometimes, him, Maureen and my daughter, Josie. Jason and I would go for long walks, looking for wild flowers on the riverbanks, listening for curlews over Fremlington Edge. Sometimes we'd go fishing up the reservoir, or visit one of the nearby farmers and help out around the yard for an afternoon, collecting eggs or feeding the pigs. We always used to go and watch the sheep-shearing. He used to love his times up here, did little Jason."

"You mentioned his mother and his sister. What about his father?"

Frank took a mouthful of casserole, chewed, swallowed and scowled. "That long streak of piss? To be honest, lad, I never had much time for him, and he never had much time for Jason. Do you know he never listens to those records he collects. Never listens to them! Still wrapped in plastic. I bloody ask you, what are you supposed to think of a bloke who buys records and doesn't even listen to them?"

Not much, Banks thought, chewing on a particularly stringy piece of chicken. Frank was obviously going to tell his story in his own time, his own way. "Sorry to interrupt," he said. "What happened?"

Frank paused for breath before continuing. "Time, mostly. That's all. I got old. Too old to walk very far. And Jason got interested in other things, stopped visiting."

"Did he still come and see you occasionally?"

"Oh aye. Now and then. But it were only in passing, like, more of a duty."

"When was the last time you saw him?"

"He drove out here the weekend before last. It'd be just a week before he died."

"Did he ever talk about his life in Leeds? His job? Friends?"

"Not really, no. Once said he was learning about computers or summat. Of course, I know nowt about that, so we soon changed the subject."

"Did he say *where* he was learning about computers?"

"No."

"His parents told me he worked in an office."

Frank shrugged. "Could be. All I remember is him once saying he was learning about computers."

"And in all his visits," Banks went on, "didn't he ever talk about this sort of thing?" He tapped the pamphlet with his knuckle.

Frank closed his eyes and shook his head. "Never. That was why it came as such a shock."

"Why do you think he never spoke to you about it?"

"I can't answer that one. Perhaps he thought I'd be against it, until I said what I did and gave him his opening? Perhaps he thought I was an old man and not worth converting? I *am* his grand-dad, after all, and we had a relationship of a kind. We didn't say much to each other when we did meet up these past few years. I'd no idea what he was up to. Mostly he'd just have time to drop by and buy me a drink and ask if I was doing all right before he was off to his football or whatever."

Banks finished his pie. "What makes you think you gave Jason an opening to send you this pamphlet?" he asked. "What was it you said?"

"Aye, well ... We were sitting in here one day, just like you and me are now." Frank lowered his voice. "The landlord here's called Jacob Bernstein. Not that fellow there. Jacob's not in right now. Anyway, I made a remark about Jacob being a bit of a tight-fisted old Jew."

"What did Jason say?"

"Nowt. Not right away. He just had this funny sort of smile on his face. Partly a smile, partly a sort of sneer. As soon as I said it, I felt I'd done wrong, but these things slip out, don't they, like saying Jews and Scotsmen have short arms and deep pockets. You don't think about it being offensive, do you? You don't really mean any harm by it. Anyways, after a minute or so, Jason says he thinks he might have something to interest me, and a few days later, this piece of filth turns up in the post. Who else could have sent it?"

"Who else, indeed?" said Banks, remembering what David Wayne had told him that morning in Leeds. "Did you ever meet any of Jason's circle?"

"No."

"So there's no way you can help us try and find out who killed him?"

"I thought you already had the lads who did it?"

Banks shook his head. "We don't know if it was them. Not for sure. At the moment, I'd say we're keeping our options open."

"Sorry, lad," said Frank. "It doesn't look like I can help, then, does it?" He paused and looked down into his glass. "It were a real shock," he said, "when I read that thing and knew our Jason were responsible. I fought in the war, you know. I never made a fuss about it, and I don't want to now. It were my duty, and I did it. I'd do it again."

"What service?"

"RAF. Tail-gunner."

Banks whistled between his teeth. His father had been a radio operator in the RAF, so he had heard what a dangerous task tail-gunner was, and how many had died doing it.

"Aye," said Frank. "Anyroad, like I said, I don't want to make a fuss about it. I said something terribly wrong about someone I consider a friend, and it shames me, but it shames me even more when my grandson thinks I'd have the time of day for this sort of rubbish. I fought the bloody Nazis, for crying out loud. And for what? So my own grandson could become one of them?"

There were tears in his eyes and Banks feared for his heart. "Calm down, Mr Hepplethwaite," he said, putting his hand on Frank's skinny wrist.

Frank looked at him through the film of tears, then gave a small nod and took a sip of Bell's. He coughed, patted his chest and forced a smile. "Don't worry, lad," he said. "It's not quite 'time, gentlemen, please' for this old codger yet."

VI

An emergency meeting of the Albion League had been called for that Monday evening. Not everyone was invited, of course, just the cell-leaders and one or two of Neville Motcombe's current favourites, like Craig. About fifteen in all, they came from Leeds and Bradford, from Halifax, Keighley, Cleckheaton, Heckmondwike, Batley, Dewsbury, Brighouse and Elland. Skinheads, for the most part, aged between sixteen and twenty-four, racists all.

And these fifteen were the pick of the crop, Craig knew. Each cell had between five and twelve members. They were the drones—football hooligans and otherwise violent skins—and Motcombe hardly ever came into contact with them except at rallies and at other large gatherings, when he addressed them from a distance. Mostly, he relied on his cell-leaders to make sure his orders were communicated and carried out, and, maybe more important still, to make sure the cash kept trickling in. After all, the League was an expensive operation to run.

They met in the upstairs room of a pub in Bingley, and as he sat sipping his lager, Craig wondered if the landlord knew exactly what was going on up there. If he had, he might not have been so quick to let them use it. On the other hand, the prospect of selling a few extra pints on a slow Monday night might tempt even the best of us to leave our ethics and politics at the door. Nothing much surprised Craig any more. Not after what Motcombe had drawn him into.

Even though the window was half open, the place was still full of smoke. Craig could hear rain falling in the street outside. A pale street-light halo glowed through the gauze of moisture. Occasionally, a car sloshed through the gathering puddles.

Meanwhile, Nev himself, erstwhile leader of the League, clad in his usual shiny leather jacket, was on his feet whipping his members into a frenzy. He didn't need to shout and wave his arms around like Hitler; there was enough power and conviction in his regular speaking voice. Mostly it was the eyes, though; they were the kind that trapped you and wouldn't let you go unless they were certain of your loyalty. They'd even made Craig tremble once or twice in the early days, but he was too good at his job to let it get to him.

"Murdered," Motcombe repeated, disgust and disbelief in his tone. He slapped the table. "One of us. Three of them. Three to one. They say one of his eyes was hanging out of its socket by the time the Paki bastards had finished with him."

Stirrings and mumblings came from the crowd. One skin started rattling his glass on the table. Motcombe shushed him with an economic hand gesture, then pulled a slip of paper out of his pocket and started to read.

"George Mahmood," he began, with the accent on *mood*. "Asim Nazur." This time, the name sounded like a sneer. People began to snigger. "And Kobir Mukhtar. Sounds about right, that one, doesn't it? Mucky-tar?"

Sycophantic laughter came from the cell-leaders.

"And do you know what happened?"

Several of them, Craig included, shook their heads.

"The police let them go. That's what."

Howls of outrage.

"Oh, yes they did. This very afternoon. Our glorious warrior Jason is probably lying on some mortuary table, cut open from th'nave to th'chops as we speak, and the three bastards who put him there, the three *brown* bastards who put him there, are out walking the streets." He slammed the table again. "What do you think about that?"

"Ain't fair," one of the cell-leaders chimed in.

"Typical," claimed another. "Get away with bloody murder they do these days."

"What we gonna do?" asked another.

Craig lit a cigarette and leaned forward. This promised to be interesting. As far as he was concerned, Jason Fox was an evil little pillock who deserved all he got.

"First off," said Motcombe, "I want a special edition of the newsletter out pronto. Black border, the lot. And I want to see some oomph in it. Ray?"

One of the Leeds cell-leaders looked up from his pint and nodded.

"You see to that," Motcombe went on. "Now Jason's no longer with us, I'm afraid we're left to rely on your rather more pedestrian prose style. But you can do it, Ray, I'm sure you can. You know the kind of thing I want. Outrage, yes, but make sure you emphasize the *reason* this all happened, the underlying causes, what we're all about. And make sure you mention the Pakis' names. We'll send each of them a copy. If they know that the entire National Socialist Alliance knows who they are, that should give them a fucking sleepless night or two. Okay?"

Ray smiled and nodded.

"And print extra copies. Next, I'd like Geoff and Keith to start working on a memorial concert for Jason. A big bash. You've got the contacts, so pick some appropriate bands, four or five of them, rent a large space and make arrangements. Soon as you can, okay?"

Geoff and Keith nodded and scribbled some notes.

"Now, as soon as I find out the details about the funeral," Motcombe went on, "I'll be contacting several members to accompany me in a tribute of honour for our fallen hero. For make no mistake about it, Jason Fox is a *martyr*, and his murder should provide us with a rallying point. We've got a chance to turn adversity into fortune here, if we choose to seize it. By all means let us grieve and mourn our lost comrade—indeed, grieve we *must*—but let us also, as *he* would have wished, use his death to spur us on to greater things, to faster growth. You all knew Jason. You know what he stood for. Let's do credit to his memory."

A few of them nodded and muttered their agreement, then the Brighouse cell-leader asked, "Are we gonna crack some heads open, then?"

A number of "ayes" went up, but Motcombe shushed them again. "Don't worry," he said. "That'll be taken care of. In time. But for the moment, we'll just publish their names and leave it at that. Let's think of the long-term mission, and let's use our golden opportunity to gain a bit of public sympathy. Think of the hundreds of blokes at home just sitting on the fence right now. They know we're right, but they don't want to make that final move and admit it. Something like this could increase our membership tenfold. Nice, pure, Aryan lad, with his whole future ahead of him, murdered by Paki immigrant scum. That'll turn a few fence-sitters in our direction."

Several members murmured in agreement. "But we can't leave Jason's murder unavenged, can we?" one of them said. "They'll think we're weak."

"Sometimes you have to postpone your vengeance for the greater good, Mick. That's all I am saying. And there's strength in that, not weakness. Believe me. There'll be plenty of time for revenge down the road. Remember, the bastards who killed Jason got away with it because our corrupt legal system is on their side. But what would happen if one of us got picked up for clobbering a Paki right now? Eh? Answer me that one." No-one did. They all looked as if they knew the answer already. Motcombe looked at his watch. "Now, I'll have to be on my way soon, I've got a lot to attend to, but there's no reason why you lot can't stay and enjoy a wake for Jason if you like. You've all got your orders. Meeting adjourned."

Then Motcombe tossed back the rest of his orange juice. Unlike the others, Craig had noticed, he never drank alcohol or smoked. People got up and moved around the room, some of them heading down to the bar to buy more pints. The last Craig saw of Motcombe, he was walking out of the room with two Bradford cell-leaders, an arm draped over each one's shoulder, deep in quiet conversation.

Liked his private meetings, did Nev, keeping the left hand and the right hand separate. Whatever he was talking to them about or asking them to do, you could bet it would have nothing to do with what he and Craig had been talking about over the past few weeks.

Craig tossed his cigarette out of the window into the rainy night, took a deep breath and went over to mourn Jason's death with Ray from Leeds and Dog-face Russell from Horsforth.

VII

It was late when Banks got home that evening, after stopping off at the station on his way from Lyndgarth, and he was tired.

Sandra was sitting at a table at the back of the living-room sorting through some transparencies, holding them up to the desk light, scrutinizing each one in turn, her long blonde hair tucked behind her ears.

"Drink?" Banks asked.

She didn't look up. "No, thanks."

Fine. Banks went to the cocktail cabinet and poured himself a finger of Laphroaig, thought about it for a moment, then added another finger. He picked up the evening paper from the coffee-table and sat on the settee.

"Hard day?" he asked.

"Not bad," Sandra said, without looking away from the transparency she was holding. "Busy."

Banks looked at the paper for a few minutes without taking anything in, then went over to the stereo. He chose a CD of arias by Angela Gheorghiu. A few seconds into the first one, Sandra looked over and raised a dark eyebrow. "Must you?"

"What's wrong?"

"Do we really *have* to listen to this?"

"What harm is it doing?"

Sandra sighed and turned back to her transparency.

"Really," Banks pressed on. "I want to know. What harm is it doing? Is it too loud?"

"No, it's not too loud."

"Then what's the problem?"

Sandra dropped the transparency on the table a little harder than necessary. "It's bloody opera, is the problem."

It was true that Sandra had once taken a magnet to one of his *Götterdämmerung* tapes. But that was Wagner, an acquired taste at the best of times. Who could possibly object to Angela Gheorghiu singing Verdi? Sandra had even been with him to see *La Traviata* on their season tickets last month, and she said she enjoyed it. But that was before last Saturday.

"I didn't think you found it *that* offensive," Banks said, walking back to the stereo.

"No, leave it," Sandra said. "You've put it on. You've made your point. Just leave it."

"What point?"

"What point? You know what point."

"No, I don't. Enlighten me."

Sandra snorted. "Opera. Bloody opera. The most important thing on your agenda. In your life, for all I know."

Banks sat down and reached for his Scotch. "Oh, we're back to that again, are we?"

"Yes, we're back to that again."

"Well, go on, then."

"Go on, what?"

"Get it off your chest."

"Oh, you'd like that, wouldn't you?"

"What do you mean?"

"You'd like me to get it off my chest. Let the little lady yell at you for a couple of minutes so you can tell your mates what a bloody fishwife she is. Pretend to listen, be all contrite, then just carry on as if nothing had happened."

"It's not like that," Banks protested. "If you've got a problem, tell me. Let's talk about it."

Sandra picked up another transparency and pushed a few loose strands of hair back behind her ears. "I don't want to talk about it. There's nothing to talk about."

Angela Gheorghiu had moved on to the "Aubade" from *Chérubin* now, but its beauty was lost on Banks.

"Look, I'm sorry," he said. "I didn't realize it was that important to you."

Sandra glanced sideways at him. "That's just it, isn't it?" she said.

"What is?"

"You never do. You never do consider how important something might be to me. It's always your needs that come first. Like bloody opera. You never bother asking me what I might want to listen to, do you? You just go straight to your bloody opera without even thinking."

Banks stood up again. "Look, I said I'm sorry. Okay? I'll take it off if it bothers you so much."

"I told you to leave it. It doesn't matter now. It's too late."

"Too late for what?"

"Oh, Alan, give it a rest. Can't you see I've got work to do." She gestured at the transparencies spread out across the table.

"Fine," said Banks. "Fine. You're pissed off, but you don't want to talk about it. You hate opera, but you want me to leave it on. I'm the one who never considers your needs or feelings, but right now you've got work to do. Well, just bloody fine."

Banks tossed back the rest of his Laphroaig, grabbed his coat from the hall stand and slammed the front door behind him.

FOUR

I

Banks was first to arrive at Tuesday morning's CID meeting in the "boardroom" of Eastvale Divisional Police HQ, shortly followed by DC Susan Gay, Superintendent Gristhorpe and, finally, Sergeant Hatchley.

Having been warned by Susan, Banks was dreading that Jimmy Riddle himself would show up. Riddle was a notoriously early riser, and the thirty miles or so of country roads from Regional HQ to Eastvale at such an hour would mean nothing to him. Especially if it gave him an opportunity to cause Banks grief.

Banks knew he would have to face the CC before long—Gristhorpe said he had already received *his* bollocking for letting his DCI too far off the leash—but he just didn't want it first thing in the morning, never his favourite time of day. Especially since he'd gone down to the Queen's Arms in a huff after his argument with Sandra the previous evening and had a jar too many.

He hadn't handled that situation well, he knew. He hadn't been at all reasonable. He had lived with Sandra long enough to know that when she lashed out like that—which was rare—it meant she had something important on her mind. And he hadn't bothered to find out what it was. Instead, he had stormed out like a petulant teenager.

As luck would have it, Jimmy Riddle hadn't turned up by the time coffee and biscuits were served. That probably meant he wouldn't come, Banks thought with relief; usually Riddle liked to be first there, sparkling and spotless, to get a jump on everyone.

"Right," said Gristhorpe. "What have we got so far? Alan, have you talked to the lab?"

Banks nodded. "Nothing yet. They're still trying, but they haven't found anything on the shoes or clothes we sent over for analysis. There's a lot of mud on George Mahmood's shoes, consistent with walking over the rec in the rain, and some sort of substance that looks a bit suspicious. But the lad was wearing trainers, for Christ's sake. Hardly what you'd choose if you were intending to kick someone's head in."

"But we don't know that he was *intending* to do anything, do we?" Gristhorpe pointed out.

"True. Still, it'd be difficult to kick someone to death wearing trainers. Dr Glendenning specified heavy boots. Or Doc Martens, something like that."

"Wouldn't the rain have washed any traces of blood away?" Susan asked.

"Lab says not. If there's enough of it, which there was, and if it gets in the stitching and seeps between the sole and upper they say it's damn near impossible to get rid of."

Susan nodded.

"Vic Manson's working on fingerprints, too," Banks said to Gristhorpe, "but he doesn't hold out a lot of hope."

"Fingerprints from where?"

"The broken bottle. According to the post-mortem, there were fragments of broken glass embedded in the back of Jason Fox's skull, and they match the fragments we found near the body. It looks as if he was hit with a bottle and then kicked. Anyway, Vic says the rain has probably buggered up his chances, but he's busy spraying SuperGlue into aquariums and lord knows what else."

"What did you find out yesterday?" Gristhorpe asked.

"Quite a lot." Banks told them in detail about Jason Fox's losing his job, his false address in Leeds, and the Albion League. "I also checked out this Milly and her boyfriend," he went on. "The West Indian woman Jason insulted at work. Seems she's gone back to live with her family in Barbados."

"Chalk up one victory to Jason Fox, then," said Gristhorpe. "Any idea where Jason lived when he wasn't at his parents' house?"

Banks smiled and produced an address in Rawdon.

"How did you find out?"

"Telephone directory. It doesn't seem as if Jason was making any particular secret out of where he lived. He just neglected to let his parents know he'd moved."

"For eighteen months?"

Banks shrugged. "Jason's relationship with his parents obviously wasn't close. There's a lot they don't know about him. I'm not entirely sure whether they didn't want to know, or whether he didn't want them to. From what I've seen so far, the Foxes aren't a particularly close family."

"How did he make his living these past two years?" Gristhorpe asked. "Do we know that?"

Banks shook his head. "No. But according to the DSS he wasn't on the dole. His grandfather mentioned something about him studying computers, too, so that might be something he's got into more recently. I've asked Ken Blackstone to give us a hand down there, checking the local college courses. And we can check tax records, see if he got another job somewhere."

Gristhorpe nodded. "Know anything about this Albion League?"

Banks's only experience with neo-Nazis was with the National Front in the seventies, when he was a young copper on the Met. He had read about the more recent, smaller and tougher groups, like Combat 18 and Blood and Honour, with all their concomitant white-power rock bands and magazines, but he hadn't actually come across any of them in the line of duty. "Not yet," he said. "And nobody else around here seems to have heard of them, either. Anyway, I faxed the Yard. They've got a special squad dealing with neo-Nazi groups."

"Let's keep our fingers crossed. Have you got anything to add, Sergeant Hatchley?"

"The uniformed lads canvassed the whole Market Street area again yesterday," said Hatchley. "Pubs, cafés, fish and chip shops, bed and breakfasts, the lot. Some people remember Georgie Mahmood and his two mates in the fish and chip shop, all right, but no-one saw them heading for the ginnel. And no-one remembers seeing Jason and his mate. We've managed to get an artist's impression of the lad who was with Jason, but I wouldn't expect too much." Hatchley scratched his nose. "I'm wondering if it was something to do with drugs, sir, The Jubilee being the sort of place it is. A deal gone wrong, maybe?"

"Have we got anything from the Drugs Squad on the victim or suspects?"

Hatchley shook his head. "No, sir. I've already checked with records. But still ..."

"Well, we'll bear it in mind, anyway. Anything else?"

"Aye, sir. I had a chat with a couple of Jason's team-mates from Eastvale United. He had a jar with them after the game, right enough, but none of them admit to seeing him Saturday night, and none of them recognize the lad in the artist's impression."

"Why hasn't Jason's mate come forward?" Gristhorpe mused aloud. "Does he even know what's happened?"

"It's possible he doesn't, sir," said Hatchley. "If he lives far off, like, doesn't watch much telly or read the papers."

Gristhorpe nodded and turned to face everyone. "Either that or he did it. Let's dig a little deeper into the background here. First off, find out if George Mahmood and Jason Fox really did know each other better than George is letting on. Maybe they'd crossed swords before. Let's also find out what we can about Asim Nazur and that cousin of his, Kobir ... what's his name ... ?"

"Mukhtar, sir," said Susan.

"Right. Someone get in touch with Bradford CID and find out if they've got anything on Kobir Mukhtar."

"I've already done that, sir," said Susan. "There was nothing on the computer, so I put in a request for information while we still had them in custody, just before ... before the CC came round yesterday, sir."

"And?"

"Nothing, sir. Seems clean."

"All right." Gristhorpe frowned. "Susan, don't I recollect something about an incident involving the Mahmoods recently?"

"Yes, sir. About a month ago. Someone stole a brick from the building site by Gallows View and lobbed it through the Mahmoods' window. They'd covered the shop windows with wire mesh a while back after a previous incident, so the yob responsible chucked this brick through the bedroom window."

"Anyone hurt?"

"Mrs Mahmood, sir. She was undressing for bed at the time. The brick missed her head by several inches, but a long sliver of glass broke free and sliced into her upper arm. She was bleeding pretty badly when her husband hurried her to Eastvale General. It took fourteen stitches, and the doctor insisted they call the police."

"They weren't going to?"

"They were reluctant, sir," Susan said. "Her husband said it would only cost them time and trouble, and they didn't expect any results in return. Apparently, this kind of thing had happened before, when they ran the shop in Bradford, and nobody ever did anything about it."

"Well, this isn't bloody Bradford," said Gristhorpe. "Any leads?"

"They'd had a customer, a teenage girl, earlier in the day who complained about getting the wrong change. When Mrs Mahmood insisted she was right, the girl swept the newspapers and sweets off the counter and stalked out. We finally tracked her down, but she was in Penrith by the time of the incident. After that, nothing."

"Could it have been Jason Fox, given his views on immigrants?"

"I suppose so," Susan said. "It happened about half past ten on a Saturday night, and we know Jason came to Eastvale on weekends. But we didn't know that then. I mean, we'd no reason to suspect him. And George Mahmood couldn't have known it was him."

"Couldn't he? Maybe he had his suspicions. Maybe he even *saw* him. But you're right, we should avoid too much speculation at this point. Perhaps you should have another word with Jason's family, Susan, see if they're a bit more forthcoming. After that, you can try the Mahmoods again, then the Nazurs at the Himalaya, see if they can tell you anything else about what happened on Saturday night." He looked at his watch, then smiled at Susan. "Time it right, lass, and you might be at the Himalaya just around lunch- time."

Hatchley laughed, and Susan blushed.

"That just about covers it." Gristhorpe rubbed his bristly chin. "But wherever we go," he said, "we tread carefully. On eggs. Remember that. Chief Constable Riddle is taking a personal inter- est in this case." He cleared his throat. "By the way, he apologized for not being with us this morning."

Banks overheard Hatchley whisper to Susan Gay, "Breakfast television."

Gristhorpe ignored them. "What we've all got to bear in mind at this point," he said, "is that while this case looked simple at first, things have changed. It's got a lot more complicated. And however odious a character Jason Fox is beginning to sound, remember, he didn't get a chance to fight back. That's voluntary manslaughter, at the very least, and more than likely it's murder. And don't forget, we've got all the ingredients of a racial incident here, too: white victim, handy Asian suspects picked up, interrogated and locked in the cells overnight. When you add to that the fact that Jason Fox was a racist, George Mahmood is busy exploring his Muslim roots and Asim Nazur's dad is a pillar of the community, then you've got a powder-keg, and I don't want it going off on my patch, Jimmy Riddle or no Jimmy Riddle. Now let's get to it."

II

It was quicker to walk to the Leaview Estate than to drive around Eastvale's confusing one-way system, so Susan nipped out of the fire-exit and took the winding cobbled streets behind the police station down to King Street. She passed the infirmary, then the Gothic pile of Eastvale Comprehensive on the right, with its turrets, clock and bell tower, and the weedy, overgrown rec on her left before entering the Leaview Estate. The weather was overcast today, windy, too, with occasional drizzle, but at least it wasn't cold.

The Foxes' garden looked less impressive in the dull light, Susan thought as she rang the doorbell, yet the roses still seemed to burn with an inner glow of their own. She felt like picking one to take home, but she didn't. That wouldn't look good at all. She could just see the headlines: PoliceWoman Steals Prize Roses From Grieving Family. Jimmy Riddle would just love that. His pate would turn scarlet. And bang would go her promotion.

Josie Fox had her hair tied back today, and her face looked pale and drawn, lips bloodless without make-up. She was wearing a baggy olive jumper and black jeans.

"Oh, it's you. Come in," she said listlessly, standing aside.

"I'm sorry to intrude," Susan said, following her into the living-room. "But I have a few more questions."

"Of course. Sit down."

Susan sat. Josie Fox followed suit, folding her long legs under her. She massaged the bridge of her nose with her thumb and fore-finger.

"Where's your husband today?" Susan asked.

She sighed. "Steven's at work. I told him not to go in, but he said he'd be better off with something to do rather than just being stuck in the house all day. I can't say I'm not glad to see the back of him for a few hours. I couldn't face going in, myself. My daughter's come down from Newcastle to stay with us, so I'm not alone."

"Is she in at the moment?"

"Upstairs, yes. Why?"

"Will you call her down, please?"

Josie Fox frowned, then shrugged and went to the bottom of the stairs to call. A minute or so later, Maureen Fox joined them. Susan's first impression was of a rather bossy, probably very fastidious sort of girl. She was attractive, too, in a sort of bouncy blonde, healthy, athletic way, with a trim figure that looked good in the tight jeans she wore, and symmetrical features, plump red lips, a creamy complexion.

Though Maureen Fox was obviously grieving, there was still a kind of energy emanating from her that she couldn't hide; it showed itself in the way her foot kept tapping on the floor, or one leg jerked when she crossed them; in her constant shifts of position, as if she were uncomfortable no matter how she sat. Susan wondered if Jason had been at all like her. Probably not, if Susan's own family were anything to go by: her brother the stockbroker, who could do no wrong, and her sister the solicitor, apple of her father's eye. Susan had nothing in common with either of them, and sometimes she thought she must have been a changeling.

"Why did you let them go?" Josie asked. "You had them in jail, the ones who did it, and you let them go."

"We don't know that they did it," Susan said. "And we can't just keep people locked up indefinitely without evidence."

"It's because they're coloured, isn't it? That's why you had to let them go. It would've been different if you thought Jason had killed one of *them*, wouldn't it?"

"Mother!" Maureen cut in.

"Oh, Maureen. Don't be so naïve. Everybody knows what it's like these days. The authorities bend over backwards to help immigrants. You ought to know that, being in nursing. It's all opportunities for ethnics, not for decent, hard-working white folks. Look what happened to your dad."

"What did happen to Mr Fox?" Susan asked.

"Oh," said Maureen, with a flick of her head, "Dad got passed over for promotion. Blamed it on some Asian bloke."

"I see. Well, you're right in a way, Mrs Fox," Susan went on, looking at Josie. "The police *do* have to be very careful about how they treat people these days, especially visible minorities. We try to handle everyone the same way, no matter what colour they are." She knew it was eyewash. In the overall scheme of things, racism, along with sexism, was alive and thriving in the police forces of the nation. But, damn it, that was what *she* tried to do. "In this case, though," she went on, "we simply have no evidence yet to connect the suspects to the crime. No witnesses. No physical evidence. Nothing."

"Does that mean they didn't do it?" Josie asked.

"It raises doubts," said Susan. "That's all. I'm afraid I can't say any more about it at the moment."

"You haven't given up, have you?"

"Certainly not. We're investigating a number of leads. That's why I'm here." She paused. "I'm afraid we turned up a couple of disturbing facts about your son."

Josie Fox frowned. "Disturbing? Like what?"

"Did you know about Jason's racist views?"

"What do you mean?"

"Did he never talk about his opinions to you?"

"He never really talked about anything much," she said. "Especially not these past few years."

"Were you aware of what he thought about Asians and blacks?"

"Well," said Josie Fox, "let's put it this way. I knew he had some opinions that might be unpopular, you know, about foreigners, immigrants and such, but I wouldn't say they were particularly extreme. Lots of people think the way Jason does and it doesn't make them racists."

That was a new one on Susan: having racist views doesn't make you a racist? "Did Jason ever mention belonging to any sort of an organization?" she asked. "A group of like-minded people?"

It was Maureen Fox who broke the silence. "No. Jason never mentioned it, but he did. Belong to a group, that is. We only found out about it yesterday."

"Maureen!"

"Oh, Mother. Jason was a creep and you know it. That's why he could never keep a girlfriend. I don't care if I am speaking ill of the dead. I could never stomach him even when he was at school back in Halifax. All his talk about bloody racial purity making the country great again. It made me want to puke. It was those skins he hung around with at school, you know, them and their masters, the ones who prey on schoolkids in depressed areas. You should have done something, you and Dad."

"Like what?" Josie Fox beseeched her. "What could we have done to change him?"

"How do I know what you should have done? But you're his parents. You should have done *something*." She turned to Susan. "Yesterday we went to visit my granddad," she said. "He showed us a pamphlet he thought Jason had sent him in the post. He was very upset about it."

"The Albion League?"

"You know?"

Susan nodded. "Your grandfather told DCI Banks yesterday evening."

Maureen looked at her mother. "There. I told you Granddad wouldn't be able to keep it to himself." She turned to Susan. "Mum thought we should keep it in the family, to protect the family name, but ..." She shrugged. "Well, the cat's out of the bag now, isn't it?"

"I still don't see what this has to do with anything," Josie Fox protested. "Now you're making out my Jason was the villain, but he was the victim. Are you suggesting those boys might have killed him because of his beliefs?"

"Could they have known?"

"What do you mean?"

Susan paused for a moment, then continued softly, "Jason wasn't here very often, Mrs Fox. He didn't put down roots, didn't get to know people. Could those boys have known about him, about what he ... believed?"

"They could have found out somehow, I suppose. They're Asians, so I suppose they have their own gangs, their own networks, don't they? Maybe he did talk to one of them, that one in the shop."

"Do you know if he ever shopped there?"

"I don't know, but he might have done. It's not far away, especially if you go to the bus stop down on Cardigan Drive."

"But Jason had a car."

"Doesn't mean he never took the bus, does it? Anyway, all I'm saying is he *might* have gone in the shop. It wasn't far away. That's all."

"Do you remember about a month ago, when someone threw a brick—"

"Now, wait a minute," said Josie. "You're not going to blame that on our Jason. Oh, no. Be nice and easy for you, that, wouldn't it, blaming a crime on someone who can't answer for himself, just so you can make your crime figures look better, write it off your books."

Susan took a deep breath. "That's not my intention, Mrs Fox. I'm trying to establish a link between Jason and George Mahmood, if there is one. Given Jason's feelings about Asians, it doesn't seem entirely beyond the realm of possibility that he chucked the brick and George knew about it."

"Well, you'll never know, will you?"

Susan sighed. "Perhaps not. Do you know if Jason gave out any of those pamphlets to anyone on the estate?"

Josie Fox shook her head. "I shouldn't think so. No, I'm fairly certain he didn't. I'd have heard about it."

I'll bet you would, Susan thought. "Did any of Jason's colleagues ever call here?"

"I told you the other day. No. We didn't know his friends." For a moment, Susan had imagined a scene like the one in the Krays' east London home, the boys upstairs planning murder and mayhem while good old mum comes in with a tray of tea and biscuits, beaming at them. Obviously not. "You'd almost think he was ashamed of us," Josie Fox added.

"Or of them," said Susan. "Look, he was seen drinking with this lad in The Jubilee on Saturday night." She turned to face Maureen again and showed her the picture. "We're trying to trace him. He might be able to help us find out what happened. Have you ever seen Jason with anyone like that?"

Maureen shook her head. "No."

"Mrs Fox?"

"No."

"You told us Jason was working at a plastics factory in Leeds. Did you know that he left there two years ago, that he was asked to leave because of his racist views?"

Josie Fox's jaw dropped and she could only shake her head slowly, eyes disbelieving. Even Maureen paled.

"Do you know where he went after that?" Susan pressed on.

"No," said Mrs Fox, her voice flat, defeated. "As far as we knew that's where he worked."

"Did he ever mention anything about studying computers?"

"Not to me, no."

"Do you know where Jason lived in Leeds?"

"I gave you the address."

Susan shook her head. "He hasn't been living there in eighteen months. He moved to Rawdon. Did you never visit him?"

Again, she shook her head. "No. How could we? We were both working during the week. Jason, too. Besides, he came to visit us at weekends."

"Did you never telephone him?"

"No. He said it was a shared telephone, out on the landing, and the people in the other flats didn't like to be disturbed. He'd usually ring us if he wanted to tell us he was coming up."

"What about at work?"

"No. His boss didn't like it. Jason would always ring us. I don't understand. This is all ... Why didn't he tell us?"

"I don't know, Mrs Fox," said Susan.

Tears welled in Josie Fox's eyes. "How could he? I mean, where did it come from, him joining such a group, not telling us anything? We used to be such a close family. We always tried to bring him up properly, decently. Where did we go wrong?"

Maureen raised her eyes and sat rigidly, arms folded over her chest, staring at a spot high on the wall, as if she were both embarrassed and disgusted by her mother's display of emotion.

Where did we go wrong? It was a question Susan had heard many times, both in the course of her work and from her own parents when they complained about her chosen career. She knew better than to try to answer it.

A lot of prejudices were inherited. Her father, for example: to all outside appearances, he was a decent and intelligent man, a regular churchgoer, a respected member of the community, yet he would never eat in an Indian restaurant because he thought he was being served horse-meat, dog or cat, and that the hot spices were used to mask the taste of decay.

Susan had inherited some of his attitudes, she knew, but she also knew she could fight against them; she didn't have to be stuck with them forever. So she went to lots of Indian restaurants and got to love the food. That was why Superintendent Gristhorpe's crack about having lunch at the Himalaya had made her blush. It was exactly what she had been thinking at the time: onion bhaji and vegetable samosas. *Mmmm*.

Whatever she did, though, it was always there, at the back of her mind: that feeling, inherited from her father, that these people weren't *quite like us*; that their customs and religious beliefs were barbaric and primitive, not Christian.

Where did we go wrong? Who knew the answer to that one? Giving up on the Foxes for now, Susan closed her notebook and walked back out onto Daffodil Rise. It had started to rain again.

III

The traffic on the Leeds ring road wasn't too bad, and Banks made it to Rawdon by eleven o'clock. Number seven Rudmore Terrace was an uninspiring, stone-clad semi just off the main road to Leeds and Bradford Airport. It had a small bay window, frosted-glass panes in the door and an overgrown garden.

First, Banks headed for number nine, where he noticed the lace curtains twitch as he walked up the path. Of course, when he knocked and a woman answered, she made a great pretence of being surprised to receive a caller, and left the chain on as she checked his warrant card and invited him in.

"You can't be too careful, these days," she said as she put the kettle on. "A woman in the next street was attacked just two weeks ago. Raped." She mouthed the word rather than speaking it aloud, as if that somehow lessened its power. "In the middle of the day, no less. I'm Liza Williams, by the way."

Liza was an attractive woman in her early thirties, with short black hair, a smooth, olive complexion and light blue eyes. She led Banks through to the living-room, the carpet of which was covered with children's toys. The room smelled vaguely of Plasticine and warm milk.

"Jamie's taken the twins over to their grannie's for the morning," she said, surveying the mess. "To give me a breather, like. Two two-and-a-half-year-olds can be a bit of a handful, Mr Banks, in case you didn't know that already."

Banks smiled. "I didn't know. There's a couple of years between my boy and girl. But believe me, *one* two-and-a-half-year-old was bad enough. I can't imagine two."

Liza Williams smiled. "Oh, it's not so bad really. I complain but … I wouldn't want to be without them. Now, I don't suppose you came here to talk about children. Is it about that woman in the next street?"

"No. I'm North Yorkshire CID," said Banks. "That'd be West Yorkshire."

"Yes, of course. I should have noticed the card." She frowned. "That just makes me even more puzzled."

"It's about next door, Mrs Williams."

She paused, then her eyes widened. "Oh, I see. Yes, that's so sad, isn't it? And him so young."

"I'm sorry?"

"You mean about the boy who was killed, don't you? Jason. In Eastvale. That's North Yorkshire, isn't it?"

"You knew?"

"Well we *were* neighbours, even if we weren't especially close ones. They say good fences make good neighbours, Mr Banks, and you need a big one to keep that ugly garden of his out of view. But fair's fair. He was quiet and considerate and he never complained about the twins."

"Look, do you think we could just back up for a minute and get a few things straight?"

"Of course."

"Jason Fox lived next door, at number seven, right?"

"Yes. That's what I was telling you."

"Okay. And you read in the paper that Jason was killed in Eastvale on Saturday night?"

"Saw it on telly, actually. How else would I know? Soon as I heard it was him you could have knocked me over with a feather."

"How did you know it wasn't some other Jason Fox?"

"Well, it's not that common a name, is it, and even if the sketch they showed on the news wasn't very good, I could still recognize him from it."

The kettle boiled and Liza Williams excused herself to make tea. She came back with a tray, a pot and two mugs.

"Why didn't you call the police?" Banks asked.

She frowned. "Police? But why should I? Did I do something wrong?"

"No. I'm not accusing you of anything. Just curious."

"Well, I never thought. Why would I? I didn't really know anything about Jason. Anyway, I was really very sorry to hear about what happened, but it didn't have anything to do with me, did it? It's none of *my* business. I mean, I've never even *been* to Eastvale."

"But didn't you think the police might want to have a look around the house where Jason lived, maybe ask you a few questions about him?"

"Well ... I ... I don't know what to say. I'm sorry. I just assumed if the police wanted to ask me anything, they'd have asked me when they were round earlier. I thought you'd done what you had to do. I don't know what happens to people's houses after—"

"Just a minute," said Banks, sitting on the edge of his seat. "Did you say the police have already been around?"

"Yes. Plainclothes. Didn't you know?"

"Obviously not, or I wouldn't be asking you all these questions." Liza Williams didn't look or sound like a stupid woman. What could she be thinking of? "When was this?"

"Sunday morning. Before I'd even heard what happened. Why? Is something wrong?"

"No. No. It's all right." Banks scratched the scar beside his right eye. Liza poured the tea, meeting his eyes as she did so and splashing a little tea on the tray. She handed Banks a steaming mugful. "Did they talk to you?" he asked.

"No. They just went into Jason's house. Two of them. They seemed to have a key, seemed to know what they were doing."

"How did you know they were police?"

"I didn't. I just assumed, the way they seemed so purposeful. Then, later that night, when I saw about Jason on the telly ... It seemed to make sense."

"What time was this, when they came?"

"Must have been about ten o'clock. Jamie had just come back from the newsagent's with the papers. We don't have them delivered bec—"

Banks tuned her out. At first he had considered the possibility, however remote, that West Yorkshire had been playing left hand to North Yorkshire's right. But Susan Gay hadn't even discovered Jason Fox's identity until lunch-time on Sunday, and the Foxes hadn't officially identified him until after that. So who had known who the victim was before the police did? And how had they found out?

Banks blew on his tea, took a sip, then leaned forward again. "This is very important, Mrs Williams," he said. "Can you tell me anything about these men?"

IV

Steven Fox clearly wasn't expecting Susan, and his face showed surprise and suspicion when she turned up in his office at the building society.

"Time for a word?" she asked, smiling.

He looked at his watch. "I suppose so. It's almost lunch-time anyway."

"My treat," said Susan. She sighed inwardly, realizing she'd have to forego the Himalaya.

Steven Fox put on his raincoat, and they walked along York Road to the El Toro coffee bar on the opposite side of the market square from the police station. The El Toro, with its dim lighting, castanet-clicking muzak, bullfight posters and smell of espresso, wasn't renowned for its food, but the sandwiches were decent enough: Susan treated herself to prawn and tomato and Steven Fox settled for ham and cheese.

Once they had taken a bite or two and sipped some coffee, Susan began: "Would you be surprised to hear that Jason was no longer working where you told us he was?"

Steven Fox paused and rubbed his glasses, steamed up by the coffee. "To be honest," he said, "nothing much would surprise me about Jason. He was a law unto himself."

"His mother was surprised."

"Maybe she had more illusions."

That might explain, Susan thought, why Steven Fox had seemed quicker to accept that Jason might have met a violent end than Josie had been.

"And you?" she asked.

"Jason was a peculiar lad. We never had a very close relationship. I don't know why."

"Did you know anything about his affiliation with the Albion League?"

"Not until yesterday, no." Steven Fox shook his head slowly. "When Jason left home," he said, "that was it. We never really knew what he was up to after then. Still, I don't suppose it's the kind of thing you do tell your parents, is it? I mean, can you imagine your son sitting down at the dinner table one night and saying, 'Guess what, Mum, Dad, I joined a neo-Nazi party today'?"

"Not unless he thought you shared his views."

Steven banged his coffee cup down on the saucer, spilling some. "Now, hold on a minute, that's quite an allegation. I resent that. I'm not a racist."

Susan held her hand up. "I'm not alleging anything, Mr Fox. I simply want to know."

"Well, he didn't get it from me or his mother."

"Do you have any ideas as to where he did get it from?"

"Well, that kind of thing … Do you really think it's as simple as … you know, just picking up or imitating someone's mannerisms or figures of speech?"

"No, I don't. But he had to start somewhere. What about this promotion business?"

"Josie told you about that?"

"Maureen, actually."

Steven Fox shrugged. "Back in Halifax, I lost out on a promotion to a fellow from Bengal. Nice chap, but … It was that, what do you call it … ?"

"Positive discrimination?"

"Aye, only giving jobs to immigrants and women. Sorry. But I had more experience. And I'd put in more years. Anyway, it gave us some hard times, not enough money coming in, that sort of thing. I think Jason took it more to heart than I did, maybe because he already had some problems of his own at school. There were a lot of Asians there, recent immigrants for the most part, some of them with poor language skills, and Jason got into trouble once for suggesting to a teacher that they were holding back the rest and ought to be put together in a special class."

"How long ago was that?"

"In his last year there. Just before we moved."

"Didn't that concern you?"

"Well it … I mean, in a way, I suppose, he was right, wasn't he? Maybe he should have put it more diplomatically. Lord knows, as I said, I'm no racist, but it seems to me that if you keep on catering for the demands of foreign cultures and other religions over your own, then you do sort of ... weaken ... your own, don't you? For crying out loud, they don't even sing a hymn and say the Lord's Prayer at morning assembly any more."

Susan moved on quickly. "Do you know the people who run the shop on Gallows View? The Mahmoods?"

"I know who you mean—I've nipped in there for a tin of soup from time to time—but I can't say I *know* them."

"Remember about a month ago when someone chucked a brick though their window?"

"I read about it in the local paper. Why?"

"Was Jason up that weekend?"

"Oh, come on," said Steven. "Surely you can't imagine he'd do something like that?"

"Why not?"

"He wasn't a hooligan."

"But he *was* a racist."

"Still ... anyway, I don't remember if he was here or not. And aren't you supposed to be looking for his killers?"

"Every little bit helps, Mr Fox. He wasn't living at the address you gave us in Leeds. Did you know that?"

"Not living there?" Steven Fox shook his head. "Bloody hell, no. I just assumed ... I mean, why would he lie about that?"

"I don't think he lied. He just omitted to let you know. Maybe he thought you weren't interested."

Steven Fox frowned. "You must think us terribly neglectful parents."

Susan said nothing.

"But Jason was over eighteen," he went on. "He led his own life."

"So you said. He still visited home, though."

"He came home on weekends to get his washing done and get a free meal, like lots of kids do."

"You said earlier that you and Jason were never close. Why was that?"

"I don't know really. When he was younger, he was always more of a mother's boy. Then, in his teens, he got involved in football. I've never been much interested in sports, myself. I was never very good at games at school. Always the last one to be picked, that sort of thing. I suppose I should have gone to watch him play, you know, shown more support ... enthusiasm. It's not that I wasn't proud of him." He shook his head. "Maybe I was selfish. I had my record collection to catalogue. Jason had his football. We just didn't seem to have anything in common. But I couldn't see where any of it was leading. How could I know?" He looked at his watch. "Look, I really do have to get back. I can't tell you anything more, honestly. If those boys really did kill Jason, you know, those immigrants you had to let go, I hope you find some evidence against them. If there's anything else I can do ... ?"

And he got up to leave. Susan nodded, more than happy to see the back of him. For the second time that day she'd had to restrain herself from screaming that George, Asim and Kobir weren't immigrants, that they'd been bloody-well born here, and their fathers before them. But she didn't. What was the point?

And now she had to go to the Himalaya and talk to Asim Nazur and his parents. They would certainly be thrilled to see her. Still, wicked though it sounded, maybe she still had room for a small samosa, after all. Just the one. For a simple pub fight gone wrong, she thought, this case was turning into a hell of a confusing affair.

V

The little pane of glass in the front door smashed easily enough when Banks applied his elbow. He stuck his hand through carefully and turned the lock. He had a warrant to search the place and, as Jason's pockets had been emptied of everything, including his house keys, this seemed the easiest way to get in.

Inside, the house was so quiet that all he could hear was the hissing of blood in his ears. There wasn't even a clock ticking. He imagined it wasn't always like that, not with the twins next door.

He started in the living-room, to his right. Three-piece suite, upholstered in tan corduroy, wallpaper with thin green and brown stripes, mirror over the mantelpiece, fake-coal electric fire. Television and video. Selection of tapes, mostly science fiction and horror by the look of them. A few paperbacks: Ayn Rand, Tom

Clancy, Michael Crichton. And that was it. There was a sideboard against one wall and in one of the drawers Banks found a couple of bills addressed to Jason Fox. Nothing else.

The kitchen was spotless, dishes all in cupboards, mugs hanging from hooks over the counter. Very little in the fridge: a tub of *I Can't Believe It's Not Butter*, Cheddar cheese turning blue at the edges, sliced white bread, boiled ham, limp celery, lettuce, tomatoes. More the kind of stuff for sandwiches than hot meals. Maybe Jason did most of his eating out.

There were three bedrooms, one no bigger than a cupboard really. That one was completely empty, the other two showed some signs of occupation. Just as at the house in Eastvale, Jason's bed was tightly made, and a similar selection of clothes hung in the wardrobe. The dresser drawers were full of socks, underwear and T-shirts, along with an unopened box of condoms and a bottle of aspirin. The third bedroom looked like a guest room, with a single bed, empty drawers and not much else.

Except the computer.

But Banks didn't trust himself not to screw something up if he started messing around with that, so he made a note to get someone else in to give it the once-over.

Back in the hall, Banks could only marvel at the sheer *emptiness* of the place. There was no personality. You'd expect, if Jason were a member of a white-power organization, at least a few Skrewdriver CDs and maybe one or two copies of *The Order* strewn around the place. But it was as if someone had been there and stripped away all signs of character, if there had been any. And maybe someone had.

Two men, Liza Williams had said, and they had left with some cardboard boxes. Unfortunately, it had been raining in Leeds that Sunday morning, and they had both been wearing flat hats. Black or navy blue. One of them wore a black leather jacket and jeans, the other a donkey jacket. The one in the leather jacket was taller than the other.

No, Liza admitted, they weren't particularly well dressed, but then she watched a lot of police programmes on telly, so she didn't expect real policemen to be any better dressed than their fictional counterparts. No, she couldn't say how old they were, hadn't seen their faces, but she got the impression by the way they moved that they were probably fairly young and fit.

And that was about all she could say, she was sorry. She had, after all, only glimpsed them, and as she noticed they used a key to get in, she didn't worry about them being burglars or rapists. She first thought they were friends of Jason's—he sometimes had friends to stay—and then, after she heard of his death, she just assumed they'd been policemen come to return his belongings to his family or something. No, her husband hadn't seen them; he had already settled down with the Sunday papers, and once he did that ...

The only thing she *had* noticed was a blue car parked outside, which she thought belonged to the men. But she didn't know what make it was, let alone the number. She did say it was clean, though.

Banks sighed as he closed the door behind him. He would have to get someone from West Yorkshire to fix the pane of glass he'd broken, and perhaps to question some of the other people in the street. Whatever they'd noticed, he hoped it would be more than Liza Williams.

VI

By mid-afternoon, Susan was wet, tired and no further ahead than she had been in the morning. The Nazurs and the Mahmoods had been sullen and uncommunicative, as expected, and she had flinched at the clear accusations of racism in their eyes. No, Jason Fox had never been in the Mahmoods' shop, as far as they knew, and the Nazurs had never seen him in their restaurant. And they knew nothing about any Albion League.

Sergeant Hatchley was still out pounding the streets, so at least she got the opportunity to warm herself up with a cup of coffee and take a little quiet time for herself.

She had just put her cold wet feet on the radiator to warm them when one of the staff from the murder room came in bearing a fax. "Just arrived," he said.

Susan thanked him and looked at the single sheet. All it said was:

THE ALBION LEAGUE

along with a telephone number. A London number.

Curious, Susan picked up the phone and dialled. She remembered that Banks had faxed a request for information about the Albion League to Scotland Yard, so she wasn't surprised when someone there answered. After a bit of shuttling around and a lot of waiting, she finally got to someone who knew what she was talking about when she mentioned the Albion League. His name, he said, was Crawley.

"Is your boss there, love?" he asked.

Susan bristled, gripping the receiver tightly, but she said nothing.

"Well?" Crawley repeated.

"I'm afraid Detective Superintendent Gristhorpe is out of the office at the moment," Susan finally managed, between gritted teeth.

"And you're DC Gay?"

"Yes." At least he didn't make any cracks about her name.

"I suppose you'll have to do then."

Not her day. "Thanks a lot," she said.

"Don't take offence, love."

"I'll try not to, sweetie pie. Now how about the Albion League?"

She heard Crawley laugh at the end of the line, then he cleared his throat. "Yeah, well, it's a neo-Nazi organization, white power. That's why we're interested, see, in why you want to know."

"I'd have thought it was a simple enough enquiry," Susan said.

"True enough, love, but nothing to do with those bastards is simple. They're flagged."

"Flagged?"

"Any time their name comes up, certain people have to be informed."

"That sounds very mysterious."

"Does it?"

"Yes. Anyway, don't worry. I'm sure DCI Banks will send you a full report—he's heading the field investigation—but would you mind, just for the moment, humouring a poor DC? Could you give me some general idea of what this particular neo-Nazi organization is all about, what they want?"

She heard another brief chuckle down the line, then Crawley said, "Want? That's easy. Same as all the rest of them, really. The usual things. Racial purity. Repatriation of immigrants and all ethnics. Keep Britain white. Oh, and they want the trains to run on time, too."

"Some hope of that."

"Tell me about it. Seriously, though, love, it's not so much what these people *want*—that's usually predictable enough—but what they're willing to do to get it—what means they'll use, how they're organized, what connections they have with other groups, whether they're armed, what international links they have, if any. That sort of thing. See what I mean?"

"Yes," said Susan. "And the Albion League, how do they fit into all that?"

There was a pause. Then Crawley said, "I'm sorry, but I'm really not authorized to tell you any more than that. Have your boss give me a bell when he comes in, will you, love?"

And the line went dead.

VII

By the time Banks had finished co-ordinating with West Yorkshire Police, it was late afternoon. He decided to drop by Tracy's residence and see what she was up to. She had only been at the University of Leeds for a little over two weeks, but already he missed her. Maybe he could take her for a spot of dinner or something. That way he would also avoid the rush-hour traffic on the way home.

And spending time with Tracy might also make him forget about his problems with Sandra for a short while.

When he got to the student residence building beside Woodhouse Moor, he was pleased to find that not just anyone could walk in. You had to know whom you wanted to see. Banks found a porter on duty, showed his identification and said he'd like to visit his daughter.

Impressed with Banks's credentials, the garrulous porter—who said he had been a policeman himself some years ago, before a leg injury forced him to retire—let him in.

As Banks walked up the two flights of stairs, he wondered if he should have announced himself first. What if Tracy were with a boy or something? Having sex? But he dismissed the idea. He couldn't imagine his daughter doing that. Either she'd be out at a lecture, or she'd be studying in her room.

When he got to her door, he knocked. He could hear music from down the hall, but not a sound from Tracy's room itself. He knocked again, more loudly this time. Nothing. He felt disappointed. She must be at a lecture.

Just as he was about to walk away, the adjacent door opened and a young tousle-haired girl stuck her head out. "Oh, sorry," she said in a husky voice. "I thought you were knocking on *my* door. Sometimes you can't tell, if you've got some music on or something." Then her eyes twinkled. "Hey, you *weren't* knocking at my door, were you?"

"No," said Banks.

She made a mock pout. "Pity. You looking for Tracy, then?"

"I'm her father."

"The detective. She's talked a lot about you." The girl twisted a tendril of red hair around her index finger. "I must say, though, she never told me you were quite so dishy. I'm Fiona, by the way. Pleased to meet you."

She held out her hand and Banks shook it. He felt himself blush. "Any idea where Tracy might be?"

Fiona looked at her watch. "Probably in The Pack Horse with the others, by now," she said, with a sigh. "I'd be there myself, 'cept I'm on antibiotics for my throat, and I'm not supposed to drink. And it's no fun if you can't have a *real* drink." She wrinkled her nose and smiled. "It's just up the road. You can't miss it."

Banks thanked her and, leaving the car parked where it was, set off on foot. He found The Pack Horse on Woodhouse Lane, close to the junction with Clarendon Road, not more than a couple of hundred yards away. He felt too formally dressed for the place, even though he had taken off his tie and was wearing casual trousers and a zippered suede jacket.

The pub had the polished wood, brass and glass look of a real Victorian ale house; it also seemed to be divided into a maze of rooms, most of them occupied by noisy groups of students. It wasn't until the third room that Banks found his daughter. She was sitting at a cluttered table with about six or seven other students, a pretty even mix of male and female. The jukebox was playing a Beatles oldie: "Ticket to Ride."

He could see Tracy in profile, chatting away over the music to a boy beside her. God, she looked so much like Sandra—the blonde hair tucked behind her small ears, black eyebrows, tilt of her nose and chin, the animated features as she talked. It made his heart ache.

Banks didn't like the look of the boy beside her. He had one of those expressions that always seem to be sneering at the world: something to do with the twist of the lip and the cast of the eyes. Either Tracy didn't notice, or it didn't bother her. Or, worse, she found it attractive.

As she spoke, she waved her hands about, stopping now and then to listen to his response and sip from a pint glass of pale amber liquid and nod in agreement from time to time. Her drink could have been lager, but Banks thought it was most likely cider. Tracy had always enjoyed non-alcoholic cider when they'd stopped for pub lunches during family holidays in Dorset or the Cotswolds.

But this glass of cider was probably alcoholic. And why not? he told himself. She was old enough. At least she wasn't smoking.

Then, as he stood there in the doorway, a strange emotion overwhelmed him. As he watched his daughter talk, laugh and drink, oblivious to her father's proximity, a lump came to his throat, and he realized he had lost her. He couldn't go over to the table and join the crowd—simply couldn't do it. He didn't belong; his presence would only embarrass her. A line had been reached and crossed. Tracy was beyond him now, and things would never be the same. And he wondered if that was the only line that had been crossed lately.

Banks turned away and walked outside. The wind made his eyes water as he went in search of somewhere else to enjoy a quiet smoke and a drink before setting off back home.

VIII

That Tuesday night, the Albion League was holding one of its regular bashes in a small rented warehouse near Shipley. Dim and cavernous, it was the same kind of place people went to for raves, but without the Ecstasy. Here, Craig guessed, the only drugs were the lager that flowed from the kegs like water from a hosepipe, nicotine and, maybe, the odd tab of amphetamine.

But one way or another everyone was pumped up. Guitars, drums and bass crashed at breakneck pace, simple three-chord sequences, interrupted occasionally by a howl of unplanned feedback from the amps. The Albion League themselves were playing tonight, a makeshift white-power band consisting of whoever felt like picking up the instruments at the time. At the moment the lead singer was growling,

White is white.
Black is black.
We don't want 'em.
Send 'em back.

Subtle. Craig wished he could wear earplugs.

From his table, Craig watched Motcombe work the room. He was good, no doubt about it. Slick. There must be at least a couple of hundred people in the place, Craig guessed, and Nev was walking around the tables patting a back here, leaning over for a smile and a word of encouragement there.

It was a miracle he managed to make himself heard with the band making so much bloody noise. Some of the older members, chronically unemployed factory workers and ageing skins, had settled into a far corner, as far away from the source of the racket as possible. What did they expect, Craig wondered, the Black Dyke Mills Band playing *Deutschland über Alles* or Wagner's *Ring* cycle? It was the rock bands that got the kids in, *and* got the message across through sheer volume and repetition.

The real trouble with this gig, Craig thought as he looked around, was that there was no chance of a bit of nooky. For some reason, girls didn't have much to do with white-power freaks, and most of the kids, in turn, seemed content enough with a celibate existence, fuelled by sheer race hatred alone.

The only females Craig could see tonight were a few peroxide scrubbers, like superannuated biker-girls, hanging out with the older crowd, and a table of skinny birds with shaved heads and rings through their noses. He sighed and drank some lager. Can't have everything. A job's a job.

The music stopped and the singer said they were going to take a short break. Thank God for that, thought Craig. Trying to keep one eye on Motcombe, he turned to the three skins at the table with him.

Christ, he thought, they couldn't be more than sixteen. One of the Leeds cell-leaders had spotted them causing a bit of aggro to a telephone box on their way home from a football match. He had joined in with them, then invited them to the show. Thick as two short planks, all three of them.

"What did you think of that, then?" Craig asked, lighting up.

"Not bad," said the spotty one, who went by the name of Billy. "I've heard better guitar players, mind you."

"Yeah, well," Craig said, with a shrug, "they're pretty new, need a bit more practice, I'll admit. See, with this lot, though, it's the words that count most. Trouble is, most rock bands don't really pay any attention to what they're saying, know what I mean? I'm talking about the message."

"What message?" the slack-jawed one asked.

"Well, see, if you were listening," Craig went on, "you'd have heard what they were saying about that we should send all the Pakis and niggers back home and get this country on its feet again."

"Oh, yeah," said Billy. "'White's white, black's black, we don't want 'em, send 'em back.'"

"That's right." Craig smiled. "So you *were* listening. Great. That's what I mean, Billy. Most rock music is self-indulgent crap, but this is real music, music with a purpose. It's truth-telling music, this is. It tells it like it is."

"Yeah," said slack-jaw. "I think I see what you mean."

In your fucking dreams, thought Craig. From the corner of his eye, he saw Motcombe about five tables away whispering in someone's ear. He couldn't make out who it was. How many irons did this one have in the fire? Even though the band had stopped playing, music still blared out of a sound system and the level of conversation was loud.

"So what do you think?" he asked. "The message?"

"Well, yeah," said pointy-head, speaking up for the first time. "It sounds all right. Send 'em all back, like. I mean, it sounds good to me." He grinned, showing bad teeth, and looked around at his friends. "I mean, kick the fuckers out, right? Eh? Send the black bastards back to the jungle. Kick the fuckers out."

"Right," said Craig. "You've got it. Thing is, there's not much a person can do by himself, all alone, if you see what I mean."

"Except wank," grinned slack-jaw.

Ah, a true wit. Craig laughed. "Yeah, except wank. And you don't want to be wankers, do you? Anyway, see, if you get organized, like with others who feel the same way, then there's a lot more you can achieve. Right?"

"Right," said Billy. "Stands to reason, don't it?"

"Okay," Craig went on, noticing the band picking up their instruments again. "Think about it, then."

"About what?" Billy asked.

"What I've just been saying. About joining the League. Where you get a chance to *act* on your beliefs. We have a lot of fun, too."

A screech of feedback came from the amp. Billy put his hands over his ears. "Yeah, I can see," he said.

He was clearly the leader of the three, Craig thought, the Alex of the group; the others were just his droogs. If Billy decided it was a good idea, they'd go along with him. Craig noticed Motcombe glance around the room then walk out of the fire-exit at the back with one of the Leeds cell-leaders. He stood up and leaned over the three skins. "Keep in touch, then," he said, as the music started again. He pointed. "See that bloke at the table there, over by the door?"

Billy nodded.

"If you decide you want to sign up tonight, he's the man to talk to."

"Right."

He patted Billy on the back. "Got to go for a piss. See you later."

Casually, he walked towards the toilets near the front door. The band had started their tribute to Ian Stuart, late leader of Skrewdriver who, Blood and Honour claimed, had been murdered by the secret service. And now the Albion League had a martyr on their hands. He wondered how quickly someone would write a song about Jason Fox.

Anyway, the toilets were empty, and most people were either talking loudly or listening to the band, so no-one saw Craig nip out the front door. Not that it mattered, anyway; the room was so hot and smoky that no-one could be suspect for going out for a breath of fresh air.

Instead of just standing there and enjoying the smell of the cool, damp night, he walked around the back of the building towards the big car park. Glancing around the corner, he saw Motcombe and the Leeds skin standing by Motcombe's black van talking. The car park was badly lit, so Craig found it easy enough to crouch down and scoot closer, hiding behind a rusty old Metro, watching them through the windows.

It didn't take long to figure out that they were talking about money. As Craig watched, the Leeds skin handed Motcombe a fistful of notes. Motcombe took a box out of his van and opened it. Then he placed the bills inside. The skin said something Craig couldn't catch, then they shook hands and he went back inside.

Motcombe stood for a moment, glancing around, sniffing the air. Craig felt a twinge of fear, as if Motcombe had twitched his antenna, sensed a presence.

But it passed. Motcombe opened the box, took out a handful of notes and stuffed them in his inside pocket. Then he squared his shoulders and strutted back in to work the crowd again.

FIVE

I

"The Albion League," said Gristhorpe in the boardroom on Wednesday morning, his game leg resting on the polished oval table, thatch of grey hair uncombed. Banks, Hatchley and Susan Gay sat listening, cups of coffee steaming in front of them. "I've been on the phone to this bugger Crawley for about half an hour, but somehow I feel I know less than when I started. Know what I mean?"

Banks nodded. He'd spoken to people like that. Still, some had said the same thing about him, too.

"Anyway," Gristhorpe went on, "they're exactly what they sound like in their pamphlet—a neo-Nazi fringe group. Albion's an old, poetic name for the British Isles. You find it in Chaucer, Shakespeare, Spenser and a lot of other poets. Anyway, according to Crawley, this lot took it from William Blake, who elevated Albion into some sort of mythical spirit of the race."

"Is this Blake a Nazi, then, sir?" Sergeant Hatchley asked.

"No, Sergeant," Gristhorpe answered patiently. "William Blake was an English poet. He lived from 1757 to 1827. You'd probably know him best as the bloke who wrote 'Jerusalem' and 'Tyger, Tyger.'"

"'Tyger tyger, burning bright'?" said Hatchley. "Aye, sir, I think we did that one at school."

"Most likely you did."

"And we sometimes used to sing the other one on the coach home after a rugby match. But isn't Jerusalem in Israel, sir? Was this Blake Jewish, then?"

"Again, Sergeant, no. I'll admit it sounds an ironic sort of symbol for a neo-Nazi organization. But, as I said, Blake liked to mythologize things. To him, Jerusalem was a sort of image of the ideal city, a spiritual city, a perfect society, if you like—of which London was a pale, fallen shadow—and he wanted to establish a *new* Jerusalem 'in England's green and pleasant land.'"

"Was he green, then, sir, one of them environmentalists?"

"No, he wasn't."

Banks could see Gristhorpe gritting his teeth in frustration. He felt like kicking Hatchley under the table, but he couldn't reach. The sergeant was trying it on, of course, but Hatchley and Gristhorpe always seemed to misunderstand one another. You wouldn't have thought they were both Yorkshiremen under the skin.

"Blake's Albion was a powerful figure, ruler of this ideal kingdom," Gristhorpe went on. "A figure of which even the heroes of the Arthurian legends were mere shadows."

"How long have they been around?" Banks asked.

Gristhorpe turned to him, clearly with some relief. "About a year," he said. "They started as a splinter group of the British National Party, which turned out to be too soft for them. And they think they're a cut above Combat 18, who they regard as nowt but a bunch of thugs."

"Well, they're right on that count," Banks said. "Who's the grand Pooh-Bah?"

"Bloke called Neville Motcombe. Aged thirty-five. You'd think he'd be old enough to know better, wouldn't you?"

"Any form?"

"One arrest for assaulting a police officer during a BNP rally years back, and another for receiving stolen goods."

"Any connection with George Mahmood and his friends?" Banks asked.

Gristhorpe shook his head. "Other than the obvious, none."

"Surely the Albion League isn't based in Eastvale, sir?" Susan Gay asked.

Gristhorpe laughed. "No. That's just where Jason Fox's parents happen to live. Luck of the draw, as far as we're concerned. Their headquarters are in Leeds—an old green-grocer's shop in Holbeck—but they've got cells all over West Yorkshire, especially in places where there's a high percentage of immigrants. As I said before, they're not above using the yobs, but there's also that element of a more intellectual appeal to disaffected white middle-class kids with chips on their shoulders—lads like Jason Fox, with a few bob's worth of brains and nobbut an a'porth of common sense."

"How strong are they?" Banks asked.

"Hard to say. According to Crawley there's about fifteen cells, give or take a couple. One each in smaller places like Batley and Liversedge, but two or three in a larger city like Leeds. We don't really know how many members in each cell, but as a rough estimate let's say maybe eighty to a hundred members in all."

"Not a lot, is it? Where does this Motcombe bloke live?"

"Pudsey, down by Fulneck way. Apparently he's got a nice detached house there."

Banks raised his eyebrows. "La-de-dah. Any idea how they're financed—apart from receiving stolen goods?"

"Crawley says he doesn't know."

"Do you believe him?"

Gristhorpe sniffed and scratched his hooked nose. "I smell politics in this one, Alan," he said. "And when I smell politics I don't believe anything I see or hear."

"Do you want Jim and me to have a poke around in Leeds?" Banks asked.

"Just what I was thinking. You could pay the shop a visit, for a start. See if there's anyone around. Clear it with Ken Blackstone first, make sure you're not treading on anyone's toes."

Banks nodded. "What about Motcombe?"

Gristhorpe paused before answering. "I got the impression that Crawley didn't want us bothering Mr Motcombe," he said slowly. "In fact, I think Crawley was only detailed to answer our request for information because they knew down there that we'd simply blunder ahead and find out anyway. The bull-in-a-china-shop approach. He was very vague indeed. And he asked us to proceed with caution."

"So what do we do?"

A wicked grin creased Gristhorpe's face. "Well," he said, tugging his plump earlobe, "I'd pay him a visit, if I were you. Rattle his chain a bit. I mean, it's not as if we've been officially warned off."

Banks smiled. "Right."

"One more thing before you all go. These letters at the bottom of the Albion League's flyer." Gristhorpe lifted the pamphlet from the table and pointed. "*Http://www.alblgue. com/index.html*. Now you all know I'm a bloody Luddite when it comes to computers, but even I know that's a Web page address. Don't ask me what a Web page looks like, mind you. Question is, can we do anything with it? Is it likely to get us anywhere? Susan?"

"It might do," said Susan Gay. "Unfortunately, we don't have access to the Internet over the station computers."

"Oh. Why not?"

"I don't know, sir. Just slow, I suppose. South Yorkshire's even got their own Web page. And West Mercia."

Gristhorpe frowned. "What do they do with them?"

Susan shrugged. "Put out information. Community relations. Crimestoppers. Chief Constable's opinion on the state of the county. That sort of thing. It's an interface with the community."

"Is it, indeed?" Gristhorpe grunted. "Sounds like a complete bloody waste of time to me. Still, if this Albion League thing's worth a try, is there some way you could have a peek? Or should I say surf?"

Susan smiled. "Browse, actually, sir. You surf the Net, but you browse the Web."

"And is there any wonder I've no patience with the bloody machines?" Gristhorpe muttered. "Whatever you call it, can you get a look at it?"

Susan nodded. "I've got a hook-up from home," she said. "I can certainly give it a try."

"Then do it, and let us know what you find. Alan, did those lads from West Yorkshire find anything on Jason Fox's computer?"

Banks shook his head. "Clean as a whistle."

"Clean as in somebody washed it?"

"That's what they said."

Gristhorpe grimaced as he shifted his bad leg and shook it to improve the circulation before standing up. "Right then," he said. "That's about it for now. Let's get cracking."

II

Susan enjoyed the unexpected surprise of being able to go home during working hours, even though she knew she was there to work.

First, she kicked off her shoes and put on the kettle. Then she looked through her collection of different tea varieties and settled on Autumn, a black tea dotted with small pieces of apple, perfect for the drizzly, blustery day. On impulse, she put a pinch of cinnamon in the pot, too. While the tea was brewing, she put on her CD of Andrew Lloyd Webber's greatest hits, smiling as she thought how much Banks would hate it, then she poured herself a cup of tea and got down to work.

The computer was in her bedroom because her flat was so small. It was the one room where she never received visitors. At least not yet. But she wasn't going to allow herself to think about DC Gavin Richards right now.

Cup of apple-and-cinnamon-scented tea steaming beside her and "Don't Cry for Me, Argentina" drifting in from the living-room, Susan curled her feet under her on the office chair and logged in. Then she typed in the address from the flyer and clicked her mouse.

The screen remained blank for a long time as the various bits and pieces of the document coming in over the telephone line added up, then suddenly it turned black.

Next, a multicoloured image began to appear, line by line from the top of the screen down, and soon the Albion League's emblem, a swastika made out of burning golden arrows, appeared in full. Probably, Susan thought, remembering Superintendent Gristhorpe's words and the Blake song, it was some sort of image of Blake's "arrows of desire."

Around the top of the swastika, the words THE ALBION LEAGUE curled in a semi-circle of bold Gothic script.

It took a couple of minutes for the rest of the document to transfer. When it was complete, Susan started browsing through it. "Memory" floated in from the living-room.

Unlike pages in a book, Web pages have an extra dimension provided by hypertext links, highlighted words or icons you can click on to go to another, related site. At first, Susan ignored these links and concentrated on reading the text. It was much the same as the pamphlet she had seen, only there was more of it.

The first paragraph welcomed the reader to the page and explained that the Albion League was a fast-growing group of concerned citizens dedicated to ethnic purity, freedom of speech, law and order, and the establishment of the true English "homeland."

After that came a number of links. Some were closely related sites, such as the British National Party's home page or Combat 18, and some were American or Canadian, such as Stormfront, Aryan Nation and the Heritage Front. They varied from the fairly literate to the downright unreadable, but some of the graphics were imaginatively conceived. Susan had never thought members of white-power groups to be particularly creative or intelligent. She had to remind herself that, these days, you didn't have to be an Einstein to work a computer. Almost any kid could do it.

She opted for the League's "News" icon and was soon treated to a number of recent stories from the unique perspective of the Albion League.

The first item concerned the amount of public money being channelled towards the huge new mosque under construction between Leeds and Bradford, and contrasted it with the shocking state of disrepair of most of Britain's churches.

The second contended that a leading academic had "proved" humans were actually descended from pale-skinned northern tribes rather than from "hairy Africans."

And so it went on: a Tory MP known for his stand on morality and family values had been surprised by a police raid on a homosexual brothel in Sheffield, wearing only a blonde wig and a tutu; Leeds City Council had voted to rename one of the city's streets after a black revolutionary "scum" ... example after example of government hypocrisy, just deserts and cultural decay.

One story concerned a white schoolboy who had been stabbed just outside the gates of a Bradford comprehensive school by three members of an Asian gang. It was a sad enough tale—and Susan remembered reading about it in the *Yorkshire Post* only a couple of weeks ago—but according to the Albion League, the tragic stabbing had occurred because the local council was dominated by "ethnics" and by their brainwashed, politically correct white lackeys, who had all known about the school's problems for years but had never done anything. The victim could, therefore, be seen as "a sacrifice to the multiracial society." Susan wondered what they would make of Jason Fox's death.

She paused and took a sip of cold tea to soothe her stomach. The Lloyd Webber had finished ages ago and she had been too absorbed to go into the living-room and put something else on. Though she hadn't actually learned much more about the Albion League and its members from the Web page, she had learned enough to make her question how she felt about freedom of speech. These people would claim all attempts to silence them violated their basic democratic freedom. Yet given any power at all, they would silence everyone but straight white males.

At the end of the League's page, Susan found, as with many sites, a hypertext link to the page's designers. In this case, the name was *FoxWood Designs*.

Curious, Susan clicked on the name. Again she was disappointed. She had expected names and addresses, but all she got was a stylized graphic image of a fox peering out from some dark trees, along with an e-mail address.

Still, she thought, as she made a note of the address, there was a slight chance that if one-half of the team was Mr Fox, then the other half was Mr Wood. And if she could track down Mr Wood, then she might just find *one* person who knew something about Jason Fox's life. And his death.

As soon as Susan hung up her modem, the telephone rang.

It was Gavin.

"Susan? Where've you been? I've been trying to phone you all morning. I bumped into Jim Hatchley in the station and he told you were working at home."

"That's right," Susan said. "What do you want?"

"Charming. And I was going to invite you to lunch."

"Lunch?"

"Yes. You know, that stuff you eat to keep you alive."

"I don't know ..." said Susan.

"Oh, come on. Even a hard-working DC needs a spot of lunch now and then, surely?"

Come to think of it, Susan *was* hungry. "Half an hour?"

"If that's all you can spare me."

"It is."

"Then I'll take it."

"And you're paying?"

"I'm paying."

Susan grinned to herself. "Right. See you at The Hope and Anchor in ten minutes."

III

The old greengrocer's turned out to be a former corner shop at the end of a street of back-to-backs between Holbeck Moor and Elland Road. The windows were boarded up with plywood, on which various obscenities, swastikas and racist slogans had been spray-painted. Drizzle suited the scene perfectly, streaking the soot-covered red brick and the faded sign over the door that read "Arthur Gelderd: Greengrocer."

Banks wondered what Arthur Gelderd, Greengrocer, would have thought if he knew what had become of his shop. Like Frank Hepplethwaite, Arthur Gelderd had probably fought against Hitler in the war. And forty or more years ago, before the supermarkets, this place would have been one of the local neighbourhood meeting-places, and a centre of gossip; it would also have provided Gelderd and his family with a modest living. Now it was the head-quarters of the Albion League.

Banks and Hatchley looked the building over in the slanting drizzle for a moment. Cars hissed by on Ingram Road, splashing up dirty rainwater from the gutters. The window in the shop door was protected by wire mesh, and the glass itself was covered with old adverts for Omo and Lucozade, so you couldn't see inside. In the centre was a cardboard clock-face to show the time the shop would next be open. It was set at nine o'clock, and it would probably be set at that time forever.

Sergeant Hatchley knocked with his ham-like fist; the door rattled in its frame, but no-one answered. He tried the handle, but the place was locked. In the silence after the knocking, Banks thought he heard a sound inside.

"What do we do?" Hatchley asked.

"Knock again."

Hatchley did so. Harder this time.

It did the trick. A voice from behind the door shouted, "What do you want?"

"Police," said Banks. "Open up."

They heard someone remove a chain and turn a key in a lock, then the door opened.

For some reason, the new occupants hadn't removed the bell that hung on its pliant arc of metal at the back of the door, and it jangled as Banks and Hatchley walked in. The sound reminded Banks of childhood errands to his local corner shop, the way he used to watch, hypnotized, as Mrs Bray turned the handle on the machine and the bacon swung back and forth in the slicer, making a whooshing sound every time the whirling wheel-blade carved off a slice; he remembered the smoky smell of the cured meat in the air, mingled with fresh bread and apples.

What he smelled when he walked in now soon put such nostalgia out of his mind—burned carbon from the photocopier and laser printer, recent paint, smoke and fresh-cut paper.

The place didn't even resemble a shop any more. What must have been the counter was covered with stacks of paper—more copies of the flyer, by the looks of it—and a computer hummed on a desk beside a telephone. On the walls were a framed poster of Adolf Hitler in full spate, addressing one of the Nuremberg rallies, by the look of it, and a large image of a swastika made out of burning arrows.

A short young man with lank black hair, antique National Health glasses and a spotty face shut the door behind them. "Always happy to help the local police," he said with a stupid grin. "We're on the same side, we are."

"Fuck off, sonny," said Banks. "What's your name?"

The young man blinked at the insult and stepped back a pace. "There's no need—"

"Name?" Banks repeated as he and Hatchley advanced, backing the young man up against the counter.

The kid held his hands up. "All right, all right. Don't hit me. It's Des. Des Parker."

"We're just going to have a little look around, Des, if that's all right with you," Banks said.

Des frowned. "Don't you need a search warrant? I mean, I know my rights."

Banks stopped and raised his eyebrows. He looked at Hatchley. "Hear that, Jim? Des here knows his rights."

"Aye," said Hatchley, walking towards the telephone and picking up the receiver. "Shall I do the honours, sir?"

Des looked puzzled. "What honours? What's he doing?"

"Getting a search warrant," Banks explained. "In about half an hour we'll have fifty flatfoots going over the place with a fine-tooth comb. Sergeant Hatchley and I will stay here with you until they arrive. Maybe you'd like to inform the building's owner—if it's not you—while we wait. He might want to be here to make sure *his* rights aren't violated."

Des gulped. "Mr Motcombe ... He wouldn't like that."

"So what?"

"What's going on, Des? Who the fuck is this? Is there a problem?"

The new speaker came out of the back room, zipping up his fly, accompanied by the sound of a toilet flushing. This one looked a few years older than Des Parker and at least fifty brain cells brighter. Tall and skinny, he was wearing black T-shirt, jeans and red braces, and his dyed blond hair was cut very close to his skull. He also wore a diamond stud in one ear and spoke with a strong Geordie accent. Definitely not the lad who'd been in The Jubilee with Jason Fox last Saturday.

"No problem at all," Banks said, showing his warrant card again. "We'd just like a quick shufty around, if that's all right with you. And you are?"

The newcomer smiled. "Of course. We've got nothing to hide. I'm Ray. Ray Knott."

"But, Ray!" Des Parker protested. "Mr Motcombe ... We can't just let—"

"Shut it, Des, there's a good lad," said Ray with another smile. "As I said, we've nothing to hide." He turned to Banks. "Sorry about my mate," he said, pointing to his temple. "He's none too bright, isn't Des. Few bricks short of a load."

Banks picked up a copy of the flyer. "What's this, then, Ray? The Albion League? A new football league, perhaps? Out to rival the Premier, are you?"

"Very funny," said Ray. But he wasn't laughing.

"Tell us about Jason Fox," Banks prompted.

"Jason? What about him? He's dead. Kicked to death by Pakis. You lot let them go."

Hatchley, still poking around, brushed against the huge stack of pamphlets on the counter. They fell to the floor, scattering all over the place. Ray and Des said nothing.

"Sorry," said Hatchley. "Clumsy of me."

Banks marvelled at him. Full of contradictions and surprises was Jim Hatchley. While he'd pin photos of half-naked women on his cork-board—at least he did before Susan moved in—he hated pornographers; and while he'd join in with lads laughing at racist jokes, and was certainly a casual bigot himself, he didn't like neo-Nazis, either. Of course, none of it seemed like a contradiction to him. The way he put it, he wasn't prejudiced, he hated everyone.

"We're not sure who killed him yet," said Banks. "Where were the two of you at that time?"

Ray laughed. "You can't be serious. Me? Us? Kill Jason. No way. He was one of us."

"So it won't do you any harm to tell me where you were, would it?"

"I were at home," Des said.

"By yourself?"

"No. I live with me mum."

"And I'm sure she's really proud of you, Des. Address?"

Des, stuttering, told him.

"What about you, Ray?"

Ray folded his arms and leaned against the counter, one leg crossed over the other, big grin on his face. "Drinking in my local."

"Which is?"

"The Oakwood. Up Gipton way."

"Witnesses?"

Ray grinned. "Six or seven at least. Local darts championship. I won."

"Congratulations. What about Sunday morning?"

"Sleeping it off. Why?"

"Alone?"

"Yes."

Banks made some notes, then said, "There was no contact address on your flyer. You're not a secret society, are you?"

"No. But we have to be careful. We have a position we want to get across, and we know it's not popular with a lot of people. So we don't exactly go around shouting about our existence to everyone."

"I'll bet you don't."

"Not everyone understands."

"I'm sure they don't. How does a person join, then?"

"Why? You interested?"

"Just answer the fucking question."

"All right. All right. No need to get shirty. Just my little joke. We recruit people."

"Where?"

Ray shrugged. "Wherever we can find them. It's no secret. Schools, youth clubs, football matches, rock concerts, the Internet. We vet them pretty thoroughly, too, of course, if they express any interest."

"Tell me, Ray, what are *your* duties?" Banks asked, pacing around the small room as he talked. "How high up the totem pole are *you*?"

Ray grinned. "Me? Not very high. Mostly, I hand out pamphlets. And I'll be doing some of the writing now Jason's dead."

"Propaganda? Was that his job?"

"One of them."

"The Goebbels of the group, eh?"

"Come again?"

"Never mind, Ray. Before your time. Anything else?"

"I do some training."

"What sort of training?"

"Country weekends. You know, survival skills, camping, hiking, physical fitness, that sort of thing."

"Real Duke of Edinburgh's Award stuff?"

"If you like."

"Weapons?"

Ray folded his arms. "Now, you *know* that would be illegal."

"Right. How silly of me to ask. Anyway, Ray, back to Jason Fox. How well did you know him?"

"Not very."

"You mean the two of you didn't share your ideas on immigration policy and sing the occasional verse of the Horst Wessel song together after a couple of jars?"

"No," said Ray. "And you can sneer all you like. I'm getting fed up of this. Look, why don't you go get your search warrant and call in your bully boys. Either that or get the fuck off our property."

Banks said nothing.

"I mean it," Ray went on. "I'm calling your bluff. Either bring in the bluebottles or bugger off."

Banks thought for a moment as he engaged Ray in a staring match. He decided that there was nothing more to be learned here. Besides, he was getting hungry. "All right, Ray," he said. "We've finished with you for the time being. Jim?"

"What? Oh, sorry." Sergeant Hatchley managed to knock over a half-full mug of tea on the counter. Banks turned and watched as the dark stain spread around the bottom few pamphlets and began to rise up as the paper absorbed it. Then, with Hatchley behind him, he opened the door and they headed out to the car. The drizzle had stopped now and a brisk wind had sprung up, allowing the occasional shaft of sunlight to slant through puffy grey clouds.

"We didn't *have* to leave, sir," Hatchley said as they got in the car. "We could have leaned on them a bit more."

"I know that. We can always go back if we need to, but I don't think we'll find any answers there."

"Think they had anything to do with Jason's death?"

"I don't know yet. I can't honestly see why he would."

"Me neither. What next?"

Banks lit a cigarette and slid the window down a couple of inches. "We'll have a word with Neville Motcombe this afternoon," he said, "but before that, how do you fancy lunch with Ken

Blackstone? There was something young Adolf said back there gave me an idea."

IV

When Susan got to The Hope and Anchor, just around the corner on York Road, Gavin was already looking over the menu, a full pint beside him. Susan waved, stopped at the bar for her usual St Clement's and went over to join him. She put the copy of *Classic CD* that she'd bought at the newsagent's on the bench beside her.

"What brings you to town, then?" she asked.

"I had a couple of boxes of stuff to deliver to your records officer. It's not all computers, you know."

The place was fairly quiet, and soon they had both ordered the lasagna-and-chips special. Gavin raised his glass. "Cheers."

"Cheers." Susan smiled at him. A little over six foot, and only a couple of years older than her, Gavin was a good-looking fellow with a strong chin, soulful eyes and a mop of shaggy chestnut hair. He played fullback for the police rugby team.

"So," Gavin said, "you are the sergeant when a call is received that there is a small nuclear device in the Swainsdale Centre. A validated code word has been given, it is a busy time of day, and you have twenty minutes to hand over every packet of Rice Crispies in Eastvale at a designated spot. What do you do?"

Susan laughed. "Get in my car and drive like hell out of there."

"Sorry, DC Gay, you fail."

It was a running joke between them. They had met just after doing their boards, and since then they had been coming up with progressively more absurd versions of the scenarios they had been given to solve.

"What's that?" Gavin asked, pointing at the magazine.

"Just a music magazine."

"I can see that. Bring it along in case the conversation gets boring, did you?"

"Idiot." Susan grinned. "I picked it up on the way. I thought I might have to wait for you."

Gavin picked up the magazine. "Classical music? With a free compact disc? Cecilia Bartoli. Sir Simon Rattle. I say. Alan Bennett plays are one thing, but I didn't know you were such a culture vulture."

Susan snatched the magazine back. "It's something I picked up from DCI Banks," she said. "I get to hear a lot of classical stuff travelling in the car with him and I thought ... well, some of it's really interesting. This is just an easy way of finding out more about it, that's all. You get snippets of things on the disc, and if I like them, sometimes I'll go and buy the whole thing."

"Ah, the ubiquitous DCI Banks. I should have known his hand would be in this somewhere. And where might golden boy be today?"

"He's gone to Leeds. And I told you not to call him that."

"Leeds? Again? Know what I think?" Gavin leaned forward and narrowed his eyes. "I think he's got a fancy woman down there. That's what I think."

"Don't be absurd. He's married."

Gavin laughed. "Well I've never known that to stop a bloke before. What about this violinist you told me about? Is Banks bonking her?"

"You're disgusting. Her name's Pamela Jeffreys, and she's a violist not a violinist. For your information, DCI Banks is a decent bloke. He's got an absolutely gorgeous wife. She runs the art gallery at the community centre. I'm certain he's faithful to her. He wouldn't do anything like that."

Gavin held his hand up. "All right, all right. I know when I'm beaten. If you say so. He's a saint."

"I didn't say that, either," Susan said through gritted teeth. Then she glared at him.

Their food came, and they both tucked in. Susan concentrated on her lasagna and tried to ignore the chips. Not entirely successfully.

"I'll tell you one thing, though," Gavin said, "your Banks is definitely not a saint in Chief Constable Riddle's books."

"Jimmy Riddle's a pillock."

"That's as may be. But he's also Chief Constable Pillock, and your golden boy has been pissing him off mightily of late. Just a friendly word of warning, that's all."

"Are you talking about those Asian kids we brought in?"

Gavin nodded. "Could be something to do with them, yes. That and near causing a race riot."

"A race riot? In Eastvale?" She laughed. "It was a storm in a teacup, Gavin. I was there. And we'd good reason to detain those three kids. They're still not off the hook, you know. The lab found something suspicious on George Mahmood's shoe. They're still working on it."

"Probably dog shit. I think you'll need a lot more than that to convince the CC."

"They think it might be blood. Anyway, you know as well as I do that Jimmy Riddle only ordered their release because of political pressure."

"Don't underestimate political pressure, Susan. It can be a powerful motivator. Especially in a person's career. Even so, you're probably right about his reasons." Gavin pushed his empty plate aside. "To be honest, I can't say I've ever heard the CC have a good word to say for darkies in private. But the public face is another matter. Sure they only got off because they're coloured. This time. And because Mustapha Camel, or whatever his name is, is some big wallah in the Muslim community. But there's a large section of the public—especially some of the more liberal members of the press—who say that they were only arrested in the first place because they were coloured. Take your pick. You can't win. Anyway, you might just want to warn DCI Banks that the CC is on the warpath."

Susan laughed. "What's new? I think he already knows that." She glanced at her watch.

"Maybe *that's* why he's gone to Leeds?"

"DCI Banks isn't scared of Jimmy Riddle."

"Well, maybe he should be."

Susan wasn't certain from his expression whether Gavin was being serious or not. It was often difficult to tell with him. "I've got to go," she said, standing up.

"You can't. You haven't finished your chips."

"They're fattening."

"But I've not had my full half-hour yet."

"Isn't life unfair," Susan said, smiling as she pecked him on the cheek and turned to leave.

"Saturday?" he called out after her.

"Maybe," she said.

SIX

I

DI Ken Blackstone, West Yorkshire CID, was already waiting when Banks and Hatchley arrived at the pub he'd suggested over the telephone, a seedy-looking dive near Kirkgate Market, at the back of the Millgarth police headquarters.

Most days there was an open-air market near the bus station, behind the huge Edwardian market hall, and today in the drizzle a few lost souls in macs wandered around the covered stalls, fingering samples of fabric and fruit, thumbing through tattered paperback romances and considering the virtues of buying that "genuine antique" brass door-knocker.

But no-one showed much enthusiasm, not even the vendors, who were usually keen to sing out the praises of their wares and draw customers to their stalls. Today most of them stood to the side, wearing flat caps and waxed jackets, drawing on cigarettes and shuffling from foot to foot.

The pub wasn't very busy inside, either. Blackstone had assured them the cook did a decent Yorkshire pudding and gravy, and luckily it turned out to be true. In deference to duty, Banks and Blackstone drank halves. Hatchley, unwilling to miss what was a rare opportunity these days, had a full pint of Tetley's bitter. A giant jukebox stood in one corner of the lounge bar, but it was silent at the moment, so they didn't have to shout.

"Well, Alan," said Blackstone, echoing Gavin Richards's sentiments, "you've been spending so much time down here this past year or two I'm surprised you're not thinking of moving."

Banks smiled. "I won't say it hasn't crossed my mind. Oh, not seriously. Well, maybe just a little bit seriously. With both Brian and

Tracy gone, the house just seems too big, and much as I love Eastvale ... I think Sandra misses big city life. And I wouldn't mind being a bit nearer Opera North." When he mentioned Sandra, he felt a pang. They hadn't talked since their argument the other night, and Opera North had certainly played its part in that.

Blackstone smiled. "It's not such a bad place. You could do a lot worse."

Banks looked at Hatchley, who had done a stint on the West Yorkshire force several years ago. "Jim?"

"He's right," Hatchley agreed. "And it might not be a bad career move." He winked. "It's a long way from Jimmy Riddle. We'd miss you, of course."

"Stop it, you'll make me cry," Banks said, pretending to reach for a handkerchief.

"All right," said Hatchley. "We won't miss you, then."

"Anyway," Banks asked, "how's crime?"

"Much the same as usual," said Blackstone. "We've had a spate of 'steamings' lately. Five or six young lads will go into a shop, then, when the shopkeeper's got his cash register open, they rush into action, create chaos all around while they grab what they want from customers and till alike. Kids for the most part. Fifteen and under, most of them. They've also taken to doing building societies and post offices the same way."

Banks shook his head. "Sounds American to me."

"You know how it goes, Alan. First America, then London, then the rest of the country. What else ... ? We've had a few too many muggings at cash dispensers, too. And to cap it all, it looks like we're heading for another drug war in Chapeltown."

Banks raised his eyebrows.

Blackstone sighed. "Bloke goes by the name of *Deevaughan*. Spelled like the county: Devon. Anyway, Devon came up from London about a month ago and sussed out the scene pretty quickly. Already it looks like we can put down one murder to him."

"Can't prove anything, of course?"

"Course not. He was in a pub with twenty mates when it happened. This one's bad, Alan. Crack, cocaine, the usual stuff, of course. But word also has it he's a big heroin fan. He spent the last few years in New York and Toronto, and there's rumours of death follow him around wherever he goes. Still want to move here?"

Banks laughed. "I'll think about it."

"Anyway, you didn't come to talk about my problems. How can I help you this time?"

Banks lit a cigarette. "Know anything about Neville Motcombe? Runs a white-power group called the Albion League. Lives out Pudsey way. Offices in Holbeck."

Blackstone shook his head. "I've heard of him, but I can't really say I know much, not off the cuff. Bit out of my bailiwick, to be honest."

"What is? Neo-Nazis or Pudsey?"

Blackstone laughed. "Both, I suppose." With his thinning sandy hair, still enough left to curl around his ears, wire-rimmed glasses, long, pale face and Cupid's bow lips, Blackstone reminded Banks more of an academic than a copper. Except that he was always well dressed. Today, he wore a dazzling white shirt, its brightness outdone only by his gaudy tie, and a pinstripe suit that looked tailor-made, not off the peg, with a silk handkerchief poking out of the top pocket. Banks didn't even wear a suit and tie unless he had to, and he always kept the top button of his shirt undone. Today he was wearing his favourite suede jacket again, and his tie hung askew.

"How did you come to hear about him?" Banks asked.

Blackstone laughed. "Bit of a joke around the station, actually. Seems he tried to flog a stolen stereo to one of our off-duty PCs at a car-boot sale last year. Luckily for us, it was one of our honest PCs, and he traced it to a Curry's break-in a couple of months earlier."

"What happened?"

"Nothing. Motcombe swore blind he'd bought it at the market and we couldn't prove otherwise. Got a light rap on the knuckles, and that's the lot."

"Did you know about the Albion League?"

"I've heard of it, yes. I try at least to stay abreast of possible troublemakers."

"And you think they're likely ones?"

Blackstone pursed his lips. "Mmm. I'd say they've got potential, yes. We've had a few unattributed racial incidents this past year or so. We can't tie them in to him and his group yet, but I have my suspicions."

"Anything in particular?"

"Know that big mosque they're putting up out Bradford way?"

Banks nodded.

"There's been a few small acts of sabotage. Nothing much. Stolen building materials, spray-painted racist slogans, slashed tires, scratched paintwork. That sort of thing."

"And you suspect Motcombe's lot?"

"Well, it'd be surprising if there weren't some sort of organized group behind it. What really worries me is what level of violence they're likely to rise to."

"A bomb? Something like that?"

Blackstone shrugged. "Well, if the IRA can do it ... Anyway, it's just speculation at the moment. Want me to dig around a bit more?"

Banks nodded. "I'd appreciate it, Ken. Right now anything is better than nothing. We're getting nowhere fast."

"What about those Asian lads you had in custody?"

"They're not off my list yet."

"You said earlier you had an idea," Sergeant Hatchley prompted Banks.

"Ah, yes." Banks stubbed out his cigarette and looked at Blackstone. "It's probably just a minor thing, really. We talked to two of Motcombe's cronies in Holbeck. Ray Knott and Des Parker."

Blackstone nodded. "We know Ray Knott," he said. "Used to be a dab hand at taking and driving away."

"Used to be?"

Blackstone shrugged.

"Anyway," Banks went on. "At one point, Knott let slip that the Albion League, or Motcombe himself, actually owned the property. I'm wondering if that's true or whether it was simply some sort of figure of speech. You know, the way someone might say 'Get off my property' even if it's only rented?"

"And you'd like me to check it out?"

"If you would."

"May I ask why?"

"Because I'd like to know if money's involved. If Motcombe owns property and lives in a nice house in Pudsey, maybe there's some scam involved."

Blackstone nodded. "Hmmm. Good thinking. I'll do what I can. As a matter of fact, I've got a couple of mates in the town hall, and they owe me a favour or two."

Banks raised his eyebrows. "What's this, Ken? Have you been tipping them off when their brothel's going to be raided?"

Blackstone laughed. "Not exactly."

"There's an address in Rawdon I'd like you to check, too, if it's not too much trouble. Jason Fox lived there. As far as we know, he hasn't been employed this past couple of years, so we'd like to know how he could afford it."

"Will do," said Blackstone. He looked at his watch. "Look, I should get back to the station. I can make a couple of phone calls, get working on it pretty much straight away."

"We should be moving along, too," said Banks, looking at Hatchley, who started swigging the last of his ale in expectation of an imminent departure. "We're going to pay Mr Motcombe a visit. And there's another thing, Ken."

Blackstone raised his eyebrows.

"We still haven't been able to track down the lad Jason Fox was drinking with the night he was killed. If the Albion League, or Neville Motcombe himself, does actually own the Holbeck build-ing, or the Rawdon house, do you think you could check and see if he owns any other property in the city? Who knows, it might lead us to Jason's mystery pal."

"Who may or may not know something?"

Banks smiled and nudged Hatchley. "Ever the optimist, our Ken, isn't he, Jim?"

Hatchley laughed. "West Yorkshire does that to you."

"Can do," said Blackstone, standing up. "I'll call you soon as I get anything."

"Appreciate it," said Banks. "I owe you one."

"I'll remember that if you ever transfer here."

II

After lunch, Susan's Wednesday afternoon was becoming every bit as frustrating as Tuesday. She had telephoned the service provider that gave Internet and Web access to FoxWood Designs, but she couldn't get a name and address out of them over the phone. A court order would see to that, of course, but what grounds had she to seek one? A vague hunch that it might lead her to someone who might know something about a mysterious death?

Every once in a while she left her computer terminal, stretched, and paced around the flat for a while. She put on the disc that came with her magazine, and arias followed solo piano pieces, which in turn followed symphonic movements, from Monteverdi to Maxwell Davies. It was all very confusing.

Like Banks, she wondered about George Mahmood and his mates. Had they done it? They certainly could have. And maybe not many people would blame them. The reporters had been around the station in droves, of course, and there was sure to be an article on police racism in the weekly *Eastvale Gazette*, due out on Friday.

Susan turned back to her desk. Still working on the assumption that if "Fox" was Jason Fox, then "Wood" might turn out to be a real person, too, she phoned directory assistance and discovered, as she suspected, that in Leeds alone there were pages of "Woods."

Well, she supposed, she *could* try them all. And what would she say? Ask each one if he knew Jason Fox? If this Wood person didn't want the police to know he knew Jason, he would hardly be likely to tell her over the telephone, would he?

There had to be an easier way. Tax records? Business registries? Maybe FoxWood Designs was incorporated, or had registered their design as a trademark.

Suddenly she realized there might be an even easier way than that. Subterfuge.

She hurried back to the computer, where she typed away for a few minutes, then sat back to survey her handiwork. Not bad. She made one or two small changes, correcting a typo here and an awkward phrase there. When she had finished, the message read:

TO: FoxWood Designs

FROM: Gayline Fashions

I have just started my own fashion-design business and I'm looking for ways to find a wider audience for my products. I noticed your work recently on a Web page and was very impressed by what I saw. I realized that the Web is an ideal way to achieve my aims and from what I saw I realized your company would be more than capable of handling the graphics necessary for the sort of page I have in mind. I would really like to talk to you about this as soon as possible. Do you think you could supply me with your address so that I could come around and discuss the possibility of our working together? I would much appreciate the opportunity to get myself established on the World Wide Web without delay.

Susan Gay.

Sole Proprietor: Gayline Fashions.

Susan read it over. It wasn't perfect—English had never been her strong point at school—but it would do.

She saved the message and logged in again. Then, when all the preliminaries were done with, she took a deep breath, pressed enter, and sent her message bouncing around the world's computer systems to the e-mail address she had taken from the bottom of the FoxWood Designs page.

III

Before Banks and Hatchley even had time to ring Motcombe's doorbell, they saw the figure approaching through the frosted glass.

"Mr Motcombe?" said Banks, showing his identification.

"That's me," said Motcombe. "I'm surprised it took you so long. Please. Come in."

They followed him through to the living-room.

"You've been expecting us?" Banks asked.

"Ever since Jason's tragic demise."

"But you didn't bother to call us?"

Motcombe smiled. "Why should I have? I don't know anything that can help you. But that doesn't keep *you* away from *me*, does it? Sit down. Please."

Hatchley sat in one of the deep armchairs and took out his notebook. Banks walked over to the window at the far end of the room. The house was perched on a hillside; the back window looked over towards the village of Tong, not much more than a mile away, past Park Wood. The smoking chimneys of Bradford stood to the right and Leeds sprawled to the left.

"Yes, it's impressive, isn't it?" Banks heard Motcombe say behind him. "It's one of the things that helps me remember what we're fighting for. That all isn't lost." Motcombe was standing so close that Banks could smell peppermint toothpaste on his breath.

Banks turned and walked past him, glancing around at the rest of the room. The furniture looked solid and well crafted—a table, chairs, sideboard and a glass-fronted cabinet, all dark, shiny wood. While there were no posters of Hitler or swastikas on the bright floral wallpaper, inside the cabinet was obviously Motcombe's collection of Nazi memorabilia: armband, bayonet, German officer's cap—all bearing the swastika—a series of dog-eared photographs of Hitler, and what was probably a wartime edition of *Mein Kampf*, again with the swastika on the front.

"Hitler was an inspiration, don't you think?" Motcombe said. "He made mistakes, perhaps, but he had the right ideas, the right intentions. We should have joined forces *with* him instead of sending our forces against him. Then we would have a strong, united *Europe* as a bulwark against the corruption and impurity of the rest of the world, instead of the moth-eaten rag-bag we do have."

Banks looked at him. He supposed Motcombe was imposing enough. Tall and gaunt, wearing a black polo-neck jumper tucked into matching black trousers with sharp creases, and a broad belt with a plain, square silver buckle, he had closely cropped black hair—shorter even than Banks's own—a sharp nose and lobeless ears flat against his skull. His eyes were brown, and there was a gleam in them like the winter sun in a frozen mud puddle. A constant, sly smile twitched at the corners of his thin, dry lips, as if he knew something no-one else did, and as if that knowledge made him somehow superior. He reminded Banks of a younger Norman Tebbit.

"That's all very interesting," Banks said at last, resting the backs of his thighs against the table. "But, if you don't mind, we've got some questions for you."

"Why should I mind? As far as I'm concerned, we're on the same side." Motcombe sat, crossed his legs and put his hands together in front of him, fingertips touching, as if in prayer.

"How do you work that one out?" Banks asked, thinking it odd that was the second time he'd heard that today.

"Easy. Jason Fox was killed on your patch. You did your job as best you could under the circumstances. You found his killers quickly. But you had to let them go."

He narrowed his eyes and gazed at Banks. Just for a moment Banks fancied he saw a gleam of something in them. Conspiracy? Condescension? Whatever it was, he didn't like it.

"How that must have sickened you," Motcombe went on, his voice a low, hypnotic monotone. "Having to bow to political pressure like that. Believe me, I *know* how your hands are tied. I *know* about the conspiracy that renders our police ineffective. You have my every sympathy."

Banks took a deep breath. It smelled like a non-smoking room, but at this point he didn't care. He lit up anyway. Motcombe didn't complain.

"Look," said Banks, after he blew out his first mouthful. "Let's get something straight from the start. I don't want your sympathy. Or your opinions. Let's stick to the facts. Jason Fox."

Motcombe shook his head slowly. "You know, I half-expected something like that. Deep down, most people agree with us. Just listen to the way they talk in pubs, the jokes they tell about Chinks, Pakis, Niggers and Yids. Listen to the way *you* talk when you let your politically correct guard down." He pointed towards the window. "There's a whole silent nation out there who want what we want but are afraid to act. We aren't. Most people just don't have the courage of their convictions. We do. All I want to do is make it possible for people to look into their hearts and see what's really there, to know that there are others who feel the same way, then to give them a way they can act on it, a goal to aim for."

"A white England?"

"Is that such a bad thing? If you put your prejudices aside for just a few moments and *really think* about it, is that such a terrible dream to pursue? Look at what's happened to our schools, our culture, our religious trad—"

"Didn't you hear me the first time?" Banks asked, his voice calm but hard. "Let's stick to the facts."

Motcombe favoured him with that conspiratorial, condescending smile, as if he were regarding a wayward child. "Of course," he said, inclining his head slightly. "Please, Chief Inspector, go ahead. Ask your questions. And there's an ashtray on the sideboard just behind you. I don't smoke myself, but my guests occasionally do. Second-hand smoke doesn't bother me."

Banks picked up the ashtray and held it in his left hand while he spoke. "Tell me about Jason Fox."

Motcombe shrugged. "What is there to say? Jason was a valued member of the Albion League and we will miss him dearly."

"How long had you known him?"

"Let me see, now ... about a year. Perhaps a little less."

"How did you meet?"

"At a rally in London. Jason was flirting with the British National Party. I had already left them, as they didn't adequately serve my vision. We talked. At the time, I was just about to start setting up the League, making contacts. A few months later, when we got going, Jason and I met again at a conference. I asked him, and he joined us."

"Were you close?"

Motcombe tilted his head again. "I wouldn't say close, no. Not in the personal sense, you understand. In ideas, yes." He tapped the side of his head. "After all, that's where it counts."

"So you didn't socialize with him?"

"No."

"What was Jason's speciality? I heard he was your Minister of Propaganda."

Motcombe laughed. "Very good. Yes, I suppose you could put it like that. He wrote most of the pamphlets. He also handled the computer. An essential tool in this day and age, I fear."

Banks showed him the vague drawing of the boy Jason had been drinking with the night he was killed. "Do you know him?" he asked. "Is he one of yours?"

"I don't think so," Motcombe said. "It's almost impossible to tell, but I don't recognize him."

"Where were you on Saturday night?"

Motcombe's black eyebrows shot up and he laughed again. "Me? Do you mean *I'm* a suspect, too? How exciting. I'm almost sorry to disappoint you, but as a matter of fact I was in Bradford, at a tenants' meeting. In a block of council flats where some people are becoming very concerned about who, or should I say *what* they're getting for neighbours. Crime is—"

"You can prove this, I suppose?"

"If I have to. Here." He got up and took a slip of paper from the sideboard drawer. "This is the address of the block where the meeting was held. Check up on it, if you want. Any number of people will vouch for me."

Banks pocketed the slip. "What time did the meeting end?"

"About ten o'clock. Actually, a couple of us went on to a pub and carried on our discussion until closing time."

"In Bradford?"

"Yes."

"Have you ever been to Eastvale?"

Motcombe laughed. "Yes. I've been there on a number of occasions. Purely as a tourist, you understand, and not for about a year. It's a rather pretty little town. I'm a great lover of walking the unspoiled English countryside. What's left of it."

"Have you ever heard of George Mahmood?"

"What a ridiculous name."

"Have you ever heard of him?"

"As a matter of fact, I have. He's one of the youths responsible for Jason's death."

"We don't know that."

"Oh, come on, Chief Inspector." Motcombe winked. "There's a big difference between what you can prove and what you *know*. You don't have to soft-soap me."

"Wouldn't think of it. Did Jason ever mention any racial problems in Eastvale?"

"No. You know, you're lucky to live there, Chief Inspector. As I understand it, these Mahmoods are about the only darkies in the place. I envy you."

"Then why don't you move?"

"Too much work to be done here first. One day, perhaps."

"Did Jason ever mention George?"

"Once or twice, yes."

"In what context?"

"I honestly don't remember."

"But you'd remember if he said he chucked a brick through their window?"

Motcombe smiled. "Oh, yes. But Jason wouldn't have done a thing like that."

For what it was worth, it was probably the first positive link between Jason Fox and George Mahmood that Banks had come across so far. But what *was* it worth? So Jason had noticed George in Eastvale and mentioned him to Motcombe. That didn't mean George knew Jason was a neo-Nazi.

And everything Motcombe said could have come from the newspapers or television. There had been plenty of local coverage of the detainment and release of the three Asian suspects. Ibrahim Nazur had even appeared on a local breakfast-television programme complaining about systemic racism.

"What about Asim Nazur?" he asked.

Motcombe shook his head. "Doesn't sound familiar."

"Kobir Mukhtar?"

Motcombe sighed and shook his head. "Chief Inspector, you have to understand, these do not sound like the kind of people I mix with. I told you I remember Jason mentioned a certain George Mahmood once or twice. That's all I know."

"By name?"

"Yes. By name."

The Mahmood part, Jason might have known from the shop sign. But George? How could he have known that? Perhaps from the report in the *Eastvale Gazette* after the brick-throwing incident. As Banks recollected, George had been mentioned by name then.

If Motcombe were lying, then he was playing it very cautiously, careful not to own to knowing *too* much, just enough. Obviously a story of a full-blown conspiracy among the three Asians to attack Jason Fox would be even better for propaganda purposes, but it would be much more suspicious. A jet flew across the valley, a bright flash of grey against the grey clouds. Suddenly, someone else walked into the room. "Nev, have you got—Sorry, didn't know you'd got company. Who's this?"

"This," said Motcombe, "is Detective Chief Inspector Banks and Detective Sergeant Hatchley."

"And now we've got that out of the way," said Banks, "maybe you'd care to tell us who you are?"

"This is Rupert," said Motcombe. "Rupert Francis. Come in, Rupert. Don't be shy."

Rupert came in. He was wearing a khaki apron, the kind Banks had to wear for woodwork classes at school. His hair was cut short, but that was where his resemblance to Jason's mystery friend ended. In his mid to late twenties, Banks guessed, Rupert was at least six feet tall, and thin rather than stocky. Also, there was no sign of an earring and, as far as Banks could make out, no hole to hang one from.

"I'm a carpenter, a cabinet-maker," said Motcombe. "Though it's more in the form of a hobby than a true occupation, I'm afraid. Anyway, I've converted the cellar into a workshop and Rupert helps me out every now and then. He's very good. I think the traditional values of the craftsman are very important indeed in our society, don't you?"

Rupert smiled and nodded at Banks and Hatchley. "Pleased to meet you," he said. "What's it about?"

"It's about Jason Fox," said Banks. "Didn't happen to know him, did you?"

"Vaguely. I mean, I saw him around. We weren't mates or anything."

"Saw him around here?"

"Down the office. Holbeck. On the computer."

Banks slipped the drawing from his briefcase again. "Know this lad?"

Rupert shook his head. "Never seen him before. Can I go now? I'm halfway through finishing a surface."

"Go on," said Banks, turning to Motcombe again.

"You really must try believing us, Chief Inspector," he said. "You see—"

Banks stood up. "Are you sure there's nothing else you can tell us? About Jason? About his problem with George Mahmood?"

"No," said Motcombe. "I'm sorry, but that just about covers it. I told you when you first came that I couldn't tell you anything that would help."

"Oh, I wouldn't say you haven't helped us, Mr Motcombe," said Banks. "I wouldn't say that at all. Sergeant."

Hatchley put his notebook away and got to his feet.

"Well," said Motcombe at the door, "I suppose I'll see you at the funeral?"

Banks turned. "What funeral?"

Motcombe raised his eyebrows. "Why, Jason's, of course. Tomorrow." He smiled. "Don't the police always attend the funerals of murder victims, just in case the killer turns up?"

"Who said anything about murder?"

"I just assumed."

"You make a lot of assumptions, Mr Motcombe. As far as we know, it could have been manslaughter. Why are you going?"

"To show support for a fallen colleague. Fallen in the course of our common struggle. And we hope to gain some media coverage. As you said yourself, why waste a golden opportunity to publicize our ideas? There'll be a small, representative presence at the grave side, and we'll be preparing a special, black-border pamphlet for the event." He smiled. "Don't you realize it yet, Chief Inspector? Jason is a martyr."

"Bollocks," said Banks, turning to leave. "Jason's just another dead Nazi, that's all."

Motcombe tut-tutted. "Really, Chief Inspector."

At the door, Banks did his Columbo impersonation. "Just one more question, Mr Motcombe."

Motcombe sighed and leaned on the doorpost, folding his arms. "Fire away, then, if you must."

"Where were you on Sunday morning?"

"Sunday morning? Why?"

"Where were you?"

"Here. At home."

"Alone?"

"Yes."

"Can you prove it?"

"Is there any reason I have to?"

"Just pursuing enquiries."

"I'm sorry. I'm afraid I can't prove it. I was alone. Sadly, my wife and I separated some years ago."

"Are you sure you didn't visit number seven Rudmore Terrace in Rawdon?"

"Of course I'm sure. Why should I?"

"Because that was where Jason Fox lived. We have information that two men went there on Sunday morning and cleaned the place out. I was just wondering if one of them happened to be you."

"I didn't go there," Motcombe repeated. "And even if I had done, I wouldn't have broken any law."

"These men had a key, Mr Motcombe. A key, in all likelihood, taken from Jason Fox's body."

"I know nothing about that. I have a key, too, though." He grinned at Banks. "As a matter of fact, I happen to own the house."

Well, Banks thought, that was one question answered. Motcombe *did* own property. "But you didn't go there on Sunday morning?" he said.

"No."

"Did you give or lend a key to anyone?"

"No."

"I think you did. I think you sent some of your lads over there to clean up after Jason's death. I think he had stuff there you didn't want the police to find."

"Interesting theory. Such as what?"

"Files, perhaps, membership lists, notes on upcoming projects. And the computer had been tampered with."

"Well, even if I did what you say," said Motcombe, "I'm sure you can understand how I would be well within my rights to go to a house I own to pick up property that, essentially, belongs to me, in my capacity as leader of the Albion League."

"Oh, I can understand that completely," Banks said.

Motcombe frowned. "Then what ... ? I'm sorry, I don't understand."

"Well, then," Banks said slowly. "Let me explain. The thing that bothers me is that whoever went there went before anyone knew that the victim was Jason Fox. Anyone except his killers, of course. Bye for now, Mr Motcombe. No doubt we'll be seeing you again soon."

SEVEN

I

It was a long time since Frank had worn a suit, and the tie seemed
to be choking him. Trust the weather to brighten up for a funeral,
too. It was Indian summer again, warm air tinged with that sweet,
smoky hint of autumn's decay, sun shining, hardly a breeze, and
here he was in the back of the car, sweat beading on his brow
despite the open window, sitting next to Josie, who was dressed all
in black.

The drive to Halifax from Lyndgarth, where Steven had picked
him up, was a long one. And a bloody ugly one once you got past
Skipton, too, Frank thought as they drove through Keighley. Talk
about your "dark Satanic mills."

He had wondered why they couldn't just bury the lad in
Eastvale and have done with it, but Josie explained Steven's family
connections with St Luke's Church, where his forebears were
buried going back centuries. Bugger yon streak of piss and his forebears, Frank thought, but he kept his mouth shut.

Nobody said very much on the journey. Josie sobbed softly
every now and then, putting a white handkerchief to her nose,
Steven—who for all his sins was a good driver—kept his eyes on
the road, and Maureen sat stiffly, arms folded, beside him, looking
out the window.

Frank found himself drifting down memory lane: Jason, aged
four or five, down by The Leas one spring afternoon, excited as he
caught his first stickleback in a net made out of an old lace curtain
and a thin strip of cane; the two of them stopping for ice-cream one
hot, still summer day at the small shop in the middle of nowhere,
halfway up Fremlington Hill, melting ice-cream dripping over his

knuckles; an autumn walk down a lane near Richmond, Jason running ahead kicking up sheaves of autumn leaves, which made a dry soughing sound as he ploughed through them; standing freezing in the snow in Ben Rhydding watching the skiers glide down Ilkley Moor.

Whatever Jason had become, Frank thought, he had once been an innocent child, as awestruck by the wonders of man and nature as any other kid. Hang onto that, he told himself, not the twisted, misguided person Jason had become.

They arrived at the funeral home on the outskirts of Halifax with time to spare. Frank stayed outside watching the traffic rush by because he could never stand the rarefied air of funeral homes, or the thought of all those corpses in caskets, make-up on their faces and formaldehyde in their veins. Jason, he suspected, would have needed a lot of cosmetic attention to *his* face.

Finally, the cortège was ready. The four of them piled into the sleek black limousine the home provided and followed the hearse through streets of dark millstone grit houses to the cemetery. In the distance, tall mill chimneys poked out between the hills.

After a short service, they all trooped outside for the grave-side ceremony. Frank loosened his tie so he could breathe more easily. The vicar droned on: "In the midst of life we are in death: of whom may we seek for succour, but of thee, O Lord, who for our sins are justly displeased? Thou knowest, Lord, the secrets of our hearts …" A fly that must have been conned into thinking it was still summer buzzed by his face. He brushed it away.

Steven stepped forward to cast a clod of earth down on the coffin. The vicar read on: "For as much as it hath pleased Almighty God of his great mercy to receive unto himself the soul of our dear brother here departed …" It should have been Josie dropping the earth, Frank thought. Steven never did get on with the kid. At least Josie had loved her son once, before they grew apart, and she must still feel a mother's love for him, a love which surely passeth all understanding and forgives a multitude of sins.

All of a sudden, Frank noticed Josie look beyond his shoulder and frown through her tears. He turned to see what it was. There, by the line of trees, stood about ten people, all wearing black polo-necks made of some shiny material, belts with silver buckles and black leather jackets, despite the warmth of the day. Over half had skinhead haircuts. Some wore sunglasses. The tall, gaunt one looked older than the rest, and Frank immediately guessed him to be the leader.

They didn't have to announce themselves. Frank knew who they were. As sure as he knew Jason was dead and in his grave. He had read the tract. As the vicar drew close to the end of his service, the leader raised his arm in a Nazi salute, and the others followed suit.

Frank couldn't help himself. Before he could even think about what he was doing, he hurried over and grabbed the leader. The man just laughed and brushed him off. Then, as Frank attempted to get at least one punch in, he was surrounded by them, jostling, pushing, shoving him between one another as if he were a ball, or as if they were playing "pass the parcel" at some long-ago children's party. And they were laughing as they pushed him, calling him "granddad" and "old man."

Frank flailed out, but he couldn't break away. All he saw was a whirl of grinning faces, shorn heads and his own reflection in the dark glasses. The world was spinning too fast, out of control. He was too hot. His tie felt tight again, even though he had loosened it, and the pain in his chest came on fast, like a vice gripping his heart and squeezing.

He stumbled away from the group, clutching his chest, the pain spreading like burning needles down his left arm. He thought he could see Maureen laying into one of the youths with a piece of wood. He could just hear her through the ringing and buzzing in his ears. "Leave him alone, you bullies! Leave him alone, you fascist bastards! Can't you see he's an old man? Can't you see he's poorly?"

Then something strange happened. Frank was lying on the ground now, and gently, slowly, he felt himself begin to float above the pain, or away from it, more like, deeper into himself, detached and light as air. Yes, that was it, deeper into himself. He wasn't hovering above the scene looking down on the chaos, but far inside, seeing pictures of himself in years long gone.

A number of memories flashed through his mind: flak bursting all around the bomber like bright flowers blooming in the night, as Frank seemed to hang suspended above it all in his gun turret; the day he proposed to Edna on their long walk home in the rain after the Helmthorpe spring fair; the night his only daughter, Josie, was born in Eastvale General Infirmary while Frank was stuck in Lyndgarth, without even a telephone then, cut off from the world by a vicious snowstorm.

But his final memory was one he had not thought of in decades. He was five years old. He had trapped his finger in the front door, and he sat on the freshly scoured stone step crying, watching the black blood gather under the fingernail. He could feel the warmth of the step against the backs of his thighs and the heat of his tears on his cheeks.

Then the door opened. He couldn't see much more than a silhouette because of the bright sunlight, but as he shaded his eyes and looked up, he *knew* it was the loving, compassionate, all-healing figure of his mother bending over to sweep him up into her arms and kiss away the pain.

Then everything went black.

II

"Ah, Banks. Here you are at last."

As soon as he heard the voice behind him on his way back to his office from the coffee machine, Banks experienced that sinking feeling. Still, he thought, it had to happen sometime. Might as well get it over with. Gird his loins. At least he was on his own turf.

Their enmity went back for some time; in fact, Banks thought it probably started the moment they met. Riddle was one of the youngest chief constables in the country, and he had come up the fast way, "accelerated promotion" right from the start. Banks had made DCI fairly young, true, but he had made it the hard way: sheer hard slog, a good case-clearance record and a natural talent for detective work. He didn't belong to any clubs or have any wealthy contacts; nor did he have a university degree. All he had was a diploma in business studies from a polytechnic—and that from the days before they were all turned into second-string universities.

For Riddle, it was all a matter of making the right contacts, mouthing the correct buzzwords; he was a bean-counter, at his happiest looking over budget proposals or putting a positive spin on crime figures on "Look North" or "Calendar." As far as Banks was concerned, Jimmy Riddle hadn't done a day's real policing in his life.

Hand on the doorknob, Banks turned. "Sir?"

Riddle kept advancing on him. "You know what I'm talking about, Banks. Where the hell do you think you've been these past few days? Trying to avoid me?"

"Wouldn't think of such a thing, sir." Banks opened the door and stood aside to let Riddle in first. The chief constable hesitated for a moment, surprised at the courtesy, then stalked in. As usual, he didn't sit but started prowling about, touching things, straightening the calendar, eyeing the untidy pile of papers on top of the filing cabinet, looking at everything in that prissy, disapproving way of his.

He was immaculately turned out. He must have a clean uniform for each day, Banks thought, sitting behind his rickety metal desk and reaching for a cigarette. However strict the anti-smoking laws had become lately, they still hadn't stretched as far as a chief inspector's own office, where not even the chief constable could stop him.

To his credit, Riddle didn't try. He didn't even make his usual protest. Instead, he launched straight into the assault that must have been building pressure inside him since Monday. "What on earth did you think you were doing bringing in those Asian kids and throwing them in the cells?"

"You mean George Mahmood and his mates?"

"You know damn well who I mean."

"Well, sir," said Banks, "I had good reason to suspect they were involved in the death of Jason Fox. They'd been seen to have an altercation with him and his pal earlier in the evening at The Jubilee, and when I started to question George Mahmood about what happened, he asked for a solicitor and clammed up."

Riddle ran his hand over his shiny head. "Did you have to lock all three of them up?"

"I think so, sir. I simply detained them within the strict limits of the PACE directive. None of them would talk to us. As I said, they were reasonable suspects, and I wanted them where I could see them while forensic tests on their clothing were being carried out. At the same time, Detective Sergeant Hatchley was trying to locate any witnesses to the assault."

"But didn't you realize what trouble your actions would cause? Didn't you *think*, man?"

Banks sipped some coffee and looked up. "Trouble, sir?"

Riddle sighed and leaned against the filing cabinet, elbow on the stack of papers. "You've alienated the entire Yorkshire Asian community, Banks. Had you never heard of Ibrahim Nazur? Don't you realize that harmony of race relations is prioritized in today's force?"

"Funny, that, sir," said Banks. "And I thought we were supposed to catch criminals."

Riddle levered himself away from the cabinet with his elbow and leaned forward, palms flat on the desk, facing Banks. His pate seemed to be pulsing on red alert. "Don't be bloody clever with me, man. I've got my eye on you. One false move, one more slip, the slightest error of judgement, and you're finished, understand? I'll have you back in Traffic."

"Very well, sir," said Banks. "Does that mean you want me off the case?"

Riddle moved back to the filing cabinet and smiled, flicking a piece of imaginary fluff from his lapel. "Off the case? You should be so lucky. No, Banks, I'm going to leave your chestnuts in the fire a bit longer."

"So what exactly is it that you want, sir?"

"For a start, I want you to start behaving like a DCI instead of a bloody probational DC. And I want to be informed before you make any move that's likely to ... to embarrass the force in any way. *Any* move. Is that clear?"

"The last bit is, sir, but—"

"What I mean," Riddle said, pacing and poking at things again, "is that as an experienced senior police officer, your input might be useful. But let your underlings do the legwork. Let them go gallivanting off to Leeds chasing wild geese. Don't think I don't know why you grab every opportunity to bugger off to Leeds."

Banks looked Riddle in the eye. "And why is that, sir?"

"That woman. The musician. And don't tell me you don't know who I'm talking about."

"I know exactly who you're talking about, sir. Her name's Pamela Jeffreys and she plays viola in the English Northern Philharmonia."

Riddle waved his hand impatiently. "Whatever. I'm sure you think your private life is none of my business, but it is when you use the force's time to live it."

Banks thought for a moment before answering. This was way out of order. Riddle was practically accusing him of having an affair with Pamela Jeffreys and of driving to Leeds during working hours for assignations with her. It was untrue, of course, but any denial at this point would only strengthen Riddle's conviction. Banks wasn't sure of the actual guidelines, but he felt this sort of behaviour far exceeded the chief constable's authority. It was a personal attack, despite the cavil about abusing the force's time.

But what could he do? It was his word against Riddle's. And Riddle was the CC. So he took it, filed it away, said nothing and determined to get his own back on the bastard one day.

"What *would* you like me to do, then, sir?" he asked.

"Sit in your office, smoke yourself silly and read reports, the way you're supposed to. And stay away from the media. Leave them to Superintendent Gristhorpe and myself."

Banks cringed. He hated it when people used "myself" instead of plain old "me." He stubbed out his cigarette. "I haven't been anywhere near the media, sir."

"Well, make sure you don't."

"You want me to sit and read reports? That's it?"

Riddle stopped prowling a moment and faced Banks. "For Heaven's sake, man! You're a DCI. You're not supposed to be gadding off all over the place interviewing people. Co-ordinate. There are plenty more important tasks for you to carry out right here, in your office."

"Sir?"

"What about the new budget, for a start? You know these days we've got to be accountable for every penny we spend. And it's about time the Annual Policing Plan was prepared for next year. Then there's the crime statistics. Why is it that when the rest of the country's experiencing a drop, North Yorkshire's on the rise? Hey? These are the sort of questions you should be addressing, not driving off to Leeds and treading on people's toes."

"Wait a minute, sir," said Banks. "Whose toes? Don't tell me Neville Motcombe's in the lodge as well?"

As soon as the words were out, Banks regretted them. It was all very well to want his own back on Riddle, but this wasn't the way to do it. He was surprised when Riddle simply stopped his tirade and asked, "Who the hell's Neville Motcombe when he's at home?"

Banks hesitated. Having put his foot in his mouth, how could he avoid not shoving it down as far as his lower intestine? And did he care? "He's an associate of Jason Fox's. One of the people I was talking to in Leeds yesterday."

"What does this Motcombe have to do with the lad's death, if anything?"

Banks shook his head. "I don't know that he does. It's just that his name came up in the course of our enquiries and—"

Riddle began pacing again. "Don't flannel me, Banks. I understand this Jason Fox belonged to some right-wing, racist movement? Is that true?"

"Yes, sir. The Albion League."

Riddle stopped and narrowed his eyes. "Would this Neville Motcombe have anything to do with the Albion League?"

No flies on Jimmy Riddle. "Actually," Banks said, "he's their leader."

Riddle said nothing for a moment, then he went back and resumed his pose at the filing cabinet. "Does this have anything to do with the Jason Fox case at all, or are you just tilting at windmills as usual?"

"I honestly don't know," Banks said. "It's what I'm trying to find out. It might have given George and his pals a motive to attack Jason."

"Have you any proof at all that the three Asians knew Jason Fox belonged to this Albion League?"

"No. But I did find out that Jason knew George Mahmood. It's a start."

"It's bloody nothing is what it is."

"We're still digging."

Riddle sighed. "Have you got *any* real suspects at all?"

"The Asians are still our best bet. The lab hasn't identified the stuff on George's trainers yet because there are so many contaminating factors, but they still haven't discounted its being blood."

"Hmm. What about the other lad, the one who was supposed to be with Jason Fox in the pub?"

"We're still looking for him."

"Any idea who he is yet?"

"No, sir. That was another thing I—"

"Well, bloody well find out. And quickly." Riddle strode towards the door. "And remember what I said."

"Which bit would that be, sir?"

"About tending to your duties as a DCI."

"So you want me to find out who Jason's pal was at the same time as I'm reading reports on budgets and crime statistics?"

"You know what I mean, Banks. Don't be so bloody literal. Delegate."

And he walked out, slamming the door behind him.

Banks breathed a sigh of relief. Too soon. The door opened again. Riddle put his head round, pointed his finger at Banks, wagged it and said, "And whatever you might think of me, Banks, don't you ever dare imply again that I or any of my fellow Masons fraternize with fascists. Is that clear?"

"Yes, sir," said Banks as the door closed again. *Fraternize with fascists*, indeed. He had to admit it had a nice ring to it. Must be the alliteration.

In the peace and silence following Riddle's withdrawal, Banks sipped his coffee and mulled over what he'd been told. He knew Riddle had a point about the way he did his job, and that certainly didn't make him feel any better. As a DCI, he should be more involved in the administrative and managerial aspects of policing. He *should* spend more time at his desk.

Except that wasn't what he wanted.

When he had been a DI on the Met and got promoted to DCI on transferring to Eastvale, it was on the understanding—given by both Detective Superintendent Gristhorpe *and* Chief Constable Hemmings, Jimmy Riddle's predecessor—that he was to take an active part as investigating officer in important cases. Even the Assistant Chief Constable (Crime), also since retired, had agreed to that.

Recently, when the powers that be had considered abolishing the rank of Chief Inspector, Banks was ready to revert to Inspector at the same pay, rather than try for Superintendent, where he was far more likely to be desk-bound. But it had never happened; the only rank to be abolished was that of Deputy Chief Constable.

Now Jimmy Riddle wanted to tie him to his desk anyway.

What could he do? Was it really time for another move?

But he didn't have time to think about these matters for very long. Not more than two minutes after Riddle had left, the phone rang.

III

Susan arrived ten minutes late for lunch at the Queen's Arms, where the object was to discuss leads and feelings about the Jason Fox case over a drink and a pub lunch. An informal brainstorming session.

Banks and Hatchley were already ensconced at a dimpled, copper-topped table between the fireplace and the window when Susan hurried in. They were both looking particularly glum, she noticed.

She stopped at the bar and ordered a St Clement's and a salad sandwich, then joined the others at the table. Hatchley had an almost-empty pint glass in front of him, while Banks was staring gloomily into a half. They scraped their chairs aside to make room for her.

"Sorry I'm late, sir," she said.

Banks shrugged. "No problem. We went ahead and ordered without you. If you want something ..."

"It's all right, sir. They're doing me a sandwich." Susan glanced from one to the other. "Excuse me if I'm being thick or something, but it can't be the weather that's making your faces as long as a wet Sunday afternoon. Is something wrong? I feel as if I've walked in on a wake."

"In a way, you have," said Banks. He lit a cigarette. "You know Frank Hepplethwaite, Jason's granddad?"

"Yes. At least I know who he is."

"Was. I just got a call from the Halifax police. He dropped dead at Jason's funeral."

"What of?"

"Heart attack."

"Oh no," said Susan. She had never met the old man but she knew Banks had been impressed with him, and that was enough for her. "What happened?"

"Motcombe took nine or ten of his blackshirts to the grave side and Frank took umbrage. Made a run at them. He was dead before his granddaughter could get them to back off."

"So they killed him?"

"You *could* say that." Banks glanced sideways at Hatchley, who drained his pint, shook his head slowly and went to the bar for another. Banks declined his offer of a second half. Smoke from his cigarette drifted perilously close to Susan's nose; she waved her hand in the air to waft it away.

"Sorry," said Banks.

"It doesn't matter. Look, sir, I'm having a bit of trouble under-standing all this. It sounds like manslaughter to me. Are we press-ing charges against Motcombe or not?"

Banks shook his head. "It's West Yorkshire's patch. And they're not."

"Why not?"

"Because Frank Hepplethwaite attacked Motcombe, and his lot were merely defending themselves."

"Ten of them? Against an old man with a bad heart? That's not on, sir."

"I know," said Banks. "But apparently they didn't punch or kick him. They just pushed him away. They were protecting themselves from him."

"It still sounds like manslaughter."

"West Yorkshire don't think they can get the CPS to prosecute."

The Crown Prosecution Service, as Susan knew, were well known for their conservative attitude towards pursuing criminal cases through the courts. "So Motcombe and his bully boys just walk away scot-free? That's it?"

Hatchley returned from the bar. At almost the same time, Glenys, the landlord's wife, appeared with the food: Susan's sandwich, plaice and chips for Hatchley and a thick wedge of game pie for Banks.

"Not exactly," said Banks, stubbing out his cigarette. "At least not immediately. They were taken in for questioning. Their argument was that they were simply attending the funeral of a fallen comrade when this madman started attacking them and they were forced to push him away to protect themselves. The fact that Frank was an old man didn't make a lot of difference to the charges, or lack of them. Some old men are pretty tough. And they didn't know he had a bad heart."

"Isn't there *anything* we can do?" Susan turned to Hatchley.

He shook his head, piece of breaded plaice on his fork in mid-air. "It doesn't look like it." Then he glanced at Banks, who looked up from his pie and nodded. "It gets worse," Hatchley went on. "We're in no position to charge Motcombe, it seems, but Motcombe has brought assault charges against Maureen Fox, Jason's sister. It seems she attacked him and his mates with a heavy plank she picked up from the grave side and cracked a couple of heads open, including Motcombe's."

Susan's jaw dropped. "And *they're* charging *her?*"

"Aye," said Hatchley. "I shouldn't imagine much will come of it, but it's exactly the kind of insult Motcombe and his sort like to throw at people."

"And at the justice system," Banks added.

There were times, Susan had to admit, when she hadn't much stomach for the *justice system*, even though she knew it was probably the best in the world. Justice is always imperfect and it was a lot more imperfect in many other countries. Even so, once in a while something came along to outrage even what she thought was her seasoned copper's view. All she could do was shake her head and bite on her salad sandwich.

In the background, the cash register chinked and a couple of shop-workers on their lunch-break laughed at a joke. Someone won a few tokens on the fruit machine.

"Any more good news?" Susan asked.

"Aye," said Hatchley. "The lab finally got back to us on that stuff they found on George Mahmood's trainers."

"And?"

"Animal blood. Must have stepped on a dead spuggy or summat while he was crossing the rec."

"Well," Susan said, "this is all very depressing, but I think I've got at least one piece of good news."

Banks raised his eyebrows.

Susan explained about the message she had left with the FoxWood Designs page. "That's why I was late," she said. "When I first checked, the reply hadn't come through, so I thought I'd give it just a few minutes more and try again."

"And?" said Banks.

"And we're in luck. Well, it's a start, anyway."

Susan brought the folded sheet of paper out of her briefcase and laid it on the table. Banks and Hatchley leaned forward to read the black-edged message:

Dear Valued Customer,

Many thanks for your interest in the work of FoxWood Designs. Unfortunately, we have had to suspend business for the time being due to bereavement. We hope you will be patient and bring your business to us in the near future, and we apologize for any inconvenience this may have caused you.

Yours sincerely,
Mark Wood

"*Mark Wood*. So we've got a name," said Banks.

Susan nodded. "As I said, it's not much, but it's a place to start. This *could* be the lad who was with Jason in The Jubilee. At the very least, he's Jason's business partner. He ought to know something."

"Maybe," said Banks. "But he still might prove to have nothing to do with the case at all."

"But don't you think it's a bit fishy that he hasn't come forward yet, no matter who he is?"

"Yes," said Banks. "But Liza Williams didn't come forward, either. Jason's neighbour in Rawdon. She didn't see any reason to. Nor did Motcombe."

"Well, sir," Susan went on, "I still think we should try and find him as soon as possible."

"Oh, I agree." Banks reached for his briefcase. "Don't mind me, Susan. I'm just a bit down in the dumps about what happened to Frank Hepplethwaite."

Susan nodded. "I understand."

"Anyway," Banks went on, "there's one thing we can check, for a start. I got a fax from Ken Blackstone listing Motcombe's properties and tenants. I haven't had time to have a good look at it yet." He pulled the sheets of paper out and glanced over them. "Seems Motcombe owns a fair bit of property," he said after a few moments. "Four houses in addition to his own, two of them divided into flats and bedsits, the semi where Jason Fox lived, and a shop with a flat above it in Bramley. He also owns the old grocer's shop where the Albion League operates from, as we thought." Finally, a few seconds later, he shook his head in disappointment. "There's no Mark Wood listed among the tenants. Maybe that would have been *too* easy."

"I wonder where Motcombe got his money from," Susan said.

"Members' dues?" Hatchley chipped in.

"Hardly likely," said Banks, with a grim smile. "Maybe he inherited it? I'll get in touch with Ken again, see if he can work up some more background on Mr Motcombe for us."

"You don't really think he did it, do you?" Susan asked.

"Kill Jason? Honestly? No. For a start, he doesn't seem to have a motive. And even if he did have something to do with it, he certainly didn't do it himself. I doubt he's got the bottle. Or the strength. Remember, Jason was a pretty tough customer. But let's have a closer look at him anyway. I don't like the bastard, or what he stands for, so any grief we can give him is fine with me. Even a traffic offence. Besides, I'd look a right prat if we overlooked something obvious, wouldn't I? And that's the last thing I need right now."

"The chief constable?" Susan ventured.

Banks nodded. "Himself. In the flesh. So I'd better get back to my desk and *co-ordinate*."

IV

Banks felt bone-weary when he arrived home that evening shortly after six o'clock. He was still upset about Frank Hepplethwaite's senseless death, his run-in with Jimmy Riddle was still niggling him, and the lack of progress in the Jason Fox case was sapping his confidence. Well, he'd done the best he could so far. If only the lab boys or Vic Manson could come through with something.

Sandra wasn't home. In a way, that made him feel relieved. He didn't think he could deal with another argument right now. Or the cold shoulder.

He made himself a cheese omelette. There wasn't any real cheese in the fridge, so he used a processed slice. It tasted fine. Shortly after eight, when Banks was relaxing with *Così Fan Tutte* and a small Laphroaig, Sandra got back. Anxious to avoid another scene, Banks turned the volume on the stereo very low.

But Sandra didn't seem to notice the opera playing softly in the background. At least she didn't say anything. She seemed distracted, Banks thought, as he tried to engage her in conversation about the day.

When he offered to take her out for a bite to eat—the omelette not having filled him up nearly as much as he'd hoped—she said she'd already eaten with a couple of friends after the arts committee meeting and she wasn't hungry. All Banks's conversational

gambits fell on deaf ears. Even his story of Jimmy Riddle's bollocking failed to gain an ounce of sympathy. Finally, he turned to her
and said, "What's wrong? Is this because of the other night? Are you
still pissed off at me about that?"

Sandra shook her head. The blonde tresses danced over her
shoulders. "I'm not pissed off," she said. "That kind of thing is
always happening with us. *That's* the real problem. Don't tell me
you haven't noticed how little we see of one another these days?
How we both seem to go our separate ways, have our separate
interests? How little we seem to have in common? Especially now
Tracy's gone."

Banks shrugged. "It's only been a couple of weeks," he said. "I've
been busy. So have you. Give it time."

"I know. But that's not it. We're always busy."

"What do you mean?"

"Work. Yours. Mine. Oh, that's not the real problem. We've
always been able to deal with that before. You've never expected a
dutiful little wife staying at home all day cooking and cleaning,
ironing, sewing buttons on, and I thank you for that. But even that's
not it." She took one of his cigarettes, something she did so rarely
these days that the gesture worried him. "I've been thinking a lot
since the other night, and I suppose what I'm saying is that I feel
alone. I mean in the relationship. I just don't feel I'm part of your life
any more. Or that you're part of mine."

"But that's absurd."

"Is it? Is it, really?" She looked at him, frowning, black eyebrows
crooked in the furrow of her brow. Then she shook her head
slowly. "I don't think it is, Alan. What was Saturday all about, then?
And the other night? I think if you're honest with yourself, you'll
agree. This house feels empty. Cold. It doesn't feel like a home. It
feels like the kind of place that two people living separate lives use
to sleep and eat in, occasionally passing one another on the landing
and saying hello. Maybe stopping for a quick fuck if they've got
time."

"That's not fair, and you know it. I think you're just feeling
depressed because both the kids have grown up and flown the
coop. It'll take time to get used to."

"Next thing, you'll be saying I'm feeling this way because it's that time of the month," said Sandra. "But you're wrong. It's not that, either." She thumped her fist on the arm of the chair. "You're not listening to me. You never really *listen* to me."

"I *am* listening, but I'm not sure I understand what I'm hearing. Are you sure this isn't still about last Saturday?"

"No, it's not about last bloody Saturday. Yes, all right, I admit I was angry. I thought for once you might just forsake your sacred bloody opera to do something that *I* thought was important. Something for *my* career. But you didn't. Fine. And then the other night you go and put your opera on the stereo. But you've always been selfish. Selfishness I can deal with. This is something else."

"What?"

"What I've been trying to tell you. We're both independent people. Always. That's why our marriage worked so well. I wasn't waiting and fretting at home for you to come back from work. Worrying that your dinner might get cold. Worrying that something might have happened to you. Though, Lord knows, that was something I never could put out of my mind, even though I tried not to let on to you too much. And if I was out and there was no dinner, if your shirt wasn't ironed, you never complained. You did it yourself. Not very well, maybe, but you did it."

"I still don't complain when dinner's not ready. I made a bloody processed-cheese omel—"

Sandra held her hand up. "Let me finish, Alan. Can't you see what's happened? What used to be our strength—our independence—now it's driving us apart. We've led separate lives for so long we take it for granted that's how a relationship should be. As long as you've got your work, your music, your books and the occasional evening with the lads at the Queen's Arms, then you're perfectly happy."

"And what about you? Are you happy with your gallery, your photography, your committee meetings, your social evenings?"

Sandra paused a long time, long enough for Banks to pour them both a stiff Laphroaig, before she answered. "Yes," she said finally, in a soft voice. "That's just it. Yes. Maybe I am. For a while I've been thinking they're all I do have. You just haven't been here, Alan. Not as a real factor."

Banks felt as if a hand made of ice had slid across his heart. It was such a palpable sensation that he put his hand to his chest. "Is there someone else?" he asked. On the stereo, Fiordiligi was singing quietly about being as firm as a rock.

Suddenly Sandra smiled, reached out and ran her hand over his hair. "Oh, you sweet, silly man," she said. "No, there's no-one else." Then her eyes clouded and turned distant. "There could have been ... perhaps ... but there isn't." She shrugged, as if to cast off a painful memory.

Banks swallowed. "Then what?"

She paused. "As I said, I've been thinking about it a lot lately, and I've come to the conclusion that we should go our separate ways. At least for a while." She reached forward and held his hand as she spoke, which seemed to him, like the smile, an out-of-place gesture. What the hell *was* wrong?

Banks snatched his hand back. "You can't be serious," he said. "We've been married over twenty years and all of a sudden you just decide to up and walk out."

"But I *am* serious. And it's not all of a sudden. Think about it. You'll agree. This has been building up for a long time, Alan. We hardly ever see one another anyway. Why continue living a lie? You know I'm right."

Banks shook his head. "No. I don't. I still think you're overreacting to Tracy's leaving and to Saturday night. Give it a little time. Maybe a holiday?" He sat forward and took her hand now. It felt limp and clammy. "When this case is over, let's take a holiday, just you and me. We could go to Paris for a few days. Or somewhere warm. Back to Rhodes, maybe?"

He could see tears in her eyes. "Alan, you're not listening to me. You're making this really difficult, you know. I've been trying to pluck up courage to say this for weeks now. It's not something I've just come up with on the spur of the moment. A holiday's not going to solve our problems." She sniffled and ran the back of her hand under her nose. "Oh, bugger," she said. "Look at me, now. I didn't want this to happen." She grabbed his hand and gripped it tightly again. This time he didn't snatch it away. He didn't know what to say. The icy touch was back, and now it seemed to be creeping into his bones and inner organs.

"I'm going away for a while," Sandra said. "It's the only way. The only way both of us can get a chance to think things over."

"Where are you going?"

"My parents'. Mum's arthritis is playing her up again, and she'll appreciate an extra pair of hands around the place. But that's not the reason. We need time apart, Alan. Time to decide whether there's anything left to salvage or not."

"So this is just a temporary separation you have in mind?"

"I don't know. A few weeks, anyway. I just know I need to get away. From the house. From Eastvale. From you."

"What about the community centre, your work?"

"Jane can take over for a while, till I decide what to do."

"Then you might not come back?"

"Alan, I'm telling you I don't know. I don't know what to do. Don't make it harder for me. I'm at my wits' end already. The only sensible thing is for me to get away. Then ... after a while ... we can talk about it. Decide where we want to go next."

"Why can't we talk now?"

"Because it's all too *close* here. That's why. Pressing in on me. Please believe me, I don't want to hurt you. I'm scared. But we've got to do it. It's the only chance we've got. We can't go on like this. For crying out loud, we're both still young. Too bloody young to settle for anything less than the best."

Banks sipped more Laphroaig, but it failed to warm the icy hand now busy caressing the inside of his spine. "When are you going?" he asked, his voice curiously flat.

Sandra avoided his eyes. "As soon as possible. Tomorrow."

Banks sighed. In the silence, he heard the letterbox open and close. Odd, at that time of night. It seemed like a good excuse to get out of the room for a moment, before he started crying himself or said things he would regret, so he went to see what it was. On the mat lay an envelope with his name typed on the front. He opened the door, but it was quiet outside in the street, and there was no-one in sight.

He opened the envelope. Inside he found a plane ticket from Leeds and Bradford Airport to Amsterdam Schiphol, leaving late the following morning, a reservation for a hotel on Keizersgracht, and a single sheet of paper on which were typed the words: "JASON FOX: SHHHHH."

EIGHT

I

The Dutch coast came into view: first the dull brown sandbars where the grey sea ended in a long white thread; then the dykes, marking off the reclaimed land, protecting it from the water level.

Banks turned off his Walkman in the middle of "Stop Breaking Down." He always listened to loud music when flying—which wasn't very often—because it was the only thing he could hear over the roar of the engines. And he hadn't played *Exile on Main Street* in so long he'd forgotten just how good it was. The Rolling Stones' raucous rhythm and blues, he found, also had the added advantage of blocking out depressing thoughts.

The plane banked lower over the patchwork of green and brown fields, and Banks could soon make out cars on the long straight roads, rooftops glinting in the midday sun. It was as lovely an autumn day in the Netherlands as it had been in Yorkshire.

Banks rubbed his eyes. He had spent a sleepless night in Brian's room because Sandra had insisted it would only have made things more difficult if they'd slept together. She was right, he knew, but still it rankled. It wasn't even a matter of sex. Somehow it seemed so unfair, when threatened with the loss of someone you had loved for over twenty years, that you didn't even get that one last night of warmth and companionship together to remember and cherish. It felt like all the things you had left unsaid when someone died.

No matter how long Sandra said that she had been grappling with the problem, her decision had come as a shock to Banks. Perhaps, as she had argued, that was a measure of how much he had turned his back, drifted away from the relationship, but somehow her words didn't soften the blow. Now, more than anything, he felt numb, a pathetic figure floating around in zero gravity.

When he thought of Sandra, he thought mostly of the early days in London, where they lived together for about a year before they got married. It was the mid-seventies. Banks was just finishing his business diploma, already thinking about joining the police, and Sandra was taking a secretarial course. Every Sunday, if he didn't have to work, they went on long walks around the city and its parks, Sandra practising her photography and Banks developing his copper's eye for suspicious characters. Somehow, in his memory, it was always autumn on these walks: sunny but cool, with the leaves crackling underfoot. And when they got back to the tiny Notting Hill flat, they'd play music, laugh, talk, drink wine and make love.

Then came marriage, children, financial responsibilities and a career that demanded more and more of Banks's time and energy. Most of his friends on the force were divorced before the seventies were over, and they all asked in wonder and envy how he and Sandra managed to survive. He didn't really know, but he put a lot of it down to his wife's independent spirit. Sandra was right about that. She wasn't the kind of person who simply hung around the house and waited for him to turn up, fretting and getting angrier by the minute as the dinner was ruined and the kids screamed for bedtime stories from daddy. Sandra went her own way; she had her own interests and her own circle of friends. Naturally, more responsibility for the children fell on her shoulders, because Banks was hardly ever home, but she never complained. And for a long time, it worked.

After Banks's near burn-out on the Met and a long rocky patch in the marriage, they moved to Eastvale, where Banks thought things would settle down and the two of them would enjoy a rural, peaceful and loving drift into middle age together; the kind of thing experienced by most couples married as long as they had been.

Wrong.

He looked at his watch. Sandra would be on the train to Croydon now, and whatever happened, whatever she finally decided, things would never be the same between them again. And there was nothing he could do about it. Not a damn thing.

He picked up that morning's *Yorkshire Post* from the empty seat beside him and looked at the headline again: "WORLD WAR TWO HERO DIES AT GRANDSON'S FUNERAL": Neo-Nazis responsible, says granddaughter." There was no photograph, but the basic facts were there: the Nazi salute; Frank Hepplethwaite's attack; Maureen Fox's spirited defence. All in all, it made depressing reading. And then there was the brief sidebar interview with Motcombe himself.

Motcombe deeply regretted the "pointless death" of "war hero" Frank Hepplethwaite, he began, while pointing out how ironic it was that the poor man had died attacking the only people who dared demand justice for his grandson's killers. Naturally, on further thought, neither he nor any member of his organization had any intention of pursuing charges against Maureen Fox, even though the head wound she gave him required five stitches; things had just got out of hand in the heat of the moment, and he could quite understand her attacking him and his friends with a plank. Grief makes people behave irrationally, he allowed.

Of course, Motcombe went on, everyone knew who had killed Jason Fox, and everyone also knew why the police were powerless to act. That was just the state of things these days. He was sympathetic, but unless the government finally decided to act and do something about immigration, then ...

Jason was a martyr of the struggle. Every true Englishman should honour him. If more people listened to Motcombe's ideas, then things could only change for the better. The reporter, to give her due credit, had managed to stop Motcombe turning the entire interview into propaganda. Either that or the copy editor had made extensive cuts. Even so, it made Banks want to puke. If anyone was the martyr in this, it was Frank Hepplethwaite.

Frank reminded Banks of his own father in many ways. Both had fought in the war, and neither spoke very much about it. Their racial attitudes were much the same, too. Banks's father might complain about immigrants taking over the country, changing the world he had known all his life, making it suddenly alien and unfamiliar, threatening even. And in the same way, Frank might have let slip a remark about a tight-fisted Jew. But when it came down to it, if anyone needed help, black or Jewish, Banks's dad would be first in line, with Frank Hepplethwaite probably a close second.

As unacceptable as even these racial attitudes were, Banks thought, they were a hell of a long way from those held by Neville Motcombe and his like. Banks's dad's view, like Frank's, was based on ignorance and anxiety, on fear of change, not on hatred. Perhaps in Motcombe's case the hatred sprang from an initial fear, but in most people it never went that far. Just like a lot of people have bad childhoods but they don't all become serial murderers.

The wheels bumped on the runway, and soon Banks was drifting into the arrivals hall with the crowds. He was travelling light, with only one holdall, so he didn't have to wait at the baggage claim. The place was like a small city, bustling with commerce, complete with its shops, bank, post office and tourist information desk. A colleague had told him a while ago that even pornography was on sale openly at Schiphol. He had neither the time nor the inclination to look for it.

The first thing Banks needed when he got off an aeroplane alive was a cigarette. He followed the signs to the bus stop and found he had a fifteen-minute wait. Perfect. He enjoyed a leisurely smoke, then got on the bus. Soon it was speeding along the motorway under grids of electrical wires and tall street-lamps.

The excitement of arrival pushed Banks's problems into the background for the moment, and he began to take some pleasure in his rebellion, his little act of irresponsibility. So that no-one would feel he had disappeared completely into thin air, he had rung Susan Gay and told her he was taking the weekend off to go to Amsterdam and should be back sometime Monday. Susan had sounded puzzled and surprised, but she had made no comment. What could she say, anyway? Banks was her boss. Now, as the bus sped towards the city centre, he began to savour the coming hours, whatever they might bring. It could hardly be worse than life in Eastvale right now.

He had been to Amsterdam once before, with Sandra, one summer when they were both between college and jobs. He remembered the bicycles, canals, trams and houseboats. The place was full of leftover sixties spirit back then, and they had tried it all while they could: the Paradiso, the Milky Way, the Vondelpark, the drugs—well, marijuana, at least—as well as taking in all the museums and the tourist sights.

Stationsplein looked much the same. The air was warm, tinged only faintly with the bad-drains smell from the canals. Trams clanked about in all directions. A Perspex-covered boat set off on its canal tour. Arrows of ripples hit the stone quay.

Mixed with the late-season tourists and ordinary folk were all the post-hippie youth styles: punk spikes, a green Mohican, studded leather vests, short bleached hair, earrings, nose-rings, pierced eyebrows.

Banks found the taxi rank nearby. He would have preferred to walk after being cooped up on the plane and the bus, but he hadn't got his bearings yet. He didn't even know how to get to the hotel, or how far it was.

The taxi was clean and the driver seemed to recognize the name of the hotel. Soon, he had negotiated his way out of the square and they were heading along a broad, busy street lined with trees, arcades, shops and cafés. The pavements were crowded with tourists, even in early October, and Banks noticed that some of the cafés and restaurants had tables out on the street. He opened the window a little and the smell of fresh-brewed coffee came in. God, it was like a summer's day.

The driver turned, crossed a picturesque bridge, then continued along one of the canals. Finally, after a few more turns, he pulled up in front of the hotel on Keizersgracht. Banks paid what seemed like an exorbitant amount of guilders for such a short trip, then hefted his holdall out of the boot.

He looked up at the unbroken row of buildings in front of him. The hotel was small and narrow, about six floors high, with a yellow sandstone façade and a gabled roof. It was wedged in a long terrace of uneven seventeenth- and eighteenth-century buildings that had once, Banks guessed, probably been merchants' houses. Some were built of red brick, some of stone; some had been painted black or grey; some had gables, some had flat roofs. All of them seemed to have plenty of windows.

Banks dodged a couple of cyclists and walked into the hotel lobby. The man at the desk spoke good English. Banks remembered from his previous trip that most people spoke good English in Amsterdam. They had to do. After all, how many English people bothered to learn Dutch?

Yes, the man said, his room was ready, and he was delighted to be able to offer a canal view. Breakfast would be served in the ground-floor lounge between seven o'clock and nine. He was sorry that the hotel had no bar of its own, but there were plenty of fine establishments within a short walking distance. He hoped Mr Banks would be comfortable.

When Banks pulled out his credit card, the clerk waved it away, telling him the room was fully paid for until Monday morning. Banks tried to discover who had paid for it, but the clerk became extremely coy, and his English went downhill fast. Banks gave up.

Then the clerk handed him a message: a single sheet of paper bearing a typed message that read "De Kuyper's: 16:00hr."

Banks asked what "De Kuyper's" meant and was told it was a "brown café"—a sort of Dutch local pub—about a hundred metres to his left along the canal. It was on a quiet street corner and would probably have a few tables outside. A very nice place. He couldn't miss it.

The room was a gabled attic up five flights of narrow stairs. When Banks got there, he was panting and beads of sweat had broken out on his forehead.

Though there was hardly room to swing a dead cat, and the bed was tiny, the room was clean, with black timber beams and pale blue wallpaper. It smelled pleasantly of lemon air-freshener. A blue ashtray stood on the bedside table, beside the reading light and telephone. There was also a small television set and *en suite* facilities.

The canal view more than made up for any inadequacies. Banks particularly liked the way the ceiling and the black-painted beams sloped down towards the gabled window, drawing the eye to its perspective. And sure enough, he looked down on Keizersgracht and the tall, elegant façades of the buildings opposite. If anything, the room was a little too warm and stuffy, so he opened the window, letting in hints of distant street sounds. He looked at his watch. Just after two. Plenty of time for a shower and a nap before the mystery meeting. But first, he headed for the telephone. There was always a chance that Sandra had changed her mind.

II

Susan Gay was worried about Banks. Kicking her heels back in her office with black coffee and a so-very-sinful KitKat, she thought about the brief, puzzling phone call. What the hell did he think he was doing, taking a few days off in the middle of a major investigation? Just when they were getting close to tracking down Mark Wood. All right, so it was the weekend. Or almost. But didn't he know that Jimmy Riddle would go spare if he found out? Even Superintendent Gristhorpe would be annoyed.

There had to be more to it. The way he had sounded on the phone bothered her. Abrupt. Distracted. Not like him at all.

Was it the Amsterdam thing? Is that what had him so worried? Was there some danger involved, or something illegal? Banks didn't often act outside the law, not like some coppers Susan had known, but he did sometimes—they all did—if he felt there was no other way. Was he up to something?

Well, she concluded, she didn't know, and there was probably no way of finding out until he got back and revealed all, if he did. Until then, the best thing to do was get on with her work and stop behaving like a mother hen.

She hadn't had a lot of luck so far tracking down Mark Wood. It would take her forever to check out all the listings in the telephone directory. Even then, he might not live in the Leeds area, or have a telephone. Sergeant Hatchley was in Leeds today with one of his old cronies from Millgarth, visiting the properties Motcombe owned. Maybe they would turn up something, but she doubted it.

She was just about to pick up the phone and start dialling down her list when it rang.

"Is that DC Gay?" the voice said. "Susan?"

"Yes." She didn't know who it was.

"It's Vic here, Vic Manson, from Fingerprints."

"Ah, of course. Sorry, I didn't recognize your voice for a moment. How's it going?"

"I was trying to call Alan, but apparently he's not in his office and all I could get at home was his answering machine. Do you know where he is?"

"I'm afraid he won't be in at all today."

"Not ill, I trust?"

"Can I help, Vic?"

"Yes. Yes, of course. Do you know much about fingerprints?"

"Not a lot, I'm afraid. Have you got some news?"

"Well, yes, in a way. Though it's not very good. Not as good as I'd hoped for."

"I'm listening."

"Right. Well, when I talked to Alan earlier in the week I was testing the glass from the broken bottle found near Jason Fox's body."

"I remember," Susan said. "He said something about spraying it with SuperGlue in an aquarium."

Manson laughed. "Yes. Cyanoacrylate fuming, as a matter of fact."

"I'll take your word for it."

"Yes ... well, I'm sorry, but it didn't work. We found nothing on the glass. Probably because of the rain."

"And that's it?"

"Not entirely. Do you know anything at all about ninhydrin?"

"Isn't it a chemical for getting prints from paper?"

"Sort of, yes. What ninhydrin does is it makes visible the amino acids you deposit with sweaty fingers, especially on paper."

"I see. But I thought we were concerned with *glass* here, Vic, not paper?"

"Ah, yes," said Manson. "We were. That is until it got us nowhere. But I found a couple of fragments of glass that were also covered by part of the *label* and, luckily, two of them were *under* the body, label side up, but not touching the victim's clothing, quite protected from the rain. Amino acids are water soluble, you see. Anyway, I don't want to get too technical about it, but it took a long time, and I destroyed one fragment completely, but after I brought a smudge or two out with ninhydrin treatment, I was able to get much better ridge detail under laser light."

"You got a fingerprint?"

"Now, hold on. Wait a minute," said Manson. "I told you from the start it's not a major breakthrough. What I got was a partial fingerprint. *Very* partial. Even with computer enhancement I couldn't do a hell of a lot more with it. And, remember, any number of people could have handled that bottle. The cellarman, the landlord, the bartender. Anyone."

"So you're saying it's worthless?"

"Not completely. Oh, it certainly wouldn't stand up in a court of law. Not enough points of comparison. I mean, it could almost be mine, at a pinch. Well, I exaggerate, but you see what I mean."

"Yes," said Susan, disappointed. She began to feel impatient. "Has this got us anywhere at all?"

"Well," Manson went on, "I ran it through the new computerized matching system and I got a list of possibles. I confined the search to Yorkshire and, of course, it only applies to people whose prints we have on file."

"And the print could belong to any person on the list?"

"Technically, yes. At least, as far as court evidence is concerned. I'm sorry. I can send it over, anyway, if you'd like?"

"Just a minute," said Susan, feeling her pulse quicken a little. "Do you have it in front of you? The list?"

"Yes."

"Let's try a hunch. Could you check for a name?"

"Of course."

"Try *Wood*. Mark Wood."

It was worth a try. Susan could hear her heart beating fast in the silence that followed. Finally, after what seemed like a millennium, Manson said, "Yes. Yes, there is a Mark Wood. I don't have all the details here, of course, but West Yorkshire have probably got a file on him."

"West Yorkshire?"

"Yes. That's where he lives. Castleford area. If he's still at the same address, that is."

"You've got the address?"

"Yes." He read it out to her.

"And let me guess," Susan said. "He was convicted for football hooliganism or some sort of racial incident?"

"Er ... no, actually," said Manson.

"What then?"

"Drugs."

"Drugs?" Susan repeated. "Interesting. Thanks a lot, Vic."

"No problem. And tell Alan I called, will you?"

Susan smiled. "Will do."

Although Vic Manson said the evidence wouldn't stand up in court, that didn't matter to Susan at the moment. The link between the partial print on the beer bottle and Jason Fox's Web page design partner was just too strong to be coincidence.

At first, Susan had thought the other lad must have either run away or left Jason *before* the attack. Now, though, the picture looked very different indeed. Maybe they couldn't convict Mark Wood on the basis of the fingerprint, but they could try for a confession, or some sort of physical evidence. For a start, the people in The Jubilee should be able to identify him.

But first, Susan thought, reaching for her jacket and her mobile, they would have to find him. Already she was feeling tremors of excitement, the thrill of the chase, and she was damned if she was going to be stuck by herself in Eastvale while Sergeant Hatchley had all the fun and glory.

III

With his hair still damp, Banks stepped out into the late afternoon warmth. Sandra hadn't been home when he called, hadn't changed her mind. It was what he had expected, really, though he felt a tremendous sense of disappointment when all he got was his own voice on the answering machine.

After an hour or so spent listening to some Mozart wind quintets on the Walkman, though, followed by a long hot shower, he started to feel more optimistic than he had on the plane. Sandra would come back eventually. Give her a few days at her parents' to get over the tiff, and then things would soon return to normal. Well, almost. They'd have a lot of talking to do, a lot of sorting out, but they'd manage it. They always had.

As he walked onto Keizersgracht, he still had that disconnected feeling he had experienced on arriving, as if all this—canal, bicycles, houseboats—were somehow not quite real, not connected with his life at all. Could he be living some sort of parallel existence, he wondered, another life going on at the same time as he was back in Eastvale talking over the future with Sandra?

Or was he time-travelling? After feeling as if he'd been away for a year, would he suddenly find himself back in Eastvale only seconds after he had left? Or worse, would he land back right in the middle of that terrible conversation last night, moments before the magic envelope arrived?

He tried to shake off the feeling as he admired the façades of the old buildings along the canals. Rows of bicycles were parked on the stone quay, and a couple of small houseboats were moored nearby. That must be an interesting existence, Banks thought, living on the water. Maybe he'd try it. Now he was a free agent once again, he supposed he could do whatever he wanted, live where he pleased. As long as he had a source of income, of course. There was always Europol or Interpol.

The sun had disappeared behind a gauze of cloud, giving a slightly hazy, misty effect to the light. It was still warm, though, and he slung his jacket over his shoulder as he walked.

Two pretty young girls passed him by, students by the look of them, and the one with long hennaed hair smiled. Definitely a flirtatious smile. Banks felt absurdly flattered and pleased with himself. Here he was, in his early forties, and young girls were still giving him the eye.

He supposed he must look young enough, despite the hint of grey at the temples of his closely cropped black hair, and he knew he was in good shape for his age, still lean in physique, with the suggestion of wiry, compact strength. Casually dressed in jeans, trainers and a light-blue denim shirt, he probably seemed younger than he was. And while his rather long, sharply angled face was not handsome in any regular sense of the word, it was the kind of face women noticed and liked. Perhaps because of the lively and striking dark blue eyes.

He reached a small stone bridge with black iron railings. A flower vendor stood at the corner and the musky scent of roses filled the air. It took him back to a vivid memory, the way smells do, something to do with one of his walks with Sandra many years ago, but he cut it off. He stood for a moment, leaning on the railings and looking down into the murky water, with its floating chocolate wrappers and cigarette packets scattered among the rainbows of diesel oil, then took a deep breath and turned back to the street.

There was the pub, De Kuyper's, right on the corner, as the desk clerk had said. It had an exterior of dark brown wood and smoked plate-glass windows with the name painted in large white letters. A few small, round tables stood outside, all empty at the moment. Banks glanced inside the dark wood-panelled bar, saw no-one he knew or who took any interest in him, then went out again. He patted his jacket pocket to make sure he had his cigarettes and wallet with him, then slung it over the back of a chair and sat down.

He was early for the meeting, as he had intended. While he didn't really expect any danger, not here, in the open, on a warm afternoon, he wanted to be able to cover as many angles as possible. His table was perfect for that. From where he sat, he could see all the way along the curving canal past the hotel he had walked from, and a fair distance in the other direction, too. He also had a clear view of the opposite bank. Somewhere, in the distance, he could hear an organ-grinder.

When the white-aproned waiter came by, Banks ordered a bottle of De Koninck, a dark Belgian beer he had tried and enjoyed once at Belgo, a London restaurant. With the beer in front of him, he lit a cigarette and settled back to wait, watching the people walk to and fro, laughing and talking, along the sides of the canal. He already had his suspicions about who would turn up.

As it happened, he didn't have long to wait. He had just lit his second cigarette and worked about halfway through the beer, when he noticed, out of the corner of his eye, someone coming down the narrow side street.

It was a familiar figure, and Banks congratulated himself for getting it right. None other than Detective Superintendent Richard "Dirty Dick" Burgess in the flesh. A little more flesh than on their previous meeting, by the look of it, most of it on his gut. Burgess worked for Special Branch, or something very close to it, and whenever he appeared on the scene Banks knew there would be complications.

"Banks, me old cock sparrow," said Burgess, putting on the Cockney accent Banks knew he'd lost years ago. Then he clapped Banks on the back and took a chair. "Mind if I join you?"

IV

A steady drizzle had settled in by the time Susan passed the Garforth exit, and she had to switch on her windscreen wipers to clean off all the muck the lorries churned up. Castleford wasn't far, though, and soon the enormous cooling towers of Ferrybridge power station came into sight. She found the road to Ferry Fryston without much trouble and, pulling over into the car park of a large pub to consult her map, pinpointed the street she was looking for.

Mark Wood lived in a "prefab" on one of the early postwar council estates. These were houses—mostly semis or short terrace blocks—built of concrete prefabricated in the factory then assembled on the site. In this area, they were built originally to house colliery workers, but since all the local pits had been closed during the Thatcher years, they were up for grabs, a source of cheap housing.

The houses themselves weren't up to much. They had no central heating, and the walls were damp. In the rain, Susan thought, the concrete looked like porridge.

Susan negotiated her way through the maze of "avenues," "rises," "terraces" and "drives" which curved and looped in great profusion, then she spotted Hatchley's dark-green Astra, just around the corner from Wood's house, as they had arranged over the phone.

Susan pulled up behind him, turned off her engine, then dashed over and jumped in beside him.

"Sorry if I kept you waiting, sarge," she said. "Three-car accident near the York junction."

"That's all right," said Hatchley, stubbing out a cigarette in the already overstuffed ashtray. "Just got here myself. Bugger of a place to find. Bugger of a place to live, too, if you ask me."

"How shall we play it?"

Hatchley squirmed in his seat and ran his pudgy fingers under the back of his collar, as if to loosen it. "Why don't you start the questioning?" he said. "It'll be good experience now you're going to be a sergeant. I'll jump in if I think it's necessary."

"Fine," said Susan, smiling to herself. She knew that Hatchley hated carrying out formal interviews unless he was talking either to an informant or a habitual criminal. With Wood, they just didn't know yet, so Hatchley would let her lead, then he would follow if she got somewhere interesting or fill in the gaps if she missed something.

As it turned out, Hatchley had even more reason for assigning the interview to Susan. When they knocked on the door, a young woman opened it, and Hatchley was useless at interviewing women. Susan finessed their way inside easily enough, showing her warrant card, after determining that Mark had just "nipped out" to the shop for some cigarettes and would be back in a few minutes. Good, she thought; it gave her a chance to talk to the girlfriend alone first.

Inside, the house was clean and tidy enough, but Susan's sense of smell, always sensitive, reacted at once to the mingled baby odours—warm milk, mushy food and, of course, the whole mess when it all comes out transformed at the other end—and the kitty litter. Sure enough, a black-and-white cat prowled the room and a baby slept in its cot in the corner, occasionally emitting a tiny sniffle or cry, as if disturbed by dreams. One of the walls was damp, and the wallpaper was peeling off near the ceiling.

"What's it all about?" the woman asked. "I'm Shirelle. Mark's wife."

That was Susan's first shock. Shirelle was Afro-Caribbean. And she didn't look a day older than fourteen. She was small in stature, with a flat chest and slim hips, and her pale brown face was framed by long braided black hair that cascaded over her shoulders. Looking at her sitting there in the worn old armchair, it was hard to believe she was old enough to be a mother.

"We've just a few questions to ask your Mark, love," said Susan, in as reassuring a tone as she could manage. When Shirelle didn't answer, she went on, "Maybe you can help. Do you know Jason Fox?"

She frowned. "No. I haven't met him. Mark mentioned him once or twice. They do some computer work together. But he never brings him here."

I'm not surprised, Susan thought. "Has Mark ever told you anything about him?"

"Like what?"

"What he's like, how they get on, that sort of thing."

"Well, I don't think Mark likes him all that much. They haven't been working together for long, and I think Mark's going to break with him. Apparently, this Jason has some peculiar ideas about immigrants and stuff."

You could say that again. "Doesn't that bother you?"

"I'm not an immigrant. I was born here."

"How long have they been working together?"

"A few months."

"How did they meet?"

"They were both doing a computer course in Leeds at the same time, and neither of them could get a job after. I think this Jason had a bit of money to put into starting a business. Mark was top of the class, so Jason asked if he wanted to join him. Like I say, I don't think Mark's going to stick with him. It's just a start, that's all. It's hard to get started when you don't have the experience."

"How's the business doing?" Susan asked.

Shirelle looked around her and snorted. "What do *you* think? Hardly made enough to pay for this place and you can see what a dump it is." Now she neither looked nor sounded like a fourteen-year-old.

The cat tried to climb on Susan's knee, but she pushed it away. "It's not that I don't like cats, Shirelle," she said. "But I'm allergic to them."

Shirelle nodded. "Tina, come here!" she said.

But the cat, as cats do, gave her a you-must-be-joking look and ignored her. Finally, Shirelle shot forward, scooped up Tina and deposited her in the next room, closing the door.

"Thanks," said Susan. "Have you heard of the Albion League?"

Shirelle shook her head. "What's that when it's at home?"

"Do you know where Mark was last Saturday night?"

Shirelle glanced away for just long enough that Susan knew she was going to tell a lie. Why? Had her husband told her to? Or did she want to avoid trouble with the police? With some people, it was habitual. Whatever the reason, as soon as she said, "He was here. At home," Susan asked her to think carefully about her answer.

"What time do you mean?" Shirelle asked, after a few moments' hesitation. "Because he might, you know, have nipped down the pub for a jar or two with his mates."

"Which pub would that be?"

"Hare and Hounds. At the corner. That's his local." Shirelle seemed distracted by Sergeant Hatchley, who had said nothing so far, but just sat next to Susan on the sofa watching the whole proceedings, still as a statue, occasionally nodding encouragement and making a note in his black book. She kept looking at him, then turned her large, frightened eyes away, back to Susan.

"And if we were to ask there, at this Hare and Hounds," Susan said, "then they'd remember Mark from last Saturday night, would they?"

"I ... I don't—"

At that moment the front door opened and a male voice called out, "Sheri? Sheri?"

Then Mark Wood entered the room: stocky build, muscular, short hair, loop earring and all. Early twenties. The man in the picture.

"Hello, Mark," said Susan. "We've been wanting a word with you ever since last Saturday."

When Mark saw Susan and Hatchley he stopped in his tracks and his jaw went slack. "Who ... ?" But it was obvious he knew who they were, even if he hadn't been expecting them. He put the packet of cigarettes on the table and sat in the other armchair. "What about?" he asked.

"Jason. We'd have thought you might have got in touch with us, you know, since Jason died."

"Jason what?" Shirelle burst in. She looked at Mark. "Jason's *dead*? You never told me that."

Mark shrugged.

"Well?" Susan asked.

"Well, what?"

"What do you have to say? Even if your wife didn't know, *you* knew Jason was dead, didn't you?"

"Read about it in the paper. But it's nothing to do with me, is it?"

"Isn't it? But you were there, Mark. You were in Eastvale drinking with Jason. You left The Jubilee with him shortly after closing time. What we want to know is what happened next."

"I was never there," Mark said. "I was here. At home. Now we've got little Connor, I don't get out as much as I used to. I can't just leave Sheri alone with him all the time, can I? Besides, as you can probably tell, we're a bit short of the readies, too."

"I'll bet you own a car, though, don't you?"

"Just an old banger. A van. I need it for the business."

"Designing Web pages?"

"That's not all we do. We do a bit of retail, refurbish systems, set up networks, trouble-shoot, that sort of thing."

"So you haven't been out dealing drugs for a while?"

"You know about that, do you?"

"We do our research. What do you expect?"

Mark shifted in his chair and shot a quick glance at Shirelle. "Yeah, well, it was years ago now. It's behind me. I've been clean ever since."

"Were you selling drugs at The Jubilee last Saturday night?"

"No. I told you. I wasn't even there. Besides, I served my time."

"You're right," said Susan. "Nine months, if I read the record right. It's nice to know there really is such a thing as rehabilitation. That's not what we're interested in anyway. All we care about is what happened to Jason Fox. What about the Albion League, Mark? Are you a member?"

Mark scoffed. "That bunch of wankers? That was Jason's thing. Not mine." He looked at Shirelle. "Or isn't that obvious enough to you already?"

"Did Jason ever introduce you to their leader, Neville Motcombe, or any of the other members?"

"No. He kept asking me to go to meetings, but that's all. I think he picked up that I wasn't really interested."

"But the two of you produced the Web page for them."

"Jason did that in his spare time. By himself. Thought it was a good idea to put the company's logo at the bottom. Said it could bring us more business." He shrugged. "Business is business, even if some of it does come from crackpots."

"And did it?"

"Did it what?"

"Bring in more business?"

"Nah. Not much. To be honest I think hardly anyone even looked at it. I mean, would you?"

"But you were friends with Jason, too, weren't you?"

"I wouldn't really say that."

"I understand he provided the capital to start the business?"

Mark looked at Shirelle. Susan guessed he was probably trying to work out exactly what his wife had told them already.

"Yes," he said. "I didn't have any money, but Jason put in a few hundred quid, just to get us going. Only a loan, mind you."

"So you wouldn't say you were friends?"

"No. It's not as if we actually socialized together."

"But you *were* socializing last Saturday night in Eastvale."

"I told you, I wasn't there. I was here all evening."

"Didn't you even nip out for a jar?" Susan asked. "Shirelle here said she thought you might have done."

Mark looked to his wife for guidance. "I ... I don't ...," she said. "They've been confusing me, Mark. *Was* it Saturday? I don't remember. I only said he might have gone out for a few minutes."

"*Did* you go out, Mark?" Susan repeated.

"No," said Mark. Then he turned to Shirelle. "Don't you remember, love, when we went in town shopping in the afternoon, we picked up a couple of bottles at the offie then we rented that Steven

Seagal video and we just stayed in and watched it. Don't you remember?"

"Oh, yes, that's right," said Shirelle. "Yes, I remember now. We stayed in and watched a video together."

Susan ignored Shirelle; she was lying again. And she thought it interesting that no matter how poor people seemed, how short of the "readies" they were, they always had enough money for booze, cigarettes, videos and pets. Cars, even. "So you weren't in Eastvale at all last Saturday night, then, Mark?"

Mark shook his head. "No."

"I suppose the video rental shop will have a record?"

"I suppose so. They're computerized, all the latest gear, so they ought to. I never asked. I mean, I didn't think anyone would be interested."

"But you could still be lying, couldn't you?" Susan went on. "In fact, it doesn't matter at all whether you rented a video on Saturday afternoon or not, does it? You could have gone to Eastvale on Saturday evening, met Jason in The Jubilee and booted him to death. You could have watched the video after you got home."

"I told you. I didn't do anything of the sort. I wasn't anywhere near there. Besides, why would I do a thing like that? I already told you, Jason was my business partner. Why would I kill the goose that lays the golden eggs?"

"You tell me. I understand you were going to dump him?"

Again, Mark looked at Shirelle, who stared into her lap.

"Look," he said, "I'm telling you, I didn't do anything. I wasn't anywhere near Eastvale. I've never even been there in my life."

Suddenly, Hatchley lurched to his feet, making even Susan jump. "Let's cut the bollocks, lad," he said, putting his notebook back into his inside pocket. "We know you were there. People *saw* you in the pub. And we've got a clear set of your fingerprints on the murder weapon. What have you got to say about that?"

Mark looked from side to side, as if seeking an escape route. Shirelle started to cry. "Oh, Mark," she wailed. "What can we do?"

"Shut up blubbering," he said, then turned back to Susan and Hatchley. "I want a lawyer."

"Later," said Hatchley. "First, we're going to fill a plastic bag with your shoes and clothes, then we're going to go back to Eastvale for a nice long chat in a proper police interview room. How do you feel about that?"

Mark said nothing.

Connor stirred in his cot and started to cry.

V

"Tell me one thing," Banks said. "Why the hell have you dragged me all the way to Amsterdam?"

Burgess smiled, flipped open his tin of Tom Thumb cigars and selected one. "Everything will be made clear in time. Shit, it's good to see you again, Banks," he said. "I knew I could rely on your curiosity to get you here. I can't think of a better man for a case like this." He lit the small cigar and blew out a plume of smoke.

"What case would that be?" asked Banks, who had learned, over the years, to trust Burgess about as much as he would trust a politician in an election year.

"Oh, don't be coy. The Jason Fox case, of course."

The waiter came out. Burgess asked Banks what he was drinking. Banks told him he'd have another De Koninck.

"Filthy stuff," said Burgess. Then he turned to the waiter. "Still, bring him another one, will you, mate, if that's what he wants. I'll have a lager. Whatever you've got on tap."

Banks noticed that Burgess had his greying hair pulled back and tied in a pony-tail. Bloody typical. The ageing stud look.

"Beautiful day, isn't it?" Burgess said when the waiter came back with their drinks. "Aren't you glad I got you the ticket, Banks?"

"I'm overwhelmed with delight and gratitude," said Banks, "but I wouldn't mind knowing what it's all about. Just a hint, maybe, to start with."

"That's my Banks." Burgess jerked forward—all his motions seemed jerky—and clapped him on the shoulder. "Always anxious to get down to business. You know, you could have made super by now. Who knows, even chief super. If only you weren't such a

Bolshie bastard. You never did learn to be nice to the right people, did you?"

Banks smiled. "And *you* did?"

Burgess winked. "I must've done something right, mustn't I? Anyway, enough about me. Sometime earlier this week you—or someone in your division—set off an alarm bell I'd placed on a certain file."

"The Albion League?"

"Who's a clever boy, then? Yes, the Albion League. I got a bloke called Crawley—good chap—to answer and instructed him to give away as little as possible. See, I wanted to know why *you* were so interested in the League. It's not as if they've got a big operation in North Yorkshire, after all. Then I found out about the Jason Fox killing, and things sort of fell into place."

"You knew Jason was a member?"

"Of course I bloody did. He was Neville Motcombe's right-hand man. Hotly tipped for future Führerdom himself. Now Jason getting himself killed like that was a very bad thing, because it set off all kinds of warning bells all over the place. Which is why I'm here. You, too."

A couple of young blonde girls walked by. One of them was wearing a tight T-shirt and high-cut turquoise shorts. She was pushing her bicycle as she chatted with her friend. "Jesus Christ, would you look at that ass," said Burgess, lapsing into his habitual American slang. "Gives me such a hard-on I don't have enough skin left to close my eyes." He gave a mock shudder. "Anyway, where was I?"

"Warning bells."

"Yes. I don't know how much you know about him, Banks, but Motcombe is a nasty piece of work. Just because he's a fucking fruitcake, it doesn't mean you should underestimate him."

"I'd have thought that *you* would have had every sympathy with him," Banks said. "In fact, I'm surprised you're not a member of the Albion League yourself."

Burgess laughed. "Oh, what a cheap shot. You know what, Banks, you're so very predictable. That's one of the reasons I like you. I've been waiting for a remark like that ever since I sat down."

He settled back in his chair and puffed on his Tom Thumb. "Do I think we're letting too many foreigners in? Yes. Do I think we've got a problem with our immigration policy? Damn right I do. But do I think a gang of goose-stepping football hooligans are the answer? No, I don't. Look at this lot." He waved his arm around, as if to indicate the Dutch in general. "Look at the problems they've had with their darkies. And they only have Dutch Guyana to worry about."

"Surinam," said Banks.

"Whatever."

"And I think you'll find they also colonized a lot more of the world than just that."

"Listen, Banks, stop being a bloody smart arse. That's not the point, and you know it. You can't convince me that England wouldn't be a damn sight more civilized and law-abiding if we hadn't let so many of the buggers in to start with."

"Civilized and law-abiding as in football hooligans?"

"Oh, it's no fucking use arguing with you, is it? Got an answer for everything, haven't you? Let me put it in a nutshell. While I think this Albion League might have some pretty good ideas, I don't like getting dressed up like an idiot and hanging around with skinheads and leather-fetishists without two brain cells to rub together between them. Credit me with a bit more sense than that, Banks. Whatever I am," Burgess concluded, thrusting his thumb towards his chest, "I am not a fucking loony."

Burgess was actually wearing his trademark scuffed-up black leather jacket, but Banks let that one go by.

"Anyway," Burgess went on after a long swig of generic lager, "back to Neville Motcombe. We know he's got connections with other right-wing groups in Europe and America. Over the past four years, he's travelled extensively in Germany, France, Spain, Italy and Holland. He's also been to Greece and Turkey."

"I wouldn't have thought a neo-Nazi would find much to interest him in Turkey," Banks said.

"You'd be surprised. There are plenty of right-wing Turkish groups with access to arms. Get them cheap off the Russians in Azerbaijan or Armenia. Very strategically located for lots of nasty things, is Turkey. And don't forget, Johnny Turk's a slimy bastard. Anyway, Motcombe has also visited a number of Militia training-camps in the south-western United States, and he's been spotted entering the Nazi party headquarters in Lincoln, Nebraska. That, for your information, is where most of the instructions on bombs and explosives come from. So this guy has talked to the sort of people who blew up that government building in Oklahoma City." Burgess pointed his cigar at Banks. "Whatever you do, Banks, don't underestimate Neville Motcombe. Besides, when you get right down to it, this isn't really about politics at all. There's something else."

"What?"

"Money. One of the Turkish right-wingers Motcombe has been communicating with frequently of late, via the Internet, is a suspected international drug dealer. Heroin, mostly. And we happen to know he's looking for new outlets in England. They met when Motcombe was in Turkey during the summer, and electronic traffic between them has increased dramatically over the past three weeks. The wires are hot, you might say."

"What do these messages say?"

"Ah, well, there's the problem. Our computer whizzes have been keeping an eye on these cyber-Nazis, as they're called. We know some of their passwords, so we can read a fair bit of the traffic. Until they get onto us and change the passwords, that is. Problem is, some of the really hot stuff is encrypted. They use PGP and even more advanced encryption programmes. I kid you not, Banks, these things make Enigma look like a fucking doddle."

"So you can't decipher the messages?"

"Well, maybe they're just chatting away about Holocaust denial or some such rubbish—we can't exactly decipher their messages—but knowing the Turk, I doubt it. I'd say he's found the pipeline he was looking for."

Banks shook his head. "And Jason Fox?" he said. "Do you think this could have something to do with his death?"

Burgess shrugged. "Well, it's a bit of a coincidence, isn't it? And I know you don't like coincidences. I thought you should be filled in, that's all."

"What a load of bollocks," said Banks. "And don't give me all this cloak-and-dagger shit. Encrypted e-mail. Vague suspicions. Is this what you dragged me all this way for?"

Burgess looked offended. "No," he said. "Well, not entirely. As it happens, I don't know much about it yet, myself."

"So why *am* I here?"

"Because a very important person is here, *has* to be here for at least a week. Because it's essential you talk to this person before you go any further in your investigation. And because it wouldn't do for you to be seen together back home. Believe me, he'll be able to tell you a lot more than I can. Good enough?"

"What about the telephone?"

"Oh, give me a break, Banks. If they can eavesdrop on Charlie and Di, they can bloody well eavesdrop on you. Telephones aren't secure. Quit belly-aching and enjoy yourself. It won't be all work. I mean, what are you complaining about? You've got yourself a free weekend in one of the most exciting cities in the world. Okay?"

Banks thought for a moment, watching the bicycles and cars passing by along the canal. He lit a cigarette. "So what happens next?" he said.

"Tomorrow afternoon, *I* get up to date on what's going on, then I'm off on my holidays, believe it or not. I think I'll just go out to Schiphol and take the first flight somewhere tropical. In the evening, *you* have a very important meeting." Burgess told him to be at a bar near Sarphatipark at eight o'clock, but not whom he would find when he got there. "And make sure you're not followed," he added.

Banks shook his head at the melodrama. Burgess just loved this cloak-and-dagger crap.

Then Burgess clapped his hands, showering ash on the table. "But until then, we're free agents. Two happy bachelors—and notice I didn't say 'gay'—with the whole night ahead of us." He lowered his voice. "Now, what I suggest is that we find a nice little Indonesian restaurant, shovel down a plate or two of *rijsttafel* and swill that down with a few pints of lager. Then we'll see if we can find one of those little coffee shops where you can smoke hash." He rested his arm over Banks's shoulder. "And after that, I suggest we take a stroll to the red-light district and get us some nice, tight Dutch pussy. It's all perfectly legal and above board here, you know, and the girls have regular check-ups. Tried and tested, stamped prime grade A." He turned to Banks and squinted. "Now, I know you've got that lovely wife of yours waiting at home—Sandra, isn't it?—but there really is nothing quite like a little strange pussy once in a while. Take my word. And what she doesn't know won't hurt her. My lips will be eternally sealed, I can promise you that. How about it?"

As usual, Banks thought, the bastard showed his unerring instinct for finding the spot that hurt, like a dentist prodding at an exposed nerve. There was no way Burgess could know what had happened between Banks and Sandra the previous evening. Nobody knew but the two of them. Yet here he was, right on the mark. Well, to hell with him.

"Fine," said Banks. "You're on." Then he raised his glass and finished his beer. "But first, I think I'll have another one of these."

NINE

I

"I'm sorry we had to take you away from your wife and child, Mark," said Gristhorpe. "Let's hope it won't be for long."

Wood said nothing; he just looked sullen and defiant.

"Anyway," Gristhorpe went on. "I'd like to thank you for sparing us the time." He balanced a pair of reading glasses on his hooked nose and flipped through some sheets of paper in front of him, glancing up over the top of his glasses from time to time. "There's just a few points we'd like to get cleared up, and we think you can help us."

"I've already told you," Wood said. "I don't know anything."

Susan sat next to Gristhorpe in the interview room: faded institutional green walls, high, barred window, metal table and chairs bolted to the floor, pervading odour of smoke, sweat and urine. Susan was convinced they sprayed it in fresh every day. Two tape recorders were running, making a soft hissing sound in the background. It was dark outside by the time they actually got around to the interview. Gristhorpe had already given the caution. Wood had also phoned a solicitor in Leeds, Giles Varney, and got his answering machine. You'd be lucky to find a lawyer at home on a Friday evening, in Susan's experience. Still, he had left a message and steadfastly refused the duty solicitor. Hardly surprising, Susan thought, given that Giles Varney was one of the best-known solicitors in the county. She would have thought he was way out of Mark's league.

"Yes," said Gristhorpe, taking off his glasses and fingering the papers in front of him. "I know that. Thing is, though, that sometimes when people come into contact with the police, they lie." He shrugged and held his hands out, palms up. "Now, I can understand that, Mark. Maybe they do it to protect themselves, or maybe just because they're afraid. But they lie. And it makes our job just that little bit more difficult."

"I'm sorry, I can't help you," said Wood.

Good sign, Susan noted. Gristhorpe had the lad apologizing already.

"Now," Gristhorpe went on, "the last time you got into trouble, you told the police that you had no idea the van you were driving was used for carrying drugs, or that some of the people you were involved with were dealing drugs. Is that true?"

"Do you mean is that what I said?"

"Yes."

Mark nodded. "Yes."

"And is the *statement* true?"

Mark grinned. "Well, of course it is. It's what I told the court, isn't it? A matter of public record. It's hardly my fault if the magistrate didn't believe me."

"Course not, Mark. Innocent people get convicted all the time. It's one of the problems with the system. Nothing's perfect. But with so many lies going around, you can understand why we might be just a bit wary, a little bit over-cautious, and perhaps not quite as trusting as you'd like, can't you?"

"I suppose so. Yes."

Gristhorpe nodded. "Good."

The superintendent's interview technique, Susan noticed, was in direct contrast to that of Banks, with whose style she was more familiar. Banks would sometimes needle his interviewees, and when he'd got them confused and vulnerable, he would subtly suggest possible scenarios of how they had committed the crime, and why. He sometimes even went so far as to explain to them their feelings and state of mind while they were doing it. Then, if they were new to the world of crime, he would describe in graphic detail what kind of life they could expect in jail and after. Banks worked on his subjects' *imaginations*; he used words to paint images unbearable to the hearer.

Gristhorpe seemed to concentrate more on logic and reasoned argument; he was polite, soft-spoken and unrelenting. He seemed slower than Banks, too. As if he had all the time in the world. But Susan was keen to get it over with. She had already pulled a couple of favours to get the lab working overtime on Mark Wood's shoes and clothing, and if they came up with some solid forensic evidence, or if Gristhorpe got a confession, there was a good chance they could wrap things up before tonight. Jimmy Riddle would be pleased about that.

As a bonus, she would have the weekend free, for once, and she might get her Saturday night out with Gavin. She had considered phoning him earlier—even picked up the phone—but no, she told herself, it wouldn't do to seem *too* keen, *too* easily available. Let him cajole her. Seduce her. *Win* her.

"You see," Gristhorpe went on, "that's one of our main problems, sorting out the lies from the truth. That's why we have science to help us. Do you know what 'forensic' means?"

Wood frowned and tugged on his earring. "It means science, doesn't it? Like blood types, footprints, DNA and fingerprints?"

"That's a common error," Gristhorpe said, toying with his glasses on the table. "Actually, it means 'for use in a court of law.' It's from the Latin, related to the word *forum*. So one of the best systems we have to help us tell the lies from the truth is a complex and broad-ranging branch of science dedicated solely to presenting scientific evidence *in court*. Now, of course, before we get to court, we use this forensic evidence to help us identify the people who should be on trial. And in your case, I'm afraid the evidence tells us that you should be in court for the murder of Jason Fox. What do you have to say about that, Mark?"

"Nothing. What can I say? I've done nothing."

Wood was taken aback by Gristhorpe's gentle and erudite logic, Susan could tell. But he was cool. She noticed that Gristhorpe let the silence stretch until Wood started squirming in his chair.

"Well, you must have something to say, lad," Gristhorpe went on, putting on his glasses again and slipping a photograph from the file in front of him. "This is an image of a fingerprint found on the label of a beer bottle," he said, turning it around so Wood could see it clearly. "It was developed by a very painstaking process. Forensic science doesn't produce miracles, Mark, but sometimes it seems to come close. Now, I'm sure you're an intelligent enough lad to know that fingerprints are unique. So far, no two fingers have been found to possess the same ridge characteristics. Isn't that amazing?"

Wood said nothing; his eyes were glued to the photo.

"Anyway," Gristhorpe went on, "what's particularly interesting about *that* fingerprint is that it came from a fragment of a broken bottle found at the scene of Jason Fox's murder. But perhaps I'm being precipitous in referring to it as a *murder* so soon, because that hasn't been proven yet. You do know that there's a big difference between homicide and manslaughter, don't you, Mark?"

Wood nodded. "Yes."

"Good. And there's also a big difference in jail sentences. But we won't let that detain us for the moment. Anyway, the point is that that is a close match for *your* fingerprint—one we already have on file—and that it was found in the ginnel by the rec, on a fragment of a broken beer bottle under Jason Fox's body. I'd like you to tell me how it got there."

Wood licked his lips and glanced at Susan. She said nothing. He looked back into Gristhorpe's guileless blue eyes.

"Well, er ... I suppose I must have touched it, mustn't I, if it's got my prints on it?" He smiled.

Gristhorpe nodded. "Aye. I suppose so. When might that have happened, Mark?"

"I gave it to Jason," Wood said finally.

"When?"

"When we came out of the pub. You see, I thought I wanted another beer, so I bought a bottle from out-sales as we were leaving, but then I remembered I had to drive back down the A1, so I just gave it to Jason. He said he was walking home."

"Ah," said Gristhorpe. "So you *gave* the bottle of beer to Jason when you parted outside The Jubilee?"

"That's right. I was parked just down the street the pub was on. Market Street. Is that right?"

"That's the one." Gristhorpe looked at Susan, who raised her eyebrows.

"What's wrong?" Wood asked.

Susan scratched the cleft of her chin. "Nothing, really, Mark," she said. "It's just that you've confused me a bit. When I talked to you earlier you denied being in Eastvale at all last Saturday night. Don't you remember?" She pretended to read from the paper in front of her. "You bought a couple of bottles of beer at the off-licence and rented a Steven Seagal video, which you and your wife watched that evening. You didn't even nip out to the Hare and Hounds for a quick one. That's what you said, Mark."

"Yeah, well ... it's like he said earlier, isn't it?" He looked at Gristhorpe.

"What would that be, Mark?" Gristhorpe asked.

"About people ly— About people not telling the exact truth sometimes when the police come after them."

"So you didn't tell the truth?"

"Not exactly."

"Why not?"

"I was scared, wasn't I?"

"What of?"

"That you'd fit me up for it because I've been in trouble before."

"Ah, yes," said Gristhorpe, shaking his head. "The classic fit-up. That's another one of the problems we constantly have to fight against: the public's perception of the police, mostly formed by the media. Especially television. Well, I won't deny it, Mark, there *are* police officers who wouldn't stop at forging a notebook entry or altering a statement in order to convict someone. We're all embarrassed about the Birmingham Six, you know. That's why there are so many laws now to help people in your position. We can't beat you up. We can't force a confession out of you. We have to treat you well while you're in custody—feed you, allow you exercise, give you access to a solicitor. That sort of thing. It's all covered in the PACE guidelines." Gristhorpe spread his hands. "You see, Mark, we're just humble public servants, really, gentle custodians here to see that your rights aren't abused in any way. By the way, you must be a bit hungry by now, aren't you? I know I am. How about I send out for some coffee and sandwiches?"

"Fine with me. Long as they're not salmon. I'm allergic to salmon."

"No problem. Susan, would you ask one of the uniformed officers to nip over to the Queen's Arms and ask Cyril to do us two or
three ham-and-cheese sandwiches? And have one of the lads up
front bring us a pot of fresh coffee, please."

"Of course, sir."

Susan popped her head out of the door and made the request,
then she went back to her chair.

"While we're waiting, though," said Gristhorpe, "and if you
don't mind, Mark, let's get back to what happened last Saturday
night, shall we? As I understand it, you've changed your original
story—which, quite understandably, you now admit was a lie."

"Because I was scared you'd fit me up."

"Right. Because you were scared we'd fit you up. Well, I hope
I've put your mind at rest about that."

Wood leaned back in his chair and smiled. "You're a lot nicer
than those bastards from West Yorkshire who nabbed me on that
drugs charge."

Bloody hell, thought Susan, the old man's even getting compliments out of his suspects now, let alone mere apologies.

"Well," said Gristhorpe, inclining his head modestly. "West
Yorkshire have a lot more problems than we do, being more urban
and all. They sometimes have to cut corners a bit roughly."

"You're telling me."

"But that's all behind you now, Mark, isn't it? I see you've been a
good lad since then. You took a course and then you went into
business. Admirable. But now there's just this little spot of bother,
and the sooner we get it cleared up, the sooner you can get back to
leading a normal and productive life with your family. Did Jason
ever try to interest you in the Albion League?"

"Sometimes. He'd spout a load of garbage about how the
Holocaust didn't really happen—how most of the Jews died of
typhoid and the showers were just ways of disinfecting them, like,
not really death camps at all. I must admit, it made me a bit sick.
Then I lost interest and didn't pay much attention after that. Half
the time I thought he couldn't even be serious."

"I understand your wife is Afro-Caribbean?"

"Her family's from Jamaica, yes."

"How did you manage to reconcile this with doing business with a racist like Jason?"

"I never thought much about it, really, not at first. Like I said, I thought Jason spouted a load of silly rubbish. I figured he'd probably grow out of it."

"You said 'at first.' What about after that?"

"Yeah, well, it started getting to me, Sheri being Jamaican and all. We had a couple of arguments. I was on the verge of ditching him when ..."

"When what, Mark?"

"Well, you know, he died."

"Ah, yes. Did you tell him you were married to a Jamaican woman?"

"Are you joking? And listen to him prattle on about that? He really had a bee in his bonnet about mixed marriages. No, I kept my private life and my business activities completely separate."

Gristhorpe adjusted his glasses again and took a moment or two to look over some sheets of paper. Then he looked back at Wood, held his glasses in his hand and frowned. "But you knew that Jason was doing this computer work for the League?"

The food came, and they took a moment's break to pass around sandwiches and pour coffee.

"Yes, I knew," Wood answered. "But what he did in his own time was up to him."

"Even if you didn't agree? It bore the trademark of the business you ran together, didn't it?"

"We could use all the business we could get."

"Right. So you let your name be used for neo-Nazi propaganda even though you found the idea loathsome. Your wife is black, for crying out loud, Mark. What do you think Jason Fox and his ilk would do with her if they got half a chance? What does that make you, Mark? Are you ashamed of her?"

"Now hold on a minute—"

Gristhorpe leaned forward. He didn't raise his voice at all, but he fixed Mark with his eyes. "No, Mark, *you* hold on a minute. You were drinking with Jason Fox on the night he got killed. Now, you've already lied to us once or twice, but we'll let that go by for the moment. Your latest story is that you *were* with Jason, but the two of you parted outside The Jubilee, at which time you gave him the bottle of beer you'd bought from out-sales because you remembered you had to drive home. Is that right?"

"Yes."

"And the two of you weren't close friends?"

"No. I've told you. We worked together. That's all."

"So what were you doing pubbing with him in The Jubilee? Eastvale's a long way from your normal stamping ground, isn't it? Can you explain that?"

"He said he was going up to Eastvale to play football. I felt like a night out, that's all. Somewhere different. Just for a change. Sheri knew I'd been a bit down lately, like, about the business and all, and she said she didn't mind staying home with Connor. The Jubilee gets really good bands on a Saturday night, and I like live music."

"So you drove all the way up from Castleford to spend a social evening with a business associate you didn't particularly like, someone who believed your wife and all her kind should be packed off in boats back to the Caribbean?"

Mark shrugged. "I went to see the band. Jason said he'd come along, as he'd be in town anyway, that's all. I thought it might make a change from Razor's Edge and Celtic Warrior and all that other crap he listens to. Hear some decent music for once. The Jubilee's got a good reputation all over the north. Just ask anyone. And it's not that far. Straight up the A1. Doesn't take more than an hour and a half or so each way."

"That's three hours' driving, Mark."

"So? I like driving."

"Where did you go after you left Jason?"

"I drove straight back home. I wasn't over the limit, if that's what you're thinking."

"But you still came all this way knowing you'd be drinking and having to drive back?"

Wood shrugged. "I'm not a big boozer. I can handle three or four pints over the course of an evening."

"Are you sure you didn't have more than that, Mark?"

"I had three pints. Four at the most. If that put me over the limit, charge me."

"Are you sure you didn't have too much to drink and ask Jason if you could stay at his house? Are you sure you didn't walk down—"

"No. I told you. I drove straight home."

"All right, Mark. If you say so. I do, however, have one more question for you before I leave you to think over our little discussion."

"What's that?"

"If you gave Jason the beer bottle, and he drank from it on his way home, then why didn't we find *his* fingerprints on it, too?"

II

The girl was incredibly beautiful, Banks thought. Part Oriental, she had long, sleek black hair, a golden complexion, a heart-shaped face with perfect, full lips and slightly hooded eyes. She couldn't have been more than nineteen or twenty years old.

At the moment, she was sitting on a chair bathed in the red neon glow, wearing dangling silver earrings and a black lace bra and panties. Nothing else. Her slender legs were parted slightly at the inner thighs so the plump mound of her pudendum was clear to see. She had a tiny tattoo—a butterfly, it looked like—on the inside of her left thigh.

And she was smiling at Banks.

"No," said Burgess. "Not that one. She's got no tits."

Banks smiled to himself and came back to earth. Lovely as the girl was, he could no more think of sleeping with her than he could with one of Tracy's friends. Though he was quite happy to wander around the red-light district window-shopping with Burgess, he had never intended to buy anything on offer there. Nor, he suspected, did Burgess, when it came right down to it. And after three or four *pils* with *jenever* chasers, it was doubtful whether either of them was even capable of much in that direction anyway.

Amsterdam was especially beautiful at night, Banks thought, with the necklaces of lights strung over the bridges mirrored in the canals, and the glowing, candle-lit interiors of glass-covered "Lovers" tour boats spilling Mantovani violins as their wake made the reflections shimmer in the dark, oily water. He wished Sandra were with him, and not Burgess. They would wander the canals all night and get hopelessly lost again, just as they had done all those years ago.

At night the red-light district also had much more of an edge than during the day, when it was basically just another stop on a sightseeing tour. Most tourists stayed away at night, but as far as Banks could tell it wasn't any more dangerous than Soho. His wallet was safely zipped up in the inside pocket of his suede jacket, and he had nothing else of value. And if it came to violence, he could handle himself. Though he felt a bit light-headed, he wasn't drunk.

They wandered along, jostled by the crowds, stopping to look into the occasional window and surprised, more often than not, by the beauty and youth of the prostitutes on display. At one point someone bumped into Burgess and Banks had to step in and prevent a fight. Wouldn't go down well, that, he thought: SENIOR SCOTLAND YARD DETECTIVE ARRESTED FOR ASSAULT IN AMSTERDAM'S RED-LIGHT DISTRICT. Maybe, he thought with a smile, he should have let it go on.

After a while the crowds began to feel claustrophobic, and Banks was thinking of going back to his hotel when Burgess said, "Fuck it. You know what, Banks?"

"What?"

"Hate to admit it, but I probably couldn't even get it up if I tried. Let's have another drink. A nightcap."

That seemed like a good idea to Banks, who fancied a sit-down and a smoke. So they nipped into a bar on a street corner, and Burgess promptly ordered *pils* and *jenever* again for both of them.

They chatted about mutual friends on the force over the loud music—some sort of modern Europop, Banks thought—and watched the punters come and go: sailors, punks, prostitutes, the occasional dealer shifting some stuff. When they'd finished their drinks, Burgess suggested another round but Banks said they should find somewhere nearer the hotel while he could still remember his way.

"Fuck the hotel. We can take a taxi anywhere we want," Burgess protested.

"I don't know where the nearest taxi rank is. Besides, it's not far. The walk'll do you good."

Burgess was truly over the top by now. He insisted on just one more *jenever*, which he downed in one, and then, after a bit more grumbling, he agreed to walk and stumbled out after Banks into the street. They soon got out of the red-light district and onto Damrak, which was still busy, with Burgess meandering from side to side bumping into people. Banks remembered that Dirty Dick's second nickname on the Met was "Bambi" on account of the way his physical co-ordination went all to pieces when he was pissed.

"Got a joke," Burgess said, nudging Banks in the ribs. "This bloke goes into a pub with an octopus, and he says to the lads in the band, 'I'll bet any of you a tenner my pet here can play any instrument you care to give him.'"

They took one of the narrow streets that crossed the canals towards Keizersgracht. Banks found his attention wandering, Burgess's voice in the background. "So one of the lads brings him a clarinet, and the bloody octopus plays it like he was Benny Goodman. Another bloke brings him a guitar and it's Django fucking Reinhardt."

Banks fancied a coffee and wondered if he could get one at the hotel. If not, there was bound to be a café nearby. He looked at his watch. Only ten o'clock. Hard to believe they'd done so much in such a short time. A small café would actually be better than the hotel, he decided. He would dump Burgess, pick up his Graham Greene and find a place to sit, read and people-watch for a while.

"Anyway, this goes on for ages, instrument after instrument. Bongos, trombone, saxophone. You name it. Bring him a ukulele, and it's George Formby. The octopus plays them all like a virsh ... a virsh ... a virt-you-oh-so. Finally, one of the musicians says he's had enough and he goes out and finds a set of bagpipes. He gives them to the octopus and the octopus looks at them, frowns, turns them every which way then back again. 'Looks like you're about to lose your tenner, mate,' the musician says. Christ, I need a piss."

Burgess tottered towards the quayside, hands working at his fly, head half-turned to look back at Banks, a crooked smile on his face. "So the guy says, 'Hang on a minute, mate. When he finds out he can't fuck it, he'll play it.' Get it? Argh! Shi-it!"

It happened so quickly that Banks didn't even have a chance to take half a step. One moment Burgess was pissing a long, noisy arc into the canal, the next, he had toppled forward with an almighty splash, followed by a string of garbled oaths.

TEN

I

By Saturday morning, Susan guessed, Mark Wood must be feeling like one of those mice that has wandered into a humane trap; it can't find its way back out, and it is just beginning to realize that it's in a trap. Even when the mice do get released, she realized, they generally find themselves a long way from home.

"Your solicitor, Mr Varney, rang," said Gristhorpe. "He's sorry, he was out last night. Anyway, he's on his way up from Leeds. What can we do for you in the meantime? Coffee? Danish?"

Wood reached forward and helped himself to a pastry. "I don't have to talk to you until he gets here," he said.

"True," said Gristhorpe. "But remember that caution I read you yesterday? If you don't say anything now, it could go very badly for you later when you try to change your story again."

"What do you mean?"

"You know what I mean. You're a liar, Mark. You've already given us half a dozen old wives' tales. The more lies you tell, the lower your credibility rating falls. I'm offering you a chance to sweep the board clean, forget the lies and tell me the truth once and for all. What happened after you and Jason Fox left The Jubilee last Saturday night? Your solicitor will only give you the same advice. Tell the truth and I'll turn on the tape recorder."

"But I've already told you."

Gristhorpe shook his head. "You lied. The bottle. The fingerprint, Mark. The fingerprint."

Susan hoped to hell that Gristhorpe did get somewhere before Giles Varney arrived, because he'd milked that fingerprint for far more than it was worth already. They couldn't be certain it was

Wood's, and Gristhorpe had framed his references to it with great care when the tapes were running, saying it was a "close match" rather than an identical one.

Even "close match" was pushing it a bit. One of the first things Varney would do was look at the forensic evidence and tell his client just how flimsy it was. Then Wood would clam up. Susan had phoned the lab just a few moments ago, and while they said they might get some results before the morning was out, it certainly wouldn't be within the hour.

Even then, she knew, these would only be preliminary results. But they might, at a pinch, at least be able to determine whether there was human blood on Wood's clothing and whether it matched Jason Fox's *general* type. For more specific and solid evidence, such as DNA analysis, they would have to wait much longer. Even a general grouping, Susan thought, along with an identification and statement from the landlord of The Jubilee, would be more than they had right now. And it might be enough to convince the magistrates to remand Wood for a while longer.

"Nobody touched that bottle but you, Mark," Gristhorpe went on. "The fingerprints prove that."

"What about the bloke I bought if off? Why weren't his finger-prints on it?"

"That's not important, Mark. What matters is that *your* finger-prints were on it and Jason's weren't. There's no getting away from that, solicitor or no solicitor. If you tell me the truth now, things will go well for you. If you don't ... well, it'll be a jury you'll have to explain yourself to. And sometimes you can wait months for a trial. Years even."

"So what? I'd be out on bail and you can't prove anything."

True, Susan thought.

"Wrong," Gristhorpe said. "I don't think you'd get bail, Mark. Not for this. It was a vicious murder. Very nasty indeed."

"You said it might not be murder."

"That depends. The way things are looking now, you'd have to *confess* to make us believe it was manslaughter, Mark. You'd have to tell us how it really happened, *convince* us it wasn't murder. Otherwise we've got you on a murder charge. Concealing evidence, not coming forward, lying—it all looks bad to a jury."

Wood chewed on his lower lip. Susan noticed the crumbs of pastry down the front of his shirt. He was sweating.

"You're a clever lad, aren't you, Mark?"

"What do you mean?"

"You know all about computers and the Internet and all that stuff?"

"So?"

"Now, me, I don't know a hard-drive from a hole in the ground, but I *do* know you're lying, and I *do* know that your only way out of this tissue of lies you've got yourself well and truly stuck in is to tell me the truth. Now."

Finally, Wood licked his lips and said, "Look, I didn't kill anyone. All right, I was there. I admit it. I was there when it started. But I didn't kill Jason. You've got to believe me."

"Why do I have to believe you, Mark?" Gristhorpe asked softly.

"Because you do. It's true."

"Why don't you just tell me what happened?"

"Can I have a smoke?"

"No," said Gristhorpe. "After you've told me. If I believe you." He turned on the dual cassette recorder and made the usual preamble about the time, date and who was present.

Wood sulked and chewed his lip for a moment, then began: "We left The Jubilee just after closing time, like I said. I had a bottle with me. Jason didn't. He didn't drink much. In fact, he had a thing about drink and drugs. Into health and fitness, was Jason. Anyway, we took the short cut—at least that's what he told me it was—through some streets across the road, and where the streets ended there's a ginnel that leads between two terrace blocks to some waste ground."

"The rec," said Gristhorpe.

"If you say so. I didn't know where the fuck we were."

"Why were *you* also heading in that direction? I thought you said your car was parked on Market Street."

"It was. Jason asked me back to his place for a drink. That's all. I know I shouldn't have been drinking so much when I was driving, but ..." He grinned. "Anyway, it was like you said yesterday. If I thought I'd had too much, I would've stopped the night."

"At Jason's house?"

"His parents' house, yes."

"Carry on."

"Well, the ginnel looked a bit creepy to me, but Jason went ahead. Then all of a sudden, they came at us, three of them, from where they'd been waiting at the other end. The rec end."

"Three of them?"

"That's right. Asian lads. I recognized them. Jason had had a minor run-in with one of them earlier, in the pub."

"What happened next?"

"I dropped the bottle and scarpered fast. I thought Jason was right behind me, but by the time I looked back he was nowhere in sight."

"You didn't see what happened to him?"

"No."

"And you didn't go back?"

"No way."

"All right. What *did* you do next?"

"I kept going until I got to the car, then I drove home."

"Why didn't you call the police?"

Wood scratched his neck and averted his eyes. "I don't know. I suppose I didn't think of it, really. And I'd been drinking."

"But your friend—sorry, your business associate—was in danger. He could at least expect a severe beating, and all you could do was scarper. Come on, Mark, you can't expect me to believe that. Surely you've got more bottle, a fit lad like you?"

"Believe what you want. I didn't know Jason was in danger, did I? For all I knew he'd run off in a different direction. I'd have been a proper wally to go back there and get my head kicked in."

"Like Jason."

"Yeah, well. I didn't know what happened, did I?"

"Did you really believe that Jason had got away too?"

"He could have done, couldn't he?"

"Okay. Now tell me, if you'd done nothing wrong, why didn't you come forward later, after you *knew* Jason had been killed?"

Mark scratched the side of his nose. "I didn't know till I read it in the papers a couple of days later. By then I thought it would look funny if I came forward."

Gristhorpe frowned. "Look funny?"

"Yeah. Suspicious."

"Why?"

"Because I hadn't said anything at the time. Isn't that something that makes you blokes suspicious?"

Gristhorpe spread his hands. "Mark, we're simple souls, really. We're just thrilled to bits when someone decides to tell us the truth."

"Yeah, well ... I must admit I wasn't too proud of myself."

"What for? Running away? Deserting your mate when he needed your help?"

Wood looked down at his hands clasped on his lap. "Yes."

"Any other reason you kept out of it?"

"Well, if they killed Jason, whether they meant to or not ... I mean, I've got a wife and kid. Know what I mean? I wouldn't want to put any of us in danger by testifying if there were likely to be ... you know ... recriminations."

"Recriminations? By the three attackers?"

"By them, yes. Or people like them."

"Other Pakistani youths?"

"Well, yeah. I mean, they stick together, stand up for one another, don't they? I didn't want to put my wife and kid at risk."

Gristhorpe shook his head slowly. "This isn't making any sense to me, Mark. You look like a strong lad. Why didn't you stay and fight with Jason, give him a bit of support?"

"I told you, I was thinking of Sheri and Connor. I mean, how would they manage without me, if I got hurt, put in hospital?"

"Same way they'll have to manage without you when you get put in jail, I suppose," said Gristhorpe. "You're telling me you ran away out of concern for your wife and child?"

Wood's face reddened. "I'm not saying that's what I thought straight off. It was instinctive. I didn't have much choice, did I? And like I said, I thought Jason was right behind me. It was three against two."

"It was three against one after you ran off, Mark. What sort of choice did Jason have? The two of you could have taken those three easily. I'd have put *my* money on you."

Wood shook his head.

"Are you telling me you're a coward, Mark? Strong-looking lad like you? Bet you lift weights, don't you? Yet when it comes to the crunch you bugger off and leave your mate to die alone."

"Look, will you shut up about that?" Wood leaned forward and banged his fist down. The metal table rattled. "The point is that I *didn't do anything*. It doesn't matter whether I ran away. Or why I ran away. All that matters is that I didn't kill Jason!"

"Calm down, Mark." Gristhorpe raised his hand, palm out. "What you're saying is true. Technically, at any rate."

"What do you mean, technically?"

"Well, if what you're telling us is the truth at last—"

"It is."

"—then you didn't kill Jason in any legal, criminal sense of the word. But I'd say you're morally responsible, wouldn't you? I mean, you could have saved him, but you didn't even try."

"I told you to stop it with that. You can't prove it would have done any good if I'd stayed. Maybe I'd have got killed, too. What good would that have done anyone? I don't care about fucking *morality*. There's nothing you can charge me with."

"How about leaving the scene?"

"That's crap, and you know it."

"Maybe so," Gristhorpe admitted. "Nevertheless, deserting your mate the way you did ... That's something you'll have to live with forever, isn't it, Mark?"

Gristhorpe went to the door and asked the two uniformed officers to come in and take Wood back to his cell, then he and Susan picked up their coffees and left the stuffy interview room for Gristhorpe's office. Up there, in a comfortable chair, with plenty of space and clean air to breathe, Susan felt herself relax.

"What do you think of his story?" Gristhorpe asked.

Susan shook her head. "He's certainly a bit of a chameleon, isn't he? I hardly know what to think. I'll tell you one thing, though, sir, I think I caught him in at least one more lie."

Gristhorpe raised his bushy eyebrows. "Oh, aye? And which lie would that be?"

"Mark told us that when they left The Jubilee, Jason invited him back to his house for a drink, and maybe to stop overnight. Jason wouldn't have done that. His parents insisted he *never* brought his friends to their house."

"Hmm. Maybe they're the ones who are lying?"

"I don't think so, sir. Why should they? If you think about it, Jason lived most of his life in Leeds. He only came home on weekends occasionally, mostly to play football for United, spend a little time with his parents, get his washing done, maybe visit his granddad. He never told any of them what he was up to in Leeds. It's easy to see why he wouldn't want to mention Neville Motcombe or explain how he got fired from the plastics factory. And that meant he couldn't mention the computer business either. He could have simply lied from the start, told them he'd left the factory of his own free will for something better, but he didn't. Didn't want to face the questions, I suppose. After that, all the lies became interconnected. Who knows what Mark might have let slip to Jason's parents?" She shook her head. "Unless Mr and Mrs Fox are lying, which I doubt, then it's hardly likely Jason would suddenly decide to take one of his Leeds mates back to the Eastvale house on a whim. Too risky. And there's another thing. Jason didn't keep anything to drink at the Eastvale house. In fact, according to all accounts, he hardly drank at all."

"Maybe he was intending to give Mark some of his dad's Scotch or something?"

"It's possible, sir," Susan said. "But as I say, I doubt it."

"And maybe he would have bent the rules a bit if his mate had had too much to drink and needed somewhere to sleep it off? That might also explain why he didn't drive down from Market Street to Jason's place."

"Again, sir," said Susan, "it's possible."

"But you're not convinced. Do you think he did it?"

"I don't know, sir. I just don't trust his story."

"Make that *stories*. All right, I'll bear your reservations in mind. I can't say I like them much, either." He shook his head slowly. "Anyway, we'd better arrange to bring in George Mahmood and his pals again."

"Even though the forensic evidence supports George's story?"

"Even so."

"Chief Constable Riddle will love that, sir."

"The way I see it, Susan, we've got no choice. Mark Wood says he saw three Asian lads attack Jason Fox. Unless we can prove he's lying, it doesn't matter what we think. We *have* to bring them in."

Susan nodded. "I know, sir."

"And give the lab another call. Ask them to get their fingers out. If all they can tell us is there's human blood on the clothes, I'd be satisfied for the time being. Because if we don't get something positive soon, Mark Wood is going to walk out of here in less than an hour and I'm still not happy with a word he's told us."

II

Banks made it down to breakfast with just minutes to spare before the nine-o'clock deadline, getting a frosty look from the stout waitress in the hotel lounge for his trouble. First, he helped himself to coffee from a table by the window, then he sat down and looked around. A large "No Smoking" symbol hung over the lace-curtained window.

He doodled away at yesterday's *Yorkshire Post* crossword while he sipped the rich, black coffee and waited. Eventually, the waitress returned, and with a dour glance, she deposited a glass of orange juice and a plate in front of him. On the plate lay a few slices of cold ham, a chunk of Edam cheese, a hard-boiled egg, a couple of rolls and some butter. The Dutch breakfast. Banks tucked in.

He felt fortunate in having only the mildest of hangovers. The slight ache behind his eyes had been easily vanquished with the aid of two extra-strength paracetamols from his traveller's emergency kit, and he suspected that the minor sense-disorientation he felt was still more due to being in a foreign city than to the residual effects of alcohol. Whatever the reason, he felt fine. At least physically.

Only as he sipped the last of his coffee did he realize he hadn't thought of his domestic problems at all last night. Even now, in the morning's light, everything felt so distant, so disembodied. He could hardly believe that Sandra had really gone. Was it a question of not being there to see the tree fall in the woods, or was it what the psychologists of grief called denial? Maybe he would ask his psychologist friend Jenny Fuller when she got back from America. Jenny. Now, if Sandra really had gone, did that make him a free agent? What were the rules? Best not think about it too much. Maybe he would ring home again before going out, just to see if she had come back.

He was the only person sitting in the spotless lounge, with its dark wood smelling of polish, its lace doilies, ticking clock and knick-knacks stuffed in alcoves. As he had hoped, Burgess had either breakfasted earlier or hadn't even got out of bed yet. Banks suspected the latter.

Thank the Lord a passer-by had stopped to help him haul Burgess out of the canal last night. Dirty Dick had stood there dripping the foul water and complaining loudly about the canal-building Dutch engineers—most of whom, according to him, had only one parent, a mother, with whom they had indulged in unspeakable sexual relations.

Banks had finally managed to persuade him to calm down and walk back to the hotel before the police arrived and arrested them.

That, they succeeded in doing, and their arrival had attracted only a puzzled frown from the man on the desk as they traipsed through the lobby. Burgess had trailed dirty canal-water as he went, his shoes squelching with every step. He had held his head high, like W.C. Fields trying to pretend he was sober, and walked with as much dignity as he could muster. After that, he had gone straight up to his room on the second floor, and that was the last Banks had seen or heard of him.

After breakfast, Banks went all the way back up to his room and phoned home again. Still nothing. Not that he had expected Sandra to get the *first* train back home, but one lives in hope. He didn't leave a message for himself.

As he trod carefully back down the steep, narrow stairs, tiptoeing over the landing near Burgess's room, he reflected on how he had enjoyed himself last night, how, against all expectations, he had enjoyed his night of freedom. He hadn't done anything he wouldn't normally have done, except perhaps drink too much and get silly, but he had *felt* differently about it.

For the first time, he found himself wondering if Sandra weren't, perhaps, right. Maybe they both did need a little time to manoeuvre and regroup after all the changes of the past few years, especially Sandra's new and more demanding work, and the loss of the children.

Not children now, Banks reminded himself. Grown-ups. He thought back to that evening in The Pack Horse only a few days ago, when he had watched Tracy with her friends and realized he couldn't cross the lounge to be with her; then he remembered a telephone call he had once made from Weymouth to his son in Portsmouth, realizing then for the first time how distant and independent Brian had become.

Well, there was nothing he could do about it. Any of it. Except to make damn sure he kept in touch with them, helped them the best he could, became a friend and not a meddlesome irritation to them. He wondered how they would take the news of their parents' separation. For that matter, who would tell them? Would Sandra? Should he?

He walked out onto Keizersgracht. The sun glinted on the parked bicycles on the quay and on the canal, making a rainbow out of a pool of oil. Reflections of trees shimmered gently in the ripples of a passing boat.

His mysterious meeting was set for eight o'clock tonight. Well, he thought, in the meantime, on a day like this, tourist map in hand, he could walk the city to his heart's content.

III

"You've got to admit, superintendent, that your evidence is pretty thin."

Giles Varney, Mark Wood's solicitor, sat in Gristhorpe's office later that Saturday morning, staring out over the market square as he talked.

Outside, a sunny morning had brought plenty of tourists to the bustling open market, but now it was clouding over and, to Susan's well-trained nose, getting ready to pour down before the day was out. She had already seen the gusts of wind that would later bring the rain clouds billowing the canvas covers of the market stalls.

Varney wasn't a pinstripe lawyer like the one they'd had to deal with last year in the Deborah Harrison murder. He was casually dressed in jeans and a sports shirt, and his very expensive light wool jacket hung on a stand in the corner. He was young, probably not much older than Susan's own twenty-seven, in good shape, and handsome in a craggy, outdoorsy kind of way. He looked as if he were on his way to go hang-gliding.

There was something Susan didn't like about him, but she couldn't put her finger on it. An arrogance, perhaps, or overconfidence. Whatever it was, it put her on her guard.

"I realize that, Mr Varney," said Gristhorpe, "but I'm sure you can see our predicament."

Varney smiled. "With all due respect, it's not my job to see your predicament. It's my job to get my client out of jail."

Supercilious prat, Susan thought.

"And it's our job," countered Gristhorpe, "to get to the bottom of Jason Fox's death. Your client admits he was at the scene."

"Only *prior* to the crime. He couldn't have had any knowledge of what was going to happen."

"Oh, come off it, Mr Varney. If three kids came at you in a dark alley, I think you'd have a pretty good idea what was about to take place, wouldn't you?"

"That's beside the point. And since when has saving your own skin been regarded as a criminal act? Technically, my client is not guilty of any crime. I expect you to release him immediately. I trust you have the real criminals in custody?"

"On their way. Again," muttered Gristhorpe.

Varney raised an eyebrow. "Yes, I understand you had these same chaps in custody once before and let them go?"

"Had to," Gristhorpe said. "No evidence. You'd have approved."

Varney smiled again. "Not having much luck with evidence these days, are you, superintendent?"

"There *is* one other small matter," said Gristhorpe.

Varney glanced at his Rolex with irritation. "Yes?"

"Your client has now become an important witness. I trust you'd have no objection to his remaining here in order to identify the suspects when we've brought them in?"

Varney narrowed his eyes. "I don't know what you're up to, superintendent. But something smells. Still, how could I have any objection? And I'm sure my client will be more than willing to help sort out this mess for you. As long as he's released from his cell this very minute and treated as a witness rather than as a criminal. He also has to know that he's free to go home whenever he wants."

Susan breathed a sigh of relief. She knew that Gristhorpe was playing for time, trying to find some reason to keep Mark Wood in Eastvale until the lab came up with something—or with nothing. This way, at least they might get another hour or so out of him, especially if they had him write another formal statement *after* the identification. Maybe a lot more time than that if they put together an identification parade, which would mean importing a few more Asians of similar build to George, Kobir and Asim.

As it turned out, they hardly had to wait at all. Just as Gristhorpe was about to leave the office and take Varney down to release Mark Wood, the phone rang. Gristhorpe excused himself, picked up the receiver, grunted a few times, then beamed at Susan. "That's the lab," he said. "They've found traces of blood between the uppers and the soles of Mark Wood's Doc Martens, and it matches Jason Fox's blood group. I'm afraid, Mr Varney, we've got a few more questions for your client."

Varney sniffed and sat down again. Gristhorpe picked up his phone and called downstairs. "Bert? Have young Mark Wood brought up from the cells, would you? Yes, the interview room."

Giles Varney insisted on having a private talk with Mark Wood before the interview. Susan waited with Gristhorpe in his office, where they went over all Wood's previous statements, planning their strategy. The rags of cloud had drifted in from Scotland now and the air that blew in through the partially open window was beginning to smell like a wet dog. Susan walked over and watched some of the tourists looking at the sky, then heading for the pubs or for their cars.

"Hungry?" Gristhorpe asked.

"I can wait, sir," said Susan. "A few less calories won't do me any harm."

"Me neither," grinned Gristhorpe. "But at my age you don't worry about it so much."

There was a brisk tap at the door and Giles Varney walked in.

"Finished?" Gristhorpe asked.

Varney nodded. "For the moment. My client wishes to make a statement."

"Another one?"

"Look," said Varney, with a thin smile, "the blood evidence isn't much to write home about so far, you have to admit, and the finger-print rubbish is even less. You should be grateful for what you can get."

"In a few days," Gristhorpe countered, "we'll have DNA on the blood. And I suspect your client knows that will prove it's Jason Fox's. At the moment, I think we've got enough to hold him."

Varney smiled. "That's what I thought you'd say. What you hear might change your mind."

"How?"

"After a certain amount of reflection, on the advice of his solic-itor, my client is now willing to explain exactly what happened last Saturday night."

"Right," said Gristhorpe, getting up and glancing over at Susan. "Let's get to it then."

They went into the interview room where Mark Wood sat chewing his fingernails, went through the preliminaries and turned on the tape recorders.

"Right, lad," said Gristhorpe. "Mr Varney here says you wish to make a statement. I hope it's the truth this time. Now what have you got to say?"

Wood looked at Varney before opening his mouth. Varney nodded. "I did it," Wood said. "I killed Jason. It was an accident. I didn't mean to."

"Why don't you tell us what happened, Mark?" Gristhorpe coaxed him. "Slowly. Take your time."

Wood looked at Varney, who nodded. "We were going back to his place, like I said before. Jason was going on about those Pakis back in The Jubilee, what he thought should be done with them. We started arguing. I told him I didn't like that racist crap. Jason was going on about how I was really a racist deep down, just like him, and why didn't I admit it, join the group. I laughed and told him I'd never join that band of wankers in a million years. I was pretty mad by then, so I told him that my wife was from Jamaica. Then he started insulting her, calling her a black bitch and a whore and calling little Connor a half-breed mutant. We were getting near the ginnel now and Jason was really laying into me. Really crude stuff. Like I'd betrayed the white race by marrying a nigger, and shit like that." Mark paused and rubbed his temples. "I'd had a few drinks, more than I admitted, and more than Jason at any rate, and sometimes I ... well, I've got a bit of a temper when I'm pissed. I just lost it, that's all. He came at me. I had the bottle in my hand and I just lashed out with it and hit him."

"What happened next?"

"He didn't go down. Just put his hand to the side of his head and swore, then he came at me again. He was strong, was Jason, but I reckon I'm probably stronger. Anyway, we started fighting, but I think the head wound had sort of weakened him and I managed to knock him down. I thought about what he'd said about Sheri and Connor and I just saw red. The next thing I knew, he wasn't moving, and I ran off."

"And left him there?"

"Yes. I didn't know he was fucking dead. How could I? I thought I'd just put him out of action for a while."

"Why did you empty his pockets?"

"I didn't. Why would I do that?"

"Because the whole thing was a lot more deliberate than you're saying? Because you wanted to make it look like a mugging? You tell me, Mark."

"Superintendent," Varney chipped in. "My client is offering a voluntary statement. If he says he didn't empty the victim's pockets, then I suggest you believe him. He has no reason to lie at this point."

"I'll be the judge of that, Mr Varney," said Gristhorpe. He looked at Mark again.

Mark shook his head. "I don't remember doing that. Honest."

Gristhorpe sniffed and riffled through some sheets of paper in front of him. "Mark," he said finally. "Jason Fox's injuries included a fractured skull and a ruptured spleen. Yet you say you only kicked him a couple of times?"

"That's how it happened. I admit I lost it, I was in a rage, but I didn't mean to kill him."

"All right, Mark," said Gristhorpe. "Is this the statement you want to make?"

"Yes."

"My client will be pleading to the charge of manslaughter, superintendent," Varney said. "And I think there might be some room for mitigating circumstances."

"Plenty of time for charges later," said Gristhorpe. "Let's just go through the story again first." Gristhorpe turned to Susan and sighed. "Susan, go and make sure George Mahmood and his friends are released immediately. The poor sods won't know whether they're coming or going."

Susan nodded and got up. As she left the interview room, she heard Gristhorpe say wearily, "Right then, Mark, once more from the top."

IV

Using a street map he'd bought that afternoon, Banks walked to the address Burgess had given him. Though he felt silly doing it, he had looked over his shoulder once in a while and taken a very circuitous route.

It was another brown café, this one on a street corner by Sarphatipark. The park itself was a dark rectangle wedged between blocks of tenements. It looked familiar. He was sure he had seen it before, with Sandra. It reminded him of the kind of square you'd find in Bloomsbury or Edinburgh. The café itself wasn't the kind of place listed in the tourist guides. The wood was dark and stained with years of tobacco smoke, and most of the tables were scratched and blackened here and there where cigarettes had been left to burn.

One or two locals sitting at the bar, working men by the look of their clothes, turned and glanced at Banks as he walked in and found a table in the far corner. One of them said something to the man behind the bar, who shrugged and laughed, then they paid him no further attention. Only a few tables were taken, and only one of those by a young man and a woman. It was pretty much of a men's pub by the look of it. Accordion music was playing quietly behind the bar. Welcome to hell.

The table wobbled. Banks took a beermat and placed it under one leg. That helped. Not wanting a repeat of last night, he decided he was going to stick with beer, and not even drink many of those. That *jenever* could be deadly. He ordered an Amstel, lit a cigarette and settled down to wait, back to the wall, eyes on the door. After a day spent walking around the city, stopping only at a café now and then for a coffee and a cigarette, Banks was also glad of the chance to rest his legs.

As he waited, he reflected on the curious and unsettling experience he had had that afternoon. One of the places he'd walked by was a canal-side coffee house he remembered visiting with Sandra all those years ago. The kind of place that also sold hash and grass. It didn't seem to have changed at all. At first he had thought it couldn't possibly be the same one, but it was. Curious, he had turned back and wandered inside.

At the back, where it was darker, piles of cushions lay scattered on the floor. You could lie back, smoke your joint, look at the posters on the wall and listen to the music. He had noticed a young couple there, in the far corner, and for one spine-tingling moment, in the dim light, he had felt he was looking down on himself and Sandra when they were young. And he hadn't even smoked any hash.

Shaken, he had walked out into the sunshine and gone on his way. It had been a good five or ten minutes before he could get rid of the spooky feeling. He and Sandra had smoked hash there with some Americans, he remembered. Dylan's *Blonde on Blonde* album had been playing, the long "Sad-eyed Lady of the Lowlands." Later, they had made love in their sleeping-bag in the Vondelpark, hidden away from other nighthawks by some bushes. Memories. Would he never escape them?

Just as he was lighting another cigarette, someone walked through the door. And for the second time that day Banks felt gobsmacked.

If he wasn't mistaken, it was the man he had last seen in Neville Motcombe's house: Rupert Francis, the tall, gangly woodworker.

He obviously noticed Banks's surprise. "You can close your mouth now, sir," he said. "It really is me."

Banks shook his head slowly. "So I see. Rupert Francis, right? And what's with the 'sir'?"

"Actually, I'm DS Craig McKeracher, sir," he said, shaking hands. "That makes you my senior officer. Pleasure to make your acquaintance." He smiled sheepishly and sat down. "I'm sorry about all the cloak-and-dagger stuff, sir, but if they found out who I really am they'd kill me."

Banks shook hands and collected his thoughts. The waiter came over and Craig ordered a beer.

"I think we can drop the 'sir,'" said Banks.

Craig nodded. "If you like. I must admit you gave me the shock of my bloody life when I saw you at Nev's place the other day. I thought the game was up right there and then."

"You didn't have to show yourself."

"I know. But I heard voices, so I thought up an excuse and came up to see what was going on. Part of my brief, after all, to keep my eyes and ears open. Just as well you'd never seen me before."

"How long have you been undercover there?"

"About five months. Nev trusts me. 'Rupert Francis' has an impeccable background with the neo-Nazi movement. BNP, fringe groups, the whole kit and caboodle. He's even been done on firearms and explosives charges. In addition to that, he's got a long and varied criminal record. Assault, burglary, drugs. You name it. That's something Nev also trusts."

"How would he know about your record?"

Craig sipped some beer from the bottle before answering. His Adam's apple bobbed in his skinny throat. "He's got a man on the inside somewhere. West Yorkshire. Some PC or DC sympathetic to the cause. Believe me, there are plenty of blokes on the Job who'd have no axe to grind with Neville Motcombe's ideas.

However he does it, he has no problem checking out criminal records."

"So it's you who wants me here, not Burgess?"

"Yes. After I'd seen you, I got in touch with Dirty—with Superintendent Burgess soon as I could. He's my controller, but with things getting so hot lately we've not had the chance for much more than minimal telephone contact. And you've got to be really careful over the phone. Anyway, I told him I wanted to talk to you as soon as possible, but I didn't want to risk doing it locally. Then I thought this would be a perfect opportunity. Know why I'm here?"

"Haven't a clue," said Banks.

"I'm helping to organize an international conference on race and IQ, if you can swallow that. Anyway, Superintendent Burgess said not to worry, he'd make the arrangements." Craig grinned. "In fact, he said he'd enjoy it. You should have heard him when I told him you'd walked right into Nev's front room. I gather the two of you know each other? You and the super, that is?"

Banks stubbed out his cigarette and sipped some beer. "You could say that."

"He likes you. Honest, he does. Respects you. That's what he told me. I reckon he thinks you're a bit naïve, but he was glad to hear it was you on the Fox case and not someone else."

"Maybe we should start a mutual admiration society."

Craig laughed.

"Anyway," Banks asked, "why all this interest in the Albion League?"

"Because of Neville Motcombe and his contacts with known international terrorists. When he left the BNP and decided to start his own fringe group, we thought it'd be a good idea to keep an eye on him."

Banks sipped some Amstel. "And did he live up to your expectations?"

"In some ways, yes. In others, he exceeded them. The Albion League's nowhere near as politically active as we thought it would be. As Combat 18 are, for example. I'm not saying there haven't been violent incidents, there have, and I've even heard talk of a pipe-bomb to sabotage the mosque opening. Now we know about that possibility, we can tighten security and make sure it doesn't happen. But mostly, as far as revolutionary action is concerned, they've been pretty tame so far. More like a fucking boys' club than anything else."

"I wondered about that. What is it with Motcombe and these young boys? Is he gay or something?"

The waiter came over and they ordered two more beers. When he had gone again, Craig said, "No. No, Nev's not gay. I'll confess I had my own suspicions when I first met him and he invited me down the cellar to help with his woodwork. Like, come and see my etchings. But he's not. If anything, I'd say he was asexual. His wife left him. If you ask me it was because he spent more time licking envelopes than licking her. He's that kind of person. Power is more important to him than romantic or sexual relationships. The youth thing is just part of his shtick. He actually used to be involved in church groups, youth clubs, that sort of thing. He was even a Boys' Brigade leader at one time. Always did like paramilitary organizations and uniforms."

"What happened?"

"He got kicked out for trying to recruit kids to the BNP. Anyway, a big part of his thing is the emphasis on the old British values and virtues: war games in the Pennines, crafts, camping, hiking, survival techniques, a healthy mind and healthy body. That sort of thing."

"Baden-Powell with swastikas?"

"If you like. He even throws in a bit of environmentalist stuff to hook the greenies. You know—preserve the traditional English village against pollution, that sort of thing. Thing is, to him pollution isn't only a matter of destroying the ozone layer and the rain forests or what have you, it includes most non-Aryan racial groups. Perhaps Nev's only saving grace as a human being is that his over-riding trait is greed."

"What do you mean?"

Craig rubbed his cheek and frowned. "Just an observation of mine. Haven't you sometimes thought that people's vices are often the only things that make them interesting? As a pure neo-Nazi,

Nev would simply be a bore. A sick and dangerous bore, perhaps, but a bore nonetheless. Predictable. It's the other stuff that's interesting, the stuff we didn't expect."

"Burgess mentioned drugs. Is that right?"

Craig nodded, finished his beer and slid the bottle aside. "Fancy walking?"

"Why not."

They paid their bill and walked outside. There were still plenty of people on the streets, especially along Albert Cuypstraat, where they walked through the debris of that afternoon's market—wilted lettuce leaves, a squashed tomato, chicken bones, a piece of cardboard that said f4.50 on it. The smell of fish still infused the evening air. Now Banks knew why Sarphatipark had felt so familiar. He and Sandra *had* been there; they had spent an hour or two one afternoon wandering through the market stalls.

"Like I said," Craig went on, "Nev got to trust me, take me into his confidence. I think he liked the fact that according to my criminal record, I didn't mind doing anything as long as it was profitable. And it didn't take me long to work out that Nev likes profit more than anything."

"So it's money with him, not politics?"

"Mmm, not entirely. Maybe it's both at the same time, if he can get it that way. If not, then I'd say money comes out distinctly on top. Like I said, Nev's a greedy bastard. Greedy for power and greedy for cash. First thing I found out when I got involved was that he was organizing some of his younger and thicker recruits into groups of thieves, turning their gains over to him, of course, for the good of the League."

"And they did this?"

Craig snorted. "Sure they did. Let's face it, most of these kids are pretty dense. Five or six of them would go into a shop, say, and as soon as—"

"Steaming?"

"You know about it?"

"I've heard the term. And I know it's been a problem for West Yorkshire CID recently. Along with muggings at cash dispensers. I didn't know Motcombe was behind it."

"Some of it. I'm sure there are plenty of freelancers out there, too. But what Nev does is, he takes these kids' anger and channels it. He gives them someone to hate. He gives their rage some structure and provides them with real targets rather than nebulous ones. So they end up believing they're committing theft, assault and vandalism for a good cause. Isn't that what terrorism is basically all about, anyway? Add a few *olde worlde* patriotic values, a lot of guff about the 'true English homeland' and a bit of green to the mix and it makes them feel like downright responsible and virtuous citizens, the only ones who really care about their country."

"You make it sound easy."

They turned right, towards the neo-Gothic mass of the Rijksmuseum, dark and solid against the night sky. Street-lights cast long shadows. A breeze stirred, wafting a smell of decay from the canal. Banks could hear music in the distance, see TV screens flickering through people's curtains.

Craig shrugged. "It's not as hard as you think, that's the sad thing. Recruiting isn't, anyway. Take rock concerts, for example. Invitation only. Makes people feel privileged and exclusive right off the bat. Then the white-power bands get the kids all worked up with their rhythm and energy, and someone like me moves in to bring the message home. And they target schools, particularly schools that have a large number of immigrant pupils. They hang around outside in the street and pass out leaflets, then they hold meetings in different venues. They also hang out in the coffee bars where some of the kids go on their way home. You know, start chatting, give them a sympathetic shoulder for their problems with Ali or Winston. They get a surprising number of converts that way."

"Some of whom Motcombe organizes into gangs of thieves?"

"Some, yes. But not all." He laughed. "One or two of the lads in the know have nicknamed him Fagin."

Banks raised his eyebrows. "'You've got to pick a pocket or two,'" he sang, a passable imitation of Ron Moody in *Oliver*. "I imagine he'd just love that."

Craig smiled. "I'll bet. Thing is, though, there's a lot of money to be made, one way or another. Steaming and mugging are just part of the bigger picture. These right-wing political groups finance themselves in any number of ways. Some deal in arms and explosives, for example. Then there's the rock angle. These bands record CDs. That means people produce, record, manufacture and distribute them. That can be big business. And where there's rock, there's drugs. There's a lot of money to be made out of that."

"Motcombe has an arrest for receiving, doesn't he?"

"Yes. His one big mistake. A couple of his lads broke into a Curry's and ran off with a few videos and stereos under their arms. They didn't tell Nev where they'd got the stuff from. Anyway, since then, it's been cash only. And he skims off the top, too. I've seen him stuff the notes into his own pocket." Craig shook his head. "If there's one thing worse than a Nazi, it's a bent Nazi."

"How does Jason Fox fit in? Was he one of the thieves?"

Craig paused and leaned on a bridge as they crossed to Hobbemakade, looking down at the reflections of the lights. Banks stood beside him and lit a cigarette. It was quiet now apart from a few cars and the whir of an occasional bicycle.

"No, Jason never went out steaming. Not his style. Too smart. Jason was a thinker. He was good at recruiting, at propaganda in general. The thing about Jason was, he was basically an honest kid. A straight, dedicated Nazi."

"One of those boring fascists, without vices?"

Craig laughed. "Almost. Not exactly boring, though. In some ways he was naïve in his sincerity, and that made him almost likeable. *Almost*. But he was also more dedicated, more driven, than most of the others. Frightening. See, when you come down to it, Nev's not much more than a petty crook with delusions of grandeur. Jason, on the other hand, was the genuine article. Real dyed-in-the-wool neo-Nazi. Probably even read *Mein Kampf*."

"I thought even Hitler's most fanatical followers couldn't get through that."

Craig laughed. "True."

"Have you any ideas as to why Jason was killed? Was he involved in this drug deal?"

They moved away from the bridge and headed down the street. Banks flicked his cigarette end in the water, immediately feeling guilty of pollution.

"No," Craig said. "Not at all. Jason was violently anti-drug. In fact, if you ask me, that's where you might want to start looking for your motive. Because he certainly knew about it."

V

"Another bottle of wine?"

"I shouldn't," said Susan, placing her hand over her half-filled glass.

"Why not? You're not driving."

"True."

"And you've just wrapped up a case. You should be celebrating."

"All right, all right, you silver-tongued devil. Go ahead."

Gavin grinned, called the waiter and ordered a second bottle of Chablis. Susan felt her heart give a slight lurch the way it did when she first jumped The Strid at Bolton Abbey as a teenager. It happened the moment her feet left the ground and she found herself hurtling through space over the deep, rushing waters, because that was the moment she had committed herself to jumping, despite all the warnings. So what had she committed herself to by agreeing to a second bottle of wine?

She took another mouthful of filo pastry stuffed with Brie, walnuts and cranberries, and washed it down with the wine she had left in her glass. It hadn't even been there long enough to get luke-warm. Already, she was beginning to feel a little light-headed—but in a pleasant way, as if a great burden had been lifted from her.

They were in a new bistro on Castle Walk, looking west over the formal gardens and the river. A high moon silvered the swirling current of water far below and frosted the tips of the leaves on the trees. The restaurant itself was one of those hushed places where everyone seemed to be whispering, and food and drink suddenly appeared out of the silence as if by magic. White tablecloths. A floating candle in a glass jar on every table. It was also, she thought, far too expensive for a couple of mere DCs. Still, you had to push the boat out once in a while, didn't you, she told herself, just to see how far it would float.

She stole a glance at Gavin, busy finishing his venison. He caught her looking and smiled. She blushed. He really did have lovely brown eyes, she thought, and a nice mouth.

"So how does it feel?" Gavin asked, putting his knife and fork down. "The success? I understand it was largely due to your initiative?"

"Oh, not really," Susan said. "It was teamwork."

"How modest of you," he teased. "But seriously, Susan. It was you who found the killer's name. What was it ... Mark something or other?"

"Mark Wood. Yes, but Superintendent Gristhorpe got him to confess."

"I'd still say you get a big gold star for this one."

Susan smiled. The waiter appeared with their wine, gave Gavin a sip to test, then poured for both of them and placed it in the ice bucket. Good God, Susan thought, an *ice* bucket. In Yorkshire! *What am I doing here? I must be mad.* She had finished her food now and concentrated on the wine while she studied the dessert menu. Sweets. Her weakness. Why she was a few inches too thick around the hips and thighs. But she didn't think she could resist nutty toffee pie. And she didn't.

"Chief Constable Riddle's pretty damn chuffed," Gavin said later as they tucked into their desserts and coffee. "Sunday or not, it's my guess he'll be down your neck of the woods again tomorrow dishing out trophies and giving a press statement. As far as he's concerned, this solution has gone a long way towards diffusing racial tensions."

"Well, he was certainly keen to get everything signed, sealed and delivered this afternoon."

"I'll tell you something else. Golden boy isn't exactly top of the pops as far as the CC is concerned."

"What's new?" Susan said. "And I told you, I wish you'd stop calling him that."

"Where is he, by the way?" Gavin went on. "Rumour has it he hasn't been much in evidence the last couple of days. Not like him to miss being in at the kill, is it?"

"He's taken some time off."

"Pretty inconsiderate time to do that, isn't it?"

"I'm sure he has his reasons." Susan pushed her empty dessert plate aside. "Mmm. That pie was divine."

"How very mysterious," Gavin said. "Is he often like that?"

"Sometimes. He can be a bit enigmatic when he wants, can the DCI. Anyway, I'm glad Jimmy Riddle's happy, but this just isn't the sort of solution that makes you feel exactly wonderful, you know."

"Why not?"

"I can't help feeling a bit sorry for Mark Wood."

"Sorry? I thought he was supposed to have kicked his mate to death?"

"Yes, I know."

"Isn't that about as vicious as it gets?"

"I suppose so. But he *was* provoked. Anyway, I don't mean that. It's not so much *him* I feel sorry for, it's his family. He has a young wife and a baby. Poor devils. I can't help but wonder how they're going to manage without him."

"He should have thought of that before he killed Jason Fox, shouldn't he?"

Susan drank some more wine. It tasted thin and acidic after the sweetness of her dessert. "I know," she said. "But you should have seen where they live, Gavin. It's a dump. Thin walls, peeling wallpaper, damp, cramped living-space. And it's a dangerous neighbourhood, especially for a young woman alone with her baby. Gangs, drugs ... And it was partly because he was defending his wife, her race, that he ended up killing Jason."

Gavin shook his head. "I never took you for a bleeding heart, Susan. You can't allow yourself to start getting sentimental. It'll make you soft. He's a villain and you've done your job. Now let's just hope the court puts him away where he belongs. Poverty's no excuse. Plenty of people have it tough and they don't go around booting their pals to death. My dad was a miner, and more often out of work than in. But that doesn't give me an excuse to go around acting like a yob. If you want anything in this life, you go out and get it, you don't idle around moaning about what a bad hand you've been dealt."

"I suppose so," Susan said. She refilled her wine glass and smiled. "Anyway, enough of that. Cheers."

They clinked glasses.

"Cheers," Gavin said. "To success."

"To success," Susan echoed.

"Why don't we pay the bill and go," Gavin said, leaning forward. His hand touched hers. She felt the tingle right down to her toes. "I'll walk you home."

Susan looked at him for a moment. Those soft, sexy brown eyes. Long lashes he had, too. "All right," she said, her hand turning to clasp his. "Yes. I'd like that."

VI

No more than a few hundred miles away, over the North Sea, Banks and Craig McKeracher had passed the Rijksmuseum and were walking down the quiet streets towards Prinsengracht.

"Basically," Craig was busy explaining, "Nev met this right-wing loony in Turkey who had a load of heroin he wanted to shift, and he wondered if Nev could help. Nev couldn't, of course. He knows bugger all about dealing drugs. Doesn't know a fucking joint from a tab of acid. But he's always one to leave the door a little ajar, so he tells this bloke, hang on a while, let me see what I can do. Now there's only two people he knows with any brains who have ever had anything to do with drugs. One of them's yours truly, and the other's Mark Wood."

Banks paused. "Wait a minute. Motcombe knew Mark Wood?"

"Yes."

"This is Jason's business partner?"

Craig snorted. "Some partnership that'd be. There wasn't a lot of love lost between them, as far as I could see."

"Is Mark a member of the League?"

Craig shook his head. "No, he wouldn't have anything to do with them."

"Then how ... ?"

"Mark and Jason met on this computer course, and they got on well enough at first. They were both good at it, too. Anyway, when they finished, Mark couldn't get a job. I understand he's got a wife

and kid and lives in a shit-hole out Castleford way, so he was pretty
desperate by then. Nev finances Jason in the computer business—
only because he knows it's something he'll be able to use to his
advantage down the line—and Jason decides he'll take Mark on as
partner, seeing as he came top of the class. Naturally, because Nev's
putting money into the business, he's curious about Mark, so Jason
arranges a meeting. I wasn't there, but I gather Nev had got details
of his record by then and quizzed him about the drug arrest."

"What were the details?"

"Mark used to be a roadie for a Leeds band, a mixed-race band,
like UB40, and one of the Jamaicans, a Chapeltown bloke, was into
dealing in a big way. Used the group van, and got Mark involved.
They got caught. End of story. So Nev finds out that Mark has
some contacts in Chapeltown who might know someone who'll be
interested if the price is right."

"This wouldn't involve a bloke called Devon, would it?"

Craig raised his eyebrows. "Yeah. How'd you know about him?"

"Same source I heard about the steaming. Just a lucky guess.
Carry on."

"Right, well, like I said, living in this shit-hole with his wife and
kid, Mark was definitely interested in making money, even though
he didn't give a flying fuck for Nev's politics. But he made a perfect
go-between. Devon and his mates probably wouldn't be any too
happy if they knew their supplier was a fascist bastard who thought
they should all be sent home to rot in the sun, at best. But Mark got
on with the black community okay, and they seemed to accept
him. And he wasn't a member of the League."

Banks nodded. "Okay. That makes sense."

They spotted a vendor at the street corner, and as neither had
eaten that evening, they bought bags of chips with mayonnaise,
something Banks would never think of eating back in Eastvale.
Here, they tasted wonderful.

"But how did Jason square all this with his politics?" Banks asked
as they walked on. "You said he was dedicated. Straight."

"He didn't. That's the point. I'll get to it in a minute. See, in
general, neo-Nazis aren't only racist, they're also anti-drug, same
way they're anti-gay."

"Even though many of Hitler's lot were homosexuals or junkies?"

Craig laughed. "You can't expect logic or consistency from these buggers. I'll give Nev his due, though. Normally, he could make raping and murdering old ladies sound like a good thing to do for the cause. A true politician. A week or so later, when Mark's out of the way, he has another meeting with just me and Jason, and he tells us about this idea he came up with after travelling in America and talking to fellow strugglers there. What he thinks is that by providing a steady and cheap supply of heroin, you weaken and destroy the fabric of the black community, making them much poorer and more vulnerable when the big day comes, blah blah blah. It's his version of the smallpox blankets the whites gave the American Indians. Or, more recently, that newspaper story about the CIA financing the crack business in south-central Los Angeles. As a bonus, the blacks become complicit in their own destruction. That's the kind of irony Nev can't resist. And all the while he makes a tidy profit out of it, too. Couldn't be better."

"Jason fell for this crap?"

Craig kicked at an empty cigarette packet in the street. "Ah, not exactly. There's the rub. Motcombe needed one of us, someone *inside* the League, just to keep an eye on Mark and make sure everything was going tickety-boo. He didn't fully trust Mark. Jason, being Mark's partner, seemed a natural choice. But Jason wasn't interested in profit; he'd have starved for the cause. Nev seriously underestimated his right-hand man's dedication. Jason didn't fall for all that rubbish about weakening the community from within. In fact, he saw the scheme for exactly what it was— a money-making venture on Nev's part. Apparently, he already suspected Nev of skimming for his own gain, and there was quite a little power struggle brewing between them. They argued. Jason said he knew the organization needed money, but this just wouldn't work, that there was no way they could limit the sale to blacks, that it would spread to the white community too and sap their spirit as well. He said drugs were a moral evil and a pure Aryan would have nothing to do with them. He also said heroin wouldn't encourage the immigrants to go back home, which is what the organization was supposed to be all about, and that they'd be better concentrating on making the buggers feel uncomfortable and unwelcome than plying them with opiates."

"Impressive," said Banks. "But surely Motcombe must have suspected he'd react that way? Why did he even tell Jason in the first place?"

"I think Nev really did miscalculate the intensity of Jason's reaction. It would also have been pretty hard to keep anything like that from him. Nev fell in love with what he thought was his impeccable rhetoric, and he figured the best thing was to bring Jason in right from the start. No way, he thought, could anyone not see the absolute perfection of his logic and irony. At that point also, remember, he'd no idea how violently anti-drugs Jason was. It had simply never come up before." Craig shook his head. "I was there. Nev was absolutely stunned at Jason's negative reaction."

"What happened next?"

"They argued. Nev couldn't convince him. In the end he said he'd abandon the idea."

"But he didn't?"

"No way. Too much money in it. He just cut Jason out."

"But Jason knew?"

"I think by then he was pretty certain Nev wouldn't give up potential profits that easily, yes."

"Jason knew about the proposed drug deal and Motcombe was worried he'd go to the police."

"That was always a possibility, yes. But even more of a threat was that he'd talk to other ranking neo-Nazis. Nev's peers and colleagues. Some of whom felt exactly the way Jason did about drugs. Think about it. If Jason could convince them Nev was nothing but a petty thief and a drug dealer, then Nev would never be able to hold his head up in the movement again. He'd be ostracized. Hypocrisy reigns in the far right every bit as much as it does in most other places. There's another thing, too."

"What's that?"

"Jason had charisma. He was popular. Nev was coming to see him as a rival for power—and power meant money for Nev. So Nev was getting paranoid about Jason. It was Jason who made first contact with most of our members. It was Jason they went to when they had problems with the ideology of beating the crap out of some poor black or Asian kid. Jason who set them straight."

"So Jason was making inroads on Motcombe's position?"

"Exactly."

Banks nodded. He found a rubbish bin and dropped his empty chip packet in it. They were near Keizersgracht now, not too far from the hotel.

"What was your role in all this?"

"Like I said, Nev wanted someone close, someone in the League to keep tabs on Mark. Obviously Jason wasn't going to do it, so I was the next logical choice. I hadn't been around as long as Jason, but I *did* have an impressive criminal record, including drugs charges."

"So what it comes down to is that Motcombe had a pretty good motive for wanting Jason out of the way."

Craig nodded. "Exactly. That's why I needed to talk to you. To fill you in on it all. I don't know who killed Jason. I wasn't privy to that. Nev likes to keep his left hand and his right hand quite independent from one another. But I do know the background."

They paused at a bridge. A young couple stood holding hands and looking into the reflections of lights in the water.

"Where do you want me to go with this?" Banks asked.

"Wherever it takes you. I didn't have you brought here to tell you to lay off, if that's what you think. And it's not a competition, or a race. Whatever we can get Motcombe for is fine with me. And with Superintendent Burgess. That's why he agreed to arrange this meeting. All I'm asking is that you hold off moving against Nev until you've got something you're certain will put him away for a long time." He grinned. "Oh, and I'd appreciate it if you don't blow my cover. I value my life, and I might need to stick around a while longer to see what he gets up to next."

"When is this drug deal supposed to take place?"

"The heroin's already on its way."

They reached the door of Banks's hotel. He thought for a moment, then said, "All right."

"Appreciate it, sir."

"Coming in?"

"No. Got to go. I'm staying somewhere else."

"Take care, then."

"I will. Believe me."

They shook hands, and Craig wandered off along the canal. Banks looked up at the hotel's façade. It was still early. He wasn't tired and didn't fancy sitting in a cramped room watching Dutch television. He also had a lot to think about. Zipping up his jacket against the chill, he wandered off in search of a quiet bar.

VII

Susan put her hands behind her head, rested back on the pillow and sighed.

"Was that a sigh of contentment," Gavin asked, "or disappointment?"

She laughed and nudged him gently. "You should know. You had something to do with it."

"I did? Little old me?"

And to think that not more than an hour ago she had cold feet. When they had got back to her flat, she had asked Gavin in and one thing led to another, as she had known and hoped it would. She realized right from the start, though, that she had made her mind up when she agreed to the second bottle of wine. Committed. Like jumping The Strid. But when the crucial decision came out into the open, there was an embarrassing moment when it turned out that neither of them had any protection. Well, it was good in a way, Susan realized. It meant that he wouldn't think she was a slut, and she didn't think he had taken her out to dinner in the expectation of ending up in her bed. But it was bloody awkward, nonetheless.

Luckily, there was an all-night chemist's on York Road, not more than a couple of hundred yards away, and Gavin threw on his jacket and set off. While he was gone, Susan started to get nervous and have second thoughts. Instead of giving in to them, she busied herself tidying up the place, especially the bedroom, throwing clean sheets on the bed, and when he came back she found, after a little kissing and caressing, that her resolve was just as strong as before.

And now, as she basked in the afterglow, she was glad she had made the decision. One of Chopin's piano concertos—she didn't know which one—played softly from the living-room.

"Well, I couldn't think of a better way to celebrate," said Gavin. His hand brushed Susan's thigh and started sliding up over her stomach.

"Mmm. Me neither."

"And I'll tell you something else," he whispered in her ear. "I'll bet we're having a better victory celebration than anyone. Even golden boy, wherever he is."

Something about the mention of Banks's name gave Susan a moment of uneasiness, the way she had felt naked talking on the telephone to him when the Jason Fox case started. But it passed. She smiled and stretched, feeling a little sleepy from the wine and sex. "Oh, he's probably not having such a bad time," she said. "He does all right."

"What makes you think that? You don't know where he is or what he's doing."

"I do know where he is."

Gavin's hand rested on her breast. He had soft hands, like silk brushing her warm skin. She felt her nipple harden. "You know?" His hand moved again, downwards.

Susan gave a little gasp. "Yes. Amsterdam. He's gone to Amsterdam."

"Lucky devil," said Gavin. Then he did something with his hand that made Susan realize she wasn't all that sleepy after all.

ELEVEN

I

Finding Jimmy Riddle wearing out the carpet back at Eastvale Divisional HQ had about the same effect on Banks's stomach as the dodgy landing.

The plane had banked sharply and plunged into thick cloud. By the time Banks had seen the runway, they were practically on it, still at an awkward angle, and for one stomach-lurching moment he had been certain the pilot was coming in too steeply and would crash the plane, wing first. But it levelled out in time, and apart from a little more bouncing and swaying than usual, the landing had gone without incident.

And now, an hour and a half later, his stomach was going through the same cartwheels again.

It was late afternoon. Banks's flight had been delayed and he hadn't arrived at Leeds and Bradford until three o'clock; he hadn't even eaten lunch. Not much chance of a bite now. He hadn't intended calling at the station, but when he neared Eastvale, he couldn't face going back to the empty house immediately.

"Ah, Chief Inspector Banks," said Riddle. "I've been waiting for you. Nice of you to drop by."

"Sorry, sir," Banks mumbled, as Riddle followed him into his office.

Riddle tugged his trousers up at the knees to preserve the creases and sat on the edge of the desk, looking down on Banks. Banks supposed he took that position because he thought it gave him a psychological edge. Little did he know.

"And take the bloody smirk off your face, man," Riddle said. "Have you any idea how much trouble you're in?"

"Trouble, sir?"

"Yes, Banks. Serious trouble this time. You bugger off for a weekend in Amsterdam in the middle of a major investigation and leave your underlings to do your work for you. And it so happens that while you're away, they solve the case." He smiled. "I must admit, that does give me more than a little satisfaction."

"With due respect, sir—"

"With due *nothing*, Banks." Riddle craned his neck forward. The tendons tautened and the skin around his throat flushed. "What the bloody hell did you think you were up to? Can you answer me that?"

Banks had tried to prepare himself for a moment like this. If truth be told, though, he had expected it to come from Gristhorpe, not Riddle. And there was a big difference. It wasn't that he didn't trust Riddle. The man was squeaky clean. It wasn't even that he suspected Riddle of "fraternizing with fascists." That had only been a joke. A bad one, at that. But whereas Gristhorpe would accept Banks's explanation at face value and let things lie, Riddle was too much of an interfering bastard to do that.

If Banks told him what he had discovered from Craig McKeracher, Riddle would be on the phone to his cronies all over the place in a matter of moments. He wouldn't want to be left out. If there were any chance of glory to result from the situation, he would want his due share. And one wrong telephone call could have serious consequences for Craig. On the other hand, if Riddle could see nothing to be gained, then he would order Banks to pass on what he knew and leave it to West Yorkshire. Riddle hadn't got to be chief constable by pursuing the truth against all odds. The problem was, someone in West Yorkshire had already been leaking information to Motcombe.

A dilemma, then.

And Banks also knew that, as far as Riddle was concerned, the case was solved. Most satisfactorily solved.

So it was with carefully measured tones that he answered the question, aware even as he did so that it just wouldn't wash. "I can't tell you everything, sir," he said. "At least, not just yet. It's very delicate. But I can assure you my trip was directly related to the Jason Fox case."

Riddle shook his head. "Delicate? Too delicate for the likes of me? No, Banks. That won't do. I've already told you, the Jason Fox case was solved in your absence."

"I know, sir. I read about it in the morning paper." Banks had picked up a copy of *The Independent* at Schiphol Airport and had seen a full report on the arrest and confession of Mark Wood for the murder of Jason Fox. Including a quote from Riddle to the effect that "Fox was killed by a friend of his in a dispute after several drinks. While alcohol was certainly a factor, race was not, I am very pleased to say." Banks didn't believe it for a moment. "But I'm not sure that's how it happened," he went on.

"Oh," said Riddle. "You're not sure that's how it happened, aren't you? Maybe if you'd been here doing your job you'd have a better idea about what's going on. Well, let me tell you Banks, that is *exactly* how it happened. Your fellow officers got a confession out of Mark Wood. While you were off cruising the red-light district, no doubt."

Banks had to admit, that did hit a little too close to home. "In all fairness, sir—"

Riddle stood up and went to lean on the filing cabinet, checking for dust first. "Don't talk to me about fairness, Banks. I've been as fair with you as I can be. I've given you more latitude, more freedom to tilt at your own various windmills than I've allowed any man under my direct command. And what have you done with that freedom? You've abused it, that's what you've done. Day trips to Leeds to buy classical records and meet your bit on the side, and now a weekend in Amsterdam in the middle of a major investigation. What do you have to say?"

"If you'll allow me to get a word in, sir," Banks said calmly. "In the first place, my trip was *entirely* case related, and in the second case you haven't *solved* the Jason Fox case."

Riddle's pate went on red alert. "And I'm telling you the case is solved. *Telling* you, Banks."

"But—"

"And who paid for this trip to Amsterdam, might I ask?"

Shit. If Banks told him it was the Met, Riddle either wouldn't believe him, or he'd be on the phone trying to find out exactly who was behind it, setting off alarms like a mad cow walking through a Cambodian minefield. Besides, Dirty Dick Burgess, the only one who could really vouch for him apart from Craig, was on holiday "somewhere tropical."

"I can't say, sir," he said.

"I trust you didn't pay for it yourself, then, out of your own pocket?"

"No, sir."

"I thought not. And your wife? Did she accompany you on this mysterious case-related mission?"

"No, sir."

"Your mistress, perhaps? Or were you out there shagging the local girls?"

Banks stood up, his irritation growing. "Look, sir, I'm beginning to resent these implications. You might be my senior officer, but I don't have to put up with personal abuse from you."

Riddle stepped forward, chin jutting like the prow of a ship. "You'll put up with whatever I dish out, laddie, and right now I'm dishing out a suspension."

"You're what?"

"You heard me, Banks. I'm suspending you from your duties pending a disciplinary hearing into your activities."

"You can't do that."

"Yes, I bloody well can. Read the regulations. I think skiving off for a long weekend during an important investigation is grounds enough for an enquiry. Dereliction of duty. For crying out loud, man, you're a DCI. You're supposed to set an example."

Banks sat down again, a leaden weight in his chest. "I see. This is official, then?"

"Official as it gets."

Banks could hardly believe what he was hearing. Anger burned inside him. Red behind his eyes. Everything was fucked. His marriage. Now his job. For some reason, this idiot had decided to persecute him. It just didn't matter to Riddle that there might still be unanswered questions in the Jason Fox case; he'd put his blinkers on and he wouldn't take them off. No doubt pleasing the Muslim community *and* the general populace simultaneously.

"So that's it, then?" he said. "I'm free to go?"

"Yes. In fact, I order you to go." Riddle grinned. "You're suspended, Banks."

"Right. I can tell you've been looking forward to saying those words for some time."

Riddle nodded. "Oh, yes."

Banks got up, slipped his cigarettes in his top pocket and picked his jacket up from the coat-rack. Next he picked up his briefcase but paused in front of Riddle and laid it down on the desk again on his way to the door. "Is that your last word on the subject, sir?" he asked.

"Yes."

Banks nodded. Then he swung his arm back as far as it would go and hit Riddle hard, right in the mouth. Riddle staggered back against the flimsy desk and slid to the floor. Which was where he lay, shaking his head and wiping blood from his mouth with the back of his hand as Banks said, "And I've been looking forward to that, too, sir. Goodbye." Then he left the station, his knuckles aching and bleeding.

II

The minute Susan heard raised voices arguing about Amsterdam, she tiptoed into the corridor like a sneaky schoolgirl to listen. Then she heard a loud crash, and saw Banks stalk out of his office and out of the building through the fire-exit, without even glancing in her direction.

The chief constable hadn't left, though. Puzzled, Susan crossed the corridor and pushed Banks's office door open. Then she just stood there. Chief Constable Riddle was getting up from the floor, brushing dust from his uniform and dabbing his mouth with a blood-soaked handkerchief.

He saw her standing in the doorway, pointed and said, "Get back to your office, DC Gay. Nothing happened, you saw nothing, do you understand?"

"Yes, sir ... Er ... what about DCI Banks ... ?"

"DCI Banks is under suspension."

Susan's jaw dropped.

"Back to your office," Riddle said again. She noticed one of his front teeth was chipped. "And remember: If word of this gets out, I'll know exactly where it came from, and your career won't be worth two penn'orth of shit, sergeant's exam or no sergeant's exam."

"Yes, sir."

Back in her office, Susan leaned on her desk, took a deep breath and tried to collect the thoughts that were suddenly spinning in her mind, out of control. Had she really just seen Jimmy Riddle getting up off the floor in Banks's office, wiping blood from his mouth? Yes, she had. Was that why Banks had got suspended?

But Riddle wanted her to keep it quiet, so there had to be another reason. He could have Banks kicked off the force for assaulting a senior officer, but it would have to be made public then.

She could understand Riddle's desire for silence easily enough—he would look like a real wimp if he publicly accused one of his DCIs of assault. After all, as Susan well knew, the police force was still very much a man's world, and physical prowess was important to men. Riddle would feel humiliated by what had just happened; it would be a blow to his macho ego. The last thing he'd want known was that Banks, four or five inches shorter than him and slighter in build, had knocked him down. If that got out, people all over the region would be sniggering at him behind his back even more than they did now.

So he must have suspended Banks for some other reason.

Amsterdam? Was that it?

And then she realized something. At first, it was just a vague sense of apprehension, then the tumblers fell into position, one inexorably after the other. Then came the final click, and the door opened.

Susan looked at her watch. Just after five.

First, she drove the short distance to Banks's house. As she drove, she chewed on her lip wondering if she were doing the right thing. She wished Superintendent Gristhorpe were here to advise her, but he'd gone off to teach a two-week course at Bramshill that morning. She didn't even know what she was going to say to Banks. After all, he was her senior officer. What could she, a mere DC, do to help?

But there were things she wanted to know. She had worked with Banks for several years now and had come to know his moods pretty well. She had seen him angry, sad, hurt and frustrated, but she had never seen him like this. Nor would she ever have thought him the kind of person to do something as stupid and impulsive as punching Jimmy Riddle.

Call it woman's intuition, a term she had a lot more respect for than she would ever care to admit in front of a roomful of male colleagues, but she felt something was seriously wrong. And it wasn't only to do with Riddle. All she could think of was that something had happened in Amsterdam. But what?

She walked up the front path to Banks's semi. Standing on the doorstep, she took a deep breath, counted to three, and rang the bell.

Nothing happened.

She rang again.

Still nothing.

She waited a few minutes more, tried knocking and ringing the bell. Still nothing. Where the hell was he? Looking around, she couldn't see his car.

She dashed down the path and jumped back in her Golf. She was starting to feel angry now, not a good emotional state for driving, but at least anger would sustain her all the way and help her do what she had to. She headed out of town through the darkening countryside at a dangerous speed, crossed over the A1 and headed south-east, then hurtled through the dark, through villages where families were just settling down to tea and an evening with the telly.

Soon she was on the outskirts of Northallerton, pulling up outside Gavin's modest terrace house.

Gavin answered on the first ring and smiled when he saw Susan. "Come in," he said, standing aside. "This is an unexpected pleasure."

Susan walked into the hall and Gavin leaned forward to plant a kiss on her cheek. She jerked back and slapped him hard across the face. Gavin staggered back a step or two. "You bastard," Susan said. "You bastard. How could you do it?"

Gavin looked surprised. He held his hand to the reddening weal on his cheek. "Do what? What the hell did you do that for?"

"You know why."

"No, I don't. Look, take your coat off and come through. Then you can tell me what you're on about."

Susan followed him into the living-room but she didn't take her coat off. "I won't be stopping," she said. "I'll just say what I have to say and go."

Gavin nodded. He leaned against the wall with his arms folded. He was wearing tartan slippers, Susan noticed, and looked ridiculous. Somehow, that helped.

"All right," he said. "I'm listening. And it'd better be good after what you just did to me."

"Oh, it's good all right," Susan said. "It took me a while. I don't know. Maybe I'm thick, maybe I'm a fool, but I worked it out in the end."

"Well, you are supposed to be a detective after all. But, look, I still don't know what you're talking about. Will you back up a little and explain?"

Susan shook her head. "You're so damn smooth, aren't you, Gavin? You used me. That's what I mean."

"How did I use you? I thought you enjoyed—"

"I'm not talking about sex. I'm talking about information. All the time we were going out together, all the things I told you in private, all the station gossip. You passed it all on to Jimmy Riddle, didn't you? Even what I told you in bed on Saturday."

"I don't know what you're talking about."

But he looked away from her eyes, down at his slippers. Susan had seen that guilty gesture in enough criminals to know it meant Gavin was lying. "Yes, you bloody well do," she went on. "How else could Riddle have known everything he did? I should have twigged much earlier, then maybe none of this would have happened."

"What?"

"Riddle suspended Banks this afternoon. Don't tell me you didn't know."

Gavin shrugged. "Oh, that. Well, it's the chief constable's pre—"

"Don't give me that crap. You got me to talk about Banks in private. Shop talk. It was me who told you he liked to call at the Classical Record Shop whenever he had to go to Leeds. When Riddle mentioned that to me a few days ago, I didn't even think at the time about where he might have got it from. It was me who told you about Pamela Jeffreys, too, the violist involved in that case a couple of years ago, the one he felt guilty about. And on Saturday night, in bed, I told you Banks was in Amsterdam. My fault for being such a fool. Blame it on the wine. But you ... you ... You're beneath contempt."

"Okay," said Gavin, gazing at her coolly. "So the chief constable wanted to be informed about what was going on at Eastvale. So what? He's like that. Unlike his predecessor, he likes to be in the know. Hands on. It's easy for you. *You* don't have to work close to him, day in, day out, do you?" He pointed his thumb at his chest. "I do. And we all have our careers to consider, don't we? What's so wrong with that?"

Susan could hardly believe what she was hearing, even though it was exactly what she had expected. "So you admit it? Just like that? You used me to spy on my colleagues?"

"Well, seeing as you have the evidence, there's not a lot else I can say, is there? I can hardly deny it. Yes. *Mea culpa.*"

"I don't understand, Gavin. How could you do that?"

Gavin shrugged. "I never thought it would come to anything like this," he said. "It was only little titbits, nothing important. Like I said, Riddle just wanted to be kept informed. But that wasn't why I asked you out in the first place. That only came later. When he found out I was going out with you. And believe me, I didn't tell him. He's got quite a network, has Riddle." He shrugged. "I didn't really think it would do any harm."

"Informed about Eastvale in general or DCI Banks in particular?"

Gavin shifted from foot to foot. "Well, he *did* ask about Banks in particular. He never really approved of Banks, you know. Thought he was a bit of a maverick, if truth be told."

"I know that," said Susan. "He never liked him. Right from the start. I remember the Deborah Harrison case, when Banks upset some of Riddle's important friends. Riddle was just looking for something to use against him. And you used me to get it for him. That's what I can't forgive."

"Like I said, I didn't really think I was doing anything—"

"Oh, stuff it, Gavin. I'm not interested in your excuses. You used me to scupper Banks's career, and that's all I care about."

"If that's how you want to see it."

"Is there any other way?"

"I take it things are over between us, then?"

Susan could only look at him and shake her head. Then she turned to leave.

"What is it, Susan?" Gavin called after her. "Fancy him yourself, do you? You should listen to the way you talk about him. Like a lovesick teenager. Believe me, it wasn't very difficult to get you talking about him. The hardest thing was getting you to stop. Even in bed."

Susan slammed the door behind her and got back in her car. She couldn't move, couldn't even turn the key in the ignition. All she could do was sit there, hands gripping the steering-wheel, shaking. She took deep breaths.

And then Susan did something she hardly ever did, something she always hated herself for when it happened. She started to cry. Bloody great convulsive sobs. Because, fuck it, she said to herself, Gavin was right. She had never admitted it, but she had known it for ages. It *was* Banks she cared about; it *was* Banks she fancied. And, dammit, he was a married man, he was her senior officer, and he wouldn't look at her that way in a month of Sundays. She was just another stupid girl in love with her boss and there was no way she could stay in Eastvale now, not after this.

III

It had long since turned dark when Banks got home. For hours, it seemed, he had driven around the Dales, hardly noticing where he was, or what music kept repeating on the cassette player. His knuckles still hurt, but the shaking inside had stopped. Had he really done it? Punched Jimmy Riddle? He realized he had, and he also realized that at the moment the anger had burst out of him, it was Sandra he had been thinking of, not the bloody job.

The house was quiet and empty. A different quality of silence and emptiness than he had ever felt there before. First, he had a look around to see if anything was missing. Sandra hadn't taken very much. Most of her clothes were still in the wardrobe, the scent of her hair still lingered on the pillows, and her photograph of the misty sunset above Hawes still hung over the fireplace in the living-room.

It made him think how only on Sunday, yesterday, he had wandered the Amsterdam museums in the rain, a pilgrim marvelling at Rembrandt's *The Night Watch* in the Rijksmuseum, unsettled by *Crows in the Wheatfield* in the Van Gogh Museum, and, finally, elated by the bright, whimsical Chagalls in the Stedelijk Museum.

All the while thinking how Sandra would have loved it, and how he would like to treat her to a visit one weekend in spring.

But Sandra was gone.

He noticed the red light blinking on the telephone answering machine. Thinking it might be Sandra, he got up and pressed the replay button. One call was Vic Manson, two were hang-ups, but the next four were from Tracy. On the last one, she said, "Dad, are you there? It's Sunday now. I've been trying to ring you all weekend. I'm worried about you. If you *are* there, please answer. I talked to Mummy and she told me what happened. I'm so sorry. I love you, Daddy. Please give me a ring."

Banks stood by the phone for a moment, head in his hands, tears burning in his eyes. Then he did what any reasonable man would do in his situation. He cranked Mozart's *Requiem* up as loud as he could bear it and got rat-arse drunk.

TWELVE

I

When Banks stirred on the sofa at about four o'clock in the morning, Mozart's *Requiem* was still playing on "repeat." And a more fitting piece of music he couldn't imagine. It was playing loudly, too, and he was surprised that none of his neighbours had called the police. Still, he *was* the police. Or used to be.

Wishing he were still unconscious, he groaned, rubbed his stubble, rolled off the sofa and put some coffee on, turning the volume down on the stereo as he went. Then he stumbled upstairs and swallowed a handful of aspirins, washed down with two glasses of water to irrigate his dehydrated cells.

Back downstairs, as the coffee dripped through the filter with frustrating slowness, he surveyed the damage: twelve cigarette ends in the ashtray; no burns on the sofa or carpet; about two fingers of Laphroaig left. If he were going to keep up this rate of drinking he would have to start buying cheaper Scotch. Still, it could have been a lot worse, he concluded, especially as he remembered the bottle had only been about three-quarters full when he started.

When the coffee was ready, he decided to switch from the *Requiem* to the C minor mass, something to bring a little more light and hope into his bleak world, then he tried to collect his thoughts.

He had punched Jimmy Riddle; that was the first memory to came back. And he had skinned knuckles to prove it. Well, that had been a stupid thing to do, he realized now, and it had also probably put the mockers on his career.

Jobless, then. Also wifeless and hung over. At least the hangover would go away. It *could* be worse, couldn't it? Yes it could, he realized. He could have been diagnosed with a terminal illness. He racked his brains to see if that had, in fact, happened, but could find no memory of it. It would probably happen today the way his lungs felt after all those cigarettes.

So what was he going to do? Become a private eye? Enter a monastery? Get a job with some security outfit? Or should he just carry on and solve the Jason Fox case on his own to show up the police, run rings around Jimmy Riddle, just like Sherlock Holmes did around Inspector Lestrade? Alan Banks, Consulting Detective. Had a nice ring to it.

He poured himself a cup of black coffee and flopped back on the sofa. Looking at the misty Hawes sunset over the fireplace, for some reason he remembered Sandra telling him on Thursday that there *might have been* somebody else, but there wasn't. Remembered the faraway look in her eyes when she said it.

And that made him angry. He pictured Sandra with some strapping, bearded young artist, standing in the wind on the moors doing a Cathy and Heathcliff, looking lovingly into each other's eyes and exercising restraint. "No, my darling, we *mustn't*. There's too much at stake. Think of the children." Grand passion collides with family values and moral responsibility. It was a scene from a cheap romance. But all the same, it made Banks clench his jaw. What *might* have been. And, come to think of it, he only had her word for it that she hadn't left him to run off with someone else, someone she would only take up with publicly after a "decent" interval.

Well, two could play at that game. Banks had had his chances at infidelity in the past, too, but he hadn't taken them. He hadn't romanticized them, either. He thought especially of Jenny Fuller. There had been a time, some years ago, when something might have blossomed between them. Was it too late now? Probably. Jenny seemed to spend most of her time teaching in America these days, and she had a steady boyfriend over there. Then there was Pamela Jeffreys, the one Riddle thought was his mistress. Banks hadn't slept with Pamela, either, but it was an appealing thought.

So many choices. So many possibilities. Then why did he feel so bloody miserable and empty? Because, he concluded, none of them were what he wanted. What he wanted, when it came right down to it, was his job back, Sandra back and his hangover gone. Perhaps if he played a country-and-western song backwards ... ? He couldn't even do that, hating country-and-western the way he did. Still, taking stock of himself, he realized that, depressed as he was, he felt calmer now than when he was stuck at the airport yesterday contemplating his return home. Thumping Jimmy Riddle probably had something to do with that.

After the first cup of coffee, he realized he was hungry. He hadn't eaten anything since that snack on the plane, a million years ago now. Searching through the remnants in the fridge, he managed to throw together three rashers of streaky bacon and two eggs only a week past their sell-by date. That would have to do. The one remaining slice of bread was a little stale, but it hadn't turned green yet, and it would fry up nicely in the bacon fat. Cholesterol special. So what?

As he fried his breakfast, Banks remembered Tracy's messages. He would have to ring her today and put her mind at rest. Should he explain to her about losing his job, too? Best not, yet, he decided. It was bad enough his daughter should suddenly find herself the child of a broken marriage the minute she flew the coop, let alone the child of a disgraced copper. There would be time enough for that later. He would have to phone Brian in Portsmouth, too, and his own parents. They would all be upset.

Suddenly, the day ahead seemed full of things to do. None of them pleasant. The only bright spot was that he wouldn't have to worry about money for a while; the suspension was *with* pay. And Jimmy Riddle couldn't do a thing about that until *after* a disciplinary hearing.

He cursed as he broke an egg while lifting it onto the plate and yolk ran all over the counter. It would have to do. No more left. Carefully, he used the spatula to lift the one unbroken egg onto the fried bread, then patted the bacon with some kitchen roll to remove the excess grease and tucked in. When he'd finished, he poured another cup of coffee and lit a cigarette.

It was still just past five in the morning, and he hadn't a clue what to do to keep himself occupied until it was a decent time to start phoning people. Sleep was out of the question now, and he knew he couldn't possibly concentrate on reading a book or listening to music. He needed something completely mindless, something to keep his thoughts off his problems for a few hours. Like television.

But there was nothing on television at that time apart from something educational on BBC2 and a studio discussion on ITV, so he started sorting through the video collection, odds and sods he'd picked up over the years. Finally, he found one that would do. It was still in its cellophane wrapper, so someone must have bought him it as a present and he'd forgotten he had it.

Bridge on the River Kwai. Perfect. He remembered his dad taking him to see a revival of it at the Gaumont when he was about twelve. It would take him back to those days, when life was simple, and right at the moment he would have given anything on earth to be that innocent twelve-year-old again, grabbing his father's hand when Jack Hawkins burned leeches off with a cigarette, thrilling at the way all the birds flew up and the pool turned red with blood when they ambushed the Japanese patrol, and biting his nails to the quick as Alec Guinness made his final, dying, staggering way to the dynamite plunger. Yes, The *Bridge on the River Kwai* might just keep the dark hounds of depression at bay for another couple of hours, until daylight came.

II

Susan didn't know where she was going when she left the station around eleven o'clock that morning, only that she had to get out of the office for a while. Let Riddle suspend her, too, if he found out.

The next thing she knew she found herself on Castle Walk looking out over the formal gardens and the river, all framed in the branches of the beeches. It was the same view she'd had from the bistro with Gavin on Saturday night. Just thinking about that night made her burn with shame and rage.

Across the Swain, a belt of trees called The Green partially obscured the East Side Estate, but she could still make out a few of the light red brick terraces and maisonettes, and the three

twelve-storey blocks of flats—a crime wave in themselves—
poked their ugly heads way above the trees. Beyond the estate
and the railway tracks were the chocolate factory and a few old
warehouses, corrugated metal roofs glinting in the sun. A local
diesel rattled by and blew its horn.

She would have to leave Eastvale; there was no doubt about
that. Now that she had admitted her feelings to herself, she could
no longer work with Banks. She couldn't trust herself not to act like
a love-struck schoolgirl; nor could she go running off in tears every
time she saw him, either. And she *would* have to see him. He might
be suspended for the moment, but a disciplinary hearing would
probably reinstate him, she thought.

It also hadn't taken her long to work out that, after what she had
witnessed yesterday, Jimmy Riddle would want her as far away from
North Yorkshire as possible. At least that could be easily accom-
plished without raising any eyebrows.

Although it *did* happen on occasion, it was rare for a DC to be
promoted straight to the rank of detective sergeant within the same
station. The most likely scenario was a transfer and at least a year
back in uniform. This was supposed to be a safeguard against
corruption: senior officers offering promotion in exchange for falsified evidence.

At first, Susan had hoped the chief constable would approve her
request to stay. But being promoted within Eastvale CID didn't
matter to her now. She had to leave. And the farther away, the
better. Devon and Cornwall, maybe. She had fond memories of
childhood holidays in that part of the world: St Ives, Torquay,
Polperro.

How could she have been so stupid? she asked herself again. In
cafés, pubs and in bed she had chatted away to Gavin about Banks
and his idiosyncrasies, his love of music, his guilt over the injuries
to Pamela Jeffreys, and Gavin had turned it over to Jimmy Riddle,
who had twisted and perverted it beyond all recognition. If anyone
deserved to be suspended, it was Riddle and Gavin. Fat chance.

An old woman walking a dog passed Susan on the path and said
hello. After they had gone by, Susan paused a moment to sit on a
bench. She was facing north now and to her left she could see the

square Norman church tower, the bus station and the glass and concrete Swainsdale Centre. Straight ahead was the pre-Roman site in the distance, not much more than a couple of bumps in the grassland down by the river.

Even though there wasn't a great deal to do around the station in the aftermath of the Jason Fox case, Susan didn't think she could honestly stay away too long. After all, a call might come in, something important, and if she missed it she'd have to explain why.

And she remembered something else she had overheard yesterday: Banks expressing doubts about the solution. Though she couldn't quite put her finger on exactly what, there were things about Mark Wood's confession that rang false with her, too. Maybe she should have a look over the reports again. So with a sigh, she stood up and headed back around Castle Walk.

As she went up the stairs to CID, she told herself she would have to get a grip, lock up her feelings, keep them separate and behave like a professional. She could do it; she'd done it before. On some level, being a woman in a man's world, she did it all the time. She would also have to work out how to deal with Banks's misplaced trust in her. Should she tell him about Gavin? Could she really do that?

III

Shortly after six o'clock that evening, Banks sat in Leeds Parish Church. Though not much to look at from the outside, the interior had recently been restored to all its Victorian Gothic glory, like the Town Hall, all stained glass, dark, polished wood and high arches.

He wasn't there because his troubles had driven him to religion. In fact, he was listening to a rehearsal of Vivaldi's *Gloria* by the St Peter's Singers and Chamber Orchestra. It certainly wasn't where he had expected to be, or what he had expected to be doing, when he woke up on the sofa that morning.

Tracy had rung him much earlier than he would have thought of ringing her. At least he was feeling a bit more human by then. She was full of concern, naturally, and he tried to assure her that he would be okay. Tracy told him she was going down to Croydon for a while to stay with her mother and grandparents, but she assured him she wasn't taking sides. He told her to go, take care of her mother; he'd see her when she came back. Reluctantly, she hung up. Maybe he hadn't lost Tracy after all.

He felt the need to get out of Eastvale around noon, so he phoned Pamela Jeffreys. As it turned out, she had a rehearsal that evening, but Banks was welcome to attend. She was surprised to hear from him and said she would be delighted to see him. Someone pleased to see him? Music to his ears.

He drove to Leeds in plenty of time to browse the city centre record shops first. A couple of CDs would be paltry compensation for the miserable time he'd had lately, but they would be better than nothing. Like the toy soldier his mother always used to buy him after he'd been to the dentist's.

By half past six, the conductor seemed frustrated by the soprano section's inability to enter on time, so he ended the rehearsal early. Pamela packed away her viola, grabbed her jacket and walked towards Banks. She was wearing black leggings and a baggy black velvet top, belted at the waist, with a scoop neckline which plunged just above the curve of her breasts. Her long raven hair hung over her shoulders and the diamond stud in her right nostril glittered in the side-lighting. Her skin was the colour of burnished gold, her eyes almond in shape and colour, and her finely drawn red lips revealed straight white teeth when she smiled. Many of them were crowned, Banks knew. Looking at her now, he found it hard to believe that only a couple of years ago she had been lying in a hospital bed covered in bandages wondering if she would ever be able to play again.

Banks gave her a peck on the cheek. She smelled of jasmine. "Thank you for inviting me," he said. "Wouldn't have missed it for the world."

She turned up her nose. "We were terrible. But thanks anyway. And it's nice to see you, stranger."

"Sorry I couldn't stick around after *The Pearl Fishers*," Banks said.

"That's okay. I was knackered anyway. Long day. What did you think?"

"Wonderful."

She grinned. "For once, you're right. Everything seemed to fit together that night. Sometimes it just does that, you know, and nobody knows why."

Banks gestured around the church. "I'm surprised you have time for this."

"St Peter's? Oh, if the schedules work out all right, I can do it. I need all the practice I can get. I've been recording the Walton viola concerto, too, with the orchestra. For Naxos. Finally the viola's getting some of the respect it deserves."

"You were the soloist?"

She slapped his arm. "No. Not me, you idiot. I'm not *that* good. The soloist was Lars Anders Tomter. He's *very* good."

"I'm really glad it's all working out for you, anyway."

Pamela smiled and made a mock curtsy. "Thank you, kind sir. So, where now?"

Banks looked at his watch. "I know it's a bit early, but how about dinner?"

"Fine with me. I'm starving."

"Curry?"

Pamela laughed. "Just because I'm Bangladeshi, it doesn't mean I eat nothing but curry, you know."

Banks held his hands out. "Whatever, then. Brasserie 44?"

"No, not there," Pamela said. "It's far too expensive. There's a new pizza place up Headingley, just off North Lane. I've heard it's pretty good."

"Pizza it is, then. I'm parked just over in The Calls."

"You can have curry if you really want."

Banks shook his head, and they walked through the dimly lit, cobbled backstreets to the car. They were in the oldest part of Leeds, and the most recent to be redeveloped. Most of the eighteenth- and nineteenth-century warehouses by the River Aire had been derelict for years until the civic-pride restoration schemes of the eighties. Now that Leeds was a boom-town, they were tourist attractions, full of trendy new restaurants, usually located on something called a "wharf," the kind of word nobody there would have used twenty years ago. Canary Wharf had a lot more to answer for than vanished fortunes, Banks thought.

"It's not that I think you eat curry all the time because you're Asian," he said. "It's just that there isn't a decent curry place in Eastvale. Well, there *is* one, but I think I might be *persona non grata* there at the moment. Anyway, pizza sounds great."

"What did you get?" Pamela asked as she got into the Cavalier and picked up the HMV package from the passenger seat.

"Have a look," said Banks, as he set off and negotiated the one-way streets of the city centre.

"*The Beatles Anthology?* I never would have taken you for a Beatles fan."

Banks smiled. "It's pure nostalgia. I used to listen to Brian Matthew do 'Saturday Club' when I was a kid. If I remember rightly, it came on right after Uncle Mac's 'Children's Favourites,' and by the age of thirteen I'd got sick to death of 'Sparky and the Magic Piano,' 'Little Green Man' and 'Big Rock Candy Mountain.'"

Pamela laughed. "Before my time. Besides, my mum and dad wouldn't let me listen to pop music."

"Didn't you rebel?"

"I did manage to sneak a little John Peel under the bedclothes once in a while."

"I hope you're speaking metaphorically." Banks drove past St Michael's church and The Original Oak, just opposite. The street-lights were on, and there were plenty of people about, students for the most part. A little farther on, he came to the junction with North Lane, an enclave of cafés, pubs and bookshops.

"Here," said Pamela, pointing. Banks managed to find a parking spot, and they walked around the corner into the restaurant. The familiar pizza smells of olive oil, tomato sauce, oregano and fresh-baked dough greeted them. The restaurant was lively and noisy, but they only had to wait at the bar for a couple of minutes before they got a tiny table for two in the back. It wasn't a great spot, too close to the toilets and the waiters' route to and from the kitchen, but at least it was in the smoking section. After a while, sipping the one glass of red wine he was allowing himself that evening, and smoking one of the duty-free Silk Cuts he'd picked up at Schiphol, Banks hardly noticed the bustle or the volume level any more.

"So, have you got a boyfriend yet?" he asked when they were settled.

Pamela frowned. "Too busy," she said. "Besides, I'm not sure I trust myself to get involved again. Not just yet. How's your wife? Sandra, isn't it?"

"Yes. She's fine."

After a while of small-talk, their pizzas came—Banks's marinara and Pamela's funghi.

"How's life at the cop shop?" Pamela asked between mouthfuls.

"I wouldn't know," said Banks. "I've been suspended from duty."

He hadn't intended to tell her, certainly not with such abruptness, but it had come out before he could stop it. He couldn't seem to hold back *everything*. In a way, he was glad he'd said it because he had to confide in someone. Her eyes opened wide. As soon as she had swallowed her food, she said, "What? Good Lord, why?"

As best he could, he told her about the Jason Fox case, and about thumping Jimmy Riddle.

"Aren't you still angry?" she asked when he'd finished.

Banks sipped some wine and watched Pamela wipe a little pizza sauce from her chin. The people at the next table left. The waiter picked up the money and began to clean up after them. "Not really angry," Banks said. "A bit, perhaps, but not a lot. Not any more."

"What, then?"

"Disappointed."

"With what?"

"Myself mostly. For being too stupid not to see it coming. And for thumping Riddle."

"I can't say I blame you, from what you've told me."

"Oh, Riddle's an arsehole, no doubt about it. He even suggested that I took *you* to Amsterdam with me."

"Me? But why?"

"He thinks you're my mistress."

Pamela almost choked on a mouthful of pizza. Banks didn't feel particularly flattered. Afterwards, he couldn't tell if she were blushing or just red in the face from coughing. "Come again," she managed finally, patting her chest.

"It's true. He thinks I've got a mistress in Leeds and that's why I keep making up excuses to come here."

"But how could he know? I mean ..."

"I know what you mean. Don't ask me." Banks smiled, felt his heart skip, but went on anyway, aiming for a light tone. "It didn't seem like such a bad idea."

Pamela looked down. He could see he'd embarrassed her. "I'm sorry," he said. "That was supposed to be a compliment."

"I know what it was supposed to be," Pamela said. Then she smiled. "Don't worry. I won't hold it against you."

Please do, he almost said, but managed to stop himself in time. He wondered if she would take him home with her if he told her that he and Sandra had split up. They ate some more pizza in silence, then Pamela shook her head slowly and said, "It just sounds so unfair."

"Fairness has nothing to do with it." Banks pushed his plate aside and lit a cigarette. "Oh, sorry," he said, looking at the small slice left on Pamela's plate.

"That's all right. I'm full." She pushed hers aside, too. "This Neville Motcombe you mentioned, isn't he the bloke who was interviewed in the *Yorkshire Post* this weekend? Something to do with neo-Nazis disrupting a funeral?"

"That's the one."

"Didn't someone die there?"

"Yes," said Banks. "Frank Hepplethwaite. I knew him slightly."

"Oh, I'm sorry."

"It's okay. We weren't close friends or anything. It's just that I liked him, and I think, of anyone, he's the real victim in this whole mess. Tell me something, have you ever come across Motcombe in any other context?"

"What, you mean with me being the sort of person this Albion League might target?"

"Partly. Yes."

She shook her head. "Not really. I've been lucky, I suppose. Oh, I've been insulted in the street and stuff. You know, called a Paki bitch or a Paki slut. It's always 'Paki.' Can't they think of anything else but that?"

Banks smiled. "That's part of their problem. Severely limited thinking. No originality."

"I suppose so. I'm not saying it doesn't bother me when it happens. It does. It upsets me. But you get used to it. I mean, it starts not to surprise you as much, so you don't get shocked by it as easily. But it still hurts. Every time. Like hot needles being stuck through your skin. Sometimes it's just the way people look at you. Am I making any sense?"

"Perfect."

"I remember once when I was a kid back in Shipley—oh, this must have been in the seventies, twenty years ago now—and I was walking back from my aunt's house with my mum and dad. We walked around this corner and there was a gang of skinheads. They surrounded us and started calling out racist insults and shoving us. There were about ten of them. There was nothing we could do. I was terrified. I think we all were. But my dad stood up to them, called them cowards and shoved them right back. At first they just laughed but then they started to get worked up and I could tell they were getting ready to really hurt us. My mother was screaming and I was crying and they got my dad on the ground and started kicking him ..." She trailed off and shook her head at the memory.

"What happened?"

Pamela looked up and smiled through her tears. "Would you believe it, a police car came by and they ran off? A bloody police car. About the only time the police have ever been there when I've needed them. Must have been a miracle."

They both laughed. The waiter came by and took their plates.

"What now?" Pamela asked, after she'd wiped her eyes from the mingled tears of humiliation and laughter.

"Coffee? Dessert?"

She hit him on the arm again. "I don't mean that, idiot. I mean, you. Your future."

"Looks bleak. I'd rather concentrate on dessert."

"Just a cappuccino for me."

Banks ordered two cappuccinos and lit another cigarette.

"You're smoking too much," Pamela said.

"I know. And just when I'd managed to cut down."

"Anyway, you haven't answered my question."

"What question was that?"

"You know quite well. Your future. What are you going to do?"

Banks shook his head. "I don't know yet. It's too early to say."

"Well surely when this chief constable person has done his investigation, he'll have to reinstate you?"

"I doubt it. Even if a disciplinary hearing really does reinstate me, it doesn't matter."

"Why not?"

"Think about it," said Banks. "I hit the chief constable. Even if he does keep that just between the two of us, it still means I can't work with him any more. He'd find ways to make my life a living hell."

"I understand it might make things difficult."

"Difficult? It was *difficult* before all this. After ..." He shrugged. "Impossible, more like."

The restaurant was full of students now. They looked like an artsy, literary crowd, all talking excitedly about the latest music, arguing loudly about books and philosophy. They made Banks feel old, made him feel he had wasted his life. A waiter passed by carrying plates, leaving a trail of garlic and basil smells.

"But you can get a job somewhere else," Pamela said. "I mean as a policeman. In a different region. Can't you?"

"I suppose so. I don't mean to be negative, Pamela, I just haven't thought that far ahead yet."

"I understand." She leaned forward and put her hand on his. Candlelight glittered in her diamond stud, made shadows of burnished gold and lit the soft down between her breasts.

Banks swallowed and felt his excitement rise. He wanted to take her home and lick every inch of her golden skin. Or did he? There would be consequences, confidences shared, a *relationship*. He didn't think he could handle anything like that right now.

Pamela sat back and flipped a long tress of hair over her shoulder with the back of her hand. "What about this case you were working on?" she asked. "You seemed to imply that it's not over."

"Everyone thinks it is."

"And you?"

Banks shrugged.

She toyed with a gold bracelet on her arm. "Look, Alan, this person you talked about earlier. Mark Wood. *Did* he do it?"

"I don't know. He *might* have done. But not, I don't think, the way he said he did, or for the reason he claimed."

"Does it matter?"

"Yes. It could mean the difference between manslaughter and murder. And if someone else was behind it, say Neville Motcombe, I'd hate to see him get away with it while Mark Wood takes the fall alone."

"If you were still on the force, would you be working on this case?"

"Probably not. The chief constable's got his confession. Everybody's happy. Case closed."

"But you're not on the force."

"That's right."

"So that means you *can* still work on it if you want."

Banks smiled and shook his head. "What impeccable logic. But I don't think so. I can't do it, Pamela. I'm sorry. It's over."

Pamela sat back and studied him for a moment. He reached for another cigarette, thought twice about it, then lit up anyway.

"Remember when I was hurt?" she said.

"Yes."

"And thought I might never play again?"

Banks nodded.

"Well, if I'd taken your negative attitude, I wouldn't have played again. And, believe me, there were times when giving up would have been the easiest thing in the world. But you helped me then. You encouraged me. You helped give me some strength and courage when I was at my lowest. I'd never had a friend like ... someone who didn't want ..." She turned away for a moment. When she looked back, her eyes were deeply serious and intense, glistening with tears. "And now you're giving up. Just like that. I don't believe it. Not you."

"What else can I do?"

"You can follow up on your ideas. On your own."

"But how? I don't have the resources, for a start."

"Someone will help you. You've still got friends there, in the department, haven't you?"

"I hope so."

"Well, then?"

"I don't know. Maybe you're right." Banks gestured for the waiter and paid, waving aside all Pamela's attempts to contribute. "My idea, my treat," he said.

"So you *will* do something? You promise me you won't just sit around at home and mope?"

"Yes, I promise. I'll do something." He scraped his chair back and smiled. "Now, come on. Let me take you home."

THIRTEEN

I

The first thing Banks needed to do, he realized in the cold light of Wednesday morning, was spend a few hours going over *all* the paperwork on the Jason Fox case—especially that which had been generated in his absence. He realized he had missed a lot over the weekend, and there were things he needed to know if he were to make any progress on his own. But how could he get hold of it? Nobody was going to kick him out of Eastvale station, he didn't think, but neither could they let him just walk in and take what he wanted.

There wasn't even a crust of bread left in the house, and he didn't fancy eating Sandra's leftover cottage cheese, so he made do with coffee and Vaughan Williams's "Serenade to Music" for breakfast.

As he let the sensuous music flow over him, he thought about last night. When he had dropped Pamela at her flat, he had half-hoped she would invite him up for a drink, but she just thanked him for the lift, said she was tired and hoped she would see him again soon. He said he would call and drove off with a pang of disappointment about not getting to do something he probably wouldn't have done anyway, even if he had had the chance. But seeing her had been good for him. At least she had persuaded him to keep working on the case.

When the music finished, he picked up the phone and called Sandra in Croydon. He had been thinking of calling last night when he got in, but decided it was too late.

Her mother answered.

"Alan? How are you doing?"

"Oh, not so bad, considering. You?"

"About the same. Look, er, I'm really sorry about what's happened. Do you want to speak to Sandra?"

"Please."

"Just a minute."

She sounded embarrassed, Banks thought as he waited. Not surprising, really. What could she say? Her daughter had left her husband and come home to sort herself out. Banks had always got on well with his mother-in-law, and he didn't expect she was going to see him as a monster now, but neither was she going to chat with him about his feelings over the telephone.

"Alan?"

It was Sandra's voice. She sounded tired. He felt the icy hand squeeze his heart. Now he had her on the line, he didn't know what to say. "Yes. I … er … I just wanted to know if you were okay."

"Of course I'm okay. I wish you hadn't called."

"But why?"

"Why do you think? I told you. I need time to work things out. This doesn't help."

"It might help me."

"I don't think so."

"I spent the weekend in Amsterdam."

"You did *what*?"

"In Amsterdam. It was strange. It brought back a lot of memories. Look, do you remember—"

"Alan, why are you telling me this? I don't want to talk about it. Please. Don't do this to me. To us."

"I'm only—"

"I'm going now."

"Don't hang up."

"Alan, I can't deal with this. I'm going now."

"Can I speak to Tracy?"

There was silence for a while, then Tracy came on the phone. "Dad, it's you. I was worried."

"I'm okay, love. Your mother … ?"

"She's upset, Dad. Honest, I don't understand what's happening any more than you do. All I know is Mum's confused and she says she needs some time away."

Banks sighed. "I know that. I shouldn't have called. She's right. Tell her I'm sorry. And tell her I ..."

"Yes?"

"Never mind. Look, does Brian know about all this? I'm sorry, I haven't been very organized. Other than you, I haven't called anyone else."

"It's all right, Dad. You don't have to apologize to me. I suppose it's hard to know what to do when something like this happens. I mean, it's not exactly something you can take a course on, is it?"

God, she sounded suddenly so mature, Banks thought. Much more mature than he felt right now. "Does he?"

"Yes. We talked to him over the weekend."

"How's he taking it?"

"Cool. You know Brian. He's okay."

"When am I going to see you?"

"I'm staying the rest of the week down here. But I'll come up for the weekend if you want."

"You will?" The icy hand relaxed its grip and Banks's heart warmed a little.

"Of course. You know I love you, Dad. I love you both. I told you yesterday, I'm not taking sides. Please don't think because I came down here that I think any less of you."

"I don't. Anyway, the weekend would be great."

Tracy hesitated. "You won't be at work all the time, will you?"

"I ... er ... no, I don't think so," Banks answered. No point telling her about his suspension, he thought. The last thing he needed right now was his daughter feeling even more sorry for him from a distance. "I'll pick you up at the train station. What time does your train get in?"

"It gets back to Leeds mid-afternoon. But I'll need to drop by the residence first. There might be messages. I shouldn't really have taken off like that. I've only just started there."

"I'm sure they'll understand."

"I hope so."

"So why don't I come down to Leeds and pick you up at the student residence? Does that sound like a good idea?"

"That'd be great."

"What time?"

"About six be okay?"

"Fine. And we'll stop at the King's Head in Masham for something to eat on the way back."

"Great. And Dad."

"What?"

"Take care of yourself."

"I will. See you on Friday. Goodbye."

"Goodbye."

Banks hung onto the receiver for a while after the line went dead, then he swallowed, took a deep breath and dialled Brian's number in Portsmouth.

After six rings, a sleepy voice drawled, "Uh. Yeah. Who is it?"

"Did I wake you?"

"Dad?"

"Yes."

"Well, yeah, as a matter of fact you did. But it's all right. I should be getting up anyway. Next lecture's at ten. What's up?"

"I gather you've heard about your mother and me?"

"Yeah. It's too bad. Are you okay?"

"I'm doing fine."

"And Mum?"

"I just talked to her. She's a bit confused right now, but she'll be okay."

"Great. What's going to happen?"

"I don't know. She says she needs some time away."

"She'll come back, Dad, you'll see."

"I hope so."

"Just wait and see. She's just having a mid-life crisis, that's all. She'll get over it."

Kids. Banks couldn't help but smile. "Right. And how are you?"

"Fine."

"How's your classes?"

"All right. Hey, Dad, the band's got a couple of gigs coming up next weekend. Paying gigs." Brian played in a local blues band. Banks thought he was a pretty good guitar player.

"That's great. Just don't let it get in the way of your studies."

"I won't. Don't worry. Gotta go now, or I'll be late for the lecture."

"When are you coming up?"

"I'll try to get up to see you before Christmas. Okay?"

"Fine. If money's a problem, I'll pay for your ticket."

"Thanks, Dad, that'd be a great help. Gotta go."

"Goodbye."

"Bye, Dad. And hang in there."

Hang in there. Like a kid from some American television programme. Banks smiled as he hung up. Well, that was enough family business for the moment, he thought. He knew he should phone his own parents and tell them what had happened, but he couldn't face them yet. They'd be really upset. All these years they had loved Sandra like the daughter they had never had. If anyone was likely to blame him for what had happened, it would be his own parents, not Sandra's, he thought ironically. No, best wait. Maybe Sandra would come up with Tracy at the weekend, then he wouldn't have to tell them anything.

He poured some more coffee and put on the Beatles CD that he'd bought in Leeds yesterday. It was the second of three anthologies, and he'd been thinking of buying it ever since it came out. He went straight to the second disc: out-takes of "Strawberry Fields." His favourite. Singing along, he tidied up a little, but soon started to feel restless and caged. Somehow, it didn't feel right to be home during the daytime, watching neighbours walk back and forth with shopping and the unemployed bank clerk over the street wash his car for the second time in a week.

It was time for action. He picked up the telephone, dialled the station and asked to be put through to DC Susan Gay's extension.

She answered on the second ring.

"Susan?" Banks said. "It's me."

"Sir? Are you ... Is everything all right?"

He was sure she meant it, but her voice sounded tight and cool. "I'm fine. Is Jim there?"

"No, he's out on the East Side Estate. Another break-in."

"The super?"

"Away at Bramshill."

"Good. Sorry, I didn't mean that to sound like it did. Look, I know I shouldn't ask you this, but do you think you could do me a favour?"

"Sir?"

"I need to look over the stuff on the Jason Fox case again. All of it—from the crime-scene photographs to Mark Wood's statements. Can you help?"

"Can I ask why you're still interested, sir?"

"Because I'm not satisfied. Will you help me?"

There was a long pause, then Susan said, "Why don't you come to the station?"

"Is that a good idea?"

"It's pretty quiet here right now. The super's going to be away for a couple of weeks."

"Well, if you're certain. I don't want to get you into trouble." Banks heard a sound like a harsh cough or bark at the other end. "Are you all right?"

"Fine. Frog in my throat. That's all. It's okay, sir. Really it is."

"Are you sure? If Jimmy Riddle turns up—"

"If Jimmy Riddle turns up, I'm buggered. I know that. But there's far too much stuff to photocopy. And that would look suspicious, especially the way you have to account for every penny you spend around here these days. I'll take the risk if you will, sir."

"All right."

"But I'd still like to know why you're not satisfied."

"I'll tell you about it when I know more myself. At the moment it's mostly just a feeling. That and a few bits of information about Mark Wood I picked up in Amsterdam."

"Why don't you just come to the station as soon as you can, then. I'll be waiting." And she hung up hurriedly.

Banks grabbed his coat and left the house. It was another sunny day, with a little high cloud and a slight chilly edge. The leaves had turned a little more than last week, and some were beginning to fall already.

He needed the exercise, so he decided to walk. When he plugged in his earphones and turned the Walkman on, the Roy Harper tape he'd been listening to on the plane home came on in the middle of "McGoohan's Blues." Protest with a mystical edge; pretentiousness with a wink. Well, that would do nicely.

He walked along Market Street past the roundabout, the zebra crossing, garage and school, the local shopping centre with its Safeway supermarket and collection of smaller shops and banks. There was a lot of traffic on Market Street today and the acrid smell of petrol and diesel fumes mingled with dry dusty air.

He paused across from The Jubilee, whose large stone and red-brick frontage curved around the junction of Market Street and Sebastopol Terrace. That was where Jason Fox had spent his last evening on earth before being dispatched to whatever circle of hell was reserved for racists. Why on earth did it matter who had killed him, or why? Banks wondered as he walked on. Wasn't it good enough that he was dead? Was it only Banks's insatiable bloody curiosity that made it so important, or was there some absolute standard of justice and truth to be served?

Banks had no answer. All he knew was that if he didn't get to spin it out until he thought it was all over, then it would stay with him like a sore that wouldn't heal. And he knew that, in some way, it was the murder of Frank Hepplethwaite he was out to avenge, not Jason Fox's.

One or two pairs of curious eyes followed him up the stairs at the station, but nobody said anything. Susan was in her office waiting for him with a thick pile of papers in front of her.

"I feel like a schoolboy sneaking a look at naughty pictures," Banks said. "Can I take them to my office?"

"Of course," said Susan. "You don't have to ask *my* permission." She stood up.

"Look, I appreciate this."

"No problem."

"Susan, is—"

"Sorry, sir. I've got to go."

She dashed out and left him standing in her office. Well, he thought, it didn't take long to become a pariah around here, did it?

But he could hardly blame Susan for wanting to put a bit of distance between them. Not after all that had happened. And she *had* put herself out to help him.

Checking to see that the coast was clear, he tiptoed across the corridor to his own office with the papers and shut the door behind him. Nothing had changed. Even the desk was still at the same odd angle after Riddle had fallen back on it. Embarrassed at the memory of what he'd done, Banks straightened it, sat down with the pile of paper, packet of cigarettes and ashtray beside him, window a couple of inches open, and settled down to read.

II

What the hell am I doing here? Susan wondered, as Banks stood aside and held the door of The Duck and Drake open for her. Why did I agree to this? *I must be insane.*

The Duck and Drake was a small hideaway in Skinner's Yard, one of the many alleys off King Street. Wedged between an anti-quarian bookshop and the Victoria wine shop, it had a narrow frontage and not much more room inside. One advantage was that it was one of the few pubs that still had a snug, a tiny room handy for private conversations. The doorway was so low that even Banks had to stoop. Inside, the snug was all dark wood beams and whitewashed stone walls hung with brass ornaments. An old black-leaded fireplace took up almost one entire wall. Above it ran a long wooden mantelpiece with a few tattered leather-bound books.

They had the snug to themselves. Banks bought the drinks and sat against the wall, opposite her, a small table between them.

Sipping her St Clement's, Susan could hear the occasional kerchunk of the fruit machine and chink of the cash register coming from the other rooms. If they wanted the barman's attention, they had to ring a little bell on the bar. It was an altogether too intimate and cosy set-up for Susan, but there was nothing she could do about it. Banks had been right in that the Queen's Arms was far too public a place for them to meet. And he was clearly oblivious to her discomfort, drinking his Sam Smith's Old Brewery Bitter and chewing on a cheese-and-onion sandwich. Susan had no appetite at all. Between mouthfuls, he told her about what he had discovered in Amsterdam.

Susan listened, frowning and biting her lower lip in concentration. When Banks had finished, she said, "It makes sense, sir, but how does it change things? We already know Mark Wood killed Jason. He admitted it."

Banks finished his sandwich, sipped some Sam Smith's and reached for his cigarettes.

"Yes," he said. "I've just read through his statements. The kid's a pathological liar. He's confessed to manslaughter, but if I'm right it was murder. Premeditated murder."

"I don't see how you can prove that."

"There's the rub. According to the post-mortem report, Jason Fox was hit *on the back of the head* with the beer bottle, right?"

Susan nodded. "That's where Dr Glendenning found the most damage to the skull, and the glass fragments."

"But in his statement, Mark Wood said he hit Jason *on the side of the head.*"

"I noticed that," said Susan, "but, quite honestly, sir, I didn't think much of it. He was confused, under pressure. Basically, he was saying he just lashed out."

"Yes, I understand that. The point is, that doesn't happen in a fight."

"Sir?"

"Stand up."

Banks edged out from the bench. The room itself was just about high enough for him to stand up in. There was no-one else around. Susan got to her feet and stood close, facing him, almost close enough to feel the warmth of his body.

She concentrated on the demonstration, focusing on little details. He didn't look well, she noticed. He had dark bags under his eyes, and his face was pale. There was also a deep sadness in him that she had never noticed before.

"Pretend to hit me on the back of the head with an imaginary beer bottle," he said.

"I can't, sir," Susan said. "Not from this angle. Jason must have had his back to Wood, walking either in front of or beside him. Or he must at least have been partly turned sideways."

"Like this?" Banks turned sideways.

"Yes, sir."

Banks went back to his seat and lit a cigarette. "Been in many fights?" he asked.

"No, sir. But that—"

"Let me finish. I have. At school. And, believe me, you would never get your opponent to stand in that position. Not willingly. Not unless you'd hit him with your fist first and knocked him sideways."

"Maybe that's what happened?"

Banks shook his head again. "Listen to what you're saying, Susan. To do that, he'd have to have been holding the beer bottle in the same hand he punched Fox with and then swung back very quickly and hit him before he moved. Even if he had the beer bottle in the other hand and switched after he'd hit him, it still doesn't make sense. And remember, Jason was no slouch when it came to physical strength. You'd need every advantage to get the better of him. Let me ask you a question."

"Yes, sir."

"Was Mark Wood bruised in any way? Did he have a black eye or a cauliflower ear?"

"No."

"You'd expect something like that, wouldn't you, if he'd been in an actual fight? Especially with as tough a customer as Jason Fox. Are you telling me Jason didn't even get one punch in?"

"I don't know, sir. Perhaps he hit Wood in the body, where it wouldn't show, and not in the face? I mean, we didn't do a strip search or anything."

Banks shook his head. "I'm sorry, but it's just not on. I had another good look at the crime-scene photographs as well, and I reread Dr Glendenning's post-mortem report. It just couldn't have happened the way Mark Wood said it did."

"Well," Susan said slowly, "Superintendent Gristhorpe wasn't entirely convinced, either. But Mark said Jason Fox was goading him about his wife and kid. They needn't have faced off to start fighting. Mark probably just lashed out when he'd had enough. I suppose you saw it for yourself in the statement, but when we pushed Wood on exactly how and when it happened, he said it was all a blur, he couldn't remember."

"How very convenient. He also denied emptying Jason Fox's pockets. Two loose ends."

"That's the thing that bothered me most, sir. But we just assumed that either he lied because it would look bad for him, too deliberate, stopping to empty Jason's pockets instead of running off in a panic. Or maybe someone else came along later and robbed Fox while he was lying there."

"I'd go for the first explanation, myself. It just didn't fit with the scenario he was painting for you. But why take his keys as well, unless they might have led to easier identification? I think whoever did this wanted to keep the victim's identity from us until they had a chance to clear out the Rawdon house of any dodgy files or notes he might have kept there, and they weren't taking any chances."

"We just thought that if some opportunist came along and did it, he simply took everything. You know, just sort of scooped it all up quickly without pausing to separate the keys from the loose change." Susan shrugged. "Chief Constable Riddle didn't seem to be worried by any of this. And by then we had him breathing right down our necks."

"It's still two loose ends too many for me."

"Then I don't know where that leaves us, sir. What about motive?"

Banks told her about Mark's connection with Motcombe's drug deal, and Jason's disapproval.

"So you think Motcombe's behind it?" she said.

"I do. But proving it's another matter. Officially the case is closed. You got a confession. That pleased Jimmy Riddle. That and the opportunity to suspend me. I made a mistake there. I didn't expect you'd solve the case so quickly that he'd be buzzing round the station all weekend. To be honest, I didn't expect he'd find out where I'd gone."

"Sir," Susan blurted out, feeling her heart lurch into her throat. "Can I tell you something?"

Banks frowned and lit another cigarette. "Yes, of course. What is it?"

Susan chewed on her lip for a while, just looking at him, unsure now whether she dare speak out or not. Then she took a deep breath and told him all about Gavin's betrayal.

When she had finished, Banks just sat quietly staring down at the table. She was afraid of what he might say, especially as she could no longer deny to herself the way she felt about him. Please God, she prayed, let him never find out about *that*.

"I'm sorry, sir," she said.

Banks looked at her, a sad, crooked smile on his face. "Never mind. It wasn't your fault. How were you to know your boyfriend would run off and tell tales to Jimmy Riddle?"

"Whichever way you look at it, sir, I still betrayed a confidence."

"Forget it."

"How can I do that? Look how it's turned out."

"It isn't over yet, Susan. I'm far from finished. It must have hurt you, this betrayal. I'm sorry."

Susan looked down, into her empty glass.

"Fancy another drink?" Banks asked.

"No, sir. I'm fine. Really."

"Well, I fancy another pint."

Banks went to the bar and rang the bell. While he was waiting to get served, Susan sat, hunched in on herself, feeling miserable. No matter how bloody kind and forgiving Banks might be, she could never forgive herself for what she had done. It wasn't so much the betrayal itself, as the humiliation of letting herself be fooled and used by a bastard like Gavin.

"So what do you want to do?" she asked when he came back. "I mean about Mark Wood."

"I see from the paperwork that Wood's solicitor was called Giles Varney?"

"That's right. A real arrogant bastard. Expensive, too. It seemed a bit odd at the time, that he would get Varney to come all the way from Leeds."

"Yes."

"Wood also said something about him being Jason's solicitor, too—the one who helped them get the business set up. He didn't want a duty solicitor. He was adamant about that."

"Interesting." Banks sipped his pint, wiped his lips and said, "And fishy. You know, I wouldn't be at all surprised if Varney is Motcombe's solicitor, too, or at least works for the same firm. I'll have to give Ken Blackstone a call and check. Now, according to the reports, it was only when the blood evidence came back that Wood confessed, right?"

"Yes, sir. It would have been pretty difficult to lie his way out of that one."

"Did he have a private conference with Varney? Make phone calls?"

"Yes, sir. We did it all strictly according to PACE."

Banks nodded. "So Wood talked to Varney, then he made a telephone call, then he confessed."

"Yes, sir."

"Who did he call?"

"I don't know. It was made in private."

"We should be able to find a record of the number. I'll bet you a pound to a penny it was Neville Motcombe. I'll bet he told Motcombe he was well and truly up the creek without a paddle and Motcombe talked to Varney, who then told him to plead manslaughter."

"But why would he do that?"

"Isn't it obvious? You had him against the ropes. I mean, fine, early blood evidence doesn't necessarily mean a hell of a lot, but Wood *knew* he'd done it, and both he and Varney probably knew it was just a matter of time before we got results from DNA testing. And that they'd be positive. In the meantime, if Mark Wood admits to a lesser charge of manslaughter, denying that he's ever even met Motcombe, then the heat's off. It was just a fight that went wrong.

"And you can also bet that Varney will milk as much sympathy from the jury as he can from the fact that the fight started over Jason Fox making racist remarks about Mark Wood's wife and child. All Motcombe has to promise is that Wood will get a short sentence *and* that his family will be financially taken care of while he's inside. That and a nice bonus when he gets out. I think it's an offer I'd probably take if my balls were in the wringer like Wood's are."

"*If* he pays a penny."

"Yes. I suppose he could renege. And arrange for an accident in jail. I'm assuming he's not doing all this out of the kindness of his heart. He's doing it because Wood has something on him. Like the truth about what happened."

"What can we do about it, if you're right?"

"*We* can't do anything, Susan. Remember, you're still on the job, but you're off the case. I, on the other hand, can do whatever I want."

"But—"

Banks held his hand up. "Susan, I appreciate what you've done so far, but I don't want to risk getting you into trouble again. Even Superintendent Gristhorpe wouldn't approve if he knew what I was up to."

"He would if you told him, sir. I told you he had his doubts, too. But Jimmy Riddle just barged in and steamrollered everything."

"I know. But the super's not here. It's better this way for the time being. Believe me."

"What next, then?"

Banks looked at his watch. "Next, I think I'll get right back to basics and pay George Mahmood another visit. There's something missing from those statements. Some connection I'm missing, and it's starting to irritate me. It might be worth eating a mouthful or two of humble pie to find out what it is."

III

Banks walked down King Street towards the Mahmoods' shop. As he passed School Lane, he could hear kids shouting on the rugby pitch and was almost tempted to go and watch. He had played rugby at school and when he first joined the Met. He'd been a pretty good winger, if he said so himself. Strong, slippery and fast.

Is this what private eyes feel like? he wondered as he cut down along Tulip Street, on the northern edge of the Leaview Estate. Walking the mean streets of Eastvale? He didn't even have a licence to validate what he was doing. How did you go about getting a private-eye licence in Yorkshire? Did you even need a licence?

He did, however, still have his warrant card. Riddle hadn't got the chance to ask for it, and Banks hadn't managed the cliché of slapping it down on the table. He supposed it would be an offence to use it while under suspension, but that was the least of his worries.

The builders were busy at work in the fields around Gallows View, mixing concrete, climbing ladders with hods resting on their shoulders, or just idling around chatting and smoking cigarettes. Soon, the row of old cottages would be swallowed up. Banks wondered if they'd change the name of the street and the fields when the new estate was finished. *Gallows Estate* probably wouldn't sit too well with the local council.

For Banks, approaching the Mahmoods' shop felt like coming full circle. Not only had the Jason Fox case led him there, but his first case in Eastvale had involved the previous owner. And the way things looked, this might be his last case.

George stood behind the counter, wearing his white shirt with its Nehru collar, serving a young woman with a baby strapped to her breast. When he saw Banks, he scowled. His mother, Shazia, came over from the freezer area, where she'd been stamping prices on packages of frozen pizza.

Though she only came up to Banks's shoulders, her eyes challenged him. "What do you want this time, Mr Banks? Haven't you caused enough trouble around here?"

"As far as I know, I haven't caused any trouble, Mrs Mahmood. Not intentionally, at any rate. I have a job to do." A small lie, he realized. *Had* a job would be more like it. "I have a job to do, and it's sometimes difficult. I'm sorry if it caused you any pain."

"Oh, are you? Such as throwing my son in a cell overnight, worrying his poor parents to death?"

"Mrs Mahmood, George wasn't *thrown* anywhere, and he exercised his right to make a telephone call. If he didn't ring you—"

She waved her hand impatiently. "Oh, yes, he rang us, all right. But we still worried. A young boy being put in jail with all those criminals."

"He was in a cell by himself. Look, I don't know where you've got this from—"

"And only because of his colour. Don't think we don't know that's why you pick on us."

Banks took a deep breath. "Look, Mrs Mahmood, I'm getting sick of this. We took your son in because he and his friends had an altercation with the victim's party on the night of the killing, because they live in pretty much the same area of town, because they refused to co-operate with us and because we found something suspicious on George's trainer."

"Suspicious? Animal blood?"

"We didn't know that at the time. It *could* have been human blood."

She shook her head. "My son would never hurt anyone."

"I'm sorry, but my business isn't always as trusting as it might be."

"And what about the second time? Wasn't that persecution?"

"My colleagues turned up a witness who said he *saw* George and his two friends beat up Jason Fox. What could they do?"

"But he was lying."

"Yes. But again, we didn't know that at the time."

"So why have you come here pestering us all over again?"

"It's all right, Mother," George said, walking over. The woman with the baby seemed torn between leaving and staying to eavesdrop on the conversation. She took a long time putting her change back in her purse, then Banks gave her a sharp glance and she scurried out murmuring comforting sounds to the baby, who had started to cry.

"Can we go somewhere and talk, Mohammed?" Banks asked.

George nodded towards the stockroom in the back of the shop.

"I'm going to call a solicitor," Mrs Mahmood said.

"No need to, Mum," said George. "I can handle this."

Banks followed him into the back. The stockroom was full of boxes and smelled of cumin and shoe polish. There were no windows, or if there were, they were covered by the stacks of boxes. A bare bulb shone in the centre of the room. Banks fancied it looked rather like a film-maker's idea of one of those interrogation rooms from the old days. He'd seen a film not too long ago in which two detectives had actually sat a woman in a chair with two bright desk lights pointed at her. He'd never tried that in interrogations himself; he wondered if it worked.

"What do you want?" George said. There wasn't a trace of friendliness in his voice. Whatever friendship there had ever been, through Brian, was gone now.

"I need your help."

George snorted and leaned against a stack of crates, arms crossed. "That's a laugh. Why should I help you?"

"To find out who really killed Jason Fox."

"Who cares? From what I've heard, the racist bastard deserved everything he got. Besides, I read in the paper that his mate confessed. Isn't that good enough for you?"

"I'm not going to argue with you. Will you just answer a few straightforward questions, please?"

He shrugged. "All right. No skin off my nose. But hurry up."

"Cast your mind back to that Saturday night at The Jubilee. Why were you there?"

George frowned. "Why? To listen to the band. Why else? Kobir was up visiting from Bradford, like I said, so Asim and me thought he'd enjoy it."

"I understand The Jubilee has a good reputation for music?"

"Yeah."

"Girls?"

"Yeah, it's a good place to meet girls."

"And drugs?"

"If you're interested in that sort of thing. I'm not."

"People come from miles around."

"So?"

"And it was really busy that night?"

"Yeah. Well, Scattered Dreams are really popular. They're pretty new on the scene and they haven't got to the expensive venues yet. But they're already recording for an indie label. Pretty soon you'll be paying through the nose to go see them at Wembley or somewhere."

"Okay. Now, apart from that little contretemps you had with Jason, did you notice anything else about him and his pal?"

"Never paid any attention, really. Except that they seemed to be talking pretty intensely a lot of the time."

"Arguing?"

"Not loudly, not so's you'd notice. But they didn't look too happy with one another."

"Did they try to chat up any girls?"

"Not that I saw."

"They weren't listening to the music?"

"Not really. Some of the time. But they were sitting towards the back, closer to the bar. We were near the front, but the way the chairs were angled around the table, they were pretty much in my line of vision. When they weren't talking, the other one, the one that killed him, would seem to be listening, but the one that got killed even put his fingers in his ears every now and then."

"What kind of music was it?"

George shifted position and put his hands in his pockets. "Hard to describe, really. Sort of a mix between rap, reggae and acid rock. That's about the best I can do."

No wonder Jason had put his fingers in his ears, Banks thought. He obviously hadn't known what kind of music to expect. But Mark Wood probably had.

"Did you see either of them talk to anyone else?"

George frowned. "No. I was far more interested in the music than in those two pillocks." The shop bell pinged. "I'd better get back and help my mum. My dad's down at the cash and carry."

"Just a couple more questions. Please."

"Okay. But hurry up."

"What about those Jamaicans selling drugs you mentioned when I first talked to you?"

"What about them?"

"Was that true?"

"Yes, of course it was. I suppose I should admit I don't know for certain they were from Jamaica, but they looked like Rastas, and one of them had dreadlocks."

"And the drugs?"

"I saw a bit of money change hands now and then, then one of them would talk on his mobile. A while later he'd nip outside and bring back the Ecstasy or crack or hash or whatever from the person who was carrying it. They don't carry it on them. That's how they usually do it."

"And you saw them doing that?"

"Sure. You think I should have reported it? You think the police don't know what's going on? You told me yourself The Jube has a reputation for drugs."

"I'm sure the Drugs Squad are quite well aware of what's going on. It doesn't sound as if these lads are major dealers, though. Were they regulars?"

"I'd never seen them before."

"Doing good business?"

"By the looks of it." George sneered. "Some of the white kids think it's cool to buy from spades."

"Were they with anyone?"

"They were with the band as far as I could tell."

A few connections started to form in Banks's mind. This was the link that had been eluding him. "Were they actually playing with the band?"

George shrugged. "No, maybe roadies or something. Hangers-on." The bell pinged again. "Look, I'd better get back. Really."

"Right. Just one more thing. Did you see any contact at all between the Jamaicans and Jason, or Mark?"

"What? That would have been hardly likely, would it? I mean ... wait a minute ..."

"What?"

"Once, when I was going for a piss, I saw them pass one another in the corridor. Anyway, now I think of it, they sort of nodded at each other. Very quick, like, and expressionless. I thought it was a bit weird at the time, then I forgot about it."

"Who nodded at whom?"

"The kid who confessed. He nodded at one of the Jamaicans. Like I said, I thought it was odd because he was with the bloke who called me a 'Paki bastard' and there he was, on nodding terms with a Rasta."

"So this was *after* your little conflict with Jason Fox?"

"Yes."

"That makes sense," Banks muttered, mostly to himself. "You were very nicely set up."

"Come again?"

"Oh, nothing. Just thinking out loud." Banks followed George back into the shop. "Thanks for your time, Mohammed." He became aware of Shazia Mahmood glaring at him as he walked out onto the street.

For a moment, Banks just stood there on Gallows View as the chaotic thoughts settled into some sort of pattern, like iron filings when you hold a magnet under them. Motcombe's drug deal with the Turk and Devon, using Mark Wood as a go-between. Mark Wood's Jamaican wife, Mark's connection with a reggae band and with drug dealing. Scattered Dreams. That signal between Wood and the drug dealer. Jason's death warrant. There was a pattern all right, but now he had to come up with a way of *proving* it.

Banks set off towards King Street. A pneumatic drill from the building site broke the silence and sent a pack of scavenging sparrows spiralling off into the sky.

FOURTEEN

I

"Ken, you're a mate," said Banks, "so I want to let you know before you agree to anything that I'm under suspension."

"Bloody hell!" Blackstone nearly spilled his drink. It was Thursday lunch-time, and they were in The City of Mabgate, near Millgarth, finishing bowls of chilli. "What's it all about?" Blackstone asked when he'd recovered his equilibrium.

Banks told him.

Blackstone shook his head. "They can't make it stick," he said. "It sounds like a personal vendetta to me."

"It is. But don't underestimate personal vendettas, Ken. Especially when Chief Constable Jimmy Riddle's the one carrying them out. And for the record, I'd appreciate it if you didn't tell anyone else around here where I was over the weekend. It could mean real trouble for Craig McKeracher."

Blackstone tilted his head and squinted at Banks. "Are you hinting that one of our lads is bent?"

Banks sighed. "Look, there's no evidence, but it seems clear that someone, most likely someone from West Yorkshire, is doing a few little favours for Neville Motcombe and his league of merry men."

Blackstone's expression hardened. "Are you certain?"

"No, not certain. It just seems to be the most obvious of things. As far as I know, so far it's just been a matter of accessing criminal records. If you use the PNC, you wouldn't have to be in West Yorkshire to do that, I'll admit, but that's where Motcombe lives. Logical deduction."

"Brilliant, my dear Holmes," said Blackstone. "But *ve haff vays* of finding out who's been using the PNC, and what they've been looking for. I'll catch the bastard and have his bollocks for golf balls."

"Maybe it's a 'her'?"

"Maybe. But how many women do you find hanging around with these white-power groups? Not a lot. It inclines me to believe they've got more sense."

"Well, not many of them like playing soldiers, that's for certain. I don't know what odds I'd take against how many of them actually *agree* with some of the stuff Motcombe's lot comes out with, though. Anyway, can I ask you one more favour, Ken?"

"Go ahead. You're doing pretty well for a suspended copper so far."

"Thanks. Don't move on the mole until I've played out my hand."

"Why not?"

"Same reason I asked you to keep quiet about Amsterdam. It could jeopardize Craig's cover as Rupert Francis. Or even his life. I don't think Motcombe's the forgiving sort."

Blackstone squirmed and scratched the back of his neck. "Okay. My lips are sealed. Want to tell me more?"

Banks told him about Motcombe's gangs of steamers and muggers, then about the Turkish connection and the possible heroin deal with Devon, the deal in which Mark Wood was to play such a big part. Blackstone listened without comment, shaking his head every now and then.

"That's quite a conspiracy," he said finally. "It makes me wonder about this suspension business. Do you think there's anything more to it?"

"Like what?"

Blackstone paused a moment. "More sinister. Remember when John Stalker got taken off that investigation into the RUC's shoot-to-kill policy in Northern Ireland a few years back?"

"Yes."

"I seem to remember they mocked up some story about him consorting with criminals just to shut him up and stop him embar-rassing them. It was all political."

Banks shook his head. "A week or two ago I might have been paranoid enough to agree with you," he said. "The old conspiracy theory has its appeal. Especially when Dirty Dick Burgess appeared on the scene. And it wouldn't have surprised me if Jimmy Riddle had been in the BNP at the very least. But I don't think so. Whatever he is, Riddle isn't a card-carrying fascist. He's just a pushy, bull-headed arsehole, a frustrated headmaster with a mean streak. Put him on the inner-city streets where the real coppers work and he'd shit himself in five minutes."

"Maybe so. But you're certain there's nothing more to it?"

"Pretty much. He's been looking for an excuse to nobble me ever since he took the job, and now he thinks he's found it."

"Okay. So how can I help?"

"I'm going to ask you a couple more favours and I want to give you the chance to say no. I don't want you to stick your neck out for me. I'm giving you fair warning."

Blackstone paused, then said, "Go ahead. I'll tell you if I don't want to hear any more. Or when."

"Fair enough." Banks lit a cigarette. "The way I see it, though, is that most of what's going on here is on *your* patch anyway, so you can regard me as informant, consultant, whatever the hell you like, as far as official records go."

Blackstone laughed. "Clever bugger. Thought it all out, haven't you? You'd have made a good lawyer. All right. I'm interested. I only hope you don't expect paying, that's all."

Banks smiled. "This is for free, Ken. First off, I'd like to know whether a solicitor called Giles Varney has ever acted for Neville Motcombe. There might be some record in the paperwork on that receiving charge. Or, better still, last Thursday, after that fracas at Frank Hepplethwaite's funeral. Someone got Motcombe out of Halifax nick pretty damn quickly."

Blackstone got his notebook out. "How d'you spell that?"

Banks spelled Varney for him.

Blackstone smiled. "Well, that ought to be easy enough to do without compromising my career."

"The next request might be a bit tougher, and I'll understand if you say no. There was a band from Leeds playing at The Jubilee in Eastvale on the Saturday Jason Fox was killed. They're called Scattered Dreams. Someone who was there told me that there were a couple of Jamaicans dealing small quantities of hash, crack and Ecstasy. Apparently, they might have been with the band in some capacity. Roadies, hangers-on, what have you."

Blackstone nodded. "A lot of small dealers are mobile now they've saturated the urban markets. And it makes sense they'd target places where there's loud music and lots of kids. I think I've heard of The Jubilee. Is that the one that advertises in the *Evening Post*?"

"That's the one. I suppose the Drugs Squad keeps tabs on these bands and their itinerant dealers?"

"I hope so," said Blackstone. "Though you never quite know what the DS is up to. They're a law unto themselves half the time."

"Anyway," Banks went on, ticking off on his fingers, "Mark Wood had passing contact with one of these lads at The Jubilee. My thinking is that they might have been in this together. First off, I need to know if this band is the same one Mark Wood roadied for a couple of years back, when he was arrested on the drugs charge."

Blackstone nodded.

"And then I'd like the names of the Jamaicans who were on the fringes of Scattered Dreams that night, if you can get them. I know that might be a bit more difficult."

"I can only try," said Blackstone. "Actually, I know a bloke on the Drugs Squad who can keep his mouth shut. We did some courses at Bramshill together a few years back. Bloke called Richie Hall. He's a Jamaican himself, and he's done a fair bit of undercover work over the years. Anyway, the point is, he knows the music and drugs scene up north better than anyone I know. If he doesn't know who they are, nobody does."

"Great. There might even be a short cut. Mark Wood's wife's Jamaican. Her maiden name is Shirelle Jade Campbell. They seem to have met up around the time Wood got involved with the band, and I'm wondering if there isn't maybe a family connection. A brother, cousin or something. At least that gives you a name to work on."

"I'll pass it on to Richie. Like I said, if anyone knows, Richie does."

"You sure you don't mind doing this, Ken?"

Blackstone shook his head. "Nah. What are mates for. I'll warn you, though, you'll be bloody lucky to get anything out of these lads even if we do track them down."

"I know that. Actually, if I'm right, I was thinking of a slightly more devious approach to the truth. But let's wait and see, shall we?"

"Just as long as your expectations aren't too high. Who knows, there might even be a bit of glory in this for me."

Banks smiled. "Maybe. Whatever happens, there'll be no Brownie points for me from Jimmy Riddle. But I promise you, if there's any credit to be taken, it's yours. And lunch is on me."

"Will you do *me* one small favour, Alan?"

"Name it."

"Just be bloody careful, that's all."

II

By nine o'clock on Friday morning, Banks felt edgy and restless alone in the house. He was pleased with himself, however, for avoiding the booze completely on Thursday evening, and for actually managing to finish *The Power and the Glory* as he listened to Beethoven's late quartets. So he felt full of energy when he woke up on Friday. There was nothing else he *could* do until he heard from Ken Blackstone, except pace the floor.

When his phone rang at about half past nine, he grabbed the receiver on the first ring. "Yes? Banks here."

"Alan, it's Ken."

"What have you got?"

"Some answers for you. I hope. In answer to your first question, yes, Giles Varney is Neville Motcombe's solicitor and has acted for him on a number of occasions. Their professional relationship goes back to the time Motcombe started buying property in the Leeds area, about four years ago. It seems like they've been bosom buddies ever since."

"Does Varney have any other known right-wing connections?"

"Yes. I checked around and he's pretty well known in some of the more extreme-right circles."

"Great. That would seem to indicate that Mark Wood did a deal with Motcombe through Varney. Anything else?"

"This is where it gets a bit more complicated, I'm afraid. And you owe me. I had to spend yesterday evening in a pub with Richie Hall, and he drinks like a bloody fish. I'll be sending you the bill."

Banks laughed. "Find anything out?"

"Yes. The band Mark Wood worked with at the time of his first arrest was called Cloth Ears. They split up shortly after the drug bust. But this Scattered Dreams was formed partly from the ashes. Phoenix-like, you might say. Apparently the blokes you're interested in used to play with Cloth Ears but now they just hang around the fringes of Scattered Dreams and sell dope. Seems drugs have sapped whatever talents they might once have had, and most of the time they're too stoned to strum a chord. And you were right about the family connection. The one with the dreadlocks is Shirelle Wood's brother, Wesley Campbell, and the other's a mate of his called Francis Robertson. 'Wes' and 'Frankie,' as they're known locally. Both of them have been seen to associate with Devon recently, according to Richie."

"Low-level dealers?"

"Looks that way."

"Excellent."

"And in Shirelle Wood's favour, Richie says she's not connected with any of this. In fact she stopped talking to her brother, Wes, as soon as she discovered he was involved in getting Mark busted the first time, and she hasn't talked to him since. Cut him off completely."

Good for her, Banks thought. There were very few people he had come to have respect for in this whole business. Frank Hepplethwaite was one of them, and Shirelle Jade Wood was another. Pity about her husband. He should have followed her lead and cut off communications with Wesley Campbell, too. But no, Mark Wood thought he could make an easy fortune. And it was a sad thought that Shirelle and Connor would be the ones to suffer the most if the truth did come out.

"Thanks, Ken," Banks said. "You've done a great job."

"No problem."

"Now for the hard part."

He heard Blackstone sigh. "Somehow I had a feeling there might be more to it than this. I assume this is your 'cunning plan' for getting to the truth?"

Banks laughed. "Hear me out, Ken, then let me know if you think we can do it."

III

About an hour later, Banks drove down to Leeds alone. There was no point involving Susan Gay or Jim Hatchley with his scheme. It was risky and could backfire, then he'd have their jobs on his conscience, too. Ken Blackstone would be fine; he was simply carrying out an investigation on his own patch, based on information received. The fact that Banks was along for the ride really didn't matter.

Banks lit a cigarette and turned up the volume on Bryn Terfel's renditions of *Songs of Travel*. He looked at the digital clock. Eleven o'clock. Plenty of time to do what he had to and pick up Tracy at the residence by six o'clock.

As he pulled up behind Millgarth, he looked at his watch. Just after twelve. If Ken Blackstone had done his work, everything ought to be set up and ready to roll by now. He checked at the front desk and went straight up to Blackstone's office. In the corridor outside the CID offices, as arranged, sat Mark Wood, who had been brought in from Armley Jail shortly after Banks's nine-thirty talk with Ken Blackstone, just to answer a few more questions and help make the paperwork flow more smoothly.

Even though Wood had been sitting there for probably a couple of hours already, he hadn't asked for Giles Varney yet. If he did, they'd have to lie and tell him they couldn't get in touch. With Varney present, the plan would be useless.

Mark Wood didn't look much, Banks thought. Muscular, yes, but basically just another sullen, nervous kid chewing his fingernails in a police station.

Banks introduced himself. They hadn't met before, and it was important that Wood know *someone* from Eastvale was involved in all this. As expected, Wood looked puzzled and confused. When he asked Banks why he had come down all this way, Banks said it was nothing to worry about, he would find out in a while. He sounded like a doctor about to tell a patient he has a terminal illness.

Leaving Wood under guard in the corridor, they went into Ken Blackstone's office, where Wood could watch them through the glass partition if he wanted, though he couldn't hear what they were saying. That would make him even more nervous. Especially if they glanced his way once in a while as they spoke.

They had been standing behind the glass chatting for fifteen minutes about Leeds United's abysmal season and occasionally looking at Mark, when three large uniformed officers led Wesley Campbell and Francis Robertson along the corridor, as arranged. The two had been passive and compliant when picked up over an hour earlier, Ken said. That was either a mark of confidence that they'd be out again in two shakes of a lamb's tail, Banks thought, or they were too stoned to care. Both had been found in possession of small amounts of marijuana, and neither had time to flush it down the toilet, so they had been languishing in the charge room for a while. By now, they weren't quite as complacent.

As they passed Mark Wood, they glanced down at him, and Mark looked even more confused. His eyes widened with fear. Campbell actually struggled against his guards for a moment and tried to get closer to Wood, as if he wanted to warn or threaten him. But the guards held on. Campbell and Robertson were taken to separate interview rooms around the corner. Both seemed to know the PACE regulations by heart, and they asked to make their phone calls immediately.

At about two o'clock, after Banks and Blackstone had enjoyed a leisurely lunch across the road, it was time to start. They went back upstairs and took Mark into an interview room. It was agreed that Banks, being more familiar with the case, would do most of the questioning. Blackstone would give the occasional prod if things got slow. They weren't taping this one. There would be time for formalities later, with Banks well out of the way, if the plan worked. If it didn't, then all hell might break loose as far as disciplinary actions were concerned. Banks had already warned Ken and given him the option of staying well away, but Ken had insisted on being involved.

"Well, Mark," said Banks, "I know we haven't met until today, but I've had a great interest in you ever since I saw Jason Fox's body a couple of weeks ago."

"I've told the police all about that," Wood said. "I've pleaded guilty to manslaughter. What's all this about?"

Banks raised an eyebrow. "It's not quite settled yet," he said. "Not to *my* satisfaction, anyway."

Wood folded his arms. "I don't know what you mean. First you leave me hanging about in the corridor for hours, now you start interrogating me. I'm not saying anything. I want my solicitor."

"Mr Varney? Well, we'll see what we can do. For the moment, though, I suggest you hold your horses, Mark, and listen to me. Certain new evidence has come to light that puts an entirely different complexion on the Jason Fox killing."

"Oh? What's that, then?"

Banks jerked his head towards the door. "We've just had a long chat with Mr Campbell and Mr Robertson, and they've told us some very interesting things."

"Like what?"

"Like the truth about what you did to Jason Fox."

"I don't know what you're talking about."

"Oh, come on, Mark, surely you can do much better than that?"

"I'm not saying a word."

"Listen to me, then. According to your brother-in-law Mr Campbell, an old mate of yours from the Cloth Ears days, the two of you were commissioned by Neville Motcombe to get rid of Jason Fox. Jason had become a major risk in a heroin deal you were planning, and a serious threat to Motcombe's power. Motcombe couldn't get any of his own members to do it because Jason was too popular with them. Instead, he got two of the people who were already involved in the drug deal—one from each side, so to speak—two people who also stood to gain a lot. I should imagine

Devon wanted one or two of his own lads along just to make sure you did what you agreed, didn't he? From what I hear, he's not the kind of bloke to take undue risks. How am I doing so far?"

Wood's eyes widened. "You know about Devon? Jesus Christ, does he know about this? Does he know I'm here? Have Wes and Frankie been talking to him? Shit, if Devon thinks I'm talking to the coppers, he'll fucking kill me."

Banks ignored him. "When Scattered Dreams played at The Jubilee, it gave you the perfect opportunity. Jason was going to be in Eastvale anyway—he had a football match in the afternoon—so you told him you were coming up and that the two of you could go see the band. Maybe it would be a chance to settle your differences and talk a bit of business, try to save the partnership somehow. I'd imagine you were compliant, more than willing to make compromises. You knew Scattered Dreams weren't Jason's cup of tea, but suggested he might like to broaden his horizons a bit. Who knows, maybe you promised to go to the next Celtic Warrior concert if he gave your lot a try. Jason had been to The Jubilee before, and he had mentioned that a couple of Pakistani youths went there on a fairly regular basis. I'm only guessing at this part, but I think he'd already chucked a brick through one of their windows, and he'd said he was looking for trouble with them. Perfect for you, if something like that happened in public, wasn't it? A bonus. As long as it was just a minor incident, enough to draw just a little attention.

"Anyway, according to Mr Campbell, you accompanied Jason towards the ginnel, where he and Mr Robertson were waiting at the other end to render any necessary assistance. According to them, you whacked Jason on the back of the head with the bottle a couple of times, and he went down. After that, you managed to kick him to death all by yourself. They didn't have to do a thing. And that, Mark, with two eyewitnesses to testify against you, makes it murder."

Wood turned pale. "That's not true," he said. "It didn't happen like that at all. They're lying."

Banks leaned forward. "What didn't happen like what, Mark?"

"It was like I said. There was just me and Jason. We got into a fight. He slagged off Sheri and Connor. I didn't mean for him to die."

Banks shook his head. "I'm afraid that story's gone right down the toilet now, Mark, along with all your other stories. Let me see if I can get them right." He began counting them off on his fingers, looking towards Ken Blackstone, who nodded at each one. "First, you weren't anywhere near Eastvale the night Jason got killed. Second, you were at The Jubilee but you never went anywhere near the ginnel. Third, you *were* there and you saw George Mahmood and his mates kill Jason. And, fourth, you killed him yourself in a fair fight. How am I doing so far?"

Wood licked his lips and shifted in his chair.

"Problem is, Mark," Banks went on, "you're a liar. The only version we have any independent corroboration of is the one I just put to you, the one Mr Campbell told us about. So it looks as if that's the way it's going to go down now." He paused, then went on. "After this interview, DI Blackstone and I will be having a word with the Crown Prosecution Service about changing the charges from manslaughter to murder. That carries a much longer jail sentence, as I'm sure you know."

"You can't be serious? You can't believe those bastards."

"Why not? I certainly can't believe *you*. Look at your track record, Mark. No, I'm afraid this is the end of the line for you. You get charged with murder now, and you don't get out of jail for a long, long time. In fact, by the time you get out, your wife will have run off with another bloke long since, and your kid will have grown up and forgotten you. In the meantime, you'll be fending off the arse-bandits in Wormwood Scrubs or Strangeways. And that's *if* you last that long. I suspect both Devon and Neville Motcombe have long reaches."

Wood seemed to shrivel, to draw in on himself like a bank of ashes collapsing. Banks could tell Wood knew he was trapped. He knew lies wouldn't save him now, but he didn't know the best course of action. Time to tell him, time to give him a ray of hope. After pulling the carpet from under him, give him a foam mattress to land on.

"There's only one way out for you, Mark," he said.

"What's that?" Mark's voice was no louder than a whisper.

"The truth. Right from the top."

"How will that help?"

"I'm not saying it'll get you off scot-free. Nothing will do that. We don't have the power to make deals with criminals, reduce their sentences in exchange for information. That only happens on American TV shows. But I can guarantee it'll make things easier for you."

Wood chewed on his knuckles for a few seconds, then said, "I need protection. They'll kill me. My family, too."

"We can help you with that, Mark. If you help us."

Mark rubbed his nose with the back of his hand. "I never meant to kill him," he said. "Honest I didn't. It was those two." He was close to tears.

"Who?"

"Frankie and Wes."

"What happened, Mark? Right from the beginning."

Banks took out his cigarettes and offered Mark one. He took it with a shaking hand. "All right," he said. "But what guarantee have I got that things will go easier for me if I tell you the truth? What are you offering me?"

"You've got my word," said Banks.

"For what?"

"That you and your family will be protected and that your co-operation will be considered."

"I want relocation for me and Sheri," he said. "And new identities. The Witness Protection Programme. That's what I want."

"I've already told you, this isn't America, Mark. We don't do things that way in England. Look, like I said, I'm not telling you you're going to walk out of here a free man. You're not. One way or another, you'll serve some time. What I'm saying is that if you give us what we want, the charge can remain manslaughter, not murder."

"It doesn't sound like that good a deal to me."

"Well, it is," Ken Blackstone chipped in. "The difference is between, say, twenty-five years in a very nasty place—where you'll be vulnerable to anyone Devon or Motcombe care to send along—and maybe five in minimum security prison. Protected environment. Telly and conjugal visits thrown in." He glanced at Banks, who nodded. "Your choice, Mark. It's as simple as that."

Wood looked between the two of them and his gaze finally settled on Banks again. "What about Sheri and Connor?"

"We'll take care of them, make sure they're safe," said Banks. "You have my word. What about it?"

Wood looked at Blackstone again, who assured him that Banks was right, then he rested back in his chair and said, "All right. Okay. Neville Motcombe approached me several weeks ago and said he knew about my record for drugs offences. At first I didn't know what he was getting at, then it became clear that he'd made a contact for getting his hands on some pretty large amounts of heroin through Turkey at a rock-bottom price, and he hadn't a clue what to do about it. Drugs just weren't part of his gig, but he saw a way to make a lot of money and fuck up the 'niggers' in the bargain, as he put it. He really does talk like that. Makes you sick. Anyway, he found out about my drug bust and decided I was to be the go-between."

"What was in it for you?"

"Something in the region of fifty thousand quid over a period of a few months, if all went well. Maybe more in the future, if the supply didn't dry up." He leaned forward and gripped the sides of the chair. "Look, you can judge me all you like, but have you any idea what that would have meant to Sheri and me? It would have got us out of that fucking prefab, for a start, and it would have given me a good chance at expanding the business, buying some up-to-date equipment, making something out of it. And all I had to do was play go-between for Motcombe and Devon." He laughed. "It was a bit of a joke on Motcombe, too. He didn't know Sheri's Jamaican and that his money would actually be going to help one of the people he wanted to destroy."

"Didn't that bother you, Mark? That he was intending to cause so much suffering in the West Indian community?"

"That was just a load of bollocks he came up with for Jason's benefit. He was after profits, pure and simple."

"Takes one to know one?"

"Something like that. Anyway, once you get heroin out on the streets, there's no telling what colour your buyers will be, is there? There's no colour bar on H. Even Jason knew that. Like I said, I thought it was funny that Sheri and Connor were going to get some benefit from this."

Banks shook his head. "So you agreed?"

Wood nodded. "Under Motcombe's instructions, I met with Wes, then with Devon. They never met Motcombe, didn't know who he was. I called him Mr H. Anyway, we talked about prices, delivery schedules, methods of getting the stuff into the country, the lot. Then Devon said he'd think about it. A few days later he got in touch with me through Wes and told me to let Mr H know we were in business. I suppose Motcombe got in touch with his blokes in Turkey—I didn't have anything to do with that end of the operation—and they set things in motion. There were huge profits in it for everyone. Devon wouldn't stop at Leeds—he'd be shifting stuff to Bradford, Sheffield, Manchester, Birmingham, you name it. Somehow or other, that seemed to resolve the problems on both sides. Motcombe's about dealing with darkies and Devon's about dealing with a whitey like me." Mark snorted. "Great healer of race relations, greed, isn't it?"

"And where does Jason come in?"

"Motcombe made a big mistake there. I could have told him, but he didn't ask. He seemed to think Jason would just love the idea. I mean, I don't think they'd ever talked about drugs or anything other than League business before. But Jason was straight. Even with Motcombe's justification, he wouldn't go for it. Motcombe got worried that Jason would spread the word among his colleagues in the movement and they'd chuck him out and put Jason in charge instead. I suppose you know neo-Nazis aren't really supposed to be into drugs?"

Banks nodded.

"Then there was the matter of the money to be made. Anyway, Motcombe got paranoid, especially as Jason had gained a lot of respect in the movement and people looked up to him for guidance and leadership. Jason was fast becoming a loose cannon on the deck. So Motcombe decided things would be better all around with Jason out of the way. He knew I was desperate for the money, and he also knew me and Jason didn't get along, so he asked me if I could arrange for the Jamaicans to do away with him. That way, he said, if they happened to get caught, it'd only be two less 'niggers' to worry about. You have to give the guy credit, at least he's consistent. I didn't want to do it. I mean, I'm no killer. I know Jason and me had our problems, but I didn't want to see him dead. You have to believe that. I had no choice."

"What happened?" Banks asked.

Mark ran his hand over his head. "Like Motcombe asked, I talked to Wes and I told him Jason was involved in the Turkish end of the deal and that he was planning to rip Devon off. I also said he turned out to be a racist bastard, a member of some loony fringe group. Well, I couldn't tell him the truth, could I? I had to make something up pretty quick, and it had to cover whatever publicity might come about when you found out who Jason was. Wes went back to Devon, who ordered it done. Just like that. No questions asked. And he also stipulated that I had to be in it with them. A sort of test of faith, I suppose. I didn't want to do it. I just didn't have any fucking choice."

"There's always a choice, Mark."

"Right. Sure. Easy for you to say that. It came down to me over Jason. Sheri and Connor over Jason. What would you have done? Like I said, Jason and me weren't close, and the bastard did get on my nerves with all that Nazi shit."

"Who came up with the plan?"

"That was down to me. You know the rest. Motcombe wanted it done out of the way. I mean, he knew you'd find out who the victim was eventually, and what organization he belonged to, but he needed time to get his files out of Jason's house. He sent two of his blokes to do that. Anyway, Scattered Dreams were playing in Eastvale and Jason had mentioned possible trouble with some Pakistani kids who went there. Told me he'd already chucked a brick through one of their windows. It couldn't have been better."

"What about the actual killing? How did it happen?"

Wood swallowed. "Frankie and Wes were waiting at the other end of the ginnel, as we'd arranged, and when I hit Jason with the bottle they came forward and started booting him. I kicked him a couple of times, to make it look like I was with them all the way. But only a couple of times. And not very hard. He—" Wood stopped for a moment and put his head in his hands. "Christ, he *begged* us to stop. I just thought about Connor and the damp walls and the yobs that taunt Sheri, call her a black bitch and threaten to gang-bang her every time she goes to the shops. I didn't think about Jason lying there till it was too late. You have to believe me, I didn't mean to kill him. It was Wes and Frankie. They're fucking maniacs. They'd been out in the van smoking crack."

"All right, Mark," said Banks. "Calm down. Tell me, what happened when we first arrested you? Why did you change your story?"

Mark shifted in his chair. "Well, the evidence. It was getting pretty strong against me. I was up shit creek. So when Varney took me aside, I phoned Motcombe and basically explained the situation."

"What did he say?"

"To tell you it was just a fight between the two of us, to leave him out of it, and he'd see I got the best legal help available. He'd also take care of Sheri and Connor financially while I was inside, if it came to that. What a laugh, Motcombe taking care of a black woman and a mixed-race kid."

"But he didn't know that."

"No. And I didn't tell him."

"Have you had any contact with him since your arrest?"

Mark shook his head.

"What about Devon?"

"No. I phoned my fucking bastard of a brother-in-law, though, Wes."

"What did you talk to him about?"

"I told him who Mr H was, where he lived. Just in case something went wrong and Motcombe didn't keep up his end of the bargain. You know, like maybe when he *did* find out Sheri's black and all, then he wouldn't help them. I needed some sort of insurance."

"Okay, Mark, I need to know just one more thing before we start taking fresh statements and making this all official."

"Yes?"

"Will you testify that Neville Motcombe instigated this conspiracy to murder Jason Fox?"

Wood's lips curled. "Motcombe? Bloody right I will. No way that bastard's going to get away with it."

"And Devon?"

Mark looked away. "I don't know. That's different. I'd need some sort—"

"We'll see you and your family are protected, Mark, like I told you earlier."

"I'll think about it. Okay?"

"Okay." Banks smiled. "I think that just about wraps it up for now. Thanks, Mark, you've been a great help."

"What happens to me now?"

"You make your official statement, then you go back to Armley. Eventually, there'll be committal proceedings and a trial, but we'll cross those bridges when we get to them. In the meantime, we'll make sure your family is protected." Banks looked at his watch. Just after three-thirty. Then he turned to Ken Blackstone. "For the moment, though, I think it's about time we paid Mr Motcombe another visit."

IV

Leaving one of Blackstone's most trusted DCs to take Mark Wood's official statement, Banks and Blackstone set off in the Cavalier for Motcombe's house. Most of the journey, they talked about getting enough evidence together for the CPS to take on Motcombe.

"I'm still not sure about this," Banks said, driving along through Pudsey. "I can't help feeling I'm jumping the gun. How bloody long's Motcombe likely to get for conspiracy to commit murder? That's assuming we can prove it. Giles Varney will whittle it down to conspiracy to assault, if he's got any brains. We might be better off leaving him to the Drugs Squad. He'd get longer for dealing heroin. And I promised Craig McKeracher I'd wait till I had something really solid before I moved in."

Ken Blackstone shook his head. "At this point, I don't think we have much choice. We've got evidence we have to act on. Mark Wood has actually *named* Motcombe as one of the blokes who requested Jason Fox's murder. Now Wood's blurted it all out, we *have* to go ahead. I don't think he'll get such a light sentence. Plus this way we also get Wes and Frankie in the bargain, and maybe even Devon, too. That'd be a real bonus."

"Maybe so," said Banks. "I hope you're right."

"Besides," Blackstone added, "I'd say we're best getting Motcombe off the streets as soon as possible. And none of what we're doing blows Craig McKeracher's cover. What we've got all came from Mark Wood."

Banks turned down the hill to Motcombe's house and they got out of the car. The sky was clear and the countryside shone green and gold and silver. A chill wind from the valley whistled around their ears as they stood and knocked at the front door.

No answer.

"What's that noise?" Blackstone asked.

Straining his ears, Banks could detect a faint whining above the sound of the wind. "Sounds like an electric drill or something. He must be down in the workshop. That's why he can't hear us."

"Let's try the back."

They walked around to the back of the house, which overlooked the valley and parkland. The sound of the drill was louder now.

Banks hammered on the back door. Still nothing. Just on the off chance, he tried the doorknob. It opened.

"Mr Motcombe!" he called out as the two of them walked down the stairs to the workshop. "We're coming in." He began to feel a slight shiver of trepidation. It looked dark at the bottom, and they could be walking into a trap. Motcombe could have a Kalashnikov or an Uzi with him. He might be hiding away in a dark corner ready to start blasting away at them.

But still they advanced slowly towards where the sound was coming from. Then Banks noticed something odd. The high-pitched whine the drill was making hadn't changed the entire time they'd been there. Surely if Motcombe were working on something and really couldn't hear them, there would be variations in the pitch of the drill—when he stuck it into a piece of wood, for example. And if he were making so much noise when he worked, he would hardly leave the back door unlocked so that anyone could walk in, would he? Banks felt the back of his neck tingle.

At last, they approached the workroom and pushed the door open slowly on the brightly lit room.

Motcombe was there all right.

His body hung at an awkward angle, naked to the waist, his polo-neck tunic hanging in shreds around his hips as if it had been ripped or cut off. His left wrist had been wedged in a vice, which had been tightened until the bones cracked and poked through the flesh. Blood caked the oiled metal. The smell of blood and sweat mixed with iron filings, shaved wood and linseed oil. And cordite. The room felt crowded, claustrophobic, even with only the two of them there. Three, if you counted the dead man.

The drill lay on the workbench. Banks didn't want to touch it, but he wanted the sound to stop. He went over to the wall and pulled out the plug, using a handkerchief carefully, and hoping he wasn't smudging any valuable prints. Old habits die hard. Somehow, he doubted that there would be any. People who do things like this don't leave fingerprints.

The scene was a gruesome one. More so because of the unnaturally bright lights that Motcombe had rigged up so he could see clearly what he was working on. What Banks at first took to be bullet holes in Motcombe's chest and stomach turned out, on further examination, to be spots where the drill had been inserted. When the bit stopped spinning, he could see it was clogged with blood and tissue.

Motcombe's right arm was practically in shreds, striped with lacerations, patches of skin hanging off as if he'd been flayed. Someone had obviously shredded the flesh with a saw, cutting deep into the muscle and bone. Banks noticed the blood and chips of bone on the edge of a circular saw that lay on the floor beside the body.

The *coup de grâce* looked like two gunshot wounds to the head, one through the left eye and the other in the middle of the temple, both leaving large exit wounds.

"Well, Ken," said Banks finally, backing away from the scene. "I can't say I envy you sorting this little lot out."

"Me neither," said Blackstone, visibly pale. "Let's get outside. I don't think I can stand being in here much longer."

They stood outside the back door overlooking the valley and the peaceful village of Tong in the distance. Three large crows circled high in the blue air. Banks lit a cigarette to take the taste and smell of the workshop out of his mouth. "Want to call it in?" he asked.

"Yes. Just give me a minute."

"What do you think?"

Blackstone took a deep breath before answering. "You probably know as well as I do, Alan," he said. "Either Wes Campbell or Frankie Robertson phoned Devon the minute they saw Mark Wood at Millgarth. That was, what, over four hours ago now. This pisses Devon off mightily, and he sends a couple of lads over right away to help him vent his rage. You don't get far in Devon's business unless you're seen to act, and to act *fast*. He relies heavily on pure fear. Who knows, maybe he's even made a down payment to Motcombe and wants his money back, too? So they either torture him to find out where the money is, or they do it for fun, just to teach him a lesson. Then they execute him. Bang, bang."

Banks nodded. "Either that or they decided they didn't like Mr H's politics when Mark told them who he really was."

"It's Devon's style, Alan," Blackstone went on. "Two head shots with a .38, by the looks of it. Remember those murders I told you about in New York, Toronto, Chapeltown?"

"Uh-huh."

"Same MO. Torture and two head shots. It still doesn't help us prove anything. I don't suppose anyone can tie Devon to the scene. He'll have an alibi you can't break, and there'll never be any trace of a murder weapon."

"We've still got Mark Wood to use against him."

"If he doesn't suddenly lose his memory the minute he hears about what happened to Motcombe. I probably would if I were him."

"And don't forget Campbell and Robertson. You've got them, too. They might not be quite as tough as they seem once you put the pressure on. Especially if they're deprived of their narcotic sustenance. And I'll bet you've got records of any telephone calls they made from Millgarth."

Blackstone nodded and looked around, then he sighed. "Well, we'd better set things in motion. Can I use your mobile?"

"Be my guest."

They walked around to Banks's car at the front of the house and Banks handed him the phone. Blackstone tapped in the numbers, gave the details and requested more police, a murder van and a SOCO team.

"I'll tell you something," he said when he'd finished. "Your chief constable isn't going to like it, is he? Remember the song and dance he made in the paper about solving the murder, keeping race out of it?"

"Bugger Jimmy Riddle," said Banks. "This isn't a matter of race, it's drugs and greed. Anyway, they're West Yorkshire's Jamaicans, not ours. And I wasn't even here."

"What do you think now?" Blackstone asked, handing Banks the phone. "Still want to come and work for West Yorkshire?"

Banks stubbed out his cigarette on the wall and put the butt in his pocket to avoid contaminating the scene. "I don't know, Ken. I really don't know. I might not have much choice, might I? Anyway, right now, I think I'd better make myself scarce before the troops arrive and all hell breaks loose. You'll be okay?"

"I'll be fine. I'll catch a lift back to Millgarth from one of the patrol cars. Go. Go."

Banks shook Blackstone's hand. "Thanks, Ken. I'd be interested to hear you tell them why you're here and how you got here, but I really can't stay."

"I'll tell them I got the bus," said Blackstone. "Now be a good lad, Alan, and bugger off back to Eastvale. I think I hear the sound of sirens."

Banks got in his car. He couldn't hear sirens, but the sound of Neville Motcombe's electric drill still whined in his ears.

A mile or so down the road, the first patrol cars passed him, lights and sirens going. No hurry, Banks thought. No hurry at all. He lit another cigarette and switched on the tape player. Robert Louis Stevenson, sung by Bryn Terfel:

Now when day dawns on the brow of the moorland,
Lone stands the house, and the chimney-stone is cold.
Lone let it stand, now the friends are all departed,
The kind hearts, the true hearts, that loved the place of old.

Banks looked at his watch. Just gone half past four. Hard to believe, but they had hardly been half an hour at Motcombe's house. He still had plenty of time to go and pick up Tracy for the weekend, even with the rush-hour traffic. Plenty of time.